D0440289

TURBULENCE

THE PEGASUS PRIZE FOR LITERATURE

TURBULENCE a novel by

JIA PINGWA

translated by

Howard Goldblatt

GROVE PRESS
New York

Originally published as *Fuzao* by Zuojia chubanshe, Beijing

This Grove Press edition is published by special arrangement with the Louisiana State University Press.

Published simultaneously in Canada
Printed in the United States of America

FIRST GROVE PRESS EDITION

Library of Congress Cataloging-in-Publication Data

Jia, Pingwa.
[Fu zao. English]
Turbulence : a novel / by Jia Pingwa ; translated by Howard Goldblatt.
p. cm.
Originally published: Baton Rouge : Louisiana State University Press, 1991.
ISBN 0-8021-3972-8
I. Goldblatt, Howard, 1939– II. Title.

PL2843.P5 F813 2003
895.1'352—dc21 2002029732

Design by Glynnis Phoebe

Publication of this book has been supported by a grant from the National Endowment for the Arts in Washington, D.C., a federal agency.

Grove Press
841 Broadway
New York, NY 10003

03 04 05 06 07 10 9 8 7 6 5 4 3 2 1

PUBLISHER'S NOTE

The Pegasus Prize for literature has been established by Mobil Corporation to introduce American readers to distinguished works from countries whose literature is rarely translated into English. The translations of the prizewrinning volumes are published by Louisiana State University Press. *Turbulence,* by Jia Pingwa, was awarded the Pegasus Prize in Beijing in October 1988, after an independent committee organized by the Chinese Writers' Association selected it from among the best novels written in China in the preceding ten years. The novel, which appeared in 1987, is one of more than a score of books Mr. Jia has had published in China. Two of his volumes have won the All-China Excellent Novella Award, and three of them have been adapted into films. Several of the author's books have been translated into Japanese and French, but *Turbulence* was the first to come out in English.

The chairman of the Pegasus selection committee was Tang Dacheng, executive secretary and acting chairman of the Chinese Writers' Associate, and a well-known literary critic in China. Other members of the jury were Liu Zaifu, a scholar who specializes in the novels of Lu Xun; Ru Zhijuan, secretary of the Chinese Writers' Association and an author of short stories; Wang Zenqi, a writer of short stories, essays, critical reviews, and poems; and Xiao Qian, a journalist and writer of fiction who has lived in Great Britain and has experience as a translator both to and from English.

Turbulence presents the successes and discouragements of Gold Dog, a young peasant who becomes a tenacious journalist and a "watchdog" alert to the corruption and exploitation rampant in the bureaucracy of the unsettled period in China after Mao Zedong's death. Gold Dog works to expose the wrongs perpetrated by officials in the region along the Zhou River and to fight the inferiority complex that he has come to think is retarding his nation's progress.

His actions reflect the idea that China's salvation lies in applying to the present the wisdom of the Three Elders—Mao Zedong, Zhou Enlai, and Zhu De. The young reporter's efforts to restore one area of his country to a path that serves more than the interests of those in power and his attempts to find a stable footing for his own and others' lives occur against a figurally suggestive backdrop of natural conditions, including drought and flood. Among the personal inquietudes that Golden Dog must resolve are his relations with three women: with Water Girl, the woman he loves and who loves him, but with whom he only haltingly comes to terms; with Yingying, whose machinations make him her fiancé; and with the married Shi Hua, who seduces him but also delivers him from his peasant rudeness and in the end quite literally saves him.

Mr. Jia's novel has been translated into English by Howard Goldblatt, a gifted translator of contemporary fiction from the Chinese, most notably *The Butcher's Wife*, by Li Ang, *Heavy Wings*, by Zhang Jie, and *Red Ivy, Green Earth Mother*, by Ai Bei. Mr. Goldblatt is professor of Chinese at the University of Colorado at Boulder.

On behalf of the author, we wish to express our appreciation to Mobil Corporation, which established the Pegasus Prize and provided for the translation of this volume into English.

BOOK ONE

1

The Zhou River flows to Crossroads Township following the curves of the mountains all the way to the end, where it waters an average-sized basin. The town's main street, located on the northern bank, meanders along like the ass of a snake—no bumps, no hollows—from one end of town to the other and is bordered on both sides by black gates adorned with two large rings. The tall, narrow houses behind them are connected by eaves topped by roof tiles whose tips swoop up into the air like wings soaring above the water. The rear walls of the houses touch the rocky slopes and show several feet less from ground to roof than those in front; often there is hardly any exposed wall at all. Doors cut into the stone walls are crowned by creeping ivy, like sculptures. Clear water falls from a precipice to form a lake below. Townspeople connect lengths of bamboo to bring water into their kitchens through holes in the walls. When water is needed, they stick the hollow bamboo pipe into the hole, and when they're finished, they pull it back out. This was the first place in the mountains to have running water in the homes. The houses on the northern bank of the river are separated according to a design that has lanes running between every three or four of them and steps leading down to the riverbank, giving the vague impression of metal chains when the flagstones reflect the light from the sun or the moon. When you walk down the street, the Zhou River disappears from view, then reappears, the surrounding scenery constantly changing as you go on, as though you are walking through a storyland. The first time is always an experience like no other you've had before. A nonchalant glance down one of the small lanes brings Restless Hill into view. Naturally, there's a monastery on the hill, just one, rising high above the few houses dotting the hillside around it. The houses are set among bamboo groves and lush green elms. Sturdy wooden fences in front are covered with edible wood-ear fungus; when guests drop by, the fungus is scraped away with a spatula, rinsed, and tossed into the pot for dinner. Sunlight reflects harshly off the lime-covered markers of grave mounds behind the houses. Here lie the people's ancestors. A channel running past the foot of the hill waters the emerald profusion of bamboo, willows, poplars, elms, and parasol pines. It's impossible to tell how deep the water is, and there's such an aura of mystery about the place that you feel as though you're in a fantasyland. Amid the green shadows, now and then you see rooftops: triangular, rectangular, sloping, a montage of uncertain shapes and sizes. Roosters crow, dogs bark, wisps of smoke curl up from chimneys. This is Stream of Wandering Spirits, the largest village on the Zhou River. Yet its entrance is unbelievably narrow, at the bottom of two cliffs connected by a stone ledge over which cascades a curtain of water whipped by endless winds. Some call it a sheet of gauze, others an impenetrable mist, but it always shimmers, blinding white.

The Zhou River fortune-teller, stone glass and compass in hand, surveyed an area of over a hundred li in circumference. His pronouncement: of the two cliffs that rise above the watery entrance to Stream of Wandering Spirits, the one on the left is a green dragon, that on the right a white tiger. The stone ledge between them is a threshold. Originally the birthplace of emperors, it is, alas, on the southern rather than the northern bank of the river. If it were on the northern bank facing south, it would be a sacred place. Of that there can be no doubt. Whether or not his theory was correct, no one overlooks the unique topography of Stream of Wandering Spirits. In reverence of the stone cliffs, the people dare not disturb a single pebble or a blade of grass, so the place teems with thickets of wild dates, whose needles are as thick as a man's hand. On still nights, heavy with the surrounding darkness, the central peak of the Shaman Mountain Range, far off at the headwaters of the channel, bears down on the river's surface, congealing the water into a vast stagnant strip; two red flares shine from the stone ledge between the cliffs. They are lanterns, their light rising and falling, like shimmering will-o'-the-wisps. A call—Coming home?—is met by another: Coming Home! Calls to the spirits, prayers for good fortune—somber, frightful sounds. Then comes the snarling of dogs, as mighty as leopards, from over here and over there, long into the night. But the sound isn't really snarling dogs; it's the cry of mountain birds. All along the Zhou River, for thousands of li, these birds are called mountain watchdogs. They can be found nowhere else, only here, where they are cherished like pandas, yet are more sacred; for it is they that appear in various forms above doorframes, on beams, and on the sides of altars to "heaven, earth, gods, emperors, and ancestors."

Today, at the first call of the mountain watchdogs a boat slipped out from the white-tipped reeds along the riverbank. Han Wenju lay drunk in the bottom of his boat, looking up at a drooping willow branch and the hazy yellow moon above it. The haze caught two turtledoves perching sleepily on the branch. Han Wenju's hand shook as he tossed six copper coins onto the wooden planks, where they clanked around. He struck a match; three coins lay face up. The match went out. He struck another and picked up an ancient, thread-bound book, so dog-eared it was nearly falling apart. He found the page he was looking for. His brain was clouded, and he gave off the stench of alcohol when he said, "Another year of drought!"

Drought characterized the place. How strange are the ways of the world: there are cloudy skies and there are bright skies, there are full moons and there are crescent moons, but total satisfaction is an elusive dream. The people in the area around Crossroads Township conserved every drop of water in the Zhou River, yet for years there hadn't been enough for the fields. In the summer you could see the peaks of the Shaman Mountain Range disappear in the clouds while here the sun beat down mercilessly, turning the fields into hot embers and stinging the people's eyes. Ten li away the rain fell in buckets while the local residents could only glare in anger. "Raindrops fill the ditches of nearby furrows" was the despairing cry of Crossroads Township.

People frequently donated lamp oil to the Restless Hill Monastery. When there was plenty of it, the lamps never went out and the abbot used the excess for cooking, until even his spit glistened. Sometimes he went out to drink with Han Wenju on his boat. Drunk, his face was suffused with mysticism and his body glowed with spirituality as he intoned scriptures no one understood. He would climb to the top of a boulder beside the river and sit as if in a trance, leaning to neither one side nor the other the night long, and never once falling into the river.

Now Han Wenju was in his boat, drunk again. Awakened by the calls of the mountain watchdogs, he gazed up at the heavens and cast his coins in divination—another year of drought—before passing out again. In his stupor he spotted an old man walking slowly toward him, about five feet tall and gray haired, wearing a baggy black cassock and holding a twisted cane in his hand. Startled, Han Wenju asked the stranger who he was. The old man answered, "I know the mysteries of heaven and have fathomed the ways of the world, I control the span of human life, I determine wealth and poverty. If a man chants the scriptures, he will reap limitless good fortune, but if he is a non-believer, all that await him are sickness and death, the wrath of officials and imprisonment, rapacious outlaws, the extermination of his livestock, a home in chaos, shattered illusions, unattainable aspirations, bankruptcy, evil spirits, plague . . ." Han Wenju prostrated himself at the bottom of the boat. "Are you the earth god?" he cried. The old man vanished, and Han Wenju sobered up. He thought about how the villagers burned incense and brought oil to the monastery but neglected the tiny Temple of the Earth God, behind Stream of Wandering Spirits. Was that why the earth god had come—to remind him of that? He scrambled to his feet, left the boat, and walked straight to the home of the painter at Restless Hill to bid him to start renovating the Temple of the Earth God the next morning. But the painter was asleep, and when Han touched the metal ring on the black gate, the effects of the alcohol hit him and he collapsed on the steps like a rag doll, where he slept until daybreak.

The Temple of the Earth God was restored, with incense glowing as brightly as in Restless Hill Monastery; afterward, Han Wenju and some of his friends tattooed mountain watchdogs on their chests. But none of that had any effect on the drought at Crossroads Township—which grew poorer every year. When local girls reached marriageable age, many preferred boys from far-off villages, determined never to wed the local boys, who could offer only lives of abject misery.

The poverty of Crossroads Township was well known, even in Zhou City. But no one could deny the auspicious nature of its location. The proof lay in the eminent personages from the Gong and Tian clans who had risen to prominence by bleeding others in a quest for wealth and power. Back in the 1940s the men of the Tian clan were boatmen, as they had been for generations. One year the Guomindang forces, having come to kidnap manpower for their side, surrounded the boats at White Rock Stockade, their bullets flying like locusts. The seventh son of the Tian clan, Tian the Seventh, alertly jumped over the side, plucked a hollow reed to breathe through, and made good his escape by swimming underwater toward the reeds along the riverbank. Tian the Sixth, on the other hand, was caught by the soldiers and dragged off. For three years no one knew if he was dead or alive, but during the fourth year he reappeared out of the blue as a liaison officer sent to Zhou City by the branch of the Communist party in Northern Shaanxi, where he had fled when he escaped the Guomindang. As a member of the Communist party, he secretly began arming and organizing the boatmen, whom a bleak future had primed for rebellion. So on a starless, moonless night on the last day of the month, they sneaked over to White Rock Stockade and killed the chief of the security forces, Third Tiger Hou, on the river shoal. This sent shock waves through the area. At the time a band of local outlaws lived in an old fort on Shaman Mountain under the leadership of Gong Baoshan, a young man of proud martial bearing who was an indomitable and capable strategist, the latest in a long line of hunters. Victimized by the headman of Crossroads Township, he had torched his enemy's land. His impregnable mountain fort was defended by twenty-three Hanyang rifles, protected like liquid gold. Several times Tian the Sixth tried to recruit Gong for the revolution, but Gong invariably refused, fearing that his troops would be absorbed. He wished to operate independently. But eventually a unit of the Red Army passed by White Rock Stockade on its northward trek and sent an emissary up the mountain to try to recruit him. When the unit moved on, a small contingent of Zhou City troops from the Tian family went with it, while the remainder joined up with Gong Baoshan as guerrilla fighters, led by Tian the Sixth, with Tian the Seventh and Gong Baoshan as his deputies. Choosing Crossroads Township as their headquarters and fighting bravely, they staged a series of raids along the Zhou River from White Rock Stockade all the way to Zhou City, executing landlords and local tyrants along the way. They launched their raids after nightfall and returned to camp in the morning, bringing back straw bundles containing pistols and the riches taken from the wealthy, along with the bloody heads of their victims. As the revolution gained momentum, some of the boatmen along the Zhou River began singing a song that went, "Willow leaves are long, bamboo leaves are green. We fight our way into Zhou City, each soldier taking a student queen." One of the bloodiest raids on the city, with bodies strewn all over the ground, left Tian the Sixth a casualty. The command of the local security forces hung his head on the city gate to show its contempt, and after that the strength of the guerrillas began to decline. When Liberation came, Tian the Seventh became director of the White Rock Stockade military office, and Gong Baoshan the White Rock Stockade party secretary. The fates of the Tian and Gong clans were so intertwined during their armed struggle that Stream of Wandering Spirits became famous as a birthplace of cadres.

When relating this page in history, the people on the banks of the

Zhou River speak first of the auspicious location of Stream of Wandering Spirits. Naturally, this was before the fortune-teller had arrived at his theory of a "sacred place" that was the birthplace of emperors. And yet research showed that since the village abuts the steep and forbidding Shaman Mountain, it's only natural that it be the birthplace of military heroes. The two cliffs at the mouth of the channel belong to the same range as Shaman Mountain, enveloping the village in their embrace and lending an aura of strength to the legions of military heroes. The village faces the Zhou River, which rather than flowing straight by, curves gently around it like an encircling bay; instead of offending the spirits, its silvery waters actually bring benefits. No wonder the corps of cadres settled in Crossroads Township, which had risen across the river to serve as a huge screen to protect the village and infuse it with the proper spirit. But since the people of Stream of Wandering Spirits are divided among ten surnames, all sharing in the auspiciousness of the location, why did only the Tian and Gong clans prosper? One explanation involves the placing of ancestral grave sites: When the mother of Tian the Seventh died, the clan was dirt poor, so the two brothers wrapped her body in a straw mat and carried it up the mountain for burial. Halfway there the ties snapped, so they buried her where she fell. By sheer coincidence, that spot was the region's center of geomantic power. As for the Gong clan, a cliff suddenly gave way one day, crushing one of its ancestors, who was taking a break from his hunting. Since the Gong clan, too, was dirt poor, instead of digging him out they simply burned spirit money on the spot and went away. From that time on, many people carried their parents up Shaman Mountain, following the peaks in their search for the "dragon roost." Each family made its own search, and each settled upon a different location, but none ever managed to produce a person of extraordinary talents: fathers followed in the footsteps of grandfathers, sons followed their fathers, one generation of peasants after another plodding behind water buffaloes, whips in hand, cursing heaven and aggrieved at the earth. Since they couldn't take their anger out on the Tian and Gong clans, they vented it on their buffaloes with curses of "Fuck your old lady!" and "Screw your old man!"

Then in the 1950s a fellow named Golden Dog appeared.

Golden Dog, a native of Restless Hill, was poling a string of three rafts through the muddy waters of Whirlpool Shoals like a river dragon by the time he was sixteen. An ancestor, Heavenly Tiger, who had led the White Rock Stockade boatmen's guild at the end of the Qing dynasty, had been drawn and quartered at Crossroads Township as a result of a dispute with the court representative at the White Rock Stockade revenue office. After that, none of his descendants had been allowed to ply the Zhou River. When Golden Dog's mother was pregnant with him, she was dragged into the water by a water demon, rumor has it, as she was washing rice on a wooden bridge. The villagers scurried to her aid as soon as they heard the commotion, but she was already dead. An infant lay in her rice basket, which was floating in the water beside her corpse next to a piling. The moment the villagers fished the infant out of the water, the mother's corpse sank, and though they dragged the river for a distance of forty li, they never recovered it.

The strange circumstances of Golden Dog's birth led his father to believe the boy was possessed. He decided to place him in the monastery to become a Buddhist acolyte and to spend his life cultivating moral character and atoning for his sinful origin. But Han Wenju saw the dark mole on the infant's chest, resembling the tattoo on his own, and he insisted that the infant was the reincarnation of a mountain watchdog. Because the boy was therefore impervious to evil, there was no need to place him in the monastery. Han Wenju suggested that the child's name include the word *dog,* and when the family genealogy was consulted, it was learned that the infant belonged to the "gold" generation: he was named Golden Dog.

Golden Dog took to the water from childhood. When he went swimming with other children, he easily dived into the water from a height of ten meters. Restless Hill was sparsely populated, by families too poor to own boats, even tiny loach skiffs. So Golden Dog started hanging out at the ferry landing at Stream of Wandering Spirits, where he peeled taro for passengers on Han Wenju's boat. Once, the boatmen, annoyed with him for nagging them to take him along to Purple Thistle Pass, knocked him into the river, where he remained under so long that Han Wenju panicked: "Oh no, he drowned!" Seven or eight men dived in just as his head popped above the surface near the opposite shore. "Here I am!" he giggled. No longer did the people of Stream of Wandering Spirits underestimate him. Eventually, Han Wenju decided to take him to Purple Thistle Pass. But as the boy was sitting on the deck in front of the cabin, his father came, tied up his hands with his belt, and dragged him off. Golden Dog's father, a midget of a man, was an honest, friendly painter who was very strict with his son. He'd been hired to paint the words *Wang Xiang Ice Fishing* on the main beam of the ancestral hall belonging to the Tian clan when he heard that Golden Dog was out on the Zhou

River. Taking with him the gift of a bottle of rice wine that he had received from the head of the Tian clan, he went to see Han Wenju. With his hands clasped in front of his chest, he thanked Han for the attention he was giving the boy, before bringing an end to Golden Dog's work around the boat. Golden Dog, back home, could feel his father's eyes boring into him, so he set to work grinding black ink, mixing cinnabar, and crushing gold powder, and eventually he learned how to seal cracks with indigo, execute flowing brush strokes, draw the Buddhist swastika, even paint pictures of mountain watchdogs.

The Tian clan's ancestral hall was a stately building. As the clan grew, each generation set up house and built its own homes and compounds. Golden Dog and his father made a good livelihood out of it. Golden Dog's father could climb the scaffolds like a spider, and when he was up on a beam, he wrapped his legs around it, balancing precariously as he took out his brush, dipped it in whatever color he was using, and painted one careful stroke after another, smoothing the brush in his mouth until his lips looked like a comical rainbow and his spit was a riot of colors. Golden Dog worked below, preparing the paint. When he had a bowlful, he climbed the scaffold and handed it to his father. A member of the Tian clan, standing off to the side, once called out, "Golden Dog, do you know the 'four mucks'?"

"I know the four joys," Golden Dog replied. "Flags in the wind, fish in a school, an eighteen-year-old girl, a braying mule. But I don't know the four mucks."

"I'll tell you then. A scabby head, ulcerated hips, an old woman's cunt, and a painter's lips!"

Golden Dog shouted indignantly and flung the bowl of paint down from the scaffold, smashing it against the wall. His stunned father fell off the scaffold, and from that day on, he walked with a pronounced limp in his left leg, which made him seem shorter than ever as he hobbled down the road.

Golden Dog stopped going with his father on painting jobs. Instead, he took his woes down to the ferry landing and passed the time with the Zhou River, which flowed past, and Han Wenju, who helped him get drunk. He also liked being with Han's niece, Water Girl, who asked him if he thought the sun turned into two separate suns when it sank into the river. It was impossible to get Golden Dog to come home, no matter how his father summoned him.

On the thirtieth of the intercalary month, a moonless night, the villagers hung two red lanterns the size of bamboo baskets from the eaves of the Tian and Gong homes, the reflected light stretching far out into the river. Golden Dog and Water Girl sat in the ferryboat, looking on enviously. "Look how big their lanterns are!" Water Girl said.

"Big?" Golden Dog replied. "I'll make you a *really* big lantern!"

He went home and, without telling his father, took some brand-new window paper and made an enormous lantern, which he put in front of the Tian and Gong houses. It glowed brightly when he lit it, and he was in noisy high spirits as he compared the size and brilliance of his lantern with what the other youngsters had put up. When his father came out to quiet him, he yelled even more resoundingly, so his father slapped him, which he deeply resented. That night he went back to the ferryboat and asked to sleep there with Han Wenju and Water Girl. When he returned home on New Year's Day, his father handed him kowtow money, but he neither took the money nor kowtowed to his father.

During the second year of the Cultural Revolution, the banks of the Zhou River were astir. Day and night people from the provincial capital and Zhou City came to White Rock Stockade, while those from White Rock Stockade went to Stream of Wandering Spirits and Crossroads Township, where the commune was located. Before long, murderous fighting erupted among the groups. It was like a bandit invasion. Birds and animals were slaughtered; "ox demons and snake spirits" of all classes were attacked. Golden Dog's father stopped working, Golden Dog left school, and father and son spent their hours on edge at home. Afraid that his son might become restive, the painter bolted the door and said, "Golden Dog, everything's topsy-turvy out there, and we don't want to stir up trouble, nor do we want to let anyone make trouble for us. People are all taking sides in the struggle, but we don't want to take a position."

Golden Dog cocked his head and glowered at his father. "Chairman Mao said, 'Not taking the correct political position is the same as not having a soul.' Who am I supposed to believe?"

"Believe me. I'm your father."

"Does that mean I shouldn't believe Chairman Mao?"

Pale with anxiety, his father went to the door, opened it, looked around, and then strode back, pinning Golden Dog up against the kang, where he gave him such a severe whipping that he didn't dare say another word. That summer the area experienced a severe drought. There was no harvest in the hills, and the rice paddies beside the river were overrun by insects. When autumn came, Golden Dog and his father went into the mountains to pick wild vegetables and dig duck garlic, which they ate after scraping away the poisonous parts. Those were frightful times.

Then the rains came and the Zhou River flooded. People living on the banks waded into the muddy water to grab floating firewood and cucumbers and turnips that had washed down from the mountains. Golden Dog urged his father to join in the scavenging, but because when they reached the riverbank they saw that there weren't any more good spots, Golden Dog said, "Let's go over to Awl Crag, Dad." Awl Crag was downstream about three li from Stream of Wandering Spirits. The crag stuck out over a backwater in the river. It was at least twenty feet deep when the river was low, very deep and very dark. Now it was six feet above the waterline and topped by a foot of foam. Sure enough, there was plenty of firewood and straw, with branches floating on top of the water. The painter tried to stop Golden Dog from getting into the water, but he had already stripped and was rubbing mud over his groin. Then he pissed, drinking some from his scooped hands and rubbing some over his navel. Before his father could stop him, he slipped into the water and dragged over a pile of dried kindling, then went back for a branch just as a platoon of soldiers came into view. They were fighting men on their way back from Crossroads Township, armed with iron clubs and hammers, all mean and scary-looking. The painter, who spotted them from beneath the crag, trembled, but he was able to call Golden Dog back, and they huddled, perfectly still, between two rocks in the crag. The troops were above them, their ghostly reflections dancing on the water below as they argued about its depth. "Even if we take this son of a bitch back to White Rock Stockade, he won't come clean. I say we send him to meet his maker with a granite skull!"

"Why waste a bullet?" another said.

An argument erupted, followed, it seemed down below, by a scuffle. In the confusion, they heard some pitiful moans above them.

Finally someone appealed to the platoon leader. "We fought all last night on the western front, and lost three comrades-in-arms. For every one of us they kill, we should kill two of theirs. I say we take care of this son of a bitch now."

"Do what you want," the other man replied. "But not here. We don't want anyone from the Tian clan at Stream of Wandering Spirits to see."

"They can't see," someone said excitedly. "Let's throw him in the cooker."

The reflections in the water stirred, and something came flying over the crag. Golden Dog saw whatever it was hit the water and send up a column of water. As it floated on the surface, he could see a bulging burlap bag closed at the top. Instead of sinking right away, it swirled for a moment, then slowly settled into the water. The men on the crag looked down at the foamy water. "Spit in the water, everybody," someone said. "We don't want his spirit to come after us!"

Ptui, ptui, ptui, the sound of spitting, was followed by laughter as the men walked off. As soon as the reflections faded away, Golden Dog jumped up and looked at his father, who was wide-eyed, apparently dumbstruck. "Dad," he said, "I'm going to see what's in that bag." He dived into the water and swam straight to the bottom, where he touched the bag. Whatever was inside was kicking and felt soft and fleshy. Was it an animal or a person? He lifted it up, finding it very light, and swam with it toward the surface. At first the water was dark, but it gradually lightened, although it was still murky. Something was keeping him from breaking the surface. A ghost for sure, he was thinking. You goddamned ghost, he cursed inwardly, I'm dragging your corpse out of the water. *What are you trying to do, come back to life through my death?* His head bumped into something hard, and his arm felt as though it had been bitten. When he realized he'd risen against some wood floating on the surface, which he couldn't break through, he tied the mouth of the bag to his leg, stretched out horizontally, and began swimming away as fast as he could. He finally surfaced in the clear water at the foot of the crag and dragged the bag out of the water, which was ten times heavier than it had been. Finally he made it to one of the rocks.

"Why did you bring it up?" his father asked fretfully.

"I want to see what's inside."

"What do you *think*'s inside? When they fought at Seven Star Gorge, they dropped six into the cooker, all of them weighted down! Let's not get involved. He's dead. Toss him back into the water, and let's get out of here."

But Golden Dog opened the bag, grabbed hold of a corner, and dumped the contents onto the ground. It was a man, Tian Zhongzheng, Tian the Sixth's nephew, who served as assistant director of the Crossroads Township commune. Some time back the painter had had a dispute with the Tian clan over a private plot of land, and Tian Zhongzheng's ruling had been in favor of his own kin. The decision, which was not subject to appeal, incensed the painter, but he could only vilify the man behind his back. *Ptui! The assistant director of the commune doesn't even have the integrity to deal fairly with the people. He isn't qualified to be an official!* Naturally, whether he was in the good graces of a painter or not had no effect on his career, but from that time on the painter kept a respectful distance from him. Now Tian had been thrown into the cooker—a tough way to go. But he was dead, and that was that. It was time to clear out. As Golden Dog's father walked away, he addressed the official who had offended him: "Everybody has enemies, and everybody pays his debts. Go look for the men who did this to you! We dragged up your corpse, which is all the sympathy you deserve. You don't expect us to take you home, do you?"

"Dad," Golden Dog yelled, "he's still alive!"

This stunned the painter. He stumbled backward, then put his hand under Tian's nose to see if he was breathing. Yes, he detected some warm air. Father and son untied the rope and set to work rubbing the man's chest. Tian Zhongzheng gradually returned from the dead, his breathing grew stronger, and he coughed up a mouthful of water. Golden Dog quickly picked him up by his feet and bounced him up and down. More water. Tian's tiny eyes snapped open.

Tian Zhongzheng hid out beneath Awl Crag for the rest of the day. He was carried home secretly by his family in the middle of the night. Three days later another pitched battle at White Rock Stockade caused heavy losses on both sides, but everyone continued talking about the death of Tian Zhongzheng. His family fed the villagers' ideas by going to Awl Crag to offer wine sacrifices and throw spirit money into the Zhou River; then they put some of his clothes into a white varnish-wood coffin and buried it. On the day of the funeral, the villagers looked on as the grieving womenfolk walked by, wailing bitterly, in full-length mourning clothes, their heads and faces covered by hempen hoods. When they moved to the side of the road and parted their hoods slightly, they saw Golden Dog standing off in the distance, his eyes staring blankly, his jaw hanging slack. After a momentary pause in the wailing, they really let loose, and under their breath they whispered to the pallbearers to hurry the coffin to the graveyard.

That night, Golden Dog and his father were awakened in bed by a gentle knock at the door. Tian Zhongzheng's wife told them to light the lamp, while she covered the window with a sheet. Then she took three hundred yuan out of her bodice and placed it on the straw mat of the kang. "Worthy painter," she said, "worthy nephew Golden Dog, my husband owes his life to you. Everyone thinks he's dead, and now it's up to you and us to make sure things turn out all right."

Golden Dog's face darkened. "You must hold us in low esteem. If we saved his life, why would we do anything to harm him now?" The look on his face showed he felt he'd been insulted.

The embarrassed woman quickly explained herself, smoothing things over. The painter picked up the money, handed it back to her, and asked her to take a message to Tian Zhongzheng: Golden Dog and his father belong to neither faction; they use their mouths only for eating, not to spread idle talk. As for saving his life, what's done is done. We're not keeping it in our ledger that we saved his life, and he shouldn't keep it in his.

A year passed, and the fighting abated. As soon as everyone's weapons had been confiscated, Tian Zhongzheng came out of his basement, where he had been hiding all that time. His hair had turned white, and the skin on his face was as delicate and fair as a woman's. The people of Crossroads Township were beside themselves. How had he escaped death? they asked. He just smiled and said nothing. Golden Dog and his father kept quiet too. When, finally, peace returned to the area, Tian resumed office. Golden Dog, who had graduated from school and returned home, was the same old Golden Dog. He went into the mountains to collect firewood and down to the river to catch fish and turtles. But his father could no longer keep him from going out on the boats. When Golden Dog saw Tian Zhongzheng, if he had anything to say, he said it; if not, he just passed him by. He neither looked down on him nor put him on a pedestal, preferring to take the self-respecting, independent course.

One day, as Golden Dog and Han Wenju were roasting fish on the boat, the neatly dressed Tian walked up to the riverbank on his way to the commune. "How's your father?" he asked Golden Dog after boarding the ferry.

"He's fine."

Tian opened a foil-wrapped pack of cigarettes and handed one each to Golden Dog and Han Wenju. Golden Dog tucked his behind Han's ear. Han then passed out strips of the roasted fish and asked Tian, "How did the commune director's hair get so black?"

"I dyed it," Tian said.

"I doubt that," Han replied. "That's just how the world is: with all its twists and turns, no matter how topsy-turvy it gets, the chosen people continue to live on delicacies while little bastards like us still eat buckwheat noodles. After what you've been through, you're bound to have a bright future."

Tian Zhongzheng was won over by neither the strips of fish nor the flattery. He kept his eyes on Golden Dog. "How old are you, Golden Dog?" he asked.

"Sixteen."

"A boy of sixteen should know what getting married's all about. Who has your father got picked out for you?"

Golden Dog just shook his head. A pole had been erected on a boulder on the riverbank, and the boat slipped noisily out into the middle of the river on the cable fastened to it. Since it was dusk, the sun was setting into the river's lower reaches. As sky and water drew together, two red balls began to merge into a dazzling whole.

"Aiya!" Golden Dog exclaimed, "there really are two suns in the world!"

Three years later, in the winter, the call came for Golden Dog to join the army. He couldn't wait to join the fighting, his fear of dying having been supplanted by the dream of heroics. But he wound up in a place called Heavenly Waters, in Gansu province, where he cooled his heels for five years, starting out as a squad leader before being transferred to headquarters as a communications clerk. Since there were no battles to fight, he decided to seek admission to a military academy, hoping that someday he'd be a magnificent military officer. He was studying for the examination when the demobilization order came and he was discharged. In five years he'd seen a part of the outside world, but now he was back on the Zhou River where it all began.

But the Zhou River had changed.

The Zhou Prefecture almanac records that the source of the Zhou River is in Yang Family Channel, on the southern slope of the Qin Range, where there's a spring the size of a finger beneath a desiccated tree. Flowing into a riverbed that stretches far, the well has not dried up. Its output travels downward and picks up water along the way, through Shaanxi, Henan, and Hubei. At Hubei's Jun County it merges with the Han River to become a proud and mighty river. During the Ming and Qing dynasties, this long body of water was plied by commercial traffic from Xiangfan all the way to Zhou City, but the vicissitudes of the times produced changes and the river began to shrink as stone-paved highways on its banks widened. River traffic gradually disappeared.

When Golden Dog had left the area five years earlier, only shuttle boats, gander skiffs, ducktail skiffs, and loach skiffs plied the river; the banks of the upper reaches were well forested and accommodated several reservoirs. But as the quantity of water decreased, the ducktail skiffs from Purple Thistle Pass sailing up to White Rock Stockade began to go no farther. The only boat at Stream of Wandering Spirits was now the ferry manned by Han Wenju that crossed from one shore to the other. All the other boats were beached on the river's shoals, buffeted by the wind and baked by the sun as they rotted and lost their nails to children who sold them to the scrap-metal dealer.

People abandoned their lives on the Zhou River when they were given plots of land to work. Blessed with several years of good weather and plenty of rain, they produced harvests that brought a measure of stability to their lives. No one had lived here so peacefully, so contentedly for hundreds of years.

Golden Dog's father got even shorter as he aged. The Restless Hill Monastery, whose main worship hall had been destroyed during the Cultural Revolution, was rebuilt, and new icons were put in place. So the old painter climbed up onto the main beam and painted colorful designs. The quality of his painting was inferior, but an aura of solemnity surrounded his work. Every time he was overcome by the difficulty of his job, he gazed down at the Buddha, so serene, so dignified and majestic, and mumbled a prayer: Merciful Buddha, I'm painting this for you, so please look after Golden Dog, help him get married and start a career!

But Golden Dog remained a bachelor.

Everyone was concerned about Golden Dog's failure to wed—everyone but Golden Dog himself. His only anxiety was a lack of spending money. Once people solve the problem of necessities, they begin thinking about self-indulgences. All the young people learned to smoke, drink, buy pocketbooks, and hang out. Golden Dog's activities were no longer restricted to Restless Hill; in Stream of Wandering Spirits and Crossroads Township, he had plenty of friends with whom he went out nearly every night to drink and have a good time. They talked about good times and making lots of money, even discussed national affairs and things like the United Nations. Every few days they'd go to White Rock Stockade or Zhou City, totally neglecting their responsibilities. Once this became fashionable throughout the area, it affected all the villages on the banks of the Zhou River. Han Wenju, who lived at the ferry crossing, tapped Golden Dog on the head with his pipe and said, "Golden Dog, you rascal, you've turned all the young men around here into a pack of wild animals!"

"Uncle Han," Golden Dog defended himself, "you're getting old, and you don't have many years left. Do you want us to suffer through decades of poverty like you did?"

"How can you talk like that? Do you call this suffering? Back when we were sailing to Purple Thistle Pass . . ."

"I know," Golden Dog interrupted. "You spent all your money on that girl in the house at Purple Thistle Pass. So what good did it do you? Now you don't have a wife to warm your feet!"

Han Wenju wasn't upset by the comment. He looked over the side of the boat into the rapidly flowing water that was forming a line of eddies. He was thinking about the past and about the big-breasted girl. He laughed.

He looked up and spotted a girl walking gracefully toward them. The sun was shining on her face, and for Golden Dog the real sun ceased to exist, replaced by the sun that was her face, a sun with a nose and a pair of eyes that drew people toward it. "Water Girl," Han shouted, "come over and help your uncle chew out Golden Dog. The no-good cur is baring his fangs again."

Water Girl boarded the boat and opened the lunch basket she'd brought. In it were some noodles with cabbage and bean curd. "Uncle Golden Dog," she said, "how can somebody who's been a soldier abuse an old man?"

Golden Dog sniggered. He watched as she pulled the ferryboat for her uncle, two white, dainty hands on the cable, one over the other, making her bracelets tinkle. "Water Girl," he said, "all the girls in White Rock Stockade wear wristwatches, but you're still wearing bracelets."

"If Uncle Golden Dog thinks I'm backward, he can buy me a wristwatch." She laughed lightly.

Golden Dog teased her for calling him Uncle Golden Dog. Nearly every sentence had an *Uncle Golden Dog* in it, and it always made him laugh. Since her father had been born in an unlucky month, a fortuneteller had been brought in, who had told his mother that he'd enjoy peace only if he had godparents. Since it was customary to choose godparents on the day after the baby was born, early the next morning she carried him outside, vowing to ask the first people she met to be his godparents. Golden Dog's father, who was four years old at the time, happened to be walking his dog that morning. He met up with them, and from that day on, he was the godfather of Water Girl's father. But her parents died young, and owing to the difference in generations, she was expected to call Golden Dog *Uncle*. Like a dog atop a dung heap, he enjoyed his superior role.

When the boat reached the opposite shore, Golden Dog jumped

down. Water Girl looked at him with her fetching eyes and asked, "Where are you off to, Uncle Golden Dog?"

Seeing his reflection in her eyes, he said, "I'm off to White Rock Stockade. Can I get you something there?"

She took the bracelets off her wrist. "You can look up my granddad on South Street and have him take these to be polished. Tell him I'll be by later to clean and mend his winter clothes."

"Anything else?" Golden Dog asked her.

"No."

She blinked, and his tiny reflections disappeared. The pair of silver bracelets fell heavily from her hands. With a smile she straightened up and went back to her seat. Golden Dog gazed at the arches of her feet, like the nimble paws of a tiny animal. He didn't much like the curved openings of her white slippers.

Han Wenju pulled the ferryboat back to the shore it had left.

2

Water Girl was wearing white shoes made for her young husband.

After her parents had died, when she was still very young, she'd gone to live with Han Wenju, who, although blessed with the gift of gab, was a moody, timid man. As a youngster he'd passed up several chances to get married, and once his fortieth birthday was behind him, even though there were still opportunities, he had neither the vigor nor the desire to take a wife. He became a confirmed bachelor. Han loved Water Girl, hard liquor, his boat, and the pleasure of mercilessly teasing the women he ferried across the river. His sharp tongue, the center of his life, frequently got him into trouble when he went beyond the bounds of what was expected of a man his age. Arguing, especially with women, was what he did best, and the women liked him best when he went a bit too far. Water Girl was pleased with everything about her uncle except his freewheeling ways, his negligent attitude, and the fact that once he started drinking on the boat, he might not come home for days. So she grew up fast, like a horse that knows how to pull a cart without being trained. At the age of seven she could climb up on a stool and make noodles that were as thin as paper, and when her uncle went to the ferry landing carrying a bowlful of her threadlike noodles, he was the envy of all. People only had to praise Water Girl for him to get carried away and invite them to share a bottle. And once he started, he didn't quit until he was drunk, so that Water Girl had to go out in the middle of the night, lantern in hand, to bring him home, drunk as a lord. When Golden Dog joined the army, he went over in his new uniform to say good-bye to the Han family. Han Wenju took out a bottle, and the two of them started drinking. But before Golden Dog had a chance to get really drunk,

Han went off to bed, leaving the younger man to show off his uniform in his tipsy state. "Water Girl," he said, "since I'm going away, probably for years, how about making me some of your special noodles?"

"Since you're going out into the world, where you'll get to feast on delicacies, what makes you think my noodles are so special?"

"Whenever I eat your noodles, no matter where I am, even if it's the end of the earth, you'll be in my heart!"

"I'll be in your heart? I'll bet that once you spread your wings, you'll never return to Stream of Wandering Spirits!"

"I'm no heartless wolf."

"I still won't make them for you," she insisted.

But her resistance was all talk. She took out some dough and kneaded it until it was soft and springy. But instead of making noodles, she rolled out little round skins and made dumplings for him, putting a coin into the center of one. "You can't eat noodles before a long trip," she said, "since they'd keep your soul tied down and make you uneasy. But you can pop dumplings into your mouth to keep you safe and well. With hard work you could be like a young Tian or a young Gong!"

Pleased by her high opinion, he said, "A Tian or a Gong? Hmph. Don't compare me with the likes of them. Wait and see, I'll wear fine leather or nothing at all."

"Uncle Golden Dog, you have high aspirations. If you eat the dumpling with the coin inside, your wish will come true!"

So he ate three bowlfuls of dumplings without biting into a coin. Then he picked up a dumpling with his chopsticks and offered it to Water Girl, who immediately bit down on the coin.

Golden Dog's departure left Water Girl with no one to talk to, and Han Wenju with no one to run into town to buy liquor for him. Much of the joy went out of their lives. So Han went out and struck up a friendship with the abbot of Restless Hill Monastery, a wise man who not only knew the Buddhist scriptures by heart but was well versed in the ways of the world and skillful at telling fortunes. Seeing that Han was a literate man, he taught him the skill of divination from the *Book of Sixty-Four Diagrams*. Secure in his new knowledge, Han began taking even more liberties with the women he ferried across the river. By scrutinizing their expressions, he could, with the aid of his six ancient copper coins, tell their fortunes and predict their future, and the giggles they awarded him helped him pass the time with some contentment. Meanwhile Water Girl quietly matured in the grip of loneliness. Her arms began to flesh out, her skin grew fair, she developed a bust line and a lovely figure.

One day she carried food down to the boat for her uncle to eat in the shade while she moved the boat into the reeds along the bank and washed his clothes. Flowers were already in bloom on the tops of the reeds, beautiful pink blossoms waving in the wind. Just then someone called out from across the river for the ferryboat. It was a high-pitched call. Water Girl pulled the boat over to the other side. It was Tian Zhongzheng's niece, flashing a broad and bewitching smile, her neat white teeth gleaming in the sun's brightness.

Water Girl shouted with pleasure, "Aiya, it's Yingying! Aren't you lovely today!"

"Am I really? Then why haven't I been dragged off the street by a man? That's what I need, since I have an appetite that demands three square meals a day, one that craves bird's-nest soup while it's feasting on ginseng. And while I'm at it, maybe I'll take a bite out of his damned heart. I wonder what he'd say about that!"

With a laugh, Water Girl scolded Yingying for being so "sinful," then took her on board and pinched her playfully on the arm. "Are you going to White Rock Stockade? The men there will gobble you up the minute they lay eyes on you!"

"Ptui!" Yingying shot back. "Since we're classmates, you should know me better than that! I'm going into town to work in the co-op. Haven't you heard?"

She hadn't, and the news was very exciting. "You got a job?"

"I can't stay in the commune any longer," Yingying said. "I'll go crazy! This isn't much of a job, but at least I'll be inside, where it's cool. The next time you need some yardage, a nice piece of fabric, come see me. Don't go to anyone else. I'll be your back-door supplier. Look, Water Girl, what do you think of this jacket?"

"A little flashy for my tastes," Water Girl said.

"It's supposed to be flashy," Yingying protested. "You wear clothes for other people, not for yourself. Otherwise, who'd take any notice? Why don't you get one?" She took the jacket off and handed it to Water Girl, who tried it on. It fit perfectly. She walked up to the bow and looked at herself in the water, then quickly took it off. "I couldn't wear something like this outside. You're a worker now, but I'm still a peasant."

They chatted affectionately until they reached the shore. Yingying got off the boat, and as Water Girl watched her walking toward town along the path beside the river, she lowered her eyelids and a panicky emptiness gripped her heart. Morosely she pulled the boat back across to where her uncle, who had finished eating, was ready to board. "Is Yingying a worker now?" he asked.

"Um."

"No one in the Tian clan tends the fields anymore!"

Water Girl ignored his remark. Feeling lethargic beneath the hot sun, she sat in the bow and gazed out over the river, which was covered by a pale mist, like a blue flame, spreading farther and farther over the water, until it seemed to become a mirage. Glistening whitecaps seemed drawn to the boat, like a resplendent tide. But when the waves broke, they fell back to the same place.

A long sigh emerged from aft. Han Wenju fetched a bottle from the cabin. "Life's impossible to figure out," he said. "In school I was in the same class as Tian the Seventh. What did he learn there? He failed every test, and the teacher caned the palm of his hand so often it was usually swollen. 'This boy can't learn anything!' he used to say. So he left home, took up a gun, and joined the guerrillas, and we all laughed about how he'd never make anything of himself. But now, I operate a ferryboat while he . . ."

"Enough, Uncle, that's enough! How many times have I heard you say that!"

Han Wenju held his tongue and kept drinking. Presently he asked Water Girl to join him, but she didn't reply. Instead, she went into the cabin, leaving him alone.

Han sensed how unfair he was being to his niece. Stumbling into the cabin and sitting down beside her, he said, "Water Girl, if you won't drink, then neither will I. I know I'm useless and that I'm the reason you don't have what other girls have. But what am I supposed to do? One of these days I'll find you someone from a good family and you can enjoy a life as good as Yingying's!"

A bright red ball of fluff blown from the reeds on the shore stuck to Water Girl's braid like a little cloud. She reached out to grab it, but it floated away. She dropped her hand, and it floated down again. A glistening tear slid down her face. Resentment toward Uncle Han Wenju? Envy of Yingying? No, it didn't seem so. Just an empty feeling, a sense of unease. And now she'd made her uncle unhappy. She felt sorry for him. Getting to her feet, she smiled and said, "Uncle, you look like you have the itch to travel. What's wrong with what we have here? We have to play the cards we're dealt. I'm going home. Instead of going out drinking tonight, come home early, and I'll make you some noodles!"

Time passed, and Water Girl grew tall and lovely. She was as ripe as a soft persimmon. To the young men who saw her she was a goddess and, at the same time, a fetching little wild animal. The son of a cadre in the Gong clan from Stream of Wandering Spirits fell in love with her and shamelessly asked a matchmaker to approach her. The idea appealed to Han Wenju, who passed it on to Water Girl. But she wasn't pleased. *He may be from a well-to-do family, but he's not someone I respect. He's too frivolous!* She convinced Uncle Han, who showed his agreement by getting her engaged in the fall to a boy from Lowlands Hamlet seven li away.

This boy, a member of the Sun family, had been born in the year of the horse. Although he was a year younger and a head shorter than Water Girl, he was honest and sincere. After the *Book of Sixty-Four Diagrams* and the abbot from Restless Hill were consulted, the wedding was set for the twenty-third day of the intercalary month. Since Golden Dog was away, Water Girl asked his father to paint the phrases *Tree of Love* and *Mandarin Ducks* on walnut chests, as well as pictures of mountain watchdogs. On the twenty-second, her final night at home, she had a wedding party, the guest list for which included Grandpa Pockface, the blacksmith from White Rock Stockade. He was a notorious drunk, and when he and Han Wenju got together, they didn't stop until they were both as drunk as lords. Grandpa was still chattering away after Uncle Han had gone to bed, and when he saw Water Girl sitting at the window plucking her maiden hairs in front of a mirror, he remarked, "Just look at our Water Girl. With that jewel of a face, you'd swear she was an empress! That Sun family must have built up a lot of goodwill to be blessed with the gift of our Water Girl!"

She blushed. "Grandpa, you sure can talk when you're drunk!"

"You think I talk too much? Just wait till tomorrow, your wedding day. What chance will I have to get a word in edgewise then? Water Girl, brides always seem to cry when they get married. Why aren't you crying?"

"Grandpa!" Water Girl scolded him, as a couple of tears ran down her cheeks.

Why was she crying? Was she reluctant to leave her uncle? Or was it the boat itself she hated to leave? Or was she afraid of the boy with whom she'd be sharing her meals in the day and a pillow at night from now on? She didn't know him well enough to say what was good about him and what wasn't. Whatever the reason, her heart was troubled by an unhappiness she couldn't put into words, and even if she had been able to, it wouldn't have made any sense. She just felt like crying.

When Grandpa Pockface saw that she was weeping, he moved toward her to console her, but his legs were so shaky, his steps so staggering, that her tears quickly turned to laughter. "You'll fall!" she warned. "Be careful!" But her warning came too late. He crashed to the floor and was out, dead-drunk.

The twenty-third was a clear, beautiful day. At dawn, when the bridegroom, decked out in red, arrived, he fell to his knees in the dirt before the door, where he kowtowed to Grandpa Pockface and Han Wenju. To the sound of firecrackers, he then set out for home with his bride. Lei Dakong, Guan Fuyun, and some other of Han Wenju's young drinking buddies, who frequently kept him company on the boat, had somehow got their hands on three catties of gunpowder, a fuse, and a detonator, which they used to make a cherry bomb. They set it off in front of the door, rattling every window in Restless Hill, Stream of Wandering Spirits, and Crossroads Township. Anyone who stepped outside to see what had happened could spot Water Girl being carried down the road by a crowd of colorfully attired attendants, led by a band of musicians raising a racket with their woodwinds. The riverbank was covered with crisscrossing footprints. Water Girl was about to begin a new life as a housewife. Older women and their daughters-in-law stood there thinking back to when they'd made a similar trip, while maidens tried to imagine what their lives would be like when they made theirs. The life of a woman is a marvel: you leave this village to marry a man in another village, and someone else leaves that village to marry a man here; awaiting you are a four-by-six kang, a stone mill, and the toil of raising sons and daughters to continue the family line. Water Girl was carried to the ferryboat on the back of the bridegroom, so during the entire trip to the home of her husband's parents her feet never touched the ground. She was lifted up onto a flatbed cart waiting on the other side of the river, and from there they negotiated their difficult way down the bank heading toward Lowlands Hamlet. She looked back and waved to Uncle Han, to Grandpa Pockface, to Dakong, to Fuyun, to all the people who were seeing her off.

Han Wenju stood at the ferry landing wiping away tears of joy. According to local custom, a girl's family was not allowed to accompany her on the trip to her new home, and although Han was only her uncle, he was like a father to her. When the party disappeared beyond the shore, he said, "Water Girl's gone. Now she belongs to someone else." The melancholy in his heart appeared contagious, for Grandpa Pockface, Dakong, and Fuyun seemed to share his feelings. "Those are the ways of the world!" he said with a smile. "I guess I've done at least one good thing in my life!" He told Dakong and Fuyun to bring over some wine so they could sit in the boat and drink with old Pockface.

Water Girl made her bashful entrance at Lowlands Hamlet when the sun was already high in the sky. Her in-laws lived in a dilapidated house that had been whitewashed for the occasion. Red scrolls had been pasted on either side of the door, and homemade furniture of all sizes and of varying quality, including a wardrobe, a wooden cabinet, chairs, and stools, as well as Han Wenju's dowry of a chest, a brazier rack, a dressing table, and a washstand, was piled on the steps. Placed on top of the cabinet and chest were household necessities, like a comforter, sheets, blankets, pillowcases, and a variety of clothing. Local women stood around looking everything over. Suddenly, firecrackers went off, for the bride had arrived, and everyone gathered around to gawk. Water Girl was the center of attention and the object of a thousand wagging tongues. In her embarrassment she ran inside and climbed onto the kang, not knowing whether to be angry or to laugh or to cry or to make a show of defiance. The commotion continued until it was time for the banquet. As soon as the tables and chairs were in place, the guests sat down to eat and drink. By then, Water Girl had calmed herself enough to take in the surroundings. The ceiling had been newly covered with rushes; the walls were freshly papered with newspapers, though not very neatly. New Year's pictures were everywhere, mostly paintings of year-of-plenty cherubic little children astride golden fishes and pinups of beautiful movie stars. In the upper right-hand corner of each was written, "Wedding greetings to Water Girl and her young husband"; the names of four or five, sometimes seven or eight, well-wishers appeared in the upper left-hand corner. The calligraphy was atrocious, all black and uneven. She closed her eyes and unconsciously began to rub the bamboo mat that covered the kang. Is this where I'll do my sewing and mending for the rest of my days, she was thinking, the place where I'll raise my family? She had been born on a big kang, and she would have children of her own on a big kang. When she grew old and died, would she pass the kang on to the wives of her sons? As countless emotions flooded her heart and she let her thoughts wander, someone outside shouted, "He's passed out!" The woodwind music stopped and was replaced by the sound of hurried footsteps. Everyone in the room thronged outside. Then came the cries: Press the blood vessel under his nose! Hurry, bring him around! Get a bowl of warm baby piss. He'll revive as soon as you pour that down his throat!

What was going on? Water Girl, her heart beating wildly, followed the others outside, where she spotted the young bridegroom flat on his back in the middle of the compound, his eyes shut, his lips purple. He had been greeting the guests when all at once he felt dizzy. The buildings had begun moving round and round, the ground had risen up to meet him, and he'd keeled over. Water Girl gasped, and her legs gave out before she was completely out the door. When she lost her balance, she tumbled upon a wooden stool, knocking it straight into a big vat of bean curd, which spilled onto the ground. Amid all the confusion in the compound, someone dragged her back to the kang. Just then the clan chief brought a peach-tree switch, put a winnowing fan over the young bridegroom's head, and began whipping it. When a half hour later the young bridegroom still hadn't come to, someone took down a door, which they used to speed him to the village clinic. Water Girl trembled on the kang, frightened out of her wits. She began to sob and tried to go outside, but she was forced to stay put. Out in the compound, the clan chief said to her father-in-law, "This is strange, really strange. It must be an evil spirit!"

The father-in-law wailed, "What have I done to deserve this? Why me? Yesterday I burned spirit money for all our ancestors!"

"It's not your family's fault," the clan chief replied. "Chances are the bride is jinxed. Why else would the child take sick the minute she entered the house, and why did a good vat like that crash to the ground? We must exorcise this evil if we're to live peaceful lives again. Hurry up and put the bride on a donkey and make her ride around the village to expiate her sins!"

The father-in-law entered the house, followed by the other villagers, and told Water Girl how things stood. Offended, she demanded to know why she was being blamed, and refused to do as they asked.

"Look what's happened," her father-in-law said with tears in his eyes. "What do you think caused it? He's my son and your husband. Would you rather see him die than try to save him?"

What could she say? She began to wail.

The clan chief lost his temper and told them to drag her down off the kang. They bound her hands, put her on a donkey someone had brought, and rode her around the village. The backbone of the scrawny, shrilly braying donkey dug into her like a knife as the animal stumbled along. Four pairs of hands held her. She wept, she screamed, she called for her uncle, she called for her grandpa, she called for her mother. Several times she slid off the donkey's back, but each time she was lifted back on. A flower fell from her hair, her wedding clothes were ripped and torn.

The maid of honor, a timid woman who was the daughter-in-law of Old Seven, from Stream of Wandering Spirits, was in a state of utter consternation. As soon as Water Girl was lifted onto the donkey's back, she ran as fast as she could to the ferry landing, where Han Wenju was on his boat drinking. When he heard what had happened, the warm wine turned into a cold sweat. His highest hopes were dashed. Pockface the blacksmith, Dakong, and Fuyun met her account with a thundering rage and vowed to go immediately to Lowlands Hamlet to raise hell. But they had no sooner leaped to shore than Han stopped them. "There's nothing we can do," he said, "nothing. Water Girl has already entered their home, so she's a member of their family now. The people of Lowlands Hamlet have their doubts about her as it is. If we go over there and raise hell, she'll be a laughingstock!"

"Getting married shouldn't be like jumping into a fire!" Pockface bellowed. "Are we just going to stand by while they destroy our Water Girl?"

But Han blocked their way, weeping as he told the maid of honor to go back to the Sun home and try to protect Water Girl. Pockface the blacksmith could barely breathe. His body was wracked by cramps, his hands and feet had turned cold. Dakong and Fuyun were forced to lift him up and carry him back onto the boat, where they took turns rubbing his chest.

Water Girl cried all night long. When dawn broke the next morning, the day to begin her "home visit," the bridegroom was still at the clinic, an intravenous tube sticking in his arm. Her brother-in-law accompanied her back to Stream of Wandering Spirits, and the moment she laid eyes on her grandpa and her uncle, she collapsed into tears again. Feeling she had brought great shame home with her, she refused to see anyone and spent the full ten days in bed. The bridegroom's illness didn't break during those ten days. He lay in bed, delirious, his stool as liquid as his urine. Water Girl felt sorry for him, and since her marriage into his family was an accomplished fact, she returned to the Sun home, where she cared for him for a couple of weeks, feeding him broth, giving him his medication, helping him urinate and defecate, and telling him what a good wife she'd be after he was well. But it wasn't to be, for one day his eyes rolled up in his head and he was gone.

Dressed in funeral clothes, Water Girl threw herself on his grave and wailed. She was crying for her husband, and even more piteously for herself. After a hundred days she formally became a widow. The result of her unfortunate marriage was that she became known to others as an unlucky star. But now she could only swallow her tears.

When she returned to Stream of Wandering Spirits, she again passed the days with her uncle. Her onetime suitor from the Gong clan could smile at her expense. Once when Tian Zhongzheng was taking Han Wenju's ferryboat to Crossroads Township, he said, "I see that Water Girl's come home. Isn't the Sun family pestering you over that?"

"We've had a clean break with that family," Han Wenju answered, "so what can they pester us about? It's only Gong Maomao and his family who keep slandering Water Girl in the village!"

"They can get away with it because of Gong Baoshan," Tian said. "I've been thinking about this and I can't help feeling sorry for Water Girl. She can't just stay home forever . . ."

"Do you mean you'll find her a job?" Han was thinking back to the time Water Girl had accompanied Yingying on her way to work, and he was placing his hopes in Tian Zhongzheng.

"Finding a job these days isn't easy. But the commune is looking for a kitchen worker. It's a highly coveted job, but I've got half a mind to recommend Water Girl."

Greatly cheered, Han thanked him effusively, then went home to tell Water Girl. Three days later, dressed in freshly laundered clothes, she started work at the commune.

But she couldn't dispel her doubts. *Why are the Tians treating me so well when all the Gongs do is take advantage of me?* The truth became clear after she arrived at the commune. Back in the fall of 1952, Tian the Seventh had expected to be promoted to political commissar of the Zhou City military district. The order had already been sent down when he died suddenly of a liver disease. With his death the Tian clan lost its opportunity for high office, whereas the power of the Gong clan grew greater and greater. The two clans were soon at each other's throats. The Tians refused to give in to the Gongs, and the Gongs would do nothing that might bolster the Tians. Decades passed, but nothing changed, and Gong Baoshan was now in charge of Zhou City. Every member of his clan, young or old, had a position, but all the Tian clan could boast was the post of party secretary of

White Rock Stockade. Tian Zhongzheng was the nephew of Tian the Sixth and Tian the Seventh, but since his uncles had never married, he had served for all these years as assistant director of the Crossroads Township commune—always a bridesmaid, never a bride.

But though he was number two, he was not a man content to serve under someone else. Knowing that strength was the key to advancement, he frequently disparaged the party secretary and the commune director in front of Water Girl as she worked in the kitchen. But she didn't dare say a word to anyone.

Yingying came over to the commune often, always fashionably dressed, going without a jacket even in February and August. Under her bright red, high-collared sweater, her breasts jutted out high and full. And her hairdo was always so fancy that it created a sensation among the residents of Crossroads Township. But that didn't faze her. She did what she pleased, flirting with the young men and getting them to do all sorts of things for her, without ever repaying them by bestowing the slightest favor. In fact, she scorned them for being simpletons. She often dropped by Water Girl's room to talk up a storm and giggle, parading her femininity. She once asked, "How old are you, Water Girl, thirty-something?"

"You're twenty-three," Water Girl shot back, "and I'm two years older than you!"

"Then why make yourself look so old? Trying to act the widow? You're no widow, you're still an unplucked flower!"

"I have an old face," Water Girl replied.

"What do you mean, old? Your face is so moist you could squeeze water out of it. It's just that you don't make yourself up. Clothes on a person are like a saddle on a horse. If you made yourself up nice and sexy, you'd have plenty of suitors!"

Water Girl just smiled, blushing. Her smile was a way of saying she was no match for Yingying. What a person eats and wears is supposed to reflect her background, and being fetching wasn't in the stars for a girl like Water Girl.

"You probably think I come from a privileged background, don't you?" Yingying said. "Well, my father died young, and Mother and I had to rely on the kindness of my aunt and uncle. But the bad times just kept coming, because my aunt had a paralytic stroke. Just another unfortunate woman. During the Cultural Revolution, when Uncle was attacked, she was in perfect health and could take everything that came. Then when Uncle's position was restored, she had a stroke, and now she spends her time lying on her back, half-dead. When

Uncle and I weren't home, it was up to Mother to take care of things and look after Auntie as well. What horrible days! If I were you, I'd grab everything coming to me!"

Water Girl was aware that Tian Zhongzheng's wife was an invalid, but it never dawned on her that the Tian family could have troubles like everyone else, and she felt sympathy for Yingying's mother. "It must be hard on your mother, having to run the whole house like that. You ought to bring her to town for a little diversion once in a while."

"Mother comes in a lot," Yingying said as she took off the old sweater she was wearing and handed it to Water Girl, who refused the gift, although in her heart she was moved. I've always resented these cadre families, she was thinking, but everyone has a conscience and is born good. *All the prejudices I had toward these people stem from my own pettiness.* She began to treat Yingying like a sister and was more respectful toward Tian Zhongzheng.

On the twenty-eighth day of the intercalary month, a market day, after Water Girl had washed the breakfast dishes and while she was in the compound killing a chicken, Yingying's mother came to the commune. Water Girl smiled and said, "On your way to the market, Auntie? Why don't you come to town more often? Have you seen Yingying yet? I'll go find her for you."

Yingying's mother was a middle-aged woman who was still graceful and refined looking. She was wearing a short jacket with a light floral pattern that day and had a white jade comb in her hair. She tittered as she said, "Water Girl, you're such a clever little girl. Don't go looking for Yingying. I'm here to see her uncle. He hasn't been home for days!"

"Director Tian's a very busy man. He was just here in the compound. He's probably gone to the market. Since his door's open, why don't you go in and rest while I go find him?"

"You're too busy," Yingying's mother said. "I can't ask you to do that for me. I'll just wait for him inside."

Water Girl smiled and said, "Stay here through noontime, Auntie. I'm going to make some noodles in chicken broth and you can see what kind of a cook I am."

As Water Girl poured scalding water over the chicken to pluck it, then sliced it open and cleaned out the innards, she was thinking about how well preserved the woman was for someone who had so much to do around the house. She walked over to the building to pour a glass of tea for Yingying's mother, who was surprised to see that Water Girl was wearing white slippers. "Water Girl, are you still in mourning for the Sun family?"

Water Girl smiled, a heaviness suddenly gripping her heart.

"Why, Water Girl? That boy should have died long before, but he held on till you came along, you poor thing. You have nothing to remember him for. You're still young, and you should be thinking about your future."

Not knowing how to respond, Water Girl went back into the yard to finish cleaning the chicken, feeling very confused. The woman was right, but Water Girl had to be sorry for the young bridegroom. Besides, he'd died right after they were married. Something as unexpected as that had to be tied up with her fate. After she took the plucked and cleaned chicken into the kitchen, she came out and swept up the feathers in the yard. A strange thought came to her: Yingying's mother isn't past her prime, and she still looks wonderful, so why hasn't she remarried after all these years? Just then, Tian Zhongzheng walked into the yard with a slab of pork over his shoulder, followed by a mountaineer carrying a load of kindling. "Water Girl," he said, "why aren't you out doing your shopping? The price of meat in the market is really low!"

She went over to help the man put the kindling down on the steps. "We're a small family," she said. "Uncle bought a pig's head the other day and pickled it. That's all we need. You sure bought a lot of pork!"

"I've got a family of meat hounds!" he said. "I used to buy thirty catties, and it was gone by the fifteenth. Your uncle likes his wine, but good wine is hard to come by this year. If you want some, I'll give you a note so you can buy it."

"That would be wonderful. Thanks on behalf of Uncle! Oh, by the way, Auntie came over looking for you, but you were out."

"Auntie!" Tian Zhongzheng said. "Which Auntie?"

"Yingying's mother. She said you haven't been home for days."

"Where is she?" Tian asked. "Did she leave?"

"She's waiting for you inside."

He turned and walked to the house. Water Girl finished sweeping up the feathers, then went inside and put the chicken in the pot. When the water was boiling, she filled a vacuum bottle to take over to Tian Zhongzheng. But as she drew up to the house she noticed that the door and all the windows were shut. Just as she was about to call out, she heard a strange noise inside, then a muted woman's voice: "You're so damned eager, even in broad daylight . . ." Tian didn't reply, except for his panting. At first Water Girl didn't know what to make of this. Then all of a sudden, a chill ran up her spine. She turned and sped back to the kitchen, her heart pounding. She couldn't believe it;

maybe she only thought she had heard it. A little while later, Tian called to Water Girl to ask if there was boiled water to make a glass of tea. When she took the water over, the door and windows were wide open. Yingying's mother, flushed, was combing her hair before the mirror. A chill gripped Water Girl's heart. But without saying anything, she walked into the sun-drenched compound, where winter sparrows were raising a commotion from their perches in the eaves.

Water Girl didn't prepare noodles in chicken broth for lunch. Instead she sent the noodles over to the commune dining hall, complaining of an upset stomach, and returned to Stream of Wandering Spirits in midafternoon. That night she told her uncle she wasn't going to cook at the commune anymore. Not knowing what to make of that, he asked if she was just tired or if someone had taken advantage of her. So she told him. What else could she do?

"They're worse than dogs or pigs!" Han spit out. He added, "That man doesn't know the meaning of the word *morality,* and sooner or later he'll get his just deserts. But if you don't go back, he'll assume you know what they were up to and he'll wait for an opportunity to make us wear tight shoes. So you'd better go back. Just pretend nothing happened, and you and I can keep on living our lives the way we want to!"

She went back to the commune and worked as always, except that now she treated Tian indifferently, keeping a proper distance. When the party secretary or the commune director complained about him, her part was to remain aloof and composed though every word pained her.

Then March arrived and Tian's wife died suddenly. It wasn't much of a funeral, and since Tian and his wife had no children, Yingying smashed the mourning bowl. Yingying's mother wailed as though her heart had broken, and everyone in the village sighed over the closeness of the two sisters-in-law, commenting on the virtue of the surviving woman. Han Wenju, drunk on his boat again, grumbled, "Virtue's right. She took over *all* the duties of her paralyzed sister-in-law!"

Soon afterward, the government decreed that agricultural villages were to institute a system of individual job responsibility, which caused as much excitement as the 1958 reversion of the land to public ownership. Within a month, all the land along the Zhou River had been parceled out. Then the commune was disbanded and the settlement converted to a township government. Tian Zhongzheng's position was changed from commune director to township chief—assistant, of course. Stream of Wandering Spirits had been a production brigade, but once the land was parceled out, not all of the eighteen public buildings were needed, and since it wasn't considered acceptable to leave some of them vacant, the decision was made to sell off four of them, at 50 percent of their value, even though they were only three years old. The villagers, who couldn't wait to get their hands on them, sent in bids. But Tian Zhongzheng announced that he planned to buy them, and the last thing anyone desired was to go up against him. So they suppressed their excitement and said, If the Tian clan wants them, let them have them; at least we'll share in the profits. Tian bought the buildings all right, but he didn't pay cash. He said he was good for it, and gave an IOU as security. He tore the houses down straight off for lumber and had the brigade lay the foundation of a four-room house right next to his own; then he began to build. Naturally, there were grumblings, and some villagers were quite vocal in their complaints. Old Seven had wanted to buy a building, but though he was angry, he merely sighed over his powerlessness and went to the ferry landing with a bottle of wine to share with Han Wenju. There he ran into Lei Dakong, who was so infuriated that he cursed Tian Zhongzheng's mother and swore he was going to file a formal complaint. Han, by then drunk, told the others about Tian's adultery, and the next day Lei Dakong went to the township government office, where he filed a complaint with the party secretary, who, along with the commune director, held a grudge against Tian and had long endured the lack of evidence against him. They embellished upon Lei Dakong's complaint as best they could and sent it up to the county committee, at the same time spreading the word throughout Crossroads Township. The talk was about nothing else, and before long it was the rare villager who didn't know all about Tian Zhongzheng's sordid behavior.

But Han Wenju began to regret his indiscretion and complained to Lei Dakong: "You can't get anything done if you don't hold your tongue." Anticipating the worst, he had Water Girl quit her job, and the two of them spent one uneasy day after another at the ferry landing. When Golden Dog was discharged and came home, he tried to hearten them, and eventually they came close once again to a normal life.

3

After Tian Zhongzheng demolished the four public buildings, a half-dozen carpenters and stonemasons worked daily on the new foundation and building next to his old home. Naturally, there were plenty of volunteers to dynamite the stone faces along the banks of the Zhou River to supply the necessary building stones, which were chiseled into rectangular slabs, cleaned, and hauled to the building site by donkeys. Tian Yishen, a production manager for the county government, managed to appropriate twenty sacks of cement and eight hundred catties of lime; he also showed up nearly every day to supervise the construction, comporting himself as conscientiously as if it had been his own house that was going up. On the morning of the seventh, after a string of firecrackers was set off, it was time to put up the roofbeam. Members of the Tian clan and friends from far and near came to offer their good wishes. Some brought money, some brought grain offerings, and some brought congratulatory scrolls to hang in the main room. As for the villagers, they observed what others had brought and went out and purchased the same things in order not to call attention to themselves. Those who had nothing to give rolled up their sleeves and went to work, smiling and flattering everyone they saw. But too many cooks spoil the broth, and although they were easily able to fit the small end of the beam in, the other end, which was a foot and a half thick and extraordinarily heavy, was beyond their ability. Fortunately for them, Fuyun, who was gleaning manure at the village entrance, was slow in getting away. "Fuyun," they yelled, "taking it easy again, hmm? Aren't you going to pitch in and help Commune Leader Tian? Come over here! We can put your talents to use!"

Fuyun just stood there for a while; finally he walked over. Orphaned as a small child, he was an ugly man, stronger than most, and still unmarried at the age of thirty, so that there was no one at home to mend the tattered crotch of his trousers. Noticing that morning that everyone had headed over to the Tians', and having nothing himself to offer, he hadn't felt like joining the crowd and lending a hand. Feigning unawareness of the events, he'd gone out early with his basket to glean manure and never expected to be hailed. But now that they'd caught him, he quickly took the offensive by complaining that Yingying's mother hadn't asked him over. But he suffered the taunts of the others over this excuse: Aren't you afraid your pride will get you into trouble? Where do you get off expecting a personal invitation? That shut him up, so he took off his shirt, tied it around his neck, and put his shoulder to the beam. With grunts and yelps of exertion, he lifted the beam into place, then stood with a smug look on his face: "Where do I get off? By putting the beam in place, that's where!"

Tian Zhongzheng had one of the men climb up onto the beam to tie a yellow "auspicious sign" and a piece of red silk around it, then set off a string of firecrackers and throw down "beam eggs." Since Tian Zhongzheng was forty-five that year, he had forty-five beam eggs prepared, filled with walnuts, dates, small coins, and pebbles, and when they hit the ground, he stood laughing heartily as the children scrambled for the treats. But extreme joy often precedes sorrow. Yingying's mother ran to him in agitation and whispered something in his ear while he was still doubled up with laughter. If only he'd ignored her, everything would have been just fine. But he didn't. His face paled as he rushed into the house. She forced a smile and said to the group, "The beam's in place, for which we have the labors of our friends and neighbors to thank. I was going to prepare some drinks for everybody, but because of what has come up unexpectedly for Yingying's uncle, we'll have to thank you later!"

The stunned looks showed how disappointed the people were, but since their host wasn't going to regale them, all they could do was grouse, "The more money people have, the stingier they get," and head home.

When Tian entered his house, Cai Da'an, the credit manager of the co-op, was sitting beside the octagonal table in the living room. "Director," he said, "there's trouble. This morning as the sun was coming up I went to the township government compound latrine to shit. It was pitch black inside. While I was squatting there, the party secretary and commune director came in to piss, and believing the latrine empty, they started to talk. 'How come we haven't had any news on the report we sent up to the party discipline committee? Has it been suppressed again?' one of them said. The other one answered, 'Well, Tian Zhongzheng can manage to get land for a new house without paying for it and appropriate public materials for his personal use. That's part of it. Then there's the matter of his affair with his sister-in-law, and you can't expect the discipline committee to remain indifferent to something as serious as that, can you?' They finished and walked out. Now, I don't know the details, but things don't look good. Since I wasn't sure you knew, I came over to tell you!"

"This is terrible," Tian said. "Those two won't be happy till I'm dead and buried. Instead of reporting to the county committee, they went straight to the party discipline committee!"

He leaned back in his chair, closed his eyes, and sat there brooding. Cai Da'an, who didn't know what to do, kept glancing at Tian and wringing his hands. With Tian sitting there motionless, Yingying's mother ran sobbing to her room. Tian's mind was confused and uneasy. "What the hell are you crying about?" he bellowed. "You're going to drive me crazy!"

Her voice came from the bedroom: "You call yourself a man? You may talk tough, but at the first sign of trouble you turn to jelly! Now someone's riding your back, and maybe tomorrow they'll be rubbing their rear ends on your nose!"

Ignoring the insult, Tian sat impassively. Suddenly he turned to Cai and said, "I want you to go to White Rock Stockade this afternoon and report what you heard to Secretary Tian of the county committee. But first go to the market and pick up ten catties of wood-ear fungus, ten catties of day lily, and four bottles of Western Phoenix wine. Don't let anybody see you. Understand?"

Cai nodded, but as he headed for the door, Tian detained him. He shouted toward the bedroom, "You haven't used those three pieces of ginseng root, have you?"

"The manager of the agricultural instruments plant gave them to me for my arthritis," Yingying's mother objected.

"I'll get you some more later," Tian promised. "Give them to me. I need them *now!*"

She brought the three roots of ginseng and handed them over without a murmur. Cai cast a hesitant glance at Tian, who waved him off. Clutching the ginseng to his chest, Cai fled through the door. Since this was no time to dawdle, he raced to White Rock Stockade as soon as he'd made his purchases, which he carried in a pack thrown over his back so that no one would know he came bearing gifts. By the time he reached town, however, he was hungry and thirsty, so he bolted down a plate of chilled noodles, then bought some chives, which he added to the backpack, and headed for Secretary Tian's home.

Secretary Tian Youshan was, in a roundabout way, related to Tian Zhongzheng, as a member of Tian the Sixth's family. He was the highest ranking official in the Tian clan, and all his immediate family worked in White Rock Stockade or Zhou City; none lived in Stream of Wandering Spirits. But his relationship with Tian Zhongzheng had always been excellent. On this particular day, he had just watered the flowers and steeped some tea, which he was sipping as he gazed contentedly out the window at the new blossoms on his Chinese rose trees. In recent years he had grown so fond of his garden that he wouldn't let anyone else set foot in it. Before that, he had hung out a sign: For viewing only, no picking allowed. He sat there admiring his roses, then lowered his head, removed the lid of his teacup, and gently blew the steam off the top. That was when he noticed someone beyond the garden craning his neck to look in. "Who's there?" he demanded.

Cai Da'an, who was wondering how he'd get to see Secretary Tian, was brought up short by the question. Too timid to respond at first, he dropped his hands and stood rooted to the spot when he noticed Secretary Tian standing at the window. "It's me," he said with an embarrassed laugh. "I've come to see you, Secretary Tian."

"Is it official business?" Tian wanted to know. "If it is, take it to the office in town. They'll handle it for you."

"It's not official business, Secretary Tian," Cai said. "It's personal. Tian Zhongzheng has sent me from Crossroads Township to talk to you."

Tian looked at Cai for a moment before saying, "Well, come in."

No sooner was Cai in the door than he removed the pack from his back and laid it on the floor. Because of the heat outside he was covered with sweat, and even though it was cool in the house, the moment he laid eyes on Secretary Tian he began to sweat again. Tian Youshan offered to pour tea, but Cai said he could pour it himself. And he did, drinking it in one gulp before sitting down on the sofa. It was a big sofa, but Cai sat on the edge as straight as he could.

"No need to be so formal," Tian said. "You're in my home. I told you to go to the office if it's business because those were the orders I gave the members of the county committee. We're involved in the business of reforms these days, and it's an uphill struggle! When you're trying to implement reforms, what one person approves of, someone else doesn't. So in order to guarantee the smooth implementation of the reform work, I refuse to allow any interference. Business is to be conducted at the office, and I keep tabs through the office manager. Now what did Tian Zhongzheng send you here for? How's everything at Crossroads Township?"

Cai had no idea how to broach the subject, since he was there to grease the skids and the other man was an unknown quantity to him. He beat around the bush, his eyes fixed on Tian as he steered the conversation around to the purpose of his visit. As he'd feared, Tian's face clouded. "Out with it!" he said. "Stop mumbling, and get to the point!"

So Cai told him everything, trusting that Secretary Tian was a patient, reasonable man and that his mission would be eased. The last thing he expected was for Tian Youshan to show his temper. "I know all about Tian Zhongzheng's affairs," he said. "It makes my blood boil, and it hurts me! A member of the Communist party, especially a leading cadre at the township level, who doesn't lead the masses in working for reform and tries to enrich himself is abusing his office. Tian Zhongzheng blithely carries on his sordid affairs, even in the present climate, which shows how low he's fallen! Now someone's lodged a complaint against him, and it's stuck. This ought to have brought him to his senses. But instead he panics and sends you here. Why didn't he come himself? He's my own kin, you know, but if he came, I'd chew him out good and ask him if he knew of a single other member of the entire Tian clan who acts like he does. Go back and tell him that Tian Youshan may be his uncle, but first and foremost he's the county party secretary. Instead of trying to engineer connections, he should be correcting his mistakes and taking to heart the lessons he's learned. And he ought to make a clear distinction between what he should and shouldn't be doing. Now get out!"

Cai's heart sank. What could he say? He glanced at the pack, not daring to reveal what it contained and loath to pick it up and take it away. Then he had an idea: pretending he'd forgotten about it, he said good-bye and walked out the door; then as he skirted the garden, he quickened his pace in case Tian Youshan discovered the pack and tried to call him back.

As soon as Cai returned, he gave Tian Zhongzheng an account of what had happened. Tian moped and stewed for the longest time, sigh followed sigh, and tears appeared on his face. Complaining of ill health, he stopped going to work, and holed up at his home in Stream of Wandering Spirits. The construction of his new four-room house came to a halt. The villagers spread the word that Tian's grave error might cost him his official position. But ten days later there was still no action against him, then two weeks. The party secretary and the commune director of Crossroads Township, knowing the truth that "the longer the night, the more plentiful the dreams," went to White Rock Stockade to check with the county committee. They were told only that the issue would be resolved soon. Armed with that assurance, they returned to the village and ignored Tian. They paid a single visit to Stream of Wandering Spirits to check on his health, then assumed management of all the affairs of government for the village. The new arrangement had a positive effect on the mood of Han Wenju, who began spending more time with Golden Dog and Lei Dakong.

As the last of the snow melted and the profusion of brilliant peach blossoms announced the arrival of spring, the villagers were lighthearted as never before. Individual plots of land were distributed to be tended as the people decided, free of the coercive influence of the Gong and Tian clans. No longer did the villagers have to work like slaves only to see their harvests wind up in the hands of the Gongs and Tians. And even though they refused to kick Tian Zhongzheng while he was down, they derived considerable satisfaction from watching him sweat.

With the people free to live as they pleased and to make their own livelihood, tears began to appear in the fabric of village life. The older generation tilled their small plots in accordance with the ideals of an earlier age—of the fifties. They planted peppers and garlic so they'd have enough to eat, and tobacco so they'd have a box of leaves for guests to smoke when they dropped in. For money for the essentials they had to buy—oil, salt, soy sauce, and vinegar—they relied upon their trips up the mountain, where they cut down branches to be woven into baskets, or alpine rushes to be plaited and woven into sandals, which they sold to shops in Crossroads Township. It was an austere but stable life. But the younger generation began to take risks on the Zhou River. For years the boats had been left on the banks to rot, so they went up onto the mountain, cut down cypress trees, and carried them back to the riverbank to build new boats. Of course, these boats were smaller than the old ones, but they were sturdier, and it was easy to sail the forty li of the river just below Crossroads Township loaded with salable goods. In three days and nights on the Zhou River they could sail all the way down to Purple Thistle Pass, where the old boatmen used to go, even as far as Xiangfan, and make a tidy profit.

It was Golden Dog who started it all.

First, he shaved his head, leaving two whorls of hair on the top: "A man with two whorls tears down his house and sells the bricks." Golden Dog was no spendthrift, and he wasn't made for a life of leisure. The first skiff was finished, then the tenth, then the twentieth, and the young men, hooting and hollering, sailed down the river in a line, filling the air with their shouts. The older boatmen stood and watched them, thinking back to when they were that age and sighing over the loss of their youth. Several days later the boats returned, filled to the gunwales with sacks of tobacco from Xiangfan and white hemp from Purple Thistle Pass. Crowds were on hand to greet them. Yingying's mother, who was in reduced circumstances because of Tian Zhongzheng's fall from favor, put on the best face she could as she dumped a bucket of chicken feathers and eggshells out on the riverbank, and bantered, "Golden Dog, you're in the money again! The world sure belongs to you fellows these days!"

"Do you want to go along?" he asked her. "We'll form a partnership. You won't have to pay any shipping charges, and we'll split the profits down the middle!" There was a twinkle in his eye. The sarcasm was obvious.

Her silence showed her sorrow. She looked at the river and said, "The Tian clan started out as boatmen, and we lost a dozen gander skiffs in a hail of gunfire . . ."

"No need for them anymore," Golden Dog replied. "The fight's over, and now we're in charge."

"In charge of what?" she fired back. "When the Tians were making revolution, we were up in the mountains holding sway, even though some of our heads hung on the city wall. But now somebody else occupies the statehouse!"

Golden Dog looked at her with disgust, but he was in no mood to be upset for long. Without knowing why, he pointed his finger like a pistol and made a loud popping noise that confused the woman. "Then it's our own damned fault we're a bunch of peasants!" he said. "Tian the Sixth was the one who set your clan up. Well, we boatmen have to take out of the dragon's mouth what we can get, and that's all the more reason for us to become rich!"

As soon as the words were out, his low spirits returned. It was a shame he'd been born too late to join the fighting. Eager to wield a sword and leap into the flames of battle, he'd spent five years in the army, only to return to ply a boat on the Zhou River. And then, on top of it all, he had to contend with the envy of others!

His temper was up, and it was time to get even. "How come you stopped work on your new house? Labor shortage?"

"We were planning to move in during harvesttime . . . Then Yingying's uncle took sick. What's the hurry, anyway? The beams are in place, well out of the reach of thieves!"

With that, she turned and headed back. Golden Dog's ill-feeling had begun to subside, so he picked up a bottle and headed off to drink with Han Wenju. They drank until nightfall, when they were joined by Dakong and Fuyun, who brought two more bottles with them. Dakong dragged them over to his place to continue the drinking. He invited Water Girl along too, tempting her with some pickled pig's intestine and pig's heart to go with the wine. When the five of them were well into their spirited drinking bout, Cai Da'an knocked on the door—*banged* on it is more like it. To Dakong, who went to answer the knock, Cai said, "Secretary Tian sent me to ask you to come help him work on his new house tomorrow. Are Golden Dog and Fuyun here? Pass the word to them, will you?"

"Which Secretary Tian?" Fuyun called. "Tian Youshan?"

"No, Tian Zhongzheng!" Cai replied. "A directive came down from the county committee this afternoon. The township secretary has been transferred to the county seat. It's supposed to be a good move for him, since he's been made director of the county drama troupe! Like they say, 'If you want to let off steam, put on a play!' Yes, a good move for him. Tian Zhongzheng has been appointed acting party secretary. You know what the word *acting* implies these days, don't you?"

Dakong, whose head was spinning, didn't hear the rest of Cai Da'an's message. "I'm not going!" he bellowed.

Cai was stunned. "Dakong! Not you!"

"What about me? Let him be party secretary, and I'll keep being a common villager. If I went, it would be as a favor. And if I don't go, so what!"

Han Wenju, Golden Dog, and the others who overheard the conversation were in a deep, silent funk. Han sighed. "This world," he said, "this world . . . Ai, you might as well bow your head when the time comes. Golden Dog, go out and try to talk some sense into Dakong. You fellows had better go tomorrow."

"And should we take an offering of meat along with us?" Golden Dog asked him.

Han shook his head and morosely stepped outside. He invited Cai in for a drink and something to eat, but Cai begged off. Han took

Dakong by the arm and pulled him away. "Old Cai, Dakong's had a bit too much to drink, so forget what he said. It's just that this business about Secretary Tian's house came as a surprise. Dakong, Golden Dog, and Fuyun are supposed to go to White Rock Stockade tomorrow to pick up some nails they ordered for the boats, and it's too late to reschedule. I'll go over and help out tomorrow." It took some doing, but he managed to defuse the situation.

When Han Wenju arrived the next day, there were plenty of people there already, including the short painter. As soon as their eyes met, they smirked so broadly their faces looked like wrinkled walnuts. Since they didn't feel like being part of the crowd, they went to lend a hand at the brickyard behind Restless Hill, where there were stacks of tiles intended for the roof. Han and the painter went into the kiln and started carrying out tiles, and in no time at all became so filthy they looked more like clay figures than men. At noon, when Tian Zhongzheng told everyone to knock off for lunch, they hurried to the village, where the Tians had set up eight tables. When everyone was seated, Tian waved a wine bottle and urged everyone to drink heartily. "I see a couple of oldtimers have come over to help out. How can I show my appreciation? Yingying's mother, bring a basin of water for them to wash up!"

"That's okay," Han said. "We're going back to the kiln this afternoon, so we'll stay as we are."

"Wash up," the woman urged them. "I brought some soap."

After a couple of swipes, Han said, "With a face as dark as mine, I couldn't scrape it clean with a knife!"

Someone sitting nearby piped up, "One visit to the kiln, and I'll bet Wenju's piss will be black for three years!" Embarrassed, Han blushed to his roots and sat down at the table, his head lowered.

Tian Zhongzheng went from table to table refilling glasses, and when he reached Han Wenju and the painter he said with a laugh, "I see Golden Dog didn't come today. Is he out on his boat?"

The painter flinched. "He went to White Rock Stockade to pick up some nails for the boats. He wanted to come . . ."

Tian laughed. "Not to worry. That Golden Dog of yours is no ordinary fellow. One of these days he's going to make a lot of money from his work on the river. I wouldn't be surprised if you started building your own house next year!"

"He's a wild young thing," the painter said. "He can't stick to anything."

Tian turned serious as he refilled Han Wenju's glass. "You shouldn't sell people short. Who knows when his day will come? Look at me. I spent half my life knocking around, ripe for the picking by anyone who wanted to bring false charges against me. But I landed on my feet. Isn't that right, Wenju?"

For a moment, Han was flustered. Deep down he was thinking about all the people Tian had victimized, and he was fuming. Since Tian knew it was Water Girl who had reported him, what was his game in asking a question like that? Han wanted to kick himself for having come to help, but it was his own fault: no one had forced him.

He summoned a weak grin, then sneezed loudly and rubbed his nose to wipe away the awkwardness of the situation.

Golden Dog and his friends returned from White Rock Stockade that night and reported that the town was buzzing over the way the leadership ranks in Crossroads Township were being shaken up, and that it was all Tian Youshan's doing. The old traitor had come across as lily-white when he reproached Tian Zhongzheng in his conversation with Cai Da'an. But then he'd slipped over to the county committee and put pressure on them to reinstate Tian Zhongzheng, actually to promote him, which effectively handed all Crossroads Township over to him. Han Wenju couldn't have been more despondent, but he swallowed his pride and counseled Golden Dog and the others to put in an appearance the next day, bowing to the powers that be by giving a good day's service to the Tians. Dakong went home to get some sleep, taking a bellyful of anger with him. Water Girl also lost heart, for now that Tian Zhongzheng was back in power, he'd surely find a way to settle accounts with her. She decided to go to White Rock Stockade and help her grandfather, the blacksmith, with his bellows. But Golden Dog, who was more inflexible than ever, refused to go. In fact, early the next morning, he walked smartly past the Tians' house, loudly singing about how he was on his way to the Zhou River to set out in his boat.

Five days later, the new house stood there proudly and it was time for the painter to apply his skills. He went inside and began painting the walls white and blue. Golden Dog's boat plied the river, attracting the attention of the younger men, and before long the river was again bustling.

As the level of the Zhou River lowered, its borders expanded, and even though the stretch from Stream of Wandering Spirits to White Rock Stockade was still navigable, a trip from White Rock Stockade to Purple Thistle Pass, a distance of 170 kilometers, meant having to sail past Leather Bowl Shoals, Sheepskin Pass Shoals, Yellow Dragon-tail Shoals, Black Dragon Shoals, Hand Strip Shoals, a total of forty-six rocky shoals in all. Five out of ten trips ended in failure. The boats cracked up on the dark cliffs, and the boatmen who saw trouble coming and had quick reflexes scampered up the cliff at the moment of impact and held on to a rock or a thistle tree for dear life. Those with slower reflexes and, even worse, those who placed more value on their cargo than on their lives and were determined to keep their boats moving ahead found that as soon as the planks wrenched upward, their own limbs followed. And even if they managed to escape destruction on the doomed boat, they were welcomed by the turbulent waters below, swirling in countless eddies, where they were churned as though they'd fallen into a grinder and twisted and wedged between rocks to feed the fish and shrimp for eternity.

Within six months, eight of the new skiffs had been destroyed, and this was a powerful brake on the boldness of the people who lived on the banks of the Zhou River.

And yet, every successful trip was financially rewarding, so there was a strong incentive among the younger men to take their chances. They were fatalists: if it was your turn to go, there was no avoiding it, and if it wasn't, then you had nothing to worry about. "In this world, the brave eat themselves to death, while the cowardly check out hungry." Those who struck it rich came to the ferry landing with packages filled with meat and crocks brimming with wine, dressed their children in brand-new clothes, and shouted for Han Wenju, the rascally Dakong of the Lei family, and members of the Tian clan to come to their homes for drinking contests. They'd drink themselves senseless, until the floor was nearly covered with sleeping bodies, bringing the party to an end. Fuyun was always invited, for even though he wasn't much of a drinker, he enjoyed being part of the group. Instead of sitting at the table, he'd stand off to the side and make sure the glasses were full, and whenever someone tried to cheat in one of the competitions, he was judge and jury. If the cheater couldn't drink another drop, Fuyun would drink the penalty for him. Then once the roosters had crowed three times and it was time for the drunken guests to head home, there were shouts in the darkness: "Fuyun, help me up! Fuyun, where the fuck are you? If you don't carry me home, I'll roll into the river!"

By the time he'd managed to get all the drunks safely home, the sun would be up.

But it was different after the boats set out under the gaze of parents, wives, and children on the shore. For the next three or four days, quiet would reign in the village, and all you could hear were the barks of dogs resonating down the lanes and bouncing from walls as though emerging from deep vats. Then one day, as the sun was setting over the mountains, the first boat would sail into view and the villagers would rush to the ferry landing to pick the particular boat they were waiting for out of the haze. When the family saw it, they'd run to the water's edge. But the boatmen wouldn't say much. They'd just walk up to a woman waiting for her man and say something in a low voice. She'd begin to wail, maybe writhe on the ground, while others helped carry her home or, picking up a door panel and a grass mat, climbed into the boat and headed downriver. And a white rooster with its feet bound always shared the boat with them, flapping its wings in the dusk. By the time a freshly painted coffin was carried up the mountain behind the village, the sky would be ready to release its rain. People who died in the river were always carried up the mountain to be buried. No one knew the origins of that custom among Zhou River inhabitants, but most people assumed it had something to do with the wishes of the deceased: their death created a hatred for the water, for they knew its evils, and they never wanted to touch it again. The path up the mountain was steep, the going particularly treacherous by reason of the falling rain, and sometimes it took the pallbearers ten or twenty minutes to negotiate even a slight rise. That's when the calls for help commenced: "Fuyun, how'd you like to join the funeral banquet? Come here and hold up the front end! Fuyun, don't waste that strength of yours. Come up here!"

So Fuyun would hoist up the front end of the coffin and, gritting his teeth, help carry it to the grave site.

When the burial was completed, the people would say, as though having laid down a great burden, That's that! Utterly exhausted and utterly relieved, they'd return home for the funeral banquet—usually ground corn and pickled cabbage in a sticky soup, with plenty of wine—before lying down and sleeping through the night. In the morning the boats would set out again, short one of their previous crew but with a new man taking the dead one's place. There'd be plenty of spirit money tossed into the river by the surviving boatmen, most of them already talking about the new widow: how young she was; how, even though she already had children, she wouldn't be a widow for long; how sooner or later she'd be taken into another home.

The boatmen included Old Seven, an elderly fellow still young in spirit. He came up to Golden Dog after one of the river deaths and said, "Golden Dog, that's some young widow there. A nice round ass like that, just right for having a few more babies. Wouldn't it be wonderful if you took her home with you!"

"Age has really caught up with Old Seven," one of the other boatmen said. "His eyes are shot and his nose doesn't work anymore. Golden Dog's already hunted one down."

"Who is it?" Uncle Maozi asked. Golden Dog ignored him.

"You've got a mouth, Old Seven," someone said. "Go over to White Rock Stockade and ask Pockface Zhang, the blacksmith. I guarantee he'll heat up a pot of wine and share it with you!"

"You mean it's Water Girl?" Old Seven asked. "Now there's a tender little morsel!"

Golden Dog said, "Old Seven, you talk too much. There's wine down in the cabin if that's what you want. Water Girl calls me Uncle, so don't start stirring things up."

Old Seven laughed heartily as he walked into the cabin for the wine, and he set out to do some serious drinking. In between swigs he said, "What's this Uncle crap? What gives you the right to call yourself her uncle? Her father died young, long before you had any chance to be related to him." He tried to stand up, but his eyes clouded, his legs turned rubbery, and he nearly fell into the water. "Damn you! I tied the ropes around your coffin, so what do you want from me? You want me to take your place? Don't blame me because you died young. I've been on the Zhou River for forty years, and I'm still around!" He mumbled on before going back to the cabin to lie down and fall fast asleep.

This gang of men who skated at the edge of life suffered plenty of hardships, but they also knew how to enjoy themselves. Every time their boats docked at White Rock Stockade, they went into town to take in an opera and enjoy a good restaurant meal. But Golden Dog never joined them. There was someplace else he'd rather go. He'd walk over to South Street to visit the pockfaced blacksmith, taking a fish or a yellow-backed turtle with him. By then Water Girl had been living there for some time. All day she worked the bellows, her rolled-up sleeves exposing alabaster arms, while her maternal grandfather took the red-hot metal out of the forge and pounded it with the small hammer. "Sledgehammer!" he'd yell, and she'd pick up the sledge and bring it down hard on the cooling metal. The clang of metal on metal reverberated up and down the narrow lane like a drumbeat. When Golden Dog and his friends appeared in the doorway, she'd let out a yelp and hit nothing but air with the sledge. "What's got you rattled?" her pockfaced grandfather would grumble.

Rattled indeed, and he couldn't have been happier. He'd invite Golden Dog and the others inside, then look high and low for something to eat. But since there was usually nothing, he'd fish out a brass wine decanter and they'd begin to drink while Water Girl took the fish or the turtle into the kitchen to make a nice soup. Pockface loved to eat and he loved to drink, and Water Girl was always saying things like, "The old one gets the head, the young one takes the tail." She'd scoop out the fishhead and put it into her grandpa's bowl, then give Golden Dog and his friends the middle part of the fish, keeping the tail for herself. "See the kind of girl I've got!" Pockface would grimace. "There's no room in her heart for her grandpa!" He'd glare at Golden Dog with a twinkle in his bloodshot eyes.

No one who drank in Pockface's blacksmith shop ever left sober. After the young men were drunk, Water Girl would politely offer to let them stay over, but they always left. Golden Dog, on the other hand, refused to leave no matter how drunk he was, and didn't return to his boat. Since the blacksmith shop was equipped with a huge kang, he slept on one side and Water Girl slept on the other, with the gaunt blacksmith spread out between them. The room was pitch black, since it was wasteful to keep the lamp lit. One time Golden Dog woke up in the middle of the night and saw Pockface smoking a cigarette, which flared up for a moment, then died out. Water Girl was also watching.

The boats set out on the river the following day. No wind, calm waters. Golden Dog's companions, accusing him of pretending to be drunk the night before, pinned him to the bottom of the boat and tried to get a confession out of him. Pointing to the fireball in the sky, he swore he hadn't done anything. When they asked if he had the guts to drink three bowlfuls of cold river water to prove what he affirmed, he loped to the bow and drank not three but four.

4

Tian Zhongzheng's new house was the most modern building in Stream of Wandering Spirits. The walls were of brick, all the way to the roof, and were beautifully limed and topped off with red tiles. It was Crossroads Township's most dazzling sight. Yingying's mother had a new set of furniture made. But she and Tian frequently argued after they moved in. While his wife was alive, Tian wouldn't allow Yingying's mother to remarry. He had arranged instead for her to settle into a life as his sister-in-law, whose physical needs he took care of. Every day she carried the invalid's meals to her—breakfast, lunch, and dinner. Invariably, this reduced the poor woman to tears of gratitude, to which Yingying's mother responded with kindly words of encouragement, although a daggerlike glint in her unblinking eyes was aimed straight at the paralyzed woman. Fated not to enjoy a long life, the pitiful invalid soon left this world. The surviving woman was sure that her trials had come to an end and that happier days lay ahead, to be made doubly pleasant by her reputation of virtue. The last thing she expected was for her affair to be exposed. It was painful to her that she had become the object of scandalous rumors. So she went to Tian Zhongzheng and said, "As things are now, I'm ashamed to step out the door. Now that Yingying's auntie is dead, it's time for you to make me your proper wife. Kinship marriages are commonplace, and the only way to shut the mouths of the people is for us to become husband and wife!"

Surrendering completely, Tian promised to marry her as soon as the house was ready. But then charges had been filed against him and construction work had come to a halt, deflating him. He took his frustrations out on her until she lost the spirit to bring the subject up again. Then, to everyone's surprise, the situation turned around with

Tian's promotion, and the house was completed. Everything was coming up roses, and the only thing lacking was a strong east wind. But there wasn't a whisper from Tian about what they'd discussed before, as though the conversation had never happened. Day in and day out Tian attended meetings at the township government office or went out drinking or hunting or strolling here and there, not returning home for ten days or a couple of weeks at a time. When at last Yingying's mother forced the issue, he complained that he'd been on the job only a short time and that it was important for him to bring credit upon Tian Youshan. He insisted that they observe the yearlong mourning period for his deceased wife so he wouldn't be a laughingstock or have his reputation as acting secretary of the township party committee sullied. With growing dejection, his sister-in-law realized that with his newly acquired power Tian had raised his sights and lost interest in her. But she was not a woman to be taken lightly; despite her apparent gentility, her heart was forged of steel, and she wasn't going to take an indignity lying down. Every time Tian came home, she made herself up from head to toe, to be as seductive as possible and arouse his passion. But when he made a move, she closed the door in his face, rebuffing his advances. Although he blew up over this more than once, he discovered each time that he was outmatched by her temper. "An old hag like me," she shouted, "just what do you think you're doing? Crossroads Township is filled with nice tender cabbages! But I'm warning you, if one of your stinking whores sets foot through this door, I'll file charges against you for appropriating public property, forcing yourself on your own sister-in-law, bribing Tian Youshan with gifts. I promise you'll be a very unhappy party secretary!"

Invariably the fight went out of Tian, who fell to his knees and swore that he had every intention of marrying her. But one month led into another without developments, and he began staying away from home longer and longer.

August rolled around, time for Midautumn Festival, and Tian summoned Cai Da'an. "I recently received a letter from Secretary Tian of the county committee, in which he said he needs twenty catties of good varnish for the coffins he bought for his wife's parents. Go to Ox-King Ditch in the northern mountains tomorrow to buy the stuff, then pick up thirty catties of walnuts, ten of mushrooms, and fifty of the best kiwis in the market. At the crack of dawn the day after tomorrow, deliver everything to the county office. You can stay there a couple of days and take in a few performances of Shanxi opera by the White

Rock Stockade opera troupe." But when the time came for Cai to set out, he couldn't find a car to take him to White Rock Stockade, so he hitched a ride on Golden Dog's boat on the pretext of a family visit.

Yingying bought fruit and pastries on the night of Midautumn Festival and took them to the township office in the hope of getting her uncle to come home for the holiday. But Tian Zhongzheng begged off, saying he had a meeting that night, and sent her home alone. Then he sat by himself, nursing his boredom by trying to get drunk. This piqued the curiosity of Tian Yishen, who approached him and asked, "Aren't you going home tonight, Secretary?"

"No," Tian said. "Midautumn Festival isn't New Year's or anything, so why make so much of it?"

"Well, if you're not going home, why not come home with me?"

"No thanks, I'm not in the mood."

"Secretary Tian," Tian Yishen continued, "I know what's on your mind, and it's not worth getting upset about. Since you don't want to come to my place, why don't the two of us go over to Cuicui's? I saw her this afternoon, and she asked if you were going to spend the evening at home. You could drop by to see her, she said, if you weren't. She's concerned that you haven't been by for days, and she's afraid she's somehow offended you."

"That Cuicui knows exactly what to say," Tian replied. "What could she have done to offend me? But I'm glad you're here. Let's go over there and do some serious drinking. But I warn you, don't start spouting a lot of nonsense when you're drunk!"

"What do you mean, nonsense? Don't I always have your best interests at heart?" He smiled and glanced at Tian's midriff.

They headed over to the western end of town, where they opened the gate of a house connected to another by eaves and walked into the backyard. As soon as Cuicui and her father, who were sitting on a stone bench in the yard, saw them, they jumped up and offered the visitors a seat. "Cuicui said you'd be coming," the old man said, "so we've been waiting for you. But when we noticed the moon rise above the roof, we assumed you wouldn't make it."

"Stop that kind of talk, Daddy. The secretary had to go home to enjoy the moon with Auntie. We can't expect him to drop everything and come over here the moment night falls, can we?"

Tian Yishen grinned. "What a sharp tongue you have, Cuicui! But you're not being fair to the secretary. He didn't go home tonight. He told me to bring him over here instead for a few drinks. What do you have? Tonight I'm getting drunk!"

The old man hastened inside, opened a cabinet, and took out a bottle, while Cuicui sat down with Tian Zhongzheng and Tian Yishen to nibble on melon seeds. She spit out the husks so they'd land on Tian Zhongzheng, glancing at him provocatively. Tian returned the looks. "Cuicui," he said, wrinkling his nose, "what kind of oil do you put on your hair? It has a lovely smell."

"Lovely?" she said. "How can a poor family afford such luxuries? I was washing clothes at the ferry landing the other day when I saw the secretary's sister-in-law. She doesn't look her age. She was made up like a girl of seventeen or eighteen!"

Not knowing what to say, Tian Zhongzheng smiled. Tian Yishen took the cue. "Cuicui, you're still a pure flower. Your hair smells lovely without oil on it. I hope you won't misunderstand me, but Yingying's mother is getting on in years and all the makeup in the world can't change that!"

"Yishen," Cuicui said, "I'm sure the secretary doesn't like that kind of talk! Everyone knows there are people who'll eat anything, even steamed buns stuffed with pickled cabbage!"

The talk was beginning to make Tian Zhongzheng squirm, and his face showed his discomfort. Cuicui's father walked out with a bottle of wine on a tray, four glasses, and four plates of snacks. He filled the glasses and passed them around. "Secretary Tian," he said, "here's to you. Drink up. You know that Cuicui's mother died young and that my son failed the school entrance exams. He doesn't know how to work the fields, and he's no good in business, so he has to rely on the secretary's kindness. The reason we turned our house into a clinic was to try to ensure enough to get by on . . ."

Tian Zhongzheng emptied his glass and said, "Old Lu, how's the clinic going?"

"Well, we're not equipped like the town clinic, so I mainly dispense medicine."

"There have been reports that when workers on the national payroll come here for medicine, they get receipts for seven or eight yuan, even for as much as ten, but all they get for their money is bottled stuff and alcohol! Old Lu, you have to be more discreet. Shady dealings have to be kept under wraps. If you insist on hanging a millstone around my neck, you're going to make life very difficult for me!"

The old man turned beet red. "Secretary," he mumbled, "I don't do things like that anymore. I wouldn't be able to face you if I did. Cuicui, hurry up and fill their glasses."

Tian was pleased with the way he'd threatened the old man without losing his composure, although it wasn't so much a threat as a means of tempering Cuicui's self-confidence. This flirtatious young woman, who flaunted her pretty face and large breasts, felt superior to everyone. On the lookout for a husband since she was twenty, she'd by now rejected a small army of suitors as beneath her. The sad thing was, she was still living with her father at the age of thirty. Tian Zhongzheng had given her a few chances and had exchanged a flirtatious look or two. Did she think he was a callow lily liver she could manipulate however she pleased? Like the fabled Monkey, if you gave her a pole, she'd climb it, but then she'd grow docile when he chanted the head-tightening incantation. She drank six glasses of wine with him, and as his eyes began to glaze, he rested his foot against hers under the table, where no one could see; she smiled sensually.

Tian Yishen, noticing the turn of events, asked the old man to show him where the toilet was. It was dark and deserted when he walked out onto the street, and he started singing at the top of his lungs. Tian Yishen was surprised when he heard someone call his name. Cai Da'an ran up to him.

"When did you get back?" Tian asked. "What are you doing out so late? Looking for one of your lovers to drink with?"

"I hitched a ride back this afternoon on Golden Dog's boat and went straight to the secretary's house. But he wasn't home, despite the holiday, and Yingying's mother started bawling and screaming, taking her frustrations out on me! So I went to the office, but he wasn't there either. Where can he be? Have you seen him?"

"He's at Cuicui's house having a few drinks," Tian said.

"So," Cai said, "he's got his eye on that little fox again, has he? No wonder his sister-in-law calls him hardhearted and accuses him of ignoring her."

Tian Yishen lowered his voice. "Don't meddle in other people's affairs. Who in his right mind would pass up tender new grass for tough old weeds?"

"That's exactly what Secretary Tian Youshan was so upset about. I've got to see him. Is there anything else you want to tell me?"

"Go find him if you want," Tian Yishen said. "I'm not going to get tangled in a sticky affair like this!" He turned and staggered home, going straight to bed.

Cai Da'an strode on to the Lu home, where he found Tian Zhongzheng still with Cuicui, laughing lewdly and playing drinking games. When Tian heard that Cai carried instructions from Tian Youshan, he jumped up to return to the office. Cuicui and her father saw him out, muttering under their breath about Cai's interference and calling him the angel of death.

Back at the township office, Cai gave a detailed report of his meeting with Tian Youshan: "Secretary Tian had two things he wanted me to tell you. First, the work in Crossroads Township has caught the attention of higher-ups, and he wants you to do whatever you have to to turn things around. Otherwise, he's going to take off the kid gloves the next time he deals with you!"

"That's easy for him to say," Tian replied, "but just how am I supposed to take charge of work in times like these? Crossroads Township isn't a county seat or a hub with plenty of auxiliary occupations. And it's not a mountain village with lots of timber, fruit, medicinal plants, or varnish. If we take charge of production and parcel out the land, how are we supposed to get the people to work the fields? All we can take charge of these days is family planning. Last month we hauled four tractorloads of women to the hospital in town for abortions. That shows we're doing something!"

"The secretary's aware of the sorry state of affairs here, but he said that if all the boats on the Zhou River originate from Crossroads Township—and he knows they do, on the basis of inquiries by the relevant bureaus—why haven't they been organized under the township government? With the country embarked on reforms, the Central Committee has emphasized time and again the importance of taking charge of the rural commodity economy and not letting opportunities slip by. A leader shows his promise by developing the local economy!"

Tian Zhongzheng sat silently for a moment as he slapped his knee. His face lit up. "On this point, the secretary's shown me the light! What else did he have to say?"

Cai hemmed and hawed for a moment, but Tian insisted on hearing the whole story.

"The secretary said that even though the charges filed against you have been dropped, they've had a definite impact, and that from now on you're to be more circumspect. Your affair with Yingying's mother could offend public morality and damage the Tian clan's reputation, since it's the sort of thing that creates gossip. But since it's gone this far already, the best course is to get married. Not only will that shut people up, it'll remove any obstacles for the future."

Tian's face fell, then he broke out laughing. "Future? Is that what he said? He's letting his imagination run wild . . . I'll take care of this little matter. But what he said about organizing the boats is important, and I'm going to set up a shipping brigade. You'll be responsible for the details. Go to Restless Hill tomorrow, and see Golden Dog. I've had my eye on him, and I can tell he might become a real thorn in our side. Things will be easier to handle once we get him in our sights!"

Cai Da'an got an early start the next morning and went to Restless Hill. He was momentarily envious when he heard how much the boatmen had been making, and he could have kicked himself for having neither a boat of his own nor the will to do a little hard work. But since Tian Zhongzheng had put him in charge of organizing the boatmen, his optimism was irrepressible. He went straight to the home of Golden Dog, who had just finished breakfast and was about to take his boat to White Rock Stockade. Cai stopped him and announced the decision to put the boats under the township government. After hearing him out, Golden Dog evinced mock astonishment: "Do you mean to tell me that Secretary Tian Zhongzheng gives a damn about our boats?"

"He's the party secretary," Cai replied, "so he's concerned about everything. He says that there's a tendency among the masses to get involved in a commodity economy, and as a leader it's his responsibility to stand with the masses! That's why he wants to set up a shipping brigade, and why he sent me to talk to you."

"Let him organize one if he wants to," Golden Dog said. "As party secretary all he has to do is give the order. Who am I? Why talk to me?"

"Now you're talking sense, Golden Dog. That's exactly what I wanted to hear. And that's exactly why the secretary sent me to see you. As a former soldier, you're more conscious of realities than other people. You, of all people, should understand the decision of the township government. You boatmen are well-off, but the majority of people in Restless Hill, Stream of Wandering Spirits, and Crossroads Township remain very poor. We can't just think of ourselves, for we're still a socialist country!"

Golden Dog had a good laugh over that, so good that Cai was puzzled. Then he stopped laughing as abruptly as he'd begun and said, "If the secretary's thought it out this far, he shouldn't be an acting secretary. How's the brigade supposed to be organized?"

"As long as you take the lead," Cai said, "it'll be easy. We can discuss the details with the secretary."

He tried to get Golden Dog to go into town with him right away, but the young man begged off, saying he had to talk things over with the boat owners first. He took his leave and went to find Old Seven and the others.

The boatmen were suspicious, wondering what Tian Zhongzheng had up his sleeve. But Golden Dog analyzed the situation, arguing that even though Tian was in a position of authority, he might be trying to do the right thing for a change, in order to trivialize the charges filed against him. And even if the well-being of the people of Crossroads Township didn't concern him and he was scheming to exploit them, they could turn the tables on him if they played their cards right, and no one would be the loser. Besides, organizing a brigade of boats to enable unified purchases and a unified profit potential benefited everyone. After hearing him out, the others granted that he was making sense and nominated him as their representative to work out with Tian Zhongzheng all the details of organizing the brigade.

Golden Dog spent the day in discussions in town. It was decided that individual owners would retain the rights to their boats; those who didn't own boats but wanted to participate could invest money and share the profits in proportion to their investment. The combine was to be called the Crossroads Township River Shipping Brigade and would be under the administrative control of the township party committee.

When it came to the election of the leaders, Cai said to Tian in front of Golden Dog, "Golden Dog is a Zhou River dragon, so he should be the brigade commander. I'll take on the responsibility of purchasing agent." Tian gave his blessing to the idea at once. To prepare for the start of operations, Cai, who worked like never before, had within a few days made arrangements with some people who wanted to ship varnish seeds. On the day the cargo was shipped, Tian Zhongzheng insisted that all the boats leave together. They set out in single file, like a river dragon, with Golden Dog in the lead boat, across the bow of which hung a banner with the words Crossroads Township River Shipping Brigade. Upon the launch of the brigade, Tian called Secretary Tian Youshan in White Rock Stockade to report what was going on. Tian Youshan then held a meeting of the standing committee and led its members to the ferry landing outside the southern gate of White Rock Stockade to observe the arrival of the boats. News of the standing committee's adjournment to the riverbank to watch the procession spread like wildfire, and in no time at all the townspeople had gathered at the ferry landing in numbers that left barely room to move.

The enthusiastic welcome by the residents of White Rock Stockade gave the boatmen a heady feeling. They made a tidy profit on the varnish seeds, but Golden Dog didn't divide it up among them. Instead the money was applied to the purchase of two new boats. He then organized a group of investors without boats to build some rafts, and they and the two new boats took to the river under his leadership. After the brigade had both boats and rafts, the members no longer had to travel far and wide to find commodities. Out on the river they looked after one another, with the result of a marked decrease in casualties. There was, too, a change in the villagers' attitude toward Tian Zhongzheng. Once a couple of weeks had passed, Tian went to the ferry landing to hear Golden Dog and Cai's report and to pat them on the back. He also passed on the commendation of the county committee. "The river shipping brigade," he concluded, "is now in operation, and we must do a good job. If we fail, it will reflect unfavorably upon the county committee. In order to expand our business, I think we should put up a warehouse in White Rock Stockade. That way we'll have a fixed sales outlet and a place to transfer goods. Let's try to make every member of the brigade a rich man within a year, and to become a model for the whole county! The party committee has decided who will be in charge of the warehouse. We've chosen Tian Yishen, since he has experience in this area. And to make his job easier, he can be one of the brigade commanders."

Cai Da'an found the news unsettling. "How can one shipping brigade have three commanders? Golden Dog, what do you say?"

"It's all the same to me."

"Golden Dog has the right attitude," Tian said. "He knows the river best, and the rafts are a heavy responsibility, so from now on, supervising the rafts will be his primary job. Tian Yishen is a production cadre, and since he currently has no other duties in the village, he can take on more responsibilities with the brigade. Let's give it a try. We can make adjustments if necessary in a month or two."

Cai didn't dare say anything in front of Tian Zhongzheng, but when he and Golden Dog were alone, he bad-mouthed Tian Yishen as a sneaky, conniving dog who had weaseled his way into Tian Zhongzheng's good graces. But Golden Dog continued to smile, sensing the absurdity of fighting over the command of a little shipping brigade. On the other hand, he was interested in knowing why Tian Zhongzheng would place his trust in Tian Yishen. Cai explained how Tian Zhongzheng had planned to marry his sister-in-law but the crafty Tian Yishen had set things up between Lu Cuicui and Tian, who now wanted to marry her instead.

"Look," Cai said, "what do you make of Tian Yishen's part in all this? I went to the secretary's home, where Yingying's mother was crying and in despair, insisting that she's a decent, respectable woman. She said the secretary would throw his arms around her when he needed her but that as soon as he'd taken what he wanted, he'd simply toss her aside. She's no weak sister, and if she's backed against a wall, she's capable of doing something that'll send even ghosts and spirits running for cover! Okay, so Tian Yishen helped Lu Cuicui get her claws into the secretary. There's nothing anyone can do about that now. But he wants to marry her, and that'll really get him into hot water."

The news so upset Golden Dog that he could hardly breathe. Spotting a sow soaking up the sun at the foot of the wall, he kicked it in the belly and sent it running away squealing. "Just because the secretary runs Crossroads Township, does that mean he can have his way with anyone he damn well pleases?"

"We can say what we want behind their backs, but Tian Yishen has lost his conscience, and the secretary's lost his eyesight."

"Well, that's your affair," Golden Dog said, "so it's up to you to handle it. Now that Tian Yishen's one of the commanders, let him get on with it. We'll just do the best we can. Tomorrow is market day in town, so go purchase four thousand catties of alpine rush. I hear that the price in Purple Thistle Pass is twelve fen higher than here, and we can ship a load there on the rafts the day after tomorrow."

Their conversation over, the two men went their separate ways. Golden Dog regretted letting Tian Zhongzheng get involved in the business, but it was too late now. All he could do was be careful that neither Tian Yishen nor Cai Da'an siphoned off the profits from the business.

Six months later a warehouse had been erected in White Rock Stockade and the brigade comprised a fleet of twenty-five shuttle boats and thirty-six raftsmen. It had become a major economic force with substantial revenues. Since the river between White Rock Stockade and Purple Thistle Pass was filled with dangers, only the ten experienced boatmen worked that stretch; the others plied the route between Crossroads Township and White Rock Stockade. Rafts were thrown together when they were needed somewhere on the Zhou River, then were dismantled after reaching their destination. Golden Dog led this pack of daredevils, and even though their rafts often capsized, there were never any casualties. Once a month accounts were settled and an inventory taken, and he was always present to check the records, countenancing no discrepancies. Meanwhile, Cai Da'an kept his eye on Tian Yishen's conduct of the warehouse, and Tian kept a close watch on Cai's purchases. There were always inconsistencies in their accounts, but Golden Dog's audits, however many it took, brought them into line. He took secret delight in ensuring that the other two men never joined forces, and after he paid them what the agreement called for, he split the remaining profits among the investors. Several residents of Restless Hill, Stream of Wandering Spirits, and Crossroads Township grew wealthy as time passed, and they sang the praises of the river shipping brigade.

5

It was the summer of 1982, one of those rare years of nearly perfect weather and excellent harvests, including even the hyacinth beans. The abbot at the Restless Hill Monastery, who had come out to beg alms, was sitting at the ferry landing waxing expansive: "The harvest followed eighty-three rainfalls. In August and October of last year and March of this year, the rains came when they were needed—proof that current policies are in accord with heavenly intent. Dharma exists only in the heart, but when seen cannot be sought; therefore it exists forever. This is proof of human life on earth. Transmigration and nirvana never end, passing beyond activity and inactivity . . ." Although he was speaking in incomprehensible Buddhist homilies, the villagers still felt that he was making sense. The final years of the republic had brought only drought to Zhou City, with not a drop of rain for eighteen months, and when Han Wenju had taken his boat to Sun-Moon Shoals, he'd ordered a stuffed bun in a restaurant and bitten into a human toenail. The Nationalist government fell a few years later. In 1976, the newspapers and broadcast media told of an earthquake at Tangshan, floods in Henan, the landing of a meteor in a certain county in Manchuria. The abbot proclaimed privately that heaven and earth had turned upside down and that the nation was in for chaotic times. His prediction proved accurate, for Mao Zedong, Zhou Enlai, and Zhu De died within months of one another. And if that weren't enough, Hua Guofeng assumed power for two years, during which a hailstorm struck the banks of the Zhou River. In Stream of Wandering Spirits, the two sons of the Wang family, who had let the family buffalo out to graze on a mountain slope, were able to take refuge from the storm in a cave, but the animal went berserk as it was pelted by thousands of giant hailstones. It died in a gully brimming with water. When the storm had passed, the hailstones wouldn't melt; the larger ones were as big as human fists, the smaller ones the size of eggs, and the ground seemed covered with a layer of white rocks. The villagers didn't need the abbot to tell them that Hua Guofeng was in trouble, and sure enough, within six months another set of changes came over their world.

Rural people, who have their own brand of philosophy, often accept by nature things denied by overcivilized urbanites.

One calm, moonlit night the people of Stream of Wandering Spirits had staked out spots on the threshing floor to winnow their grain. Since nearly all the buffalo had been sold off and the millstones had been used to build pigsties, they were using all sorts of primitive, hand-held threshing racks. Once the chaff was bundled up, each family had a pile of wheat, big at the top and small at the bottom, like the hats worn by Qing dynasty officials which had been thrown defiantly to the ground. The people looked as if they were standing amid the graves of Shaolin masters outside the walls of Kung-fu temples. The men, having winnowed the wheat until they could barely hold up their arms and having watched their womenfolk go home to cook, stripped naked and lay down on straw mats in the wheat fields to smoke and talk among themselves. All the while, they could see the glowing lantern at the ferry landing. It was a barn lantern that had been lit by Han Wenju and hung above the cabin hatch of his boat.

Ever since Water Girl had gone to her grandfather in White Rock Stockade to pump his bellows, Han had all but stopped going home. He kept provisions and utensils on the boat, including a little aluminum cooking pot that he carried to the stone cookstove on the riverbank three times a day. When he finished his meal, he'd hang the pot on a transverse beam, where it clanged noisily while the boat was out on the river. As soon as his winnowed wheat had been spread out in front of the door of his house, he went back to the boat to drown his sorrows. "Water Girl," he cried out, "fry some taro strips to go with the wine!" But the words were barely out before he remembered that she wasn't there. That kind of thing happened repeatedly, day in and day out, and it always produced a feeling of emptiness as the futility of his commands became evident. Resentment concerning his niece gradually set in, although the person he really resented was the pock-faced blacksmith who was so heartless that he wouldn't let Water Girl come back even in the middle of the summer to help with the harvest.

He stood up and yelled in the direction of the threshing floor,

"Fuyun, come over for a drink! Fuyun, are you dead or something? Are you telling me you're not interested in drinking?" Fuyun's alacrity showed how pleased he was with the invitation. But three or four naked men from the field came up to the ferry landing too.

"Who invited you bunch of shit-eating dogs, ready whenever anyone calls?"

"Uncle Han," they fired back, "is that shit in your bottle, then, or horse piss? If you keep eating and drinking alone, who'll carry your corpse ashore when you croak?"

"If I croak, I've got Fuyun. He'll stuff me in that vat in my house and set it adrift on the Zhou River, where it'll float all the way down to the sea!"

But it was all friendly banter. He tossed some straw cushions off the boat for the men to sit on. Then, cursing Fuyun and telling him to find some kindling so they could boil tea, he went ashore with his bottle.

Fuyun, who'd come for the wine, was put to work making a fire and hanging the teapot on the rack above it to boil water. He poured some oil into an earthenware pot to fry the tea leaves and some aniseeds over the fire. Once the water was boiling, he filled the earthenware pot, and later he poured a cup of strong, pungent tea for each man. No one was better at this than the extraordinarily patient and uncomplaining Fuyun. By the time he'd filled their cups three times, sweat covered his face and they'd finished off half a decanter of wine.

"Uncle Han," one of the men asked, "isn't Water Girl coming to help with the harvest?"

"Old Pockface isn't human!" Han complained. "Sure, he needs Water Girl, but doesn't he realize that I'm lost without her? And she's no better. What's she scared of? Tian Zhongzheng isn't a tiger or anything, so we don't have to worry about him gobbling us up! . . . Thank goodness I've got Fuyun around to help out. Without him, the wheat would still be in the ground."

One of the men said, "Uncle Han, you may be shorthanded, but you threshed your crop faster than the rest of us. We've got wives and a pack of kids, so when we go to bed at night, the floor around the kang is covered with shoes, and when we eat, the pot's surrounded by hungry mouths. But when it's time to work in the fields, we're out there by ourselves and the wheat just keeps piling up on the threshing floor. After we're finished, we'll invite you over for some serious drinking!"

"Aren't you the considerate one!" Han said. "The wine at your place is probably sour! And who says my wheat's been taken care of? It's still lying out there on the ground!"

Their eyes widened. "But since you sleep on the boat, aren't you afraid of thieves?"

"Afraid?" Han Wenju said. "I've got watchmen."

"Who?" Fuyun asked.

"The branch secretary and the chairman of the Poor Peasants Association."

They were leery. The old fellow must have lost it. The branch secretary had died of cancer six years before, and the chairman of the Poor Peasants Association had been dead for five years. They were buried across from Han's house. *The crazy old boatman's trying to scare us with talk of ghosts and spirits!*

Han Wenju, looking very serious, refilled their glasses, secretly chuckling over his little joke. "The branch secretary and the chairman of the Poor Peasants Association were important men in Stream of Wandering Spirits. Who wasn't afraid of them when they were alive? Ever since they died, I've noticed that not even children play around their graves. When important people die, they turn into mighty ghosts. The only people who'd steal my grain are those who don't value their lives."

Fuyun said, "I hear their ghosts are always arguing. Is that true?"

"Of course it is," Han said. "I hear them every night. That's because the geomancer chose adjoining grave sites. All night long a croaking sound comes from one of the graves, and it's answered by chirps from the other. It doesn't stop till sunup."

His audience, credulous concerning ghosts, had turned pale, somber, and very anxious. But when they heard him describe the sounds of arguing, a moment's reflection told them that it had to be toads and crickets. Once they knew they were being toyed with, they jeered at Han, telling him that maggots would stop up his mouth. "So what if they're watching your grain for you?" one of them needled. "Since they're more rapacious than living people, what's to keep them from stealing it themselves? Remember those eighteen cypress trees on the rocky promontory over the river by the village entrance, the ones that served as a windbreak? Wasn't it the branch secretary who had them cut down, supposedly for use as construction material for the county? But then the damned county chief of White Rock Stockade used the lumber for a couple of coffins, one for Tian Zhongzheng's father-in-law and the other for himself. Eight big pieces of fine wood, all beautifully polished. You couldn't buy one of those for eight hundred or even a thousand!"

"All right!" Han shot back. "So the branch secretary was in the Tian clan's pocket. Didn't the chairman of the Poor Peasants Association, who belonged to the Gong clan, file a complaint with his kin in Zhou City? They'll never steal from me! Just think, both their souls are there, so they keep tabs on each other and I'll never lose a kernel of grain!"

They had a good laugh over this, calling Han Wenju a closet politician and saying that when the branch secretary and the chairman of the Poor Peasants Association were alive, he was so well behaved he wouldn't fart in front of them even though he was older than either, and that he was all smiles whenever he saw them, but that now he was getting even with them with his mean, sarcastic talk. When the chairman of the Poor Peasants Association died, the Gong clan's influence in Stream of Wandering Spirits began to wane, but the power of the Tian clan was as great as ever; sooner or later they'd make trouble for him.

"Don't you realize that times have changed? Now that the land's been parceled out, the farmers take care of themselves. I'm not breaking any laws, so nobody gives me a second look. If Secretary Tian Zhongzheng comes up to the ferry landing and I don't feel like ferrying him across, he'll just have to jump bare-assed into the water and swim!"

That was just when someone called out sweetly from the opposite bank for the ferry boat.

"You see," Han said. "Anybody who comes here has to bow and scrape to me!" He pulled the boat across the river and returned with his passenger, the abbot from the monastery, who received an enthusiastic greeting.

"Say, Abbot, where've you been off to in the middle of the night? Not carousing, I hope, or the monastery will burn to the ground again!"

Forty years earlier, the previous abbot, a sex fiend, had kept a prostitute in a cave behind the worship hall for his pleasure. When the local people confronted him, he burned the monastery to the ground. After it was rebuilt, they recruited a new abbot, a devout Buddhist who treated the people with kindness and never got upset when they took advantage of him. "Sins, sins," he'd say. "Buddha lives in people's hearts. Pure hearts cannot be invaded; depraved hearts pollute all living creatures. The elimination of desire is the destruction of evil. When evil is destroyed, it is replaced by goodness. And once goodness is in place, there is no need to look outside the heart. The hearts of people who have been enlightened by the dharma are like the sun, illuminating all around them, and doubts cease to exist."

He always dealt with awkward situations by somberly reciting Buddhist scriptures. Seeing that he was straying from the subject at hand, Han Wenju asked, "Where have you been?"

"I rode the clouds back from White Rock Stockade."

"Have they finished the harvest there?" Han asked.

"White Rock Stockade is crawling with grain merchants this year," the abbot replied. "They're paying six yuan an acre, and the people are falling all over themselves to sell. The entire crop is going into silos. It's funny when you think of it. Man is born with eyes, ears, nose, and a mouth, and the temptations are great. Sex is the king of vices; money is the root of all evil!"

Han envied the people of White Rock Stockade for the ease with which they did business, even dealing with grain merchants. But he disagreed with the abbot. "Abbot, you're a Buddhist disciple, and we mere mortals are no match for you. What are we supposed to do without money—live off the farts of the wind?"

"The heart of anyone who realizes Buddhahood, even if he lives in the human world, is in the right place, and doubts and confusion are eliminated."

Han laughed and turned to look at the torches in the fields beyond the riverbank, then grew philosophical. "Abbot, how can the harvest at White Rock Stockade compare with ours? With such a bountiful harvest this year, things should be hopping at the monastery. At year's end, you'll get fat on all the oil people donate. I'll bet even the coats of the rats there glisten!"

"Maybe not," the abbot replied. "There's a reason why they're in such a hurry to harvest their crop at White Rock Stockade. A rumor's sweeping the area that there's going to be a change in government policy. When I was at White Rock Stockade, the price of vegetables was higher than that of grain, and the townspeople were using their grain to buy eggs, a full catty for one tiny, little egg. But that's about to change. There's talk that the land's going to be taken back and that, once that happens, the farmers will work as a collective again. That will probably make the price of grain soar. Obviously, running a country and managing the hearts of the people are closely linked. The first order of business in running a country is managing the hearts of the people, and that can't be accomplished through material incentives. Buddha is cultivated without cultivation, gains entry without entering, can cause the learned to return their natural knowledge. One gets lost in the darkness but finds the plow, and sees Polaris when one looks up."

The men weren't moved by the moral the abbot drew, but the news he'd brought struck terror in them, beginning with Han Wenju. What alarmed him wasn't the prospect of a higher price for grain, since how much grain can one person eat? Both he and Water Girl were laborers, with no elders to take care of and no children to rear, so even if the cost of grain went through the ceiling, it wouldn't impair his diet. What unnerved him was that, since Stream of Wandering Spirits was under the administrative control of the Tian clan, if the land was taken back for a collective, Tian Zhongzheng would finally have a chance to get his revenge. His heart filled with apprehensions, and it was time to get the abbot to make a prediction. "Abbot," he said, "you once taught me the Sixty-Four Diagrams of Wealth, but they don't go far enough. People say you have a book called *Illuminations of Nature's Mysteries*, which chronicles the dynastic history of China from the mythical emperors all the way down. Will you check to see if a dynastic change is on the horizon. Then tonight, see if there are changes in the stars. Didn't you predict that this would be a year of good weather and that the nation would be at peace and the people contented? So why this change of wind?"

The abbot didn't have a copy of *Illuminations of Nature's Mysteries*, and when he had observed the stars that night, all he could predict was whether the next day would be cloudy or clear. Although he could add his voice to the cause, where political issues were concerned the only thing his mouth was good for was eating: "I've already got up at night to observe the heavenly bodies, but I couldn't tell if there will be changes or not . . . This matter is like the winds over the Zhou River: unpredictable. Fusing and dividing, dividing and fusing, constant change is good . . ."

"Good, my ass!" Han said. "How can things be permitted to change? If they change, the people will lose faith. We've just got a bumper crop out of the ground, which means we can eat, for a change!"

"We'll have to ask the spirits," the abbot said. "Check the Ouija board."

"I don't put much faith in that," Fuyun said.

"Fuyun," Han remonstrated, "don't talk nonsense! Don't you put your faith in spirits?"

"If the spirits' powers are boundless," Fuyun said, "then why did it take only a single order from Chairman Mao during the Cultural Revolution to demolish the temple overnight?"

The abbot said, "Bamboo emerald green, the essence of wisdom, flowers fragrant yellow, one and the same. Buddha looks straight into the human heart, for all creatures possess the Buddha nature. Chairman Mao was born a mortal, assumed the form of a human, but with greater intelligence, and was a child of the universe with a natural vitality. Therefore he, too, was a spirit. Chairman Mao's spirit was mighty enough to gain supremacy over the hundred spirits!"

The abbot stopped, conscious that his reasoning was too abstruse to win them over. He added a couple of perfunctory comments before getting up and returning to the Restless Hill Monastery. Han Wenju, who by then was extremely dispirited, was too listless to go into the cabin to replace the emptied bottle of wine, and the men just sat there feeling empty, but too wide-awake to sleep and unwilling to go home to lie on the kang and feed the mosquitoes. Eventually Han tried to cheer them up. "Enough of that," he said with a smile. "Let's talk about something else. Have you heard the story of the ghost in the Zhou River that turned into an immortal?"

"No," they replied. Han, who had plenty of experience, often regaled audiences at the ferry landing with tales of marriages between men and goblins, of the weddings of rodents, and the like; he took tales like those of *The Arabian Nights*, which had been told long before the land was parceled out, and moved them to his own boat. Since it was a chilly night, and he didn't want the abbot's comments to weigh on their minds, he decided to relate a tale of the supernatural.

When Han told tales, his listeners were drawn into the world of the narration so quickly they forgot their troubles. "Once upon a time, there was a Taoist temple in White Rock Stockade, where a ghost from the Zhou River took shelter every night. One day the ghost said to the Taoist priest, 'A man is going to cross the river at the ferry landing tonight, and the king of the underworld has ordered me to drown him so he can be my replacement ghost.' The priest didn't believe him. But, sure enough, the next day he saw a man crossing the river, and just as he reached the center, he suddenly sank beneath the surface. He then resurfaced. That night the priest asked the ghost, 'Didn't you drown him to be your replacement?' The ghost answered, 'He has an eighty-year-old mother, and if he died, she would also be left to die. Since I'm already a ghost, I might as well stick it out for a few more years.' A year passed, and one day the ghost said to the priest, 'A woman will cross the river tomorrow, and the king of the underworld has ordered me to take her to be my replacement ghost.' Sure enough, the next day a woman crossed the river, and just as she reached the center, she suddenly sank into the water. She then resurfaced. That night the priest asked the ghost why. The ghost said, 'The woman has a six-month-old child, and if she died, her child would also be left to die. I'm already a ghost, so I might as well keep at it.' Another year passed, and one day the ghost said to the priest, 'You've been a Taoist for more than sixty years. What great wisdom have you acquired?' The Taoist said, 'When water flows across land, it gets muddy. People should have lofty ideals and not concern themselves with worries of the mortal world.' The ghost shook its head, so the priest said, 'All right, since you've been a ghost for ten years, what great wisdom have you acquired?' The ghost replied, 'When a human becomes a ghost, it should be an opportunity for reflection. I've reflected for ten years, and now I know why people are afraid of us. Most ghosts bring disaster to the mortal world. Do you agree?' The priest lowered his head and said nothing. The ghost continued, 'Are you prepared to do something good for the world? In five years a plague is going to hit White Rock Stockade. Medicinal herbs grow in abundance on Shaman Mountain. If you go there and bring back enough medicinal herbs, you can distribute them to the people and save their lives. Who knows, you may see me there.' With that the ghost vanished. Five years later, a plague did indeed hit White Rock Stockade, with devastating consequences for the population. Recalling what the ghost had told him, the priest climbed Shaman Mountain to gather medicinal herbs, which he took to White Rock Stockade and distributed to the people, curing them of their illness. They were so grateful that they bestowed the title *Miraculous Physician* on him. Greatly moved, he went back up Shaman Mountain to find the ghost but had no luck even after several days of looking. As he was about to come down off the mountain, though, he heard someone calling to him from behind. Turning, he saw a figure emerging from the Earth God Temple. It was the ghost from five years ago, but now he was attired in the regalia of an immortal."

The men were listening in rapt attention. Their fear of ghosts had been replaced by good feelings.

"There's no reason to be afraid of ghosts," Han said. "When I'm sleeping on the boat alone, ghosts often drop by, but I don't pay them any mind. They can do what they want, but I'm going to sleep. A few nights ago, when the sky was overcast and there was no moon in sight, even though its rays were visible, I had to take a shit. I was so close to the ferry landing that I worried the wind would carry the stink over, so I went down to one of the shoals to do my business. When I got there, I spotted a pair of embroidered slippers placed neatly on top of a rock. I wondered who had left them. I kicked them down off the rock, and they landed, one pointing east, the other west. Well, I walked off a way, did what I'd come to do, and when I returned, the slippers had been placed neatly on the rock where they'd been when I first saw them. I looked all around, but there wasn't a soul anywhere, and I knew that a ghost was playing tricks on me. Without a word, I came back to the boat, went to bed, and fell asleep. When I woke up in the middle of the night, I saw someone in white walking along the bank toward the village, mumbling something. Pretty soon, someone came walking out of the village. It was Secretary Tian Zhongzheng. I asked him, 'Who was that woman I saw just a moment ago?' 'There was no one!' he said. When I remarked, '*Another* ghost!' Secretary Tian was so startled he turned pale. He sat on my boat until sunrise before going to the township office."

Han Wenju, loving every minute of it, laughed roundly, and was quickly joined by the others, who gazed at the surface of the river, where the bright moonlight bounced off the lapping waves as though a ghost were frolicking in the water.

"Uncle Han," one of them said, "don't try to pull a fast one on us. Are you saying that Secretary Tian's scared of ghosts? You're always seeing things, and this time I'm afraid that what you saw was Secretary Tian on his way to see Lu Cuicui."

At the mention of Cuicui, Han lowered his voice and said, "I didn't say that, you did! What about Lu Cuicui? Why would Secretary Tian be wanting to see her?"

"Don't act dumb, Uncle Han," the man said. "Tian Zhongzheng is a man who has his eye on the pot while he's eating out of his bowl. After all, Lu Cuicui's a virgin!"

"A virgin?" Han fired back. "She hasn't had a baby yet, that's all! If he does get his clutches on her, he'll have himself a female ghost, a *living* female ghost, and he can kiss his manhood good-bye!"

Now that their conversation was going again, talk ranged from the Lu family to the Tian clan; when something funny was said, they had a hearty laugh, and when something displeased them, they cursed. But Fuyun sat there the whole time, his head buried between his knees, without saying a word. Han Wenju shook him. "Fuyun, are you sleeping?"

He wasn't. All the talk of ghosts had puzzled him. He couldn't stop thinking that ghosts were all female and that one night one of them would steal into his home through a crack in the door. But he wouldn't be afraid, not Fuyun. Then when the others began talking about Lu Cuicui, his thoughts drifted to Tian Zhongzheng's sister-in-law and how it was too bad she was fated to spend the rest of her life as a widow. He wondered what kind of ghost she had been. His imagination began to run wild. A female ghost was calling him, a long, drawn-out sound, like a child who's just had a poop calling to his dog to come over and taste it.

But this ghost was a real woman, Tian Zhongzheng's sister-in-law, who came walking down to the ferry landing, shouting as she came. The naked men instinctively crossed their legs to cover up and hunched over under the hazy rays of the moon. Fuyun hastily put on his pants. "Is that you, Auntie Tian?" he shouted. "Don't come down for a minute, we're all stark naked. Where's my belt?"

She laughed and kept coming. "I'm no teenager, so don't think you can shock me."

A couple of the men who couldn't get their pants on in time slipped into the water. But Han Wenju had already gotten to his feet. His enmity toward the woman had nearly been replaced by pity. "It's late," he said. "Can't you sleep either?"

"I can't take it easy like you fellows. You rely on your muscles to bring in the harvest and get it threshed, but ours is still piled up on the threshing floor and nothing's been done with it. Yingying's uncle doesn't care enough to come home, and Yingying's work unit won't give her any time off. So where does that leave me?"

"The secretary's busy," Han said. "Social obligations, you know. Besides, with all the wage earners in your family, what difference can a little grain make?"

"How much money do you think I have?" she asked. "Yingying and her uncle's wages are fixed, so we're worse off than anyone in the village. Why, Golden Dog's almost a rich man, isn't he?"

"He may be rich," Han said, "but he's a big snake in a large hole. He's not like you, trying to make every coin work double."

No sooner were the words out of his mouth than his heart skipped a beat. He recalled what the abbot had said, and a black cloud descended over his mood. He softened his tone of voice. "Did you come to ask Fuyun to help out with the work?"

"Fuyun's a bachelor, without a care in the world. Fuyun, will you come and help me? I'll pay you well."

Fuyun smiled. "What makes you think I want to be paid? A little meat in my belly is all I need."

"Always thinking about your stomach," Han interjected. "Are you forgetting who Secretary Tian is? You think he won't pay someone for putting in a good day's work? I don't have anything to do tomorrow, so I'll come over and help you do the winnowing."

"I wouldn't dream of trying to hire someone like you!" she said. "But when Yingying's uncle comes home, he'll treat you to some good strong wine. A few days ago someone gave him a few bottles of good Sichuan stuff. That'll get you good and drunk!"

Who'd be giving him wine this time? Han was thinking. More and more people were giving out gifts these days, which could only mean there were changes in the air. "Secretary Tian hasn't heard any news, has he? There are rumors in White Rock Stockade that the land's going to be taken back. Is that true?"

"How would I know?" she said. "That's the business of the higher-ups. But I hear it's every man for himself these days, and that everyone's going crazy trying to get rich. They keep it all for themselves, while the country is desperately in need. If it keeps up like this, we're in trouble in the long run."

Han's heart froze as he realized that the abbot hadn't been spouting nonsense, and resented the fact that he hadn't made plans for himself. Things didn't look good. With a blank look on his face, he watched Fuyun walk off with the woman. "Fuyun," he barked out, "you'd better put in a good day's work!"

The others began worrying about the grain that was piling up on the threshing floor. As though a fire were singeing their eyebrows, they knew they had to get this year's harvest stored as fast as possible. That was the very least they had to do. They stood up. "It's getting late, so we'd better be heading home." They walked up the riverbank toward their homes, leaving Han Wenju alone on his boat to stare blankly at the sparks from the fires, the cloud of white smoke that settled over them, and the blackness that then swallowed it up.

The mountain watchdogs set up a howl in the early morning hours. The threshing floor at Stream of Wandering Spirits was deathly still. In the darkness, Han Wenju took out his six copper coins and tossed them onto the deck. But since the moon had nearly disappeared in the sky, he couldn't see them from where he sat, and he was too lethargic to go over and look closely. So he just sat there with his eyes fixed on the reflection of a solitary star in the water off the stern of his boat, feeling terribly anxious.

6

Han Wenju's worries proved idle. He moped around the ferry landing for several days, but things were as placid as ever. The boats of the shipping brigade continued to ply the river from White Rock Stockade to Purple Thistle Pass and Xiangfan, their contented owners getting richer and richer. Water Girl hadn't returned from White Rock Stockade and hadn't written a letter; by the look of things, there were no great changes afoot at White Rock Stockade. And if everything was all right there, then everything should be all right at Crossroads Township as well. As for the abbot, it was a case of "predicting rain at the first gust of wind." He'd thrown a scare into the men, which had come to nothing. But Han was, after all, a cautious man who viewed a situation thoroughly and calmly before deciding what to do. So he tucked a tiny bit of cleverness away, deciding to test Tian Zhongzheng and see what his attitude was.

But Tian hadn't shown up at the ferry landing for a long time.

After all the grain had been taken in, the banks of the Zhou River seemed somehow thinner. Families that had finished their harvest planted corn, then began their annual visits to friends and relatives to see the summer off, taking with them steamed buns made from the new wheat. Once the daughters and sons-in-law had paid their respects to their elders, they returned home, and there wasn't a single child who didn't bring with him scrolls given him by his grandparents. Men and women of all ages from these lucky families came up to the ferry landing every day shouting for the ferryboat, and while Han Wenju chatted with them, or traded insults, deep down he was saddened by his own troubles: a man with no children of his own, who had taken in Water Girl only to see her widowed as a youngster, thereby ruining his chances of ever enjoying the steamed buns for sending off summer and ever knowing how it feels to dote on a grandson. Tian Zhongzheng's grain was the last to be brought in, and when it was time to plant corn, the secretary called a bunch of people together to help him with the planting. One overcast, moonless night, he came to the landing to be ferried across to Stream of Wandering Spirits. Han Wenju noticed the flustered look on his face, which was darker and gaunter than before. On board, he sat silently smoking a cigarette. Han felt uneasy. When the boat reached the center of the river, where they were surrounded by mist-covered water, he said timidly, "Secretary Tian, we haven't seen you around for a long time. You must be busy at the township office."

"I'm swamped with work!"

"People envy you senior cadres, but they don't know how busy you are. The Communist party is always holding meetings, and even apart from the time and energy spent, the emotional burdens must be overwhelming. Secretary Tian, are there any changes in the air these days?"

Tian lit a fresh cigarette with the stub of the first one. "Yes, of course there are."

"Well, tell me," Han said, "is it good news or bad?"

"It's good news and it's bad, it's bad news and it's good," Tian said. He just smiled, without saying more, and when the boat reached the bank, he walked off toward the village.

If you're afraid of something, it's bound to happen. Han mulled over what Tian Zhongzheng had said. *Ambiguous, to be sure, but he's an official, and I'm just a commoner. There's no need for a man like that to sit down for heart-to-heart talks with the common folk.* The tense look on Tian's face and the strange smile were enough to rekindle Han's uneasiness.

There are two kinds of cleverness in the world: grand cleverness and petty cleverness. Grand cleverness is muddled and stupid, but petty cleverness has a way of outfoxing itself. What bothered Tian Zhongzheng was not what Han Wenju assumed. During the time he'd stayed away from home, he'd lost his appetite and had trouble sleeping, all over something that had happened to him. His sister-in-law, who was getting older all the time, was pressing him to get married. Meanwhile, the head of the county committee, Tian Youshan, had told him to forget about romance and start thinking about marrying his sister-in-law. But now Lu Cuicui was pregnant. How could a young woman like that, who was as ripe as a grape and oozed water when you touched her, get pregnant so easily? The women who should have babies can't, and those who shouldn't have them do! As soon as Cuicui discovered she was pregnant, she became fixated on the subject of marriage. Her tender charms had been replaced by the vicious attitude of a she-wolf. He wanted her to have an abortion, but she was insisting that he put his intention to marry her in writing or else she'd have the child and then they'd see whether or not this party secretary could hold his head up in society! Finding himself astride a tiger, he didn't know how to get off. As coincidence would have it, just then the county sent down a quota for apprentice journalists for the Zhou City newspaper. They were the only two journalism slots to be filled in the county, and Secretary Tian Youshan wanted to use the positions to encourage and reward Crossroads Township for the success of the river shipping brigade. Consequently, both positions were allocated to the township. Tian Zhongzheng felt like a man stranded in the middle of the ocean who'd spotted a rescue boat. Yingying was the first name that had come to mind, for nominating her would go a long way toward calming the anxieties of her mother. When he shared the news with Cuicui, she demanded that the second opening go to her younger brother. In the dealing that followed, Tian gave his word that her brother would get the position, on the condition that she terminated the pregnancy and that all talk of marriage went on hold for the time being. Upon her bending to his terms, he sought out Tian Yishen and told him to take her to Purple Thistle Pass for an abortion on the pretext of looking for commodities for the shipping brigade.

Tian Yishen and Lu Cuicui boarded a boat for Purple Thistle Pass. When Han Wenju caught sight of them getting ready to depart from the ferry landing, he glowered at Cuicui, looking her up and down. A demon-woman, he thought, three parts human and seven parts fox spirit. She reminded him of all the women he'd seen in the brothels at White Rock Stockade and Purple Thistle Pass during his youth. Disgusted, he spit into the river. Cuicui turned red with embarrassment when she saw him do that, but Han, at once mindful that evil cannot triumph over good, let his petty cleverness take over. All he could think of was humiliating the little fox. "Is that you, Lu Cuicui," he called out. "We hardly ever see you at the ferry landing. Are you going to White Rock Stockade to buy some medicine?"

There was a giddy look in her eyes. "Yes, that's where I'm going."

"White Rock Stockade's a bustling place," Han said, "a good place to take in the sights. Cuicui, I hear your daddy's running a clinic. How's business?"

"Not bad."

"No wonder you can dress up so nice. The way you look, Cuicui, some day you're going to be an official's wife!"

Tian Yishen, who was running around making preparations to get under way, heard the conversation and chided, "Old Han, you damned drunkard, I'll bet you're swacked on horse piss again. What business is it of yours what sort of husband she gets? It won't be you, that's for sure!"

"Commander Tian," Han replied, "did I say something untrue? Do you want to bet that Cuicui won't be an official's wife?"

With a stern look on his face, Tian said, "Old Han, I'm telling you, you'd better hold that tongue of yours. People are complaining about all the dangerous talk you've been spreading at the ferry landing. Didn't you start a rumor that there's going to be a change in government policy?"

"I said that, yes," Han replied, turning serious.

"Does that mean you're dissatisfied with current policy? Are you trying to stir people up? Did the rumor come out of your own head, or were you peddling somebody else's rubbish?"

Han was about to say he'd got his information from the abbot, but he didn't want to implicate him, so he said, "One of my passengers told me some things, but I don't remember his name or where he was from. He was wearing a traditional blue jacket."

"You old prick!" Tian said. "If this had happened a few years ago, you'd be up the creek by now."

A dark cloud settled over Han's heart as he watched Tian help settle Cuicui in the boat. "Commander Tian," he said as the travelers started downstream, "you don't think I'd welcome a change in policy, do you? I only asked because I'm *afraid* of a change."

Tian ignored him as the boat slowly made its way downriver, until it was no more than a black speck and finally disappeared from sight on the horizon. Han stood frozen on his ferryboat; suddenly he grew excited. *The fact that Tian spoke that way proves there won't be a change in policy, doesn't it? Hmph! As long as there's no change in policy, you, Commander Tian Yishen, might be able to control what happens with the boats in the shipping brigade, but you can't do a thing about Han Wenju's ferryboat! And neither can Tian Zhongzheng!*

His happiness regained, Han stood at the ferry landing and roared like a lion for Fuyun. Where the hell was he? *He must have died over there, or he'd be coming to chat and have a few drinks with me.* Han drank a few cups alone, but without anyone to share the wine, it lost its taste. Seeing that night had nearly fallen, and that there were no passengers at the landing, he tied up his boat and went looking for Fuyun in the village. There he learned that he'd gone with Tian Zhongzheng's sister-in-law to plow up a vegetable patch. The old ferryman was deflated, but then he thought of Golden Dog and headed to Restless Hill.

Over the previous six months or so, Golden Dog had grown increasingly attentive toward Han, and Han had adopted a more submissive attitude toward him. He was just another young fellow on shore, but as soon as he was out on the river poling a raft, he was a single-minded desperado, and Han was sure that even he hadn't taken on the Zhou River with that sort of bravado when he was young. In recent days, every time Golden Dog returned from rafting he came over to the ferry landing to sit for a while, where he'd take out a bottle of good wine and hand it to Han. "Water Girl told me to give you this," he'd say.

Han would say some nice things about Water Girl before opening the bottle and sharing it with Golden Dog. On those occasions when he got a bit tipsy, he'd say with tears in his eyes, "Water Girl treats me better than I deserve! No matter how you look at it—talent, character, or temperament—that niece of mine deserves to be happy. But fate played a dirty trick on her and made her a widow!" Golden Dog's eyes would fill with sadness, too, and he'd try to console the old man, not leaving him, to go home, until Han was asleep. His respect for Han increased until it was as great as his respect for his father, the painter. The wine continued to arrive with Golden Dog, and eventually Han asked him to take Water Girl a letter; he told her that he was fine, that he made enough ferrying passengers to keep him in wine, and that she should save the money she made at the blacksmith shop to make her life better when she found the right man. But she wrote back that she hadn't been sending him wine, and that it must have been Golden Dog's idea. Han Wenju was puzzled. Why would Golden Dog do something like that? He began to wonder if the young man had an ulterior motive. When he asked around, he was met by smiles. "Lucky you!" the others said. "If somebody bought me a bottle of wine, I'd burn a stick of incense for him!"

The next time Golden Dog pulled out a bottle of wine, Han asked, "Another present from Water Girl?"

"She said it's good for you to have a little wine every day but not to get drunk. The older you get, the harder it is to hold your liquor."

Han glared at him and said, "Golden Dog, you're a lying prick. You think I don't know that you bought this yourself?"

Golden Dog's face turned scarlet. With a flustered laugh he asked, "Does that mean you don't want it? I've been drinking your wine since I was little, so what's wrong with paying you back?"

"Level with me," Han said. "What's on your mind?"

Golden Dog's face turned even brighter. "What's on my mind?" he asked calmly. "Do you always have something on your mind when you ask me over to drink with you?"

Han thought for a moment. *He's got a point.* He suppressed the thoughts that lay at the bottom of his heart and said nothing more on the subject. They drank in silence. Then when he was nearly drunk, he said craftily, "We old people have important things to say where contemporary events are concerned, but there's no avoiding the fact that we're old and our opinions aren't much more than food for thought. It's you young people whose opinions really count, because the events really concern you."

There was a cavalier tone to his voice, but he looked to see what effect his words were having on Golden Dog, who listened carefully with an innocent look on his face. He hadn't caught the drift. "What do you mean by that?" he asked. The question dampened Han's spirits.

Han went over to Restless Hill a few days later, but Golden Dog wasn't home. He'd taken his boat to White Rock Stockade after finishing the threshing and after cleaning up the corn husks, and had already been gone for several days. His father was sitting beneath the lamp, making paint out of charcoal. Happy to see Han Wenju, he invited him to sit down. Then, his tiny eyes fixed on the man, he asked, "What did you want Golden Dog to buy for you in White Rock Stockade? If he promised, that's fine, but he'd better not dawdle. He's been gone several days already."

"What would I be asking anybody to buy for me?" Han said. "I dropped by to find out what's been going on outside the village lately!"

"What's happened?"

Han didn't know where to start. The dog outside snarled, and a flashlight beam shone in the door. Before he could see who it was, the visitor bellowed, "Aiya, so here you are, Uncle Han! I shouted for you at the ferry landing, but no answer, so I had to swim across, cursing you the whole way. I wondered what skirt the irresponsible old fart was chasing this time!"

"Commander Cai," Han said, "you and your dirty mind! Two years ago, when the river was flooded, a woman about thirty years old fell in and I rescued her. Well, she got down on her knees in front of me and kowtowed, vowing to repay me. 'How are you going to do that?' I asked her. She said she'd give me money, but I didn't want her money. Then she said she'd let me have her body. But I just patted her on the thigh, which quivered a little, and told her to put her pants back on. She got up and left. She was pretty hot stuff, but I wasn't up to it."

They all found it amusing. "Your own words were enough to make you come!" the painter gibed. "Wenju, that mouth of yours has got you into plenty of trouble, and the next time around, you'll come back as a horse or a donkey!"

Cai Da'an took a seat and had the yellow dog sit beside him. "Hasn't Golden Dog come back yet?" he asked the painter.

"Wenju came over to see him, too. It must be something important to get you out in the middle of the night."

Cai didn't say anything as he glanced over at Han Wenju.

"You two have things to talk about," Han said, "so I'll go into the bedroom and have a smoke."

"You don't have to go," Cai said. "You're close to Golden Dog's family. It's no big secret. I have good news about him, but don't go spreading it around."

Han Wenju sat back down and tried to look casual.

"You have to send someone to White Rock Stockade tomorrow to bring him back," Cai said. "The Zhou City newspaper has asked the county to recommend two people as journalists. Secretary Tian got the county committee to give him the quota because he wanted Yingying to fill one of the slots. So there's one left, and I've recommended Golden Dog, since this is the sort of thing he did in the military. It's a tailor-made position for a former soldier. But Tian Yishen is pushing for someone else."

Han Wenju had heard of cadre recruitment, but he wasn't familiar with the term *journalism*. But when they told him that it was the job of a *reporter*, a term he was familiar with, he secretly congratulated Golden Dog. Upon hearing Cai say that Tian Yishen favored someone else, he asked, "Who is it?"

"It's the sixth son of the Lu family from east of town."

"The sixth son of the Lu family?" Han repeated.

"If I tell you who his sister is, you'll know. It's Cuicui!"

The painter was confused, but Han erupted. "That little fox spirit! Aren't she and Tian Zhongzheng stuck on each other?"

Cai was shocked. "You said that, not me! How did you know?"

Han could have kicked himself for letting it slip out, and he tried to backtrack. "Don't take me seriously, I'm just talking. Somebody said so."

Cai stood up, walked over to the door, and took a look outside. Then he walked back and said in a low voice, "Since you already know, let's not hold anything back, and when I leave, it stays right here. Tian Yishen was the one who procured Cuicui for the secretary, with the idea that he'd marry her. If that isn't a case of getting our leader in hot water, I don't know what it is. Well, Cuicui got pregnant, and she's hounding the secretary to marry her. But he can't throw away his reputation over a cheap little whore! Cuicui refused to go to Purple Thistle Pass for an abortion until he agreed to let her brother fill the job opening. But this is too good an opportunity to let pass, so let's get Golden Dog back here and have him sign up at the township office. I expect them to put four or five names forward, and then someone from the newspaper will come to make the selection. Time is of the essence, and we have to move fast! The village government doesn't want this news to leak out, but you know how close Golden Dog and I are. I feel I have to do this even if they say I was wrong and punish me!"

The painter was so melted that he fell all over himself trying to show his gratitude. He withdrew to the other room and brought out some wine.

Han Wenju broke the silence. "I've known all along that Golden Dog's features show he's no ordinary fellow. If he works for the Zhou City newspaper, he'll make a name for himself and prove that the Tian and Gong clans aren't the only people in Stream of Wandering Spirits worth talking about! But if Secretary Tian gave Cuicui his word, he can't very well go back on it, can he?"

"It all depends on us," Cai said. "That's why we have to get Golden Dog back here right away. He's the most qualified person, but Tian Yishen refuses to give in. On the surface, he's all buddy-buddy with Golden Dog, but he'll do anything he can to make things difficult for him. He can't fool me!"

"Isn't your river shipping brigade making money hand over fist?" Han asked him. "And I hear that Tian Yishen is doing a terrific job at the warehouse in White Rock Stockade."

"He's a crafty fellow," Cai said, "even though he manages to keep a good reputation. It's Golden Dog and the others who supply the effort for the river shipping brigade. Go ask Tian Yishen how many times he's been out on the river and how much running around he's done. He talks a good job! All he wants is power, as though the shipping brigade were all his doing!"

The painter, who was just sitting there drinking, asked, "Doesn't Secretary Tian put a lot of trust in him?"

"That's the only thing I've got against Secretary Tian. I don't know what he's thinking of by relying on Tian Yishen. When people complained to him how dissatisfied they were with Tian Yishen and how they wanted him removed, Secretary Tian agreed to hold an election at a general meeting of the brigade to keep things from getting out of hand. That's why Tian Yishen set that sex trap. When Golden Dog gets back, tell him to unite the others not to vote for Tian Yishen. Who does he think he is? With all the economic problems we're facing now, everything's going to turn to shit if we let him keep running things!"

Han, who had little information on what was happening with the river shipping brigade, wasn't about to voice any opinions, so he kept his mouth shut. A river shipping brigade with two commanders was like two people trying to piss into the same bottle—no different from the situation several years earlier with the branch secretary and the chairman of the Poor Peasants Association. *What is it with these officials, who are on the public payroll and eat the people's food, yet can't get along with each other? Well, let them not get along, it doesn't mean shit to me!* In fact, the news made Han happy. All this arguing among the leaders of the brigade had resulted in good for Golden Dog. He picked up the decanter of wine and complained loudly that it was empty, reviling the painter for not keeping a supply of wine in the house and volunteering to go to his boat to get more. But the painter went in and got another bottle, and the three of them continued toasting one another, glass after glass.

Han Wenju, soon drunk, said, "Commander Cai, the way you tell it, Yingying's going to work at the newspaper, too, right? Doesn't she already have a job at the Crossroads Township co-op? What does she need to be on the list for, since she already has a salary? Does she even know how to write a story?"

"Wasn't it Secretary Tian who went to the county and got them to give the quota to our village? Would Golden Dog have a chance of going if it hadn't come to our village? Whatever work there is, someone has to do it, and if you don't know how, you can always learn. Sure, she has a decent job at the co-op, but what kind of future does she have there?"

Han then brought up an event of the past. "Ten years ago," he said, "a reporter from the Zhou City paper came here on a story and asked about the revolutionary activities of the Tian and Gong clans in Stream of Wandering Spirits. He left after interviewing me all morning, and a few days later they published a long story. You can be an official without talent, but not a reporter. I don't think Yingying would have much luck writing for a newspaper."

"Uncle Han," the painter said, "you're drunk again!"

Han Wenju stood up. "Sure, I've had plenty to drink, and the older I get, the harder it is to hold my liquor. Once, forty years ago, I finished off two catties of white spirits and went to the whorehouse at White Rock Stockade. That damned madam, with her rotten teeth, said I was drunk and charged me three silver dollars. I really gave her hell, then I took a whore to bed, but as I was leaving I swiped a bar of soap. I've had too much to drink today, Commander Cai, so I'd better head back to my boat. Give a hoot when you want to go back. I won't ferry anybody else, but I'll ferry you for sure, ferry you . . ."

As Han walked out the door, the painter asked him if he could make it back by himself. "I can make it," he said. "I can make it." He weaved his way down the road.

Fuyun was waiting for him in the cabin of the boat. He was covered with sweat and belching like crazy.

"What did she feed you after you worked damned near all night?" Han asked.

"Meat, like she promised," Fuyun said. "Twelve slices." His face turned crimson as he screwed up the courage to ask, "Uncle Han, what do you think of her?"

Han Wenju's drunken eyes glazed over. "You think she's all right just because she fed you some meat?" he said.

"What I mean is . . ." He didn't go on.

The perception sobered Han up a bit. "Did she offer you something even better?"

Fuyun nodded his head.

Han grabbed him. "Well, well, Fuyun, so that's what you're capable of. That woman's Secretary Tian's sister-in-law, and she's at least ten years older than you!"

Fuyun was getting even more nervous. "I didn't do anything, Uncle Han. After I plowed her garden, I went in to eat. She kept feeding me meat, and when I finished, she said I must be tired and told me to lie down on the kang. Then she took off her jacket, complaining of the heat, but I didn't dare take mine off, because I thought she'd get the wrong idea. She came over and sat down next to me, and

I got scared again, figuring it was a trick. So I said I had to go to the bathroom, and as soon as I was out the door, I came down here to the boat."

Han spit in his face. "You're goddamned useless," he cursed him. "What kind of trick could that woman play on you? If I were as young as you, I wouldn't worry about things like that. Even if it had been a trick, you could have played one back on her!"

Fuyun sat there abashed.

Han, laughing so hard he couldn't stop, collapsed on the deck. He tried to think of a way to tease Fuyun. "You're an impotent little bastard," he finally said. "Do you have any idea how many mistresses Tian Zhongzheng has? That woman's over forty, just at her peak. A wolf at thirty, a tiger at forty. First, she can't control herself, and second, she wants to get even with Tian. She doesn't come looking for me . . . I'm no good to her, while you, you coarse little bastard, don't know how to deal with women!"

He turned his head, coughed up a big gob of phlegm, and had nothing more to say.

7

Outside the southern gate of White Rock Stockade a row of run-down shacks, some tall, some low, lined the bank of the Zhou River. Having fallen outside the plans of the city construction bureau, they had just been thrown together. But they were unique and presented a picturesque sight. Artists from Zhou City, whose hair was so long you couldn't tell if they were boys or girls, frequently stopped to paint them. Since the shacks had no foundations and their walls were made of stones piled upon bricks right on the riverbank, they looked a little like blockhouses. Wooden stairs or suspension ladders tied to posts inside the houses allowed the people to climb upstairs. Where there weren't any flat rocks on the riverbank and the owners were short of building materials, they just set up a couple of stone columns, then built illegal wooden shacks on top of them. Because the windows were left open day and night, they looked like a row of ugly—or beautiful—eyes staring out over the Zhou River.

Winds swept across the surface of the Zhou River, but it was still a good river. (Whether you call a girl ugly or beautiful, her face is still fair.) Early-morning fog rose from the water and climbed to the roofs of the shacks until the town seemed to be set in a gigantic steamer with the lid open. City streetlights shone weakly, spreading a shy yellow glow over South Avenue, an old street that resounded with crisp sounds: they were either from the hard plastic heels of water carriers on cobblestones or from pigs being let into their sties, honey-bucket carriers behind them so that when the pigs raised their tails they could quickly scoop up what came out and dump it into their buckets. Wooden scoops banged rhythmically against the sides of the buckets, like night watchmen's wooden clappers of olden days. By this hour the shacks on the outskirts of the city were visible through the fog, and a resplendent morning luminosity extended out from the surface of the river, gradually swallowing up the uneven stone walls as it moved to the western bank to embrace three or four riverboats and the rafts floating on the water.

A sleepy woman in one of the wood-and-stone attics, her hair uncombed, sticks her head out the window in the morning and yells something before dumping a pan of smelly liquid into the water below. Artists from town who are regularly splashed curse this foul "miasma" on the smelly riverbank. The woman hears them, quickly lowers the window curtain, and laughs. Or the artists are painting the stone columns when they see something white squatting down and shitting into a hole at the base of one of the wooden shacks, and they wish they had a rock to throw, to elicit howls of indignation that might assuage theirs. Winter comes, and there is added to the stone columns yet other columns, of frozen shit. Peasants come to town with their hammers and attack it as though they were sculpting, then put the stuff on their rafts and sail downstream. It's a scene worth preserving, but unhappily the artists never frequent the town during this season.

At dusk, darkness begins to envelop the town, although the banks of the river are still bright. On the eastern bank, a row of rafts is being towed upriver by men shouting a cadence, their bodies bent nearly parallel to the shoreline as the rafts draw nearer the bank. Heads rest on the sills of the windows in the wood-and-stone buildings, and the banks are crowded with onlookers shouting across the river to the boatmen, "Need a place to stay? Fifty cents a night. Clean sheets plus food and drink!" Their eyes are riveted on the leather money pouches around the waists of the men, who love the attention, like soldiers returning from battle. But they're too busy to stop and answer; never pausing in their swaggering gait, they know where they're going, all except the younger, inexperienced men with innocent faces, who are soon surrounded by innkeepers, like sheep stalked by a pack of wolves, and dragged off to one of the buildings where the beds are small and the sheets are filthy. They wake up in the middle of the night feeling itchy all over and pluck fleshy objects off their bodies, which they pinch between their fingernails until they hear a loud pop. Light streams up from downstairs through the cracks in the floor, and they can see the innkeeper and his mistress wrapped around each other like contortionists. Since the men can't sleep, they gnaw on their fingernails and stroke their chests, getting up all night long.

Golden Dog never stayed at one of these places. Every time he returned, he'd bathe in the river, then hang his wet clothes on the raft to dry, putting them back on as he drew up to the shore, where he'd tie up his raft and head straight to the blacksmith shop on South Avenue. Water Girl would still the rumblings of his stomach with breakfast and wine and fill his greedy eyes with her presence. Sometimes they whispered in a dark corner before Golden Dog called out to Old Pockface, who was standing beside the furnace, "Elder Uncle, I'm going to the warehouse." He'd glance back at Water Girl, who'd be standing behind the door curtain, her face beet red.

Pockface knew everything. "Golden Dog," he'd bellow, "what did you call me?"

"Grandpa," Water Girl would say, "you're getting old. I call him Younger Uncle!"

"What do you mean, old? I want him to call me Grandpa, and he'd damn well better!"

Even Water Girl's neck was red now. She called out to Golden Dog, who was walking away, "Uncle Golden Dog, the next time you come, don't forget to bring some good wine for Grandpa."

Golden Dog never brought wine, and it was always the blacksmith who treated him. But he spent every night, without fail, in the bunkhouse of the warehouse, where he'd talk all night long with his buddies, who didn't worry about age differences or what words people used.

One day Golden Dog and Old Seven bought several thousand catties of varnish at a village ten li above Crossroads Township, which they shipped to Purple Thistle Pass, where the price was three times what they'd paid. There they took on a load of tobacco, which they could easily transport upstream to White Rock Stockade. While they were sitting in a small inn at Purple Thistle Pass sharing a bottle of wine, a stranger in his thirties and wearing black clothes stopped just outside the entrance. He spread a piece of yellow oilcloth out on the ground, then placed some red-dyed grains of wheat and a pile of little paper packets on it. On the wall behind him he hung three red silk banners with crooked black lettering: Rodent Exterminator, Rodent Enemy, Extermination Expert. Golden Dog, who was aware that you could find just about any sort of person you wanted in Purple Thistle Pass, heard the man in black clothes outside bang two pieces of bamboo together and begin his spiel: "Listen up, elders, townspeople, all you ladies. I'm a man of few talents, but with a heart bent on service to my country. These are peaceful times, times of plenty, but great harvests produce hordes of rats, those evil creatures, and I've come to this wonderful place to sell you my rat poison. This poison of mine is a secret concoction passed down through generations. Rats can't resist it, and once they've eaten it, they're doomed before they go three steps. Most peddlers are charlatans who care only for profits and have damaged the reputation of my trade. But I'm in business to drive out what harms the people! The human population these days is on the rise, and so is that of rats. The birth of people is matched by the birth of rats, and people and rats must contend for food. If the rats aren't exterminated, 70 percent of the food goes to people, 30 percent to the rats. Before I sell my concoction, I give free samples. The first packet is yours for nothing. If you feel you're being cheated, please read the banner behind me. My name is Wu Feng, and I live in Crossroads Township. I never change my name, at home or on the road. If you think you've been cheated, you can report me to the White Rock Stockade People's Court, where I'll willingly accept incarceration or punishment even if they demand my head!" When Golden Dog heard the words *Crossroads Township,* his heart skipped a beat. He had never heard of a secret concoction passed down through generations in Crossroads Township. There was something fishy here. He got up and went out the door to take a closer look. Who did he see but Lei Dakong from Stream of Wandering Spirits.

Before he could shout out, Dakong spotted him, and his eyes nearly popped out of his head. He pulled Golden Dog over to the side and said, "Don't give me away. I've just set up shop, so don't spoil it!"

"Come on," Golden Dog said. "Let's have a drink. My treat."

"Give me a few minutes," Dakong pleaded. "Let me make some sales, and I'll treat you. I need your help. Pretend you don't know me. Say you bought some of my rat poison, that the rats dropped like flies, and everything's back to normal where you live. Say you're here to buy twenty packets for your neighbors. I'll return your money."

"Don't try that," Golden Dog said. "Uncle Seven's here. Seeing a fellow villager far from home is always cause to celebrate over some wine." He gathered up Dakong's banners and medicine, and they went over to the inn, where they ordered a decanter of wine, three small dishes of pigs' knuckles, a dish of pickled vegetables, and half a bowl of peanuts. In loud voices they played drinking games as the wine began to take effect.

"Dakong," Golden Dog asked, "how come you haven't been home for so long?"

"I brought charges against Tian Zhongzheng, and what happened? He got promoted. I was so depressed I decided to go out and drift for a while. After all, with no parents and no wife and kids, I can take my meals where I want, so why should I stay there and put up with his abuse?"

"Let Tian be party secretary, and let us be commoners. He can't exterminate us! If we all left, he'd have smooth sailing and there'd be no one to keep the snake from turning into a dragon. And you, instead of leaving and doing something worthwhile, you begin hawking wares on the street, an ignoble and degrading profession!"

"It cost almost nothing to set up this business," Dakong defended himself. "For half a yuan I can buy a bottle of zinc phosphate. Then all I have to do is add ten catties of wheat grain, twenty kernels per packet, and sell them for ten cents apiece. It's almost all profit! I can hawk the stuff anywhere I go, eat where I want, roam where I please, and be as happy as a wandering immortal!"

"Does that concoction of yours really work?"

"The packet I give away does. The rest I could eat right on the spot."

Old Seven snorted, "You're terrible!"

"These days," Dakong argued, "people cheat me, and I cheat them. Who doesn't live that way? We common folk cheat a few coppers out of one another, but what about the officials? Uncle Seven, it's too bad you don't know how to read, because if you saw all the newspaper exposés of bureaucratic scandals, you'd be so angry you'd probably go out and hang yourself! And what do they suffer for their evil deeds? If they stink up one office, they're transferred to another, still officials. When one of them moves up the ladder, he takes his seven brothers-in-law and eight sisters-in-law with him! Do you think the Tian and Gong clans are any different?"

Golden Dog knew that Lei Dakong had done a lot of traveling over the previous few years, that he'd seen a lot, and that he had a quick mind. "Uncle Seven's right," he said. "You really ought to care more about integrity and principles. You're a capable man, and as long as you do an honest day's work with a clear conscience, your prospects will be fine. You can't keep this up. We're taking some rafts back to White Rock Stockade today. Come along with us."

So Lei Dakong boarded a raft. He was a water dragon, and even though he'd been drinking, he poled the raft like a pro. Seemingly immune from fear, when he spotted a hornets' nest on the shore, he soaked one of his homemade silk banners in wine, lit it, and set the nest on fire without getting stung once. Old Seven urged him to join the river shipping brigade. "The reason I took up selling rat poison," Dakong said, "was that I didn't want to be a boatman. Tian Zhongzheng made his running dogs, Tian Yishen and Cai Da'an, leaders of the river shipping brigade. Well, I'm up to here with them. Besides, if I do anything, it'll be something big, not knocking my self out on the river for a few bowls of rice!"

The rafts arrived at White Rock Stockade, and Lei Dakong went ashore to sell his wares. Old Seven and Golden Dog told the men working in the warehouse to unload the tobacco while awaiting the arrival of the other boats in the brigade. One superstitious old fellow on boat number eight always set up an altar in his cabin with a little white snake, which he called the river dragon. When he sailed into Purple Thistle Pass, he picked up the caged snake and headed straight for the main hall of the Smooth Seas Temple, where he placed the snake at the base of the idol and burned incense and kowtowed, praying for safe passage on the river. When he sailed into White Rock Stockade, where there was also a Smooth Seas Temple, he carried his snake there and burned more incense and kowtowed. Old Seven chose to participate in the ritual, but Golden Dog just laughed at them and refused to waste his time. Once the rafts were unloaded, he rushed over to the blacksmith shop on South Avenue instead. As the young man was leaving, Old Seven said, "Golden Dog, why go over there? Is Water Girl more important than the gods?"

"I'm taking a fish over to the blacksmith," Golden Dog answered.

"Golden Dog," Old Seven insisted, "you've never tasted the wrath of the river. The Smooth Seas Temple was built with money donated by your ancestor's sailors' guild. He was a hardy fellow, but he had respect for the river gods. Don't you consider yourself a descendant of the sailors' guild?"

But Golden Dog went off anyway. If my ancestor built a temple and prayed to the river gods, he was thinking, why did he end up being drawn and quartered? Golden Dog headed straight for South Avenue, and all the people along the way knew he was the blacksmith's regular guest. They smiled as he passed and said, "Pockface has gone to the tavern. He's been drinking a lot lately and is drunk half the time."

"Is Water Girl with him?"

"She's had it with his getting drunk. She used to go over and help him home. But he kept going back, and she became so disgusted that she's stopped going for him."

As long as Water Girl's home, that's good enough for me, Golden Dog thought. He couldn't say when they'd started having feelings for each other, since neither ever talked about it. But it was getting harder and harder to be away from her, and when they were together, they couldn't stop talking and laughing. Finally, Water Girl began to lose the diffidence caused by her widowhood, and Golden Dog stopped worrying about their uncle-niece relationship. All they had to do was look into each other's eyes to know their sentiments. At first, the men in the river shipping brigade were unaware of the change in the relationship and were surprised by the brightness of Water Girl's eyes whenever she saw Golden Dog. The two of them said nothing to call attention to their feelings and always assumed the proper attitude when they were around the others. Water Girl always called him Uncle Golden Dog. Then one day at the blacksmith shop, when there was no one around, he suddenly kissed her on the cheek. He tensed, and so did she. "You?" she blurted out. He was so startled that he bolted out the door and didn't have the confidence to go back. After ten days, she went over to the ferry landing beyond the southern gate of town and called out for him. His mettle returned when he heard her shout, and he was ecstatic. He let go with his eyebrows, his eyes, his speech, his actions. He was as bold as a wolf. And with his change in behavior, the other boatmen soon noticed the affection Water Girl and Golden Dog had for each other. Today, hearing that Water Girl was alone at the blacksmith shop, he made his way there eagerly. And the minute he walked in the door, he caught her off guard, wrapping his arms around her like clinging vines. She couldn't get free no matter how she struggled. Finally, she pricked his face with a bamboo needle, and he sat on the edge of the kang panting.

"How come you're so late getting here today?" she asked him.

"There weren't enough men to unload the rafts. I came straight over as soon as we finished cleaning up."

"That's what you say! Maybe you went to a restaurant first. You river men are always hungry, and you've got money in your pockets. And you'll eat anything, a dead cat or a rotten dog!"

"White Rock Stockade doesn't have anything to compare with you," he said. "If I so much as think of going to a restaurant, I hope my raft flips over at Black Tiger Shoals!"

She put her hand over his mouth, and he took the opportunity to lick the palm of her hand.

"Golden Dog," she said, "I call you Uncle, so why are you acting like that?"

"You tell me how I'm related to you. You call me Uncle, but let's hear you *say* it! Let's hear you say, 'Uncle' now!" Like a wild beast, he wrapped his limbs around her and pinned her beneath him on the kang.

Water Girl would let him do anything he wanted, anything but that. It wasn't modesty, it was her sense of right and wrong. An unmarried daughter could cross a thousand lines, ten thousand lines, but the final line was her maidenhood, and that was not to be crossed. A girl's parents alone could make that decision. Only after the match was made and a ceremony completed could she give herself to a man. She was a moral girl. "Golden Dog," she protested, "you can't do this! Your food's on the plate waiting for you, so what's your hurry? I'm keeping myself for you, but if you sneak up and do it now, what will it mean to you later?"

He paused as her words sank in, and at that moment she rolled off the kang and walked over to the doorway, laughing heartily. He chased her and grabbed her behind the door. She didn't flinch. "Water Girl," he said, "I'll do what you say, but you have to do what I say, too. We won't do *that* if you say so, but you have to let me feel you."

She was weakening. How long could she keep putting him off? So she slipped behind the door. "If you can't have the main course, will you settle for an appetizer? I'm yours anyway, so you can have a feel, but just a little one. And close your eyes!" He moved over and slid his hand under her blouse. He felt her once, and then a second time, and left his hand there.

Too embarrassed to look, she was trembling like a stalk of bamboo in the wind. "Does this make me a bad girl?"

Golden Dog didn't say anything, for he'd lost control and was no longer behaving rationally. This was the first time he'd felt a woman's body, and it was like someone on the road on a hot summer day who comes upon a woods, or a thirsty person who stumbles upon a spring. It's all right if you don't walk into the woods to cool off, but once you enter, you feel like staying there forever; it's all right if you don't drink from the spring, but once you do, you're thirstier than ever. He was like a crazed man, like a wild lion. He pulled her close and began to tear at her clothes. She was panic-stricken. She screamed his name, then bit him on the shoulder and pushed him so hard he fell to the floor. "Golden Dog," she said severely, "if you try that again, I won't be yours anymore. I'm the daughter of this house, and no one in the Han family has ever done a dirty thing like that before!"

Golden Dog sat on the floor and stared at her, his eyes gradually turning from red to green to white. The fire had been put out, and his eyelids settled slowly down. He was unrequited, remorseful, frustrated. He even fancied that an invisible barrier had come between them.

Seeing him on the floor despondent and disappointed, Water Girl began to cry. She didn't know why she was crying, but she wept as with a broken heart.

Golden Dog had no sooner picked himself up off the floor than the door opened explosively.

Pockface strode in, his face dark, his eyes clouded. "Golden Dog!" he bellowed. "Golden Dog!" Water Girl walked out from behind the door, drying her eyes. "Grandpa, you're drunk again. What makes you think Golden Dog is here?"

"Don't lie to me," he said. "I could see four feet under the door, and two of them were tanned, with splayed toes. If they don't belong to Golden Dog, what dog do they belong to?" Golden Dog jumped out from behind the door with a shout.

"Golden Dog," Pockface complained, "you wild beast!" The minute you show up, Water Girl forgets to come get me. Are you just waiting for me to die, Water Girl?"

"You don't have any room in your heart for me, Grandpa. If you did, you wouldn't drink like that!"

Pockface laughed—heh-heh—and sat down on the edge of the kang. He grabbed Golden Dog. "Golden Dog," he said, "I'm not drunk. Tell me, what do you think of Water Girl?"

"I like her, and I like you even better!"

"Your mother's ass!" Pockface shot back. "What's there to like about me? If it weren't for Water Girl, you wouldn't give me the time of day. If you like her, do something about it. If you come here without a matchmaker, you've wasted the trip! You tell me if you can find another girl like Water Girl anywhere along the banks of the Zhou River. She's capable and good-natured, and it's not our fault that the Sun family wasn't lucky enough to keep her."

"Grandpa," Water Girl said, "you've had too much to drink."

"We boatmen in the river shipping brigade have already talked to Uncle Han about it . . . "

This incited Pockface, who let loose a torrent of abuse: "Talking to Han Wenju is like farting in the wind. He's never done an honest day's work in his life. He can't even take care of himself, so how do you expect him to take care of Water Girl? If you find a matchmaker, bring her here. Isn't that right, Water Girl?"

"If Uncle Han knew you were talking about him like that, Grandpa, he'd be over here with fists flying."

"You think I'm afraid of that old bag of bones? He's been sending messages for you to go back, but you'll go back over my dead body! Golden Dog, if you're good enough to handle it, I'll teach you my blacksmith skills, and someday you can run the shop. But if you take Han Wenju's side in this, don't show your face around here anymore, and you can forget about Water Girl even to your dying day."

Annoyed that her grandpa was straying from the subject, Water Girl sniffed, but he kept talking, turning her livid. She went out and sat alone on a tree stump by the furnace and breathed heavily as she thought about her mother. Her tears began to flow.

"What are you so unhappy about?" her grandfather asked.

"Everything would be fine if Mother were alive. You're an old man, and you're always drinking, even though you're not supposed to. And when you drink, you run off at the mouth!"

Mention of Water Girl's mother had a sobering effect on Pockface, and a saddening one. It also shut him up. Complaining of a headache, he climbed up onto the kang and went to sleep. The blacksmith shop was quiet again. Golden Dog went and cleaned the fish he'd brought. By the time he was finished, his hands shiny with fish scales, Water Girl had lit the stove.

Someone called Golden Dog's name softly from outside. Though Water Girl, when she saw it was Dakong, got up and greeted him, he wouldn't come in. "Water Girl," he said, "so Golden Dog's here after all! Can I borrow him for a while? I have to talk to him about something."

"Golden Dog isn't one of my handkerchiefs. If you want him, take him! I don't like the way you talk, you bum!"

Golden Dog stepped toward him with a smile on his face. "Aren't you busy selling your goods? What do you want me for?"

Dakong didn't say a word. His tiny eyes were blinking rapidly, a signal that he wanted Golden Dog to come outside at once. Golden Dog told Water Girl to cook the fish, then went out with Dakong. "Do you want to make serious money or not?" Dakong asked when they reached the street.

"What kind of shit is that? Do you think I'm out there playing games with that boat of mine?"

"How do you expect to make serious money poling a boat?" Dakong asked him. "These days it's real work, no money; real money, no work.

I've heard of a good way to tap the well, but it depends on whether you're willing to go along."

"Where money's concerned, the more the merrier. I'm not afraid to stick my hand in, so tell me what this is all about."

"I went to a lot of privately run shops," Dakong said, "and asked them how they were doing. Well, they've got it made! Do you know how that store on South Avenue made such a killing? All their merchandise was bought in Beijing and Shanghai. It cost them a thousand yuan, and after six months of buying and selling, they've got seventy or eighty thousand! Let's open a store of our own. What do you say?"

Golden Dog's brain was overheated, as though the passions he'd been unable to release toward Water Girl had found a new outlet. "That sounds terrific! You get us started. Find a location, and get your hands on some merchandise. You can mind the store, and I'll be in charge of purchasing new stock. By poling a boat *and* running a store, I can let one job serve the other, and we can make as much money as anybody else."

"Okay," Dakong said, "I'll make all the arrangements. Since our problem now is capital I'll make a trip to Guangzhou."

"Guangzhou?"

Dakong couldn't control his excitement. "I ran into an old friend," he said, "a traveling salesman. He says that in Guangzhou a silver dollar is worth eighteen yuan. I got my hands on ten of them. What I'm saying is, ask around and see if any of the boatmen have some. We'll give them a good price."

Golden Dog was somewhat hesitant. "Isn't that illegal?"

"I thought I'd be wasting my time talking to you about this. How do you expect to open a business without capital? I went to the credit co-op to borrow some money, but that son of a bitch Cai Da'an wouldn't lend it to me. He said I'd never be able to pay it back! That's public money; it doesn't belong to him. He expected me to give him something under the table. But Lei Dakong never learned how to bow and scrape to the likes of him!"

Golden Dog just shook his head. Dakong grabbed him by the arm and dragged him over to North Avenue. When they reached a lane, they hunkered down by the road. "You were a soldier, so you're pretty straitlaced. But nowadays you can do pretty much what you please. Let me ask you this: do you know how many illegal prostitutes there are?"

Golden Dog was aware of what went on in the wood-and-stone buildings on the bank of the Zhou River, so he said, "Some of the men on the boats piss their money away on those women. But not all the women in those wood-and-stone buildings are prostitutes. Some of them are really in love with their men, and that's all they can think about."

"That shows how much you know! I'll tell you the truth. I've been there. Put a group of them together, and I can tell you which ones are in the business. As soon as it's dark, go out on the street and you'll see three or four women with new perms standing beneath a telephone pole, their lips painted like they've been drinking blood, and holding a little sheepskin fur in their hands. If you go up to them, they'll ask you, 'Want to buy some fur?' If you don't know what's going on and think they're really selling the fur and you try to bargain with them, you'll never get the price you want. So off you go. But if you know what's going on, when you ask the price, you say, 'Oh, my, I didn't bring enough. Come with me and I'll get the money.' Turn and walk off, and she'll follow you. You can take her down to the riverbank, to one of the hollows in the city wall. That's the economical way. If you want a higher class of woman, you can find them too. See that two-story building across the street?"

Golden Dog looked. It was a shop, a little one, with all kinds of clothes hanging inside. There was a vase filled with lovely flowers on the green window ledge of the second floor.

"That's one of the houses," Lei Dakong said. "They say it belongs to some unemployed high-school graduates, three men and a woman, although I don't know where they come from. You see that bright-red down parka hanging above the counter? If you know the score, you'll ask its price. The man will quote you a figure. If you think it's too high, you just go about your business. But if the price is okay, you can say you want to buy it, and he'll take you upstairs, where the woman will take care of you. When you're finished, off you go, and the red parka is hung up over the counter again. Golden Dog, if things like that can go on, what's the big deal about my dealing in silver coins?"

Golden Dog had never heard such things before. If he'd been listening to Han Wenju telling ghost stories at the ferry landing, he'd only have half-believed him. But Dakong had been roaming the countryside for a good six months and had seen just about everything. He couldn't possibly be making it all up. This White Rock Stockade is a bad place, he was thinking. *What the hell are the police doing?* He stood up, spit several times, and pointed at Dakong's forehead. "It's a dirty, low-class business, so don't get involved, like some nasty fly. Nothing good will come of it. I'm not going to touch that silver-dollar business of yours. Now, if you want to eat some fish, come to the blacksmith shop with me."

Golden Dog's reaction took Dakong by surprise. "Then how are we going to manage a store, Golden Dog?"

"We'll manage. Do you mean to say we can't do a thing without those few silver coins? Give it some thought, and I will too."

Dakong smiled helplessly. "Golden Dog, you're a decent man," he said after a moment. "I can't be angry with you if you won't go along. Just pretend I didn't say anything, and don't tell anybody else what I said." He turned and walked away.

Golden Dog walked back alone, feeling depressed. When he reached Central Avenue, caught up in his thoughts, someone grabbed him around the waist. Golden Dog swung around and looked. It was Fuyun, his head shaved clean, his face covered with sweat, like little beads. "Do you know how long I've been looking for you?" he yelled hoarsely. "When I couldn't find you at the warehouse, I went over to the blacksmith shop, but Water Girl said you went out. I've been running up and down looking for you, and you've been right here all along!"

"What's got you so excited?" Golden Dog asked.

"Come with me to Stream of Wandering Spirits," Fuyun said, "and hurry! Your father and Han Wenju sent me to look for you. They say it's urgent, so you're to get there right away! I asked them what was wrong, but they wouldn't tell me."

Golden Dog was puzzled. What could be wrong at home? He was worried. He said he'd run back to the blacksmith shop to tell Water Girl, but Fuyun said he'd already told her. He started pushing Golden Dog toward the ferry landing beyond the southern gate of town, where they boarded a boat heading upstream.

8

After Fuyun left, Water Girl waited in the blacksmith shop. She waited and she waited. As night was falling, she saw flocks of white-necked crows flying from the southern bank of the Zhou River to the roof of the Smooth Seas Temple, and she decided that Fuyun must have found Golden Dog and taken him back to the village. She felt suddenly uneasy. Grandpa Pockface, who had slept off his drunk, looked at the cold cooked fish and told Water Girl to warm it for him. When the fish was ready and she had handed it to him, she said she was going to Stream of Wandering Spirits. He couldn't stop her, since he knew there was a night boat, so he gave her a peachwood club to ward off evil and told her to come back the next day, and then he walked her to the end of the lane.

The boat was passing when she reached the river, and she called out to it. Tian Yishen and Lu Cuicui, from Crossroads Township, were already on board. Water Girl didn't know Cuicui very well. Nevertheless, after a casual greeting, she sat down with them.

"Water Girl," Tian asked, "is business still booming at your grandpa's shop?"

"It's not *that* good, but he makes some pocket money."

"I'll bet he brought you here so you could take over the shop someday."

"You're joking. How could I take over for him?"

Tian said he wouldn't be surprised if Pockface was looking for a son-in-law, and he asked her if she had a boyfriend. She averted her head and glanced at Cuicui without saying a word.

But Tian wouldn't be denied. "They're hard to find! No chance of finding someone unspoiled. Your best bet is to look for a guy going around for the second time. Someone like that has his good points,

Water Girl. He'll know how to take care of you, and you can be the boss!"

Water Girl was ruffled, but she just leaned over and talked to Cuicui, who was holding a brand-new wool blanket in her arms. "Did you just buy that? It's a wonderful color. Your family's doing fine if you can afford high-quality stuff like that!"

"You don't think this is for me, do you? I bought it for my younger brother. He's going to Zhou City, and how would it look if he used a coarse printed blanket from our mountain village? He'd be a laughingstock!"

"Is he going there for business?"

"He has a job there. At the newspaper. You read the Zhou City paper, don't you? Well he's going to be a reporter."

Tian Yishen gave an admonitory cough and Cuicui quickly shut up. Water Girl could see that they wanted to avoid saying more to her, so she refrained from further questions and just stared at the mountains on either side of the river, which looked like strange wild animals. The half-moon hanging above the mountain peaks seemed pitifully small.

It was midnight when they reached Stream of Wandering Spirits. The landing was deserted, and her uncle's ferryboat was tied up at the pier. Tian Yishen and Lu Cuicui disembarked and headed straight for Crossroads Township; the boatman tied up his boat and went off home. Water Girl stepped onto the ferry and called out, "Uncle," several times. No response. Something was wrong. She stood listening to the mountain watchdogs, which sounded particularly vicious that night; their hollow sounds echoed back and forth between the mountains before circling over the river and settling into the water. She climbed up the stone steps of the landing, each footstep producing an echo, and looked at Green Dragon and White Tiger peaks. She shivered, then ran all the way to Han Wenju's house as though a ghost were on her tail.

Han Wenju was there. So were Golden Dog, his father, Fuyun, and Cai Da'an. They were sitting around the table drinking and talking. "Yo!" they cried when they saw her, and they jumped to their feet.

"You're back," Fuyun said. "That's wonderful. Now, tell us if this news is good or bad."

Her heart leaped into her throat as she heard what was going on. Her eyes lit up. "It's good news!" she cried out happily. "Great news! I thought something terrible had happened, and my soul almost flew away. Uncle Golden Dog, how many times do you think something this good will happen to you?"

"You're right, it's good news. But if it's Tian Zhongzheng's list, Yingying will be on it for sure. That only leaves one real opening, and there are plenty of pigs at the trough, so what are my chances? Besides, I won't kiss somebody's ass for it!"

"I'm here!" Cai said. "All you have to do is sign in at the village office, and I'll do the fighting for you! Even if Tian Yishen tries to cause trouble, who the hell is he? I'll fight it out with him at the meeting, and you can get the boatmen from the river shipping brigade behind you. There's supposed to be an election, isn't there? Well, if everybody gangs up on him, that'll take care of him, won't it? Opportunity only knocks once, and if you let this get away, you'll spend the rest of your life regretting it!"

Han Wenju took a coarse cloth bundle from under his shirt and removed his six ancient copper coins and his divination book. Golden Dog tossed the coins, as Han told him to do. But Han couldn't explain what the results meant. "Tell you what. I'll do a word divination for you. Give me a word."

Golden Dog laughed. "You know that one too, hmm? Okay, *tiger*. See what you can do with the word *tiger*."

Han solemnly dipped his finger in the wine and wrote the word *tiger* on the table. "Good," he said, "that's a good word. Golden Dog, don't pass up this chance. Sign up, and the job's as good as yours! Look here, all of you. What does the top part of the character mean? It's means 'go.' That's it, then; you're supposed to 'go' to Zhou City!"

Water Girl reached over and wiped away the *tiger* her uncle had written, then turned to Golden Dog. "Commander Cai's right. You have what it takes, particularly since this is what you did in the army. And you're just the right age. Why are you hesitating? If you don't go, someone without your talent and ethics surely will, and what good will your aloofness do anybody?"

They finished off another jug of wine with hardly a word from Golden Dog. Cai kept the conversation alive by fulminating against Tian Yishen. When Water Girl got up to make some tea, she gave Golden Dog a sign, and he followed her into the kitchen. "Make up your mind," she said, "and be quick about it!"

Her words sent a surge of heat through his heart and drove out the dejection that had lain there since earlier that day in the blacksmith shop. "I'll tell you the truth, Water Girl. If you want me to be a cadre,

I'll be one. The way the world is these days, you can't do anything for yourself unless you're a cadre. And if you want to do the right thing and oppose selfishness, you still have to be a cadre. Don't think the idea of being a reporter isn't appealing. It's just that I wonder why Cai Da'an is so enthusiastic about my standing for the job. I guarantee you he's not doing it for me. He's using me to get back at Tian Yishen!"

"Well, if he's using you," Water Girl said, "what's to keep you from using him?"

"That's occurred to me. But you don't know Tian Zhongzheng. He's in his element in official circles. If Cai Da'an is trying to get at Tian Yishen by putting my name on the list, there's no guarantee that Tian Zhongzheng will go along with it. So instead of being rash, I have to get to the bottom of things."

"Nobody in the shipping brigade likes Tian Yishen, do they?"

"No. And that's why Tian Zhongzheng holds such a tight rein on it. He's a master at the political strategy of one divides into two. He knows there's trouble between Cai and Tian Yishen, so he ties them together and has them eat out of the same trough so they'll keep an eye on each other. If one steps out of line, he can push him down and raise up the other. Then if the other acts up, he can push him down and raise up the first again. That way he keeps both satellites circling around him."

Water Girl was impressed by Golden Dog's insight and grew silent for a while, before mentioning to him that, since she and Tian Zhongzheng's niece were schoolmates and got along well, she'd see if Yingying would be willing to talk to her uncle.

"Okay, we'll try the back door! After all, I've dreamed of going to Zhou City. If it doesn't work out, I'll set up shop with Dakong. Do you think Yingying will be willing to help?"

"She's a reasonable girl. I'll do my best to persuade her."

She smiled at Golden Dog, who reached out in the darkness to take her hand. But she thrust her hand in her pocket and said calculatively, "No matter what, you mustn't give Cai the cold shoulder. He's a petty man, so let him think you're together." She picked up the vacuum bottle of tea and carried it into the other room. The tiny bit of warmth that had found its way into Golden Dog's heart was extinguished by her actions, and he stood there without moving for a while before following her. He walked to the table and said, "Commander Cai, I'm touched that you'd take so much trouble for my benefit, and I want to show my gratitude. But are you sure you'll be able to persuade Secretary Tian to put my name forward?"

"I'm thrilled to hear that!" Cai said. "I don't see any problem as long as we cooperate fully. I have a plan, but I'm not sure you'll go along with it."

"I'm sure you've set a condition," Golden Dog said.

"I'm doing this for you. Why not put your army experience to good use? Our shipping brigade was set up by Secretary Tian, and now he's viewed as a model throughout the county. Secretary Tian Youshan of the county committee sets a great deal of store by him, and they say that even the district leadership has its eye on him. So why not write something that spells out why Secretary Tian took charge of the brigade, how he did it, and what the effects have been? When you've got it written, I'll have my friends at the county broadcasting station put it on the radio and get the Zhou City newspaper to run it. Don't you think that would make him happy? Even if he's in your corner all along, if what you write makes the radio and the newspaper, it will at least defuse other opposition!"

"That's a wonderful idea!" Water Girl shouted. "Write it as soon as the wine's finished. Golden Dog, there'll be no sleep for you tonight. And since you might doze off if you're alone, Fuyun, you keep him company. What do you say?"

"Fine with me!" Fuyun said.

So it was settled. Han Wenju walked back to town with Cai Da'an, then went over to the painter's, where the two of them got some incense and made their way to Restless Hill Monastery. Finding the door shut, they walked in the darkness to the Temple of the Earth God, where they lit the incense and mumbled some prayers. After that, they split up, but Han ran after Golden Dog's father and commanded, "Go home and write a couple of slips of paper with the words *mountain watchdogs* on them. We'll put one of them under Golden Dog's pillow and stick the other one in his pocket. That should keep him safe! All you ever do is paint for other people and never get around to doing a couple of paintings for your own son!"

Back at Fuyun's house, Fuyun, Golden Dog, and Water Girl were bent over the table working on the draft of the story. What to write? Water Girl suggested concentrating on Tian Zhongzheng so he could wear a bright-red hat. Golden Dog demurred, saying he couldn't write something that wasn't true. If he did, once it was on the radio or in the newspaper, he'd be lying to everyone in the county and district. If unintentionally he made it possible for Tian Zhongzheng to be promoted and to improve his situation, he'd spend the rest of his life feeling empty, even if he'd made it to Zhou City and had become a reporter. They kept on like this until the rooster crowed three times, and still they hadn't written a single word. Water Girl became upset and was soon doing nothing but complaining. She recalled her encounter with Tian Yishen and Lu Cuicui on the Zhou River. "If you don't start writing," she said, "you can kiss your chances of ever getting to Zhou City good-bye. I guarantee that Tian Zhongzheng gave Cuicui all the assurances she'd need, or she wouldn't have bought her brother a wool blanket."

"Did Cuicui really tell you her brother was going to the Zhou City newspaper?" Golden Dog asked her.

"Would I lie to you? It just slipped out, and Tian Yishen quickly shut her up! Think about it: if you don't do everything you can, with their connections that simpleton from the Lu family will get the job and likely disgrace the profession!"

Golden Dog threw his head back and laughed heartily, which puzzled Water Girl and Fuyun, who stared blankly at him. "No need to write a phony news story now! Don't you see? It's a case of dipping bean curd in brine: one subdues the other!"

Water Girl and Fuyun were more at sea than ever. But Golden Dog told them a plan, which so delighted Fuyun that he shouted out exuberantly and pounded Golden Dog with his fist. He couldn't praise his astuteness enough, saying he was a demon for sure, the reincarnation of a mountain watchdog.

Since they were wide-awake, they sat and drank more wine, and were soon in such a lighthearted mood that Golden Dog decided to liven things up a bit. But when he looked at Water Girl, his words wouldn't come. Fuyun, sensing the nature of the situation and knowing that three's a crowd, got to his feet. "It's nearly light out, so I'd better go and catch a few winks," he muttered as an excuse.

"Fuyun," Water Girl objected, "what are you up to? Everyone says how straightforward you are, but I think you're being underhanded."

Her words stinging his ears, Golden Dog reached out and kept Fuyun from leaving.

Water Girl smiled and said, "I'll tell you what. Both of you go in and stretch out on the kang while I make some hot-and-sour soup noodles. That'll perk us all up. Now don't fall asleep, Fuyun. After you've eaten, go with Uncle Golden Dog, since the woman trusts you!" She went into the kitchen, from which the sound of clanging pots and pans soon emerged.

Day broke as Golden Dog and Fuyun finished their noodles. They left the house and went to the Tian compound, arriving just as Yingying's mother, her hair still uncombed, was heading to the outhouse with a bedpan. She was so agitated when she saw them that she quickly dumped the filthy water into the cistern. After that, she invited them inside, where they sat at the octagonal table while she went into her room to wash up and comb her hair. She emerged after a few minutes, all combed and washed, a new woman. With a smile, she inquired, "What wind blew you two this way so early in the morning? Fuyun's no stranger here, but we don't see you around here very often, Golden Dog. What's up?"

"Nothing in particular," Golden Dog said. "We just dropped by. Isn't the secretary home?"

"It's a rare day that you'll find him in this house." There was rancor in her voice. She took some cigarettes out of the cupboard and handed each man one. "He's not here, and I don't know if these cigarettes are any good or not. Golden Dog, you have the world by the tail these days, always traveling up to White Rock Stockade and down to Purple Thistle Pass. When are you going to give me a ride on that boat of yours and show me a little of the world?"

As Golden Dog lit his cigarette, he looked around the new house. The light and dark seemed perfectly balanced; the room had a concrete floor, glass panes in the windows, a double-door wooden cabinet with four inlaid panes in each door, and new-styled cabinets at the base of the east and west walls. A tall, sectioned mirror stood above the wooden cabinet in the main room, and on it was the scene *Three Oldtimers Enjoying Peach Blossoms.* A pair of scrolls on either side read, "The Triad of Heaven, Earth, and Man" and, "Riches, Fortune and Longevity, Spring Blessings." Tian Zhongzheng draws his meager wages like anybody else, Golden Dog thought to himself, yet look how beautifully this new house is furnished. *I wonder what the old place must look like!*

"Auntie sure has a way with words," he said. "No matter how well off people in Crossroads Township are, nobody has it so good as you people. If you really want to see a little of the world, you're welcome on my boat any time at all. I'm just worried that Secretary Tian might think it improper."

"He's not my lord and master!" she replied. "Everybody says what a good party secretary he is, and maybe he is. But he's not so hot as a family man. Do you know the pains I've taken with this home for all these years? Now that Yingying's aunt is gone, he doesn't give a moment's thought to his home. I don't see him as much as a stranger on the street does."

"Who *does?* There must be something wrong with him, since he's off to the medical clinic on East Avenue every few days."

"Are you talking about the clinic run by the Lu family?"

"That's the one," Fuyun answered, "Lu Cuicui's house."

The woman sat down abruptly, her face darkening. She mumbled something, then looked up and, with a bitter smile, invited Golden Dog and Fuyun to have some tea. When she scalded her hand in pouring, Golden Dog was sure that she knew what was going on between Tian Zhongzheng and Lu Cuicui. "Auntie, how can you live as comfortably as this and still be down in the dumps?" he prodded. "Yingying already has one job, and now she's off to Zhou City to work for the newspaper. When she sends for you to join her, your life will be better than ever."

"How did you know Yingying was going to Zhou City?"

"Everybody's talking about it. They say she's one of those who are going and that Cuicui's younger brother is the other."

"The son of the Lu family?"

"That's right," Fuyun said, "the son of the Lu family. People say she has her sights set on the secretary . . ."

She gripped him with both hands before he could finish and demanded to know where he'd heard this and exactly what people were saying. Fuyun froze. He didn't know what to reply.

"Auntie," Golden Dog cut in, "we don't understand it either. We came to ask you. The secretary's alone now, so he ought to be looking for another wife. But Lu Cuicui? She's nothing but a fox fairy, and I don't think this house is big enough for the two of you."

A ferocious look came over the woman's face. "So that's what's been going on! I figured he was just having some fun with her. I never thought his heart was that black!"

Watching her grind her teeth in anger, Golden Dog discreetly stood up and apologized: "Auntie, we shouldn't have upset you like this. We wouldn't have brought it up in the first place if we weren't concerned about the secretary's reputation. He's more than just Crossroads Township's party secretary, after all. He also commands the river shipping brigade. Now that the brigade has built such a fine name and is regarded so highly at the county and district levels, it's time for him to make a move up the ladder. He can't give up something that big for something so small. You know that the Tian and Gong clans have never got along, and we can't let the Gongs get wind of what's going on, to use against him. We're worried as well about your reputation and what will happen to you after this. That's why we came to talk. Now, don't get upset, and don't let the secretary know what we've said to you. That would really make things difficult for us!"

She just sat there, enraged, without saying a word. When she noticed that Golden Dog and Fuyun were on their way out the door, she hastened to them and handed each another cigarette. "I'm a pig or a dog if I whisper a word of this conversation. I'm glad you wised me up. I'm just a woman, whose place is in the home, and if you hadn't told me, he could have cooked and eaten me without my knowing it. From now on, if you hear anything out there, be sure to come and tell me."

On leaving the Tian compound they had a good laugh over what had happened. Fuyun headed off to do some fertilizing; Golden Dog went to the government office at Crossroads Township and signed up for the job. Cai Da'an was there and asked for the story Golden Dog was going to write. He was disappointed that it hadn't been written yet, but Golden Dog tried to dispel his fears. There was still time if the situation warranted it, he said. Then he returned to the village as though nothing had happened, boarded a raft, and poled it down the Zhou River to White Rock Stockade.

That night, Yingying's mother went to the township office to see Tian Zhongzheng and to lay her cards on the table. She was hoping she could produce a change of heart and make him break off with Lu Cuicui. But he wasn't there. When he'd heard that the opera troupe from the provincial capital was performing at White Rock Stockade, he'd taken the car belonging to the farm implements factory and gone to town for the show. Her suspicions aroused, she asked whether anyone had gone with him. The man panicked and blurted out that the secretary had taken Lu Cuicui along. With an outburst of coarse invective, she picked up a rock and threw it through Tian's office window. As she strode off, she was still cursing loudly. Back at Stream of Wandering Spirits, she closed the door behind her, threw herself down on the bed, and bawled until her eyes looked like rotten peach pits. She bewailed the injustice done to her and remonstrated that Tian had tricked her, that after he'd taken his pleasure with her, he'd decided she was too old for him and planned to marry a tender, young thing. Poor me, she was thinking. *All that time I took care of his paralyzed wife, feeding her and everything, and making his bed, then keeping it warm for him, figuring his was the house I'd grow old in. So what happened? I not only lost the chance of a comfortable life but my reputation as well.* With hatred boiling inside her, she picked up the flour and rice jars from the cupboard and smashed them to the floor, then ripped to shreds the door curtain with the embroidered peonies, and finally kicked a couple of holes in the big standing cabinet. Collapsed, panting on the floor with a smarting foot, she turned her anger on her own stupidity: *I shouldn't be smashing the stuff in the house. It belongs to me. This is my house, and as long as there's breath in my body, Lu Cuicui won't set foot in it.* So she scrambled up, sat at the table, and wrote a letter to Gong Baoshan. This is what she was thinking: *Tian Zhongzheng is the township party secretary and the commander of the river shipping brigade, which is so highly esteemed at the county and district levels that he's probably in line for a promotion. But any promotion will completely eliminate the possibility of his marrying me. So it's time to take the firewood out of the stove and block his way up the official ladder. And the only way to do that is to write a letter to Gong Baoshan. With the bad blood between the two clans, Gong Baoshan won't pass up a chance to cut his legs out from under him.* The fury in her heart caused her hand to shake as she wrote. The characters looked like chicken scratches, and half of them she wrote incorrectly. But she kept at it, making one case after another against Tian, emphasizing his shady tactics in setting up the shipping brigade. She included details on Tian Yishen's corruption in skimming off half the profits for the benefit of Tian Zhongzheng. She put the finished letter in an envelope and sealed it, then lay down with a feeling of satisfaction and slept soundly. But when she awoke, she began to have second thoughts. Once the letter got into Gong Baoshan's hands, Tian would be finished. What chance would there be then that he'd marry her? And even if he did, their days of high living would be over, and she could never again hold her head up in Stream of Wandering Spirits. No, her plan wasn't the flawless one she needed. So she sat down and wrote a second letter—to Tian Youshan—and sent it together with the letter she'd written to Gong Baoshan, asking Tian Youshan to forward it. Of course he wouldn't send it on to Gong Baoshan, but he'd apply plenty of pressure on Tian Zhongzheng.

That morning she took the envelope with the two letters over to the Crossroads Township post office, and Tian Youshan received it that afternoon. As it turned out, Tian Zhongzheng had checked into a hotel in town with Lu Cuicui after the opera, where they'd spent a rollicking night together. The next morning he put her on the bus to Crossroads Township, then, in the afternoon, went to call on Tian Youshan, who behind closed doors gave him a merciless tongue-lashing, even showing him the letter from Yingying's mother.

Tian Zhongzheng was astonished at how much more savage a woman could be than a man. "That stinking whore!" he swore. "Wait and see what I do to her when I get home!"

"Shit!" Tian Youshan snorted. "So that's what you're good for! What are you going to do, kill her? Do you know who you're damning? Yourself, that's who! You get back there today and settle upon a date to get married. Don't wait till she raises a real stink."

That was exactly what he didn't want to hear. As the number-one man in Crossroads Township, wasn't he even free to make his own decision where marriage was concerned? "Do you actually expect me to marry a woman like that?" he said. "I don't love her, I really don't."

"How can you be so stupid?" Tian Youshan said. "If you hadn't got involved with Yingying's mother in the first place, no one would have said a word if you decided to marry Lu Cuicui. But how will it look if you go through with it now? Do you know what we'll become in the people's eyes? A herd of incestuous cattle! Are you an ordinary citizen? No, you're the Crossroads Township party secretary and the leader of the river shipping brigade."

Tian Zhongzheng hung his head in despair and rubbed his knees with his hands, then held them hard. Despondent over where his love life had put him, he cursed his own stupidity and weakness. "Does that mean a leader doesn't have the right to marry whomever he wants?" he whined. "If that's the case, I'll give up my position as party secretary and throw in the towel with the river shipping brigade!"

"Bullshit!" Tian Youshan retorted. He turned and walked into his bedroom as calmly as his anger allowed.

Tian Zhongzheng could have kicked himself for spouting off like that and getting Tian Youshan so upset. Now what? Leave? Stay? He stood there without saying a word.

Tian Youshan's wife came out of the bedroom. She was extremely young and could just as well have been his daughter. "Zhongzheng," she said with a smile, "you're acting like a child. Do you know what the river shipping brigade means these days? And do you realize how important it is that you're the Crossroads Township party secretary? Are you prepared to ruin yourself? How can you be so foolish? Look at the situation. If you retire from the fray, there goes Crossroads Township, and there goes the river shipping brigade. What do you think the Gong clan will do? Do you really think that we Tians feel our work is over?"

Tian Youshan came out of the bedroom, his manner again serene. Adopting the tone of an elder, he said, "Listen to me. Yingying's mother is getting on in years, but she's a talented woman. I've seen Lu Cuicui, and there's nothing special about her. Women are all the same, anyway, aren't they?" He had his wife see Tian Zhongzheng out.

But first she took a fine little cardboard box out of a chest and thrust it into Tian Zhongzheng's hand. "Since you're getting married, I have to give you a small present in my role of aunt. There's a necklace in there. Give it to Yingying's mother. Someone bought it for me in the capital. It's lovely!"

Tian thanked her and left through the garden. Nice-sounding words, he was thinking, "that women are all the same, anyway, aren't they?" *Then why did you divorce your first wife and marry an actress fifteen years younger than you? A woman that old wearing a necklace? Cuicui's never even worn one!*

Tian headed to the township office. Not unexpectedly, Yingying's mother came over to give him a piece of her mind. He begged her forgiveness, trying his damnedest to stay in control of events. Finally he agreed to their engagement, promising to set an early date. In addition, he consented to taking Cuicui's younger brother's name off the list of candidates for the newspaper job and putting Golden Dog's name on instead.

Yingying's mother didn't go home to sleep that night. Instead, she applied her femininity to bringing Tian Zhongzheng to the point of being absolutely drained. When he insisted on extinguishing the lamp, she asked, "Is it Lu Cuicui you have on your mind when I'm in your arms?" She had hit on the truth, but he flatly denied it. Before long he was rolling to his side, totally spent, like a man near death. "The pigs in your own home are squealing from hunger," she said. "But do you still have chaff to give them?" Tian was so cut by her mockery that he turned crimson.

The next morning, they applied for a permit to marry. The step they had taken surprised everyone, and talk about their adultery began anew. But it didn't last, since they were about to become man and wife and weren't breaking any laws. Immorality was not an issue that would dog them long. When the talk reached Tian's ears, he congratulated himself on making the right move this time, and even though he couldn't get Cuicui off his mind, he swallowed the bitter pill. The barest trace of a smile visited his face.

As they were being ferried across the river, Han Wenju said, "Congratulations, Secretary Tian, congratulations! When's the wedding? The big event in a man's life. Don't forget to throw a big party to celebrate your good fortune!"

Tian sneered, "For a couple of oldsters like us? We're not kids, you know, so there's no need for a fuss."

"No fuss?" Han responded even more spiritedly. "Don't tell me a rich family like yours can't afford a party!"

Tian was already off the boat and walking up the bank, but Han still taunted him, savoring the sweetest revenge he'd ever tasted. Feeling his oats, he made a point of telling everyone he met about going over to the Tians' when the big day came. He even went to Crossroads Township and bought a string of firecrackers at the shop across from the Lu family clinic, screaming at the top of his lungs about how he intended to set them off at the gate of the Tian compound on the day Tian Zhongzheng was married. The Lus found it so difficult to face people that they closed up shop for the day.

At noon on the tenth day, Tian Zhongzheng's marriage took place. But instead of holding a rousing good party, they merely stuck a new pair of wedding scrolls up on the doorjam and invited a few important guests—family and members of the township government. All the townspeople who carried gifts to them were turned away. Since Han Wenju didn't have a chance to set off his firecrackers at the couple's gate, he lit them on his ferryboat instead.

That night a group of curious villagers went to cause some mild mischief at the bridal home. Tian wanted to shut the crowd out, but his wife invited them in, to offer them wine and snacks. Dressed in her finest, she played the perfect hostess. After polishing off the wine, one of the company urged the others, "Let's carry the bride and groom into bed." Tian resisted, but someone else said, "Marriage is a happy event, party secretary or not! If you don't let us do what we came to do, tell us about your courtship!" The sarcasm wasn't lost on Tian, but he couldn't do anything about it, so he jumped down off the kang. They picked him up and put him right back, and this time someone called out, "If you won't tell us about your courtship, then compose a wedding couplet." The woman began, "A brand new bride and groom," and he followed with, "Old furniture in a brand new room." Shouts of "Bravo!" filled the air. "Another one, let's have another!" At the peak of the excitement, Tian Yishen squeezed into the room, and as soon as Tian Zhongzheng laid eyes on him, he tried to change the subject. "Pour some wine for Tian Yishen!" But Tian

Yishen came and whispered in his ear, and Tian Zhongzheng's face took on a strange cast. "I have a phone call," he announced. "I'll be right back. Help yourself to more wine and tea!" He walked out of the room.

There was no phone call. Instead, he headed to Lu Cuicui's house as fast as his legs could carry him.

Cuicui had been in frail health since the abortion, and after going to town to see the opera and pass a night of revelry, she'd taken sick from exhaustion. She hadn't been out of bed for several days, spending nearly all her time thinking about the fine turn her life had taken. Tian had been by to see her only once, not so much as showing his face otherwise. When she sent her younger brother to the township office to find him, Tian was always out. But then, the last time, her brother had overheard the heated exchange between Tian and Yingying's mother and had learned that they were going to apply for a permit to marry. Cuicui swooned from the shock. By the time she came to, she'd begun to hemorrhage down below and refused to take anything, even hot water. All she wanted was to see Tian Zhongzheng. Her father, observing that his daughter's condition had grown serious and that his medicine wasn't working, swallowed his pride and went to the township office to find Tian Zhongzheng. He saw through a crack in the gate, however, that the place was deserted. But Cai Da'an walked up just then. "Who's there?" he asked. "What are you doing sneaking around here?"

Old man Lu managed an ingratiating smile and inquired whether Tian Zhongzheng was inside.

"What do you want with the secretary?" Cai asked him. "He's home getting ready for the wedding and is too busy to see anybody!"

"Please, I beg you," old man Lu said, "go over to his house and tell him I have to see him on urgent business."

"What urgent business could you have? Go look for him if you want to. Who knows, maybe his missus-to-be will drink a toast to you. Me, I don't have the time. We have two candidates for the newspaper job in Zhou City, Yingying and Golden Dog, and I have to get the paperwork done for both of them!"

"Golden Dog? Isn't my son supposed to be on that list?"

Cai looked surprised. "Your son, too? Is your business your son or is it Cuicui? How come the secretary didn't tell me about this?"

Old man Lu slinked back home, disgraced. He told Cuicui exactly what had happened, and she reacted by shrieking and spitting out a mouthful of fresh blood.

Between then and the day of Tian's marriage, Cuicui slipped in and out of a coma. That night, when the lamp was lit, she was feeling well enough to roll over and get out of bed, with the help of her younger brother. She wanted to go over and see Tian, but old man Lu said, "Cuicui, you can't go over there. He's a beast in human form, and you don't think he'll let you see him on his wedding day, do you?"

"I want to confront him, face-to-face!" she said. "What can he say? He's the reason I'm like I am today, while he goes on cheerfully to take another wife. I know I won't live long, but I'm not about to let him and that old sow get married without raising a stink. If I'm going to die, I'll do it in his house!"

She took three steps and sank into a heap. Old man Lu and his son rushed to pick her up. Her eyes staring straight ahead, she spit out the words "Tian Zhongzheng!" three times before dying.

Father and son, grief-stricken, wailed over their loss. They dressed her body, washed her face, and combed her hair. Then they laid her out in the living room. When the neighbors heard the commotion, they came and helped with the preparations for the funeral. One of the busybodies, knowing what lay behind Cuicui's death, flew to tell Tian Yishen what had happened, and he barreled over to Tian Zhongzheng's house with the news.

Tian strode to the bank of the Zhou River and was ferried across. He stopped to buy some mourning paper before going to the Lu home. It was sheer chaos, with people filling the house and the yard outside, some to hear the details, some to sigh over the loss, and some just to join the excitement. A few of the women were sewing up the shroud; others were carrying an old coffin down the stairs. Old man Lu had bought the coffin years earlier in preparation for his own death, never imagining that he'd have to use it for his daughter. The tragic mysteries of life had laid him low. Barely able to stand and out of tears, he squatted in a corner, his face streaked with the stains his tears had left. "Here comes the secretary!" someone shouted. The old man got quietly to his feet, took the mourning paper from Tian with both hands, and summoned his son to bring a stool for the secretary. But the son glared at Tian Zhongzheng and ejaculated, "You killed my sister! What the hell did you come for?"

Old man Lu at once put his hand over his foolish son's mouth and told the people standing nearby to drag him outside. "Secretary," he said, "I'm so happy you came . . . This child of mine never had a chance for happiness."

Without saying a word, Tian walked over to the corpse, pulled back the shroud, and stared into the face of Lu Cuicui. She was much thinner than before, and there was a hard look on her face. Tian was transfixed, and a chill ran down his spine. He'd stood still for a long time, the other people in the room silently watching him, when he took a little cardboard box out of his pocket, opened it, and drew out the necklace Tian Youshan's wife had given him as a wedding present. He put it around Cuicui's neck.

Tian Yishen walked up. "Secretary, you'd better leave now."

Tian didn't reply. He reached out and stroked Cuicui's face, then gently slapped her as bitterness and resentment built up inside him. "Cuicui, why did you have to die? Tell me, why?" Tears coursed down his cheeks. He turned and walked out the door with his head lowered.

Everyone who saw Tian Zhongzheng's actions was deeply moved. Old man Lu began to wail noisily and threw himself on his daughter's body. Tian Yishen came and pulled him off, lugging him into the other room, where he handed him two hundred yuan from his pocket. "The secretary wants you to have this for the funeral expenses. Take it and hire a funeral troupe to ease Cuicui's soul to the other side. He also told me to say that if your family ever needs anything, you're to go straight to him."

Old man Lu took the money and declared, "It was Cuicui's great good fortune to have the secretary come see her. Please thank him for me, and tell him he's always welcome at my house!" After he saw Tian Yishen out, he took another look at his daughter's body, his grief twisting his insides into knots. "Everything's all right," he mumbled to himself. "It's all right. At least she didn't die in vain."

Tian Zhongzheng walked alone to the township office and sat at his desk like a statue, his tears flowing without restraint. When Tian Yishen arrived, he called in to the secretary, who refused to open the door. Tian Yishen tried to console him through the door, urging him not to let the woman's death undo him. The condolence was met by a string of curses, telling Tian Yishen what a rotten human being he was. Tian Yishen bore the insults in silence, and gradually the vilification was directed not at him but at Tian Zhongzheng himself, at Tian Youshan, at the entire Tian and Gong clans. Tian Yishen sat outside the closed door, too cowed to say a word and not daring to leave. Tian Zhongzheng kept up the verbal barrage for a full hour before beginning to calm down. He understood that Lu Cuicui had been lost to him for the sake of his career, and that it was he, the party secretary, who had once been privileged to have her. Now she was dead, and that was that. Since he had given up so much for his career, he was determined to work even harder for it now. He'd get everything he wanted!

He opened the door, and was surprised to find Tian Yishen still sitting there, surprised and moved, even a little apologetic. "You still here?"

"This is your wedding night, so you have to go home."

"I'm going," he mumbled, as much for his own benefit as for Tian Yishen's. "I'm going home."

At that very moment, smoke from smoldering spirit money was swirling in the air above the intersection in the eastern part of town for the sake of a departed soul. The night was dark, the burning paper like puddles of blood. Han could see it from the ferry landing, and so could everyone in Stream of Wandering Spirits.

9

Five days later, a reorganization of the river shipping brigade was carried out, with the addition of three ships and ten men. But the men were not summoned to elect a new team of commanders; instead, the cadres from the township government were brought together, along with the six group leaders from the brigade itself. Golden Dog, of course, was invited to attend as a special participant. The meeting lasted all day and all night. On the beginning morning, Tian Zhongzheng, who presided, spelled out the session's goals, emphasizing that it had been called in response to the wishes of the entire membership and encouraging everyone to speak his mind about whether the two commanders should stay in office. If they weren't considered suitable to continue, who was more qualified? Tian spoke for half the morning, then opened discussion to the floor. But no one spoke up. The participants sat with lowered heads, smoking cigarettes until the floor was littered with butts and the air so thick with smoke that three female comrades couldn't stand it and walked outside coughing. The meeting's paralysis continued until the cook, Zhao Wangshan, stood by the kitchen and declared, "Time to eat!"

Tian looked at the people around the conference table and inquired, "Are you holding yourselves back from saying things because you haven't thought the issues through? Let's take a break, and you can think them over while you're eating. We'll reconvene at noon."

They ate in the government compound, but instead of sitting on the stools around the table, they squatted on the steps beside the garden fence or around the stone chess table, rice bowls in hand. They avoided arguments by keeping clear of the issue of elections, telling each other risqué jokes instead. It was the first time Golden Dog had attended one of the meetings, and he was amused. He didn't say anything, preferring to stand back and "watch the river rise." After Tian Zhongzheng's marriage, Golden Dog reckoned that things looked pretty good for him, so he went to Lei Dakong with word that he'd changed his mind about opening a shop for business. The immediate future was going to be a critical time in his life, and he'd make the most of it. He was well aware that Cai Da'an expected to gain personally from the election by nominating Golden Dog and that he needed to keep on steady terms with Cai without making trouble for Tian Yishen in the process. His prospects for managing Tian Zhongzheng hung on being able to manage Cai Da'an and Tian Yishen, and it was important to establish himself atop the complex and subtle relationships between the three men if he was going to make it out of the village to Zhou City. So he feigned innocence and, instead of sniggering and cursing like the others, spoke coarsely and ambiguously, telling dirty jokes with considerable enthusiasm, all the while keeping a close eye on what Tian Yishen and Cai Da'an were up to.

Tian and Cai ate along with the others, laughing at the jokes as though everything was fine. Cai commented on the good relationship Tian Yishen seemed to have with Zhao Wangshan, since he had more food in his bowl than the others; Tian teased Cai about being afraid of his wife, multiplying examples until everyone was in stitches.

Cai answered, "What about that little wife of yours? I'm not bragging when I say I do whatever I please at home. I lie down on the kang, and she brings my food. She doesn't know the meaning of the word *no*. Women! They eat our food, they follow behind us, and when it gets dark they fondle our you-know-whats!"

"No more boasts, please," Tian Yishen said, "or you'll sprain your back! I went over to your place on the second of February. Do you want to tell us why your old lady was straddling you? Was she giving you a beating! All you said was, 'Old Tian, this old lady of mine's a nuisance. I'm giving her a ride into town to sell her off!'"

Golden Dog admired the way they could carry on as though they were the best of friends. He joined the others in the laughter of the moment, then walked over and played with some children who had just got out of school and were sitting at the compound gate. All about eight or nine years old, and all cute and innocent, they were bantering over who was excelling in school.

Zhao Wangshan's son said, "I'm good in math, so when I grow up, I'm going to be a math teacher."

The clerk's daughter said, "I'm good in language arts, so when I grow up, I'm going to be a clerk just like my dad!"

The son of the head of the Women's League said, "I'm going to be a boatman when I grow up! Little Dragon, your grades are low in everything. What are you going to be when you grow up?"

Little Dragon was Tian Zhongzheng's nephew and had been enrolled in the local school by his uncle. "I'm not going to study anything," he said. "Like my uncle, I'm going to be in charge of the rest of you!"

The smile on Golden Dog's face froze. He was about to reprove Little Dragon, when Cai Da'an called out to him, "Golden Dog, do you have any paper on you? I have to go to the toilet!" Golden Dog said he didn't, but he removed the cigarettes from a pack and handed it to Cai.

"How come you haven't said anything?" Cai asked him softly.

"I'm not one of the leaders," Golden Dog said, "so I didn't think I should start things off."

"What are you afraid of? Speak on behalf of the boatmen!" Seeing that Tian Yishen was walking up to them, he raised his voice: "Golden Dog, are you saving up to get married? Otherwise, why smoke cheap cigarettes like these?"

"Golden Dog," Tian Yishen said, "I hear there's something between you and Water Girl. Han Wenju's not going to let you off easy, and you'll have to come up with a nice gift! If you want to get married, at the very least you'll have to buy a couple of coffins, one for Han and one for the pockfaced blacksmith at White Rock Stockade."

Golden Dog just laughed perfunctorily.

The meeting resumed at noon, and still no one spoke up. For two solid hours, Golden Dog looked at the people around the table, seeing nothing but expressionless faces. The excitement during the meal had left no trace, and a change had come over everyone. Cai Da'an cast several glances toward Golden Dog, who pretended not to notice, keeping his eyes on the cracks between the bricks at his feet. An ant crawled out of a hole between two bricks and started dragging off a kernel of cooked rice three times its size. When it had got it to the edge of the hole, another came out and began fighting over the booty. Then they stopped, each sizing up its opponent by employing its antenna, but neither willing to begin the second round and neither prepared to retreat. Golden Dog was fascinated by the sight.

"Why isn't anyone talking?" Tian Zhongzheng asked. "Say what's on your minds!"

Golden Dog reached down and flipped the kernel of rice away with his finger, then looked up and lit a cigarette.

Cai Da'an cleared his throat. "Since someone has to begin, I guess it's up to me. This is an important and timely meeting Secretary Tian has called. All the comrades in the brigade should have been invited, but they're not here, and that's okay, since we need to reach a consensus. It's our responsibility to make sure the meeting is successful. We can thank Secretary Tian for the existence of the river shipping brigade, and the results have been excellent from the very beginning. I'm sure everyone agrees. In order to keep up the good work and make things even better, we must, in accordance with the wishes of the comrades in the brigade, strengthen the position of the leadership. At first you asked Yishen and me to assume the responsibility and, to be honest, we didn't do a bad job. But, in all candor, we have our failings. We had only limited success in purchasing and sales, for instance, and there were too many problems with the brigade's nonproductive members. I'll take the blame for that. So I don't think I'm particularly qualified for the position as commander, and I recommend adding Golden Dog to the leadership ranks."

Golden Dog never dreamed that Cai would present his name like that. He smiled out of confusion.

"All right," Tian Yishen spoke up. "Da'an has started things rolling, and he's right when he says that our leadership ranks are in need of reorganization. As for me, I share his opinion that we aren't the best ones to continue. I'm a production cadre with the village government, with plenty of duties to keep me busy. Da'an has his credit work, and neither of us has the time or energy to do everything that's needed. I want to toss in a name myself. I'd like you to consider asking Old Seven to take over."

Tian Zhongzheng laughed. "Well, what do you all say?"

Silence.

Then the coughing began. Someone spit, and three or four of the others followed, the most accomplished sending their missiles through the window. Four or five chickens scurried over and began fighting over the spittle.

Tian Zhongzheng spoke up. "I don't think either Golden Dog or Old Seven is the right man for the job. One's too young, and the other's too old. Even though our brigade is no vast army, it's nothing to scoff at. I'll give you my opinion—and, remember, I'm speaking as a private citizen, not as party secretary—we're being completely democratic here, so you don't have to accept my opinion if you don't want to. As far as I'm concerned, the two original commanders have done pretty well, and I think we ought to keep them on."

More silence.

More and more cigarette butts were accumulating on the floor. Someone gathered up a pile of them, emptied the tobacco out into a small piece of newspaper, rolled it up, and lit it. The afternoon came to an end when Zhao Wangshan announced that dinner was ready.

"You still haven't made up your minds?" Tian Zhongzheng asked them. "Well, then, keep thinking about it, and we'll continue the meeting this evening."

But that evening Secretary Tian suddenly decided not to attend the meeting and asked one of his deputies to preside. "Is everyone holding back because I'm here?" he asked. "We must be democratic, completely democratic!"

But during the evening assembly no one recommended removing either of the commanders, although a few more people were nominated. When this was reported to Tian, he was adamant: "No, keep talking. The meeting's over when a decision has been reached, and not before!"

So they sat late into the evening, still without Tian Zhongzheng. Farther into the night the complete list of candidates was given to him, but he rejected it out of hand. Showing the first signs of anger, he returned to the meeting. "Our superiors are always trying to get us to keep our meetings short, but this one's getting longer and longer! We must elect brigade commanders, and if we don't get it done tonight, we'll meet again tomorrow morning, and tomorrow afternoon if necessary. We're not going through this again!"

Golden Dog stood up. "I have a recommendation," he said. "We can't let all the candidates on our list be commanders, can we? The brigade is considered very important at the county and prefecture levels. It owes its existence to Secretary Tian, and it's become the crown jewel of our township, our very lifeblood. That's why this election is so important. But the gap between us keeps getting wider with all these names, and at this rate we won't reach a decision even if we meet for the next three days and nights. So I recommend total democracy, with secret ballots. We can vote twice, starting with eight names and choosing four. Then we vote again to elect two of the four. What do you think?"

"Good idea," several people agreed at once. "Let's do it!"

Tian Zhongzheng, lifting his empty glass, went back to the office, ostensibly for more tea.

"Golden Dog has the right idea," Cai Da'an said as they waited for Tian to return and announce his decision on the recommendation.

"The masses know what they're doing, and they'll elect the right person!"

Tian Yishen added his endorsement: "Good, a secret ballot's the way to go."

Golden Dog looked at the people around the table, and they returned his look. Just then, Tian Zhongzheng called from his office, "Golden Dog, telephone!" Golden Dog walked out of the room, wondering who could be calling him. As soon as he entered the office, Tian closed the door behind him and said, "Golden Dog, you're absolutely right, of course, but what do you think the results of a secret ballot will be?"

"I think it'll be Tian Yishen and Cai Da'an. Who else could it be?"

"The reason we're holding this election is to benefit the river shipping brigade," Tian said. "We have to elect the strongest comrades as leaders!"

"I know that," Golden Dog assured him.

When Golden Dog and Tian Zhongzheng returned to the meeting, Tian said, "Golden Dog's suggestion that we vote by secret ballot is a good one, and since everyone agrees, so do I. Our shipping brigade has accomplished a great deal, and for much of that we can thank our two original commanders. Still, nobody's perfect. If they're reelected, they'll have to take stock of their strengths and work on their shortcomings. If someone else is elected, those people must do an even better job than Tian Yishen and Cai Da'an. For the first vote, everyone is to write four names on a slip of paper, and anyone who doesn't know how to write can ask someone else for help."

The individual slips were prepared by the deputy township head and distributed. Golden Dog sat down near several men who didn't know how to write, since they wanted him to fill out the ballots for them. Cai Da'an, who was sitting across from him, nudged him under the table with his foot. Without saying a word, Golden Dog wrote Cai's name on his ballot. Tian Yishen, who was sitting off to the side, fixed his eyes on Golden Dog. "Golden Dog," he said, "I forgot my pen. Let me use yours when you're finished." Golden Dog knew exactly what he meant, so he tossed him his pen, then helped the men around him fill out their ballots.

After the ballots were collected, the deputy township head called out the votes while Tian Zhongzheng made tallies on the wall with a piece of chalk. The atmosphere grew tense, and no one so much as coughed. The results of the first vote were eleven votes for Cai Da'an, eleven for Golden Dog, ten for Tian Yishen, and eight for Old Seven.

What that meant was, barring any irregularities on the second ballot, Cai Da'an would be elected commander, with Golden Dog as his deputy. When the new ballots were distributed, Cai Da'an and Tian Yishen rose to go out and relieve themselves, unable to hold their bladders any longer. "I voted for you," Cai whispered to Tian, "so how come you got fewer votes than Golden Dog? Whatever we do, we must keep him from being elected commander! Don't vote for him in the next round, and I won't either."

Tian didn't say a word, but there was a clouded look on his face. Golden Dog had already scored a victory on the first ballot. He wanted Tian Zhongzheng to take notice of his value, but he wasn't interested in becoming commander, so just before the voting began, he said, "I'm grateful to all of you who voted for me, but I want you to know that I'll decline the job, so please don't vote for me this time!" In order to show he was serious, he asked Tian Zhongzheng to prepare the ballots of the men who didn't know how to write. But when he filled out his own ballot, instead of writing Cai Da'an's name, he wrote in Tian Yishen's, then passed his pen over to Tian, unintentionally, or so he pretended, handing his ballot with it. Tian took a quick look at Golden Dog's choice and flashed a smile his way. When the votes were counted, everyone was surprised that Tian Yishen had eleven votes, whereas Cai Da'an managed only ten, and Golden Dog seven. "Now that we've completed this democratic election," Tian Zhongzheng announced with satisfaction, "the results are the same as before. In other words, Tian Yishen and Cai Da'an are appreciated by the people, who trust them completely. Let's applaud the results." The meeting was adjourned after a round of applause.

All the participants in the meeting, which had lasted a day and a night, were in awe of Tian Zhongzheng. Tian Yishen threw a party at his home to celebrate his victory, and he made a point of inviting Golden Dog. Cai Da'an, on the other hand, was disappointed in the results and said to Golden Dog at the party, "I came in first on the first ballot, but second on the final one. I can see Tian Yishen's hand in this! On reflection, I can only conclude that he voted for himself but not for me and not for you. He's despicable! And stupid. Why didn't he let the others vote for you, and why didn't he volunteer to fill out the ballots for those who don't know how to write?"

"You were elected, so what's the problem?"

"I'm too honest for my own good," Cai said. "I should have tried to stop him. So we lost!"

Golden Dog said a few comforting words, then asked Cai about the name list for the Zhou City newspaper job. "Worthy brother," Cai said, "the old man upstairs works in mysterious ways. Don't you see what happened at the meeting? Now that Tian Yishen's the commander, and Secretary Tian has been taken in by him, there's nothing more I can do!"

That was precisely what Golden Dog had anticipated, and he knew that in the election he'd managed to avoid alienating Cai Da'an, while winning Tian Zhongzheng and Tian Yishen over to his side. He went over to Water Girl's and told her what had happened. Wanting there to be no loose ends, she went to the co-op at Crossroads Township to put in a good word for Golden Dog with Yingying, who volunteered the opinion that since Golden Dog had written news stories in the military, he must have developed considerable writing skills. She agreed to put in a good word with her uncle. Two days later Tian Zhongzheng ran into Golden Dog. "Golden Dog," he said expansively, "I see you went over and registered for the job. Now you're using your head. Can you handle the job?"

"I can handle it!"

Tian Zhongzheng laughed heartily. "You've got style, and that's what you need to get ahead! I've had my eye on you for some time. You have a quick mind, and you express your views well. You're quite a young man! Do you remember what happened in the Zhou River that time?"

"What happened?"

"If you hadn't rescued me, the grass over my grave would be as tall as you are by now."

"You recall that?"

"I'll never forget it. Naturally, rescuing me didn't just involve the two of us but demonstrated the interrelation of the masses and the cadres. If we senior cadres are the boats, then the masses are the water, and the boats are at the mercy of the water. As soon as the opportunity to send someone to Zhou City presented itself, I thought of you. What with your talent, the river shipping brigade is the loser if you go, but we have to allocate people on the basis of their abilities! I'm not doing this just because you saved my life."

Golden Dog smiled and thanked him.

Giving the impression that he and Golden Dog were fast friends, Tian asked him, "How's your marksmanship?"

"Excellent!"

"How would you like to go hunting with me? So much has been going on lately that it's time to clear my head. Interested?"

"Sure."

Tian patted Golden Dog on the shoulder. "It would be wonderful if Yishen and Da'an were more like you!"

Golden Dog took the day off to go hunting and had Fuyun stand in for him on Old Seven's boat. He waited at home for Tian Zhongzheng. In the hills surrounding a large ravine some ten kilometers behind Restless Hill there were plenty of wild rabbits, pheasants, and mountain goats, and an occasional wild boar or black bear. Tian arrived with a semiautomatic rifle over his shoulder; it belonged to the township government's military adviser. Cai Da'an came along, also carrying a rifle. "Have you noticed," Cai whispered to Golden Dog, "that Tian Yishen's out of favor again? The secretary invited me right in front of him, without inviting him!" Golden Dog smiled. Hmph, he was thinking, Tian Zhongzheng is performing a balancing act, and you haven't figured out how he's manipulating you! But what he said was, "That's great. Now you can speak up for me."

"Who do you think got you invited today in the first place?"

The three of them walked some ten kilometers down the ravine, where the mountain path became rugged and dangerous, with plenty of crags and some outcroppings in the shape of a charging tiger. The rocks were covered with white pine, all twisted and looking especially white against the black backdrop. When they reached a hollow, with rocks sticking straight up around it and filled with huge boulders covered with moss, they spotted the home of a hunting family tucked in among the boulders. The head of the family was a short, energetic man, who was lying in the grass in front of his door. A skinny nanny goat was beside him, her full teats hanging low, and he was milking it, squirting the milk straight into his mouth. When he heard footsteps, he raised his head and looked around, without the trace of an expression on his face. Then he went back to his milk.

"Panther Cub!" Tian Zhongzheng greeted the man.

He raised his head again and rubbed his eyes. "Is that you, Secretary Tian?" he asked. "We were just talking about you this morning, saying it was about time you dropped by. And here you are! There's a wild boar over on East Slope. Let's go bag him today!"

"What a life you have, Panther Cub!" Tian said. "Lying there drinking milk all day. Our stomachs are growling. Let's have something to eat first."

He'd barely gotten the words out when they heard the muffled sound of an explosion in the valley behind them. Panther Cub was ecstatic. "Secretary Tian, you are truly blessed! That gunpowder charge went off not a minute early nor a minute late but the precise moment you arrived!" He turned and yelled into the house, "Hey, Secretary Tian's here. Why haven't you put down your loom?" He ran off alone toward the valley the explosion had come from.

A woman wearing tattered clothes but with a pretty face and a graceful bearing emerged. When she saw her guests, she shouted, "Oh, no!" and fled back inside to comb her hair and put on better clothes. Tian Zhongzheng turned to Golden Dog and Cai Da'an: "Now you see the truth in the saying that deep mountains produce beauty. A tender, fresh cabbage like that in the hands of a blind pig!"

The three men entered the house, and Tian, continuing to praise the woman's beauty, stood in the middle of the room. Having freshened up, the woman came out as far as the doorway of the bedroom. "To listen to the secretary talk, you'd think that everyone in the deep mountains was special. In fact, we're so ugly we can't go out into the real world!" Her eyes flashed. She brewed tea for her guests, which she handed to them accompanied by complaints about how long it had been since the people there had seen Secretary Tian. She accused him of thinking their bowls weren't clean enough for him or that their bedding was too dirty for him to sleep in. Tian's laughter almost drowned out his own repartee. Before long, Panther Cub returned with a wild dog over his shoulder. He ranted on about the secretary's good luck in having dogmeat to go with the wine. Throwing down the carcass of the dog, whose mouth had been blown off by the explosive charge, he butchered it, then lit the stove and cooked it. When they had finished eating, Panther Cub took down a musket, filled it with gunpowder, and stuck a ramrod down the barrel. He next tore a piece of paper with red stains into four strips, which he rolled into little balls and stuffed into each man's gun barrel. To Golden Dog's question about what they were for, the little man replied, "To ward off evil."

"Golden Dog," Tian said, "aren't you the dumb one! That's the woman's menstrual paper. Nothing will happen to you if you stuff that into your gun barrel."

This so revolted Golden Dog that he refused it.

"If you don't want it," Tian said, "I'll take it. Panther Cub, you go up on the mountain behind us; Da'an, you take the one to the right; Golden Dog, you take the one to the left. Whatever the three of you flush out, drive it down this way. I'll be waiting at the mouth of the ravine. If there's anything up there today, it can't escape!"

As soon as the assignments had been made, the three men went up into the mountains with their weapons. Tian Zhongzheng remained in the house drinking his tea. Panther Cub's woman came in with a bucket of water, which she heated for washing up.

After about the time it takes to finish a couple of meals, Panther Cub's shout rent the air above the trees in the ravine. That was followed by shouts from Da'an on the right: "Oh——! Oh——!" Golden Dog gripped his rifle tightly, knowing that prey of some sort had been spotted. He crouched silently behind a dead tree and waited, not daring to blink. Suddenly, the tall grass in front of him rustled and swayed like a wave coming straight at him, and fast. "Oh——! Oh——!" he shouted. The wave stopped immediately, turned, and headed toward the ravine. Golden Dog couldn't tell what kind of animal it was. "Secretary Tian," he shouted, "coming your way!" In a flurry of excitement, he rustled the branches around him to cause a commotion, at the same time cutting off the animal's path of retreat as he moved toward the ravine. But no sound rose from down below, even after the longest time; Tian Zhongzheng, who was supposed to be at the mouth of the ravine, didn't fire. Could it have escaped? Golden Dog wondered. He darted across the mountain and ran down a thistle-covered path to the ravine, where he clambered up onto a rock. Suddenly he heard some sounds ahead. Lying on the ground and looking through the foliage, he could glimpse two women squatting in the middle of a spring, bathing. "Secretary Tian's come again," one of them said. "Didn't he go to your place?"

"Why would he come to my place?" the other woman answered. "Do I have your looks? Since he has a choice, he'll always go for the one with the pretty face"

" . . . we're not the same."

"We're not? Then that old fox of yours is a lucky man!"

"That bastard, he doesn't come home till it's dark, so I can't see a thing inside the house, and before I know it, he climbs up and starts humping away without a thought for anybody else. Then just when I start getting into the swing, he finishes and rolls over and goes to sleep, not giving a damn how I feel. But not Secretary Tian. He sits and talks to you till you start getting the itch, then he climbs up on you and even helps you get into the mood, with a touch here and some rubbing there, until you're begging him to hurry. But he's in no hurry, and while he's inside you he bumps up against everything, up and down, in and out, deeper and deeper, and damned if you don't want to just melt, just dissolve, just die . . . then, ai! That man's a cadre, and cadres and peasants are different animals!"

The other one said, "You're getting greedier and greedier. Better watch out, or your old man'll take his gun and knock you off!"

"Knock me off? That's no dead cat or mangy dog I'm with, it's Secretary Tian!"

Golden Dog, who heard everything, was so taken aback he didn't have it in him to get up, and he asked himself who the women could be. When they finished bathing, they stood up and walked off. That was the first that he saw them clearly. The pretty one was Panther Cub's woman.

His head was spinning, and everything was fuzzy. He watched Panther Cub's wife glide off through the tall grass, which swayed in the wind, alternately hiding and revealing her, until he began seeing things. First she was Yingying's mother; then she turned into the dead Cuicui . . . As his anger rose, he cursed these shameless women, then cursed, even more roundly, Tian Zhongzheng, who carried his evil ways wherever he went. He picked up his rifle and started down to the mouth of the ravine to look for Tian, resolved to give him a resounding slap and demand that he kneel down, ready to come clean about his despicable behavior. But just then Panther Cub's shouts floated down on the air: "Coming your way! A wild boar! Oh——! Oh——!"

"You've already disgraced your ancestors!" Golden Dog thundered. "And all you're worried about is shooting a wild boar!" But then his thoughts took a different tack. *Panther Cub's her husband, and if it's okay with him, why am I getting angry? Besides, even if I accused her of adultery, where's my proof? They both wanted it, so there was no rape, and the law's not going to worry about it. So what can I do?* Feeling suddenly depressed and frustrated, he stood there like a simpleton.

From a distance, Panther Cub's shouts grew louder, and Cai Da'an was shouting too. Their calls swirled above the valley. Golden Dog fell to his hands and knees and suddenly began screaming like a madman and beating the ground with his fists. He picked up his rifle, aimed it at a white pine, and pulled the trigger, firing thirteen shots, one after another, until there were no more bullets.

Cai and Panther Cub, who heard the shots, came running down the mountain clamoring for Tian Zhongzheng and Golden Dog. Golden Dog stayed on his hands and knees neither moving nor answering the shouts, until Tian ran up to him, rifle in hand. "Did you hit it, Golden Dog?" Golden Dog sank weakly to the ground, his face ghostly pale.

"Golden Dog's a softy," Panther Cub growled. "Not only didn't he shoot the wild boar, he let the damned thing scare the shit out of him!"

Golden Dog raised his head and spit in Panther Cub's face. "You're the goddamned softy!" he retorted. "If I were you, I'd jerk a hair off my balls and hang myself with it!"

Tian Zhongzheng's face turned beet red, but he quickly mastered himself and said, "Golden Dog, what the hell are you talking about? So you didn't bag the wild boar. Forget it. Let's go back to Panther Cub's house for something to eat. We can return here afterward."

Golden Dog stood up. "I wouldn't go to his house if I was starving. It'd make me puke!"

He headed home alone, but by the time he'd gone halfway, his anger had subsided, and he began to regret his outburst. In a moment of high emotion he'd offended Tian Zhongzheng and ruined his chances with him. Dusk had fallen when, dejected, he dragged himself into the house, where he was met by Water Girl, his father, and the abbot, whom they'd invited in to tell fortunes. The abbot had stuck out his left hand and was counting on his fingers to calculate months, days, and times of day. "Tell me the hour," he said to Water Girl.

"Golden Dog was born at four in the afternoon," she said. "Make it four."

The abbot chanted something and shook his hand. "Great Peace!" he said. "'Great Peace,' that's good!"

"What's so good about it?" Golden Dog's father wanted to know. "The poem goes, 'Great Peace,' everything flourishes. Wealth is found in women, lost items will be found, the home is protected and safe, the journey not yet begun, the invalid has no problem, the general has returned to the farm, and all things are inferred carefully. The newspaper job for Golden Dog is assured!"

"Read my fortune," Golden Dog said from the doorway, "and see if I'll eat today."

"What the hell are you talking about?" his father asked. "The abbot's a tremendous fortune-teller, so if he says it's assured, it's assured. What did you fellows bag today?"

"I don't just tell fortunes with diagrams," the abbot said with a smile. "Just look at Golden Dog, that protruding arch above his eyes, the shiny brows, and the reddish space between them. Those are all signs of great fortune."

"You're completely wrong," Golden Dog said. "I don't have a chance of working on the newspaper. I offended Cai Da'an, and I offended Tian Zhongzheng. Now, you tell me, what are my chances?"

The abbot chose not to say more about his prospects; after a few casual comments he left for the monastery.

"You say you offended Tian Zhongzheng?" Water Girl asked. "How?" Golden Dog told them about the hunting incident and Water Girl said, "You didn't tell them what was bothering you, so how would Tian know that the horror you showed related to him? I've already talked to Yingying, and she's very enthusiastic. She wants me to take you over for a talk with her. That's why I came here, but since you went hunting, your father fetched the abbot to tell your fortune."

Golden Dog refused to go to Yingying, and his unwillingness brought his father's wrath down on him. Touched by the old painter's outburst, Golden Dog backed down. "Okay, I'll go. I'm not afraid . . . Hell, I'd climb a mountain of knives or swim in an ocean of flames!" He and Water Girl wolfed down a couple of bowls of rice before venturing out into the night and across the river to the co-op in town.

On the way, Water Girl criticized Golden Dog: "Why do you always talk back to your father? All the old man wants is what's good for you. You hurt him with all your arguing."

"I'm worried, if you want to know the truth. Although I'm not altogether up on national events, I'm certainly for the current policy. China's in urgent need of reforms, and without them we have serious problems! Crossroads Township is Tian Zhongzheng's power base, and the river shipping brigade is a feather in his cap. He's on his way up! But the very thought makes my blood boil. I simply can't bring myself to go crawling to him. Still, what good does losing my temper do, since he's in the driver's seat? To survive you have to be a running dog like Cai Da'an or Tian Yishen, or be like my father: when somebody shits on your head, you wipe his ass with your nose. You won't catch me getting ahead like that! You have to stand up and fight! But how? Take your Uncle Han. All he does all day is complain and talk a bunch of nonsense. That's about as useful as a fart! Circumstances have forced me to put up a fight if I'm going to be better than the others. Water Girl, tell me which way I should go. I'm still young and hot-blooded. One minute my thoughts go this way, and the next minute they're someplace else. Now you see why I'm worried? When I see my father spending his time getting the abbot to tell fortunes, I can't help blowing up at him!"

She listened in silence. Understanding and sympathizing with him, she wanted to say something. But he'd thought things out so clearly, and she was struck by the realization that he was not only smart but sensitive as well. He seemed so casual on the surface, so nonchalant about everything, but he never missed a thing, nothing escaped him. He was a real man! At this point in her reflections, her cheeks felt hot. To herself she said, Uncle Golden Dog, don't you think I've got a bellyful of worries too? *I'm just a woman, and I don't have your kind of ambitions to drive me. All I can do is look after your needs.* Those were her thoughts as she looked at Golden Dog, with the sun's rays reflecting off his turned-under collar. She raised her hand, but quickly let it drop. "Uncle Golden Dog," she said, "straighten your collar. You don't want Yingying to laugh at you."

Golden Dog turned his collar out as he walked beside her. "Water Girl, do you think I'm nothing but worthless trash?"

"If you think you're worthless trash, Uncle Golden Dog, you must see the rest of us as subhuman!"

"Why are you still calling me Uncle Golden Dog?" he asked with a wave of his hand, accidentally bumping hers. He kept himself from waving it again, for he knew that if he touched her hand a second time, he'd hold on to it. But by then it was out of sight, thrust into her jacket pocket. They walked on, taking in the scenery around them. Golden Dog fell silent and moved to put some distance between them. He gazed up at the moonlit yet somehow lonely night sky.

They walked in silence for quite a while, until Water Girl felt she should say something. She didn't know what to say, so she laughed lightly and changed the subject. "Get rid of that hangdog look before we get to Yingyings's. Let me do the talking, and I'll signal what I want you to do."

When they reached the co-op, Golden Dog started to get cold feet. He took out a cigarette and lit it as Water Girl knocked on the door of Yingying's dormitory room. Yingying, who was washing up for bed, was wearing a pastel figure-hugging nightgown that showed off her full breasts. "I brought Golden Dog over to see you," Water Girl gulped. "Put some clothes on!"

"I've got clothes on!" Yingying said. "Golden Dog's no wolf, so he's not going to eat me, is he?" She laughed as she grabbed his hand and tugged him into the room.

Once she got him seated, she brought out a plate of fruit candies, then flopped on her bed and invited them to eat. She popped one into her mouth, holding Golden Dog with her flashing eyes. "I like everything about you except your haughty airs. Every time you come to the co-op you pretend you don't see me."

This comment caught Golden Dog by surprise, and he didn't like it. He was blushing.

"Uncle Golden Dog's a simple, honest man who treats everyone like that," Water Girl said. "When it was time to sign up for the newspaper job, you notice he didn't come looking for your uncle, and he wouldn't have known what to say if he had."

Yingying, who was sitting directly across from Golden Dog, opened her legs one minute and crossed them the next, raising her fancy low-heeled shoe up in the air and combing her fingers through her hair. "Simple and honest?" she said with feigned incredulity. "That's like congratulating a manure carrier for not eating his load. I've seen him out on his raft. He's like a dragon or a tiger, so why would he be afraid of my uncle? Golden Dog, my uncle thinks very highly of you. He says you saved his life once during the Cultural Revolution and he hasn't really shown his appreciation yet."

For some reason Golden Dog had good feelings about Yingying, and as he looked at the two women sitting next to each other on the edge of the kang, she appeared so much more sharp-tongued than Water Girl, so much bolder, and so much more devoid of cares. This was the first chance he'd had to observe her close up. She was just like her mother, on the plump side, but to her advantage, and she gave off a strong feminine scent. But her manner was nothing like that of her mother or of her uncle. She said what was on her mind, without the slightest affectation, and that made her very attractive.

"Tell your uncle there's no need to keep bringing that up. I didn't sign up in order to give him an opportunity to show his gratitude for being rescued back then. If that's what he thinks, I'd prefer to withdraw my name altogether."

Water Girl reached out with her foot in the shadow of the lamp and stepped on his toe. But his comment delighted Yingying. "That's the way to talk. If you were using the fact that you saved my uncle's life as leverage, you'd come across as pretty common, at least to me. I have no respect for people like Cai Da'an. I'll tell you straight out that two names have been sent forward from our village, yours and mine. They say the newspaper is going to send someone to check us out. Since you have all the talent, I'll have to learn a few things from you."

Water Girl, tickled by what she heard, shouted out, "Uncle Golden Dog, the abbot's predictions were right on the mark! Instead of going out on the river the next few days, stay home and do some reading, so that when the people from the newspaper come, you'll pass the test.

Then you can come over to White Rock Stockade and I'll throw a celebration party for both of you!"

They sat there talking like old friends, with Golden Dog livelier than usual. Yingying offered to make some noodles for everyone, so Water Girl got up and lit the stove, while Yingying picked up a bucket to go out back and get some water, asking Golden Dog to give her a hand. He said he wasn't hungry, but Yingying countered, "When we get to the newspaper, you'll be separated from your father and I'll be away from my mother and uncle. Neither of us will have any kin in Zhou City. Won't you let me make you something to eat?"

"Uncle Golden Dog," Water Girl said, "you're hopeless. You're worse than a girl!"

"Why do you call him Uncle?" Yingying asked.

"His father is my father's godfather."

Yingying laughed. "Well, if that's not a lapdog standing atop a manure pile, I don't know what it is! Brother Golden Dog is in a perfect position."

She picked up the bucket and headed out the door. Water Girl turned to Golden Dog and said, "Yingying's a little crazy, but she's a lot better than her uncle. At least she's nice to people. You must come here more often to make friends with her."

"Does that mean you don't want to come with me anymore?"

"On our way over, I was worried you'd have a hangdog look on your face while you were here, but now I can't shut you up, and you seem to get along with her better than I do!"

Yingying called for Golden Dog from out back, and Water Girl pushed him out the door. Alone in the room, she sat down, still excited, and looked at herself in Yingying's mirror. She quickly tidied up her hair, and when she heard their footsteps outside, she promptly turned the mirror around. There was a color photograph of Yingying in a pink T-shirt on the back, so she spun it around again. What a temptress! Water Girl was thinking.

The next day, Water Girl rode back to White Rock Stockade on Old Seven and Fuyun's boat to take up her work in the blacksmith shop again. She couldn't get Golden Dog off her mind, however, and couldn't wait to take a break and run down to the river's edge in order to catch the first glimpse of his face as he came to give her the good news.

10

In a comprehensive examination, Golden Dog and Yingying passed political muster and were found physically acceptable, but during the professional interview, Golden Dog passed the written and oral examinations with flying colors whereas Yingying washed out completely. The examiners, a man and a woman wearing thick glasses for their nearsightedness, didn't realize that Yingying was Secretary Tian's adoptive daughter, so when they made their report to the township committee, they were critical of her. After they announced their decision to accept only Golden Dog, Tian Zhongzheng expressed his displeasure: "These two youngsters were selected from a list of ten candidates through a long screening process, and the party committee did a great deal of background checking. It's our view that it should be a package deal: either they both go or neither goes!" The examiners, who were particularly keen on taking Golden Dog, tried to negotiate, but Tian wouldn't budge. Because of the impasse, they decided to return to White Rock Stockade to talk with the county committee before making a final decision. Yingying wept bitterly over the news but instead of divulging what had happened, when Golden Dog dropped by to see her, she just told him her uncle had gone to White Rock Stockade to work on the examination aspect of their selection. But he soon discovered the truth and asked her: "I hear they want to take only one of us and that your uncle's trying to make it a package deal. Is that right?"

His bluntness startled her. "Where did you hear that?"

"Am I right or not?" he pressed her.

She smiled. "It's just a rumor. My uncle hasn't even come back yet, so how could anything be firm?"

That was all he needed to hear to know that the rumors were true.

"Then we'll have to wait till Secretary Tian returns," he remarked as he turned and left.

Tian had to break the news to Yingying that the newspaper people were adamant in their desire to select Golden Dog; he told her that although the county committee had been supportive, the Gong clan, who ran Zhou City, stood by the decision of the examiners. Tian's hands were tied. That night, after Yingying had left home for the co-op in town, she couldn't sleep, feeling an emptiness in her heart, a sense of foreboding. Her self-confidence was battered, for the first time in her life, by this rebuff. Despite the heady success she had enjoyed throughout her years, she had to face the unpleasant realization that her uncle's power and influence were limited to Crossroads Township, that he couldn't be counted on, and that among the younger generation in Crossroads Township, Golden Dog was the force to contend with. In a night of tossing and turning, during which her mind was flooded with images of Golden Dog, she was suddenly seized by the desire to possess him. Have I fallen in love with Golden Dog? she wondered, feeling feverish and incredibly restless. She gazed out the window at the bright moon, opening herself to the impression that somehow he already belonged to her. The idea excited her, restored her self-confidence. Gripped by a devilish impulse, she took the newest dress she owned from her trunk, put it on, and sat at the dressing table to make herself up in front of the mirror. Having applied a thick layer of perfumed powder to her face and neck, she got up, opened the door, and walked into the night.

She headed for the ferry landing, where she boarded Han Wenju's ferry for Stream of Wandering Spirits. "Going back tonight?" Han asked idly.

"I forgot something at home."

Han was well aware of the effort she'd expended trying to get Golden Dog chosen for the job in Zhou City, and he was grateful to her. Just as he was about to ask how things had gone with the examiners from the newspaper, he noticed a fragrance. "What smells so good? The osmanthuses aren't in bloom, are they?"

Yingying laughed. "Uncle Han, your nose is sure working!"

He suddenly realized what it was. "I'll bet you're going looking for someone!"

"How did you know?"

"I've read some books in my time," he said, "and there's a saying that goes, 'A man will die for a bosom friend, a woman dolls herself up for someone who loves her.' With that sweet-smelling powder you're wearing, you must have your sights on someone!"

"You're right, but I won't tell you who he is." She laughed again, and was still laughing when the boat reached the bank. Han disapproved under his breath: "What a scheming little witch!" On the return trip, he fumed and fretted over his misfortune in not being able to afford perfumed powder for Water Girl.

Yingying walked up to Golden Dog's house and called at full voice for him to come out. When he saw her in the moonlight, all dolled up, he gaped.

"What's wrong?" she asked him. "Are you upset that I came looking for you at night?"

"I hardly recognize you!"

"Do I look good like this?"

"Yes, very good."

"I have something to talk to you about. Let's take a walk. If you change your mind, you can always come back and go to bed."

Golden Dog smiled and joined her outside.

They strolled down the path beneath Restless Hill all the way to Stream of Wandering Spirits, then left the stone path and walked up to the edge of the river, where they turned and headed out onto the sandbar, stepping on the rays of the moon. He had no idea what she wanted to talk about, and she skirted the issue with light banter and occasional laughter. He could smell the perfume of her powder mixed with her feminine scents. When they reached the sandbar, she confronted him, "Golden Dog, are you angry we've walked so far? Are you bored?"

"No," he said, "I could spend all night walking to White Rock Stockade."

"Great! Look how beautiful the moon is. We country folk usually turn in right after dark, so we don't give the moon a chance to touch our senses with its light."

They looked up at the moon together, so round and full, so clear and bright.

"Golden Dog, you're a sensitive man; tell me what the moon looks like to you."

"Like a jade plate."

"What else?" she asked him.

"Like a mirror."

"What else?"

"An eye in the sky."

"What else?"

He stared at the moon before blurting out, "If I had a carved seal as big as the moon, I'd stamp it on the canopy of heaven, and it would belong to me!"

Yingying was left speechless for a moment but then said, "Only a man could make a comparison like that." In excitement, she touched his forehead with her finger and said, "Golden Dog, you're a real careerist!"

He stirred at the touch of her finger, but when he saw that she was still happily looking up at the moon, he calmed down. "I guess the selection notice must have come, since you're in such high spirits."

Her eyes fell; the moonbeams darkened. But she immediately pulled herself together and said, "Golden Dog, my uncle says that they decided to take only one person, which means one of us can't go."

His heart froze. He sat on the sandbar, wordless. He knew that Tian had failed because his prestige didn't extend beyond Crossroads Township. But since his authority there was absolute, what chance did Golden Dog have of being chosen?

"I understand," he said. "You want me to share your joy tonight."

"If I was that kind of girl, I wouldn't need anybody to share my joy." She was clearly annoyed. "This business with the name list has tormented my uncle. Since he doesn't know who to send, he wants us to talk it over. We're sort of family, so we ought to be able to decide on something."

He stared at her but couldn't see what was going on behind that pretty face. Then he had an idea: maybe the newspaper had already decided on him. He'd find out.

"Then you should be the one to go," he said. "I can stay with the river shipping brigade."

"I'd love to go, but what about you? You're more qualified than I, and you're a man. Men make the world go round, and women rely on them!"

Golden Dog was suddenly aroused. Moonbeams were playing on her face; her eyes sparkled like stars. "It has to be you."

She moved closer, seductively. "And if I don't want to?"

He smiled. "No chance of that."

She gazed at him blankly. "Would you refuse if I asked you to go?"

"Would your uncle allow it? Just think how much better your life would be in Zhou City than at the co-op in town."

"But only one person will be accepted. I'd rather we both went, so we could live in Zhou City forever. Think how wonderful that would be! But only one can go, and we can't waste this opportunity. I think you should go, except you'd probably forget all about us once you left, like all the other men."

His heart was pounding as he pondered her words. He knew there was more to this than met the eye. But since he couldn't figure out what that was, he tried to interpret the hints she was dropping. If he made a mistake at this critical juncture, Tian might use his authority and not send anyone.

Disingenuously, he said, "Yingying, I'm very grateful!"

"How will you show that gratitude?" she asked coquettishly.

"I'll never forget you as long as I live!"

"Then let me give you a present. Will you take it?"

He didn't know what to say.

She took off her wristwatch and held it out in front of him.

For the first time in his life, Golden Dog's masculine decisiveness failed him. He just stood there without moving.

Yingying gazed at him with her sparkling eyes. "You won't take it?"

He accepted the challenge, and the wristwatch.

That night, Han Wenju heard voices coming from the sandbar upstream, and laughter. Since the misty moonlight prevented him from seeing who it was, he had to identify them by their voices. It was Yingying and Golden Dog. The next morning, he reported what he'd heard to the painter, as though it were big news, relating in detail what Golden Dog and Yingying had been doing on the sandbar. The painter just shook his head, assuming that Han Wenju was hearing things. Would someone with Yingying's background fall for his Golden Dog? But then at noon Cai Da'an dropped by and said that he'd come as a matchmaker at the request of Yingying and Tian Zhongzheng. The painter, astonished beyond words, invited Cai to sit with him on the edge of the kang. He thanked Cai profusely, but Golden Dog felt terrible, and it showed on his face, which was as dark as that of the god of war. The painter couldn't contain his excitement. He made tea for Cai, then stuck incense in the tripod at the base of the altar for heaven, earth, gods, emperors, and ancestors. Noticing that the drawings of the mountain watchdogs beside the altar were fading, he picked up his brush and touched them up with fresh paint.

Cai teased him, "Don't get so worked up! You're getting so much paint on your mouth, it's going to look like a baby's dirty behind. Wipe your mouth, and let's drink a few cups of wine!"

Golden Dog was sitting at the table with fire in his eyes. He sped over, grabbed the bowl out of his father's hand, and flung the paint down in front of Cai Da'an. His impulsive action stunned Cai, and the painter as well, who reached out and gave his son a resounding slap. "Golden Dog!" he shrieked. "Have you gone crazy?"

Cai just laughed and said, "I take it you're not happy, Golden Dog. I know you like Water Girl, but how can she compare with Yingying? Use your head. With Yingying, your future happiness is assured; without her, your problems have just begun. You're smart enough to know the score. Even if Water Girl were a fairy princess, what difference would it make? As long as you parlay your work into a respectable position, you'll never have to worry about women, and it won't cost you a cent!"

Golden Dog eyed Cai coldly, his turmoil showing in his hard breathing. He forced himself to calm down, and there was defiance in his voice as he said, "I think it's time for you to go. Just leave!" He stormed into the bedroom, where he lay down on the kang, holding his head, and tried to sleep. But his mind was in turmoil. He loathed Tian Zhongzheng, he loathed Yingying, he loathed himself. A decent young man who wanted desperately to pull himself out of a tough situation, who wanted to break free of the net of personal connections thrown over the Zhou River by the loathsome Tian and Gong clans, found that the more he struggled, the more entangled he became, and now he was expected to become the son-in-law of Tian Zhongzheng! At this rate, how much longer could he maintain his self-respect? How could he do the right thing where Water Girl was concerned?

He jumped down off the kang like a man possessed and bellowed at Cai, "I'm not going to Zhou City for that job! You tell Tian Zhongzheng that I'm going to be a boatman for the rest of my life and that I'll die on the Zhou River!"

This came as such a jolt to Cai that the cup in his hand went crashing to the floor. The painter impetuously picked up a straw cushion from behind the door and threw it at Golden Dog. "You ingrate, you're out of your mind!" Forcing a smile, he turned to Cai and said, "Don't take him seriously! I raised this dog, and I know his temper. He'll come around. Go tell Tian Zhongzheng that everything's fine. I'm going into town in a couple of days, and I'll buy you a pair of new shoes to show our appreciation for your matchmaking."

Cai smiled and said, "I understand young people's tempers. Tell him to use his head and get his priorities straight. I just want to say that Golden Dog's seen enough of the world to know what's up and

I'm surprised to find him acting like a child! But I'm not offended. He's mad now, but someday he'll thank me." He laughed drily once or twice, and as he turned to leave, the painter thrust a bottle of strong wine into his hand.

That night, when Golden Dog refused to come out of his room for dinner, his father squatted down by the stove and ate alone. Yingying suddenly appeared at the door. The painter at once put down his bowl and offered her a seat, then went straight into the bedroom and dragged Golden Dog off the kang. He returned to make Yingying a cup of tea. "Aiya!" he said. "This room's a mess. There's no place for you to sit. Golden Dog seems to have caught a cold, so he went to bed to sweat it out. He's fine now. You two sit here while I go borrow a flour sifter from the Lius." He walked outside, closing the door behind him, even bolting it to make sure it stayed closed.

But he didn't go to borrow the flour sifter. Instead he took his pipe and mosquito-repellent incense over to the hill across from the house, where he could see the light through the window. He sat there smoking his pipe, huddled up against the night air, thinking happily, Let the youngsters have their talk. *One of them's dry kindling, and the other's a lit torch, so maybe they'll build a fire together!*

Golden Dog sat mute on the edge of the kang, and even though he didn't look at Yingying, he could guess why she had come over. But he was a little surprised at her boldness in coming alone. Since Cai had brought their relationship into the open, it was time to hear what she had to say.

But she didn't come right out and talk about the wedding. "He says you've been sick," she said "Are you all right now?"

"I'm not sick. I just felt like sleeping."

"At least you're honest," she said with a smile. "I knew he was making it up."

Such a casual, carefree smile, as though nothing had happened. She continued where she'd left off the night before, telling him earnestly what she thought of him and how she felt, her dreams and hopes, and what had moved her to take her name off the list in favor of him. But with all her fine talk, tender emotions, and good intentions, Golden Dog detected a note of coercion and cold calculation: *It was my uncle who managed to get this opportunity, and I'm the one who's turning it over to you!* She impressed him as a strong, self-confident young woman who, like her uncle, knew what she wanted and had the courage to go after it. Golden Dog was like a man receiving a beating from a club wrapped in cotton, and he knew he was suffering internal injuries. Nevertheless, he wanted to see where things were going, so he clenched his teeth and looked into her eyes. Nothing frightened Golden Dog, certainly not a woman!

He soon found himself warming to her, and she was looking prettier by the minute. As she talked, she gazed into the mirror opposite the window, her eyes darting back and forth. She reached back and gathered her hair up to reveal the soft white skin of her neck. Golden Dog noticed a large black mole just below her ear, which he found captivating in the light of the lamp. He lowered his eyes and thought of Water Girl, who also had a mole, on her eyebrow. He'd once asked her if he could take a close look at it, but she'd pushed his hand away.

By now, Yingying seemed to be feeling right at home; she leaned her chair back and thrust her head toward him. With a glint in her eyes, she asked, "Golden Dog, how do you feel about me, anyway?"

"Good," he said, flustered by her question.

"Just good?"

"Yes, good."

He heard the sound of a cricket in a corner of the room, but he heard nothing after that. His heart began pounding as he noticed her heaving breast. A strange sensation came over him, as though he were floating in a daze, carried away by the tide. He'd felt this way before, in the company of Water Girl, but she'd always used some power he couldn't name to dam up the tide and bring it under control. The sensation held him: he had an overpowering thirst, his lips were dry, and he seemed to be breathing fire through his nose. The lamp atop the cupboard flickered a time or two, as the oil in it sputtered. "No more oil," he told Yingying. "I'll add some."

Yingying stood up and held him back with her hand, and as the lamp sputtered, he felt a pair of arms wrap around his neck; it was a snake, a snake that was nibbling at his face, biting down on his lips. The lamp flared up one last time, and an inky darkness settled over the room, which became as still as death. A whispered "Golden Dog" came through the darkness. "My uncle's very happy about you and me, and he wants me to bring you over to our house. Don't call him Secretary any more. Call him Uncle!"

Golden Dog felt intoxicated. His youthful impulses had filled him with a powerful desire to be united with Water Girl, but that was impossible; now Yingying had taken the initiative, and in his clumsiness he didn't know what to do. Her body was growing limp; she began to slip through his arms like a noodle in boiling water. "Golden Dog," she whispered, "I can't stand it anymore. I'm so wet down there . . ."

In a flash, he turned into a crazed wolf, a golden leopard, as he picked her up in his arms and laid her down on the kang, where he mounted her breathlessly and began to paw her—not the tender strokings of love but the release of savage, violent feelings. He rolled off, covered with sweat, physically gratified, his mind a blank.

After relighting the lamp, he lay quietly on the kang and watched Yingying, who was sitting on the edge. Neither of them spoke. He just looked at her.

"Don't look at me like that," she said.

But he kept looking at her as a feeling of loss slowly filled his heart. He was feeling remorse, as the first thought that entered his mind was that he'd shamed Water Girl.

"What are you thinking?" Yingying asked him.

"I never dreamed we'd do what we did."

"Do you regret it?"

"What I mean is, you're still just a young girl!"

"You've taken my virginity from me! But since it was someone I liked, I gave it willingly. It's nobody else's business!"

Golden Dog sat up, but his head felt so heavy he couldn't raise it. "Don't say any more . . . Now, you and I don't have to worry anymore!"

Yingying straightened her hair in the mirror and said she ought to go, since it was getting late. Golden Dog saw her out, then watched her walk off in the spreading moonlight. By now, he was back to normal, physically and mentally, and his mind was filled with images of Water Girl and Yingying: Water Girl was a bodhisattva, Yingying was a wild animal. People revere bodhisattvas, but they fall in love with wild animals; the holiness of the bodhisattva had steered him clear of wicked thoughts, but the seductiveness of the wild animal had forced him into a quagmire from which there was no escape.

He turned and walked silently back into the house, as two hot tears coursed down his cheeks.

The painter waited patiently until Yingying walked into the night before returning. He found his son sitting like a statue on the kang. He went over to his own kang and lay down without asking anything. But before closing his eyes, he said, "Go to sleep. You'll have to go over to the Tians' and call on Yingying's mother."

Golden Dog didn't answer. He blew out the lamp and sat there on the kang listening to the mountain watchdogs, whose calls had begun before he was aware of it. He looked out the window at the stone ledge between Green Dragon and White Tiger peaks, at the mouth of the ravine, where two lanterns swayed in the wind and the sound of spirits calling, "Coming back?" and its echo, "Coming back!" produced a feeling of desolation within anyone who heard it.

The painter slept like a baby that night, not waking up till after daybreak. By then his son was gone.

Golden Dog had taken his boat down to White Rock Stockade.

Water Girl sighted him before he pulled up to the bank. "Uncle Golden Dog!" she cried out happily. "Uncle Golden Dog!"

He had become gaunt in the space of a single night; his face was drawn and pale, his expression dulled. He climbed up onto the riverbank and strolled with her toward the blacksmith shop.

Pockface, drunk again, was slouching in front of the bellows, engaged in a conversation with a woman at a peddler's stand across the street. "What imaginable complaint might there be about Water Girl? Just let your eye follow her sometime. She always looks just right, whether she's sitting down or walking! I've lived in White Rock Stockade for forty years, where I've seen thousands of women, and only three good ones in the lot. One's Gong Baoshan's woman. When he took up office in town, he married a student fifteen years his junior, with a big, beautiful face like the consort Yang Guifei, and she went with him to Zhou City to live the good life. The second one's the bodhisattva in the Temple of the Immortal Matron. Water Girl's the third!"

The peddler woman laughed indulgently. "What a lucky man you are, blacksmith!" she said. "Who knows, when you get old, maybe you'll settle in the city with Water Girl!"

Pockface loved what he was hearing. "Maybe I will! Do you know Golden Dog? The one who writes so well? Well, the Zhou City newspaper wants to hire him as a reporter, and if Water Girl goes with him to enjoy the good life, you don't think she'll leave her old grandpa here to work the forge, do you? I've said it before: if a man has talent, no matter where he goes he can make a good living, but a woman's better off with no talent and a beautiful face, because she can go where she wants and land on a high perch even if her mother was a beggar!"

Water Girl and Golden Dog walked up just then. "Grandpa," she said, "you're drunk again, and you're embarrassing me with all that nonsense."

Pockface turned and saw them. "Golden Dog," he said, "what the hell's kept you away so long? If you become a reporter, you know who's responsible, don't you? Where would you be if Water Girl hadn't dragged you over there? So why have you been staying away? Too good for a simple blacksmith now? Well, there's a treasure in the blacksmith shop!"

Golden Dog ignored him and walked inside with Water Girl, who busied herself making tea. Pockface followed them inside and sat down, giggling irrepressibly. When the tea was brought in, Golden Dog said, "Drink some tea, Uncle. That'll sober you up."

"Still calling me Uncle? Why are you so stubborn? Everyone on the block knows I'm your grandfather now, so why are you still calling me Uncle?"

"Grandpa," Water Girl said, "you really annoy me with all that chatter! Let's talk about something important."

"Oh!" he said, as he went out to banter some more with the peddler woman across the street.

"Where do things stand with the newspaper?" she asked.

"I've been selected."

She was ecstatic. "I told you the abbot knew what he was talking about. His predictions came true! Last night I dreamed you hadn't been selected, and when I woke up this morning all I could do was sigh. When Grandpa heard what was wrong, he clasped his hands in front of himself and said that since dreams are the opposite of the truth, you were sure to be selected. But I was still worried. What do you feel like eating? Name it, and I'll make it to celebrate."

Golden Dog looked at her and smiled wryly, seemingly in a world by himself.

"What's wrong?" she asked. "Aren't you happy?"

He threw himself down on the kang, buried his head under the covers, and began to sob.

She was baffled. Usually, you couldn't drag him from her when they were together. She always looked forward to his arrival, then fretted over the possibility of their being left alone. She still carried his teeth marks on her chin, and her breast still heaved when she thought of him. But he'd suddenly lost his playfulness and seemed to be a different person altogether. She turned his face toward her and saw it was covered with tears. "What's wrong?" she demanded. "What's wrong with you?"

He told her what had happened, leaving nothing out, not even what he and Yingying had done. His recital stunned Water Girl, who stumbled backward and fell into a chair, where she sat in stupefied silence. Golden Dog's sobs stopped at once, and he watched her actions fearfully. She rose to her feet and went to the backyard, where she threw her arms around a toon tree in the corner and slumped to the ground.

Pockface smelled smoke coming from inside the house. He entered as fast as he could, to find thick clouds belching out of the stove. Scooping up a bucketful of water and dousing the flames, he shouted for Water Girl. But she was still slumped at the base of the tree, unable to get up. Terribly confused, he insisted on knowing what was wrong, but only after she overcame her tears could she tell him what had happened. He snatched up a broom, ran into the house, and began beating Golden Dog over the head. "So that's it!" he exploded. "You son of a bitch, even a wolf would be disgusted with you! Nothing but a sneak with no conscience! Why don't you love my Water Girl? All you wanted was to seduce her, to play with her. You tricked her into acting like a simpleton, and tricked me out of some damned good wine! I'm taking you to court on this! You think Tian Zhongzheng's got power? Well, I've got friends at court! And if that doesn't work, I have plenty of blacksmith friends and apprentices and I'll find a way to skin you alive!" Smack! Smack! The broom landed hard on Golden Dog's waist and thighs. He didn't raise a hand to protect himself.

Completely out of control, Pockface threw down the broom and grabbed at Golden Dog. But encountering a weight too great for him, he ran into the kitchen and picked up a cleaver. Water Girl stopped him. "Grandpa, don't!" she pleaded. "Just let him go."

"Go?" Pockface said. "Let him go? Is there no rule of law under the Communist party?"

Water Girl turned to Golden Dog. "What are you waiting for ? You want him to chop off your leg?"

Golden Dog got woodenly to his feet and cleared out.

He walked down the street like a zombi: he didn't see the crowds of people nor the peddlers' stands lining the sides. He just walked in a daze, his legs moving mechanically on the sun-drenched street, until a woman on a bicycle, her bell clanging frantically, crashed into him. "Are you blind?" she screeched. "Did a chicken peck out your eyes?" He didn't utter a word but waited until she'd had her say and had climbed back onto her bicycle. As she passed, she spit on him and got in a final "Did a chicken peck out your eyes?"

On the Zhou River, boats originating in Crossroads Township had already left the ferry landing for their downriver journey to Purple Thistle Pass; those heading in the opposite direction had left for Crossroads Township. The dark riverbank was littered with garbage, deserted of people; three or four dogs were chasing one another in the shallows. Golden Dog sat down on the riverbank to contemplate the swirling yellow water, feeling lost and alone. Some children came running up: "Hurry. Look, it's great! They're hooked together!" He looked up to see a pair of dogs on the sandbar linked together rump to rump. The children were tormenting them with sticks. He experienced an overpowering sense of shame.

Night fell, and moonlight took over. Golden Dog was too ashamed to go into town to look up friends, and didn't feel like spending the night at the shipping brigade warehouse. He'd spend the night on the bank of the river, hoping he'd freeze in the wind or that the tide would sweep him away to expiate his sins against Water Girl. He thought he heard her voice, but he didn't turn around, for he knew he was imagining things. *Water Girl, Water Girl, oh, Water Girl, I'll never hear your voice again, and I'll have to get through life carrying this illusion with me!* Have I won, he was thinking, or have I lost?

"Uncle Golden Dog!"

There it was again, Water Girl's shout, the same one he'd heard before, but gentler and sadder. He turned, and there, standing behind him, was a living, breathing Water Girl.

"You're still here?" she asked. "I knew you would be. Grandpa's drunk again. He finished off eight ounces, and he doesn't know which end is up. That's when I came out."

"Water Girl, why did you come looking for me? Someone like me doesn't deserve your attention."

"Let's go over to the sandbar."

They left the riverbank by way of the stone path and walked over to the deserted sandbar, from where they could see red and yellow lanterns in the wood-and-stone buildings off in the distance and hear strains of music from tape recorders and a stringed erhu floating above the Zhou River. The light stretched out over the water, like a writhing snake. Water Girl took off her jacket and laid it on the ground. She sat down, leaving space for him.

"Try to understand why Grandpa screamed and hit you."

"I know that, and I deserved it. When he picked up the knife, I knew I wouldn't move even if he cut me. I'd have been happy to die at his hands."

"That's no way to deal with things. My heart broke when you told me. But I wouldn't let myself weep openly, because of all the people walking by outside. What could I have said to them? Besides, Grandpa's getting old, and he loves me more than he loves himself. If he'd seen me wailing, it could have killed him, or he might have done something crazy. I hate you, hate you so much I could gnash my teeth until they shattered. But I came looking for you . . . After thinking it over as calmly as I could, I realized that Yingying's a seductress who's capable of anything. I know you didn't want to do it . . ."

"If you want to know the truth," Golden Dog said, "I was thinking of you the whole time. I wanted to hate her, get even with her, and the truth is, I wanted to get even with you to some degree . . . But I was wrong, dead wrong."

Tears welled up in Water Girl's eyes, and she began to sob. Before long, she was crying aloud.

Golden Dog stood up but then just stood there dumbly. He sat back down, thrust his hands into the sand, and didn't say a word. Seeing that she was still crying, he grabbed her cold hands and held them tightly. "Water Girl," he said with a sob, "forgive me, please forgive me. I won't go to work at the newspaper, and that way I won't have to get engaged to Yingying. I want to marry you, Water Girl!"

As her sobs faded, she slowly and quietly pulled her hands out of Golden Dog's grip. "Uncle Golden Dog, that's not possible! You fought for that job with the newspaper, and so did I. Now that things have gone this far, you must put them into perspective. I don't blame anything but my own bitter fate! Most girls in my position wouldn't come looking for you, and they wouldn't let themselves cry in front of you. I did because I know I have a place in your heart. I came to tell you to sever this thread between us so you can go to the newspaper with an easy mind."

He wept.

"Even with what's just happened, I have no regrets for the past," she consoled him. "If you still love me, do a good job and bring credit to our generation. Since it's time for us to break up, I have something for you."

"Something for me?" Golden Dog said. "What is it?"

She ripped the third button off her blouse and handed it to him. He held it in his hand, knowing that by its location this particular button symbolized her heart.

She walked down off the sandbar.

He watched her silhouette disappear into the darkness; then he ran wildly across the sandbar, stepping on those places bathed in moonlight, places where there was water, all the way to the riverbank, his feet soaked, then back up onto the beach. He didn't know how long he'd run before he was back on the sandbar; by then he wasn't sure how to return to the ferry landing. Finally, he climbed a stone embankment that served as a dike, scrambling up frantically until he was illuminated by the flashlight beam of a passerby. "Hey, who's there? What are you doing?"

"I want to get to White Rock Stockade!"

"Spirits preserve us!" the man exclaimed. "Do you think that's the road? You must be possessed by a blockhead of a ghost!" He ran up and kicked Golden Dog, then slapped him several times. That snapped Golden Dog out of it, and tears began running down his face. He climbed down to the bank and headed for town.

11

Pockface's blacksmith shop was famous in White Rock Stockade. During his youth, when his face was strong and handsome, he'd been a postman. Back then, only two kinds of people rode bicycles: stockade troops and postmen. He'd ridden a Japanese bicycle with double crossbars, wearing a green helmet as he made trips to Crossroads Township every other day, returning the following day. When the stockade troops encircled the mountain to "pacify" the troops of Tian the Sixth, he was delivering mail to Crossroads Township; the gunshots drove the townspeople to the mountains, where they crossed suspension bridges to a cave for safety. He followed them. Believing that Tian the Sixth and his troops were also hidden in the cave, the pacification troops fired a hail of bullets toward it. The people who had taken refuge tried to flee back across the bridges, planning to tear up the planks behind them, but the men in khaki uniforms were already crossing over. So the townspeople went back into the cave, where they strained to pull up the supports, sending the pacification troops tumbling down the mountain. The troops' enraged comrades at the foot of the mountain opened fire. As Pockface lay on his belly at the mouth of the cave looking down, a bullet narrowly missed him, striking a rock above his head, which shattered and struck him in the face, covering it with blood. He was never again handsome, and he never went back to the postal service. Instead he apprenticed himself to a blacksmith in White Rock Stockade. The blacksmith, who was born a pockface and had lost his wife years earlier, worked the forge with his ugly daughter. The former postman married into the family and carried on the tradition of the shop's blacksmith being a pockface. In his later years he quit caring whether or not people called him Pockface, and for years he cast the word *pock* into every piece of ironware, every knife, every pair of scissors, and every pick and ax he made, so that the young people no longer knew what his real name was. When children saw his familiar face, they called out, "Grandpa Pockface!"—to which he responded with feigned hurt, "Grandpa's good enough, so why add Pockface?" When he went to the inn at the southern gate, whose proprietor was an old friend, instead of sitting at a table he'd stand at the bar, order two ounces of wine, and drink it down in two gulps. This routine had taken on the aspects of a ritual. If he ordered more, there'd still be wine in the cup; less, and it wouldn't have been a mouthful: naturally, the proprietor wouldn't have dared to pour too little. When the wine was safely down his throat, he'd smack his lips and say, "Tell me, how much do you dilute this wine? A dishpan per barrel?"

The proprietor would reply softly, "Not so loud, you'll ruin my reputation! Here, have a couple more ounces." The second two ounces were on the house, although he always tossed some money onto the bar as he was leaving and ordered a jugful before weaving his way out the door.

The blacksmith shop had been closed for several days, the furnace shut down. Now that the place was quiet, the neighbors, who were used to hearing the sound of hammer on anvil day and night, found it impossible to sleep at night. The peddler woman across the street, accustomed to eating two eggs fried on the blacksmith's forge every morning, was reduced to making the trek to Central Avenue for a breakfast of fermented bean curd. Then one morning before the sun was up, when all the neighbors were still fast asleep, they were startled from their dreams by the clanging of a hammer. On opening their eyes, they saw a red glare through the paper covering their windows, and they knew that Pockface was back to work at his furnace. But the old, familiar sound, filled with a unique sense of cheer, suddenly seemed to them somehow different from before, harsh and grating.

When they got up, they discovered Fuyun working the hammer. They all knew him as a man who worked like an ox.

"Fuyun," someone asked, "why aren't you out on your boat?"

"Grandpa Pockface has taken me on as his apprentice."

They laughed. "Then you'd better be careful, or one day your face'll be covered with pockmarks!"

Fuyun had quit the river shipping brigade and come over on his own. When he heard that Golden Dog and Water Girl had broken up, he reviled the Tian clan and vowed never to help them again with their autumn harvest; he also reviled Golden Dog in front of the painter. He had a fondness for Water Girl but was incapable of consoling her, so he came to the blacksmith shop and volunteered to be Pockface's assistant. Although no one was aware of it, in his heart he had decided that by helping out at the blacksmith shop he could look after and lend assistance to the old man and his granddaughter, for he was strong and not afraid of hard work. But Pockface refused to take him on at first, fearing that he was too clumsy to master the skills of the trade. But Fuyun wouldn't take no for an answer. Still, the first time he picked up the hammer, he swung it so hard that he twisted his back and couldn't move for several days. When at last the local chiropractor came to treat him, he had him try to walk around the yard, and when he wasn't looking, came up behind him and kicked him in the small of the back. That hurt so much that Fuyun sank to the ground and broke out in a heavy sweat, but before he had time to groan, he was on his feet again, his back feeling much better. Inasmuch as Fuyun hadn't made a sound, Pockface then and there decided to end his probation. "You're not afraid of hard work and you have patience, the two virtues of blacksmithing. But you don't have Golden Dog's self-confidence or intelligence." The mention of Golden Dog's name brought an immediate change to Pockface's expression. He let loose a string of expletives, then took a piece of red-hot metal out of the furnace and began hammering it so hard that sparks flew.

Things gradually returned to normal, one uneventful day leading to another. Business was booming at the shop, with a steady flow of customers coming in to place orders or to pick up orders or to bring in tools for repair. It gradually occurred to Pockface that the customers were forever sneaking glances at Water Girl as they looked over the merchandise. At first he thought they were just envious of her good looks and obvious abilities; not only didn't it bother him, it gave him a measure of pride. But after a while he noticed something amiss in the way they were looking at her, something askance about it. Then one day as he was leaving the shop he spotted two men pointing to Water Girl as she was carrying a bucket of water. "That's her," one of them said, "the one who was rejected by Golden Dog, that boatman out on the Zhou River."

"She's quite a looker," the other one added. "The only reason someone would reject her is because she's used goods. I hear she's still a widow. Is there something special about a widow?" But spotting Pockface, he shut up. The two men then slipped away, swiftly, having a good laugh as they left.

Pockface became aware that the entire neighborhood knew that Golden Dog had broken off his relationship with Water Girl, and he felt humiliation. But he couldn't vent his distress on her, since she was the victim and needed compassion and solace. That very day he fell ill.

Water Girl attended her grandfather day and night. He grabbed her hand and said tearfully, "My Water Girl has such a bitter fate!" Then he vilified Golden Dog until he began spitting blood. All this time, Fuyun helped Water Girl any way he could: he fetched water, he went to the market, he bought medicine for his master, and he helped her with the customers.

She was immensely grateful. "Fuyun," she said, "you've suffered because of us! After Grandpa's better, I'll have him give you two months' wages for every month, since there's plenty of work in the shop."

"What would I do with that much money? I'm not going to build a house or buy land, and I don't need a wife and kids, so I'd just spend it foolishly. Look at Golden Dog. It was trying to find ways to make more money that ruined him."

"Fuyun, don't talk like that."

"Who are you protecting? I've said it all over Stream of Wandering Spirits: If nobody wants to become an official, all the officials will be ordinary people. When Golden Dog worked his boat, he was a good man. But as soon as he set his heart on being a cadre, things changed."

Knowing Fuyun's intensity, she dropped the subject. But he was worried that she didn't quite trust his commitment to the forge, so he went over to Stream of Wandering Spirits, where he wrapped up his affairs on the farm, rolled up his bedding, and packed several bags of dry grain, in order to move into the blacksmith shop lock, stock, and barrel.

Meanwhile, in Stream of Wandering Spirits, Tian Zhongzheng went to the painter's house to tell him that Golden Dog had been formally selected, and since he'd be leaving soon, they wanted to have some sort of engagement ceremony. "By rights this should be your responsibility, but we can skip the formalities and hold it at my place, where it's more convenient. What do you say?"

Golden Dog's my son, the painter was thinking, and a son's engagement party is his father's responsibility. *Having it at your house is the same as taking the groom into your family, isn't it?* But instead of saying what bothered him, he just nodded his assent, then went back and urged his son to get moving, going so far in the end as to help him change clothes even though he was a grown man. The old man then went and bought a gift for the Tians.

Guests filled the Tian home, all of them members of Crossroads Township's upper crust, and a party atmosphere prevailed throughout the noon hour. When Golden Dog headed out for the toilet, he ran into Old Seven and Fuyun, who were in a hurry to get to the riverbank from the village. He hailed them, but they didn't respond, so he caught up with them and asked, "Fuyun, what are you doing here? I heard you've become a blacksmith."

"Where'd you hear that? I didn't think you were interested."

"Where are you off to?"

"The blacksmith shop in White Rock Stockade."

"I'll go with you."

"You want to go there *now?* No member of the Tian clan has been out on the river for decades!"

"Who's a member of the Tian clan?" Golden Dog bellowed.

Fuyun matched his tone: "Would you want Yingying if it weren't for her uncle?"

Golden Dog doubled up his fist and hit Fuyun square in the chest, knocking him to the ground. Even with all his strength, Fuyun was afraid of Golden Dog, but he clambered to his feet to fight back. Old Seven stopped him. Golden Dog turned and walked down to the riverbank, where he jumped onto a tied-up raft.

Han Wenju, who spied him from the ferry landing, spit into the river, then began singing a boatman song from his youth, which suddenly came back to him after all these years:

What can we do but sail the Zhou River,
Punt pole in hand, legs quivering,
Three hundred li of water, four hundred shoals,
Fought over by the dragon king and the king of hell?

What can we do but sail the Zhou River,
Towlines gouging our shoulders, rocks cutting our feet,
Taxes and tyrants claiming our lives,
More worries than there are rocks?

What can we do but sail the Zhou River,
Tears in our eyes, a song on our lips,
Kidnapped by pirates, who drown us in lakes,
Cut open fish bellies to find our remains?

Nothing but the sound of labored breathing came from Golden Dog. Fuyun jumped onto a raft, ignoring him. "Uncle Seven," he said, "let's get under way!" He tossed off the rope, pushed off with his pole, turned the raft around, and let the current take him downstream. Golden Dog took off his jacket and his pants, and poled his raft so hard he soon overtook Old Seven's raft.

"Golden Dog," Old Seven said, "you shouldn't be out on the river today."

"It's my last time on the rafts."

"Since you'll be leaving soon, we should get together for a few drinks. But you'll be the Tians' son-in-law. Things are happening almost too fast."

"I know," Golden Dog said.

"I don't know anything about romance, but when I was a young man, I knew a woman in Purple Thistle Pass, and I still dream about her even though she worked in a brothel. Have you and Water Girl broken off for good?"

"Yes."

Old Seven sighed as he sat down at the rear of the raft without a word, pulled out a jug, and took a drink. Fuyun asked for a drink, but Old Seven turned him down. "People today only think of themselves, so why should I be the generous one?" he asked peevishly. "If you feel like drinking, go buy your own wine!"

Fuyun wasn't upset by this display, but Golden Dog felt his cheeks burning.

The rafts moved slowly down the river. No one spoke. Golden Dog hadn't experienced such a frigid atmosphere in all the time he'd sailed a boat or poled a raft. He knew that Old Seven resented him, and so did Fuyun, but what could he say to them? All he could do was stand speechless on his raft, nervously staring ahead as he tried to wipe his mind free of the flood of chaotic thoughts. The Zhou River flowed calmly down its riverbed, sometimes forming a broad, watery road as it snaked its way close to the northern bank, exposing the sand and stones of the southern bank, then shifting toward the southern bank, raising the southern course up to the overhanging cliffs and revealing dry sandbars on the northern bank, where there were newly planted rice paddies. Where the river flowed straight, it made its way down three or four separate paths. This was the hardest section to navigate, since the boatman had to determine quickly which of the paths ran deep, which ran shallow. Golden Dog invariably chose the right one, on the basis of the color of the water and the height of the spray. Once this section was passed, the riverbed sloped downward and the water flowed steadily along. The slanting rays of the afternoon sun made the surface of the water appear like an oil painting. By looking at the ripples on the water, Golden Dog knew where the whirlpools were, where there were boulders jutting up from the bottom. He knew there were dangers all around and that if he let down his guard for even a moment, the tranquil-looking surface could pull a raft toward it like a magnet, spinning it around and sending it to the bottom, where it would disappear for all time. The river narrowed at Seven-Li Gorge, where eight mountain spurs jutted out menacingly from the banks and the river began a series of seven treacherous twists through a wall of trees whose overhanging branches blocked out the sunlight. Dead trees showed up white amid the surrounding green, their trunks wrapped in creepers and grapevines that hung from the branches like ropes swaying above the water. Black, oily boulders rose from the banks in secluded inlets where dense grass and wolf-fang brambles grew. Golden Dog's heart was in his throat as he poled his raft frantically, first this way, then that, sometimes striking the bank and causing both raft and man to shudder and groan. Trees rooted in the river had been cut off at the water level, and the waves frequently exposed stumps as tall as a man. He was carefully negotiating the raft past them when he heard a sudden crash and felt the raft lurch to the side before stopping dead in the water.

"Submerged tree!" he shouted.

Old Man Seven and Fuyun, who were behind him looking on icily, appeared to relish the trouble he'd got himself into. Instead of rising to their feet, they casually put away their wine jug. "Bad luck!" Old Seven said. "That tree never snagged a raft before! Fuyun, go down and take a look. See if there's a ghost down there that's snagged it!"

Fuyun picked up a curved knife, stripped off his clothes, and dived into the water. A row of air bubbles followed his descent. Then he surfaced. "Uncle Seven, you're right, there is a ghost! A tree branch is stuck up through a gap in the raft."

"A woman hanged herself on that very tree a couple of weeks ago," Old Seven said. "Her tongue was hanging down a couple of feet through the hair that covered her face. That son of a bitch Stony pulled her pants down with his pole, but instead of going after him, her ghost is taking it out on us!" He spit three times into the river and had Fuyun do the same, in order to drive the evil away. They all dived into the water to unsnag the raft but couldn't budge it. It was held fast. Old Seven examined its bottom. "Our knives are useless in the water," he said when he resurfaced. "Get a saw, so we can cut the branch away." Fuyun fetched the saw and was about to dive into the river, when Golden Dog snatched it out of his hand and dived in himself. For ten minutes, then twenty, Golden Dog kept bobbing to the surface, his face flushed from exertion, gasping for air. Fuyun wanted to spell him, but he dived under again. His head broke the surface after the time it took to have a smoke. "It's nearly sawed through. Let's all go down and give the raft a push."

The three of them went into the water, where they tied a long vine around the branch, then shoved the raft with all their might. Snap! The branch broke in two, and the raft bobbed to the surface as the vine was stretched taut. Old Seven climbed up onto his raft, where he stood on the bow and called out, "Everybody up!" Fuyun climbed up, and when he looked down to see Golden Dog casually washing his feet in the river, he reached down and cut the vine in two. Golden Dog's raft shot forward without him and floated quickly downstream, around a bend in the river and out of sight.

"Fuyun," Old Seven fretted, "why'd you do that? We can't leave him out in the middle of nowhere. What'll he do when night falls?"

"Let him spend the night with the ghost of that woman!"

"Pull up alongside the bank," Old Seven said, "and we'll wait for him there."

"Let him suffer. It won't kill him. Let's get out of here."

Golden Dog swam over to the riverbank and stood there. When Fuyun stranded him, there was murder in his eyes. He felt like diving back into the water, swimming after the raft Fuyun was on, and tearing the man limb from limb. But his fury passed, and he laughed. If the cruelty would lessen Old Seven and Fuyun's animus toward him, spending the night here was a small price to pay. He suddenly felt more at peace than he had for days, and a smile creased his face. Fortunately for him, before long a boat came sailing downstream, and the boatman, who knew him, stopped and let him aboard. Dusk had fallen by the time they were heading toward White Rock Stockade.

The boat negotiated the river quickly, since it was so light, and when they were five li past Seven-Li Gorge, Golden Dog spotted Old Seven and Fuyun's raft in the distance. He went into the lean-to so they wouldn't see him, but when the boat was within half a li of the raft, the boatman suddenly cried out, "Oh-oh! That raft ahead of us is in trouble!" Golden Dog flew out of the lean-to just in time to see a wire from a downed telephone pole stretched across the river. Fuyun had tried to lift it over the raft with his pole, but he was too late: it caught him at the waist and dumped him into the river. The raft then ran over the wire, which snapped in two, whipping several loose branches from the raft into the water.

"Fuyun!" Old Seven screamed pitifully. "Fuyun!" Panicking, he poled the raft up to the riverbank. Golden Dog was as worried as the old man, for he knew that Fuyun was only an average swimmer, and that the raft had passed over him as soon as he hit the water and had certainly pushed him into the water trough. So without waiting for the boat to stop, he dived in and swam to the scene as fast as he could. Just as he'd foreseen, when Fuyun bobbed to the surface in the water trough he was immediately pulled back down. Golden Dog swam to him and grabbed him by the hair as the boat drifted up to them. The boatman held out a bamboo pole, which Fuyun grabbed to climb onto the boat. Then it was Golden Dog's turn, but before he could grasp the pole, he felt himself being pulled backward. It was a whirlpool. All he could do was shout, "Help!" as the force of the whirlpool sucked him in and deposited him in a crevice between two dark boulders. Old Seven was already in the water and was swimming toward the rocks. He homed in on Golden Dog, grabbed him by the legs, and pulled with all his might until he'd yanked him free. But the force dislocated one of Golden Dog's shoulders, leaving him in such excruciating pain that he couldn't move. Fuyun picked him up and put him on the raft, where he begged forgiveness for what he'd done.

"That's enough," Golden Dog said. "I don't hold a grudge against you, Fuyun. I know you stranded me because of the way I treated Water Girl, and I don't blame you."

Fuyun and Old Seven tried to force his arm back into the socket, but it wouldn't go, and his upper arm began turning dark and ugly and started to swell up. They'd have to take him to the doctor at White Rock Stockade.

"Golden Dog," Fuyun said to him, "Why don't you want Water Girl? Did she do something to hurt you?"

"No."

"Then why?"

He knew he had to tell everything, and when he did, they were agape. They sailed along for a couple of li without speaking. "Fuyun," Golden Dog said, breaking the silence, "even if things fall through with Yingying, it'll never work out between Water Girl and me. I want to say something, but I don't know if you're willing to hear it or not."

"What's that?"

Golden Dog's eyes were watery even before he began. "Water

Girl's a good woman. Life's been hard for her, with no parents and only Uncle Han, who's negligent and a confirmed bachelor, not the sort of person whose love is a big help. Grandpa Pockface looks after her, but he's getting old, so it's up to you to help out. I know you've gone over to the blacksmith shop, and for that I'll thank you for the rest of my life!"

Fuyun, an honorable man, was moved by Golden Dog's words and nodded his head.

It was dark by the time the raft pulled up to White Rock Stockade, and the three men made their way to the doctor's office, where Golden Dog's arm was put back into the socket. When they returned to the raft, all the houses were lit by lamps.

"Golden Dog," Fuyun said, "let's go to the blacksmith shop. You can't put it off any longer, the way things are now."

"Don't think I don't want to go," he said with an anguished look on his face. "But Grandpa Pockface won't let me set foot in the place. And more arguing will just sadden Water Girl more."

Fuyun knew he was right. Old Seven took Fuyun aside. "Go tell Water Girl to come here, and let the two of them talk things over on the raft. He came with us today even though it's his engagement day, so that proves she's still on his mind."

Fuyun offered Golden Dog the excuse that he was going to get some wine for Old Seven and ran up the beach toward the blacksmith shop.

Grandpa Pockface was still sick, and Water Girl had taken ill as well. Her head ached, her chest ached, and she had no appetite at all. Grandpa Pockface, worried to distraction, dragged himself over to the pharmacy to buy some pain-killer. But it had no effect on her. He then went to get a sorcerer from the western suburbs, who took one look at her and pronounced, "She's possessed!"

"I've heard of people being possessed by spirits of the dead," Grandpa Pockface said, "but can someone be possessed by a spirit of the living?"

"Of course," the sorcerer said. "Even if someone's still alive, his soul can possess someone else, and it's far worse than when it's the spirit of someone who's dead."

Pockface damned Golden Dog. The sorcerer wrote a charm on two slips of yellow paper, putting one under the straw mat on the kang and pasting the other above the door. Peace would return to the family within a day, he assured, and all illness would be driven away. But Water Girl continued to feel that her body weighed a ton, and she did nothing but cry. Fuyun arrived to find the shop closed. He could hear Water Girl weeping inside. When he went in to comfort her, she sat up and forced a smile, asking him how things were in the village, without mentioning Golden Dog.

"Don't cry any more," Fuyun said to her. "That can't change the way things are. Everybody on the boats and in the village is concerned about you. They know who did what to whom, and no one's on Golden Dog's side."

"Don't hate him. It's not easy for him either."

"I know that," Fuyun said. "I got even with him on the raft today, but he wound up saving my life, and getting a dislocated shoulder in the bargain. He sheds tears when he talks about what happened, but that doesn't make him right. Even if he had to be a peasant for the rest of his life and die on a mountain or in the river, he had no right to behave as heartlessly as he did!"

"He's here? Where?"

"He had his arm set already. He's out on the raft. I told him to come with me, but he didn't feel he should. I came over to fetch you without telling him, but you're sick!"

She jumped down off the kang and hastily brushed her hair. "Let's go, I want to see him."

Fuyun was taken aback as he watched her get off the kang like someone who wasn't sick at all. "Can you manage it?" he asked. "Are you sure you're all right?" She was already out the door.

When they reached the ferry landing at the southern gate, the raft was bobbing quietly on the river. Old Seven was sitting on the raft, but there was no sign of Golden Dog.

"Golden Dog," Fuyun called. "Golden Dog!"

Old Seven walked over and said softly, "There's no need to shout. He left."

"Where did he go?" Fuyun asked.

"After you went off, he asked where you were really headed. I told him. His eyes brimmed when he said he didn't think he ought to see Water Girl. That was why he came, but he lost his nerve. As he walked up the shore, I asked him if he was going over to the warehouse, but he said no, he didn't know where he was going. He told me to leave him alone."

Water Girl stood as though in a trance, gazing up at the setting sun, off in the distance above the Zhou River, whose twisting rapids were half hidden in the dying rays. "Maybe it's better this way," she mumbled, "maybe it's better."

BOOK TWO

12

The evening of the fifth was especially depressing. A mountain watchdog at Stream of Wandering Spirits had begun howling at dinnertime the night before, and soon all the mountain watchdogs in the area had joined it, their howls blending with the cries of other birds to form a foul, hollow din that drowned out even the evening bell at Restless Hill Monastery. Han Wenju, who was eating dinner at home, felt that something strange was happening, and he was sweating profusely as he ate, his anxiety mounting by the minute. He was assaulted by a horde of mosquitoes, which kept him relentlessly busy swatting his legs and face until the palm of his hand was spotted with blood. The endless buzzing sounded like a gong. He put down his bowl, but, since he was too lazy to clean the pot, he walked down to the ferry landing, where there were no mosquitoes, although the howling of the mountain watchdogs was even louder. He went into the cabin of his ferryboat to fetch his tattered copy of the ancient book. After tossing his six copper coins onto the deck, he looked up at the moon, chillingly white, framed in a wide halo of clouds, almost as though the sky were the Zhou River; it formed a hole in the surface through which swirling water seemed to pour out in a torrent. "Is it going to rain?" he asked himself. "I hope so; we sure need it." He walked back into the cabin, lay down, and went to sleep.

His expectation was right on the mark, for later that night the heavens opened and rain fell in a deluge. The storm woke him, but the rain cooled the night, making it perfect for sleeping, and he drifted off again. By sunrise the river had risen so high that his boat had shifted downstream and was nestled against the bank. Fortunately he had tied it to a willow tree that bent against the pull but kept the boat from being swept along. Men were out on the riverbank gathering driftwood for kindling. "Uncle Han," one of them called, "how come you weren't driven down the river—all the way up to heaven? Afraid somebody will take your place at the landing?"

"Your old lady's ass, that's why! Boat people aren't afraid of the water. High currents just lift a boat higher!"

"Boats can float on the water," the man replied, "but they can flip over in the water too. You live and die by your profession. You just wait. You survived it this time, but if the river rises any higher, you're a goner!"

"My name's not Tian, and it isn't Gong," Han fired back, "so I have nothing to be ashamed of. Why would the dragon king want me?" But when he went up onto the bank to look at his rope, which was rubbing against a boulder, he was disturbed to see that all that rocking and bobbing had nearly cut it in two. He retied it around the tree. "You think some more water will finish me off?" he said when he'd finished. "If you had any sense, you'd look at the sky and see that the rain's almost over. You worry about your driftwood, and watch out you don't wind up gathering rocks in the river!"

The driftwood gatherers returned to their work. There was little usable wood in the river; mostly there were dead branches and some dry leaves that had been caught up in the foam of whirlpools as they floated downriver. The rain, however, kept falling, more and more heavily, and the wind picked up. The men on the bank were soaked to the skin, so intent on reaping their tiny reward that they didn't bother to go home as their piles of kindling grew. But before long the water had risen dangerously, and one of them shouted, "Hurry. Let's get out of here. The water's already up to our feet!" They had barely fled the spot when the surging tide engulfed their piles of kindling and carried everything back to the river, where it continued its way downstream. The sight so tickled Han Wenju that he broke into laughter, for which he was rewarded by a mouthful of windblown water. The rising water made it necessary for him to retie his boat higher on the trunk of the willow tree before running to the village on the heels of the others.

The rain fell for two days and two nights; it was as though Mother Nature were releasing years of pent-up anger, unwilling to rest until it was all spent. The rain fell the whole length of the Zhou River watershed, filling every tributary of the Qin Range; water flowed into the valleys, then spilled over into streams, which emptied into the Zhou River. One urgent telephone call after another was fielded at Crossroads Township: The reservoir upstream has breached its banks! Such-and-such village is completely under water! Zhou City itself is threatened! Word came down to the lower precincts of the river to prepare for an emergency. Fortunately, Crossroads Township was situated on high ground, so the water wouldn't reach its streets. The villagers took satisfaction in their own safety, and when they looked out over the river, flooded as it hadn't been in the recent decades of drought, they saw huge branches and saplings, and dead cattle and pigs, and they dashed forward to turn their strength and good fortune to profit. They managed to retrieve a considerable number of the smaller pieces, but all they could do was watch helplessly as the larger branches tossed and bobbed in the middle of the river on their course downstream. Then someone shouted, "Where's Golden Dog? He always wants to make a killing, and he's the only one who'd take on the river!"

But Golden Dog was nowhere on the riverbank. At that very moment he had reached the outskirts of Zhou City.

During the final years of the Qing dynasty, boats from White Rock Stockade could navigate the river all the way to Zhou City. But then the river became clogged with deposits and too shallow for boat travel, and a highway that followed the curves of the mountain range through several counties was the only public road. Golden Dog had boarded a bus for Zhou City the day before the rains came, but his trip was halted in the county town just before Zhou City because the road was washed out. He stayed there for two days and nights; at a little after four in the afternoon on the third day the bus continued on.

Zhou City was a onetime border town with a long history. It had acquired a far-reaching reputation as the only city in the province completely surrounded by a well-preserved city wall. Built on the bank of the Zhou River, it was constructed neither of rammed earth nor of brick but of black stone, which was covered with moss that made it glisten in the sunlight. Wild grasses, ivy, even holly bushes, grew in profusion in the cracks between the stones, making it a perfect nesting place for crows. When dusk fell, flocks of them returned to their nests, filling the air with the din of their cawing and covering the surface of the stones with a gleaming white blanket of their droppings. As soon as Golden Dog emerged from the bus station, he heard the dull roar of the Zhou River. He walked briskly to the northern wall tower, which rose above the riverbank; it was, in fact, the river embankment at that spot. He had barely climbed the twelve stone steps to the top of the tower when, looking behind the adjacent bulwark, he saw men scurrying back and forth with hempen baskets filled with earth, which they carried to the northeast corner of the city wall. "What are they doing with all that earth?" he asked someone beside him.

"Repairing the wall. A twenty-foot slab of stone fell from the northeast corner!"

He raced along the top of the wall to see for himself, and sure enough, there in the northeast corner was a gaping hole that was being filled with layers of mud—twelve so far—in hempen baskets, which were anchored in place with a net of wire. He stood listening to the urgent discussions of the workers, and he learned how, earlier, the townspeople had viewed the rising river as offering sport. They had clambered up onto the wall to watch the spectacle of the river rising higher and higher. Some even dangled their feet in the water to wash them off, jesting about how they could wash up without getting athlete's foot. No one at that point believed the water presented a danger to the wall, since some forty years earlier, during the autumn when Tian the Sixth had led a guerrilla attack on the city, the river had flooded, sending water over the northwest corner, but there hadn't been any trouble with it since. They were convinced that the Zhou River would never again overflow its banks, and that the walls of this onetime border town would stand forever as a historic relic. But when twenty or thirty feet of the northeastern stone face collapsed, the onlookers went into a panic. They ran home to protect their families and property, and municipal workers came forward to repair the damage. Luckily, the river rose no higher.

As Golden Dog listened to the talk, he too was surprised that the Zhou River, normally so placid, could flood with such destructive power. He stared at the surface, then at the vast expanse of water farther up that gave the impression of flowing down from heaven itself. Waves crashed, one on top of the other, forming a murky yellow panorama of ridges, pushing ever forward and striking the walled embankment, crashing and merging in thousands of whitecaps. The people roared as each wave struck, covering their ears with their hands and screaming for Golden Dog to step back so as not to lose his balance and fall into the river. But he didn't retreat, for he was too absorbed in thought about the possible effects of the flood on Stream of Wandering Spirits and Crossroads Township; he wondered if the villagers were still out gathering firewood. If he hadn't left, he'd probably be swimming into the heart of the river like a water sprite, to tow in the large pieces of wood. The sky grew bright and clear after that, as the sun reappeared, sending its golden rays in all directions and forming golden arches around the clouds in the sky. This imparted a yellow hue to the surface of the water as it ate away the corner of the city wall, which itself had taken on a bronze cast. Then the sun floated atop the river, dipping occasionally beneath the surface like an enormous red ball riding the water or like a bloody fetus emerging, the river assuming the appearance of a mother in the throes of an agonizing delivery. Golden Dog was suddenly struck by the robust beauty of the scene before him. In all the years he'd been sailing the Zhou River, he'd never seen anything like it, and the arresting thought occurred to him that the forces of nature were dredging the Zhou River of its rocks and shoals, making it easy sailing for the boats and rafts.

Thoughts of sailing boats and rafts stimulated him, but he knew he'd no longer be involved in navigation, that his life on the water had come to an end, superseded by new vistas. He hung his head and walked silently back along the top of the wall until he regained the wall tower. He didn't give the Zhou River a parting glance.

After returning to the tower, he walked down the twelve stone steps and emerged onto North Avenue, which was lined by squat, ancient houses and dirty stalls crowded together; a thick blanket of rain-fed moss covered the roof tiles and walls of the buildings. Standing in the filthy water at the roadsides were peddlers with baskets on shoulder poles, who were haggling with customers over prices. Zhou City was divided into Old Town and New Town, and this was Old Town. After you passed down this street, taller buildings and broad thoroughfares took over, with flower stands, traffic lights, colorful shop windows, and fashionably dressed men and women; this was New Town. Golden Dog walked straight ahead, his bedroll thrown over his shoulder, and he was greeted by scenes of revelry and beauty. Once the Zhou River stopped rising, even though twenty or more feet of stone had been washed away from the northeastern corner of the city wall, the flood was no longer a threat to the city itself. The populace was enjoying its first peace after a time of fear, and there was a tape recorder in the door of nearly every shop from Old Town to New Town blaring out popular songs, including the frenetic rhythms of disco music. Salesgirls with powdered faces and reddened lips sat like ice sculptures or swayed their tiny waists and full shoulders to the beat of the music. After making his way by seven or eight shops, Golden Dog noticed posters pasted on the walls, including ads for kung fu movies on videocassettes, all described in vivid detail to grab the attention of passersby. People in pedicabs and pushing bicycles were hawking newspapers and magazines with lurid stories of murder, spies, and sex. The citizens of the capital had their own aesthetic preferences, and Golden Dog, thrust into their midst, was stirred by the newness and strangeness of it all. He stopped to ask the way to the newspaper office of a group of men and women, who looked him over, dissolved into laughter, and walked off. They were mocking the country bumpkin, feeling he was beneath their concern. His face turned pink with discomfort, but he went on to laugh an unspoken rejoinder, thereby wresting his dignity from an initial self-loathing. *Do you think the capital belongs to you alone? The man who runs this town, Gong Baoshan, is a country bumpkin too! Now Golden Dog's arrived, and you just wait and see!*

When he reached the busiest intersection in New Town, where people swarmed, he held his head high and walked proudly down the middle of the street, looking straight into the face of everyone he saw, returning smug looks with smug looks of his own. Girls with powdered faces and painted lips turned and gave him quizzical looks. A row of three horse-drawn carts emerged from a nearby lane and crossed the intersection into another lane. The carts were piled high with sand for one of the city's building sites. The high-pitched nasal commands of the drivers, all from the countryside, drew upon horses and drivers alike the curses of the locals on their bicycles. The drivers shouted timid apologies, but the locals, unappeased, tried to obstruct the horses' progress and hit the drivers. Outraged, Golden Dog lost no time in coming to the assistance of the drivers. He pulled the locals away roughly. A man in a Western suit hurled shrill taunts: "Hey, you hick, where do you get off coming to town and acting like that? Is this the kind of spunk you've picked up from all those years of good harvests?"

Golden Dog sneered back, "You little runt, maybe it is. Why are you so skinny? Can't you afford decent food on your pittance?"

The man in the suit became livid. "Who the hell do you think you are? Are you looking for trouble?"

Golden Dog came at him and slapped him—smack! "How's that for a little decent nourishment? What are you going to do about it?"

The man, knowing his bravado had been seen through, was daunted and hard pressed, but he needed to save face. Golden Dog threw down his bedroll, grabbed a spade from the horse cart, and blustered, "Come on, we country folk love nothing more than visiting the city to test our strength!"

The man stopped in his tracks, without the mettle to step forward.

"Okay, hick," he said, "I'll see you in the Zhou City *Daily* 'Drum Tower'!"

The "Drum Tower" was a column that carried social criticism contributed by the general public. Golden Dog was delighted. "Go ahead and write something. Then send me the draft, and I'll correct your mistakes!"

The man was baffled. "He's *from* the newspaper!" one of his friends suggested.

Golden Dog laughed—heh-heh—and quickly relaxed from his fighting stance. "Country folks know how to do more than drive carts and haul sand, don't they!"

The locals climbed onto their bicycles and rode off, bringing the episode to an end. The cart drivers thanked Golden Dog, who responded somberly, "When you come into the city, hold your head high, sure of your right to be here. If you cringe in front of these people, they'll treat you like dogs." He turned and walked away. But he hadn't got far before his indignation subsided and he had to laugh: he'd admonished the carters regarding their sense of inferiority, but wasn't his disquiet over the incident more or less the same thing? *Golden Dog, oh, Golden Dog, when you were out on the river, Zhou City was an unattainable dream; now that you're to be a resident of the place and work for the Zhou City newspaper, what does your new environment hold for you? Will you fit in? Will you be able to give full play to your talents here?*

He was assigned to one of the editorial offices, where he did odd jobs while he learned the ropes and practiced his skills as a writer. The office staff consisted of five people under the direction of a long-faced man in his fifties who made demands on him in the same way he might have on a son. Golden Dog did what he was told with alacrity; arriving early each morning, he brought water into the office, mopped the floor, and took out the trash. After he'd been there awhile, he realized that he was the only person on the staff the director had any control over. The young man in blue jeans was the brother-in-law of the chief of the Zhou City organization department, and it didn't take much for him to get into a heated exchange with the director. The young woman was the daughter of the district cultural commissioner; a charming, pretty young thing, she never missed an opportunity to call the editor in chief or managing editor Uncle. The bespectacled Old Gong had come to the newspaper at the same time as the managing editor and held his superior's background and knowledge in contempt; he frequently told his fellow workers how the managing editor had fallen in love with a student after arriving in the city in the fifties and had abandoned his village-born wife. The remaining co-worker was a widow of thirty-nine who had been observed coming out of the editor in chief's office late one night. "Handing in a report," she'd said. The walls of the tiny office were plastered with newspapers, the cabinets crammed full of manuscripts. The telephone rang every three or four minutes, and writers of all kinds were constantly coming to ask about their articles, seek advice, or find out why their work hadn't been published. Bearers of gifts were frequent: a packet of sunflower seeds, a carton of cigarettes, a bag of dried persimmons, even a bundle of low-cost fancy underpants brought by someone writing for a garment factory, one pair for each person in the office. When the hustle and bustle died down, the office door was closed and the workers might discuss this or that stupid writer, or someone's hairdo or figure, or an affair between employees—the last topic, naturally, requiring the absence of the widow. When such themes were exhausted, all the workers bent over their desks to deal with the stories they were working on, the men smoking cigarettes, the women sipping tea.

"Golden Dog," the widow said, "you're from White Rock Stockade, aren't you?"

"Stream of Wandering Spirits," he answered.

"A nice name! Where did you work before you came to the newspaper?"

"I was a peasant. I worked on a raft."

"Oh! You have a relative in the capital?"

"No."

"No? Keeping it a secret, I see!"

Without responding, he bent over and busied himself with a story, respectfully asking the others' opinions when he encountered doubts or difficulties. On raising his head, he invariably found the daughter of the cultural commissioner in his line of sight. Always in stylish attire, as though she were a fashion setter for the whole city, she changed into a completely new outfit every few days. She was at this time wearing a bright red tie, and when Golden Dog lowered his eyes again, there persisted the image of a blazing red streak across his eyes. Because of it, he looked up again, rather blankly, but just then she saw she was being observed, and asked him what he thought of her clothes. He didn't know what to say, so he just nodded his head.

"Golden Dog," she said, "you don't know a thing about clothes. Tell us about the strange people and weird happenings on the Zhou

River. The stories I'm working on are giving me a headache, and I need some sort of relief."

Her request took Golden Dog's thoughts back to the river, to the boats and rafts, and with a shyness in his voice, he began talking about what it was like to ride a boat through the waves and about the strange noises you heard in the middle of the night which the old boatmen said were the shrieks of water sprites. He told his co-workers how scary it was to walk on the sandbars on a summer day, when you could suddenly be possessed and end up trying to bury your head in the sand until your nose and mouth were filled and you died of suffocation. He told them about a certain family that had lived on the riverbank, how the wife became involved in an adulterous relationship with a boatman, and how, when the villagers discovered it, she was hung up naked from the branch of a tree and whipped. Afterward, the two lovers ran off together, and their bodies were found on Sun-Moon Shoals, wrapped so tightly in each other's arms they couldn't be pried apart. But mainly he spoke of the flood on the Zhou River: how the boatmen risked their lives to rescue people swept into the water, how a dozen or so boats combined their efforts to rescue one that had overturned, how a boatman had gone upriver to gather firewood and had spent the night in the home of a mountaineer, sleeping on an overheated kang, the hostess to the east, the boatman to the west, and the host in the middle, with the lamp left on all night and each of them having noisy recourse to the large bedpan on the floor. He spoke with obvious excitement, gesturing to embellish his narrative. But as he was talking, his thoughts drifted to the blacksmith shop in White Rock Stockade and to the girl who operated the bellows, and he soon brought his narrative to an end.

When he left the Zhou River, all thoughts of Yingying simply vanished. As he saw it, the pleasures they had taken from each other that night served as a small punishment to the Tian family, and he derived a certain amount of satisfaction from the difficult situation in which it had placed Yingying. But the image of Water Girl shadowed him wherever he went. At first he assumed that his feeling of guilt would gradually lessen and eventually disappear with separation from the Zhou River traffic and his departure from Stream of Wandering Spirits and White Rock Stockade. How could he have anticipated that the farther away from Water Girl he was, the greater would be the sense of remorse eating painfully into his heart like a boring insect? Every day since his arrival in the city he had been exposed to beautiful fashions, which he couldn't help admiring: when he was in the courtyard of the newspaper office, he saw many chic young women, and out on the street he was treated to the sight of gorgeously decked out girls. He understood at last the words he'd so often come across in classical books: *Like a flower, like a cloud.* Two opposing images accompanied him: one of Water Girl, the revered bodhisattva, an image that inspired guilt in him; the other of much fashionable beauty, which fired masculine urges. After extended contact with the city girls, each of them different, he began to think, If Water Girl could only come to the city and wear clothes like that, she wouldn't take a backseat to anyone. His thought grew in intensity, until he began to fantasize that Water Girl and the modish city girls were one and the same and his fantasy began to affect his mood. Thus, after he'd spoken, somewhat impulsively, about events on the Zhou River at the office, he'd slink off to the bar across from the newspaper and drink alone. When he returned, he'd be utterly uncommunicative for hours.

Golden Dog's comrades in the office began to talk about him: When he was in a talkative mood, there was no shutting him up, but when he wasn't, you couldn't pry a word out of him. There was no figuring him out!

Then something happened at the office. Several people noticed that their letters were arriving late, with the appearance of having been opened. Golden Dog had been receiving a letter from Yingying every three days or so. It was always four or five pages long, filled from beginning to end with revolutionary talk, like an essay by a high-school student, and written in an ornate, cliché-ridden style. But her letters always began with a vulgar "Dearest Elder Brother" and ended with "Your Little Sister." When she wrote about what had happened that night in his house, his face burned, he broke into a cold sweat, and he felt deeply depressed and remorseful. He burned her letters after reading them, apprehensive that someone else might see them. He began going to the mailroom as soon as he arrived in the morning. After hearing that someone appeared to be opening other people's mail, he carefully examined Yingying's letters and found that the flap of one of them was still moist. For the next two nights he hid in a dark corner near the mailroom to uncover what was going on. And sure enough, at two o'clock on the second night he saw someone sneak in, gather up all the incoming mail, and take it away. Two hours later, when the same person tiptoed in to return the letters, Golden Dog jumped from his hiding place and threw his arms around the mail thief's waist. It was a sixty-year-old editor from one of the other offices. The investigation that resulted revealed that he'd been opening the mail with a razor blade, reading it, and then resealing the envelopes and putting them back in the middle of the night. His bitter fellow workers insisted on knowing the seamy political reason behind the thefts, but his behavior turned out to be a case of emotional instability. After the investigation, Golden Dog learned from the others that this editor was a graduate of one of the top colleges and that even though he'd escaped being capped as a rightist in 1957, his injudicious comments had labeled him a pawn of certain elements. From then on he had seldom voiced an opinion. During editorial meetings, when his turn to speak came around, he'd take out a short prepared statement and read it, word for word, always ending with some slogan like "Forge ahead with a red banner held high!" He'd married a woman much younger than he, who had taken charge of everything at home: politics, economics, external affairs—the last manifested in a long-term adulterous relationship with one of the deputy editors in chief. More than once the older man had come home and caught them in the act. On such occasions he just sat down sullenly and picked up a newspaper to block out the disgraceful scene. "Despicable!" he'd mutter. "Despicable!" But during meetings, the deputy editor in chief frequently singled the older man out for the low quality of his work: he'd once rejected a story that the author had gone on to submit successfully to *People's Daily*.

This incident had a tremendous effect on Golden Dog, who realized that if someone's soul is perpetually tortured, sooner or later his self-confidence will go and he'll begin to lose his bearings and see himself reduced to a worthless wretch. As a result, Golden Dog achieved a better understanding of himself. He recognized that the path to personal salvation was hard work and complete devotion to his job. It was the only way to drive the pain out of his heart.

Three months later he was transferred to the reporters' section, where there was a lot more going on. The young reporters tucked their ID cards into their jacket pockets just far enough so the red letters could still catch people's attention. Golden Dog learned the ins and outs of news gathering from an older reporter, who also taught him how to deal with complex situations, how to socialize with various kinds of people, and how to act like a reporter. He forced himself to get the upper hand on his peasant mentality, in order to display the proper manners. He brought himself to where, no matter whom he met or where he was, just knowing that he was a reporter dispelled his timidity. The true power of a reporter became clear: if you call someone powerless, he has nothing; if you call him powerful, he has everything. Invitations for reporters came daily, and telephone requests were virtually endless. A certain enterprise was having a grand opening, or a certain company was holding a forum, and they wanted a reporter present. At mealtime there were seven dishes, eight dishes: squid, sea cucumber, white tree fungus, mushrooms, sorghum wine, sweet wine, beer, soft drinks—a riot of colors, seemingly endless. There were inscriptions, photographs, a nice gift—everything from an electric warming glass, an electric iron, a rice cooker, or other kinds of electrical household amenities, to high-quality merchandise like bed sheets, wool blankets, wool fabric, or a briefcase. The next morning's paper would have a piece on the enterprise or the company, and without having to pay for advertising, businesses would have won prospective buyers' confidence and many orders, thereby saving the concerns money, making reputations, and moving products. Golden Dog was staggered by the power of the press, and by all the strange things that went on at the office.

On one occasion, the manager of a privately run restaurant came to the office to seek the newspaper's support, claiming that he was the victim of bureaucratic extortion. Golden Dog and another reporter went to investigate. They learned that from the time the owner received permission to go into business until the grand opening he had hosted over a hundred free meals, to the tune of two thousand yuan. Tax collectors, a free lunch; health inspectors, a free lunch; the water department, a free lunch. Everyone demanded a free lunch. Four people arrived from the electric company, and before they'd finished their meal, two more came by, saying that the first four were responsible for service within the restaurant while they were in charge of electricity coming *into* the restaurant. The manager just smiled, invited them in, and set up another table. Even a grimy old man from the sanitation department showed up. He stood in the doorway and charged vocally that someone had dumped a load of trash before construction of the restaurant was finished. "Let's see your license to dump trash! No license? Well, that's good for a fine!" He whipped out his citation book. "That'll cost you three hundred! I'll give you a receipt." All the manager could do was acknowledge the mistake and beg leniency. The old man raised his voice: "Are you aware that I'm in charge of trash in this area?" Set another table. When he'd finished his free meal, he took out a lunchbox and said, "I have a good-for-nothing son at home. How about some leftovers for him?" What could the restaurateur do? Fill the box with some fresh rice and good food, that's what. Golden Dog was fighting mad and swore to expose this extortion.

"Wonderful," the manager said. "Sit down and have something to eat. It's all ready."

It was a feast. When they finished, the other reporter went to pay the bill. After he returned, Golden Dog asked him, "How much?"

"Nothing."

"Nothing?" Golden Dog tensed. "You mean a free lunch? We're here to investigate the free lunches others have forced them to provide, and we're guilty of the same thing?"

"What could I do?" his partner asked. "If we don't go along, he'll think we aren't in his corner."

Golden Dog thought to himself, How could a good and proper society like ours let things get out of hand like this? *I used to think that Crossroads Township was bad, and that White Rock Stockade was bad, but now I see that Zhou City's no better!* He was fit to be tied. Blood rushed to his face. His partner only laughed. "Getting upset just shows how naïve you are! Society—what is it? It's what you're looking at! We reporters have no official rank, but officials are afraid of us. We could use our status to get a little something for ourselves, but we don't, because of our conscience. All we can hope is that we'll get a chance to use our position to do something for the people once in a while. Let's go back and write a piece for the paper. We can bring an end to this extortion setup once and for all."

Golden Dog couldn't refute this logic, but he still didn't think it was right. Yet, after their story appeared in the paper and engaged the attention of senior officials in Zhou City, a campaign was waged against the "water tyrants," "electric tyrants," "tax tyrants," and "road agents." When the manager of the restaurant came to the newspaper to express his gratitude to them, Golden Dog finally reconciled himself to the idea that, although impulsiveness and passion, and fair-mindedness and sternness, were the stuff of heroes, times like his weren't for heroes; not only did too much machismo prevent your accomplishing what you set out to do, it often promoted the opposite of what you wanted, making it truly worse than useless. By hanging around some of the older reporters, Golden Dog realized why they were held in such esteem and enjoyed such fine reputations, and what they could do to accomplish things for the people. Their lives were filled with the humor of "living ghosts turning the world upside down."

At the end of the month the newspaper needed a reporter to do a series on mountaineers in Dongyang County who had been getting rich. The assignment had evolved out of a visit to the newspaper from the Dongyang County party secretary himself. He had sketched out the general situation in his county, which had filled the editor in chief with enthusiasm, for he saw an opportunity to write the kind of story that would present an instructive model. But when the assignment reached the news section, several of the older reporters begged off, pleading conditions at home that required their presence. In recent years, because reporters had become reluctant to go on assignments in far-off mountain counties, local news bureaus had been set up where reporters were required to serve one-year stints. But since those assigned always looked for ways to be exempted and those who were unable to evade the posting put in their time grudgingly, eventually most of the bureaus had to be staffed by locals who made the switch from being support personnel for the newspaper to being full-fledged reporters. Dongyang County was the most remote and the poorest county in the area, and no reporter willingly went there on assignment. But on the other hand, neither the party secretary nor the editor in chief trusted the articles written by the local Dongyang reporters. The upshot was that Golden Dog volunteered. Coming from the banks of the Zhou River, he knew how hard it was for mountain people to become wealthy; if, as he hoped, the experience in Dongyang County was positive, he would pass information about it on to people in his hometown, to use as an example.

Another letter from Yingying arrived on the day before his departure. Longer than the others, it lacked the fervid excited tone of its predecessors. She seemed to be pleading with him, though she included a barb or two: Why, she wanted to know, hadn't he answered her letters? No matter how busy he was, he ought to be able to find the time to drop her a line or two. She ended by saying she knew that his feelings for Water Girl had not disappeared, but she asked what, since he'd already disappointed one woman, would be served by breaking another heart. The letter softened Golden Dog enough that he decided to write. But all he mentioned was what he'd been doing at the newspaper. He told her he was about to leave for an assignment in Dongyang County. When he'd finished, he composed another letter to the blacksmith shop in White Rock Stockade. That helped him maintain his emotional equilibrium. In writing to Water Girl, he refrained from using words like *dear* and told her about the feelings of guilt and pain he was suffering. After dropping both letters into the mailbox, he went alone that night to the wooded area beyond Southgate, for he needed a quiet place to sort out his feelings. But when he got there, he found young couples sitting on stone benches, or under trees, or in grassy hollows. He noticed two bicycles sparkling in the moon's rays and the light of distant streetlamps, and he concluded that there was a lover's lane nearby. He skirted the area and kept walking, his heart troubled. All around him were whispers and giggles, even some heated arguments, along with sobs and the sound of an occasional slap. What in heaven's name is love? There, in the giggles, was the sweetness of love; but the hypocrisy, the deception, the vulgarity, the ugliness of love was in the sobs and the arguments. A nameless fire began to fill his heart, and there was no getting rid of it.

Suddenly someone shrieked, "Stop that hooligan!" There were sounds of a struggle. Like a feral tiger, Golden Dog sprang forward and pounced on a fleeing young man, knocking him to the ground with a flurry of punches. The young rowdy, it turned out, had been hiding behind a tree eavesdropping on the conversation of two youthful lovers when, undone by a fit of envy, he smashed a rock into the man's shoulder. Golden Dog threw him back onto the ground, watching him whimper for mercy as blood oozed from his mouth and nose; then he too slumped to the ground like a deflated balloon.

13

Water Girl hadn't seen Golden Dog after the flood—which people were still talking about for days afterward, finding it hard to believe that their placid river had nearly swamped Zhou City and White Rock Stockade. Had Golden Dog been in the village when it came? For a long time, no one ventured to tell her, and she couldn't very well ask. After a while, though, someone from the shipping brigade brought some fish and crabs to the blacksmith shop and she learned he'd already gone to Zhou City.

From then on she never went out without her jacket with the missing third button; even if the wind whistled straight through to her heart, she wouldn't put on something warmer or sew on another button. In the emotional blur in which she lived, she felt her heart had vanished along with the button. She became so absentminded that she'd forget things she'd gone to get and lose the drift of conversation with her grandfather and Fuyun. At times like this she hated Golden Dog, but the rancor would pass and she'd hope that her feelings would bring him no harm. Then she'd begin to wonder if she'd been wrong about him and wrong to love him, but she'd quickly drive those thoughts from her mind. Sometimes, when she was alone, she'd say, "Golden Dog, you're not the same good person I used to know," but then she'd start fretting that her thoughts might become prophetic. She never could abandon her love for him, even though he'd left her for another woman. How could she? Her feelings were so pure, so sincere, always renewing themselves. They would always be there to sustain her. Since he could never love her again, some might say she was foolish, maybe even shameless, yet she'd come to realize what a joy it is to be loved by someone, and to return that love. She wrote him three letters, but didn't mail them. Even her lovesick anguish filled her with a sense of joy.

Even knowing there was no hope, she woke from her sleep every morning with the first thought in her head, surprising even to her, that he'd suddenly sent her a letter.

But he never did.

This sad state of affairs made Grandpa Pockface and Fuyun miserable, and it frightened them. They wanted desperately to find a way to console her, but she insisted she was all right. Finally, she forced herself to act naturally around them; except when working the forge or eating, she kept up a steady conversation to lull them into forgetting their concern, and to lull herself at the same time. On the wedding day of the son of the shop owner across the street, the lane was filled with people, and Pockface and Fuyun went out to join the festivities. Water Girl stayed inside, trying to ignore the engaging sounds of the musical instruments and the exploding firecrackers. But she looked through the window and saw the bride and groom entering the gate, to be showered with confetti; as a sentimental reaction, her tears began to flow. Just then, Fuyun came inside, and she abruptly turned her back to the window. "Water Girl," he said, "why weren't you watching?"

"I was. Isn't it exciting?"

"What's wrong with your eyes?"

"Are they red?" she asked, sorry that he had seen. "I must have rubbed too hard to get a bug out. The bride sure is pretty. Let's go over and tease them tonight."

Fuyun wasn't so dense that he didn't know she was covering up, and he wished he'd kept his mouth shut. Instead of saying more, he turned and walked into the backyard, sighing softly.

With the intention of keeping Fuyun from seeing through her, she began humming a flower-drum aria, but it was too much for him and he came back inside. "Water Girl, don't sing that. Let's take a walk by the river this afternoon. I haven't been over there for a long time, and I miss the boatmen."

She agreed readily. His train of thought was so clear and so ingenuous that she was nearly moved to tears.

When they went to the riverbank that afternoon, no Stream of Wandering Spirits boats were tied up at the ferry landing, so they walked down to the bend in the river. Wanting to cheer her up, but not knowing what to say, Fuyun asked, "Water Girl, do you like crab?"

"I love it," she answered.

He picked up a big rock at the river's edge, where he caught several crabs and brought them over to her. Then he went back and picked up the rock again, but she stopped him. "We're not southerners, who can never get enough of those. These few are plenty, we'll just play with them for a while."

"Didn't you say you like crab?" he asked her. "I can catch all you want!" Squatting down and lifting the rock, he was soon covered with water and sweat.

Just then someone came walking out of the village by the bend in the river. He was wearing a long black cassock, and his head was shaved. He sort of floated over.

"Fuyun, isn't that the abbot from Restless Hill Monastery?"

It was he, all right, and they invited him to join them.

"What are you doing here, Abbot?" Water Girl asked him.

"Amita Buddha," the abbot said. "I was out begging alms when some villagers asked me to tell their fortunes, and before I knew it I'd been there nearly all day."

Fuyun was delighted. "Abbot, everyone says you tell fortunes the best. Tell Water Girl hers."

"Why does she need her fortune told? Isn't everything just fine with her?"

"Of course it is! But you can tell her exactly how fine a life she's going to have. I'll pay you. Here, take these crabs."

"A sin—that's a sin! How could you kill things like that?"

Fuyun tittered in embarrassment, and quickly tossed the crabs back into the river to show the abbot his good intentions.

"Please, Abbot," Water Girl said, "tell my fortune. I know whatever you say will come true."

The abbot looked at her. "What sign were you born under? What's your birthday?"

"The year of the goat. I was born late at night on the tenth day of the ninth lunar month."

The abbot moaned softly for a moment before saying, "Born under the sign of the goat, a weak-fated maid, a September goat, grass and leaves fade . . ."

This unsettled Fuyun. "Abbot," he said, "see how her marriage will work out."

"Everything about Water Girl is just right, except for that little mole on the bridge of her nose. Even that would be all right if it were a little to one side, or a little lower. But right in the middle is a sign of weakness. She'll have better luck than most people, but a perfect contentment will just elude her."

An ungrateful look spread across Fuyun's face. "How can you say something disheartening like that?"

"Let him speak," Water Girl said. "I want the truth, whatever it is."

The abbot stared blankly for a long moment, then his eyelids slowly began to close. He reached up and fingered the beads of the rosary around his neck as he began to intone a chant. "The pipal was not a tree at first, the shiny rock was not a mirror, the Buddha-nature is pure and vacuous, how could it be tainted with dust?" Water Girl and Fuyun had no idea what he was saying and were about to ask for an explanation, when a sublime look spread across his face and, with an "Amita Buddha" on his lips, he walked off into the distance.

Utterly dejected, Fuyun stared at the abbot's retreating back and grumbled, "That bald donkey's playing games with us, with all that nonsense!"

But Water Girl sat there calmly and mumbled, "It's my fate, Fuyun; it's my fate."

Now that she'd heard her future, and believed it, she grew extraordinarily calm. She harbored no more resentment toward Golden Dog and suffered no more anguish over his departure. Her appetite returned, as did her pleasure in talking and laughing with others. She was back to normal. Fuyun didn't know what to make of the transformation. At first he groused about the "bald donkey" from time to time as they worked in the blacksmith shop, but when he noticed how she was putting on weight and how her face seemed to glow, his reproaches of the abbot turned to praise. Water Girl's recovery of her equanimity brought renewed strength to Fuyun. He worked at the shop as never before, and the atmosphere never seemed so steady and tranquil.

One night, as he lay sleeping on the bed in the kitchen after swinging his hammer in the shop all day, he was suddenly roused by a call for Water Girl at the front door. He heard the door being opened, and after that Water Girl's exclamations: "Yingying! What a wonderful surprise! What are you doing here?" Then he heard her call her grandfather: "Grandpa, wake up. Look who's here! It's Yingying, my schoolmate from Stream of Wandering Spirits! This is her first time here at the shop. Where did you put the melon seeds? Have you eaten dinner yet, Yingying?"

"This late? What do you think? People around here are so poor that the first thing they ask when they see you is whether or not you've eaten. Is this your grandfather the blacksmith? I've heard such good things about you, and I'm glad to have a chance finally to meet you. Were you in bed already?"

Pockface cleared his throat: "Well, so you're Yingying, Tian Zhongzheng's niece!"

"Do you know my uncle?"

"Do I know him? Who doesn't?"

"Just as I was leaving, he told me to send his regards."

"Wonderful," the old man said. "Just wonderful." Louder coughs.

"Grandpa isn't well," Water Girl interjected, "not well at all. Have a seat. The shop's so small and cluttered you probably don't want to sit down."

"It's fine," Yingying assured her. "Have you been making starchy vegetables? Do the people here eat them, too?"

"Yes, I have. The smell's strong even in the shop, isn't it? But let me make you some tea. Fuyun! Are you up? Yingying's here. Come here and boil some water so we can offer her tea!"

Fuyun was wondering what had brought Yingying to their door. Didn't she know about Water Girl and Golden Dog? Maybe she came as a victor, to mock Water Girl. Pretending that Water Girl's shouts had wakened him, he got up, put on his clothes, and joined the others in the room.

"Well!" Yingying said. "What are you doing sleeping here? Did you come over from the river?"

"I left the shipping brigade a long time ago," he said. "I'm Uncle Pockface's apprentice now. But, Yingying, what's a girl like you doing in our neighborhood so late at night?"

"Water Girl and I are schoolmates, and dear, dear friends. She used to come to my place all the time. We made noodles together."

Water Girl thought back to the one time that she, Yingying, and Golden Dog had eaten noodles at Yingying's home. "Yingying, how's Uncle Golden Dog?" she asked softly.

Pockface spit loudly from the kang.

"He's fine!" Yingying gushed. "He's in Zhou City now, a carp that's jumped through the dragon gate. He's there to bring glory to Stream of Wandering Spirits, Crossroads Township, and White Rock Stockade!"

"That's wonderful," Water Girl said. "He can look to a bright future." She stepped into the shadows of the lamp and straightened her bangs, surreptitiously rubbing her nose, which had begun to ache, then wiping her hand on the sole of her shoe.

Fuyun boiled water for a couple of glasses of tea, one of which he handed to the blacksmith, placing the other in front of Yingying. "Yingying, you're quite a woman," he said. "With him as a big reporter, you'll be a working couple, and when the baby comes you won't have to worry about making a living up on the mountain or out on the river."

"That's because you all helped him so much!" Yingying replied. "I have Water Girl to thank that he came to my place. Even though Cai Da'an acted as matchmaker, it was really her doing, and someday I'll tell Golden Dog to recompense her with a pair of leather shoes!"

Grandpa Pockface in his agitation was sweating profusely on the kang. "Are you implying that my Water Girl's so poor she has to go around barefoot?"

Yingying didn't deign to notice his comment and kept talking about Golden Dog. "It wasn't easy for him to become a reporter, and everybody knows that now that he has the chance he'll really make something of himself. But there are some envious people who say he went through the back door. They don't have anything good to say about him, and I'm worried that their talk may hurt him if it gets to the newspaper office."

"What do you mean by that, Yingying?" Fuyun asked. "Who begrudges Golden Dog his success? He may have got the job by being on your uncle's list, but he's a talented writer."

"That's precisely why I came over tonight," Yingying confessed. "I want you to be on guard against those people. Don't let them start rumors that will make things hard for him."

"Now that he's at the newspaper office," Water Girl conceded, "we don't know what's going on. What are they saying?"

"Water Girl, you're sophisticated enough for me to speak the truth to you. I was planning to take you aside, but there's no need to keep secrets from Grandpa and Fuyun. I've heard that you and Golden Dog used to be very close. Is that right? I had no idea. If I had, I'd have tried to get you together. But I don't think you bear me ill will for the way things have turned out. Over the past few days there's been talk here in White Rock Stockade and all the way down to Crossroads Township that you and Golden Dog were so close you couldn't tell where one ended and the other began. They say that ever since he went to the newspaper you write to each other every two or three days . . ."

Grandpa Pockface sat up on the kang and remonstrated, "Yingying, did you come to insult my Water Girl? She's a poor girl with a bitter fate, but she's got too much dignity to do anything of the sort!"

Seeing her grandfather fuming, Water Girl pleaded, "Grandpa, don't be like that. Let Yingying say her piece."

She took Yingying by the hand and led her into the kitchen, closing the door behind them. "Yingying, that's nothing but a rumor. Golden Dog and I used to be close, but since his engagement to you, he and I haven't had a thing to do with each other. He hasn't written to me, and I certainly haven't written to him. All that talk is intended to tarnish my reputation!"

Tears ran down Yingying's cheeks. "I didn't believe it for a minute, but ever since our engagement, Golden Dog's heart has been somewhere else, not with me. He hasn't written since he went to Zhou City, even though I've sent him nine or ten letters, spilling my heart to him. Not a word back! I stewed for days before coming to see you. But I can't lose Golden Dog! We're engaged, so he belongs to me. What do I have without him? Nothing like this has ever happened to the Tian clan, so how could I face people?"

Water Girl was trembling from head to toe, as every word cut to the quick. She was shaken that Yingying had the effrontery to seduce Golden Dog and then come over and say things like this to her. She felt faint, her breath was short, her heart seemed about to burst. But polite form wouldn't let her turn her guest away with a sharp answer, so she forced herself to calm down. "Yingying," she said, "if you treat Golden Dog right, he'll come to love you. Who am I? I don't want anything from him. I just wish him the best and hope that in time he makes something of himself."

Pockface was pounding on the kitchen door. "Yingying, you little fox spirit!" he bellowed. "Get the hell out of here! There isn't a decent person in your whole family. Why don't you take a piss and look into it to see just what you're like! Where do you get the brass to come harrying my Water Girl?"

Water Girl opened the door but blocked Grandpa Pockface's entrance. "Grandpa, what's wrong with you? You're a sick man. Keep out of this!"

He spit in her face. "Don't you have any shame?" he shouted. "How can you defend a rotten piece of goods like her?"

Yingying looked straight at Pockface and sneered. "Grandpa, curse me if you want to. I figured that might happen when I decided to come over. You love your little Water Girl, but it never dawned on you that I have to love myself, too, did it? You're a sick man, Grandpa, so you ought to take care of yourself. Look, it's getting late, and I'd better be leaving."

Pockface was fit to be tied. He picked up one of the tea glasses and threw it at Yingying as she was walking out the door. It barely missed her, shattering as it hit the doorjamb. Fuyun was both seething and stupefied. He just stood there, not knowing what to do. Hearing a sudden thump, he turned to see the old man crumpled on the floor. He scooped him up and took him to the kang. Water Girl dashed over, babbling through her sobs. Hardly able to breathe, the old man spit in her hand. When she saw that the spittle was mixed with blood, she turned ashen and directed Fuyun to run for the doctor.

The tumult lasted until well past midnight, when the doctor checked Grandpa Pockface's pulse and gave him a sedative to help him sleep. Water Girl and Fuyun saw the doctor off, then went back to the kitchen and sat silently on their stools. Fuyun broke the silence: "That Yingying doesn't have an ounce of shame, sleeping with Golden Dog before they're married! Then she has the gall to come over and raise a stink with you! You can't tell the difference between her face and her ass!"

"She only did it because she wanted Golden Dog for herself!"

"But he isn't writing to her, so she's getting what she deserves. The best thing of all would be if he didn't marry her."

Water Girl didn't say anything more. She disliked Yingying for intimidating and humbling her, but she understood that Yingying's inability to consider the effects of her actions made her what she was. In a way, she began to admire her. As for herself, she had come to understand that she was in her sorry state not because Golden Dog had forsaken her but because *she'd* lost Golden Dog. Although she was jealous of Yingying, she had to respect her, all the while growing dejected over her own weakness and timidity. As she pondered Yingying's predicament, she couldn't help sighing, "Yingying's heart is broken too."

Fuyun was befuddled. He stared at her. "*Her* heart's broken? She tore yours to pieces!"

Water Girl sighed. "Fuyun, enough. I can't alter my fate."

After a couple of days, Grandpa managed to climb down from the kang and move around a little. Water Girl was still carrying a heavy emotional burden. She knew that Yingying had come to pressure her and regain control of Golden Dog by driving a wedge between him and her. She had no choice but to examine herself, and it didn't take long for her to forgive Yingying. Since Yingying was Golden Dog's fiancée, she had the right to do what she did. Golden Dog should have been Water Girl's, but she'd lost him through lack of courage. The way things were now, she could only give the two of them her heartfelt blessing. Regretting ever having fallen in love, she castigated herself for behaving so correctly that night on the beach when she and Golden Dog parted. She even began to berate and laugh at herself for trying to hold on to a one-sided love. It now seemed positively immoral. Clenching her teeth, she vowed to drive every thought of Golden Dog out of her heart.

After making up a story so Grandpa wouldn't worry and telling Fuyun her plan, she sneaked off to Crossroads Township, where she went straight to Yingying's room at the co-op dormitory and told her everything, leaving out nothing. She hoped Yingying would understand and absolve her, and she wished the two of them a lifetime of happiness. The next day, while she was at Stream of Wandering Spirits washing Uncle Han's clothes, a boatman came down the river with news that Yingying was spreading word that Water Girl had come to apologize to her. The boatman went to the blacksmith shop, and when Pockface heard his account, he groaned, "Oh, God!" and collapsed in a faint. He was revived with some starchy water, but for the next seven days he lay on the kang in a trance, eating and drinking scarcely at all. When Water Girl was informed of what had happened, she lost no time in returning to the shop—only to receive abuse from her grandfather: he called her feckless, accused her of disgracing herself, and demanded to know what got into her that she had to go crawling to someone like that. He was soon sobbing and appealing to his long-deceased parents. After crying himself out, he tried to talk some sense into Water Girl. Finally, he lay down, his eyes staring straight ahead, and for the next two days ate and drank nothing, not saying anything more about Water Girl and her troubles. By sunset on the third day the color returned to his face and he could sit up. When he said he was hungry, she fried four eggs for him, which he gobbled up. "Everything's okay now," he said as he lay back down. Later that night he rolled out of bed. Water Girl jumped up to help him up, but it was too late. He was dead.

With the death of Pockface, White Rock Stockade was without a blacksmith and the inn at the southern gate had lost a customer. In olden days, old men would walk up and down the cobblestone streets and lanes announcing the time with wooden clappers, bringing a sense of security to the neighborhood. When the blacksmith shop had opened, the fire from the furnace was like a light that always burned, keeping thieves away. Now the nights were so quiet and peaceful it frightened the residents nearby. Adults slept right through the sunrise, and, of course, so did the children, who woke too late to get to school on time. Afraid of their teachers' reprimands, they refused to go to school at all, and their parents had to chase them through the streets with feather dusters. Women in the neighborhod complained to one another, "Ai, who are we going to blame for this? Now that Pockface is dead, there are no more bangs and clangs to wake us up!" While he was alive, he had been to them just the blacksmith—Pockface, a man who didn't worry about differences in age, who liked to drink and loved to tell tales. But now that he was gone, they felt the void in their lives. They brought funeral wreaths, and papier-mâché "gold mountains" and "silver mountains." Several families got together to buy six or seven reams of paper and thirty feet of black funeral satin to bless his entrance into heaven. But Pockface had left no heirs. Since he had no family in town, Water Girl proposed that they take his body to Stream of Wandering Spirits for burial next to her parents. That way he wouldn't be alone in the netherworld.

On the day of the autumnal equinox, in the seventh lunar month, a shuttle boat arrived from Stream of Wandering Spirits. Han Wenju was there to receive Pockface's coffin. Surrounded by neighborhood women, Water Girl burned spirit money and drank funeral wine at the head of his bier, then kowtowed to his spirit. She then prostrated herself in front of the people to express her gratitude to elders and contemporaries alike. She got to her feet and followed the coffin down to the river, reaching the sky with her wails.

A group of boatmen from Crossroads Township who were to play the funeral dirge were on the boat waiting. For years they had worked the Zhou River, and nearly all of them had gone to pester the blacksmith at his shop at one time or another, drinking his tea, eating his food, and enjoying his strong wine. But their host had never ridden in one of their boats; thus it was fitting that he ride one in death. They tooted their woodwinds, put their bows to their fiddles, and sang mourning songs to make his journey down the river a happy one. Water Girl, dressed in white, carried a basket filled with spirit money, which she scattered over the surface of the river. She was so frail, so tragic-looking, that everyone who saw her felt their noses ache. But no one said anything, though they all had their thoughts: *What a bitter fate she has. Golden Dog broke her heart, making her suffer every conceivable misfortune, yet she went to Yingying's and poured out her heart to her; and still she keeps going. She is pure and innocent, and so is Golden Dog. All this talk is nothing but lies and rumors! Why else would someone as hale and hearty as Pockface just up and die like that? His heart was so filled with her that when he heard her insulted it simply gave out.*

Pockface's grave had been dug deep into the ground behind those of his daughter and her husband, Water Girl's mother and father. As the coffin was to be lowered, Water Girl, crazed with grief, jumped into the hole and refused to come out. People tried to pull her out, but she sobbed and said, "Grandpa died because of me, so let me warm the earth for him!" She lay at the bottom of the grave, soaking the earth with her tears. Unable to bear looking at her, the assembly fell to the ground by the hole and cried along with her. By the time Han Wenju and Fuyun lifted her out, she had fainted.

After Pockface was buried, Water Girl lay on her kang for ten days without waking. The third week of mourning came and went, and she slowly improved, but she refused to return to White Rock Stockade. Every day she went down to the ferry landing at Stream of Wandering Spirits to cook for Han Wenju and wash his clothes and sit and talk with him. Now that Pockface was gone, she was back with Uncle Han, and that qualified his grief over the old man's death. He ate what she cooked him by himself, and he drank alone. But one day, after finishing half a jug of wine, he called for her to come and drink a few cups with him. When he realized that she was nowhere in sight, he left the cabin and found her sitting on a rock on the riverbank, gazing blankly at the river.

"Water Girl," he said, "I've been calling you. Didn't you hear me? Come have some wine with me. Do you like me less than Grandpa Pockface?"

Tears came to her eyes as she thought of Grandpa's kindness. Sure, he'd been a big drinker, but even when he was drunk, every word showed his love for her.

Han knew he shouldn't have asked that. "Water Girl, that was wrong of me. I shouldn't have added to your grief. I've been alone so long I don't know how to act around people. But that doesn't mean I don't love you. I know how painful it is for you just to sit around the house all day, and I've been giving that a lot of thought recently."

Water Girl didn't budge.

"I'm not bragging," he said, "but in Crossroads Township I'm considered a man of letters, even though I never studied anything useful. I may have spent my life poling a ferryboat, but I know the ways of the world. The way it looks, the Tian clan is going to hold on to power, and so is the Gong clan. For someone like Golden Dog, the only way to make it is by becoming the son-in-law of one of those families . . ."

She could barely keep from laughing. She stared at his thick lips and wondered how they could manage all that talk.

But he wasn't through yet. "Golden Dog was born not as a mountain watchdog but as a lapdog! He hurt you, and he hurt Stream of Wandering Spirits and Crossroads Township. But I'm not going to say anything more about that. What I'm saying is that people fated to live lives of power and property should be left alone to live them, and people like us, who are born to poverty, should be left alone to live their lives of poverty. When Golden Dog was still here, he fought openly with the Tians and they hated him for that, hated and feared him. So they hated and feared us too. Now that he's made his peace with them, they shouldn't have any more reason to hate us or fear us, should they? Officials don't have any love for the people, but without the people, who would need them? That's why I've decided to go to Tian Zhongzheng with my head bowed and see if he'll admit you into the river shipping brigade. Even if you can't pole a boat, you can work in the warehouse at White Rock Stockade. We don't have the money to buy into the brigade, but there's always your grandpa's two-room blacksmith shop at White Rock Stockade, which could be made into a second warehouse."

Believing that this was just one more drunken pipe dream, she had been tuning him out, but when she heard him spell out concrete plans, she became upset. "Uncle, so that's your plan, to buy a share with Grandpa's blacksmith shop! Do you think I want to join the shipping brigade?"

"If you were home, I'd always have somebody to talk to. But I can't ignore that hangdog look that's always on your face. I can't change the way things are, and I won't live forever. You can't spend the rest of your life always having people feeling sorry for you. The shipping brigade is doing a land-office business, and if it gets any bigger—who knows?—maybe the county will take over. When that happens, you might have a chance to do something really important for the nation."

"I'd rather die than go to the Tians with my head bowed!"

"I'll talk to them if you don't want to! What do I care about them? I'm always talking, and I've given Tian hell before. Everybody knows that when I'm drunk, there's no way to stop up this mouth of mine."

Having heard enough on the subject, Water Girl stood up and walked from the riverbank, heading for home.

Stung by the rebuff, Han lifted the jug and drained it, getting drunker and drunker until his tongue couldn't form words, though he couldn't stop thinking. *Why do I talk so much? They say it's the mouth that gets you into trouble. It was this mouth of mine that offended the Tians and made things so tough for us.*

He fell asleep after a while, not waking until noon. The thoughts he'd gone to sleep with were still on his mind. So without a word to his niece, he walked to the government compound at Crossroads Township to look for Tian Zhongzheng. Tian wasn't there, but Yingying was in the compound washing her uncle's clothes.

"Yingying," Han called to her, "when did you get a perm? You look like a real modern girl!"

"I had it done at White Rock Stockade a few days ago. Do you like it?"

Like it? You look like a pug-dog! was what he felt like saying, but he complimented her instead: "It's beautiful. It makes you look six or seven years younger. Where's your uncle?"

"He had a meeting in town. What do you want him for? This is the first time you've ever come here looking for him, Uncle Han, isn't it?"

"Your uncle's a very busy man, and I hate to add to his troubles. But today it's important to talk to him. It's about Water Girl, and I may need your help, as well."

"What do you mean, it's about Water Girl?"

"You and she were schoolmates and close friends. You know how much she's suffered over this business concerning Golden Dog. She even came here to explain things to you personally, didn't she? She did very well by you. Now that her grandpa's gone, she can't stay in White Rock Stockade, and all she does is mope around the house. Do you think you could talk to your uncle and try to get her assigned to the river shipping brigade?"

Han didn't say anything about turning the blacksmith shop over for a warehouse. Assuming that Yingying would be willing to help out, they might be able to hold on to their two-room shop.

"I'll do what I can," Yingying promised. "I feel so sorry for Water Girl. Will she be home for the next few days?"

"Yes." Then he added, "All she does is cry."

"Since my uncle's in town for the meeting, he probably won't be back until after Grownups' Day. That's a holiday for me, so I'll go see her then."

"Grownups' Day?" Han blurted out. "Is it that time again? The time's passing so fast my poor head's swimming!"

Grownups' Day is the only temple festival on the banks of the

Zhou River. After New Year's and the fifteenth day of the first lunar month, it is the major local event, more important than Grave-Sweeping Day and the Midautumn Festival. Han Wenju was distressed by the quick passage of time but excited by the prospect of the festival. He thanked Yingying, feeling very lighthearted. Since Grownups' Day was only two days off, he decided to buy something for Water Girl to show how much he cared for her. So he went to the co-op and bought a blouse; then he stopped by a café, where he ordered a bowl of egg-flavored glutinous rice before heading back to the ferry landing, singing all the way.

That evening, when Water Girl brought his dinner over, he gave her the new blouse and told her to try it on. "Perfect," he said. "Just perfect! Clothes for people, saddles for horses. My little Water Girl's as pretty as a flower. Grownups' Day is the day after tomorrow. I'm muddleheaded. Did you forget, too?"

"No, I didn't forget. I bought some incense and put up couplets yesterday. Didn't you get anything for yourself, Uncle?"

"What do I need? Water Girl, the third week of mourning for your grandpa is past, so you don't have to wear those white slippers anymore. They won't bring him back to life, and the living have to go on with their lives. We'll have a decent memorial for him on the first anniversary. Go to the temple in your new blouse the day after tomorrow and light some incense. Who knows, something good might happen after the festival!"

"What good could happen to me?"

Han was on the verge of telling her what he'd asked Yingying to do, but he just laughed contentedly and said, "You'll know when the time comes. All Grandpa Pockface could do was love you like a kitten. But he was an illiterate man who could only see what was right in front of his eyes. He never gave a thought to your future."

Two days later, on the morning of Grownups' Day, the banks of the river were packed with people setting off firecrackers. Old women, middle-aged women, young maidens, and even little girls crowded up to the ferry landing, calling out to Han Wenju to ferry them across to Restless Hill Monastery. Han felt as though his troubles had vanished, and when he saw all those people, his chatter flowed like the river. "Hey, there!" he teased the women. "Grownups' Day means all grownups, not just you ladies."

"Wenju," one of them said, "it looks like you've lived for nothing all these years. What would Grownups' Day be if not for us? Where would the rest of you be?"

Not to be outdone, Han fired back, "Hah! I suppose all you women have to do is breathe the wind and drink the water to have your babies! Do you have any idea what kind of monastery this is at Restless Hill? After Nüwa repaired the heavens, she came down to earth to rest here at Restless Hill. What if the heavens came crashing down after all my work? she thought to herself. *I can't go on working myself to death.* So she dug up some mud from the Zhou River and made a female figure out of it. But how come she didn't stop there? She said it herself, Women aren't enough! So she made a male figure and put both of them down on the riverbank. Now, she said, when the river floods and wipes out Zhou City, these clay figures will come to life!" He paused to keep his listeners in suspense, picked up his wine jug, and took a drink.

"That's a bunch of nonsense," one of them said. "There weren't any people then, so how could there be a Zhou City?"

"Maybe there wasn't a Zhou City then," Han answered, "but the land where Zhou City would be built was there. So later on, whenever the Zhou River flooded, Zhou City was wiped out, a major event! I've read the prefecture records, and they record the year when King Chuang invaded Zhou City. The river flooded that year. And in the year of Tian the Sixth's guerrilla raid on Zhou City the river took away a corner of the city wall, didn't it?"

"According to you," the passenger countered, "this year's floods were even bigger, since they tore twenty feet of stone from the city wall. Does that mean we can expect a big event?"

Discomfited for just a moment, he quickly jumped to his own defense: "Of course that's what it means! Don't you think the unrest in the farming villages is a big event? I hear lots of peasants have come into Zhou City and White Rock Stockade to do business. Don't tell me there isn't a lot of potential among them. So, like I said, after Nüwa left, the river began to rise, Zhou City was flooded, and the two clay figures turned into flesh-and-blood humans. Then when they got together, the sons and grandsons started coming. Later on, the people built a monastery at Restless Hill and settled upon a date for Grownups' Day. But now you women think the world belongs to you and that Grownups' Day is your day. Is that right? The township government is working like crazy on planned parenthood, and I don't know why they don't make me the chairman. Then I'd pass out a diaphragm to every woman I ferried across the river!"

The women rained blows down on his head until he was laughing so hard he could hardly breathe. "Han Wenju," one of them chided him, "with the nonsense that comes out of your mouth, no wonder the old man upstairs hasn't given you a wife. That thing you've got down there is about as useful as a little chick. Some night when you're sleeping, a cat will come and enjoy three or four ounces of tasty meat!"

Realizing he was no match for them, he started rocking the boat. "Since I'm so useless, I think I'll just tip this boat over and drown myself!" The women dealt him blows and grabbed his ears to force him to pole the boat to the opposite shore.

While Han Wenju was teasing and carrying on with the women on his boat, Water Girl changed into her new blouse at home and, following the custom of Grownups' Day, was frying two large flatcakes for each of the people in the household, one to be tossed up onto the roof, the other to be thrown down the well. When they were ready, she lit incense in front of her grandfather's spirit tablet, and some more in front of her parents' spirit tablets, then took two of the flatcakes outside and stood just beyond the doorway. "This ones's for Uncle," she said, throwing the first of them up into the air, where it spun like a platter and floated like a handkerchief before landing in the trough of the tile roof. "And this one's for Water Girl." The second flatcake soared in the air and landed squarely on the ridgepole. As she was standing on her tiptoes to see just where they'd alighted, someone called out from behind her, "The third one's for me!" She turned to see who it was. It was Yingying.

Water Girl was still angry at Yingying for spreading it around the village that she'd come to explain herself, and embellishing on it at that. But now that Yingying was there to see her, it wouldn't be right to make her uncomfortable. "Are you going to the monastery, Yingying?"

"Sure I am," she said, "but first I wanted to see you."

Water Girl's heart froze. What does she want to see me for? she wondered. *Is she still worried that there's something between Golden Dog and me?*

"I wanted to say hello, but I also have some good news for you."

"What good news could you have for me?"

"Didn't Uncle Han tell you? He asked me to put in a good word for you with my uncle so you could be assigned to the river shipping brigade. My uncle came back this morning, earlier than planned, and gave his approval for you to work in the warehouse."

She felt like screaming at her uncle. "I'm not going to go, Yingying," she said. "My uncle was just talking, that's all."

Yingying stood there for a moment not knowing what to make of this. "You won't go? It's a wonderful chance! Now that Grandpa Pockface is gone, you're all alone—which not only means more work but means that you'll be depressed all the time. Lots of people work in the warehouse, so there's always something going on. Why won't you go?"

Water Girl just shook her head and bit down hard on her lip.

"You don't want to work for my uncle—is that it? He does some things I don't like either, but he's not so bad as they make him out to be. You can believe that or not; it's up to you. But at the warehouse you won't be working directly for him. Or is it that you're still angry with me? I've said some shameful things about you in the past, but I've had problems, too, you know!"

Water Girl was moved by Yingying's candor. "Don't talk like that, Yingying. That has nothing to do with it. I don't want to go anywhere. I'm not holding a grudge, not against you and not against Golden Dog. The only person I hate is me. I'm just going to stay at home and lead a peaceful, uneventful life."

Yingying stared at Water Girl for the longest time and shook her head in exasperation.

Sensing the awkwardness, Water Girl smiled wryly and asked, "Did you fry flatcakes today, Yingying?"

"I don't believe in that nonsense! Mother got up this morning and fried several of them. She told me to toss them up onto the roof, including one for Golden Dog, but I refused. Well, she got mad at me, and I didn't want to argue with her, so I stuffed them into my handbag and told her I'd done what she'd asked. I figured I'd take them with me to the monastery to have something to eat when I get hungry." She laughed impishly as she took two large flatcakes out of her handbag.

"You shouldn't have done that," Water Girl said. "Maybe it's just a silly superstition, but there could be something to it. Even if you don't throw one of them for yourself, you ought to throw one for Golden Dog. Now that he's away, he needs the protection of the spirits more than ever!"

"Well, if you say so!" With a flick of her wrist, she hurled one of the cakes up into the air; it landed on the ridgepole of Water Girl's house. Water Girl looked up and saw that it had landed right smack on top of her own. The sight made her heart ache.

They chatted a while longer, then Yingying set out for the monastery to take part in the observance there. As Water Girl watched her walk off, she felt pangs of envy over the other girl's good fortune. Listless, she dragged herself over to the well with the two remaining flatcakes. It was deep, very deep, and all she could see was a glimmer at the bottom. Such a quiet, mysterious world down there. As she gazed at the shimmer, it looked to her like a human figure. She dropped the flatcakes down into the darkness and heard two muffled thuds, then continued gazing at the shattered, blurred glimmer of light. Grownups' Day, she thought to herself, Grownups' Day. *Everybody fries flatcakes, but not everybody grows up the same.*

She decided not to go to the monastery at Restless Hill after all.

When Fuyun dropped by at dusk, he asked if she'd gone to the monastery. She said no. "Why not? Weren't you going to light incense for the gods? The place was packed, and when I squeezed in to light some incense, the smoke nearly choked me."

"I don't think lighting incense will change anything."

"Don't talk like that. Uncle Han's always saying how lives change. Who knows? You could have good times in your future. Let's go over tonight. Last year almost a hundred women spent the night there singing, and it was wonderful. There might even be more this year."

He finally managed to sway her, and they went together after nightfall. There weren't as many people inside as there had been during the day, but the floor was covered with ashes and the remains of firecrackers and burned-out incense sticks. Red and yellow banners proclaiming the redemption of vows hung on both walls of the Spirit Hall, and the altar was piled high with food and daily necessities, including dozens of plastic containers holding vegetable oil. Fifty or sixty people were seated cross-legged on the floor before the altar, one of whom was leading the others in song. The hall vibrated with their singing, causing the flames in the oil lamps on the altar to flicker and blur. Water Girl walked up to get a better look. They were all older women in shabby clothes, their thinning hair mussed, their arms wrapped around their knees or holding their bound feet in their hands, their eyes half-closed, as they sang and sang and sang. Neither Fuyun nor Water Girl knew what they were singing. Maybe the *Canon for Daughters* or a Buddhist sutra, but the words weren't clear enough to tell. The women never missed a beat, as the melodies rose and fell, flowing beautifully, the flickering lamplight dimly illuminating their wrinkled, gaunt, sweaty faces. Water Girl leaned against the doorway of the hall and watched them, feeling a chill at first, and terrified, as though she'd entered a dark, ghostly world. She began to shiver. But the more she listened, the clearer the words of the songs became, and she realized that these women who were nearing the end of their lives were singing about womanhood. They were relating the story of how Nüwa made clay images after heaven and earth were separated, how women then gave birth to children, with all the blood and water, the stench of the birthing fluids, and how children began to grow—one year old, two years old, three years old, diapers, the first words, the first steps, falling, bawling, reaching adulthood, tilling the fields, reaping the harvests, wolves coming to look for meat, lice drinking their blood, sickness, injury, suffering, worries and anguish, then marriage, intercourse, pregnancy, childbirth, followed by the dimming of sight and the loss of hearing as their children grew, mistreatment at the hands of their own young, and finally, after years of trials and tribulations, and strife and struggles, being laid out as, breathing their last breath, they were seized by the angels of death and taken to the court of King Yama in hell to be tried . . . On and on they sang, as though in tearful complaint of all the bitterness they'd tasted in a long lifetime. When their tale ended, they started again from the beginning, and before Water Girl knew it, she was swept up in the song, her mood in union with theirs. When Fuyun told her it was time to go, her face was covered with tears.

They walked out of the monastery grounds in the darkness, neither saying a word. As they were negotiating the slope of Restless Hill, they came upon an earthen ridge as tall as a man. Fuyun jumped over it, but just as Water Girl was on top of the ridge, off in the distance mountain watchdogs called—a shrill, soul-stirring sound. She softly spoke Fuyun's name.

"Does the sound of the mountain watchdogs frighten you?" he asked.

"Yes."

"They ward off evil," he said. "Their howls keep ghosts and spirits at bay! Jump down."

"Give me a hand."

He reached up, but instead of helping her down, he put his hands on the ridge, forming a ladder with his arms so she could get down on her own. She stepped on his arms and jumped down, right into his embrace. He tried to back away at once but was grasped tightly by a demon holding on to him for dear life and breathing heavily. The demon was Water Girl.

"Water Girl, Water Girl!" Not knowing what she was up to, he called her name in a panicky voice.

A mouth pressing up against his own cut off his shouts. It was sweetness such as he'd never tasted before. He was holding something cottony in his arms, so soft and warm, the curvaceous body of a young woman, which gave off a delicate, fleshy aroma, exciting him, making him giddy. By the time he'd pulled himself together and touched Water Girl's face, it was soaked with tears.

In the darkness of this Grownups' Day, on a deserted slope in Restless Hill, as far-off mountain watchdogs cried out and the faint, neverending song of life drifted over from the monastery, Water Girl poured out her heart to Fuyun. She wanted to marry him, to spend her life with him, so they could grow old together. He was caught completely off guard, and his courage left him. He stood there dumbstruck, completely at a loss. How was a clumsy man like him going to handle this? What was he going to do with this woman who wasn't acting like herself? Meanwhile, she had taken the initiative. With no misgivings and with the courage to sacrifice everything, she held him close, having him lie on top of her then lying on top of him, letting him kiss her, fondle her, bite her, then kissing him, fondling him, biting him. She drew her fingers across his back, leaving deep scratches; she bit him on the neck and cheeks, leaving deep marks. She knew now, as she'd never known before, that she'd lost Golden Dog, that he hadn't abandoned her, and now she wanted a man, not caring that she would be righting a wrong with the naïve, dull, and ugly Fuyun. She wasn't getting even with Golden Dog; it was a show of strength by a weak young woman. She let her animal nature, so deep-seated and natural, take over.

"But . . . ," Fuyun stammered. "But . . ." She took herself to task for her stupidity, she took him to task for his stupidity. "I want to live like a human being," she said softly yet with determination. "I want to live like a human being!"

They were married a month later.

They would make their home in Fuyun's three-room house. Of course, Han Wenju was in charge of all the arrangements. On the day of the wedding, many villagers came to offer congratulations, and if there was no shower of blankets or comforters or satin quilt covers, everyone came with firecrackers, which they set off in the doorway, filling the air with their din. Three or four families pitched in to buy a pair of wedding couplets for the walls, which were soon covered with red and green paper.

Even Yingying came over to congratulate them, bringing Fuyun up short with surprise. He had been running around the neighborhood borrowing tables and chairs and stools for the guests, and while he was arranging the furniture he looked up just as Yingying walked in the door. He froze. She was dressed in her fashionable best: smart black slacks, open-toe shoes. She was holding a satin quilt cover in her hand. "Fuyun," she said with a pert smile, "aren't you going to welcome your guest?"

He just stood there.

"All this happiness has made you muddleheaded! Where's Water Girl? How come she didn't tell me? Here. I picked this up on the way over."

Water Girl came into the room when she heard Yingying's voice and pulled her over to one of the chairs. "I was going to tell you, but I was afraid you'd have to work and I didn't want to bother you."

"I'd have come no matter how busy I was! This quilt cover is a gift from Golden Dog and me. You're such a lucky girl, getting married before me—even if you are older than I."

Hearing the name Golden Dog brought a momentary jab to Water Girl's heart, but she held her smile fixed on her face. Still, she nearly knocked Yingying's glass over as she was pouring tea.

Fuyun saw it all. Yingying was Tian Zhongzheng's daughter, he was thinking, and he'd be proud of the way she was handling this, making sure the villagers noticed her arrival and seeing her treat Water Girl like a sister, to show she hadn't stolen Golden Dog like a mean, selfish hussy. All poor Water Girl could do was bite her tongue and swallow her suffering. Fuyun went over and said to Yingying, "Will you join us at the banquet?"

"I'll just sit here on the kang and keep the bride company. Don't worry. I'll take good care of her."

The other guests found seats in the living room or out in the yard, the older ones at tables, the youngsters and women in the yard on overturned baskets around tables made of door panels. The cold appetizers were brought out, water and wine was poured, and the air filled with the sounds of their talking, their eating, and their drinking games. Water Girl sat on the kang, as custom dictated, with two chaperons and Yingying. The four of them sat with their legs crossed, facing one another as they ate. Water Girl was smiling modestly; the two chaperons, inhibited by Yingying's presence, said very little. Yingying was clearly the liveliest of the group. She drank several glasses of wine without a hint of redness coming to her face, then filled a glass to the brim and handed it to Water Girl. "A toast!" she said.

"I've had too much already," Water Girl objected, her face bright red. "You know I can't hold it!"

"Don't worry. This toast is on behalf of Golden Dog. Now will you drink?"

Water Girl took the glass and gulped the wine so fast she nearly choked. With panic in her heart, she asked, "How is he?"

"He's fine. He's been transferred to the reporters' section. In his last letter he said he'd been assigned to Dongyang County to write a series of articles for the paper. You can imagine the impact those pieces will have on local agricultural production. He'll be famous!"

Water Girl looked at Yingying in astonishment, a look of overwhelming excitement in her eyes. "Is that true?"

Yingying reached into her pocket and took out a three-page letter. She shook it open. "Here's his letter. Read it!"

Water Girl took the letter from her but, on second thought, handed it back.

"There's nothing there you shouldn't read. What do you think he wrote? All that gossip a while ago, saying Golden Dog was such a shady character. But now the facts are known. You were a proper maiden, and now you're a happily married woman. Isn't that right? I'll bet all those gossipy men and women won't so much as fart from now on!"

Water Girl didn't know what to say. She lowered her head and said nothing. Finally she said, "Come on, let's all drink. I hope and pray that Golden Dog is a great success, that he meets people's highest expectations as a reporter, and that the two of you will get married soon."

They raised their glasses and drank. Water Girl refilled the glasses and toasted each of her companions in turn. Then Yingying refilled Water Girl's glass and toasted her again. After that, they took care of their own glasses. The chaperons kept glancing back and forth at Water Girl and Yingying, sensing that something wasn't quite right. "Aiya!" one of them said, "I've had too much!"

"Drink up!" Water Girl urged her. "You won't get drunk." She held out her own glass and then drained it.

Growing fearful, one of the chaperons climbed off the kang and went out to talk to Fuyun. "Something's up between Water Girl and Yingying today. They're drinking much too heavily. They've nearly polished off a jug of wine."

"That damned Yingying!" Fuyun said angrily. "The weasel's come to pay the hen its respects! She's here to humiliate Water Girl again!" His anger rising, he turned on his heel, determined to throw Yingying out of his house.

Han Wenju interceded just in time. "Are you crazy?" he whispered. "Have you forgotten what day this is? Her presence has given you standing. Even if she's trying to humiliate Water Girl, that doesn't mean you can cause a scene."

Han went into the bedroom, where he found Yingying laid out on the kang mat, glassy-eyed drunk.

"Uncle," Water Girl said, "I grew up as an orphan, and I owe everything to you, including this wedding. And I haven't even toasted my gratitude to you yet. Fuyun, Fuyun! Come in here and join me in a toast to Uncle."

She got to her feet, wineglass in hand, only to keel over, bumping a corner of the table. The glass fell from her hand and shattered on the floor.

14

The bus pulled into the Dongyang County depot, where a car from the county committee was waiting for Golden Dog. As he rode through the crowded streets of the city, the driver laid on his horn, but it did no good, and the people kept turning their heads to look into the car. Golden Dog tried to get out and walk, but his host restrained him. "Please don't be offended," he explained, "but these mountain folk aren't very civilized!" He rolled down the window, stuck his head and torso out, and screamed at the people. Eventually, the car made it to the county committee compound, where the party secretary, whom he'd met at the office, greeted him with an enthusiastic handshake and led him to a row of low buildings at the rear.

A slim, nimble young man bounded up with two vacuum bottles of water, one hot and one cold. He poured hot water into a small basin, tested it with his finger, added cold water, tested it again, added some more hot water, then said, "Here. You can wash up." After washing his face, Golden Dog picked up the basin to dump the dirty water, but the young man took it from him and dumped it himself. He poured some tea and handed it to Golden Dog, then offered a cigarette and lit it for him.

Golden Dog was feeling a little awkward, but the party secretary said, "Let him do it; that's his job." He asked about Golden Dog's trip and whether he'd been to Dongyang before. "The mountains are tall here," he said, "and the valleys great. The cadres have a saying: 'The rivers and mountains of China are beauties, all except Dongyin and Dongyang counties.' Dongyin's south of here. The bus ride from the city frightens the wits out of some of the women."

"It didn't bother me," Golden Dog said. "I slept the whole way. I'm from the mountains myself: White Rock Stockade County."

"You're from White Rock Stockade? Where exactly?"

"Stream of Wandering Spirits."

The party secretary was impressed. "No wonder! Some splendid people have come from there." He proceeded to tell Golden Dog about his relationship with the Gong clan and what good friends he was with Secretary Tian of White Rock Stockade. They chatted for about half an hour before the secretary took Golden Dog over to the dining hall, where they had set a full table, mostly local things. Golden Dog was especially intrigued by a baby fish and some cold noodles made of taro. The secretary told him they raised the fish in the region and had turned the wild taro into a major product. Owing to rising prices and the high nutritional value and medicinal properties of the taro, outsiders had come in droves to buy it. So they'd cultivated it and made it into the county committee's greatest contribution to the public weal.

Golden Dog enjoyed the meal immensely, and his initial impression was that this remote little county was blessed with considerable resourcefulness and great learning, if the cultivation of a simple thing like taro could bring prosperity to the entire district. When the meal was over, he and the secretary had a long, rewarding discussion about the county. He admired the eloquence of the man, who had him hanging on every word even though the speaker was only a middle-school graduate. That night and the following morning and noon, Golden Dog talked to local cadres, who showed up on time for each discussion and were eager to speak, though not without prepared notes. The table was supplied with sweets and cigarettes, and Golden Dog noticed that the men were always smiling. He was so braced by the gatherings that he filled two notebooks from these discussions, and when they were over he asked for permission to look around the villages to get some firsthand impressions.

"That's just what you ought to do," the secretary replied. "We're developing so fast around here that you have to see for yourself. You'll fall in love with this place! But there's no hurry. I'm going to make an inspection tour in a couple of days, so you can come with me. What do you say?"

Golden Dog decided to stick around town, reading the reams of information the county committee sent to his room, as the outline of a story began to take shape in his mind.

The county committee compound, which wasn't particularly large, included a row of single-storied rooms; the party secretary lived in No. 4, which was unfurnished, since his wife and child were back in Zhou

City. Was it that he planned to work here for only two or three years, or did he feel it would be hard to concentrate on his work if his family were with him? In addition to the secretary's quarters, there were a TV room, a conference room, and a recreation room equipped with Chinese chess and mah-jongg sets. The remainder of the rooms were reserved for visiting VIPs. After Golden Dog woke up in the morning, the young attendant would come with water for him to wash up. After dumping the water outside, he'd return to mop the floor and dust the furniture. It was immediately obvious to Golden Dog that they were taking good care of their visitor, and even better care of the party secretary, and it embarrassed him. Whenever he offered the attendant a cigarette, the young man waved it off, smiling agreeably. The secretary was always at some meeting or other, and his table was piled high with documents to read and approve. Golden Dog was reluctant to disturb him. So he stood beneath the leafy banana tree in the compound for a while, then walked alone into town, where there were two main streets, one of the old type, the other modern and prosperous. When he squeezed into a crowd of people in front of one of the shops on the street, he saw the crowd had formed around hawkers of rat poison and food supplements for pigs. Someone else was running a monkey show, and a peddler of wool shirts was proving that his product was the genuine article by lighting one of them with a match, to the excited ejaculations of his audience. There were also dirty-faced girls with tangled hair performing deep-breathing exercises; dressed in tattered clothes with thick wires wrapped around their necks, they were ugly and pitiful as they held straw hats for handouts from the crowd. Golden Dog couldn't bear to watch things like that, and he wondered why the county government allowed them. He walked, dejected, into a café, ordered some wine, and sat down to drink it alone, just as an ugly man with a face as black as soot walked in and leaned his carrying pole against a table. He had strips of leather tied around his waist. Having ordered a bottle of strong wine and a large flatcake, he began eating and drinking. In no time, the wine was gone and the flatcake finished, and he began singing a drum song as he picked up his carrying pole and walked out the door. He slumped to the ground the minute he was outside.

"He's out!" the waiter declared. "Another one's out!" He dragged the drunk off the steps, then came back with a grin on his face. "This one was able to sing a drum song—pretty good too."

Golden Dog didn't understand. He inquired who the man was. A mountain man, came the answer. He asked about the way the man had wolfed down his food and wine. The answer bewildered him even more: "Those men have no families and no personal property. They chop down kindling on the mountain and sell it in town. Then they come over to eat and drink until they're roaring drunk. They go back up into the mountains at nightfall and are back selling kindling and getting drunk the next day." Not keen to hear any more, Golden Dog stepped outside, where the drunk was still passed out beneath the steps. His pants were torn to shreds, his grimy asshole showing through.

At that moment three more men with carrying poles brushed by Golden Dog on their way into the café. "Three bowls of wine," one of them called out, "and make sure it's good stuff! If it's been diluted, I'll grab you by the arm and drag you over to see Secretary You-Know-Who!"

Golden Dog walked back to the county committee compound, where the secretary was taking a break after one of his meetings. He had moved the chess table out under the banana tree and was playing with three of his underlings. Obviously pleased with his game, he kept tapping the table with one of the pieces he'd won. He grinned at his opponents, each of whom he beat in succession to loud and enthusiastic compliments. The secretary invited Golden Dog to play him a game, and after begging off a time or two, the reporter sat down, only to discover that the secretary was a mediocre player at best. He made short work of him. The three underlings returned to the table, and the secretary started off like a house afire, but before he knew it, he'd lost. Golden Dog understood that they routinely let the secretary win. He sneered inwardly but didn't let on that he knew.

That night, the best player of the three chess-playing staff members came over to challenge Golden Dog to a match.

"It must be tough not having any strong opponents," Golden Dog commented.

"The secretary isn't bad, but it's no fun playing with him."

"I'm a reporter from Zhou City. Okay. Let's see you beat me."

The man colored and smiled diffidently, without saying anything, before beginning. Their game was about half over when he asked Golden Dog, "What did you come here to write about?"

"You're a public servant here, so you know what's going on. Suppose you tell me what I ought to write about."

"About the secretary, naturally, and how the people have grown wealthy under his leadership. That's what they all write."

"If local officials can point to real accomplishments, they should of course be written up. What else should I write about?" He told the man about the drunks he'd seen that day at a local café and asked for the dope on that.

"How did you run into them? It's very complicated, and we've looked into the matter. Those people are in difficult circumstances, but they're lazy and uncultured and they've given up on themselves."

"How many people are there like that in the county?"

The man hemmed and hawed awhile, several times seeming about to speak but then appearing to think better of it. Finally he said, "There's documentation in the office. Would you like to see it?"

Golden Dog pushed the chess table away and asked him to fetch the evidence. The man returned in no time with a stack of mimeographed papers, all investigative reports by him and his colleagues. A family of three in a certain township had contracted to work a plot of land but ran into production problems. They neither plowed enough land nor got their planting done in time. So they decided to plant beans but fried the seeds and ate them instead, leaving the land fallow the whole year. A crippled mother and her retarded son in a certain township harvested some of their wheat before it was ripe, took it home, and turned it into flour, so that when harvest time came, they reaped only a bushel and a half. Within a month they were in the street begging. The people in a certain township had a decent harvest but no money to transport it and no belongings of their own. They dressed in tatters and were ashamed to go outside, so that they spent the winter indoors beside the stove . . . Golden Dog leafed through the documents, which concluded with the observation that the mountain people were uncultured, lazy, and incapable of taking care of themselves. His forehead was furrowed deeply. "What's the county doing to solve these problems?" he asked.

"The problems have a long history," the man replied. "Of course, it's not this bad everywhere, and there are even more examples of people growing wealthy. Gorky once said, 'The brighter the light, the easier it is to see the filth.'"

Golden Dog knew exactly the kind of blameless duplicity the man was practicing, so he dropped the subject, asking if he could hold on to the documents. But the man insisted on taking them back. "I didn't plan to let you see these. Just remember that it wasn't me who let you read them!"

Golden Dog nodded. "I didn't see a thing!"

They resumed their game of chess and went on to play others, not quitting until two in the morning, with Golden Dog losing every time.

After daybreak he set out for the countryside in the party secretary's car, visiting three townships in all, and in each being greeted with a sumptuous meal at the government office and then taken to visit well-to-do entrepreneurs and people in specialized professions.

"Well?" the secretary said. "Not bad, hmm?" He asked the people to brief Golden Dog, and they all said essentially the same thing: they owed their success to sound government policies, excellent leadership, and socialism in general. Yet every time the car stopped in a village or little town, it was immediately surrounded by a crowd of people lodging complaints with the party secretary, and the local officials had to shout, sometimes even scuffle to ward them off. One old fellow lay down in the road under the wheel, and the village cadre had to drag him away physically before the car could drive off. The embarrassed secretary said, "The damage done by the Gang of Four was severe, and their pernicious influence still exists in society. Since you're not familiar with this county, you don't know how terrible the local customs are. One party secretary after another has been unable to keep his position. The masses all say that Dongyang County consumes party secretaries! The people are professional malcontents. All they do is complain! They're the same as people who have plenty of food but are used to begging. Like they say, if you've been a beggar for three years, you wouldn't be emperor even if you could. By then you're hooked."

The secretary rattled on, his disconcertion soon giving way to magnanimity. Before long, casual and relaxed again, he was laughing. Golden Dog smiled thinly, though he was heartsick. Complaining of motion sickness, he leaned against the car door so that he could escape further chatter.

They drove on to another township, where Golden Dog decided to stop for a while, unwilling to visit additional villages with the secretary, who was left puzzled by the way he was acting. "I don't travel well in automobiles," Golden Dog lied. "I get terribly light-headed. It'll be best for you to carry on without me. I'll just stroll around until nightfall, then take the bus back to the county office."

"You can't ride in cars?"

Golden Dog chuckled. "I guess I'll never become an official!"

The secretary roared. "People think we officials have it easy, riding around in cars all the time. In fact it's murder! But it's part of our job, day in and day out, sometimes for three or four days straight. The roads here are pretty bad, and I'm beginning to wonder if my belly's so big because of all the bumping around. Well, okay, if riding in the car bothers you, you can take the bus back to the county office. I'll have someone stay with you."

"No need for that. We reporters are used to running around by ourselves. The others can go with you."

They said good-bye, with Golden Dog remaining in the township. First he went to a café and had something to eat. Later, he planned to take a stroll through some of the nearby villages in order to get a truer picture of how people were getting along in these mountains. He didn't expect to return to the county office for three or four days.

No sooner had he finished his meal, however, than he bumped into a fellow named Stone Tiger. The two men shook hands heartily in the café doorway. Stone Tiger and Golden Dog were army buddies who had been demobilized at the same time, and Stone Tiger had been assigned as a clerk in this township. Running into Golden Dog after all these years, Stone Tiger pressed him to put up at his home, where they talked about how frequently they'd thought of each other since going their separate ways, and related their frustrations and difficulties since returning to civilian life. Stone Tiger envied Golden Dog his position as a reporter and the opportunity he had to use his pen to express views about society. But Golden Dog shook his head slowly and explained how he used to think that way too before beginning work at the newspaper but how as a reporter he had been forced to recognize that the scope for doing good was more limited than it seemed. He told Stone Tiger about his assignment in Dongyang County and how the actual situation didn't square with what the local leadership was saying. That, after all, was why he'd decided to look around on his own. Stone Tiger gamely volunteered to serve as Golden Dog's guide and recommended several villages where he could see for himself the difficulties the mountain people faced. They set out right after dinner.

On the way to the first village, Golden Dog stopped at a shop to buy a box of matches. Then he asked Stone Tiger to take off his jacket and let him wear it. Stone Tiger looked perplexed. "When they see me in this jacket they'll know I'm from the city—that and my cigarette lighter. I'll never be able to get close to the masses that way."

Stone Tiger grinned. "That's where you're wrong. These mountain people have changed. If they see you wearing tattered clothes like theirs, they'll know you have no official status and can't solve their problems. Instead of respecting you, they may see no reason to tell you the truth."

Upon entering the village, they came across four men sitting under the eaves of a three-room house that backed against a mountain wall. The sun seemed closer here, its rays lighting up the valley. It was noon; the chickens were silent, the dogs were just lying around, and the only sounds were the gurgling stream in the distance, flowing over its rocky bed, and the occasional lowing of a cow in a nearby pen. It was gloomily quiet. The men were drowsing in the sun, their arms crossed. Actually, they weren't asleep; they had noted the approach of the two visitors but continued sitting as if they hadn't. Golden Dog and Stone Tiger walked up and squatted beside them, asking for a light before engaging in casual conversation.

"Not going out today?"

"Where? Up to heaven?"

"Out into the fields."

"The planting's done. Should we go watch the rats fight?"

"Isn't there some line of business you might try?" Golden Dog asked.

"How do you propose we do that without money?" came the surly response.

Their apathy and their way of responding to every query with a sarcastic question of their own antagonized Stone Tiger, who jumped up and growled, "Have you been eating gunpowder? I'm from the township government, and this man's a reporter from the Zhou City newspaper!"

The men's eyes popped. They took in Golden Dog and Stone Tiger, then exchanged looks among themselves without a word. When one of the four stood and walked off, the others got to their feet and followed, ceding their spot beneath the mountains to the warm sunlight and a row of rocks. A filthy sow being suckled by six or seven piglets rolled over sleepily in the grass at the foot of a wall, snorted once or twice, and lumbered away.

After an awkward, self-deprecating laugh, Stone Tiger explained, "They're stubborn cusses. It's hard to talk to them. I'll take you to a family I know in a valley nearby."

The natural setting of the valley was spectacularly lovely, with a gully surrounded on three sides by hills. The house was right in the middle, and there was a bend of the stream in front, where two people were weeding a patch of beans. Stone Tiger called to them. The old man, stripped to the waist, looked up briefly, then silently returned to his work. The old woman, wearing a dress that came down below her knees, arched her hand over her eyes and looked hard for a moment. "It's Clerk Stone Tiger!" she squealed. "Ayia! It's been two years since you were here if it's been a day, and we thought you'd forgotten us for sure. I guess you only like the rich people now—and hang the poor!" She shuffled up to them. A real hag, she prattled on without a hint of fear.

"What kind of nonsense is that?" Stone Tiger asked her. "Who said I like the rich over the poor? Government policy allows for some people to get rich before the others, and you folks ought to . . ."

"Aren't we supposed to be getting welfare relief?" she asked him. "You gave me this dress out of welfare money two years ago, but since then we haven't seen hide nor hair of any of those big-shot bastards, and not a single penny. Look at this dress, it's falling apart! No money to buy an ox, which means no fertilizer. The only way we can eat three square meals a day is to plant some decent crops. Look at my face. It looks plump, but it's actually puffy. And look at my legs!"

She pushed her finger into her leg, and when she took it away, the indentation remained too long before springing back. She grabbed hold of Stone Tiger's shirt and refused to let go, as though she were expecting to reach in and pull out some welfare money for herself. The sight of the two of them standing there, the old woman asking, Stone Tiger answering, the old woman complaining, Stone Tiger consoling, at first struck Golden Dog as comical, but presently a sadness set in and he walked over to the yard in front of the house. It was a mess, covered by stagnant water, rotting weeds, chicken droppings, and pig shit. The stench in the hot sun was enough to bowl him over. He pushed the front door open and peered inside, but it was too dark to see. As his eyes gradually adjusted, however, he discovered that the place was nearly empty, except for a large stone bin against one of the walls that was filled with wheat, corn, and potatoes; a millstone beside the bin, with a stove behind it, on top of which were an astonishingly large griddle and two unwashed bowls; and a kang behind the door, with a filthy comforter folded at the head. But what really surprised him was the portrait of Chairman Mao on the northern wall, showing the effects of the ten or more years it had hung there. A new scroll was hanging on either side of the portrait, but each of them was decorated not with words but with five large circles imprinted in ashes by the rim of a bowl.

It took Stone Tiger a good half hour to tear himself away from the old woman. He came over to Golden Dog. "People who have seen a bit of the world say what's on their minds. But so do people who haven't seen anything of the world. These mountain people don't know much, so they have nothing to fear. If they ran into a national leader, they'd talk his ear off!"

"No matter how you look at it," Golden Dog said, "they're just too poor!"

"That they are," Stone Tiger agreed.

What else could they say? Not trusting their composure enough to look at each other, they glanced into the distance, where a solitary crow sat on the branch of a dead tree.

Stone Tiger took Golden Dog to four villages over the succeeding two days, where he met thirteen families. While they were all different and lived in varying circumstances, the obvious conclusion was that in this remote, impoverished mountain area, a significant portion of the peasantry continued to live hand to mouth, far differently from the lowlanders around the county town, let alone the residents of Zhou City. The more he observed the area, the more confused he grew. He had no idea how he'd carry out his journalistic mandate this time, and he was worried that nothing would come of his efforts, that in the end he'd fail.

Stone Tiger asked at one point, "Have you decided on the angle your story will take?"

"Of course I could write about how representative Dongyang County is with regard to wealth, but precisely because there are areas all over China where the same thing is happening, there are plenty of other provinces and counties that are just as representative, and the situation could be more clearly reported from many of them. It seems to me that what really stands out in Dongyang County is the segment of the population that's so wretchedly poor."

Stone Tiger was dubious. "Can you write something like that?"

Golden Dog didn't know. He was well aware of the function of a newspaper, and even more aware of how contemporary society was structured and of the psychology of the people living in that society. A story like the one he had in mind would not easily find its way into print, might even be killed outright. But the problems he'd discovered in Dongyang County grieved him deeply. Instead of trying to solve the problems, the county committee kept them hidden from their superiors and boasted of how it was leading the people along the road to wealth. This situation, with people at one level painting a false picture for those at the next, had grown pernicious. Meanwhile, the peasants were left to struggle to keep their heads above water in a sea of poverty.

Golden Dog worked out an approach and angle for his story, and filled three pages with an outline. He stayed with Stone Tiger for three days and nights, during which Stone Tiger's wife fixed him three lavish meals a day, taking the children out of the room with her while the men ate. At first he couldn't figure out why she was doing that, but during one meal, when they were eating dumplings, it all became clear. Golden Dog had wolfed down two bowlfuls, and Stone Tiger had gone to fetch some corn noodles and fish, which he said he loved. When his wife brought in more dumplings, Golden Dog put them into Stone Tiger's bowl. But Stone Tiger ate only about half before complaining of a stomachache and commanding his wife to take the rest away. To Golden Dog's question whether the pain was bad, he merely smiled: "It's just a little problem of mine. I'll be fine in no time." And he was. But then Golden Dog went into the kitchen for a match. The children were dividing up their father's leftovers, counting how many dumplings each had in his bowl. He knew at once what that meant. Back in the other room, he reproached his friend, "Stone Tiger, what do you take me for, stuffing me like that with the best food? Are you trying to make me choke on others' hunger?"

Pain spread its shadow across Stone Tiger's face, and he mumbled words Golden Dog couldn't make out. Then, sighing, the young father buried his head in his hands.

Golden Dog decided that it was time to move back to the government compound so he wouldn't make life any harder for his friend's family. But Stone Tiger wouldn't let him. "Old friends should never allow things to get to this point. I don't care if you laugh at me, but from now on, we'll all eat simple meals. But I won't have you moving into the government compound. I've read your outline, and if you plan to write something like that, there'll be trouble if you stay there. Anyway, they'd know you stayed here first, and that would get me in hot water."

Golden Dog was momentarily speechless. "Stone Tiger," he said, "are you worried that the party secretary of the county will conduct an investigation afterward?"

"The mountains of Dongyang are high, and the emperor is far away. It's not like White Rock Stockade. The party secretary is the power in this county; he's our Mao Zedong! I don't think you ought to write what you're planning. I showed you around so you and others like you could know what was really going on here. But don't write about that in your story. After all, Dongyang is a socialist county, and it's not right to expose its dark side!"

Golden Dog heard his friend out impassively and didn't try to explain his position. That afternoon he caught the bus back to the county offices in Dongyang. Unable to dissuade him from leaving, Stone Tiger tearfully implored his friend not to be angry over what he'd said and not to be disappointed in him. He apologized for being a poor host.

"I understand perfectly," Golden Dog said. "And I wouldn't want to put you and your family at risk. I've learned a lot, thanks to you, but I won't implicate you. Trust me." As they shook hands, he stuffed thirty yuan into Stone Tiger's pocket.

Back at the Dongyang County offices he stared at his three-page outline but was unable to get on with the article. He knew he could write a story about what he'd seen in the villages without mentioning that Stone Tiger had accompanied him, but would it ever get into print? How would it be received at the newspaper? What would the reaction be in Dongyang County? And what would the reaction be by political, economic, and cultural circles in Zhou City? He brooded, growing confused, perplexed, sad, and angry. It would be best to leave Dongyang County as quickly as possible and report to the paper. If he got the green light, he'd write his story.

But a letter arrived that afternoon that made it necessary to stay in Dongyang County. It was from Yingying, and the sly fox had written directly to the Dongyang County offices. She thanked him for his letter in the most effusive terms, and for the first time wrote things like, "I send you a kiss," and ended with, "Our relationship will forever be close and intimate. No one will ever come between us again. Did you know that the pockfaced old blacksmith at White Rock Stockade will never again hate or yell at you, because he died? And that Water Girl has become Fuyun's wife!" The fulsome contents of her letter burned their way into Golden Dog's heart like a red-hot brand. But he didn't raise a clamor, he didn't storm around. He just silently tossed the letter aside and sat for the longest time without moving, as though in a trance. His mind was blank. He couldn't remember what the pockfaced blacksmith looked like, or Water Girl. He just stared at the whitewashed walls and smiled strangely. "That makes everything fine," he said.

He lit a match and casually burned the letter, then picked up his washbasin and went outside to get some water to wash his face. But as he stepped out the door, he slumped to the ground.

The compound was deserted, so instead of getting to his feet right away, he lay there and wept mournfully. In his tears and sighs, images of the pockfaced blacksmith and of Water Girl, one after the other, flashed through his mind. He felt unbearable sadness and regret. Pockface's death and Water Girl's marriage were the cruel retribution and chastisement he deserved, and he would have to bear them forever. Ever since beginning his relationship with Yingying, he'd known that Water Girl would marry someday, and he'd hoped that would be soon, in order to lessen his remorse and free her from her suffering. But now that it had happened, it was more than he could bear. The old man was dead and gone, and Water Girl would never belong to him—all because of him, Golden Dog! He and his career had cost them too much, far too much; yet Yingying seemed exultant, and the only feelings he had for her were of abhorrence.

That night, he went to a nearby shop with a sheaf of manuscript paper under his arm, bought a string of firecrackers, and headed off alone to the hill behind the town. In the hazy moonlight, the trees gave off eerie shadows as he set the paper on the ground, took a ten-yuan note from his pocket, and placed it on top. He lit the pile for the pockfaced blacksmith and prayed for the peaceful journey of his soul. Then he lit the string of firecrackers for Water Girl, hoping with all his heart that she'd live a happy, healthy life in her new home. The loud pops of the exploding firecrackers didn't really register on him; his attention was riveted to the sparks and the shreds of paper floating in the air. The last firecracker exploded in his hand, taking a chunk of flesh with it. It matched the pain in his heart.

Later that night he returned to his room, where he wrote to Water Girl, assuming she was still at the blacksmith shop in White Rock Stockade. In it he described how things were going with him and congratulated her. He said he hoped she'd hate him always but that she'd find a way to understand him. Then, reciprocating her earlier gesture, he reached up and tore the button off his shirt next to the third buttonhole, wrapped it in a piece of red satin, and put it into the envelope. He walked out into the night and stuffed the letter into a mailbox, then went back to his room, picked up his pen, and began writing his story about Dongyang County. His heading was "Don't Forget the Mountain Areas Where Peasants Still Live a Marginal Existence," followed by "An Investigative Report on Dongyang County." The responsibilities of a reporter, a young man from Zhou City, weighed heavily on him: the pockfaced blacksmith and Water Girl had met their fates because of him, and it was they who had pushed him to become a spokesman for the common people. He was a reporter now, a man with a voice, and it was time to let it be heard!

All night long he wrote, not stopping until sunup.

At noon he received a phone call from one of the villages; it was the party secretary. He asked Golden Dog when he'd returned, what he'd seen in the countryside, and what tack he anticipated taking in his story. "Are you getting along all right? Sorry to have put you through so much inconvenience. If there's anything you'd like to eat, just tell the office manager. I already called him, and he'll do everything he can for you."

"Secretary," Golden Dog said, "everything's just fine. I've already started writing, but I do need some more material."

"Go talk to the clerks. They write all the documents. Tell them I said to give you whatever you need!"

So Golden Dog talked to each of the clerks, seeking from them the documents they had. But for the material he needed the most, all those confidential papers about the poor of Dongyang County, he went to the cadre who had beaten him in chess, informing him of the secretary's instructions. The man handed over twelve mimeographed reports on the poor. Golden Dog congratulated himself on his cunning, on having learned to use subterfuges to correct an unhealthy situation. The next day he boarded the bus back to Zhou City.

15

When Golden Dog showed up at the newspaper office, the editor in chief commented on how tan and thin he was, and asked about his progress on his article. When Golden Dog handed him the long, neatly written story, the editor in chief's face lit up and he told him to go for a bath, get a haircut, and take a couple of days off. But the very next morning, Golden Dog was summoned to the editor in chief's office.

"Golden Dog, what's your opinion of this story of yours?"

"I think it's the best thing I've ever done. Of course, there are a few stylistic problems to be ironed out."

"What was your assignment?"

"To write about the status of economic reforms in the villages of Dongyang County."

"And what did you write?"

"I wrote about problems existing among the reforms. And they aren't unique to any particular district but can be found throughout the mountain villages. If they're not given serious consideration, they'll never be resolved, and what good will it do to talk about reforms then?"

The editor in chief tapped the desk with his finger and gave Golden Dog his sternest look for a moment before saying, "What's the function of this newspaper? We're a party organ, the voice of the party, which isn't the same as a private newspaper in Hong Kong, which can publish anything it pleases to serve its own private interests! Comrade Golden Dog, I'm not going to make this incident public, and nothing will happen to you. Who's to blame for this? You are, but so are we. Those of us in leadership positions haven't done enough to improve the political thought of the people who work here.

I shouldn't have given a cub reporter such an important story. You weren't ready for it."

Golden Dog had figured all along that the editor in chief wouldn't approve his story, but since anything was possible, he wanted to appear honest and sincere in the conversation and to answer all the editor in chief's questions straightforwardly. But when he knew the effort was failing, he put a cap on his hopes. "What you're saying is you won't be able to use the story; is that right?"

The editor in chief gently slid the manuscript over to Golden Dog so he could see the comment written in red on the first page: "We must adopt a correct attitude toward the status of economic reforms in agricultural villages, drawing attention to their intrinsic nature and main trends. Stories have been circulating recently that there must be changes in government policy, which shows there are people in society who are opposed to reforms. Is the author aware of this?"

A smile tugged at the corners of Golden Dog's mouth. He picked up the manuscript, rolled it up, and thrust it into his pocket. "Thank you for the thoughtful concern you've given this." He turned and went back to the dormitory.

Instead of destroying the manuscript, he sent it that evening to *People's Daily*.

Would *People's Daily* publish it? A month passed, and he heard nothing. Every time the editor in chief met him, he asked if he'd destroyed the manuscript or held on to it. He also mentioned that he'd received several phone calls from the Dongyang County committee asking when the story would be published, so that the paper had to send someone else—a veteran reporter—to get the job done. He patted Golden Dog on the shoulder and advised him to read some more theory textbooks. "Golden Dog," he said, "you have the right spirit except that it's too turbulent. You mustn't let so much turbulence find its way into your work!"

By this time, Golden Dog had despaired that his story would see the light of day, and his whole outlook had soured. He closed himself up in his dormitory room and started drowning his sorrows in drink, which left him feeling still lower. On his benders he frequently threw up all over the place.

Oh, how he wished for a letter from Water Girl. Then one day what he'd written her from Dongyang County was returned with the notation "Not at this address." Suspecting she'd refused to accept the letter, he wrote her three more, and all of them were returned unopened.

Soon afterward, he fell sick. His face grew waxen, he had no energy and no appetite, his belly began to swell, and he ran a steady fever. Worried that he had hepatitis, his fellow workers took him to the hospital for a blood test, which turned out positive: his amino-acid count was up to 180, and his illness was diagnosed as hepatitis B. He looked the disease up in a medical book, which described it in frightening terms: 70 percent of hepatitis B cases led to cirrhosis of the liver, and 70 percent of those cases led to cancer of the liver. He refused to believe he had hepatitis, but not because he was afraid of dying. He believed that wasn't possible, since he couldn't accept that he'd spent his days on earth without accomplishing a thing. So he began taking Chinese medicine, three doses daily of a bitter liquid that made him shudder. Often waking in the middle of the night, overcome by indefinite fears, he'd try to go back to sleep but strange apparitions of bizarre birds and beasts and ghostlike figures with animal faces would keep flying back and forth in front of his eyes. Someone said there were evil spirits in the room, that there'd been a well beneath it before Liberation. Back then, after the puppet military authorities had surrounded the forces of Gong Baoshan behind Restless Hill, they had captured four of his soldiers despite the troops' valiant resistance and their determination to protect their commander—who had managed to escape. The captors, after gouging the four men's eyes out and ripping their hearts from their chests, threw them down the well. Golden Dog wasn't convinced. Why be afraid of ghosts? If living, breathing people didn't frighten him, he wasn't going to be intimidated by ghosts. What tortured him was only how he was going to deal with Yingying, the one ghost in his life he couldn't get rid of.

She received her second letter from him, a very brief one. Since he'd contracted an incurable illness and didn't want to get her involved, she was free to break off their engagement, he told her. She cried pitifully after reading the letter.

Tian Zhongzheng, who dropped by her dormitory that day, saw her crying, and when he asked what was wrong, she let him see the letter. He collapsed into a chair as though hit by a thunderbolt.

Tian had been walking on air after Yingying's engagement to Golden Dog, though he tried not to show his euphoria. He'd seen a lot of people in his life, and he knew that Golden Dog was no ordinary man. It pained him to acknowledge that an inconsequential dwarf like the painter could produce a son like Golden Dog. After he and his sister-in-law were married, he had found out about Golden

Dog's machinations to bring about the marriage, and he had despised him for them. But Golden Dog had managed to get a job at the Zhou City newspaper through him even though, Tian knew, he himself was no match for the Gongs, who held the power in Zhou City, whereas his own influence extended no farther than White Rock Stockade County. Moreover, by getting Golden Dog out of Crossroads Township, he could pretty much have things his own way there. When Yingying told him she wanted to marry Golden Dog, he was at first furious. But in the end he gave his blessing and even arranged for Cai Da'an to act as matchmaker. He was obliged to her, and secretly complimented her, for enabling him to do something he couldn't accomplish on his own. Since, with the exception of members of the Gong clan, Golden Dog was the only person from Stream of Wandering Spirits who had position and weight in Zhou City, Tian could snatch victory out of the jaws of defeat by having the influential reporter part of the family. He was forever pressing Yingying over whether she'd got a letter from Golden Dog and what he was saying about the situation at the newspaper. Could she get him to write a story about the shipping brigade? He even inquiried if Golden Dog sent regards to him in his letters. Yingying discreetly kept the truth from her uncle, making up what was needed to satisfy him, including the words she attributed to Golden Dog in expression of his best wishes. Beaming, Tian frequently spoke of his son-in-law in the township compound.

Now there'd been a letter saying how sick Golden Dog was and consenting to a termination of the engagement.

"Who doesn't get sick once in a while? How can hepatitis be that bad?"

"You don't understand, Uncle. Read between the lines!"

His eyes bored into her. "Are there problems between you?"

Her response was another round of tears.

Tian became exceedingly suspicious. How was their courtship going? he wanted to know. And just who was courting whom? He demanded a full account of what Golden Dog had written in his letters, wanting to judge whether the young man's feelings were sincere or if he'd had a change of heart. And he insisted on being told what had caused the current troubles. He was worried that Golden Dog was manipulating Yingying the same way he had manipulated him in order to get the newspaper job in Zhou City. If that was the case, it was time to break off the relationship and let everyone know how the young reporter had manipulated them. They could send a letter to the newspaper and expose him. They could level charges against him. They could ruin his reputation and cost him his job.

But Yingying, acting like a woman possessed, bellowed at her uncle. "Stop saying that! And keep your nose out of my business! It's all your fault, anyway!" Her crying started anew, and she called for her mother and her father. When she heard herself summoning her father, her grief redoubled.

The entreaty to her father had a mellowing effect on Tian, who didn't have the heart to say another harsh word. Silently he watched her cry until the sobs subsided. "Yingying," he said, "don't cry over your father any more. Do you really think I'm lukewarm about your marriage? I've always let you have your way. More than anything else I want you two to get together. If Golden Dog isn't as bad as I just made him out to be, there's no reason to be so sad. He's young; he'll get better. He's just too busy to recuperate like he should. Write and tell him to come back for treatment. I'll go to White Rock Stockade and get the best doctor to see him."

"I want to go to Zhou City and see him in person!"

The next day, she took a boat into White Rock Stockade, where she boarded a bus for Zhou City. She wore new clothes and brought a number of gifts. As soon as she arrived, she asked how to get to the newspaper. But Golden Dog wasn't there.

"Where is he?" she asked the doorman.

"He's at a correspondents' meeting at the guesthouse."

"But he's sick, isn't he?"

"It's not serious. What do you want him for?"

"I'm his fiancée."

The doorman immediately sent a courier to get Golden Dog.

The message surprised Golden Dog. He never imagined that Yingying would come to town by herself, and he became conscious that she was not someone to take lightly. Everyone at the meeting had learned that he had a fiancée and that she was in town at that very minute. Shouting ebulliently, they cajoled him to buy some wedding candy so they could celebrate with him. When some of the more vapid of the women chided him for keeping the good news a secret, he didn't know whether to laugh or to cry. He headed wearily back to the newspaper office.

As soon as he entered the compound, he spotted her wearing an overcoat with the collar and sleeves buttoned tight. Her perm made her look older than she usually did. Compared with the girls in town, who dressed more casually and had a livelier air, she wore clothes and a hairdo that struck him as vulgar and coarse. Apparently she'd gained weight, and from the side she looked a lot like her mother.

"What are you doing here?"

"Why shouldn't I be here?"

"You should have written to tell me."

"Would you have written back if I had? Is this the way to greet someone who's traveled hundreds of li to get here?"

"Why are you screaming? Are you afraid somebody might not hear you?"

"I want them to hear me! I want everybody to see whether you're going to act like somebody who's engaged. Don't think I'm some daffy woman. I know you're closing your heart to me. You wrote to say you were sick, so I came to see if that's true. If it's not, I'll be on the next bus out of town!"

They rode to the dormitory without exchanging a word.

Once Golden Dog's colleagues at the newspaper knew that his fiancée was on the scene, they came knocking at his door. He had no choice but to see what they'd ask for. Some said they wanted to borrow a book; others wondered if he had any tea in his pot. As they poured the tea, they'd sneak a look at Yingying. He felt terribly awkward, but she didn't seem to mind. Eventually she just threw open the door and said, "Look. You're newspaper people. Why are you beating around the bush? If you want to see what I look like, why not admit it? I'm not a flower or anything!" Golden Dog's colleagues at first tittered, but then guffawed. When they sat down, they had no problem striking up a conversation with Yingying, who was unusually ebullient. She laid out all the regional goodies she'd brought and plied her visitors with them, fretting that Golden Dog was sick, without anyone to look after him: "Our Golden Dog is all alone here, and who's he going to rely on if not you folks? I'd be forever grateful if you'd take care of him for me!"

"Would you just look at the pains Golden Dog's fiancée takes concerning his welfare!" one of his colleagues remarked.

Golden Dog was speechless with rage; his face was livid. After he'd shown the guests out, he protested, "How could you show off like that? Why didn't you just go ahead and tell them exactly what happened between us?"

"I will if I feel like it! Afraid you'll lose their esteem?"

"Okay, you win. Your coming to town means you've won. But you came because you thought I was faking illness, not because you were worried I was sick. What do you think now?"

"Whatever you say. I'm only a good-for-nothing. I traveled hundreds of li without stopping for a bite, just to be humiliated by you! Now that you've become a reporter in the big city, you're not the Golden Dog I used to know, and it's clear you've got someone else on your mind. But since I'm here, let me tell you something. Water Girl's married now. She's sleeping in Guan Fuyun's warm bed as his wife."

The words were like bullets, and his heart swelled with rancor. But he simply gazed steadily at Yingying and sneered. "You already told me that!" he said in a strained voice. "What else do you have to say? She's married, and that's great news. I didn't marry her, and you're not getting any younger, are you? Hmm?"

Yingying's lips quivered as she hugged her knees tight. Tears trickled down her cheeks.

Golden Dog stood up and spoke impassively: "Don't cry. What good will that do? There's a meal ticket in the drawer. The cafeteria opens at six. It's right behind this building. You pay for what you eat. I have water here, so drink some if you're thirsty. And if you feel tired, you can sleep on my bed. I have to be getting back to the meeting."

He took his leave, closing the door behind him, and strode off like a conquering hero, his arms swinging freely at his sides. He heard the sound of a fist pounding the table in the room behind him, followed by a crashing sound. Yingying was bawling away. "Golden Dog," she sputtered, "you have no shame, no shame at all!"

On the way to the assembly hall, Golden Dog had an attack of excruciating pains in his liver. He went into the room reserved for him in the guesthouse and lay down for some sleep. One of the other journalists came by at dinnertime, and when he saw how bad Golden Dog looked, he asked, "Are you sick, Teacher Golden Dog?"

"Old Xi, you're five or six years older than I, so don't call me Teacher! You go ahead and have dinner. I don't feel like eating. My liver's acting up."

"Is it hepatitis?" the man called Old Xi asked him. "Have you seen a doctor?"

"I've taken thirty doses of herbal medicine, but I'm not getting any better."

"I'll get you another doctor, one who specializes in this," Old Xi said as he darted out, toward a room across the hall. "Shi Hua!"

A young woman, fresh from her bath, came hurrying across the hall. Her long black hair cascaded over her shoulders, her fair skin had a reddish tinge. Golden Dog immediately recognized the resemblance to Water Girl, although this woman carried herself with more poise. He sat up and leaned against the wall, embarrassed to be seen lying down.

"What's wrong, old man?" the woman said. "Aren't you going to dinner?"

"Let me introduce you," Old Xi said. "This is my wife. Her name's Shi Hua. We used to work in the same market. Her father's a practitioner of traditional medicine, and he has a centuries-old cure for hepatitis."

Shi Hua shot a glance at Golden Dog, then smiled: "Do you want to see a doctor?"

"This is Golden Dog, a reporter," Old Xi said. "I told you about him, didn't I?"

A light flashed in Shi Hua's eyes as she reached out to shake Golden Dog's hand. "Oh, I didn't picture you as so young. I thought you'd be a balding old man! You must be from the countryside, since you still go by a nickname."

The man beside her gave her a sign with his eyes, but she held her own obstinately, "What's wrong with that? I'm just a worker, after all. I'm not genteel like you fellows, with all that printer's ink in your veins!"

Golden Dog smiled, marveling at her frankness. He expressed his gratitude for their concern and urged them to go to dinner before it was too late.

"Old man," Shi Hua said, "I drew on your privileges when I came to the guesthouse for a bath, but I don't have the nerve to go over there for dinner. You go, and bring some back for Teacher Golden Dog and me, okay?"

After Shi Hua's husband returned with the food, Golden Dog noticed how they ate. She'd fish around in his bowl one minute and put some of her food into it the next, continually calling him "old man." Golden Dog was intrigued. Shi Hua kept up a steady patter, as though she and Golden Dog were longtime friends, telling him all sorts of family history. Her husband was eight years older than she and looked even older than that. He'd been employed by the Zhou City Agricultural Instruments Company and on an inspection tour to Xiyang County had met her when she was looking for a job after having worked in a production team in the provincial capital. After exchanging forty letters, they decided they were in love. But once married, they were forced to live apart for a long time, and it wasn't until the winter before the previous one that he'd managed to get her transferred to Zhou City.

"Teacher Golden Dog," she said, "leave it to me. I guarantee your illness will be cured. My father's here with me, so it's no problem at all. If you're not going anywhere this evening, come over to our home so he can examine you."

Knowing it would be ungracious to decline, Golden Dog assented. But instead of accompanying them, he said, "You go on ahead. Give me your address. There's some business I have to take care of first."

The man chuckled. "Teacher Golden Dog's fiancée is in town, and he has to make sure she's taken care of."

"Oh!" Shi Hua said. "Then, for me, her name will be Teacher's Wife! I'll go with you, Teacher Golden Dog. I'd like to see what sort of beauty a big-time reporter like you has picked out to wed. She's a lucky girl! Old man, you go home and fix dinner."

Golden Dog dredged for every excuse imaginable in order to talk her out of going with him, but she was determined to go to the dormitory to invite Teacher's Wife to her home. His excuses exhausted, he took her along, but when they got to his room, Yingying was gone. He turned on the light and spied a note on his desk: "I came to see you in good faith, but I'm not going to put up with your insults! I know you can't forget Water Girl, even though she's married. That shows how despicable you are! At first I figured I'd have it out with you, once and for all, but since you're sick, I've decided to leave! (Don't try to find out where I'm staying tonight, because you'd just be wasting your time. I doubt you'd try, anyway.) I don't need to remind you how you landed this job at the newspaper. I may not be as talented as you, but I'm not a woman to look down on, either! I want you to know that I don't regret this trip to Zhou City, because now I know the direction my life is going to take. Your contempt for me has opened my eyes, for which I'm grateful!"

He crumpled the note and sat down in his chair with a dark look on his face.

"What did she have to say?" the curious Shi Hua asked.

He didn't respond right away, but after a moment he looked up and forced a smile on his lips. "My relationship with her was a mistake from the very beginning. Let's go."

It was a cool, clear night, with a light breeze, as they rode their bicycles to Shi Hua's home. When they passed through an intersection, they saw young couples with their arms entwined strolling beneath the vapor street lights, and they heard the shouts, some loud and some soft, of food peddlers. Golden Dog slowed down and said, "Shi Hua, how about a bowl of dumplings?"

"The food here's unsanitary," she replied. "Are you hungry? The old man will have something ready for us at home."

The owner of the dumpling stall, seeing them approach, had removed the lid from his pot. "Here, have a bowl!" He hawked. As they rode past, he bantered, "None for you? Young lovebirds talking over a bowl of dumplings; you can't beat it!"

Golden Dog heard Shi Hua snort contemptuously, and he forced himself not to smile. They came upon a movie theater that had been converted into a dance hall. There were so many people they had to dismount and walk through the crowd. Large numbers of young people were holding money up in the air and braying, "Tickets, who's got tickets?" Some of them held their money in Golden Dog's and Shi Hua's faces. "Any tickets, comrades?"

Golden Dog was about to tell them they weren't there for the dance, but Shi Hua checked him: "These kids don't know what they're doing. Since we're a couple, even if we did have tickets, they'd be wasting their time." As they squeezed past the theater entrance, Shi Hua inquired, "Teacher Golden Dog, do you like to dance?"

"I don't know how," he admitted.

"You don't? How can you be a reporter and not know how to dance? I'll teach you someday."

He smiled and said, "Shi Hua, please don't call me Teacher any more."

"All right, I'll call you Golden Dog! Now that you're a hotshot reporter in Zhou City, you have to learn how to dance. It's a form of social interaction. Get rid of your inhibitions. No more peasant mentality!"

When they arrived at Shi Hua's home, Golden Dog discovered that her father lived in a building across the way. He looked like an old practitioner of traditional medicine, lively yet inscrutable. He checked Golden Dog's pulse and felt the area above his liver; then he examined the palms of his hands and looked in his eyes. He shook his head and said it didn't look like hepatitis. Suspecting an inflamed gallbladder, he told him not to eat anything the following morning and go to the hospital to have his gallbladder checked.

Shi Hua was delighted. "That's wonderful! When Father suspects something, 90 percent of the time he's right!" She dragged Golden

Dog to her home, where her husband had prepared a simple meal. They took turns urging Golden Dog to eat as much as he could. Relieved at the practitioner's diagnosis, he wound up eating two more bowls of food than usual.

After undergoing examinations at a number of hospitals, Golden Dog had his condition diagnosed as indeed an inflamed gallbladder, and after twenty doses of the herbal medicine prescribed by the old practitioner, he was cured. To show Shi Hua his appreciation, he dropped by every two or three days. When he visited, her husband occasionally asked him to look over the stories he'd written, and a close relationship quickly developed between the three.

But Old Xi's talents were clearly not up to the mark, and no matter how hard he tried, his stories always seemed to miss the point and were filled with clichés. Shi Hua was sitting beside them one day while they were talking; with fire in her eyes, she put the question: "What do you think, Golden Dog? Does the old man write a decent story? If not, tell him to give it up and concentrate on his job, then come home to cook and do the sewing. You may not know it, but this old man of mine is a wonderful tailor. See this blouse I'm wearing? Well, I designed it, and he made it. I don't buy clothes in shops. There's no variety there. Everyone dresses alike. I get the same pleasure out of designing clothes that you fellows get out of writing your stories. What do you think of this blouse? Not bad, hmm?"

Golden Dog made flattering comments about how special her blouse was and how well it suited her. Yingying could never wear clothes like that, he continued, and even if she did, she wouldn't look as if she belonged in Zhou City. But Shi Hua certainly did.

"It's as much who wears something as it is what the person wears," Shi Hua said. "The peasants have got rich in recent years, and they've started paying attention to what they wear. But when you see them in Zhou City, you can always tell they're peasants. Don't misunderstand me, Golden Dog: I'm not slandering the peasants. But take the men, for example. Over the past few years they've started wearing black wool tunics. But if you look at the collars, you'll see they're filthy! The women wear different things, too, and everything's nice and neat. But they still look like local products done up in Western packaging!"

"That's enough of that kind of talk," Old Xi interrupted. "We were discussing something important."

"Okay, old man," Shi Hua said. "Writing news stories takes talent. Golden Dog's an accomplished reporter even though he's still young. It doesn't look like you'll ever make the grade, even after you have a flowing white beard. Golden Dog, how much money do you make from your stories? You must be rich by now!"

"I don't make any money from my stories!" he protested.

"Don't worry, I'm not going to hit you up for a loan!"

"Writing for a living is a far cry from running a business," Old Xi corrected Shi Hua. "Why all the talk about money?"

"What's wrong with money? Do you demean yourself when you talk about it? Everything costs money these days!" With a look of excitement, she nestled her foot in her husband's lap. He quickly lifted it off and cast a mortified glance at Golden Dog as he stood up. "What are you afraid of?" Shi Hua asked him. "I didn't rest it on *him!*" She laughed so hard that every tooth showed.

At first Golden Dog thought she had gone too far, but he had to laugh. "Quite an atmosphere you keep here," he said.

"Everybody says my old man's wrong for me, but he's just what I like. Except for cooking the meals, everything else around the house is my job, from mopping the floor to washing the clothes. Isn't that right, old man?"

Through his contact with this family, Golden Dog found himself less gripped by his sorrows. It was almost as though he were using the place as an escape from himself. As time passed, he grew particularly fond of Shi Hua, to the point where he was beginning to adore her. She was only semiliterate, and when she left him a note, her writing was a childish scrawl. But she was a virtual almanac on the things she enjoyed—like movies, TV, and pop singers. She became eloquent when she spoke of them. She knew how to sing and dance and was very adept in applying cosmetics. On Sundays she penciled her eyebrows and dressed up in bright, even outlandish, clothes, until she looked like a girl in her early twenties. On more than one occasion young idlers bowed and scraped to her, but she just walked arm in arm with her old man, like a show-off. The young men were so incited by this that they'd have liked to beat her husband half to death. But she didn't let herself be bothered. She was outspoken and fearless, and when she flew off the handle, as she did frequently, anyone might be the target of her outburst. She'd curse an official for being corrupt, she'd curse the rising prices at the market, she'd curse these shameless young men whose eyes followed her, and she'd curse editors who refused to publish her husband's stories. She was particularly concerned about Golden Dog, frequently reproving him for not bathing often enough or for wearing clothes that were either too small or too baggy. One Sunday she went out on her bicycle to buy him a cap.

To find what she had in mind, she had to go to eighteen different shops.

Golden Dog started getting more and more phone calls, and without asking, he always knew that it was she on the phone. "Come over after work, Golden Dog."

"I can't come today. I have a story to write."

"Whatever you earn from your writing doesn't make it worth ruining your health! Do you know what today is?"

"No, what is it?"

"It's your birthday, you silly bookworm. I've made you some long-life noodles."

Golden Dog was troubled. Had he told her when his birthday was? His thoughts drifted back to the blacksmith shop and Water Girl. But he hastened to Shi Hua's home, where they had prepared dinner and were waiting for him. He and Old Xi clinked their glasses in a toast; then she toasted him. After dinner, when Old Xi went into the kitchen to wash the dishes, she stayed behind to scold him for letting his hair grow so shaggy. She sat him down and did as good a job cutting his hair as any barber in town.

Golden Dog was feeling a little abashed, but she said, "Like it or not, I'm a woman, and women are supposed to take care of men. After you and Yingying get married and she gets transferred to Zhou City, I won't take care of you anymore. I'll even let her wait on my old man!"

Since the newspaper employed a great number of people, and there was always plenty going on—too much for someone writing a major story—Shi Hua and her husband told him he could do his writing at their place. They both left for work in the mornings, and no one was there after that to bother him. Then, when they came home, they cooked him a nice meal. One day Shi Hua stayed home from work and sat quietly off to the side knitting a sweater. After he'd been writing for most of the morning, she said, "Why don't you take a break? Aren't you tired?" He said he wasn't. So she walked over and took the pen out of his hand and told him she wanted him to talk to her, to read her what he was writing. As he was reading, he sensed a warmth beside his ear. He spun around to find her standing next to his chair, breathing down his neck as she tried to read his manuscript. Their eyes met, and he noticed a glimmer; it was like a brilliant net gathering him into it. Those dark, shimmering eyes were like pools, the downy lashes like reeds on the edges. He knew he'd walked into the net and was being swallowed up . . . At some point they merged into a single person, and the thing that should never have happened did.

Afterward, Golden Dog was panic-stricken. He couldn't understand why she'd done it, and he began to have doubts about her. Had she laid a trap for him? Did she have an ulterior motive?

"How could I have done it?" he said with dismay.

By then she'd washed her face and was putting on some face powder, penciling her eyebrows, applying lipstick. "What's the big deal?" she said. "If you're upset, have a glass of hot water with some sugar and you'll feel better."

He was shaken by how casual she was. "I'm not good-looking or anything!" he said uncomprehendingly.

She smiled to comfort him. "No, you're not good looking. And I'm not after your money. I haven't taken a penny for all the meals you've eaten or the nights you've spent here. And it's definitely not because you're a reporter and I want your help in getting my husband's stories published. I'm always throwing cold water on him and his so-called talents as a writer!"

His face was bright red when she came over and threw her arms around him. Deep down he felt unspeakably dirty. He rubbed her hand, so soft, the fingers so long; there was a tiny scar he'd never noticed. "Did you get that in a fall?"

"A bite."

That surprised him. "Who would bite you that hard?"

Shi Hua spoke contemptuously of the culprit. "It was the personnel section chief where I worked. I'd just been transferred to Zhou City from the county seat, and he was very helpful—for which I was grateful. He said he wanted me to divorce my old man and marry him. That showed he didn't think very highly of me. When I went into his office to conclude the transfer, he closed the door, placed his official seal on the papers, then said he couldn't stand it any longer and wanted to have an affair with me. Did he really think I'd fall for him? Well, he grabbed my hand and started kissing it. Kissing it? He looked like he was trying to swallow it. When I tried to pull it back, he sunk his teeth in, like he was gnawing on a damned pig's foot!"

Golden Dog fell silent as yet another seed of doubt was planted. "Have you done it with other men?" he asked wide-eyed.

"I figured you'd ask me that. I can tell you I've never met another man who's aroused me. You're the first. Lots of men have fawned over me and treated me well, but all they ever wanted was to get inside my pants. I'm no slut! You believe that, don't you?"

Although he didn't say so, he believed her.

"Say something," Shi Hua said. "Do you regret what we did? Do you think it's a slap in Yingying's face?"

Golden Dog shook his head at the mention of Yingying. He didn't feel he owed Yingying anything, but he was astonished that he could have taken that step. Had it been a sort of escape? Was it degenerate? Or could it have been a reappearance of his hidden love for Water Girl?

He returned to the newspaper, his mind filled with thoughts of what had just happened. He could recall every word that Shi Hua had said, every expression on her face. But before long, a heaviness came over his heart, and he felt more panicky, more nervous than he had after he and Yingying had foolishly gotten involved that time. Early the next morning he called Shi Hua and asked her if she'd told her husband—or if he'd found out on his own. She told him that there was no way either could happen but that even if her husband knew, it wouldn't make any difference. Then, with impatience, she invited him over again and, as though their comradely relationship had been shattered, gave him a pet name: Little Dog.

He went over, but when they saw each other, uncomfortable feelings washed over them, for they both realized that they had committed a sin of sorts against the old man. Golden Dog regretted what he'd done. Nonetheless, every time he called on the couple, he lost control. He knew that at that rate his worries would gradually disappear, only to be replaced by new and greater ones. But his growing reserve was met by increased boldness from her. She continued to treat her husband as well as ever and kept nagging him playfully in front of Golden Dog; and she spoke as caustically to Golden Dog as she had before. Her husband scolded her for her corrosive remarks and smiled at Golden Dog to compensate for them. Golden Dog, alive to the unbearable awkwardness of the situation, smiled weakly and went off to attend to other matters.

He didn't know what else to do.

16

What rescued Golden Dog and infused him with new vigor was a Central Committee directive.

He, his editor in chief, the other reporters, and all the editors at the Zhou City newspaper were taken by surprise when his story on Dongyang County was published in *People's Daily* in a restricted-circulation issue on domestic matters; it elicited an immediate response from the Central Committee of the party, which directed officials in the political departments of every province, municipality, and autonomous region to pay strict attention to problems that had arisen in conjunction with the accumulation of wealth in rural villages, to organize relief efforts for citizens in remote mountain districts, to avoid inflated and exaggerated claims, and to solve subsistence problems in impoverished areas. The directive singled out Golden Dog for commendation.

Provincial authorities wasted no time: first the party secretary and governor made separate inspection trips to several mountain districts; then they sent teams of cadres to begin the necessary grass-roots work for putting the peasants on the road to wealth. Zhou City's senior officials came to the newspaper to call on Golden Dog, and for the first time he met Commissioner Gong Baoshan, a small, slight old man with a gentle demeanor and a winning smile. The commissioner addressed a meeting of all the reporters and editors concerning the prefectural party committee and the prefectural commission's plans to implement fully the Central Committee directive. First, agricultural taxes in remote mountain districts were being reduced or eliminated to give the people a respite from their burdens. Second, large numbers of cadres were being sent to undertake grass-roots work. Third, construction materials were being distributed to the peasants so that they could build and repair roads into the city. Fourth, farmland and forest areas were being returned to the peasants, and rural enterprises diversified. Fifth, cotton goods were being distributed, and each person was to be given thirty yuan of immediate aid. Sixth, educational systems were being strengthened. Gong Baoshan's speech fired an enthusiasm in his listeners, and during the forum that followed, the reporters embraced and praised the proposed measures. Golden Dog spoke up at the forum, and even though Gong Baoshan's program had included nothing that wasn't already in his own story, the action of one of the area's leaders in spelling out concrete plans emboldened him to make several recommendations of his own, on the basis of his experiences in the countryside. He pointed out the problems of an egalitarian approach by relating an actual case. When Dongyang County officials requested assistance for mountain districts higher than a thousand meters above sea level, the provisions, cotton goods, chemical fertilizers, and machinery had all been delivered to lowland villages, since the districts at the higher elevations were considered too poor to benefit from short-term assistance. Instead, wealthy model villages in the lowlands were created for the sake of appearances. As a result, in at least one of the high-elevation districts the number of oxen available to till the fields had fallen to five; the people had no money to buy chemical fertilizer; the annual harvest sank to two hundred catties per mu; and the district's sole industry, touch paper, was wiped out when the river flooded. The average annual income in the area was a paltry four yuan. Since it had been decided to aid the impoverished mountain districts, the first order of business should be to concentrate on setting up new industries: mining, forestry, animal husbandry, fisheries, and land cultivation. Next, technicians should be sent to the areas, and they should be followed by teams of cadres, each to be responsible for a prescribed number of households.

Golden Dog's recommendations had his listeners looking at each other in blank wonder. He had proved his familiarity with the situation in the rural villages and won his listeners' admiration through the considered, innovative nature of his views. Even Gong Baoshan was impressed. He led the others in applause when Golden Dog finished. "Comrade Golden Dog's recommendations are excellent!" he said. "You sound like an expert on village work. Where are you from? What's your background?"

"Commissioner Gong, I knew your name when I was a child. You'll be surprised to learn that I'm from Stream of Wandering Spirits!"

"You are?" Clearly Gong Baoshan's interest was captured. "Who's your father?"

"The painter at Restless Hill."

"Well, it looks like the son of the short painter has grown up!"

For a period after the departure of Commissioner Gong, the Zhou City paper published a series of stories dealing with efforts to resolve the problems of impoverished households, and Golden Dog became a local hero and was thought of as a famous reporter who had rendered outstanding service. The comment "The son of the short painter has grown up," uttered by the respected Gong Baoshan, began to bring luster to Golden Dog's background and family history.

But he quickly discovered that his fame put him at a certain disadvantage, though he couldn't admit that publicly. A noticeable lack of sincerity marked his colleagues' discussions with him, and whenever he went out on a story, particularly to other counties, the local officials wined and dined him, never letting him out of their sight. He understood that this was their way of keeping him from discovering dark secrets they didn't want exposed in his stories. In addition, the close monitoring of his activities by the people assigned to accompany him had the effect of forming an impenetrable net around him. It became impossible to grasp the reality of the places he visited, for all he heard were the empty talk, officialese, platitudes, and useless chatter of interview comments. After returning dispirited to the newspaper, he'd discover that his hosts had sent a letter to his bosses, praising him for his down-to-earth manner of seeking truth from facts.

At about this time he began receiving letters from Yingying again. One filled with recriminations would be followed by one dripping with sweet talk.

As he grew increasingly depressed over his two predicaments, he began spending more and more time at Shi Hua's home, where the outcome had become a routine . . . He began to adopt Shi Hua's lifestyle, let his hair grow long, wore fancy shirts, and learned how to dance. He forgot everything when he was with her, but when he was in bed back at the dormitory, he would be overcome by dejection, feeling that in his new life something frightful was taking over his mind. He wondered if he'd lost the simple mountain-village qualities he had so venerated.

He shared these thoughts with Shi Hua, who poked him on the forehead with her finger and said, "You're the son of the short painter, all right!"

"How did you know my father's a painter?"

"That's what they're saying at the office. What kind of painting does your father do?"

"He's a craftsman who specializes in rural folk art, restoring temples, engraving tombstones—things like that, nothing special."

"The kind who straddles a beam while he paints a ceiling, and wets his brush in his mouth until it looks like a baby's asshole?"

Golden Dog's eyes grew wide. He hit the table with his fist and yelled, "Damn you! How dare you talk about him like that!"

This sudden outburst stunned Shi Hua, who in all the time she'd known him had never seen him lose his temper. The glass top of the desk had shattered under the blow and cut his hand. But when she tried to wrap it with her handkerchief, he pushed her arm away and stormed out the door.

It didn't take long for him to regret his show of spleen to Shi Hua, but the outburst had cleared his mind. He was the son of a painter from a small township, a man whose life-style was no different from that of any of the other villagers in Stream of Wandering Spirits or Crossroads Township. What had he been doing in Zhou City that would cause him to forget all that? Reminding himself that he had a job to do, he decided to stop seeing Shi Hua. How could a man like him fall under the spell of a flowery skirt and nearly lose his way?

After having offended Golden Dog, Shi Hua made a special visit to the newspaper to apologize to him, and she had Lao Xi go over every two or three days to invite him to their home. Softened by her concern and Lao Xi's kindness, he finally acquiesced. On the way over he was hoping he'd find her home alone, but the minute he laid eyes on her, he was relieved to find that Lao Xi was home; they talked in a relaxed mood and chatted about world events. When the conversation turned to family matters, Golden Dog showed him Yingying's latest letter, in which she'd congratulated him on his newfound fame and passed along Tian Zhongzheng's views on what was happening: he was of the opinion that moderation was called for in affairs like this. He'd heard that as a result of Golden Dog's article the Dongyang County party committee had been reshuffled and the party secretary reassigned to organizational duties. He wondered whether Golden Dog "had considered the fact that a man's family had been ruined in the process."

"So a party secretary's family was ruined!" Golden Dog fumed. "I wonder if she's considered how the peasants are supposed to get by!"

Seeing that Golden Dog's anger was up, Lao Xi tried to soothe him, granting Yingying's flaws but, as a man experienced in such matters, telling him that the first requirement of a prospective spouse was a good heart. "Take Shi Hua, for example," he said. "I'm perfectly satisfied. Her cultural level may not be very high, and she's always been pampered, but she's not a vulgar woman, and I have no cause to be concerned about her behavior at home or regarding family finances. A wife's a wife. She shouldn't be some low-class witch, nor should she be a politician!" Golden Dog blushed, and he was too unsettled to look the other man in the eye. Complaining of a headache, he went into the bedroom to lie down.

The next time Shi Hua and her husband came by the newspaper office to ask Golden Dog to spend Sunday with them, they discovered he'd left, having requested a transfer from Zhou City to be resident correspondent at the White Rock Stockade bureau.

Shi Hua stood there overwhelmed, her eyes clouded. He was gone, and all because of her! She'd lost him, and with him the genuine love of a real man!

Two or three large tears fell from her eyes. "He's gone," she murmured.

"He's gone," Lao Xi echoed her. "How could he leave without telling us?"

Golden Dog was back in White Rock Stockade, where the atmosphere and the work at the bureau office suited him perfectly. Once again he walked down familiar streets and lanes. On his first afternoon in town he went to the blacksmith shop on South Street. The door was locked. The strange stare from the neighbors made him feel as closed-in as if he'd fallen into a pile of wheat chaff. Forcing himself to bear up under the stares, he asked about Water Girl and was told that she'd gone home to Stream of Wandering Spirits upon the death of her grandfather. She hadn't been back since. This news made Golden Dog realize that she'd never received his letters. With a deep sigh, he turned and left wordlessly. But on several nights after that, his feet brought him back to stand alone in front of the shop and stare at the brick foundation of the forge and the lonely wooden anvil base. He should have forgotten Water Girl after his relationships with Yingying and Shi Hua, but instead, in his mind she'd become a saintly, sublime image. He'd chosen to leave Zhou City and return to White Rock Stockade to do the work for which he was trained and to participate in the life over which he'd been brooding, which had at last dragged him from the perfumed temptations of the city. He was confident that this was where he could engage the Tian family in a test of strength. But he needed moral support, and only Water Girl came to mind. He stood silently in front of the shop until his legs ached, then turned and walked over to the bank of the Zhou River beyond the southern gate. All the boats were tied up at the ferry landing, and the boatmen were asleep. The water had a gray cast under the light of the moon, silence reigned, and even though he was feeling melancholy, his nostrils were filled with the smells of the river and of the rotting water weeds. The boats and the people who plied the river were extremely familiar to him, and he started to wonder when the day would come for Fuyun and his wife to be riding one of the skiffs.

Golden Dog didn't tell his father or Yingying that he'd been reassigned to the local bureau office. Instead, he wrote to her on newspaper stationery to tell her that they must break off their engagement since there was no way they could be happy as man and wife.

Before long, a letter was forwarded to him from the newspaper. Yingying had written to Golden Dog's boss, accusing the reporter of unconscionable behavior in abandoning his hometown fiancée after going to Zhou City, and demanding that the organization either subject him to criticism and reeducation or send him back to his village. His boss enclosed a letter of his own in which he admonished Golden Dog to get his thinking in order and not to act like someone who feels above personal obligations. He reminded Golden Dog that he valued the correspondent's talents and for that reason had answered Yingying's letter with a promise to investigate the situation but also with frank indications that there was no possibility of Golden Dog's being sent back to his village. When Golden Dog had finished reading the letters, he went out and bought a bottle of wine, which he drank alone. "Yingying," he said with a laugh, "now you've shown your true colors!"

He returned to Restless Hill the next day.

The painter was delighted to have his son home again. The news of his arrival came while the old man was painting cloud patterns on a newly erected mausoleum; he dropped everything and ran home. "Now that you're a hotshot reporter on the national payroll," he needled his son, "I'm surprised you even remembered you have a father. What are you doing back here? I didn't figure you'd come home even if I dropped dead!"

Golden Dog smiled and took out of his bag the new clothes he'd bought for him. "Is that all?" his father asked him.

"You expected more?"

"Didn't you buy anything for Yingying? And what about some nice tobacco for her father?"

"She's her, and I'm me. Why should I buy her anything?"

"Shit on you! She came over and complained about how you were treating her. What kind of family do you think she comes from? And what kind of woman do you think she is? After you left, she dropped by every week or ten days to give me a hand with one thing or another . . . I'm telling you, in order to get a wife in this township you have to pay a certain amount of money to her family and do a certain amount of work for them. That's what other people do, and that's what you're expected to do. Don't think that just because you've got a job, you don't have to go through the forms for getting a wife or that you can humiliate Yingying any time you feel like it. If you want to act like Chen Shimei in the play, who abandoned his wife for another woman, the people will scorn you and spit in your face! Now you listen to me. Go to the co-op and buy her something, then get yourself over to the Tians. I saw her walking home from town this morning."

Golden Dog refused to stir.

The news that he was back was delivered to Tian Zhongzheng at the township office in Crossroads Township while he was drafting a report for the county committee about the experiences of the river transport brigade. When he was told that Golden Dog had arrived on a boat from White Rock Stockade, where he said he'd been reassigned, Tian mulled the news a short while before setting his report aside and going to see his niece.

Yingying had already heard what he was coming to tell her and was making her face up in the mirror. Even though she'd been bullied by Golden Dog, she'd managed to learn a thing or two during her trip to Zhou City. The girls there penciled their eyebrows thin and long, which made their eyes seem especially lively, and they didn't perm their hair like the local girls. As a result, she bought a curling iron, which she used every morning as soon as she was out of bed, and she'd begun plucking her bushy eyebrows. She'd just finished with the tweezers and had plugged in her curling iron when Tian came in with the tidings that Golden Dog had returned.

"I wonder what made him give up the bright lights of Zhou City?" she asked.

As he watched her pick up the curling iron and work on her bangs, Tian knew that she'd already heard about Golden Dog's return, and panic set in. "Do you know where he was before he came home?" he asked her. "He was in White Rock Stockade. He's working at the bureau office there."

Her hand froze, and the curling iron began to singe her bangs, giving off a burning smell. She turned and looked absently at her uncle. "White Rock Stockade? Has he been sent down to remold himself?"

Not knowing what more to say, they just stared at each other.

Shortly after returning from Zhou City, Yingying had told her uncle everything, and the information had come as a shock. It happened that Golden Dog's story was just then being circulated throughout the country as a directive, bringing sudden fame to its author. Tian came over to see Yingying and tell her not to be swayed by her emotions and to do whatever was necessary to patch up her relationship with him. That was why she'd fired off those letters to him after leaving Zhou City in a huff. But his silence was proof that she hadn't prevailed, and his resistance enraged her to the point that she rampaged around the house, smashing plates and bowls. After reflecting on the situation, Tian concluded that Golden Dog's mind was made up and that, now that he enjoyed position and prestige in Zhou City, he had no more use for Tian Zhongzheng, let along Yingying. So on his advice, she'd written to Golden Dog's boss at the newspaper in an attempt to damage his reputation, calling him a modern-day Chen Shimei; she hoped to make it impossible for him to stay on at the Zhou City newspaper. This time she'd followed her uncle's advice to the letter, never dreaming that Golden Dog had already requested reassignment to the bureau office at White Rock Stockade.

She threw down the curling iron and burst into tears.

"Yingying," Tian said, "what are you crying for? Pull yourself together and go over and sound out Golden Dog's attitude."

"This was all your idea!" she pouted. "How do you expect me to go over there now? If he knows I wrote that letter, he'll hate me till the day he dies!"

"Maybe not. Now that his prestige at the newspaper has suffered, he might have a change of heart. As I see it, his boss has put pressure on him and taken disciplinary action. Even though he's been sent to a local bureau, he's still a reporter, and that's reason enough to go through with the wedding."

Yingying's sobs slowly abated.

Tian left, but after he'd walked a way down the road, he turned and came back. "Yingying," he said, "listen to me. I know I'm right this time. Go see him right away, and invite him to our house. I'll talk to him myself. Now I'll go get some groceries and wait for the two of you."

After Tian left, the letter from Golden Dog's boss arrived. Yingying, admiring her uncle's acumen in weighing the situation, put the finishing touches on her hairdo and headed over to Stream of Wandering Spirits to find her fiancé.

When Golden Dog and his father left off arguing, the painter's son, feeling utterly bored, went alone to Stream of Wandering Spirits. Seeing the distant red-tiled roof of the Tian compound, he sneered and headed for Fuyun's three-room house. Just before he got there, a woman gathering edible fungus with a spatula from the fence in front of her doorway noticed him. "Is that you, Golden Dog?" she exclaimed. "My god, when did you get back?"

"How are you, Auntie? I got back this morning. That's quite a crop of fungus you have there. Expecting guests?"

"How am I, you ask? How could I be? Just look at you. Everybody ought to go out into the world and do something. You've turned into a real dragon! No wonder Yingying's mother came by a while ago to buy some fungus from me. She said she was going to entertain her new son-in-law! Are you looking for Fuyun? He and Water Girl went into town early this morning. Shall I send someone to look for them?"

Golden Dog insisted he hadn't come only looking for Fuyun and Water Girl but that he wanted to know where the pockfaced old blacksmith's grave was so he could go take a look.

As the woman was giving him directions, she suddenly raised her sleeve to dry her eyes. "Golden Dog," she said, "you're a good man. You haven't forgotten the pockfaced old man. You ought to go see him. They say he died with his eyes open . . ."

A sadness came over Golden Dog, and his legs felt as if they were weighted down as he walked up the mountain, one slow step at a time. The grave was overgrown with weeds. He fell to his knees and laid his head on the ground as the tears began to flow.

That was all he could do, shed the tears stored up inside. He was back where he belonged. The sky was the same, and so was the ground, but those who had gone on were gone forever and those who had left had left for good. As he knelt in front of the desolate, lonely grave, he thought about the distant past and found a measure of peace in spite of the tangled confusion before him.

It was getting dark, and cries of the mountain watchdogs began to emerge from the forest high up on the mountain. He didn't feel like going home after coming down off the mountain, for he wasn't keen to hear his father's complaints and grumbles. He wanted to see Water Girl, but he didn't know if she and Fuyun had returned from town yet, and he certainly wasn't about to follow his father's urgings to call on the Tians. Without thinking about it, he went down to the ferry landing to see Han Wenju.

Han stepped out of the cabin when he heard someone calling him. He couldn't believe his eyes; he thought he was dreaming. Golden Dog called his name again, and the old man sat on the deck as though the starch had gone from him. "You're back?"

Golden Dog jumped aboard. "Uncle Han, I know you don't like me, I know you hate me, but still I came to see you!"

By this time, Han had snapped out of his confusion and reached over to pull Golden Dog down next to him. "You're okay, Golden Dog," he said as he looked him over carefully. "How could I hate you if you came to see me? Marriages are made in heaven, so how could I force a union between you and Water Girl? I'm not the pockfaced old blacksmith, who never did see things straight. When did you get back?"

"This morning. Do you have any wine, Uncle Han?"

"Aha!" Han blurted out. "You may have become a hotshot reporter, but you haven't forgotten Han Wenju's wine! Of course I have wine. Since you became a reporter, I've often mused out here on the boat how hard it was for one of the families of Stream of Wandering Spirits unrelated to the Tians and Gongs to produce a Golden Dog, and I think about what you and Water Girl had for a time. I was afraid you'd forget all about us. What's it like out there? Anything like our Crossroads Township? After you left, there was no one in the shipping brigade who could stand up to the bosses, and now it's all Tian . . ."

He didn't finish. Instead he blinked and said, "Since you work for the paper now, how about sending a few copies of your newspaper for me to look at? I know how to read, and I can do some publicity work for you."

Golden Dog could see that Han had changed, that he was no longer the man who'd taken him in as a friend, talking and fulminating without holding anything back. Golden Dog responded in platitudes: "I see you're as concerned as ever about what's going on in the country. What's happened in Crossroads Township over the past six months? How are things with the shipping brigade?"

"If you want to know about local events, your father-in-law is still the headman. But it's not in just an acting capacity anymore. He's the boss, and he knows everything. The brigade's in great shape! Here, drink up. I've got plenty! Fuyun brings me a new supply every month."

"How are Water Girl and Fuyun doing these days?"

"Fine." Han suddenly raised his voice. "They're doing just fine! A loving couple, happy and contented. I've never heard them have an argument and never seen one of them raise a hand against the other. Naturally, they're not as talented as you, but they get by, and what else can a person ask? As long as your mind's at peace and you get along with each other, cool water can satisfy like wine."

Han kept glancing over at Golden Dog with his tiny eyes, which were filled with pride and contentment. That's the real Han Wenju, Golden Dog was thinking. But he was happy for Water Girl, even if he felt sorry for himself.

Soon someone called out from the bank, "Uncle Han, is Golden Dog there with you?"

When Han stepped out of the cabin, he saw it was the painter. "He's in here drinking with me. Come join us."

"Golden Dog," the painter whined, "what's the idea of hanging around here instead of coming home?"

Han's face darkened. "Shorty, why yell at him like that? He's a reporter now, an important man. People will poke fun at you."

Shorty was implacable. "Yingying came over looking for him this afternoon and said her uncle was waiting for them at home. She's still at my place, and I've been halfway around the world trying to find him!"

Han turned and looked into the cabin. "Haven't you been over to the Tians since you got back?" he asked Golden Dog.

"I'm not going over there!"

"Golden Dog," Han said, "that's not right. You're going to be his son-in-law, so you should have gone over to pay your respects the minute you got back. Go on, now. I won't keep you."

Golden Dog never thought he'd hear Han talk about the Tian family like that or treat him this way. He jumped ashore and went back with his father. When they reached the doorway, the painter turned aside and walked over to the hill across the way, in order to give Golden Dog and Yingying a chance to talk alone.

Yingying, who had been waiting a long time, was dozing beside the kang. She stood up when she saw Golden Dog enter and gibed, "It must have taken a powerful genie to get you to finally come home!"

"Well?"

"Why didn't you come over when you got back? Did you figure that since you're a reporter, the Tian home's too small for you?"

"Who'd dare consider the Tian mansion beneath his dignity? Secretary Tian's pinky is thicker than anyone else's waist! But I'm my father's son, so naturally I wanted to see him first."

"But you'll soon be a member of the Tian family! Uncle and Mother have been wondering if you think they're beneath you."

Golden Dog maintained a cool arrogance. "Did you show them my letter?"

"Yes."

"What did they say?"

"They wouldn't agree."

"Yingying, you're one of Crossroads Township's smart young women, so you ought to be able to figure out what it would be like to be in a loveless marriage."

"I knew that before you! But I want to know why you didn't tell me you didn't love me when you were working on the boat."

He laughed mirthlessly. "You tell me why you've been so spiteful."

"What are you talking about?"

"What I'm talking about is that someone sent a letter accusing me of things they thought would get me into hot water!"

She was speechless. After a long pause, she said, "So you're living in White Rock Stockade now?"

"So you've heard, have you?"

She lowered her voice. "Golden Dog, maybe I was wrong. I wrote that letter in a huff . . . Since it's already done, you can get as mad as you like . . . Maybe it's all for the better. As long as you have a change of heart, I can get it back."

It suddenly dawned on him that she thought he'd been transferred because of her letter. "No need for that. It's right here!" He took it out and tossed it down on the kang.

Yingying dissolved into tears, and as her sobs faded, she said, "Golden Dog, I want to ask you a simple question: Do you know what you're doing?"

"You should know the answer to that."

She threw herself on him like a madwoman. "You ravished me, Golden Dog!" she screamed.

"Go ahead and file charges."

Yingying, who was shaking all over, raised her fists against Golden Dog, who didn't move a muscle. Suddenly losing strength, she grabbed her own hair with both hands and collapsed to the floor, wailing.

The painter, who was still sitting on the hill across from the house, heard the shrill sound and knew that things were out of hand. He could barely resist the impulse to make a beeline for Golden Dog in order to beat him. But he knew his son was too obstinate to obey a father's wishes, and besides, now that he was a hotshot reporter, how could he beat him in front of Yingying? Then in his distress, his thoughts ran to Tian Zhongzheng. Maybe Golden Dog would listen to him. *If I ask him to help, he won't be able to complain that we didn't show him the proper respect.*

Tian Zhongzheng and his wife had spent the afternoon preparing a meal and waiting for Golden Dog. But he still hadn't shown up, nor had Yingying. Tian Zhongzheng was mightily upset, since he knew that things must have gone badly. "Well, they're not coming!" he said. "Let's eat." But he changed his mind after Yingying's mother brought the food in from the kitchen. He decided to wait a bit longer.

"This is a great loss of face," she said. "Nothing like this has ever happened in our family before!"

The dejected Tian Zhongzheng simply said, "We'll just have to put up with it. He's not the Golden Dog we used to know. He's a reporter now!"

"He may be a reporter," his wife said, "but you're a party secretary!"

This really set Tian off: "What the hell do you know? Do you think it's easy being a party secretary? How much influence does a goddamned township secretary have even in prefectural affairs—forget about provincial and national? Go over and invite him personally."

But she refused, and an argument ensued. The short painter walked in on them just as things were reaching the flash point. In a muted voice he explained the situation to Tian, complaining that Golden Dog was too young to know anything, and simpleminded to boot. He begged Tian to accompany him home to help patch things up between the two youngsters.

Tian's face was livid as he listened to the painter speak his piece. When he had finished, Tian picked up his pipe and sat smoking for several moments before saying, "I don't believe in getting involved in young people's affairs. All we can do is give them advice. But Golden Dog and Yingying were getting along so well. How could things turn out like this? His thoughts seem to have undergone a change, and it appears he now considers himself better than the rest of us. Sure, he's a talented reporter, but even if he were governor of the province, in our eyes he'd still be a member of the younger generation and he shouldn't forget his place, should he?"

"You're absolutely right," the painter said. "Golden Dog wouldn't have stood a chance of landing a job with the Zhou City newspaper if it hadn't been for you."

"No need to bring that up now," Tian said. "The way things are between them now isn't good for either one of them, and it's our responsibility as adults to step in and try to talk them around."

"That's exactly why I came over to ask your help. With your position in the community, your words carry a lot more weight. If you go over and put pressure on Golden Dog, he'll have to listen. If he doesn't, I'll beat him to death!"

Tian Zhongzheng agreed to go along to the painter's home; since he'd never been there before, he had the painter show the way and instructed him to make sure no one saw them. When they arrived, Tian told him to shut the gate and the front door, then ordered Golden Dog and Yingying to sit down. Yingying was still sobbing.

"What are you crying for? Do you want us all to be humiliated?"

She stopped crying.

"I'm glad you came, Secretary Tian," Golden Dog said.

With a strained look on his face, Tian said, "Golden Dog, I'm not here as party secretary to resolve a dispute between citizens under my jurisdiction."

"Regardless of what you say," Golden Dog replied, "you're the only one who can straighten this out. I know how busy you are with official matters, and I'm sorry to have to add to your troubles, but in this matter I'm afraid there's no other way."

"All right," Tian said. "Now that we're together, let's have a family parley. I've never come up against a problem in Crossroads Township that I couldn't resolve, even though it's a big place with a large population. I'd be a laughingstock if I couldn't handle a simple domestic dispute in my own family, wouldn't I? Even though you've turned famous, Golden Dog, I can't believe you've lost all respect for your father and me."

Golden Dog just gave a laughing snort.

"Golden Dog!" the painter cut him off.

Golden Dog's derision had distracted Tian Zhongzheng, and instead of picking up his thread right away, he fished around in his pockets for a pack of cigarettes. Golden Dog quickly took out a pack of filter cigarettes. "Try one of these!" He brought out his lighter and lit it. Since it would have looked ungracious to refuse, Tian took a cigarette and began puffing furiously. Silence reigned in the room.

"Breaking the engagement was your idea, Golden Dog," Tian finally continued, "and I'm not going to interfere. If you two can work things out, fine. If not, then break it off. You can probably find a better wife in Zhou City, and I don't believe that Yingying will remain a spinster all her life."

"Golden Dog wouldn't dare!" the painter said. "Golden Dog, you listen now. Your uncle's the township party secretary, and I want you to listen to him. Remember, when things between you and Yingying improve, we'll have a big wedding. Wouldn't that be wonderful this winter?"

"Let's not talk like that," Tian said. "In the long run, they have to work things out for themselves. Since things appear to have got out of hand, let's hear what they have to say. What exactly is the problem?"

"Fine," Golden Dog said. "Let Yingying speak first."

So Yingying related how Golden Dog had grown indifferent toward her after leaving for Zhou City. She told how many letters she'd written him and how many replies she'd received, how she'd gone to Zhou City to see how serious his illness was, how he'd greeted her so frostily, and finally, how he'd written to demand that they break off the engagement. As Golden Dog watched her, he began to experience pangs of sympathy, but the way she'd made herself up repelled him: since she was a country girl, why did she have to try to look so modern? As a country girl she was no match for Water Girl, and as a modern girl she couldn't compete with Shi Hua. Neither fish nor fowl! But what bothered him most was the arrogant tone of voice so characteristic of the Tian family. When she'd finished, he simply said that they were temperamentally and emotionally incompatible, and he refused to talk about anything else, including her letter of complaint.

Looking gloomy, Tian asked him, "What are your plans?"

"His plans?" the painter interrupted. "What we have to do is resolve their problems here and now. We don't need to talk about the future, except for the wedding arrangements. All this talk about emotions. Once they're husband and wife and start a family, the emotions will come around in time!"

Tian didn't build on the painter's comment; instead he looked at Golden Dog, then said coolly, "Golden Dog, you've been reassigned to White Rock Stockade, haven't you?"

"Yes, White Rock Stockade."

Tian smiled. "The main office is in Zhou City. If you were doing so well there, why have you been transferred to White Rock Stockade?"

"Uncle," Yingying interrupted, "don't ask him that!"

Tian wasn't aware of what lay behind her objection. "Why not? It's important."

"You want me to tell you about that letter, don't you?" Golden Dog said. "Well, here's what happened. I could have stayed in Zhou City as long as I wanted. It was my idea to return to White Rock Stockade, because that's where my roots are. I'm familiar with the way things work around here, which will make it easier for me to do my job. Shortly after I arrived in White Rock Stockade, a letter was forwarded to me from my boss, and he told me to take care of it. I just gave it back to Yingying, its author, for safekeeping."

Tian Zhongzheng, who had been sitting on the edge of the kang, jumped to his feet but then sat down again, gave a chortle, and said in a soft voice with a hateful edge to it, "Golden Dog, I've never been to the newspaper office, but the reporters have made calls on the local government offices, and I've seen them. A reporter's ID card is no magic sword!"

"Of course not," Golden Dog replied. "When a reporter sees a cadre handle a matter justly, all he can do is write a story and praise him with words."

Seeing that the atmosphere was turning sour, the painter interjected, "Golden Dog, don't try to divert the East River past West Crossroads. I want you to tell Uncle Tian and me exactly what you're going to do about your wedding!"

"What am I supposed to do if we can't work things out?"

The painter picked up a pillow from the kang and threw it at his son, hitting him squarely on the head. Then he glanced over at Tian, whose face looked like a crumpled gunnysack. The painter began to pour him some tea, but Tian told him not to bother with that on his account and said he had to go to the toilet. He left the room, which grew silent as they waited for him to return. But when, after a spell, he still hadn't come back, the painter went looking for him. The gate was open, and Tian was nowhere in sight. Seeing that her uncle had left, Yingying followed, again in tears. The painter was so dismayed he couldn't stop oohing and ahing, and he was about to strike out at Golden Dog again when he caught himself and said, "Okay, okay, he's gone, which means we're in disgrace. How could you talk to him like that? No one has ever made him that mad. You and I are going over to his house, where I want you to hold your tongue except to ask his forgiveness and admit you were wrong. Tell him you'll never behave like that again."

Golden Dog remained as defiant as ever, until his father fell to his knees in front of him. That made him feel so sorry for the old man that he picked him up and, for his sake, agreed to go with him to the Tian home in Stream of Wandering Spirits. But the gate was closed when they got there, and no one inside responded to their knocks and shouts. Father and son kept at it for nearly an hour, but though they heard someone cough inside, no one came out.

"Father," Golden Dog finally asked, "why should we be so submissive? You're my father—which means that you and Tian are of the same generation. In fact, you're several years his senior. We've been calling to them all this time, but they won't open the gate or answer our cries. What else are we supposed to do?"

They returned home, Golden Dog helping his father as he hobbled along execrating his son every step of the way.

"We don't need somebody like Yingying in our family," Golden Dog said. "She wants to marry me, but she doesn't really love me."

"Nonsense! Would she have let you be first in line for the job if she hadn't loved you?"

"That was all part of their scheme. The people at the newspaper told me what went on behind the scenes. They hadn't wanted her in the first place."

The painter, nursing his low spirits, said, "Even if it was a scheme, you were engaged for such a long time. How can you break it off with just a word?"

"We hardly ever wrote to each other; then she fired a letter off to my boss as soon as a problem arose. She demanded that I be sent back to my village!"

"Is that the truth?"

"Would I lie to my own father? My boss wasn't ready to believe her, so he forwarded her letter to me."

When the painter heard this side of the story, he began to recover his trust in his son and to thunder against Yingying's cruel streak: "How could she be so malicious? After all it took for you to land that job, where does she get off thinking she can act like that just because things didn't work out between the two of you?"

Father and son walked the remaining distance without speaking, and the silence continued once they got home, where they sat quietly across from each other until they heard the crowing of a rooster.

"Get some sleep, Golden Dog," the painter said. "No matter what you say, this business was your fault in the first place. The Tian family occupies a high position, higher than most people can climb. I guarantee you that Tian Zhongzheng won't let this matter drop. Just you wait. Sooner or later he'll find a way to get even with us. The only talent your father has is daubing paint on things, a job people look down on. I don't care if Tian Zhongzheng makes a target of me, but you have your whole life ahead of you. You'll have to be careful!"

Golden Dog helped his father over to the kang to get some sleep. All night long he listened to his father sigh and grumble, "You haven't seen much of the world, and don't know enough about human relations!" His tears in the darkness soaked the pillow.

It was midnight; the mountain watchdogs were howling.

17

March. A downpour fell on the banks of the Zhou River for several days; it was the beginning of the spring rains. After letting up for a while, the embarrassed skies opened up again, as though suddenly angered, sending down sheets of threadlike rain that covered the surface of the river like a gauze net anchored by the wild peach trees dressed in their spring reds on the banks. Han Wenju was forced to tie up his ferryboat at the rocky landing and go over to Fuyun's to eat and while away the hours playing dominoes. The stakes were two ounces of strong wine per match; Han, who won far less than he lost, cursed the bad omens of the year: "I must have rubbed the nun's cunt!" He went over to the monastery at Restless Hill to have the abbot tell his fortune.

The abbot was in meditation and would not be disturbed, so Han squatted down on the steps of one of the outer buildings and chewed the fat with the short painter.

"Shorty," he said, "why make your life any harder than it is? During the rainy season you should stay home sleeping all day instead of coming out to slave away for somebody. Maybe you don't care about your own image, but aren't you afraid of what you're doing to that of your son, the reporter?"

The painter merely smiled. Ever since the relationship between Golden Dog and Water Girl had fallen through, he'd done his best to avoid Han Wenju, whose rapierlike tongue would have made him feel miserable. Sure enough, Han hit him where it hurt: "Shorty, has Golden Dog decided now that he doesn't want Yingying either? I guess that since he's a hotshot reporter, he plans to bring home a fancy girl from town."

The painter swallowed a mouthful of multihued saliva and said,

"Uncle Han, how can anyone wield control over young people these days? Since you're not going out on the river, why don't you stop by my place for a drink sometime?" He gathered up his brushes and paints and walked off.

"What's your hurry, Shorty?" Han called out after him. "Do you have a new wife waiting at home? I want to ask you something. Has Golden Dog mentioned anything about changes coming down from above? You folks are closer to the makers of government policy!"

The painter tried to get away as quickly as possible.

But Han wasn't through. "Where are you going?" he shouted. "Guilty conscience? I'm Han Wenju, not the local party secretary or some hungry animal!"

The news that Golden Dog had broken off his engagement with Yingying had struck Han like a bolt from the blue. He was utterly agape. How could Golden Dog *not* want a girl from the Tian family? And how could Tian Zhongzheng condescend by going to Golden Dog's place to try to mend matters? After the initial surprise, however, he began to feel happy about the way things had turned out. If an alliance were struck between the local party secretary and a reporter from town, life would become very difficult for everyone else and Han would no longer feel free to speak his mind. By the look of things, Golden Dog really didn't fear the Tians; three mountains facing one another—the Tians, the Gongs, and Golden Dog, just the way it was during the Three Kingdom period. The situation around the Zhou River might turn very chaotic, or things might really settle down. And so little measures of disrespect crept into Han's dealings with the Tians, and he made a point of ragging the short painter whenever he saw him.

The abbot had completed his meditation. "Wenju," he said when he emerged, "what a sinner you are! Are you trying to make life impossible for Golden Dog's father? The Buddha is embodied in the green stalks of the bamboo, the bodhi is found in lush yellow flowers!"

"What kind of weird talk is that, Abbot? No one knows what you're saying."

"The world of mortals is a killing field! This business of Golden Dog's marriage has offended both the Han and the Tian families. A few days ago Secretary Tian's daughter was so upset she went into a frenzy in front of the painter."

Han laughed loudly. "It's their own fault! They're no match for us

Hans! Tell me what harm I did to Shorty by asking an honest question about government policies."

"You're too interested in worldly affairs. I wonder when you'll finally lay down your killing knife and become a Buddha! Four words—*everything is but emptiness*—are enough to define the mortal world! Why are you always looking for trouble?"

"You monks are always talking about emptiness. But what do you mean by it?"

"Emptiness takes many forms. There is inner emptiness, outer emptiness, inner-outer emptiness, the emptiness of activity, the emptiness of inactivity, the emptiness of no beginning, the emptiness of essentiality, the emptiness of nothingness, the emptiness of original meaning, the emptiness of emptiness, and the great emptiness. Wenju, you should come over more often and let me instruct you in the scriptures."

"But I'm not one of your monks," Han said. "I've got Water Girl and Fuyun. If we have to deal with all this emptiness, what's the use in living?"

"That's where you're wrong. It's worldly affairs that are empty. Buddha, scriptures, monks, and enlightenment embody constancy, joy, self, and purity, and unnamed emptinesses."

"Don't talk to me about that stuff, Abbot. You can brag all you want about your monks, but you won't see me becoming one. I've seen pictures of the Central Committee in the newspaper, and their faces radiate the spirit of an orderly world. We'll not see war and chaos again as long as I live! Water Girl and Fuyun are good to me. Too bad they don't have greater aptitudes. All Fuyun knows how to do is pole his raft up and down the river, and it doesn't look like the good times are coming. What bothers me is that even though there's nothing particularly wrong with current government policy, the mood of the people couldn't be worse. Our leaders are going to have to come up with something to turn that around!"

"Okay. Let's forget about Buddhist affairs for the moment," the abbot said, "and talk about worldly affairs. Wenju, you've forgotten what you're supposed to be doing. You're a ferryman!"

Han was taken aback momentarily and merely lowered his head to drink the tea the abbot had steeped for him. "But look what's happened these past six months," he finally said. "The people are like black-eyed chickens. The rich get richer, and the poor get poorer. Tian Zhongzheng talks about helping the people get rich, and the shipping brigade has done well. But Fuyun takes out his rafts, and either there's no cargo to bring back or when he brings some back, he can't sell it. That Cai Da'an is burying us alive. The taxes are exorbitant, and everyone has his hand out. Once the money is handed over, the person gives you a receipt and leaves. The Tian family say their power is nearly exhausted, but their authority remains, and meanwhile they're getting rich. Do you know how much Tian Zhongzheng's taken out of the shipping brigade? Just look at the new tiles on his roof and you'll see: his house looks like your monastery! Look at the history of promotions in his family. Nearly every one of them has an official position in White Rock Stockade. Yingying told someone at the ferry landing that if her uncle weren't so old, he'd probably already be working in the county government. I remember what it was like in the old days, and I've seen statues of Chiang Kai-shek. Awesome-looking? You bet he was! But he still fell from power. I read once that the Chiang dynasty fell for two reasons: first, his petticoat influences ruined officials at all levels; and second, there was runaway inflation. You're a learned man, Abbot. Does that make sense to you?"

The abbot was listening attentively to Han Wenju, a literate man who had seen a great deal on his boat and was a good talker. They had always got along well. Setting aside Buddhist concerns for the moment, he said, "Wenju, life has not been good to you. Did you ever act in plays as a young man?"

"Yes, I did. I played a high prefectural official, a man in a peacock hat!"

The abbot brought his hands together and said, "That's what I'm talking about. You have the ability to be an official, but you ruined your chances by going on the stage!"

That threw Han deeper into his gloom. "I've had an unsuccessful life," he said dejectedly, "and I've passed it on to Water Girl. The geomancy of Stream of Wandering Spirits favors the Gong and Tian families—plus the Han family, of course. Abbot, look at my face and tell my fortune. Is there any hope for someone with a forlorn look like this? Even in dominoes all I ever do is lose!"

The abbot did as he was bid, concluding bluntly that great riches were out of the question. But happily Han Wenju had a mole above the corner of his mouth, which the abbot called an "absorbing mole."

"That's right on the mark," Han said. "I never let a day pass without absorbing wine, mostly as penalties when I lose at dominoes. I've drunk more penalties than anybody else. I told Water Girl and Fuyun that even if someday they were so poor they had to go out begging, they'd never cut my drinking down."

There was more he felt like getting off his chest, but he heard some muted shouts and poured himself another glass of tea, never thinking the shouts had anything to do with him. Before long, a young cowherd stuck his head in the door and called, "Uncle Han, has all that tea ruined your hearing? Someone's yelling for you at the ferry landing. They've just about shouted themselves hoarse!"

"Why shout for me?" Han growled. "Can't they see how high the river is? Do they want me to come over and climb into their mother's bed?"

But growl or no, he strolled out of the monastery, and when he reached the grassy knoll of Restless Hill, he spotted a wild rabbit, its ears sticking straight up as it shook the water off its body. It scurried off at the sight of Han. If he could only catch it, he was thinking, it'd sure go nice with a little wine.

He reached the ferry landing, where he saw on the opposite bank three or four people headed to a birthday party at Tian Zhongzheng's. Hearing that the guests had arrived there, Tian's wife had come down to the ferry landing and was lavishing greetings on them. Han showed up in a foul mood. *In all my years no one's ever come to celebrate my birthday. Tian's only in his fifties, but he has a birthday party every year, with seven or eight tables of guests. An official's life is a bowl of cherries!* But what irritated him most was that during all those years, when the wine was flowing, Tian had never once invited him to join the fete. *Am I supposed to sell my soul for a few cups of his wine? I've got wine of my own!* So every year on this day he invited some of the villagers in to drink the night away; they'd see who could get more guests falling-down drunk. When he saw Tian's wife standing at the landing, he said, "The river's too high to put the boat out. Maybe my life's not worth anything, but you don't want to take chances with your guests."

"Forget the boat. Dakong's carrying them over on his back!"

He looked down into the water, where he saw two bobbing heads, one well above the water in front, a woman, and another, shaved clean, behind at the water line: Lei Dakong. "That's fine with me!" Han fired back, although he cursed Dakong for risking his life to get into the family's good graces.

Dakong had returned from Guangzhou a couple of weeks earlier, where he'd traded in silver and rare herbal medicines, expecting to make a killing. But he'd been picked up on the train, and the silver he was carrying in a bag around his waist had been confiscated; a gold ring he was hiding in his mouth had also come flying out, along with one of his teeth, as the result of a resounding slap. Not only had he lost his entire investment, he'd spent two weeks in jail and was released without a cent in his pocket; he was reduced to hitching rides and begging for food as he made his way home, looking more like a ghost than a man. He promptly became the butt of the villagers' jokes, but he went on looking, unsuccessfully, for another way to make a living. Those were trying days. Han was shocked by the sight of Dakong carrying the woman out of the water and onto the riverbank, for he was as naked as the day he was born. The woman, who was still young, was shivering as she emerged from the water, and she covered her face with her hands. Tian Zhongzheng's wife stood ready to throw a blanket around her, then ran into the village with her. Lei Dakong drank some wine from a bottle, wiped the water from his belly and crotch, then dived back into the water and swam across for the next person.

"Dakong!" Han Wenju expostulated. "You damned sinner. What's wrong with you, carrying her without wearing a stitch of clothing?"

Dakong smiled from the middle of the river. "Jealous, Uncle Han? She had to choose between seeing me naked and staying on the other side of the river—between modesty and Tian Zhongzheng's party! How I got her across was my business, and she had to pay what I asked."

He carried two men over, then went back for the other woman, a virginal, lovely young thing. When they were halfway there, she suddenly screeched, and everyone, in turning to look, saw both heads sink beneath the surface. After they bobbed up, there were no more screeches. She didn't make another sound. But once out of the water, she turned and let go at Dakong: "Pervert!" Dakong snapped back in the filthiest language he could think of. Tian Zhongzheng's wife interposed, threw five yuan down onto the bank, grabbed the guest's hand, and led her toward the village. Han handed Dakong his clothes so he could get dressed and asked why she'd used the epithet she did. Dakong smiled. "I just wonder why she's so eager to help Tian Zhongzheng celebrate his birthday," he said after a moment. "I'd like to know if she calls Tian a pervert when he sticks it to her!"

Han Wenju invited his friends in to drink with him that night, as always, and Lei Dakong was among them. He was wearing a pair of trousers made from a devotional flag he'd stolen from the monastery and dyed. But the dye hadn't completely covered the words on the flag; there on one of the legs the word *request* showed up clearly; the seat of his pants sported the words "grant my." Water Girl doubled over with laughter. "Elder Brother Dakong," she said, "you're quite the fellow. Is this how you're planning to get through life?"

Dakong wasn't fazed. "Do you know what I wore in Guangzhou? A Western suit! But when my luck ran out, I sold everything to get home. But you wait. I'm going to put another stake together and get back on the road. This isn't the real Dakong you're looking at. On my next birthday, I'm going to have a banquet with eight or ten tables and become the second Tian Zhongzheng!"

"Where are you going to get your stake?" Water Girl asked. "Why don't you show Fuyun how you do it."

"I'm not sure at the moment."

That brought a laugh from everyone.

"Dakong," Han said, "remember what I'm about to tell you. In the ways of the world, a little fish in your bowl is better than a whopper out in the river. You have to start out small and go from there!"

"Enough of that, Uncle Han," Dakong said. "I know that better than you do. But where am I supposed to start? If I said I wanted to help you on the ferryboat, would you take me on?"

Han wasn't sure what to say.

When the meal was ready, Water Girl started frying some pickled cabbage, then stepped outside to pick some garlic shoots.

It was getting late by then, and the moon was bright and clear. As Tian Zhongzheng, who was seeing his guests off, passed by, his eye rested on the hips of a girl bending over to pick garlic shoots. From what he could see, she was full figured and lovely. Dazzled by the sight, which reminded him of Lu Cuicui, he stopped in his tracks. For whatever reason, since Golden Dog and Yingying had broken off their engagement he couldn't get his mind off Cuicui. He still nursed a grievance against Golden Dog, who'd set in train the events that led to his casting her aside; then she'd been taken from this world. At the birthday party earlier that evening, he'd no sooner got a bit tipsy than he began cursing Golden Dog, soon turning his ire on Cai Da'an. When his wife tried to placate him, he slapped her in annoyance in front of everyone. Now he stood entranced by the woman in front of him, and he was about to call out Cuicui's name when a dog ran barking out the door. Water Girl straightened up and noticed Tian Zhongzheng. "Is that you, Secretary Tian? Where are you headed so late at night?"

Brought back to earth, he just sighed, although he couldn't help thinking again how much she resembled Cuicui. Water Girl repeated her question after she observed the blank look on his face.

"I had to see Yingying's eldest uncle home," he said after a moment. "He had so much to drink he could barely walk. I couldn't tell who you were at first, Water Girl. Over the past six months or so you've . . . grown up, without my realizing it." He nearly said, "filled out," as his eyes roamed across her shoulders, her breasts, her buttocks. He walked up to her. But the family dog snapped at him, and he squatted down as if looking for a rock. The dog retreated a few steps, but moved forward again as soon as Tian stood up. "Is he yours, Water Girl? He's mean! Why raise a vicious dog like this?"

An official's just another person to a dog, and this one had already sunk its teeth into Tian's heel, ripping the shoe if not breaking the skin. Water Girl laughed good-naturedly and finished picking the garlic shoots. "Dog!" she shouted "What's the big idea of biting Secretary Tian? You had lots of guests tonight, Secretary Tian, and you've had a bit too much to drink."

After putting his shoe back on, Tian stared at her and said, "Not that much, not much at all. How come you didn't stop by for a few drinks?" He took a few more clumsy steps forward, and the dog rushed him again, barking fiercely.

"With the sort of people who were over at your house, I'd be a real disappointment!" she said. "Uncle's inside drinking with some friends. Would you like to join them?"

"I'd better not, since he has guests. Water Girl, it's a good thing you got married. Now that you're married, you can . . ." He walked off with a limp.

Water Girl went inside with the image of Tian's nauseating condition stamped in her mind. She picked up a pig's ear from the table and tossed it to Dog as a reward for its sense of duty. "Dogs can tell good people from bad!" she said.

The men in the room were arguing with Lei Dakong, who was bewailing all that had happened to him. When Han Wenju heard Water Girl's comment, he asked her, "What are you grumbling about?"

"You have sharp ears, Uncle. I ran into Tian Zhongzheng outside, and the dog bit him."

"Why didn't you invite him in to have a look at the wine we've got?" Han asked her. "He could have watched us get drunk, and then he'd know what a real party is! Dakong, forget about striking it rich for now, and concentrate on drinking!"

"Uncle Han, you're in rare form today," someone commented. "Aren't you afraid of Tian Zhongzheng?"

"I'm afraid of people when there's reason to be, and not when there isn't. Why should I be afraid? I think these things out."

"Is it because you've noticed that Golden Dog is squaring off against the Tians again?"

"Fuck you! What's he done? You tell me how many times he's shot his mouth off at anyone in the Tian or Gong family. But me, except for eating three meals a day and drinking my wine, all this mouth of mine does is curse people at the ferry landing."

Water Girl carried the fried pickled cabbage in. "Uncle," she said, "you're a real chatterbox. Can't you talk about something serious?"

"Like what? I'd suffocate if I couldn't get this out of my system."

Ignoring him, she turned to Dakong and said, "If you're really interested in doing something, I've got an idea. Why not join up with Fuyun? With your mind and his work ethic, you could do fine and split the profits down the middle. What do you say?"

"Sounds good to me. Would you take me on, Fuyun?"

"Well, I am shorthanded, and Water Girl and I have talked about this before. We didn't say anything to you because we didn't think you'd be willing."

"Dakong," Han said, "my son-in-law's an honest man, so don't take advantage of him!"

"I'm not that evil," Dakong said. "And I'm no rabbit that eats the grass around its burrow. Instead of splitting the profits down the middle, we should each take thirty percent and let Uncle Han use the remaining ten to buy wine!" He picked up his glass and toasted Han.

The bird now had two heads. Fuyun and Dakong poled the rafts together. Fuyun, the older of the two, was a good-hearted man who wasn't afraid of hard work. The ingenious Dakong, grateful to his friends for coming to his aid when he needed it most, devoted himself to the business side of their enterprise, using his glib tongue to buy goods cheaply, then selling them at a high price; their profits far exceeded what they would have earned individually. Han was in an excellent mood now that he had plenty of wine and the knowledge that Fuyun wouldn't suffer at the hands of others out there. The ferryman spent his time at the landing talking with the abbot about the vicissitudes of life and the ways of Buddha.

One day, when he'd had more to drink than usual and was sleeping on his boat, he woke with a start and, in his befuddlement, saw two dogs standing far off on the beach. One was as black as ebony, the other as white as snow, and they had their heads together as if talking. How strange. Are dogs like people? he wondered. *What could they be talking about?* He listened carefully, and even though their barks and growls sounded like human speech, he couldn't make out a word. "Hey there!" he yelled, startling the dogs, who dived into the river and swam downstream. They disappeared from sight in no time, and the next thing he saw was a skiff coming toward him. Old Seven was standing on the prow.

"Old Seven!" He shouted. "Why didn't you fish those dogs out of the river?"

"What dogs? The only dog I see has a beard and is drinking wine in his cabin!"

Han didn't let the matter pass as a joke. When the skiff had tied up alongside, he asked, "You really didn't see any dogs? Two of them, one white and one black. They were standing on the beach talking, but as soon as I yelled at them, they jumped into the river and swam away."

Old Seven was holding his box with the white snake inside, and as Han went on, his face darkened. "Did you see it clearly? That's a bad sign! You're a literate man. Haven't you read that book *Tales of Yue Fei?* I heard it from a blind storyteller in White Rock Stockade twenty years ago. When General Yue Fei was in danger, he dreamed he saw two talking dogs, so he sought out a fortune-teller, who told him two talking dogs are the ideograph for prison, which signifies the calamity of imprisonment. Later on, that's exactly what happened to him. General Yue only dreamed he saw them, but you saw them with your own two eyes. Why did you have to see something like that?"

Frightened by what Old Seven had revealed, Han thought immediately of Fuyun and Dakong out on their raft. He himself worked the ferry, and when there were passengers, he took them across, but when there weren't any, he kept his boat tied up. He charged them five fen and entertained them with his chatter and his jokes, without arguing with them. He didn't want to go to prison, and there wasn't much chance he'd ever have to. But Fuyun now had Dakong on his raft; and who knew what might happen in that guy's dealings with other people? Han was too distraught to speak. Looking at the box in Old Seven's hands, he noticed that the white snake was slithering around inside, trying to get out onto the deck. He reached over and shoved it back. "Old Seven," he said, "you haven't seen Fuyun, have you? They took a load of varnish seeds to Purple Thistle Pass, and they should have been back today."

"I haven't seen them," Old Seven said. "Wenju, I told you long ago that you ought to try to get Fuyun and Dakong into the shipping brigade. That might not increase their profits, but they could sail under its protection. If they're on their own, and they run into . . . well, Fuyun's not very smart, and you can't depend upon Dakong. Now, if it were Golden Dog, you wouldn't have anything to worry about."

"Don't talk to me about him!"

"Okay, I won't. But don't tell anyone you saw a couple of talking dogs. The abbot's a friend of yours, so go over and light some incense and ask him to do an exorcism."

Han Wenju, who wasn't in as high spirits as he'd been in recent days, said, "I'll go right away. Would you lend me your river god? Fuyun and Dakong are still young, and I hate to think that something might happen . . ."

After an awkward pause, Old Seven said, "All right, but with this river god, halfhearted offerings aren't enough. When Fuyun and Dakong get back, they can take it to White Rock Stockade and perform kowtows at the Smooth Seas Temple, then go to Purple Thistle Pass and do the same thing at the Smooth Seas Temple there. I'll come for it in five days."

Han was extremely grateful. He fell to his knees and held the box with both hands, then took it to the Restless Hill Monastery, where he asked the abbot to intone a chant, spray it with clear water, and draw three tallies, one to paste above Fuyun's door, one to put inside his jacket pocket, and the final one for Dakong's jacket pocket. When he was finished, the abbot said, "You see how many calamities exist in your mortal world?"

"It's because of all the ghosts sent down from the Buddhist heavens!" Han said. "Living people have enough goddamned problems, but since we've lived this long, what's the purpose in killing yourself by banging your head against a wall? It's lucky for us you're here at Restless Hill, and I hope you'll keep us on the straight and narrow."

Fuyun and Dakong had returned by the time Han got home. When he told them what had happened, it made Fuyun very nervous. "Dakong and I have just begun enjoying the fruits of our cooperation, and we sure don't need any trouble now! Dakong, we haven't disturbed the natural order of things, have we?"

"How could we disturb the natural order of anything by making a living by the sweat of our own brows?"

"Then why do you think Uncle Han saw something as strange as that?"

"I don't believe in that stuff! It was all a figment of his drunken imagination."

"Then why did the abbot draw up those tallies?"

"That bald-pated donkey doesn't do anything all day long but read the scriptures and go around telling fortunes and drawing tallies! I've seen plenty of fortune-tellers in Purple Thistle Pass, and I've seen the books they use. They divide people into nine categories. When you add the year, month, and day of birth together and divide by nine, that number determines the category. There's a saying that goes, Objects are divided into categories, people are brought together in crowds. Now, there might be something to dividing people into categories, but that doesn't tell me anything I don't already know. I can tell you all about people by their appearance. If somebody looks like an ox, you treat them like an ox, and if they look like a rat, you treat them like a rat. It never fails. Oxen, horses, pigs, dogs, rats, and snakes are all animals, and so are people, so what's the difference? Do you believe that? Uncle Han says he saw some dogs talking. Well, of course dogs talk. It's just that we can't understand what they're saying. You say dogs talk like humans? Well, humans talk like dogs, too. Bow-wow. Isn't that dog talk? How can somebody come up with the wild idea that that signifies prison? In Chinese, the word *good* is made up of the characters for 'female' and 'person.' Does that mean that all female people are good? How about Yingying and her mother? The word *male* is made up of the characters for 'field' and 'strength.' Does that mean that all men work the fields? Tian Zhongzheng and Gong Baoshan haven't worked in the fields a day in their lives. Does that mean they're not male? It's all bullshit!"

"Dakong!" Han Wenju grumbled. "You roamed from place to goddamned place for years, and you can outtalk me. Don't believe in this sign if you don't want to. But Fuyun, as my son-in-law, is supposed to do what I tell him. Anyone who doesn't listen to his elders is in for a rude comeuppance!"

Not venturing to disobey his father-in-law, Fuyun stuck the tally in the sack beneath his shirt.

For ten days running, the river was calm and the rafts sailed it without incident. Han's worries gradually diminished.

Some time later, Fuyun and Dakong bought two raftloads of unfinished hemp in the upper reaches of the Zhou River, which they brought back, and left in the shallow water beneath the ferry landing until it began to decay and stink. The poles on which it was hung started to rot, and Water Girl spent the better part of every day pounding it with a mallet on a rock at the water's edge, then washing it off and hanging it up as clean hemp threads to dry in the sun.

One particularly hot day she took off her jacket, tied her hair and let it hang down her back, and stood barefoot in the water, bending over at the waist. She heard someone shouting for her uncle, and when she looked toward the ferry landing, the blinding rays of the sun blurred whoever it was. "Do you want to cross the river?" she shouted. "Uncle went home to get something. You'll have to wait a few moments."

"Is that you, Water Girl?" the person said as he walked toward her. It was Tian Zhongzheng. Ever since discovering the resemblance between Water Girl and Lu Cuicui, he experienced a twinge every time he saw Water Girl. The loathing he felt for Golden Dog was somehow inverted into a strange compulsion to talk to Water Girl. He asked her if the water was cold, and what price the hemp would command in Purple Thistle Pass.

"According to Fuyun, it will sell for thirty-six fen a catty," she said. "It's a good profit, but I've had to put a lot of time into pounding and washing it."

"That Fuyun sure has a racket. He goes off to White Rock Stockade with the profits, to fill his belly with good food and wine, and leaves you here working yourself to an early grave."

"Fuyun's too good a man to do something like that."

"Dakong would do it, even if Fuyun wouldn't. You learn from the people you're with. It's different in the river shipping brigade, where everybody works under supervision. Don't let him take advantage of you, Water Girl!"

She assumed he was just making conversation and didn't take him seriously. She continued pounding and washing the hemp as they talked, when she suddenly noticed a candy wrapper floating in the water. She looked up at Tian and saw that he had a piece of candy in his mouth.

"Water Girl," he said, "here's one for you. It comes from Zhou City. It has a liqueur center. Try it, it tastes just like a liqueur."

He tossed her a piece of candy, and as she caught it, she could tell that he was transfixed by her naked calves. She quickly moved into deeper water and said, "My teeth are no good. I can't eat candy." She pitched the offering back to him.

Tian sat down dejectedly and gazed over at the ferry landing.

"Water Girl," he said, "come see me any time your family has problems. After all, I'm the party secretary and I can do more for you than Fuyun can. Just come see me."

"We have no problems," she maintained, keeping her head lowered.

Han arrived at the ferry landing and bellowed that he was ready to take the boat over, so Tian stood up and went aboard, singing a sappy flower-drum aria. After docking on the return, Han came and helped Water Girl gather up the clean, dried hemp and store it in a rickety shed at the landing. "What was Tian Zhongzheng talking to you about just now?" he asked her.

"Nothing," she said. "Uncle, after we sell this hemp, I'm going to make you a new set of clothes."

Han looked at his niece tenderly. "If you hadn't said anything, I'd have asked you for some clothes. But since you've said it, I don't want any. What do I need nice clothes for? Buy some clothes for yourself. You're still young, and you don't want people making snide remarks." The two of them, belonging to different generations, seldom had intimate talks, so they turned to a discussion of things like provisions for the house. But the fleeting demonstration of their mutual attachment had nearly brought tears to their eyes. Finally, she sat quietly beside the old man on the boat and watched the sun sink beneath the horizon upriver, leaving behind a colorful blaze. Just as night was about to fall, a fog spread out from the foot of the mountain.

"Water Girl," Han said, "I'm a man of few skills, and when I see the Tian family wearing fancy clothes and eating so well, I feel I've let you down."

"Don't talk like that, Uncle. Things are a lot better these days, and provided nothing happens to Fuyun's raft, someday we'll be as well off as the Tians."

That reminded Han of the sight of the talking dogs, and he drifted into melancholy.

Water Girl, who was walking up the riverbank, told him to come along home since there'd be no more passengers that night. But he sat there thinking.

"What's wrong"? she asked.

"Nothing," he replied with a smile, as he got up and headed off with his niece.

18

The hemp was sold in Purple Thistle Pass at a good price, to the delight of all. Fuyun returned home after dark, immediately undressed, and climbed up onto the kang. "Water Girl," he said, "come over here. I have some good news for you."

"Get some sleep," she said. "You must be tired."

"It's about Golden Dog," he said.

She pricked up her ears but kept her back to him and didn't betray her interest.

"Dakong and I ran into him today in White Rock Stockade. He hasn't changed a bit. He took us both out to lunch."

Water Girl rolled over. "You let him buy you lunch? You have money of your own. You're hopeless!"

That didn't sit well with Fuyun, who said, "What's wrong with you? Still mad at him? I don't care what you say, he's a good man."

Fuyun's reaction stilled Water Girl's qualms, but she couldn't help thinking about his "rival" of times past; a few hot tears slid silently down her cheeks. She held him tightly. "As long as you understand him, I'm happy. He is a good man, he really is, but I don't want you to mention him again."

"Are you afraid I'll be upset over your relationship with him? We grew up together, so of course I understand him. That's why I got so mad when he visited Uncle on his boat after he came home but didn't come see us."

"I'm glad he didn't come see us," she said after a long pause. "On the way back from town that night, Second Auntie Wang told me he'd returned, and I seriously considered going to see him. But I didn't. I was afraid to. I wouldn't have known what to say. Fuyun, let's not talk about the past."

"We don't have to talk about the past, but you have to admit he's done well. You know it was his story that was responsible for the provincial government's sending cadres into the poorest mountain districts. He's made the people of Stream of Wandering Spirits proud. He took us to lunch so we could meet a cadre who's been assigned to the Shaman Mountain area."

"I heard about that man," Water Girl said. "A few days ago, at the ferry landing, I saw dozens of men with walking sticks over their shoulders on their way to Crossroads Township. They said they were from Shaman Mountain."

"That's what I'm talking about. Those mountain folk never knew the meaning of the word *commerce*. They just ate what they planted, and when outsiders came to see the local products, they fed them and gave them what they wanted and wouldn't take their money for it. They believed that respectable people didn't engage in buying and selling. They were so poor they couldn't even buy salt. But after the cadre was assigned there, the first thing he did was take a group of them into Crossroads Township and White Rock Stockade to let them see for themselves; then he had them cut down branches for walking sticks and take them to Crossroads Township to sell. But the market there is extremely limited, so when we told Golden Dog we needed more goods to haul, he introduced us to the resident cadre of Shaman Mountain. We struck a deal right off, and he's going to have the mountain folk deliver their walking sticks to the ferry landing. We'll buy the whole lot and ship them to White Rock Stockade and Purple Thistle Pass. The mountain folk will make a profit, and so will we."

"Is that true?" Water Girl sat up and asked excitedly.

"If I'm lying, I hope I'll drown in the Zhou River!"

She pouted and told him not to say things like that. Her eyes flashed in the darkness as she mumbled, "I'm glad Golden Dog went to work at the newspaper. But he was doing so well in Zhou City. What's he doing back in White Rock Stockade?"

"When I asked him, he just smiled and said that being at the White Rock Stockade bureau gives him a greater understanding of what's really going on. The office is located on Western Avenue. You know the place. Reporters have a lot of power. The party secretary of Dongyang County was thrown out because of that story of his, and people in White Rock Stockade are beginning to say that a reporter's pen is a sword that can vanquish evil!"

"If he can topple the party secretary of Dongyang County, why can't he do the same to the Tian family?"

"Dakong says that's precisely why Golden Dog came to the local bureau. Maybe he's hit the nail on the head."

Water Girl closed her eyes to get some sleep, but there were too many things on her mind. "What else did you and Golden Dog talk about?"

"He wanted to know what was going on in the village and how we were doing. When your name came up, he apologized for the way he'd treated you and said he'd sent three or four letters to the blacksmith shop but that they'd all been returned unopened. He wanted to buy a wedding gift but was afraid it would bring back painful memories for you."

"Painful memories? He probably forgot all about me." She had begun to sob.

Fuyun reached out to wipe away her tears with his rough hand.

"What else did you talk about? Tell me," she went on.

"He told me to love you with all my heart. As if I needed him to tell me that! And he said he hoped we'd come see him the next time we're in White Rock Stockade. Why don't you ride over there someday on the raft?"

"I don't think that's a good idea . . . Did he say if he'd found a wife yet?"

"No, and when I asked him, he changed the subject."

"He's not getting any younger. How long does he plan to put it off?" She rested her head against Fuyun's chest and stared into the dark.

Their pillow talk continued late into the night, until they finally fell asleep. Early the next morning they went down to the ferry landing to wait for the men from Shaman Mountain to come with their walking sticks. At breakfast time twenty mountaineers showed up, dressed in tattered clothes and presenting a look of simplicity and guilelessness. Each was carrying a thick bundle of sticks over his shoulder, and their shirts were soaked with sweat. The price they charged for the walking sticks was twenty-five fen apiece, and when the hard cash exchanged hands, the mountaineers beamed and marked their tallies by wetting their fingers with saliva. When the sale was completed, they took off their their worn-out straw sandals and threw them away, then boarded Han Wenju's ferryboat to go to Crossroads Township to buy new shoes, new clothes, salt, and oil. When they returned from their frenzied shopping trip, many of them were wearing plastic rain boots. "You mountain folk are really something," Han said. "Why did you buy those? Don't they roast your feet?"

The rain boots were causing feet to sweat in the heat, and some of the men poured water into them, so that they made a squishing sound with each step. "These are great!" one of them said. "We can wear them when the sun's out *and* when it's raining! If you keep buying our walking sticks, we'll be able to afford real leather shoes in another six months!" They strode off triumphantly.

As Dakong watched them go, he said, "Uncle Han, those mountaineers in their plastic rainboots are a real sight. They're so hot they have to keep pouring water in them. They sure haven't seen much of the world!"

"Seeing them like that breaks my heart," Han replied. "We complain about how poor we are, but compared with them we're on easy street. They're so far behind everyone else. I wonder why it took them so long to learn a thing or two about commerce. They're just starting to wake up."

"And only because of the cadre sent there to organize them," Dakong said. "At this rate, though, they'll be rich someday. Let's take these walking sticks to White Rock Stockade and Purple Thistle Pass so we can make our share."

"Dakong, how did you manage something as lucrative as this?"

"With Golden Dog's help. His great instincts and his access to information were what let us pull it off."

The name was enough to spark an outburst that hit even the short painter. Han vowed never to seek help from either father or son, no matter how bad things got.

"Uncle Han, you don't still hate Golden Dog, do you?" Dakong asked. "He isn't Tian Zhongzheng's son-in-law, so it doesn't make sense."

"It does when you consider what he did to my Water Girl."

"You're being spiteful, Uncle Han. Aren't you satisfied with Fuyun? Hasn't he been bringing you wine? You can make a sworn enemy of Golden Dog if you want to, but he's helping us turn a profit, and that's good enough for us. Are you afraid the money will get between us?"

Han Wenju laughed. "Dakong, everybody says I've got a mouth like a steel trap, but it's no match for yours! As soon as you see Golden Dog, you lay it on about how I'm always badmouthing him, and tell him he doesn't scare me."

"How could anyone scare somebody who brags as much as you do? Uncle Han, you've got a mouth of steel and a rubber asshole!"

The sale of the load of walking sticks produced a tidy profit, and that was followed by several more trips. After Water Girl set up a ledger, a man from the township revenue bureau came to collect the taxes, the village chief came to collect local school taxes, the village cadre bureau claimed its fees, and the people's school tax came due. Fuyun erupted in anger: "The damned turnip's being sliced from both ends. How are we going to make a profit? The money goes so fast there's nothing left for us!"

"How can you say that?" the man from the revenue bureau asked him. "Schools are part of social welfare!"

"First we support the local teachers; then we have to give money to the schools. But I don't have any children at all, let alone kids in school. And since it's welfare, how come you collect from every household?"

It was the other man's turn to get angry. "Rich people in other areas give tens of thousands to the schools, knowing that in the long run it'll pay off. But you're not willing to make the slightest investment in the future."

"Who said I'm rich? Are you conferring the title on me?"

Things were clearly getting out of hand, so Water Girl pulled Fuyun away with an apologetic smile to the revenue man and even invited him to stay for lunch.

With their expenses mounting, Fuyun and Dakong worked day and night. But then one day the men from Shaman Mountain stopped bringing their walking sticks down to the ferry landing, and the shipping brigade transported loads of them for several days running. When Dakong asked around, he learned that Cai Da'an and Tian Yishen had discovered the source of Fuyun's profits and had decided to cut themselves in. They quietly made an agreement with the mountaineers and set up a procurement station in a village behind Restless Hill. The mountaineers were happy to put their trust in a collective, and the agreement saved them from making the long trip to the river. Incensed, Fuyun and Dakong raised the price they'd pay for the walking sticks to twenty-seven fen, and once again the people from Shaman Mountain sold their wares to them.

While they were poling downriver to Purple Thistle Pass with their load of walking sticks one day, Dakong spotted Tian Yishen on the bank and sang out from his perch on the lead raft, "Rafts on the river . . . !"

But Fuyun didn't echo his taunt from the rear.

"Why aren't you shouting?" Dakong called to him.

"Dakong, Tian Yishen's mad enough already, and if we get too insolent, he'll find a way to get even with us."

"How's he going to do that?" Dakong asked him. "Offer thirty fen apiece? The boatmen in the river shipping brigade are already upset with him for stealing business from us, and if he raises the buying price, they'll rebel. I hope I make him so mad he explodes!" Once again, he shouted from the prow, "Rafts on the river . . . !" and this time he was echoed by Fuyun on the stern: "Rafts on the river . . . !" Then they started chanting in unison, sometimes loud, sometimes soft, sometime slow, sometimes fast, keeping up a steady rhythm.

Tian Yishen and Cai Da'an reported the provocation to Tian Zhongzheng, who was so angry he could barely speak. "It's my own fault for losing our strategic advantage and leaving an opening in the dragon gate for Golden Dog to swim through. It's obvious he's come back to tangle with me!"

"Since they found this source of commodities," Tian Yishen said, "let them have it. We can find one of our own."

"Just what do you think you're going to find?" Tian Zhongzheng shot back.

"If we fail, then let the damned river shipping brigade break up!" Tian Yishen said. "We've already made plenty."

"Quit talking through your ass!" Tian growled at him. "Now that you've made a tidy sum for yourself, you're talking about disbanding the shipping brigade. Well, if you get the boatmen mad, you'll be sorry! The county government is banking on our making a success of the shipping brigade, so if we disband it, what will we say to the county committee? I've sent a report on the experiences of the brigade up to it, and it's planning a big public meeting for us. How in the world do you think we could disband it?

"All right," Tian Yishen said, "so they plan to hold a public meeting. But if we can't find a source of goods and don't turn a profit, what are we going to say at the meeting?"

"That's why we have to increase our income. I want you two to come up with something."

After the dressing-down by Tian Zhongzheng, Tian Yishen and Cai Da'an spent a worried night over a bottle of wine but couldn't put together a workable plan. All they did was get good and drunk. The next morning, Tian Zhongzheng summoned them to the township government office. They were both sleeping off their drunk when the messenger arrived, but they jumped out of bed, stuck their finger down their throat to clear their head, and rushed over to the government office. When Tian asked what plan they'd contrived, they were tongue-tied.

"Just as I expected," he said with a grin. "So I devised a plan of my own during the night, one that will cut off Fuyun and Dakong's source of goods without affecting our profits."

As soon as he had spelled out the details of his plan, Tian and Cai took steps to put it into action.

Three days later, on market day at Crossroads Township, the men from Shaman Mountain showed up without their walking sticks, bringing instead a load of lumber to sell. Tian Yishen and Cai Da'an had announced that in order to build some houses, the township government would buy up all the available lumber. From then on, every three or four days the men brought a load of lumber down from the mountain and piled it high in the government compound. Fuyun and Dakong smelled something fishy and wondered what sort of buildings the government had in mind that required so much timber. When they asked the men from Shaman Mountain to restore the supply of walking sticks, they balked: "We get as much for one load of lumber as we did for three or four loads of walking sticks!" There was nothing Fuyun or Dakong could do. Later that day, Han Wenju came by to tell them that some boats from the shipping brigade were heading downriver piled high with lumber.

"That fucking Tian Zhongzheng has stuck it to us again!" Dakong screamed. "Well, all right, if he can deal in lumber, so can we! Since the law's being broken, we might as well break it right along with Tian Zhongzheng."

"You can't do that," Han said. "Old Seven says they've set up an inspection point at the White Rock Stockade landing, and the lumber agents won't even talk to you without a permit. The river shipping brigade's using permits issued by the township government. How are you going to get one?"

At their wits' end, all Fuyun and Dakong could do was bemoan their fate and vilify Tian Zhongzheng.

"What good does that do?" Water Girl asked them. "What they're up to is illegal, and we're not going to get involved in skulduggery like that. But we won't allow them to get away with it either. Go get Golden Dog. Since he's a reporter, listen to what he has to say."

That night Fuyun and Dakong sailed for White Rock Stockade.

Golden Dog had already heard that the county committee was planning to hold a public meeting, but he didn't have grounds for interfering, no matter how angry or worried he might be. But when he heard that the shipping brigade was dealing in lumber, he smiled.

"What do you say?" Dakong asked him. "As a reporter you can bring charges against the Tian family, can't you?"

Golden Dog replied, "Now that I know what's going on, you can head back and feel easy about obeying the law yourselves."

"We don't have anything to ship," Dakong said. "If we have to go back empty, we might as well dismantle our rafts."

"Here, I'll give you a note to a Mr. Zhang at Hotel Number Two, near the western gate. He's a purchasing agent for Zhouville who came to see me a couple of days ago to check on the economic news and to tell me he'd bought some porcelain but didn't know how to ship it home. It's very fragile. Can you handle it?"

"No big deal," Dakong boasted. "We'd handle gold and silver if we had the chance."

"I knew you'd say that," Golden Dog encouraged them with a grin. "But be careful. It's a six-day round trip, and when you get back, be sure to come see me. I'll treat you to a flower-drum opera."

"Are we supposed to drop the matter of Tian Zhongzheng and the lumber?" Dakong asked. "If you find a way to get him on this one, I'll treat *you* to the opera!"

Golden Dog laughed. "It's a deal. Fuyun, you're my witness."

After they left, Golden Dog went straight to the White Rock Stockade industrial and commercial management bureau, where he was enthusiastically received by the young bureau chief as soon as he saw the reporter's ID. In response to the functionary's helpfulness, Golden Dog mentioned that he'd already heard about the young man's recent assignment and that, since everyone was talking about the improved situation, he'd come to interview him for a story. After the formalities had been dispatched, the bureau chief called in a group of grass-roots cadres to tell Golden Dog about the industrial and commercial management work they were involved in. Golden Dog took careful notes. "You're doing a fine job," he said when they had finished, "and a lot of your experiences are very much worth publicizing. The markets are flourishing these days, our market economy is running smoothly, and now that the river is wide open, things are really humming. But as your workload increases, how do you find time to oversee some of the smaller private industries?"

The bureau chief said, "We have that well in hand. I'll give you an example. In the past, the purchase of mountain products was state-controlled, and the system was just too cumbersome. Now that policies have been relaxed, the peasants are being encouraged to participate in the business end. The scope of their activity is sometimes too small, though, and we've taken it upon ourselves to furnish them with information. But we deal harshly with those who don't pay taxes or who get involved in illegal activities. We can't turn a blind eye to that."

"That sounds wonderful!" Golden Dog exclaimed. "It's a good way to strengthen market management."

"But market management by itself isn't enough," the bureau chief said. "Take lumber, for instance. Government policy permits the peasants to buy and sell a certain amount in the market, but under no circumstances are they permitted to ship it out of the area of origin without permission. We've set up checkpoints to inspect all vehicular traffic. But since some people set out in the middle of the night with their loads, we're working with the lumber companies to man the checkpoints day and night."

"Where have you set up the checkpoints?" Golden Dog asked him.

He gave the names of several spots. Golden Dog directed a look of puzzlement at him. "Those are all on highways. Don't you have any on the river?"

The bureau chief turned to his subordinates, who replied that there weren't any.

"According to my information," Golden Dog said, "traffic on the Zhou River has been on the rise in recent years, and you're planning on setting up a water transport company, I believe, with checkpoints at several strategic ports. Several public-spirited fellows came to the newspaper bureau the other day with information that some boats are transporting lumber. I wonder if they have permits to ship it out of their area."

The bureau chief and his subordinates exchanged glances, and he dressed them down for neglecting their duty to keep him informed, and for not going about their work seriously. "You reporters are on top of everything!" he flattered. "I'm embarrassed that you have to keep us on our toes. We'll send someone to the landing at the southern gate right away, and if someone's shipping lumber illegally, we'll confiscate their cargo! The next step will be to devise a concrete maritime management policy. Comrade reporter, we'll give you a complete report on how this turns out, and I hope you'll drop by frequently with your advice." Golden Dog smiled and said he'd be back to write his story, which he'd submit to the responsible bureau officials for approval.

After leaving the industrial and commercial management bureau, Golden Dog went straight to the bus station to buy a ticket for Shaman Mountain. The town there wasn't that far from White Rock Stockade, but the roads were bad and there was only one bus a week—on Saturdays. Told that there was no bus until then, he went to the transport company, to see the manager. Identifying himself and explaining his predicament, he asked if any trucks had consignments for Shaman Mountain. Fortunately, one was taking a load of fertilizer that day, so he hitched a bumpy, three-hour ride up the mountain, arriving just before nightfall. All the local cadres lived in the government compound, and when Golden Dog saw one he knew, he asked about changes in the local situation. The man eagerly gave a complete report, and when Golden Dog asked if there were any particular problems, he invited Golden Dog to his apartment. "People living deep in the mountains never used to know a thing about commerce, but now that they've had a taste of it, some have got carried away. We outside cadres and the local government officials don't see eye to eye on some matters. Today we had a meeting that lasted all day."

"At first you organized the peasants to sell walking sticks to the outside. Why aren't they selling them any longer? Now they're dealing in lumber!"

"That's what the meeting was about. Has it caused a stir?"

"It sure has. How else would I know about it?"

"They had been excited about selling walking sticks, but then some people from Crossroads Township came to buy lumber, which is a lot more profitable. When one person starts selling, ten more tag along to see what's going on. Now all the families have begun cutting down the trees on their land—which is legal. But the area is beginning to look like it's been razed, and we can't allow that to happen! The local officials are willing to do anything to remove the yoke of poverty from the Shaman Mountain people, so they refuse to stop it, drawing the line only at forest areas belonging to the collective. But the people's eyes are filled with greed, and once they've cut down their own trees, they start secretly cutting down the collective's. A lot's already been lost. Long-term benefits are being jeopardized for the sake of quick profits. After discussing the matter, we outside cadres have decided to put a stop to it right away. If the local officials remain indifferent to the problem, we're going to report them to our superiors."

"I'll help you put a stop to it," Golden Dog said. "Could you write up a report for me, giving an approximate count of how many trees have been cut down?"

The following day the cadre took Golden Dog on an inspection tour of every village, from which it transpired that eight hundred trees belonging to the peasants had been cut down, in addition to three hundred, without approval, from the forest belonging to the collective. The number roughly corresponded to what had been taken into Crossroads Township and sold, minus the trees from which the peasants were in the process of removing the bark and trimming off the branches. Three peasants from two separate households had fallen over a cliff in the middle of the night while they were cutting trees illegally. One suffered a broken leg, the other two suffered head gashes, and all were home in bed. That very day, Golden Dog hitched a ride back to White Rock Stockade, numbers in hand, where he stayed up all night writing a story about the positive results attained by the industrial and commercial management bureau. In the morning he went over to the bureau, his eyes red from lack of sleep, and asked to see the bureau chief.

When the bureau chief saw him, he thought he was sick and inquired about his bloodshot eyes. Golden Dog asked him to read the story he'd written, acknowledging that he'd stayed up all night to write it. The bureau chief was moved by the reporter's effort. He told Golden Dog that his information was extremely accurate, that over the previous two days and nights they had detained seven boats hauling lumber, all belonging to the Crossroads Township River Shipping Brigade. The cargo was being held while they figured out what to do with it. Golden Dog felt so exultant that he nearly let out a whoop. He asked the bureau chief to give him a written account, then asked him to approve with his seal the story he'd brought for clearance, so he could send it off at once to the Zhou City *Daily News*.

The bureau chief seemed constrained. "There are still problems with our work," he said. "The things you've written—I'm wondering if they'll . . ."

"Everyone has problems," Golden Dog assured him. "No need to mention this particular matter. I wrote positive things in order to stimulate people to work even harder. Besides, you've already improved your management of river transportation, haven't you?"

After the bureau chief applied his seal, he saw Golden Dog out to the street.

Armed with the two reports, the one he'd written and the one the bureau chief had supplied, Golden Dog composed a restricted-circulation story headlined "Tree Cutting on Shaman Mountain Reaches Serious Proportions: Crossroads Township River Shipping Brigade Deals in Lumber." When he finished, he took the story and the reports to Party Secretary Tian Youshan.

He entered the party secretary's office just as a tailor from the clothing factory was measuring Tian's waist. "Ah, it's you, Golden Dog," Tian greeted him. "Have a seat!"

"Having some new clothes made, Secretary Tian?"

"Look at the size of this paunch. I can never find anything to fit me in the stores, so I have to have my clothes made."

"With a paunch that size, Secretary," the tailor commented, "Western suits are more appropriate. I'm sure you'll be happy with what I make for you."

Golden Dog laughed. "Are you wearing Western suits now?"

"I'm getting old. Time to try for a little fashion. All the members of the Central Committee are wearing them these days, and Mao jackets are out. How about you, Golden Dog, would you like one, too? He can measure you while he's at it."

"I don't have a paunch like you," Golden Dog said. "Maybe what I wear doesn't have a debonair look, but anyway I can buy my clothes in the stores."

"This wasn't my idea. It was my wife's. She's always saying how shabby I look when I go to meetings. And she's right! Tailor, this suit has to be ready in ten days. I want to wear it at the public meeting in Crossroads Township!"

"A public meeting in Crossroads Township?" Golden Dog queried. "Is it being held for the river shipping brigade? If you show up in this new suit, it'll be a perfect example of 'returning home in silken robes'—a true success story."

Tian Youshan laughed. "You're a reporter, all right, Golden Dog. Words flow from your mouth as from the pen of a master."

The tailor left with his measurements, and Tian poured Golden Dog a cup of tea. "We haven't seen you for a long time. Why haven't you been over to the house? Since you're still a bachelor, I'll have my wife cook you something—anything you want."

Golden Dog smiled and said he'd take him up on his offer.

"So you know about the public meeting, do you? Have you been to Stream of Wandering Spirits lately? The shipping brigade has been in business now for a year or two, and it's been a remarkable success. It looks like our reforms are working magnificently. They're what the party and the people want. The Chinese people are all right. Reforms are needed, so they pull together. But the key to success lies with the cadres. Does Tian Zhongzheng have his faults? Sure he does. He has a poor work ethic, and there are plenty of people he doesn't get along with. But he knows how to make breakthroughs, and he has a keen sense of ideology. We need more pioneers like him. He created the Crossroads Township River Shipping Brigade single-handedly and kept after it from the very beginning. Now the profits are really rolling in. It's a wonderful model for enriching the peasants by organizing them. The county government has been pushing for a public meeting for some time, but I've always blocked it, saying, Let's give them a chance to keep developing. If you're going to show your hand, make it a fist! Now the brigade has come into its own. I expect you, as a reporter from Crossroads Township, to give us plenty of good publicity!"

Golden Dog listened without saying a word, but when Tian Youshan was finished, smiled and said, "I was there when the brigade was launched, so I know what went on. But I sort of lost touch after going to Zhou City. If things are really like you say, I'm duty-bound to publicize it."

Tian grasped him by the shoulder. "You're all right, Golden Dog. You've brought glory to Crossroads Township. But that isn't why you came today, is it?"

"I wrote a restricted-circulation story I'd like you to read."

"What do you mean, restricted circulation?"

Golden Dog handed him the story and the two reports. Tian's smile vanished when he saw the headline. He quickly took out his reading glasses and read the story. "Is what you've written here true, Golden Dog?"

"Read the two reports I've attached. They came in the mail, and I was appalled when I read them. I went there to verify their accuracy, and they both checked out. The authors asked me to write the story up for the newspaper and said if I didn't, they'd send their reports directly to the paper. So I decided to write a story for restricted circulation to avoid any possible adverse effects on society. But our superiors will want to see it, at least, and I thought I'd let you read it first."

The color began to return to Tian Youshan's face. "Golden Dog," he said, "you did the right thing. To think that the people on Shaman Mountain got so carried away with cutting trees! And the shipping brigade is really muddled on this one. Don't they know it's illegal to ship and deal in lumber?"

"Secretary Tian, do I have the go-ahead to publish this?"

Tian raised his head and looked at Golden Dog. "It's completely up to you."

"I think it would be better not to, as long as the county government handles the matter skillfully and discreetly. In your opinion . . ."

"Then here's what we'll do," Tian said. "You go on back, and after I've looked into things, if what you've written is true the county will take strong measures. Tomorrow I'll tell you what I've found."

Later that afternoon, Tian Youshan called Tian Zhongzheng, to get to the bottom of things. Since Tian Zhongzheng's lumber had been confiscated, he had no choice but to entreat Tian Youshan to intercede with the industrial and commercial management bureau. That was a mistake. Tian Youshan was so distraught he shrieked at Tian Zhongzheng before slamming the receiver down.

The following day he sent for Golden Dog. "Everything you wrote is true. It's beyond belief. The county committee is debating what to do at this very minute. The incident was caused by a few greedy boatmen who tried to pull the wool over Tian Zhongzheng's eyes, and when I called to tell him what had happened, I could hear him pound the table in exasperation."

"Oh!" Golden Dog replied. "A single rat can spoil the soup! Now that the boats with the lumber have been detained in port, everybody in town knows about it. I guess that means you'll have to cancel the public meeting."

"That's the worst part of it," Tian said dispiritedly. "We'll have to postpone the meeting, and if you send your story in, I don't know what we'll say to our superiors. Golden Dog, this county work is hard on a person. There's always something to make life difficult for an insignificant official like me, always something to tire me out!"

It was time for Golden Dog to say his piece: "Secretary Tian, I'm not going to publish the story. That's the only copy, so go ahead and burn it. You and I are the only ones who know, and that's all that matters."

Secretary Tian picked up the article and held it out to Golden Dog, who lit it with his cigarette lighter.

The moment he stepped out of the county committee compound, Golden Dog felt relieved. He nearly floated down the street, and the pedestrians he passed seemed to be smiling at him. Feeling the need for a drink, he stepped into the first bar he saw, laid a ten-yuan note on the bar, and said, "Give me half a liter and a plate of sliced pig's liver!"

Before he'd finished the half-liter he was lying face down on the bar, dead drunk.

Six days later, Fuyun and Dakong came sailing back from Zhouville, and Dakong bought three tickets for the flower-drum opera *Liu Hai Taunts the Golden Cicada*. "Golden Dog," he whispered during the performance, "I'll never doubt you again. If this were a bandit stronghold, you'd be the bandit chief and I'd be your henchman. And if it were an opera, you'd be the generalissimo and I'd be your advance scout. Now we'll see what tricks Tian Zhongzheng has up his sleeve!"

"Don't underestimate him. He's not about to give up. He wants to use the shipping brigade as his stairway to the top, so maybe we ought to try to knock that stairway out from under him. You two pole those rafts for all you're worth. The fine the brigade is going to have to pay might just frighten a few of its members into asking to join up with you."

That's exactly what happened. Even though the county committee didn't punish the boats whose lumber had been confiscated, a heavy fine was levied by the industrial and commercial management bureau, which made the boatmen so uneasy that several of them quit and joined up with Fuyun. Tian Zhongzheng was sufficiently shaken by these developments that he washed his hands of the Crossroads Township River Shipping Brigade and stormed off to hunt for a couple of weeks. Hunting is a good way to let off steam, and he stewed away deep in the mountains until his eyes turned fiery red and he pumped seven bullets into a goat he mistook for wild game.

He returned from his hunting trip utterly dispirited, refusing to attend meetings and disdaining even the newspapers. He just moped around in town or in the village, and sneaked over to Lu Cuicui's grave several times.

Water Girl was alone at home one day when she heard the dog bark threateningly in the doorway. By the time she could see what was going on, the dog had its teeth in Tian Zhongzheng. She yelled at the dog, but it wouldn't let go. Tian was scared, his face covered with sweat. "Is that dog blind or something? Can't he spot a friend? Is Fuyun home?"

"Come in and sit down, Secretary Tian. Fuyun's out on the river. Do you need to see him about something?"

"That simpleton Fuyun has had pretty good luck poling his rafts. He must have made plenty lately!"

"He's not afraid of hard work," Water Girl said.

"That's the key to making a living. Those men in the river shipping brigade want to get rich without working for it. Where do they think they're going to find a free meal? I want to invite Fuyun to join the brigade to spur the other boatmen on. Let everybody make a decent living."

Water Girl felt a momentary panic. But she smiled and said, "Fuyun's a slow, clumsy man, and I don't think he'd fit in. I'm pretty sure we'd do best to forget the whole idea, Secretary Tian, but we certainly appreciate your concern."

Turning Tian Zhongzheng down like that made her uncomfortable, and it took some effort to keep a smile on her face. She made tea and even laid out some persimmon cakes with walnut centers for him.

"As an official, I have to take the well-being of the entire community into consideration," Tian said. "But I can't force you to participate if you don't want to. Don't bustle about so, Water Girl. Please, let's just sit and talk for a while. Believe me, I didn't come to sample your snacks."

She settled down on the kang, feeling extremely edgy with Tian's eyes fixed on her. Reminded of the time by the river, she hoped the dog would come in and scare him off. But when she called the animal inside, he was still shying because of the scolding, and he curled up in a corner and didn't stir. To hide her anxieties, she got up to pour some water. When she came up to refill Tian's glass, he said, "Here, I'll do that," letting his hand brush against hers.

"Secretary Tian!" she said forcefully as she put back the teapot and returned to the kang. "Since this is the first time you've been inside my house, let me fry you a couple of eggs." She walked outside.

She was drenched in sweat as she stepped out the door, wishing someone would come to aid her. Seeing the abbot making his way down from Restless Hill, she bleated, "Abbot, where are you off to? Come in for a cup of tea! You can keep Secretary Tian company."

He returned her salutation just as Tian Zhongzheng strolled outside and objected, "Water Girl, I've got no use for that bald-headed donkey, and I'm not about to sit and chat with him! I have some things to attend to, so I'll come back some other time."

Fuyun and Dakong were still out on their rafts.

Since the men from Shaman Mountain had recommenced selling Fuyun and his partner walking sticks, lack of stock had ceased to be a problem, and Water Girl no longer had to beat and wash hemp in the river or weave baskets out of twigs or alpine rushes. But there was plenty of housework to keep her busy, what with seeing to it that Han Wenju's clothes were mended and clean and making sure that Dakong had a wearable padded jacket in the winter and an unlined one in the summer. Fuyun and Dakong frequently ran into Golden Dog, to whom they brought mountain peaches, or cherries, or peas, and when they returned they talked about what he was doing. "He's getting real

Westernized," Fuyun commented one day. "He's let his hair grow long, and his room doesn't have a stick of furniture in it. The sheet on his bed is covered with patches."

Dakong added, "I'll bet he doesn't make as much as a reporter as he did out on the boats. And everything's more expensive these days. Except for parking your bike, which is still two fen, everything—food, clothing, whatever you need—has nearly doubled in price."

Water Girl, who was washing and starching yarn to make some clothes for Fuyun and Dakong, couldn't help overhearing them. How could he not even have a decent bed sheet? she wondered. "Since you two see him all the time, why don't you feel him out about his marriage prospects? He doesn't know how to manage his money—just like a man. He probably makes eight or nine hundred a month and doesn't have a thing to show for it."

"Every time we broach the subject, he just shakes his head and says he hasn't found the right girl."

"He can't go through life as a bachelor," Water Girl said.

Fuyun didn't say a word. Given the earlier relationship between Water Girl and Golden Dog, he felt that by becoming her husband he was responsible for the way life had gone for Golden Dog. He sat despondent in the doorway, smoking a cigarette.

The next time they were about to sail to White Rock Stockade, Fuyun said to Water Girl, "You haven't been to White Rock Stockade for a long time. Come have a look at things."

She knew what he was aiming at. "Can't you see I'm busy?"

"Come along and try to talk Golden Dog around. He can't live alone for the rest of his life. Every time I run into the abbot, he tells me that the painter is forever at the monastery praying that the gods will look after his son and help him find a wife. Nothing we say has any effect."

She looked into his face, which was filled with sincerity, and said, "I think I'd better stay home. But you must go see him more often when you're in White Rock Stockade. Tell him I'm weaving some material to make him a nice checkered bed sheet. And say to him that if he doesn't hurry up and get married, I'll come over to the bureau office and give him a piece of my mind!"

After Fuyun left, Water Girl set up her loom, sat down, and began working the treadle. She flung the shuttle back and forth until it was humming resonantly, and in the first day she wove nearly two yards of cloth. She wove even more the second day. At noon of the third day, Uncle Han left for the ferry landing after lunch, and she put the dishes in the sink to soak so that she could get back to her loom. The afternoon sun rested sleepily in the doorway, its rays making it difficult for her to see the cloth she was weaving. So she turned the loom around until it was facing away from the door, letting her benefit also from the light breeze blowing in through the door; her thoughts drifted to Fuyun, who was out on the river, and Golden Dog, who was away in White Rock Stockade. She wondered if Fuyun had gone to see Golden Dog. She slowed the pace of weaving, and then the shuttle fell to the floor.

When she bent over to retrieve it, someone walked up from behind and wrapped his arms around her. He picked her up.

"Are you out of your mind? In broad daylight!"

He said nothing as he carried her over to the kang.

"Aren't you tired after poling your raft all day?" she grumbled lightly. "You said you'd be away for four days. Put me down! What's wrong with you?" She turned her head and was floored to find that the man holding her was Tian Zhongzheng. "You!" she screamed. "What do you think you're doing? What a paragon of a party secretary you are!"

"Isn't this exactly when I ought to be here?" Tian said. "When that dolt Fuyun's not home? You're right, of course. A party secretary is only human." He lifted her onto the kang and pressed his mouth against hers.

She reached up and scratched his face. He released her and fetched some chicken feathers from the corner of the room to staunch the blood. But still he didn't leave. "Water Girl," he said, "don't put on an act with me. Yingying told me that you and Golden Dog did it before you married Fuyun. Don't act the innocent with me. If you can do it with one man, what's to keep you from doing it with two? Or three? You've already given Fuyun great pleasure just by being with him. What are you afraid of?"

Shaking with fury, she stood in front of the cupboard holding an earthenware jar. "That's enough rubbish from you," she said. "Yingying and I were classmates, and we're the same age. Aren't you ashamed of yourself? Now get out of here, and don't you ever come into my house again. As a favor to your reputation, I'll let it go this time. But if you ever set foot in my house again, I'll let you have it with this jar. If you're not afraid of losing your position as party secretary, I'm not afraid of dying!" Her arched eyebrows showed that her threat was not made idly.

Tian was momentarily at a loss for words, but then he smiled and said, "Water Girl, don't try to cow me. I've seen plenty of women like you. All right, I'm not going to force you like some young pup. It's not worth it. But think it over. I'll come back tonight, and if not tonight, tomorrow night, and if not tomorrow, there's always the day after. I'm not bragging when I say that there isn't a single woman anywhere in my jurisdiction who won't let me snuggle up to her if that's what I want." He took ten yuan out of his pocket and placed it on the loom.

After he'd left, Water Girl sank weakly to the floor in front of the cupboard, and her wrath gave way to a terror that made her scalp itch and forced tears down her cheeks. After a while, the dog, which had been outside roaming, came in and snuggled ingratiatingly beside her. But she began hammering her fists on him and screaming, "Where the hell have you been? You're never around when I need you! Do you think I'm just keeping you around to feed you?" The poor animal, having no idea what was behind the violence, slinked over to the corner and whimpered.

Uncle Han came back for dinner at dusk, and from the panic on Water Girl's face he knew that something was wrong. She wanted to tell him everything, but she stopped herself. How can I tell him what happened? she was thinking. *Besides, Tian is human, and so am I, and he's not about to kill me. And even if he does try to use force, I can handle him.* "It's nothing," she said. "Are you going to the landing tonight again?"

"Yes."

"How long did Fuyun say he'd be gone? Was it four days?"

"Yes, four days. How much cloth have you finished?"

"Over five yards so far. Uncle, since Fuyun isn't home, don't leave the ferry landing. Keep your eyes open, and when no one is there to cross the river, don't drink too much. I don't want to see you drunk. If someone is ready to cross and doesn't get any response, you'll make them angry." She hoped her warning was sufficiently strong that if something happened at home and she called out, he'd be sober enough to hear her. After dinner she walked him down to the river.

When she returned, she noticed that there was still a bit of evening light, so she put the dog out, tied him up to keep watch, then closed the door and bolted it from inside. She even propped the poker used for the fire burning under the kang up against it. Only then did she climb onto the kang to go to sleep. But sleep wouldn't come, as she was constantly pricking her ears to listen for sounds in the night. She heard the heavy sounds of a bell at Restless Hill and assumed that the abbot was chanting his evening prayers; then she heard the drawn-out lowing of an ox, and a woman yelling for her child, who was playing outside: "It's dark out. Why the hell aren't you inside getting ready for bed?" Then there was silence, except for the scuffling and gnawing sounds of rats in the attic. All of a sudden, she heard footsteps outside the door. The dog barked once. Someone was jiggling the door handle.

"Water Girl, open up. What are you doing in bed so early?"

She recognized the voice: it was Fuyun, and he was home! She jumped out of bed and asked in a quaking voice, "Fuyun?"

"Of course it's me. Can't you tell by my voice?"

She opened the door and fell into his arms, hugging him tightly. Her passionate welcome delighted him, and he kissed her, grazing her face with his heavy beard. But he was somewhat at sea. "What's with you tonight? I've only been gone three days. Now let me go. Dakong will be here in a minute."

She blushed. "I thought you said four days. What are you doing back so early? Did you have some sort of premonition? I'm glad you're home, but why so early?"

"What's with you, Water Girl? Is something wrong?"

She teared up immediately and fell back into his arms, lightly pounding and pushing him for not being affectionate enough. She told him that she'd suddenly realized how important a man was and that as long as he was home, no matter how dull-witted he was, she could rely upon him, her mainstay. She wanted him to promise he wouldn't go out on the rafts anymore and would stay home with her.

Fuyun laughed. "What'll I do if I don't go out on the rafts? We've already had a go at being a couple of old stay-at-homes . . . !"

She told him what had happened that day. He was beside himself after she spilled the story. "Tian Zhongzheng, you motherfucker! Rabbits don't eat the grass around their own burrows. How dare you play around like that in the village!"

Dakong walked in the door just then, and when they let him in on what had happened, he cursed eight generations of the Tian family. "You're back now," Water Girl said, "so everything's fine. I'm not afraid anymore. Let him just try to come over now."

"If he comes over, just ignore him. Don't even offer him tea. His face can burn up for all I care!"

"That's letting him off too lightly," Dakong said. "You mustn't go easy on people like that, since all they understand is toughness. We have to see that he gets his due. Even if he isn't inclined to pull any more of his rotten stunts at our house, he's likely to do it somewhere else."

"What are you thinking?" Water Girl asked him.

Dakong shared his plan with them.

A short time later, the dog started barking outside. Fuyun and Dakong exchanged glances and immediately hid behind the cupboard, just in time to hear Tian Zhongzheng say, "Who are you trying to bite? Here's a meat dumpling for you." Then there was a knock at the door.

"Who is it?" Water Girl asked.

"It's me. Open the door."

She went over and opened the door. "I wasn't sure you'd let me in," Tian sniggered. "By doing that, you've shown you're at least 50 percent convinced. Did you tuck that ten yuan away?"

"It's on the table," she said.

The bill was held there by a pair of scissors. Tian walked over, picked up the scissors, then looked straight at Water Girl and started saying filthy things to her. She hurled invective back, but he contented himself with saying, "Go ahead, get it off your chest. When you're finished, it's me you'll be thinking about." He bounded across the room and wrapped himself around her.

There was a noise, and Fuyun and Dakong jumped out from behind the cupboard. "So this is how a party secretary acts!" Fuyun said icily.

The openmouthed Tian stood there like a statue. Fuyun lashed out at him so hard that he crashed to the floor and blood began oozing from his mouth and nose. Fuyun was about to hit him again, but his rage denied him the strength.

"Fuyun," Dakong said, "sit down and let me teach this hooligan a lesson!" He jerked Tian to his feet and yelled in his face, "You shameless, rotten pig, you think that just because you're a party secretary, you can have your way with the wife of anybody you please, right? If we don't take care of you now, this habit of yours will only get worse!"

All the blood had drained from Tian's face, and he started babbling for mercy.

"Okay," Dakong said, "tell us what we ought to do."

"I'll give you anything you want. I'll do anything you tell me to do," Tian said.

"I want that nose of yours!" Dakong said as he picked up a razor and made as if to cut off Tian's nose.

"Dakong, you'd ruin me forever! You might as well kill me!"

"Okay, then I'll just take a finger. Stick out your hand and tell me which one you want me to cut off!" He picked up the cleaver and banged it down on the table.

Tian kowtowed and clasped his hands beseechingly, saying he was, after all, the party secretary, and how would it look if he stood up at a meeting and had only four fingers?

"All right," Dakong said, "since you're an official, you need all your fingers, but no one has to look at your feet, so I'll cut off one of your toes instead! You're not going to get away without losing something. If I cut off one of your toes, you'll think twice before chasing after somebody else's wife!" He pulled Tian's foot over and with one chop severed the little toe.

After Tian had fled, Fuyun and Water Girl started getting nervous. "Dakong, isn't what you did against the law?"

"How can it be? He came to your house, we didn't go to his. We were just acting in self-defense. Don't worry. Get some sleep. I'd better be going. I'll come get you tomorrow morning so we can make another trip to Xiangfan and earn a few hundred yuan." He picked the bloody toe up off the floor, wrapped it in a leaf, and put it into his pocket as he left.

But instead of going home to sleep, he went to the ferry landing, bursting with excitement and self-satisfaction over a job well done. He boarded the ferryboat and told Han Wenju to break out a bottle of wine. "You've already drunk half of what I had!" Han beefed. "What are you, my foster son?" He fetched a bottle, reprehending him all the while.

"I've just rid your family of a scourge," Dakong said, "so instead of considering it charity, you should be giving me this wine out of gratitude!"

In the light of the lamp, Han could see the excitement in the muscles of Dakong's face. "You rid my family of a scourge? I have a cat at home, so I don't need that bogus rat poison of yours!"

"Uncle Han, I cut off one of Tian Zhongzheng's little toes!"

Han laughed deeply. "A big man like you should have cut off his head! If you'd cut off his ears, at least we'd have something to go with our wine!"

Dakong reached into his pocket and pulled out the blood-soaked toe, which he laid on the table. "Since you don't believe me," he said, "tell me what this is!"

Han gasped; the jug fell out of his hand to the floor. "You really cut off his toe?" he exclaimed, fright in his voice.

Pleased with the reaction, Dakong told him what had happened. Han's face was as pale as a sheet of paper. "This is horrible!" he lamented. "You're really asking for trouble this time!" Leaving Dakong alone, he jumped down onto the bank and stumbled into the village, heading straight for Tian Zhongzheng's home.

A dog inside the compound was barking, but the gate was shut tight. Han banged on it for a time, but there was no response, so he peeked in through a crack and sighted some moving shapes inside the house. Something terrible had happened, all right, and his legs seemed to turn to rubber; he couldn't utter a word. By the time he returned to his boat, late that night, Dakong was gone, and no matter how hard he tried, he simply couldn't get to sleep. As dawn broke, he thought he heard the sound of water, then in the dim light saw some people getting a boat ready below the ferry landing and lifting something up onto it. "Who's that setting out so early?" he called. No answer. As the boat got under way, he saw someone standing on the bank, someone very fat. It looked like Tian Zhongzheng's wife. So he's on his way to White Rock Stockade to have his injury taken care of, Han thought to himself. They were ignoring him, hoping to keep their secret safe.

19

Three days passed, then five, and nothing had changed at Stream of Wandering Spirits. Water Girl and Fuyun said to Han Wenju, "Don't worry. After the shameless thing he did, he won't say anything." But Han couldn't shake his fears.

On the eighth day, Fuyun and Dakong poled their rafts down to White Rock Stockade, where there was a dark line of boats tied up at the landing at the southern gate. They'd brought a load of touch paper to the warehouse from Purple Thistle Pass, and virtually all the boatmen had gone into town for some fun. Old Seven was washing down a boat with a large brush and talking to a man on the boat: "Dongsheng, you're not that kind of man, so don't grandstand as if you were. Women aren't a novelty to you. You've been married seven years now, and you've got a couple of babies. You'll be home tomorrow. Can't you wait that long? Your woman wanted you to make this trip so you could bring back some material for clothes for your children. And look at you, now you've lost your ten yuan, and you didn't even see a single pussy hair!"

The man called Dongsheng was from Crossroads Township, a gaunt, skinny fellow who was so indignant he was foaming at the mouth. "I'm going to give that pimp a taste of my fists!" he said. "He cheated me out of my money!"

"If it had been Dakong," Old Seven said, "no pimp would have dared cheat him. But who's afraid of a runt like you?"

"Who cheated Dongsheng?" Dakong asked.

Old Seven nearly doubled over with laughter. He told Dakong that when Dongsheng had seen someone take a woman to a house by the western gate for some fun, he'd picked up another for himself and given her five yuan. But the pimp there demanded five yuan for the room. Dongsheng and his woman went on in, but he'd barely pulled down his pants when the pimp outside shouted, "Run quick! The police are here!"

Dongsheng was so scared he jumped out the window. But after he got away, he nosed around and found that no police had been anywhere in sight, that it was all a trick by the pimp. So he returned to ask for a refund, but the pimp just said, "Okay, bring her back." She was, of course, long gone, and Dongsheng had no idea where to find her. He made his way to the boat grumbling over the loss of ten yuan.

The whole thing struck Dakong as funny, but it made him angry as well, and he railed at Dongsheng for not using better judgment in spending his money and dealing with women. "What kind of man are you?" He said he'd go get the money back.

Old Seven stopped him. "Why cry over spilled milk? A streetwalker like that's not worth getting heated up over. Look at Lumpy Shi there. He's got a real looker and goes to her place to snuggle up in bed without paying a cent. She even feeds him and gives him wine. Now that's what you call getting it done!"

"Shacking up with a widow doesn't come free," Dongsheng objected.

"But she's faithful to him. Every time I come here, she asks, 'Where's Lumpy? Has he got himself a wife?'"

"That fellow Lumpy, does he live in town?" Fuyun asked.

"No, at Teahouse Bay. He poles a raft. He's got a birthmark on the right side of his face." He straightened up and hollered toward a hut built of stone on the riverbank, "Hey, Lumpy Shi! Hey, Scarface! Haven't you had enough? There's a regulating committee for shipping now, and they're going to want their tax. Get down here fast!"

A head poked out through the window in the hut; it was a man with a rough-looking face and a big birthmark on the right side. "Old Seven," he said, "I'll be right down. I've just started to drink a nice cup of tea, and I'll be there as soon as I'm finished." A few minutes later he came down the bank, his eyes all puffy.

"You scarfaced beast," Old Seven greeted him, "you sure know how to enjoy yourself, even having me to wake you up when you sleep in. But don't think what you've got up there is the soft, easy life. That'll tire you out faster than poling your raft past a shoal. It's just that you don't realize it."

Scarface said, "She wouldn't let me leave and wouldn't stop crying. What was I supposed to do?"

Dongsheng said enviously, "Lumpy, how can an ugly man like you have some widow crying over you? You lucky stiff!"

Lumpy Shi said smugly, "She's wonderful to me and keeps begging me to marry her. That puts me in a tough spot. Have you had tea? I've got some block tea from Yunnan up there. It picks you right up. I'll have her throw some down." He negotiated his raft to a position opposite the hut, from where he yelled and whistled. A woman appeared at the window, about thirty years old with a nice, clean face. Dakong was amazed that a pretty young widow would fall for someone like Scarface. They exchanged a few words; then she tossed down a chunk of tea wrapped in paper. "Lumpy," she said, "button up your shirt so you won't catch cold. Don't forget that the wind can blow right through you."

While they were steeping the tea, several of the other boatmen drifted over, having returned from town, where they'd spent nearly all the money they'd earned on their latest trip down the river. Their talk generally centered on the high cost of things in town. "Motherfucker, everything's going up, everything, that is, except my body and my status! We talk about what we earn for the shipping brigade, and that's true enough, but how much of that trickles down to us? Why does Tian Yishen need all those purchasing agents and all those women? Cai Da'an is the credit manager as well as a brigade commander—a cadre on the national payroll getting two salaries and strutting around like a cock of the walk. He's even raising a wolfhound! One of these days I'll throttle that mutt and we'll all eat dogmeat!"

Old Seven said, "Our shipping brigade is better than nothing at all. All we have to worry about is operating our boats. What gets my goat is that we do all the work while Tian Zhongzheng and his group take all the credit. Someone in town said that if we're going to have a strong township government, Tian Zhongzheng's the only one we can count on. They say he's providing a model by organizing the peasants and improving their lives. It looks like he's on his way up. Motherfucker, what difference does it make to us who's on his way up and who's on his way down? Except that the Gong family is losing its grip on power."

"All the officials in the Tian family are rank seven or below," someone said, "and the power of the Gong family is concentrated in Zhou City. I hear that the work in White Rock Stockade isn't considered very highly there."

"What the hell are you worried about?" Dongsheng said. "Fuyun, have you seen Golden Dog lately? He can get the higher-ups to pay attention to the problems of poor families, but does he know he's responsible for Tian Zhongzheng's becoming a hero in the struggle of the poor to escape poverty?"

"Do you have any idea why the county government canceled plans for their public meeting?" Fuyun asked him. "Look, good is rewarded with good, and evil with evil. Tian isn't going to have a chance to get too cocky!" Reminded of how they'd taken care of Tian, he had a powerful urge to tell everyone what had happened that night.

But Dakong gave him a nudge with his foot, and Fuyun exercised discretion. "Golden Dog would have been in charge of the shipping brigade if the rest of you had pushed harder. Now he's gone off to become a reporter and can't get directly involved with the brigade. Tian wants us to join the brigade, but who'd join, the way it's being run now? The only way we'll join is if Dakong's put in charge. Dakong, when you become successful, I expect you to help those of us who aren't named Tian or Gong!"

Dakong smiled but kept quiet.

"Dakong," Old Seven said, "it looks like you've got your mind set on becoming a cadre. But without a solid foundation, your hopes don't mean shit. You're too quick to say what's on your mind, and you don't have that spark that Golden Dog has. No, I don't think you've got what it takes to be a cadre."

"And what if I become one?" Dakong said.

"Someone like you," Old Seven said, "is fine for a bit player, but if you were playing the lead, not only would these fellows who go out on the river with you not get a break, they'd be in worse trouble than they are now. Do you believe that? An official position is a strange thing. Anybody, no matter how decent he is, changes as soon as he's got it."

Dakong laughed. "Okay, Uncle Seven, I'm going to become an official, and my first act will be to kill you!" He suddenly started sneezing. What does this stupid talk achieve? he thought to himself. *Everybody else has already gone to town and bought what they wanted.* He turned to Fuyun. "Instead of wasting our time bullshitting with Uncle Seven, let's get ourselves into town."

They jumped down off their raft and were on their way. Dakong bought a package of salt and a bottle of vinegar and some noodles, which he planned to cook back on the raft. When they passed a theater on South Street, where the Shaanxi opera *The Orphan of Zhao* was playing, Fuyun decided to buy a ticket. "Go see it if you want,"

Dakong said. "I've seen enough opera. I'll wait for you on the raft. Come back as soon as it's over, since we have to get under way before sunup tomorrow." He walked off with his groceries, looking very pleased with himself.

Fuyun returned to the raft as soon as the opera was over, but he couldn't find hide nor hair of Dakong. When he asked around, he learned that Old Seven and the others had all retired to the warehouse for a nap. The man who'd stayed behind to watch the cargo said that some policemen had suddenly appeared and surrounded the landing. When Dakong, who was enjoying a jug of wine, saw Tian Yishen and Cai Da'an with the police, he raised his glass and shouted, "Out catching criminals? Come on over and have a drink!" Tian and Cai boarded his raft and had a drink but then grabbed him and held him down for the police, who snapped handcuffs on his wrists. Dakong put up a fight. "What's this for?"

The policeman said, "For trying to wreck the reforms by physically attacking a cadre in the forefront of the reform movement!"

"It was self-defense!" Dakong protested. "Tian Zhongzheng came over . . ."

Tian Yishen knocked him unconscious before he could finish and dragged him off the raft.

Without uttering a sound, Fuyun sank to the floor of the raft. Later that night, he paced back and forth for a while in front of the police station, but since the gate was shut tight, he decided to go across the street, where he crouched beneath the eaves of a building, never taking his eyes off the metal gate glistening darkly under the two light bulbs that burned on the building behind it. His face was streaked with tears born of his realization that he was powerless to save Dakong. He didn't know a soul in White Rock Stockade who'd be able to do anything, and all he could do was blame Tian Zhongzheng, and blame Tian Yishen and Cai Da'an. Suddenly it dawned on him: there was someone. He went straight to a building in a tiny compound on West Avenue. When no one came to the gate, he backed out onto the street and shouted up toward a third-floor window. The window opened, and Golden Dog leaned out. "Golden Dog," Fuyun shouted, "Golden Dog . . . !" Then he broke into tears, too overcome to utter another word.

Golden Dog, who had been working against a deadline that night, hadn't put down his pen and gone to bed until two in the morning. Dimly, he sensed that someone had come into his room. He strained to see who it was: it was Water Girl, Fuyun, and Dakong. She was wearing white mourning clothes; Fuyun and Dakong were dressed in black. They were all so young and attractive. They came over and took his hand, gesturing for him to follow them down to the river and out on the rafts. He accompanied them willingly all the way down to the landing at the southern gate, where Fuyun's raft was tied up. They boarded the raft and slipped out into the river. Water Girl was looking at him with her big, passionate eyes. He returned her look, but at once turned his eyes away in confusion. *What am I doing?* He gazed down at the water and said, "The Zhou River is so deep!"

"Don't sit so close to the edge," Water Girl cautioned him. "The water's too turbulent!"

Just then a strong wind came up, and the raft began to rock violently in the cresting waves. "Dakong," he said, "let me pole the raft."

Dakong laughed and said, "Don't you trust me? You're a Zhou River dragon, but so am I. I know how to swim!"

"Stop bragging," he said. "Have you ever poled a string of three rafts during a flood?"

"Just watch!" Dakong said. But just then the raft listed violently, and Dakong and Fuyun were thrown into the murky water and sank beneath the surface.

With a bellow, Golden Dog lurched forward—and discovered he was sitting up in bed. His covers were on the floor, and he was drenched in sweat. It had been a bad dream. His eyes swept the four walls, on which something was swaying, growing bigger and then smaller. He shuddered, but when he looked more closely, he realized it was the light from a distant streetlamp causing the branches of a parasol tree to cast shadows on the wall. Not one easily overcome by fear, he lay back down to sleep, but sleep wouldn't come. He was gripped by the curious dream. After he and Water Girl broke up, he'd often gone to bed hoping he'd dream about her, but he never did. Recently that desire had become less insistent, and now, inexplicably, she'd appeared as clear as life in a dream. More surprising was the fact that she'd been wearing white mourning clothes whereas Fuyun and Dakong had been dressed all in black. "Men look best when black is worn, women look best wearing white to mourn." Was this the result of his wishing them happiness all this time? What about the capsized raft? The thought of Fuyun and Dakong submerged in the river disturbed him. Back home he'd heard the abbot say it was a bad sign when people sank beneath murky waters. Was this an omen? He talked himself out of that possibility: don't people say that dreams are the reverse of reality and that if you dream that someone is dead, they're bound to enjoy a good life? Calmed by such thoughts, he gradually drifted off to sleep.

When he heard Fuyun's call from outside, he assumed he was dreaming again. Then another call, and a third; he recognized Fuyun's voice, although it was more strained and urgent than usual. It gave him a fright. He called to Fuyun to come up, and the minute he walked into the room demanded to know what was wrong.

Fuyun was sobbing in gasps that kept Golden Dog from making sense of what he was saying. He broke out in a cold sweat, shook Fuyun, and insisted, "What's happened to Water Girl? Tell me! Say something!" But Fuyun still couldn't get the words out, and since Golden Dog could see he was nearly in shock, he slapped him. With an intake of air, Fuyun went from sobs to whimpers. Then he told Golden Dog what had happened, from start to finish.

Golden Dog took the news calmly. He pulled out his cigarettes, handed one to Fuyun, and lit another for himself, then smoked it silently until it burned his fingers, before crushing it violently and saying, "Okay, Tian Zhongzheng, now you've gone too far! The police are an instrument of the national dictatorship, not your private watchdogs, and Stream of Wandering Spirits isn't a private playground where you can commit your outrages!" He pushed his story to the edge of the desk, picked up his pen and a clean sheet of paper, and wrote out a formal complaint to the police, with Fuyun and Water Girl as litigants. Fuyun, who was illiterate, leaned over the desk and watched, tears welling up and beginning to spill onto the paper as he answered Golden Dog's questions.

"Fuyun," Golden Dog consoled him, "don't become too discouraged. Dakong did overreact in taking a toe, but that's not to say that Tian didn't get what he deserved. Even breaking his back, forget about cutting off a toe, wouldn't have quelled Dakong's hatred. The mistake you made was in not handing Tian over to the authorities right away, to let the people of Stream of Wandering Spirits know what he'd done. If you had, he wouldn't have dared go around arresting people."

"We figured that since he was party secretary, we'd be able to buy his silence by letting him keep his face."

"You were worried about his face, and now he wants your lives. What about Water Girl? Is she okay?"

"She's fine. She's at home making you a bed sheet. I'll bring it with me next time."

Golden Dog's eyes began to mist over, and his pen hovered above the paper without moving. When he tried to write, he scratched a hole in the paper and the words got all jumbled up. The sun was lighting up the sky by the time the complaint was finished, so he handed it to Fuyun and sent him to the police station. "When you get there go straight to the man in charge and ask why Dakong was arrested. Once you've determined the charges against him, give a complete account of what really happened and hand the man this complaint. I'll be here waiting for news."

Fuyun turned and left, and as Golden Dog watched his chunky body move down the lane and disappear at the intersection, his eyes filled with warm tears. If Golden Dog were Water Girl's husband, and not Fuyun, how would he protect his wife? *You're a real son of a bitch, Tian Zhongzheng! You tried to have your lustful way with a decent woman, and now you're using your position to crush someone else. Fuyun and Dakong may not be able to stand up to you, but I'm not the same Golden Dog who used to be under your jurisdiction. I'm a reporter now, one who doesn't have to answer to anybody in Crossroads Township or White Rock Stockade!* He waited at home for Fuyun to return, unable to dispel the anxiety that filled his heart. When he couldn't wait another minute, he went and took a seat in a little bar across the street from the police station, where he sat and drank, his mood as dark as the tall metal gate he was watching as he waited for Fuyun to emerge.

The gate opened, and Fuyun stepped out onto the street. His straw hat was missing and he looked utterly dejected as he stumbled across the way. Golden Dog shouted to him to come into the bar; he turned, careered into the bar, and collapsed onto a stool.

"Well?"

"It looks bad," Fuyun said. "It's been blown up into a major incident. They say Dakong's charged with undermining the reforms and assaulting a senior cadre. They say he attacked Tian with a rock in a vegetable plot east of Crossroads Township and severed his toe in the process. They showed me some eyewitness reports—one from the owner of the vegetable plot, an old man named Wu Mingren, and another from Lu Cuicui's simpleton brother. They both swore they'd witnessed the incident."

"That bastard!" Golden Dog exclaimed. "How could the police chief believe that?"

"I couldn't find the chief," Fuyun said. "I had to talk to an investigator."

"What did you say to him?"

"I don't know what I said. He was a mean-looking man in a policeman's hat, with acne all over his face. As soon as I opened my mouth, he banged the table and even pulled out his pistol and slammed it down on the table . . . I left my hat in his office."

Golden Dog could see that the affair had scared the wits out of Fuyun, and he knew the kind of temper those policemen had; he also knew how an honest fellow like Fuyun might be so rattled he could barely speak. With a grunt he picked up his glass and drained it. "Did you hand him the complaint?"

"He took it, and I told him to make sure he gave it to his boss. When he asked me who wrote it for me, I told him I paid somebody I didn't know to write it. I didn't say it was you."

"You could have told him it was me."

Fuyun stayed at Golden Dog's for the next three days, going to the police station every day to determine the reaction to the written complaint. But each time he got only as far as the reception office just inside the gate, where he was told it was still being studied. He asked to see the chief—which got a laugh out of the man he spoke to, who said his boss was too busy to play games with just anyone off the street. Emboldened, Fuyun reminded the man that in classical operas there was always a big drum in the main hall that anyone who had been misused could beat to summon the magistrate to the hall to hear his complaint. Fuyun mused aloud over the oddity that in a modern society it was so difficult to see a local police chief. What was he so busy doing? Was it a "game" that an innocent man was in jail? The police clerk lost his temper and called Fuyun a local rowdy, a scoundrel, and an antisocial element. When he tried to steer the complainant out of the station, Fuyun held on to the doorframe and stood his ground, until four or five policemen picked him up bodily and deposited him outside the gate, which they slammed shut behind him.

Seeing how Fuyun had muffed the filing of the complaint, Golden Dog sent him back to Stream of Wandering Spirits to reassure the others. The only way to catch this scoundrel Tian was to gather all the evidence against him and uncover how he'd suborned the witnesses.

At home, Fuyun talked things over with Water Girl and Han Wenju, and they decided to wrap the cleaver in a rag to protect it as evidence. Fuyun and Water girl suggested looking for the severed toe at the ferry landing, but Han told them he'd fed it to the dog. The unavailability of this piece of evidence worried them all. That night, when Han went to his boat, he was still berating himself for not keeping the toe safe. Instead of sleeping, he sat up drinking and brooding, and as soon as morning came, he went into town to buy some more wine. Walking along the beach, he heard someone call his name softly. When he turned toward the voice, he saw an old man hobbling down to the beach from behind a tree. It was Wu Mingren, who lived on the eastern edge of town. Han began castigating him the minute he saw who it was. "Wu Mingren, you bastard! What did an old man like you have in mind in helping Tian Zhongzheng engineer such a raw deal for a decent man? Aren't you worried that an evil spirit will come dogging you after what you've done?"

Instead of defending himself, the old man fell to his knees and said, "Go ahead, give me the dickens, Uncle Han. Hit me if you want to. After what I've done, I look at my sixty-six years and see only a wasted life! I've wanted to see you because I heard that Dakong's been arrested and I haven't been able to sleep a wink for three nights. I came over last night, but I didn't have the guts to face you, and I've been hiding behind the tree over there ever since. The testimony I gave was false. Tian Yishen made me give it, Uncle Han!"

Seeing how overwrought Wu was, Han helped him to his feet and over to his boat, where he said, "Well, you came on your own, and that's to your credit. Tell me why Tian Yishen mixed you up in this and how he got you to lie."

The old man explained about his family's pitiful housing and how he'd been saving building materials for years in order to erect a new structure, but at the crucial moment had his permit to lay a foundation suspended by the township government. He went to see Tian Yishen, who promised redress provided that he attested to an eyewitness report that Tian wrote out and read to him. He knew he was doing wrong in affixing his fingerprint to it, but he saw his behavior as a relatively harmless deception that would let him lay the foundation of his house. It didn't seem like a big deal to say he'd seen Dakong in a fight, and he never dreamed it would come to this. Now the town was buzzing over the incident, and his children were pointing fingers at him. He couldn't live under this cloud. "Uncle Han, I have to recant my eyewitness testimony even if it means that my application for the permit will be denied. I can't let myself drown in people's spit and die with the expectation that my body will go unburied!" Han took out a sheet of paper and wrote down everything Wu Mingren had said, then read it to him, after which he mixed up some ashes and asked the old man to place an impression of his fingerprint on the paper. Wu gave him all ten.

By the time Han saw Wu Mingren off, he'd forgotten about wanting more wine. He made a beeline for home and handed Fuyun the new evidence, without admitting that Wu Mingren had come looking for him. Instead, he said he'd gone to Wu Mingren's and persuaded the old bastard to tell the truth, in order to compensate for his own error of destroying the evidence of the severed toe.

Fuyun and Water Girl were delighted, of course, and tried to think of a way to induce Lu Cuicui's brother to come clean as well, in order that Dakong might be cleared of all charges. Han didn't have any ideas, but Water Girl said, "Uncle, go down to the ferry landing and get the raft ready. We have to go to White Rock Stockade tonight!"

"Do you think the two of you can get the Lu boy to give you the statement we need?" Han asked her.

"I'll give it a try," Water Girl said. "Fuyun, bring a pen and some paper."

Han had his doubts, but not so many as Fuyun, who accompanied Water Girl skeptically to Restless Hill. The Lu boy was a contract ranger for the township forestry service, a good-paying job that required virtually no work. All he had to do was take a walk around the hills behind Restless Hill every day and come back at night to sleep in one of the small buildings at the rear of the monastery. An intellectual lightweight, he had a mind seldom troubled by thoughts. After the abbot completed his evening prayers, he had him help the young monks fetch water, plant vegetables, and gather dead branches and twigs on the mountain for firewood. He'd then listen to the abbot tell ghost stories that kept him awake into the night. He was out on an inspection round when Water Girl and Fuyun reached the monastery. As Water Girl told the abbot what had happened, the normally placid, quiet monastic gnashed his teeth. He knew about Lei Dakong's arrest but was unaware of the conspiracy that had put him behind bars, and he was sickened that the Lu boy, who slept and took his meals in the monastery, could give false evidence, thereby sullying the purity of a house of Buddha.

"Pure thoughts lead to heaven; evil thoughts lead to hell," he said. "A man of mercy becomes a bodhisattva; a man of evil becomes a beast. Leave everything to me. As soon as he returns, I'll get him to write a new affidavit."

"Although you're confident of winning him over," Water Girl cautioned him, "remember that no matter how stupid he is, he's still smart enough to know he's better off fearing Tian than fearing you. And don't forget our urgency. We must have the new testimony by this afternoon."

"Give me time to think," the abbot said as he closed his eyes and sat in rigid meditation.

Growing impatient at the sight of him meditating, Water Girl said, "Go ahead and think. Meanwhile, we'll find him and bring him back." She dragged Fuyun off toward the mountain behind them, where the Lu boy was sleeping in a grassy opening among the trees, his arms and legs stretched out and his hat pulled down over his face. Fuyun walked up, hoisted him to his feet, and administered several resounding slaps. Fully awakened by the unexpected violence, the ranger was both angry and alarmed. He stared at Fuyun but, knowing it would be useless to resist, just squawked, "What did you hit me for?"

"Why shouldn't I hit you after what you did? Now I'm going to spill some of that black blood of yours!"

Growing more panicky by the minute, the Lu boy ran over and knelt before Water Girl, pleading for help.

She had a sudden inspiration. "Did you or didn't you write an eyewitness report for the police?" she asked.

"I didn't write anything," he said.

Fuyun came up and struck him again. Blood oozed out of his nose and the corner of his mouth.

"Don't hit him any more," Water Girl said. "He has enough trouble as it is. Since he helped Tian Zhongzheng frame Dakong for that arrest that's been overturned, Tian's trying to shift the blame to him, in the investigation by the authorities. If this guy won't talk to us, let him tell his story at the police station."

The boy turned deathly pale at what he'd heard. "It's not my fault," he said plaintively. "Tian Zhongzheng made me write it. How can he denounce me?"

"Is that the truth?" Water Girl demanded.

"If it isn't," the boy pleaded, "may the spirits strike me dead!"

"All right," she said, "now that Dakong's released, he's been looking everywhere for you in order to take you to the police station. Everything will be all right if you tell us what happened."

"I'll tell Dakong myself," the boy insisted.

"The first thing you'll see of Lei Dakong is his fists. You're better off writing out what happened and letting us show him your account. We can put in a good word for you."

"How can I write without a pen and paper?"

Water Girl drew out the pen and paper and handed them to him. He sprawled on the ground, using a flat rock as his writing surface. When he'd finished he dipped his finger in the blood dripping from his nostril and affixed his fingerprint to the paper to prove that what he'd written was the truth. With the new evidence that Water Girl and Fuyun had extorted, the couple couldn't help laughing in contentment as they left the woods.

"Water Girl, you were terrific!"

"Those slaps of yours did the trick!" she said.

Back at the monastery the abbot had decided on his course of action. "Fuyun, I've figured out what to do. Bring him here, and I'll tell his fortune, trapping him into divulging exactly what happened."

"No need for that now," Water Girl said. "He's already given us what we want."

The abbot was exultant when they told him what had happened. He marveled at Water Girl's wiles, which had put his to shame.

Late that night, a raft conveyed the two eyewitnesses to White Rock Stockade. Water Girl brought the bed sheet she had made with her, but when she saw Golden Dog, she experienced bashfulness, anger, and sadness, all at the same time. Her eyes brimmed with tears. Golden Dog read the exciting new evidence carefully and sent it to the police station with Fuyun before the sun was up. After hearing nothing for three days, they began to worry. Golden Dog said it was time for him to take matters in hand, and he suggested that Fuyun go with him to see the police chief.

"Let me go in Fuyun's place," Water Girl said. "He may be a man, but this is no job for him. I can talk to people better than he can. I'm not afraid—not when things have reached this stage." So Golden Dog coached her on what to say to the chief, and the two of them left together.

Golden Dog showed his reporter's ID in the reception room of the police station and demanded to see the man in charge. The underling, not daring to toy with a reporter, informed him that the police chief had gone to Secretary Tian's home that morning. Perfect, Golden Dog thought. *We'll go over and file charges with the secretary.* He and Water Girl set out for Secretary Tian's home.

Ever since Golden Dog had written the restricted-circulation story that had halted the public meeting in Crossroads Township, Tian Youshan was aware that Golden Dog's arrival in White Rock Stockade was not the beginning of a run-of-the-mill journalistic posting. "Golden Dog's like a member of the family," he said to a subordinate. "He's not a dog that goes around biting people but one that doesn't make a lot of noise while he's giving you a boost up or sinking his fangs into you. The Dongyang County party secretary fell because he didn't take precautions against him! He has a way of putting things together, so you mustn't divulge county committee secrets to him. But don't just be careful around him; be sure to get on his good side as well." As for Golden Dog, he knew all about Tian Youshan's various stratagems. After the restricted-circulation story, he'd written a number of reports commending the efforts of various specialists, nearly all of which he'd cleared with Tian Youshan. Tian always had a smile for Golden Dog, and if there was a banquet for a visiting VIP, Golden Dog's name was sure to be on the guest list. But whenever Tian Youshan tried to get Golden Dog to send his party credentials to the county committee, the reporter told him they were at the newspaper office; he'd left word at the office that they weren't to be sent to the county, since he didn't wish to be at the mercy of the county committee, for that would have compromised his integrity and effectiveness.

Once inside Tian's front door, Golden Dog and Water Girl confronted three sweaty-faced men around a table that held a big spread. The sight made Water Girl weak, for two of them were raising their glasses to toast the third, their host: the guests were the police chief and Tian Zhongzheng.

"Well!" Tian Youshan greeted them. "Better late than never! Leave it to Golden Dog to smell out a good meal! Come in, let me introduce you. This is Golden Dog, a well-known journalist from right here in White Rock Stockade, a writer par excellence. And this is . . ."

Even though Water Girl was from Stream of Wandering Spirits, she'd never met Tian Youshan, and he didn't know who she was. "My name's Water Girl," she said. "You know Han Wenju, don't you? He's my uncle."

"Know him?" Tian replied warmly. "Of course I know him! Does he still run the ferryboat? To think that a dark, skinny old man like that, with skin like leather, could have a fair-skinned niece like this! When I was there about ten years ago, I saw you at the ferry landing. You were still a playful little girl then, with a pigtail like a garlic top.

Ai, I'm getting old, but that's what happens. The babies grow up, and the years pass for me the same as for them. Sit down, Water Girl; have a drink!"

Golden Dog was already seated and digging in with his chopsticks, but she didn't move, preferring to stand in the doorway and keep her gaze fixed on Tian Zhongzheng, who was too abashed to look up. He thrust his chopsticks into the plate of beef and tomatoes with quail eggs in front of him as though the food were the only thing on his mind. After coming up empty on his first two stabs, he managed to spear some food on the third try, but his hand was shaking so that the egg dropped back onto the plate, splattering tomato sauce over the table.

"Zhongzheng," Tian Youshan said, "what's wrong with you? Can't you even manage to get an egg in your mouth?"

Water Girl laughed mirthlessly through clenched teeth.

"Why aren't you eating, Water Girl?" Tian Youshan asked.

"Because watching how the township party secretary is struggling to keep eating is satisfying enough," she replied coolly.

Tian Youshan was uncomfortable.

"Secretary Tian," Golden Dog said, "Water Girl's here to file a complaint."

"A complaint? What sort of complaint? Whatever it is, it can wait till we've eaten. As long as I'm party secretary, no one's going to take advantage of one of my villagers!"

Golden Dog turned to Water Girl. "Secretary Tian's made himself clear, Water Girl, so sit down and dig in. With his reputation for fairness, you can be sure he'll make things right for you. If you won't eat, at least come over and drink a toast to the secretary."

She approached the table and picked up a glass. "That's better," Tian Youshan said. "Everybody, a toast!" Water Girl reached over and clinked Tian Youshan's glass, then did the same with the police chief, but snubbed Tian Zhongzheng and drank the wine in one gulp.

Tian Zhongzheng, his face drained of color, banged his glass on the table, spilling wine.

"Don't you know Tian Zhongzheng?" Tian Youshan asked her.

"I'd recognize him if he were burned to a crisp! Secretary Tian, your question convinces me that I can rely on you. You folks go ahead and eat. We'll talk when you're done." She stepped away from the table.

"Ah!" Tian Youshan sighed. "It looks like she's indeed come to file charges. Tell me, who are they against? So much has been happening in Stream of Wandering Spirits lately. We've just cleared up an assault case, and now this!"

"Are you referring to the assault on the township party secretary?" Water Girl asked. "I'm responsible for that."

Her comment made Tian Youshan fidget; he bobbed and swayed for a moment without responding.

The police chief stood up. "You're responsible? What's your relationship to Lei Dakong?"

"He's a friend of my husband's."

"Are you aware that he's been arrested? Are you going to take the rap for him? You people assaulted a senior cadre, but instead of waiting for me to come for you, here you are, creating a scene! When I saw you glowering at Tian Zhongzheng a minute ago, I knew there was bad blood between you."

"Secretary Tian," Tian Zhongzheng piped up, "as soon as she walked in the door, I could see that she wanted to make a scene in front of you and the police chief. I've made her and her husband and Lei Dakong toe the mark, because they were profiting from the reforms. For that, they ganged up and assaulted me. I didn't bring charges against her, because she's a woman, but now she has the audacity to come and bother you."

"Police Chief," Water Girl said, "Tian Zhongzheng told you that the three of us ganged up on him, so you can arrest me too. But I can add that not only did we assault him, we cut off one of his toes! We can't show it to you, since our dog ate it, but I brought along the cleaver we used."

She reached under her jacket and pulled out the cleaver, which she banged down on the table.

"Great!" the police chief said wryly. "May we consider you to be turning yourself in?"

"Only on the condition that the township party secretary comes clean about why we lopped off his toe."

Tian Zhongzheng, harried and beset, said, "Where do you think you are, Water Girl Han? You're out of line with histrionics like that here!"

"Where do I think I am? At the home of the county secretary of the Communist party, that's where! You came to my place with rape on your mind. Fortunately for me, my husband and Lei Dakong had returned, and taking your toe was nothing more than self-defense. Admit it! What was it you said when you were down on your knees? It's incredible that you'd try to frame us as opposing the reforms and that you'd accuse us of assaulting you for doing your job. Dakong's in jail, but every time my husband goes to the police station with an appeal, the chief here refuses to see him, and I'll bet he hasn't even read the appeal. Have you read the new testimony from the eyewitnesses? A bad man does evil things, for which he's protected by the authorities: is that the law of the Communist party? I took our case to the newspaper because it was the only avenue open. But I hope that the secretary will rise in support of fairness and redress this injustice!"

Tian Zhongzheng abruptly threw his wineglass to the floor, smashing it. "Lies, all lies!" he declaimed. "You're lying to the county leader and to the representative of the police!"

"That glass belonged to Secretary Tian," Golden Dog pointed out. "Water Girl is accusing you of entering a citizen's home at night with rape on your mind, and you've accused her and the others of ganging up on you. The discrepancy is easily judged. Stick out your foot, and let them see if you have all your toes."

Tian's foot was still wrapped in gauze. He tried to stand up with the aid of a cane but stumbled and returned to his chair. "I'm missing a toe because they smashed it with a rock! I have affidavits from eyewitnesses!"

"Oh!" Golden Dog said. "That's easily judged too. The wounds from a severed toe and from one that's been smashed are different. And the eyewitnesses you refer to—would they be the old man Wu Mingren and the boy from the Lu family? They've submitted new affidavits. Here, take a look. These are photocopies."

Tian Youshan was astonished at the pass matters had come to, and his face clouded over as, summoning his authority, he said, "That's enough, all of you. This isn't a court of law! We'll never get to the bottom of things by shouting and arguing. If a crime's been committed, the offender will not get away. But also, we'll never permit false accusations. Are we going to let things get out of control in White Rock Stockade? Now sit down, all of you. Golden Dog, did you put Water Girl up to coming here?"

"Here's what happened," Golden Dog replied. "She asked the newspaper in Zhou City to publicize what's happened, and I was ordered to investigate. Because of how well the incident of the shipping brigade's illegal traffic in lumber was handled, the newspaper thought we could avoid a scandal. I too hoped we could handle this quietly and settle the business without bringing disgrace on anyone, so I brought her here."

Tian Youshan laughed. "Golden Dog, you've got quite a head on your shoulders!"

The police chief pounded the table. "Put it in the papers if you want to! Our young scholar here has time on his hands, it seems. Why should we be in awe of some blasted newspaper?"

"Shut up!" Tian Youshan bellowed. "Let him finish."

Golden Dog sat down and sipped his wine, then continued, "A newspaper is the voice of the party, and it can't be written off as easily as the police chief would have us believe. When Water Girl made her complaint, here's what my thinking was. White Rock Stockade is a county where the work is done well at all levels, and I've written plenty of stories demonstrating that. If this matter makes the papers, it wouldn't be good for the county, for our township, or for you gentlemen here. It was wrong for Water Girl and the others to cut off Secretary Tian Zhongzheng's toe, even in self-defense. But it was, if I may speak bluntly, a case of rape turned upon itself. As for his missing toe, it is, after all, only a toe, and doesn't affect his appearance or his ability to walk. Nobody else knows about his loss, so why blow it up into a public scandal? Wouldn't that just make it harder for him to carry out his duties?"

"How did a country girl like her know she could take a complaint to the newspaper?"

"Secretary Tian," Tian Zhongzheng interrupted, "it's a conspiracy. They're setting a trap for us. Handling this matter quietly and putting it to rest sounds fine, but does that mean I've lost a toe and no one pays? If villagers can get away with injuring a township party secretary, why can't a county cadre injure the county secretary or a Central Committee cadre injure the president?"

"Don't go off the deep end, Zhongzheng," Tian Youshan said. "Lie down in the back room for a while. Go on!"

Tian Zhongzheng hobbled out of the room on his cane.

"Secretary Tian," Water Girl said, "I'm a middle-school graduate, so I know the functions of a newspaper. I first went to the police station with my complaint, but the chief wouldn't see me, and I went to the Zhou City newspaper only because there was nothing else I could do."

Tian Youshan chuckled. "So that's it. Now that I know what's what, it's up to me to act. Golden Dog, you can take her home. I'll convene a meeting of the standing committee to study the matter. I'll get back to you as soon as possible. I truly applaud the way you've handled things so far, and in the future feel free to bring anyone who feels he's been treated unjustly to see me. During a period of reforms, unusual cases are bound to occur, and as party secretary I'm the one to deal with them. In the movie *The Minor Official,* set in feudal times, there's the slogan 'An official who doesn't help his people out of jams might as well go home and plant some yams!' That's even more true of a secretary of the Communist party!"

Golden Dog expressed his gratitude and left with Water Girl.

As they were walking along the flower garden, a panful of dirty water splattered on the ground behind them. Water Girl spun around just as Tian Zhongzheng's head disappeared from the window. "The minute I give him a chance, he throws dirty water on us!" Water Girl said sadly. "God, how he must hate me!"

Golden Dog didn't even turn around. "The world would be a strange place if people like that *didn't* hate us. You were really spectacular in there today, Water Girl!"

"I wouldn't have had the courage if you hadn't been with me," she said. "Did I say anything terribly wrong? Once I found my pluck, my mouth just took over! That police chief tried to buffalo me, but I wasn't going to give him an inch in front of those people. Tian Youshan seems all right."

Golden Dog laughed.

Two days later, Secretary Tian Youshan told Golden Dog over the phone that it was decided after careful consideration that Lei Dakong would not be formally charged but would be detained for fifteen days. Golden Dog argued that there was no reason for the detention since Lei Dakong had acted in self-defense; he asked whether the decision had anything to do with Tian Zhongzheng's being a senior cadre, and whether the arrest was considered appropriate and correct. His insistence on approaching the case logically increased the strain on Tian Youshan, who intimated his awareness of the relationship between Golden Dog and Water Girl, as well as between Golden Dog and Tian Zhongzheng. He urged Golden Dog "not to do anything that might get people saying he was out for personal revenge." Golden Dog seethed when he heard this and was about to let fly a torrent when he heard the line go dead.

Since the decision seemed firm, Golden Dog returned to Crossroads Township as a reporter for the Zhou City newspaper to interview people about any wrongdoing by Tian Zhongzheng. Meanwhile, Fuyun and Water Girl began stirring up public opinion, vowing to go to Zhou City to accuse Tian Zhongzheng of attempted rape and of falsifying evidence to frame the innocent. Cai Da'an and Tian Yishen were quaking, since they were the ones who had arranged the falsified evidence. They set out at night to see Tian Zhongzheng in White Rock Stockade, and he went directly to seek support from the county secretary. But he ran into a buzz saw: "Now that things have come this far, you're finally worried, are you? Go on home. I'll tell the police chief to release Lei Dakong, and that'll be the end of it. Now listen carefully. Golden Dog is no longer the nobody he used to be. It's easier to make enemies than to win them back as friends, so you'd better learn how to treat him with kid gloves!" When Tian Zhongzheng returned to Crossroads Township, he had Cai Da'an take two bottles of Tiger Bone wine to the painter's house; Cai Da'an's instructions were to work on the painter in whatever ways might win his goodwill. The next day, Dakong was released from jail with a clean record.

20

When Lei Dakong returned to Stream of Wandering Spirits, he headed to Fuyun's house, where Golden Dog was telling the others about Cai Da'an's visit to his father with the wine, and musing on its significance. The wind had changed, he was pretty sure, but he was still surprised to see Dakong walk in the door. They'd got what they wanted, and they could be happy. The painter reached out and pushed away the six copper coins Han Wenju had laid out on the table and said, "Golden Dog, now that Dakong's back with no mark on his record, let's forget about making more trouble for that thief Tian Zhongzheng. Let's have a celebration dinner here. I'll go home and get those two bottles of Tiger Bone wine." After fetching the wine, he went into the kitchen with Water Girl and Fuyun to prepare a meal of bean curd in casserole, Four Happinesses meatballs, fried beef and alfalfa sprouts, and a clear soup. When it was ready, the six of them ate and drank heartily.

They waited until the meal was over to ask Dakong how it had been in jail. He took off his shirt to show the scars on his back, and he thundered against the men who had whipped him. Sick at heart, Water Girl reached for the scars, but she didn't know what to say that would bring any relief.

"Now don't get all upset," Dakong anticipated her. "Spending a few days in jail was good for me! At first I was frantic, and I spent most of my time pounding the walls with my fists or banging my head against the bars. I damned near went crazy! But I stopped screaming after a while, since all it did was make me hungry."

Tears streamed down Water Girl's face. "It's all my fault," she said. "You were so strong and husky, and now . . ."

"All they gave us was a steamed bun and some thin soup at each meal," he continued, "and at first I gave half of mine away. But after ten days or so, I was so damned hungry that when I went to bed, all I could think was, I'm not going to die, at least not before enjoying some of Water Girl's wonderful noodles!"

Everyone laughed except Water Girl, who kept putting food in his bowl, which he wolfed down as though trying to consume in one meal all the food he'd missed in jail.

"Take it easy, Dakong," Han said. "There's plenty. You didn't starve in prison; now don't eat yourself to death here at home!"

They laughed again and began playing drinking games. Dakong started off with a guantong, a two-handed ploy, and his excitement mounted quickly and vocally. Only Han was a capable adversary for him at this game—but he was so capable that Dakong drank one penalty after another. "I don't mind losing," he exclaimed. "In jail just the thought of wine nearly did me in. Every loss means that much more wine, and there's nothing wrong with that!"

"That's the spirit, Dakong," Han said. "The promise of drink was what motivated me to learn the game. But once I mastered it, I started to win regularly, and I wound up drinking hardly anything."

Dakong, whose eyes were turning bloodshot, didn't find Han's boasts to his liking. He rolled up his sleeves and said, "Let's go another dozen rounds. If I lose, we'll play Cantonese style!"

"Cantonese style?" Han asked. "What's that?"

"You mean you don't know how to play Cantonese style? How about Japanese style, then? How's your Japanese?"

"You really did pick up a thing or two in that goddamned jail!" Han said. "So you think I don't know Japanese? Your, lotsa dead peoples you have, *bakayaro!*"

They all burst out laughing. "That's enough," Golden Dog said. "You guys are usually models of decorum, but when you get a few drinks under your belt, all you want to do is outbrag each other. Let's all play the same style, so we don't have to sit here and watch the two of you. Dad, come sit with us."

The painter had been standing off to the side watching the fun and filling their plates and glasses. "I'm not much of a drinker," he said to his son. "And I don't know the first thing about drinking games. You go ahead without me."

They got to playing the "tiger, club, chicken, insect" game. Dakong gobbled up Fuyun's chicken with his tiger, then Han beat Dakong's tiger with his club, but Golden Dog ate Han's club with his insect. They were so evenly matched that no one got the upper hand,

and the game went back and forth as the food and wine kept disappearing and the laughter increased. They were having a riotous time. Golden Dog was feeling particularly unreined. "If only we had a tape recorder, we could preserve this drinking party. It'd make a terrific story. I wonder who invented the terms in this game. They perfectly represent the social order."

"How's that?" Han Wenju asked.

"Tigers eat chickens, chickens eat insects, insects eat clubs, clubs hit tigers: every prey has its predator, so they keep one another in check."

"Are you thinking about the way Tian Zhongzheng took advantage of us but had to answer to the county committee, which is under the jurisdiction of the prefecture committee?" Fuyun asked.

Water Girl exulted, "Everybody says Fuyun's not very bright, but he's right on the mark! The cards are stacked against us common people, and if it hadn't been for Uncle Golden Dog, Dakong would have had to spend three to five years in jail."

"Right!" Uncle Han said. "And why was Golden Dog able to take care of things? Because of his reporter's ID card, that's why! Officials have influence, but Golden Dog's ID is the real power!"

Dakong teased, "All his life Uncle Han's been reviling officials behind their back, but to their face he's the soul of deference."

"Who isn't?" Han replied. "Before Tian Zhongzheng became an official, he didn't have a kind word about officials, either, and once he became the township secretary, he never failed to complain about how stupid his superiors at the county level were. When you told Tian Youshan you were going to take your case up to the prefecture level, he caved in. Is Tian Youshan afraid of Gong Baoshan? You bet he is! Does he despise him? So much that his teeth bleed from gnashing them so much! Don't assume I don't know the score just because I spend my days at the ferry landing. The way I see it, Golden Dog despises those officials, but he's not above trying to get on their good side. And that's how he was able to rescue Dakong. Am I right, Golden Dog?"

Golden Dog scowled at Han; his cheeks were distended, and the tendons in his neck were taut. Water Girl was sure he was about to blow up at her uncle, but he didn't say anything. Instead he grabbed the jug and filled his glass with wine.

"Uncle," Water Girl said, "we're here to drink and have a good time, not to be lectured at by you. You owe us all a drink."

Golden Dog was the first to drain his glass, but still he didn't speak, and the atmosphere around the table had become chilly. Han tried to revive the party by urging everybody to drink, but the enthusiasm of just a moment before had been lost. It was Golden Dog who finally stood up and said, "Come on, everybody, drink up. Dakong, let's have another of your guantongs. I'm a little dizzy, so I'm going to lie down for a minute. But I'll be back to take you on again later."

"What's wrong with him?" Han asked after he had left the table and gone into the other room. "What did I say? I was complimenting him. How did I offend him?"

"Don't take me wrong," Dakong said, "but Golden Dog's got it all over you when it comes to finesse. If it had been you out there instead of him, I'd still be cooling my heels in jail! Let him get some rest. All this flurry on my behalf has tired him out, and the wine hasn't helped him any. Come on, let's go a few rounds!"

Golden Dog lay spread out on the kang, with a splitting headache. Han's casual remark had hit home, reactivating all the anguish and distress he'd experienced for days on end. Even though he'd succeeded in frustrating Tian Youshan's plan for a public meeting about the river shipping brigade and had rescued Dakong, his successes hadn't brought him the joy they had Water Girl, Fuyun, and Han Wenju, for he sensed a personal defeat in both incidents. He'd violated his own code of ethics by writing positive stories about the industrial and commercial management bureau, by saying exactly the things he knew Tian Youshan loved to hear, by browbeating and intimidating the police chief, and by threatening to take his case to the prefectural government, to bring pressure on Tian Youshan. All his complex scheming had been at a cost to his self-esteem. He wanted desperately to do something important, but he couldn't deny that he'd become a sly fox; to the son of a peasant, turning out that way seemed to fly in the face of everything that was decent.

Water Girl entered the bedroom, aware that something was bothering him but not knowing what it was; she manifested her feminine tenderness and concern by bringing him soup, which she told him to drink while he told her what he was brooding about.

"Don't let Uncle's words upset you. You know how he is when he's drinking."

"Uncle Han was right."

"But so were you. No matter how you look at it, we won."

He shook his head and poured out his anguish, including the doubt weighing most heavily on his mind. Could he, alone or in concert with others, ever bring people like Tian Zhongzheng into line or successfully complete the struggle against bureaucracy, he asked skeptically.

What was she to say? She could only remind him that this was the way the world was and that he had to work with human nature as it is. "Drink this soup. It'll sober you up and make you feel better."

He drank the soup, which was cool and sour; it neutralized the effects of the alcohol. After spitting up a mouthful of phlegm, which helped clear his mind, he looked up at her and asked, as much for her benefit as for his own, "If that's the case, am I going about it the right way?"

She had no answer.

They were looking at each other wordlessly as Dakong and Han's banter drifted into the room. Dakong had lost again, and Han was stridently demanding that he drink.

"Feeling better, Golden Dog?" Dakong yelled. "Come in here, and go a few rounds of guantong. I can't believe we young men are no match for Uncle Han!"

Golden Dog and Water Girl left the bedroom just as the dog started barking outside and Cai Da'an and Tian Yishen strode into the house, greeting everyone with clasped hands and saying they'd come to pay their respects to Dakong.

The turmoil Golden Dog had just managed to suppress broke through again. "Well, well!" he exclaimed. "Our two commanders. First you have him arrested, then you come to pay your respects!"

Dakong leaped to his feet and raised his glass. "I'm glad they're here!" he said. "I don't hold it against you, since you were only following orders. Here, let me toast you gentlemen!"

Cai and Tian sat down, picked up glasses, and accepted the toast. "Dakong, we had to do it; we were forced. Now that everything's worked out, we're here to apologize. Secretary Tian sent us to tell you that if you have any problems with your raft, just let him know. There's plenty of business for the river shipping brigade these days, and he's giving you the consignment of a load of alpine rush."

Dakong laughed uproariously. "I'm sorry as hell about that, because I don't want to earn my living on the water anymore. I'm going into business. The only way a powerless man like me can keep from being knocked around is to make a fistful of money. I don't guess Secretary Tian will object to that, will he?"

Cai and Tian were embarrassed. "Of course not," they said softly. "Of course he won't. In this period of reforms, if you became a rich man, he'll do nothing but commend you." After a few more rounds of wine, Cai and Tian began to grow uneasy and got up and left the party.

"Dakong," Han said, "you say you want to get as much out of life as possible and make your fortune. What do you have in mind?"

"I'm going to open a store! Before Golden Dog went to Zhou City, I was hoping we'd go in together. But I gave up the idea when he left. Truthfully, I haven't found anything else over the past few years that's as much up my alley, so I've decided to strike out in a big way. I know I'll never be able to handle a pen like Golden Dog, but if I can get my hands on some capital, I'm sure I can outdo the Tians financially. Then we'll see what happens."

"Money can rescue a man," the painter said, "but it can also ruin him!"

"You might be right, Uncle, but you might be wrong, too. What I need now is to be rescued. The best way to manage that would be to become a cadre, but who's going to let me do that? Or I could hire some guns and go into the mountains as a bandit chief. But this is a socialist country! Golden Dog, are you with me?"

Golden Dog, who was listening intently, pounded the table and said, "I'm with you! Give it everything you've got. If they want power, then we'll go after money! What do you have in mind?"

"First I need some capital; then I need a business license."

"Even if we pool our resources, we won't come up with much, and I doubt that you can borrow much outside. Why not set your sights as high as possible and borrow the money from the credit co-op? Cai Da'an wouldn't dare turn you down now. He's a greedy customer, but you can cut him in."

"I know," Dakong said. "I'll take care of raising the capital, but how can I get a business license?"

"Leave that to me," Golden Dog said. "We expect a lot from you this time, since it's our best chance to crush Tian's river shipping brigade."

"The shipping brigade? Hmph!" He gave the thumbs-up sign and spit on the ground. "Just you watch!"

As a bachelor, Dakong had a single possession, his old three-room shack, with its few pieces of furniture. He lived hand to mouth, his days alternating between bitter lows and excessive highs. Now that he was determined to strike out big, he took to the village credit co-op the seven yuan he'd been given as restitution upon his release from jail, and the co-op approved a loan for seventy yuan; then he took the seventy yuan to Cai Da'an, who approved a loan for seven hundred. The seven hundred he deposited with the district credit co-op, where he borrowed seven thousand. Finally, he took that to White Rock Stockade, where he received a loan of seventy thousand yuan. When he returned to Stream of Wandering Spirits, he dumped the money onto the table and said excitedly, "Water Girl, Fuyun, look at that. Do today's co-op officers belong to the Communist party or the Kuomintang? In the past I couldn't borrow a cent, but now in less than two days I've come up with seventy thousand yuan!"

Water Girl and Fuyun were amazed. "Where did you learn how to do this?" Fuyun asked.

"I was too naïve before," he said. "But my time in jail wised me up. One of my cellmates shared his experience with me. He has a real head for business, and we agreed that as soon as we got out of jail, we'd take the money we were given and set up a store together. The signboard's important these days, and we have to be called Something-or-Other Company. Water Girl, help me out!"

"This is no game, Dakong. Is your cellmate reliable?"

Dakong said, "Heroes die from overeating; cowards starve to death! You can tell how important money is these days by the ease with which I made all these loans. Money talks. With what I have between my ears, this time I'll make it. Golden Dog said he'd get me a business license, so my only worry now is finding a building. How about renting the blacksmith shop to me? I'll give you ninety yuan a month. What do you say?"

"The place is empty," Water Girl said. "So it's yours if you want it, as long as you don't mind its run-down condition. And it's rent-free, since you'll be looking after it for me. But what if things don't work out? It'd take you the rest of your life to pay back seventy thousand yuan!"

"I've thought this out from every angle," Dakong said. "Don't worry, I'm going to show all those people who've made life tough for me what I'm really made of! As for the shop, here's what we'll do. Since you're not asking for rent, we'll refurbish the place; then when we start turning a profit, we'll pay you a monthly rent."

Water Girl's doubts persisted. "Dakong, you're a changed man, and I'm not sure you can make a go of this. I'm all confused. Go to White Rock Stockade, and talk it over with Golden Dog. As a reporter, he knows a lot more than you or I."

Dakong assented, but when he arrived in White Rock Stockade, he picked up the business license Golden Dog had secured for him but didn't go to see him. He and his cellmate quickly did the shop over from top to bottom, and fifteen days later hung out their sign: White Rock Stockade City and Country United Trade Co.

Lei Dakong was manager of the new company, while the cellmate, Liu Zhuangzhuang, was assistant manager. They dealt in many kinds of goods, and although the small, two-room building housed the shop, in reality most of the profits came not from sales there but from large-volume trade in the surrounding area: they bought up local products and wholesaled them to outlying regions; they established connections with suppliers of assembled items like TV sets, bicycles, and sewing machines and sold them in nearby villages; and later on, they began dealing in larger manufactures like steel and automobiles, where each transaction ran to tens or even hundreds of thousands of yuan. As Dakong had predicted, rivers of money flowed in, and their momentum built so quickly that within a few months they had bought the three rooms next to the blacksmith shop, which they also refurbished. By this time their business put state-run stores to shame. No one had much of an idea of what the partners were involved in, but every few days Dakong, dressed to kill, could be seen entertaining guests in White Rock Stockade's biggest retaurant, on West Avenue, where business deals were made. Lei Dakong had become the talk of the town.

Once, after Golden Dog had sent an urgent dispatch to the newspaper and was finished for the day, he went out to buy some cigarettes and bumped into a man along the way. Giving the man only a passing glance, he continued walking. "Elder Brother Golden Dog!" the man called after him.

Golden Dog stopped and took a closer look. "Dakong, is that you? I didn't recognize you!"

Dakong, wearing a Western suit and sunglasses, looked very urbane. "How do I look, Golden Dog? I have to dress like this. Saddles make the horse, but clothes make the man. People don't trust businessmen who look like beggars."

"Packaging is all the rage these days," Golden Dog allowed. "For a native product, you're packaged pretty well! When did you come to town? What brought you here?"

"I was in Lanzhou. I heard that a unit desperately needed some steel, so I went there to see them. I just got back today."

"All White Rock Stockade is buzzing over how well you're doing. Dakong, you're really hot stuff! Now that you're on a roll, keep it going. The more people who know about you, the better, and the more money you make, the better. I'd like to see the looks on their faces. The first phase of your victory is complete. No one believed you had it in you!"

"Just like you. Who could have predicted that you'd become a hotshot reporter? People these days are recognizing their own worth, and they're cashing in on their own intelligence and abilities. I read that in that newspaper of yours."

"Oh, so you're reading newspapers now, and starting to mouth the slogans!"

"Of course. Information is money! Our company has two subscriptions to your paper."

"You say you made a deal to sell some steel. Do you have the steel?"

"I shouldn't be divulging company secrets to you . . . Where would I get steel? I just resell it. But that stimulates trade between the city and the countryside. I've been meaning to look you up, since you hear things at the newspaper and get the news first. Let me know if you hear anything I might be able to use. We deal in anything. If you hear of a unit in need of some manufactured product, put us in touch with them and you'll get a cut."

"That's out of my line," Golden Dog said with a laugh. "But I'm in the market for some good rat poison, if you have any. That old house of mine is rat-infested."

Dakong hooted long and hard over this. He remarked on how stupid he'd been back then, selling rat poison for a few fucking pennies. "But it was good experience, since I learned how to make a sales pitch. In my business you have to be a smooth talker."

They said good-bye after sharing a few more reminiscences and anecdotes. Three days later, when Golden Dog had returned to White Rock Stockade, he had to go to the east bank of the Zhou River for a story, and on the way back, as he was passing the southern gate, a car pulled up beside him and stopped. Dakong opened the door and invited him to hop in. In the car, Golden Dog asked him what was up.

"It's still that Lanzhou business," Dakong said. "I'm picking up someone to show him the steel."

"Where is the steel?"

"At the municipal construction bureau warehouse at He Family Bay east of town."

Golden Dog was skeptical. That steel belonged to the municipal construction bureau. How could Dakong get his hands on it? Dakong smiled. "If you're not busy, why not come along? But don't say anything. Just call me Manager."

The car pulled up at a hotel, where they picked up three guests from Lanzhou and drove to the warehouse at He Family Bay. The warehouse guard, a bald, doddering fellow, smiled at Dakong and called him Manager. Dakong just nodded to him as he opened the door, like a high-ranking cadre, and handed him a State Express cigarette before leading the three guests into the compound behind the warehouse, where there was a small mountain of steel. "Here it is. What do you say? Does that put your mind at ease?"

His customers were as content as clams. "We trust you completely. Completely. We'll sign the contract tomorrow, all right?"

The car sped back to the hotel, where the customers were let off. Golden Dog, of course, realized what was going on. "Dakong, you're stalling them by letting them see somebody's else's goods, aren't you?"

"That's the only way I can ease their anxieties and get the contract signed quickly."

"And does the municipal construction bureau let you get away with that?"

"I came over yesterday and had a talk with the warehouse guard, promising him eighty yuan if he'd let me have a look at their steel. Money talks with Old Baldy, too!"

Golden Dog was taken aback. "Isn't that a bribe?"

"When I wanted to open the store, didn't you recommend giving Cai Da'an a cut? People like that are always on the take."

"But you have to know when to do it and when not to," Golden Dog exclaimed censoriously.

Dakong pulled a notebook out of his pocket. "You're a man of letters, but this is the only means of power I've got. How would I manage without it? Here, take a look."

Golden Dog opened the notebook, which was filled with entries in a small, compact hand:

xx/xx/xx tape recorder to Mr. Li of the tax bureau

xx/xx/xx four hundred ¥ to municipal police precinct

xx/xx/xx one 18″ Hitachi color TV to Mr. Zhang of Zhou City planning commission

xx/xx/xx sold car, gave county purchasing agent 780 ¥

xx/xx/xx electric fan and 50-bottle case of Western Phoenix wine to White Rock Stockade planning commission

xx/xx/xx Cai Da'an, 500 ¥ for delivering goods

xx/xx/xx forestry investigation team, one 14″ b/w TV

xx/xx/xx Party Secretary Tian, one tape recorder (value 1,300 ¥) for marriage of third son

Golden Dog was speechless. He'd heard about "entertaining guests and giving gifts," but he'd never dreamed it had reached this point. This wasn't the Lei Dakong of old. How could he have changed so fast? Was this what being in jail had done to him? Golden Dog wanted to keep reading, but Dakong took the notebook from him and volunteered, "This is what society taught me. Golden Dog, some of these gifts I gave on my own. Each layer of the bureaucracy has its lord in charge, someone who trades his authority for cash. Some of them demanded gifts, and if I hadn't come across, I'd have been out of luck. Current policy is like a yam. If you know the person, the yam is baked and soft; if you don't, it's raw and hard. How do you soften people up? With cash, that's how."

Golden Dog could see that Dakong was far more daring and hardened than he, for he had been ashamed of compromising himself in order to be effective. It was tempting to adopt Dakong's ways. But he quickly reminded himself of the risks. He had known from the start what Dakong was like, and he began to wish that he'd never encouraged him to move in this direction. He took a long look at Dakong, who stood smugly beside him, and realized that, things being as they were, only people like Lei Dakong were answering the call of the times.

"Dakong," he said, "I've had something in mind that I've wanted to say to you ever since we ran into each other several days ago. When you take steps like yours to accomplish something, you must be absolutely sure it's the only way, and you mustn't confuse means with ends. As a businessman, you must keep one principle firmly in view: Never compromise your humanity for riches. I don't need to impress on you that during every historical period, in all societies, economic crimes have been dealt with severely. That's doubly true for a socialist society like ours!"

"Chickens don't piss," Dakong said, "but the stuff gets out somehow. Official circles are involved in constant infighting. You became a reporter because you love to read and write. But what about me? How am I supposed to make my mark? Don't think I haven't considered the risks. That's why I've kept this record. When the day comes, we'll all go down together if necessary. This is my little cache of dynamite. By wrapping my legs around theirs, I'll take them with me when it goes off."

Golden Dog puffed his cigarette deeply without saying another word.

"You probably think I've turned bad, don't you? I admit that what I'm doing is wrong, but I'm as pure as the driven snow compared with those power-hungry officials. Sure, I make a lot of money, but you have no idea what kind of pressure I'm under day and night, or how exhausting all this traveling is. Even though you and I nursed at different breasts, as far as I'm concerned we're closer than brothers. I'd never have got out of jail if it hadn't been for you, and I'll make it up to you someday. What's mine is yours, and if there's trouble, you won't be implicated."

Golden Dog didn't know what to say.

Dakong and his three customers from Lanzhou signed the contract the following day, in a restaurant, and Dakong telephoned Golden Dog afterward to request his presence at the banquet. He declined the invitation.

A couple of weeks later, Water Girl and Fuyun rode their raft down to White Rock Stockade. She was several months pregnant by then and beginning to show. No sooner was she on the raft than she began throwing up. Dakong had written to say that he was shorthanded and that, remembering their kindness, he wondered whether Fuyun would be willing to help out at a monthly salary of a hundred yuan. Delighted that Dakong had finally become somebody, they packed some native delicacies and set out for White Rock Stockade, not even stopping to sleep along the way. After tying up at the pier, Fuyun wanted to cut the raft loose and let it drift downstream, but Water Girl couldn't bear the thought and recommended trying to sell it. So he picked up his chopper and cut the binding ropes, then put the wood up for sale, cheap. The people living in the huts along the river came and fought over the lumber. Among them Fuyun spotted a familiar face and whispered to Water Girl, "Look over there; that's Scarface's girlfriend."

"She's very pretty."

Fuyun walked over and said, "What are you doing here? A few

pieces of wood can't mean much to a river dragon like Scarface."

"How can I pass it up at this price? We're planning on renovating that house of mine."

"Are you getting married?" Water Girl asked.

"We haven't set the date yet. But a young thing like you may not understand. You probably think I'm pretty foolish!"

"If you're going to get married," Water Girl said, "the sooner the better. For a happy occasion like that, we don't want your money for this little bit of wood. It's a wedding present."

The woman was embarrassed but delighted. "Why are you getting rid of a nice raft like this? Are you quitting the river?"

"A friend of mine has opened a business," Fuyun said, "and he's asked us to work for him and take things a little easier. Maybe you know him: Lei Dakong!"

"Lei Dakong?" the woman exclaimed. "Who doesn't know him? This is a wonderful break for you."

Water Girl moved closer and confided, "You have a kind face, sister, and you're making plans for your own wedding. I've felt I could trust you since the minute I laid eyes on you. May I ask a favor?"

"Of course," the woman said. "I can't guarantee anything, though, except that I know everybody in White Rock Stockade."

"I have two elder brothers," Water Girl explained. "Lei Dakong is one. The other's name is Golden Dog. They're both talented and good-looking, but neither's married. I'd appreciate it ever so much if you asked around for a couple of dependable, attractive girls. I'd bring the boys over to meet them."

"No problem," the woman said. "Leave it to me." She pointed out her house and told them her name was White Fragrance.

Fuyun and Water Girl walked into town in animated conversation about White Fragrance. "Water Girl," he said, "why are you putting so much trust in a woman you've just met? And why did you turn down her money? After all, it was your idea to sell the wood!"

"I like her."

"Her relationship with Scarface has damaged her reputation."

"She's doing exactly the right thing."

Fuyun wasn't clear what she meant.

They went first to the bureau ofice, where they told Golden Dog why they'd come to town. But instead of receiving the news with the joy they had expected, he sat deep in thought for the longest while. What could he say about the White Rock Stockade City and Country

United Trade Co.? He certainly could tell them that Dakong was a competent businessman, but he also had to say that he was taking too many chances. Golden Dog offered two reasons that they shouldn't join Dakong: first, the job wasn't quite right for an honest, artless man like Fuyun; second, since Water Girl was pregnant, she needed someone around to look after her. Water Girl insisted that she didn't want Fuyun tending her. But after hearing Golden Dog out, she began to worry about Dakong and urged the reporter to see that the new tycoon walked the straight and narrow and kept out of trouble. After they'd talked things out Fuyun went to get Dakong to join them.

The idea of seeing his friends again delighted Dakong. "Water Girl," he shouted from the foot of the stairs, "guess what I brought you!" He marched into the room and thrust a bag into her hands. When she opened it, she saw dried apricots, just what every pregnant woman craves. That association of the gift wasn't lost on her, and her face turned crimson. After they'd talked about the ache of being apart, Dakong announced that he was taking them to a highly acclaimed restaurant on West Avenue that specialized in dumplings like those served in the imperial palace. Forty-two varieties were on the menu, and the price of a meal was figured by the table. He ordered a sampling of all forty-two varieties, which were brought out, one steamer after another, including Flying Dragons in the Snow and Four Happinesses and Riches. Water Girl had heard of the place when she was working at the blacksmith shop, and Grandpa Pockface had promised to take her there, but he'd never got around to it. The table was piled with dumplings, and she exclaimed, "How can four of us eat all this? Dakong, tell them to take some back. It's too wasteful!"

"Eat as much as you can, worthy sister-in-law. It's time you had a real treat. These are called Imperial Concubine dumplings, named after Yang Guifei, the imperial concubine. Tradition has it that they were her favorites. If the Yang woman could eat them, Water Girl Han ought to be able to do the same! But it wasn't her liking them that got them named after her. Rather, it's because they're stuffed with the meat from chicken wings and drumsticks. Wings are for flying, *fei*, and drumsticks are for kneeling, *gui*, and together that's *guifei*."

Water Girl tried one but couldn't discern anything special about it. "My taste buds aren't subtle enough. It doesn't seem out of the ordinary to me."

"Forget how it tastes. What's important for you now is the nutrition," Dakong said.

Fuyun was eating with real gusto. He barely chewed before swallowing. "This must be costing you nearly a hundred yuan!" he said.

"Nearly a hundred?" Dakong harrumphed. "This is the best the place has to offer. Two hundred a table!"

Fuyun, who had just stuffed a dumpling into his mouth, spit it out in horror. "My god!" he exclaimed. "The food's worth more than we are!"

"Everything's expensive here. Take this plate of cold cuts and the beer, for example. In other places the cold cuts sell for eighty fen; here a plate goes for two-twenty. And beer that usually costs one yuan and eight fen is three yuan here. You wonder how business could be this good, with everything so expensive. Well, people are rich these days, and they pay these prices to prove their status."

"You mean they're just showing off their wealth?" Water Girl said.

"How many times in a lifetime do you think wealth comes your way?" Dakong asked. "We have the money now, so if we can't eat like this, who can? Tian Zhongzheng? Hmph! I seriously doubt that he could afford a meal here. We might as well flaunt it. I just made a cool forty-eight thousand without doing anything!"

Fuyun gaped in astonishment and asked how it was possible to make that much without doing anything. Had Dakong found a pot of gold?

"That's exactly what it was, a pot of gold six or seven meters wide, six or seven meters long, and as deep as you want it to be! Golden Dog knows what I'm talking about. It's the steel I sold to Lanzhou. The contract stipulated that they had to send a money order for 280,000 within a week to make the purchase, with a 20-percent penalty for late payment and a 25-percent penalty I'd have to pay if my delivery was late. The day after the contract was signed, I drove straight to Zhou City and boarded a plane for Lanzhou, where I prevailed on friends in the bank and at the post office to make sure that the payment wasn't received in White Rock Stockade within the week. I gave each of them a thousand yuan. The payment arrived late, so I made an easy forty-eight thousand, and I had an excuse not to deliver the steel. Now, wouldn't you call that making a profit without doing anything?"

Water Girl and Fuyun were so perturbed by what they were hearing that they couldn't eat. They glanced at Golden Dog, who had been listening quietly to Dakong and sipping his beer with an air of dejection. "Dakong," he said sternly, "we've talked about this before, and

I'm not going to repeat myself in front of others. But the only business that company of yours engages in is speculation, and you're in for big trouble if you keep it up!"

"Golden Dog works in the public sector, so that's exactly what he's supposed to say. But I want you all to know that everything's fine—no problems at all. I've left myself an escape hatch. Come on, enough of this talk. Drink up. It's too bad Uncle Han isn't here. That would really liven things up. Drink up, Golden Dog. I know you're worried about me, and I won't forget it, not as long as I live. Here's a toast to you; drink up!"

He filled his own glass halfway with strong, clear liquor, tipped his head back, and drained it. Then he just sat there, as though dazed, his bloodshot eyes staring straight ahead.

"Dakong," Golden Dog said, "you don't have to listen to me if you don't want to, but in my opinion, even though asking Fuyun to come work for you was well intentioned, I don't think it's a good idea. It's no place for him. Besides, since Water Girl's pregnant, she needs him around . . ."

"I didn't ask Fuyun to be a buyer," Dakong objected. "I just wanted to give him a chance to make some decent money. But you have a point. Fuyun, Water Girl, what do you think?"

"Maybe we'd better hold off for a while," Water Girl said.

"All right, that's fine," he said as she picked up the bottle and filled his glass halfway again. After he'd drunk it down, it was clear he wasn't holding the liquor well.

"You've had enough, Dakong," Golden Dog warned him. "You know I have your interest at heart. And, of course, I want what's best for Fuyun and Water Girl. Let's leave; what do you say? We can continue at my place."

They stepped out of the restaurant, with Fuyun helping Dakong, who said, "You're right, Golden Dog. Fuyun has Water Girl to take care of, and she's going to present us with a nephew. I don't want to add to their burdens. I know I'm constantly on the razor's edge, and I could lose my footing at any time. But, for me, so what, since I don't have a wife or children? I'd go down with no regrets. But I want you to do something for me, Golden Dog. I want you to place an announcement in the Zhou City newspaper saying that you have no dealings with me. Of course, that's for other people's benefit. We'll still share the profits, but if something goes wrong, the ax will fall on my head alone!"

"Bullshit!" Golden Dog said savagely. "If I hear any more of that nonsense, I'll stitch your mouth shut!"

"You're drunk, Dakong," Water Girl said. "We tried to keep you from drinking so much, and now look at you!"

Dakong fell to his knees in front of Golden Dog and pleaded, "Golden Dog, I beg you, place that announcement, for my sake!"

Golden Dog slapped him.

But Dakong didn't flinch. "Go ahead, slap me again! I deserve it. I won't raise a hand against you!"

Seeing the bad turn events had taken, Fuyun walked up decisively and lifted Dakong onto his back, to carry him to the bureau office. All of a sudden, Dakong emitted a wild laugh from his perch. He was laughing so hard he nearly choked. By the time they reached Golden Dog's place, the laughter had turned to wails, and he had begun cursing himself: was he a man or a devil or a half-man/half-devil? He implored them not to despise him. Since he'd let things go this far, all he wanted, he said, was to smash his head against the southern wall and knock it down. Then he began throwing up, covering the floor with the filthy detritus of the food he'd just eaten. In no time at all, he was snoring like a pig.

While Fuyun and Water Girl were outside getting dirt to throw on the mess, Golden Dog picked Dakong up and carried him to the bed; five wrapped condoms fell out of Dakong's pocket. This left Golden Dog no doubt that Dakong was whoring around. But when Water Girl and Fuyun returned with the dirt, Golden Dog picked the things up and, making an excuse to go outside, tossed them into a garbage can.

21

Water Girl and Fuyun returned to Stream of Wandering Spirits from White Rock Stockade in low spirits. They'd gone with such hopes and returned so disheartened. And the raft that had been their livelihood was gone. They spent their days at home stewing and watching boats and rafts sail up and down the river. Fuyun sometimes went out to tend the fields, but his heart was set on getting back on a raft. Water Girl didn't approve of his goal, nor did Han Wenju.

"After Dakong left," she said, "all the boatmen we'd sailed with rejoined the river shipping brigade, and I'd worry too much if you tried to go it alone. You're a good sailor, but where are you going to get cargoes, and how will you sell what you get? And that's only part of it. What will the Tian family come up with to make life difficult for you?"

Fuyun began to lose his appetite, and when the yellow dog tried to jump playfully up to his lap, he gave it an impulsive kick.

Han Wenju took umbrage. "Fuyun, kicking the dog like that—whose benefit was that for? Is that your way of showing you're peeved with me? Does it irk you that I keep drinking even though I don't have an income?"

"Don't read too much into it, Uncle. It's me I hate!"

"You ought to hate yourself! Now that Dakong's made it big, he's willing to give you a salary of a hundred yuan a month. But you're afraid his money will soil your hand—is that it? So you go around complaining about being broke!"

Water Girl resented it when her uncle talked like that. "It was Golden Dog's and my idea not to work for Dakong!" she fired back. "Don't go blaming Fuyun!"

"Why not work for him?" Han asked her. "Is he a stranger, some outsider? When he was in jail, all we could think about was getting him out, so what's wrong with cashing in on his success now? Besides, we're not asking for a handout!"

"You hang around the ferry landing all the time, so what do you know? It's out of the question, and I've told you so more than once! But you have to keep bugging us about it. You won't be happy until you cause a row, will you?"

Han Wenju wasn't ready to let it drop.

"So you let Golden Dog make your decisions for you now. How come he forgets us, then, when things get bad?"

She stood up offended and walked out, and when Fuyun saw her go, he followed her. Han was beginning to regret his nagging and, with a hangdog look, headed down to the boat to drown his sorrows.

The days passed like that until one day, when Old Seven was about to sail for White Rock Stockade, he came looking for Fuyun to try to talk him into joining the river shipping brigade. The idea made Fuyun uneasy, but Han urged him to go ahead, singing his refrain about how Golden Dog and Dakong had proved themselves superior to other men and were surely a match for Tian Zhongzheng. But a minor official nearby is a greater threat than a high official far away, Fuyun could see, and Crossroads Township was, after all, under Tian Zhongzheng's jurisdiction. Han recommended accepting what can't be changed and joining the shipping brigade. Old Seven told Fuyun that it was, in fact, Golden Dog's idea, and when Water Girl thought it over, she realized that, since the differences between Golden Dog and Tian Zhongzheng were irreconcilable, the reporter probably figured that this was the only possible move. So, for the moment, she decided not to oppose it, particularly since Tian might take a refusal as a slight that he'd someday want to avenge. Old Seven went and talked things over with Tian Yishen, who didn't approve of the idea, but Old Seven joined with ten other boatmen in threatening to leave the brigade if Fuyun were blackballed. So once again Fuyun was a member of the river shipping brigade as a hand on Old Seven's boat.

On his first day back on the water, Water Girl went to the shore with her husband and rolled up his sleeves for him and made sure his belt was tightly fastened. "This isn't going to be permanent," she said to him. "I'm sure Golden Dog is trying to come up with something better, or if we can ever stop worrying about Dakong, you can work for him. When you're out on the boat, be a little more assertive. Don't bully anyone, but if someone tries to bully you, let him know he can't get away with it!"

Fuyun nodded as he pushed the boat away from the rocks and began sailing it downstream.

At home, Water Girl spent her time worrying about Fuyun, and even more about Dakong. She sent a message through Fuyun to Golden Dog at White Rock Stockade, reminding him that Dakong had a wild streak because of being orphaned. That, she thought, combined with his cultural disadvantages, made it hard for him to control himself. She exhorted Golden Dog to keep trying to talk sense into him, and if that didn't work, to try verbal abuse or even to take physical measures—whatever was needed to bring him to heel.

As the seventh lunar month approached, Water Girl recalled that the eleventh day of it was Dakong's birthday, his thirty-fifth. That means he'll be thirty-six next year, she mumbled to herself, another threshold year. *Those are critical stages, and most people have trouble getting past them. Since he's in such a dangerous profession, he's bound to run into all kinds of problems next year.* Growing increasingly apprehensive, she said to Fuyun the next time he was scheduled to sail to White Rock Stockade, "Go see Golden Dog and tell him that Dakong's going into his threshold year and that on the eleventh you and I are going to give him some red underwear and a red belt."

"He won't be thirty-six till next year, so why worry now about his threshold year?" Fuyun wanted to know.

"A person's threshold year occurs during the year preceding his thirty-sixth birthday," she explained. "Don't you know anything?"

In White Rock Stockade, Fuyun passed the message on to Golden Dog, who sighed over Water Girl's thoughtfulness. He went to the White Rock Stockade City and Country United Trade Co. to find Dakong, but he wasn't there. As he walked through the front door of the refurbished building, he noticed that the office was located in what had been the shop's kitchen. But that was the only trace of anything familiar. There was a third again as much space inside, the walls had been papered, the ceiling painted, and there were overhead lights, carpets on the floor, and a sofa up against one of the walls. Golden Dog's first impression was that the place put the conference room at the office of the White Rock Stockade county committee to shame. Assistant Manager Liu was talking to someone. Golden Dog had met Liu, but he didn't know the other man, who was wearing a flashy sport shirt with a tie. The cordovan shoes he had on, one foot in the air, since his right leg was crossed over the other, had a dazzling shine. Golden Dog was about to leave, when Liu Zhuangzhuang rose and turned on the sweet talk. "Here's our reporter. Long time no see! Every official in the county has dropped by, but this is the first time this deity has honored us. You bring glory to our humble establishment!"

This sort of eyewash always made Golden Dog shudder. He asked tersely, "Is Dakong in?"

"Have a seat," Liu said. "Pour our reporter a soft drink, Little Wang."

A fashionable young woman appeared almost at once with a glass of lemon soda, which she placed on the tea table in front of Golden Dog. "Are you here to write a story about our company?" she asked him, smiling sweetly.

"I'm here to see someone." Reminded of the condoms that had fallen out of Dakong's pocket, he turned his eyes away from the young woman.

Liu handed Golden Dog a cigarette and said emphatically, "Dakong's not in, but you've come at just the right time. Let me introduce you. This is Golden Dog, a reporter from the White Rock Stockade newspaper bureau. This is Manager Yang of the Shangzhou branch of the Zhou-Shen Limited Company."

"The Zhou-Shen Limited Company?"

"You've heard of it, haven't you? It's a Zhou City–Shenzhen joint-venture company. An impressive name, isn't it? Manager Yang is Commissioner Gong's son-in-law."

Gong Baoshan's son-in-law? Golden Dog pondered the arrangement with disquiet. People like that were always looking for an advantage. Hostility welled in his heart. Hostility toward whom? Dakong? Yang? Gong Baoshan? He couldn't say. "Oh!" he stammered as he reached to shake Yang's extended hand.

Liu Zhuangzhuang laughed. "A meeting of two VIPs!" he said.

"Manager Liu, you have the tongue of a businessman. How's business, Manager Yang?"

"Not bad."

"When did you come to White Rock Stockade? What sort of business do you have here?"

"We don't have anything here for him," Liu interjected. "Manager Yang only gets involved in big deals. Since you're Dakong's friend, I don't mind telling you that Manager Yang is here to discuss matters advantageous to both our companies."

"There's no reason to keep economic cooperation a secret, is there?" Golden Dog asked with a smile.

"I've been thinking for a long time," Manager Yang said, "that commercial reforms throughout the area have created an opening for a united front, and that, if possible, the White Rock Stockade City and Country United Trade Co. ought to become an affiliate of the Zhou-Shen Limited Company. In an age of information like this, that's the way to spark the economy. I came here specifically to talk this over."

"That sounds impressive," Golden Dog said encouragingly. "If you can work it out, you'll be a power!"

"You came to see Dakong," Liu said, "and we're hoping he comes back soon, too. He went to the provincial capital and sent a telegram saying he'd return tomorrow. He has to approve all the company's major decisions, and if we're to become an affiliate, there's a lot he'll have to take into consideration."

Golden Dog exchanged a few more pleasantries with the men and asked Gong Baoshan's son-in-law a few casual questions, then returned to the bureau office.

He was assailed by misgivings all the following day, unable to shake the image of the insufferable arrogance and the domineering of the Gong family son-in-law, with that broad smile that seemed to presage the gathering of dark clouds: he had the look of a wolf, or a lion, or a monster, or an evil spirit. Golden Dog had the presentiment of danger for Dakong and for himself. He felt compromised by and ashamed of Dakong's activities. He began calling the company early in the morning but didn't reach Dakong until noon. When he asked to see him at once, Dakong replied that he couldn't leave because of the important questions he had to attend to. Golden Dog, losing his temper, pointed out that those important questions were his reason for wanting to talk right away. Dakong consented to come over, but when he walked in, he met a Golden Dog who sat stonily looking ahead and who showed no inclination to pour tea or to offer a cigarette. Golden Dog just stared at Dakong, with no indication of what was passing through his mind.

"Don't ogle me like that," Dakong said. "It scares me."

"I understand you've hooked up with Gong Baoshan's son-in-law," Golden Dog said, "and that you're going to become an affiliate of his Zhou-Shen Limited Company. Earning profits isn't enough anymore, and you've now set your sights on preferment in the public sector—is that it?"

Dakong's expression changed. "Where'd you hear that?"

"Am I right or not? Has Gong Baoshan's son-in-law left?"

"Who do you take me for? Do you really think I'd let myself become a lapdog for the Gong family? I know who I am, and I haven't come this far only to get swallowed up by the Gong family! It's like this. When we set up the company, I sent gifts to Tian in White Rock Stockade to make sure everything went smoothly. That's how we were able to make it this far. You and Water Girl and Fuyun were right when you urged me to know just how far I could go and to leave myself a way out. Tian seemed mollified by what we gave him, but there was always the chance he'd turn on us, so we had to take the long view and get political clout on our side. That's why I sought out Gong Baoshan's son-in-law as a patron. Their company is far more successful than ours, and they've been trying to extend their influence into White Rock Stockade. I'm just trying to participate in their success."

"So that's what you're doing! You think that with the Gong family on your side you can stand up to the Tian family. It's a fine-sounding theory, but what's really going to happen? You know better than anyone what kind of business you're involved in, so you ought to know how the Zhou-Shen Limited Company operates and how much better they are at it than you. They want to unite the companies throughout the province to create an economic bloc that serves their own power and profit. Where will you fit into their plans? Is this what you call participating in their success? You'll wind up being an accomplice without being a beneficiary."

"That's a pretty incredible scenario, Golden Dog!" Dakong said, shaking his head.

"Whether it's incredible or not is debatable. It's the possibility of it that's got me worried. There may be nothing I can say to sway you, but I can't help feeling that you've got some blind spots and that you're racing headlong to quicksand. I may as well speak bluntly, no matter how it sounds. If you keep on as you're going, I won't have anything more to do with you, and you can forget about having anything more to do with me!"

Dakong sat there, his face going first pale then red, as beads of sweat dotted his forehead. "'If that's how it is, Golden Dog . . . I'll take your advice, regardless of what I think. I'll cancel our agreement to become an affiliate."

"Do what you think is right. I have a message from Water Girl and Fuyun that the eleventh is your thirty-fifth birthday and next year is a threshold year for you. So they're coming to town to celebrate your birthday and ally themselves with you against the troubles you face next year."

"My birthday's on the eleventh? I forgot, but she remembered!"

"The people of Stream of Wandering Spirits want to see you succeed," Golden Dog said with compassion, "and they couldn't bear it if they had to turn against you in the process."

Dakong's nose began to ache. "When are they coming?"

"Around the tenth."

"Golden Dog, what grieves me more than anything is the way I've treated Water Girl and Fuyun. Are you aware that when I asked them to come work for me, and you talked them out of it, they gave their raft away? Things are tough for them these days. With both you and me away from the village, they have to be completely self-reliant. I offered them some money, but they wouldn't accept it . . ."

"I advised Fuyun to join the river shipping brigade."

"The shipping brigade? Are you crazy? Without anyone to look after him? You've delivered the lamb into the jaws of the tiger!"

"There was no other way. I don't think Tian will try anything funny for now . . . If you ran your business on the up and up, the shipping brigade would be the last place he'd have gone."

Dakong swallowed hard but didn't say anything.

Golden Dog walked Dakong to the street and before turning back said, "If you've got time over the next few days, come tell me everything you know about the Zhou-Shen Limited Company."

"What do you want to know that for? Planning an exposé?"

"I'm thinking about it."

Dakong hesitated for a moment, murmured, "Okay," and walked off.

Golden Dog waited two days, then a third, but Dakong didn't show up.

Water Girl and Fuyun, on the other hand, did come to the bureau office. She was wearing a pastel blouse with a Western collar that showed off the fair skin of her neck, and a pair of trousers that made her legs look particularly long. As usual, she had on cloth shoes, but not those she'd made herself: the black velvet tops contrasted beautifully with her white stockings. Fuyun was dressed in a clean polyester shirt and a new straw hat.

"Fuyun," Golden Dog greeted him with pleasure, "you're dressed to kill today!"

Water Girl laughed. "He refused to put them on until I said I wouldn't let him come to White Rock Stockade unless he did. I told him that not only would he embarrass me but he'd embarrass you and Dakong as well."

"I can barely walk dressed up like this!" Fuyun complained.

They were carrying an armload of packages, which they emptied as soon as they were inside. They'd brought a fish cooked in noodles, a red cotton stomacher, a red belt, two sets of red underwear, and edible fungus, chrysanthemum, walnuts, and chestnuts. Golden Dog surveyed it and said it looked as if they were going to hold a little boy's birthday party for Dakong. He asked what the noodles and fish were for. The birthday for a threshold year was the same as starting anew, Water Girl assured him. Then he turned in amusement to the stomacher, wondering why it was so red, and asked if she thought Dakong would wear it. He'll wear it whether he wants to or not, she said. Besides, it's worn under the clothes, not outside. She took out some red underwear and said, "This pair's for you!"

He held them up and shook them. They were bright red, and huge.

"I'm wearing a pair too," Fuyun said. "This place is full of evil spirits, but these keep them away."

Golden Dog laughed again and said, "You're dressing us up so we look like something between men and women, between adults and children."

"What about Dakong?" she asked. "Did you tell him to come today?"'

"I told him several days ago. He must be sore at me, because he hasn't been over since."

"Did the two of you have an argument?" Water Girl asked anxiously. "How's he been lately?"

If only she hadn't asked. For with her question, Golden Dog's vexation returned. He recounted the upsetting story of Dakong's relationship with Gong Baoshan's son-in-law. Just as they were taxing Dakong with being stupid, he walked in the door. It was plain to him that they were talking about him. "Golden Dog's bad-mouthing me again, I see!"

"Nonsense!" Water Girl objected. "Uncle Golden Dog was just telling us about you, not bad-mouthing you. I was going to ask you about yourself anyway. But why didn't you come the other day when Golden Dog asked you to?"

"I was going to, but I wasn't sure what to say. He's going to write an exposé about the company owned by the Gong family, and I don't know what my part in that should be. I decided to wait till you came so we could talk it over together."

"Dakong," Golden Dog said, "it's as clear as day. When you're with us, you're a human being, but as soon as you're back in the office, you turn into a demon."

"I admit that the Zhou-Shen Limited is a shady company, but we're already tangled in some of their activities, and if you expose them, I'll be caught in the middle."

"See there!" Golden Dog exclaimed. "I said you'd slide right into it, but you wouldn't believe me! But so help me, I'm going to expose them anyway."

Dakong shrugged his shoulders and looked at Water Girl. She pleaded, "At least don't do it just yet, Golden Dog. Dakong, you must separate yourself from them right away!"

"If I don't heed your advice, may I drop dead during my threshold year!"

"Stop that talk!" Water Girl rebuked him. "Why do you think we came? Okay, let's change the subject. We're here to celebrate your birthday. Uncle Golden Dog, come with me to buy some groceries. Then you three can get good and drunk together!"

"I've made reservations at a restaurant," Dakong interjected.

"Not today," Water Girl said. "We can't talk freely there, and they won't let us sit and eat for as long as we want."

Acceding to her, Dakong took out a hundred yuan for the groceries. "I know you've got money," she said, "but we'll use our own. We're giving you a birthday party, not the other way around. You stay here and put on your red stomacher and red underpants, and put on that red belt. I know you'd rather deck yourself out in gold and silver, but you can do that next year, when it's safe. Do you hear me?"

Later that day, they ate until the sun went down. By then, Golden Dog, Dakong, and Fuyun were roaring drunk. At first they were boisterous, but they became more subdued when they started throwing up. Water Girl was kept busy taking care of first one, then the other, giving them water to rinse their mouths and wash their faces, and cleaning up their messes. But she didn't so much as shake her head. She was a bodhisattva, a protecting angel, a mother hen. As the cool night breeze came through the window, she looked up into the black sky and could see the first three stars in the handle of the Big Dipper. Just then she felt the stirrings of the tiny life inside her belly.

Golden Dog wouldn't let Water Girl and Fuyun leave immediately for Stream of Wandering Spirits. He made arrangements for them to take in several operas, while he tried to learn as much as he could about the company run by Gong Baoshan's son-in-law. By coincidence, a reporter from the Zhou City newspaper, who had been sent to a neighboring county on a story, passed through, and when Golden Dog spoke to him about what he was doing, what the man told him put him into a deep depression. Golden Dog knew that the company was nominally a joint venture of organizations in Zhou City and Shenzhen, but he hadn't been aware that Gong Baoshan's son-in-law was an employee of the provincial capital who had taken unpaid leave to work for a company whose manager was one of the children of a certain high cadre on the provincial committee. He'd gone from there to Zhou City to open his own company and had made contact with a business in Shenzhen that had connections with a member of the Central Committee. One thing led to another, until the Zhou-Shen Limited Company was formed.

Golden Dog knew he had a problem. How was he going to write an exposé under these circumstances? Although he'd been able to topple the party secretary of Dongyang County, it would be a different matter altogether to smash a web of relationships as intricate and complex as this. And as Dakong had said, if he exposed the Zhou-Shen Limited Company, Dakong himself would be undone in the process. The last thing Golden Dog wanted was to cause injury to Dakong.

He was asleep in bed by the time Water Girl and Fuyun returned from the theater. The sight of his face, dark and clouded in sleep, alarmed Water Girl, who assumed he must be sick. But when she felt his forehead with her hand, he woke up and insisted he was fine. She kept her eye on him through dinner, however, and asked what was wrong as soon as she saw him put down his chopsticks after finishing only one bowl of rice. He didn't want to talk about it, and that nettled her. "If you're not sick, and you say there's nothing wrong, why are you acting like this?"

What could he answer? He knew that telling them wouldn't relieve his own worries and would only add to theirs, so he managed a self-deprecatory laugh and returned to the rice, forcing down another bowlful.

Water Girl and Fuyun were sufficiently disturbed that they went to ask Dakong what was weighing on Golden Dog, but he didn't know. That night Golden Dog slept elsewhere so that Water Girl and Fuyun could have his room. They talked about him in bed. "No matter what we ask him," Fuyun said, "we don't get anywhere. Do you think . . ."

"Think what?"

He didn't finish. After a long pause, he mumbled, "We're using his bed while he's out there all alone."

Water Girl echoed, "All alone," but didn't say anything more.

"What do you think?" Fuyun asked her.

"What do I think about what?"

"I'd better go back tomorrow," he said. "Tian Yishen will make trouble if I spend too much time away from the shipping brigade."

"Then we'll go back together."

"Why don't you stay a few days longer?" he asked.

She knew what he was thinking, and she pummeled him with her fists. But after a moment she threw her arms around him and hugged him tight. She cried for her good and decent husband, and she cried for Golden Dog, who was sleeping somewhere else.

The next day, the two of them made their way to the buildings near the southern gate, but White Fragrance didn't have good news for them. Even though she'd thought of several girls, either they already had boyfriends or they had some sort of character flaw. But she promised to keep looking. From there they went to the bureau office, only to find that Golden Dog was out. Fuyun commented, "Even if White Fragrance finds someone, there's no guarantee Golden Dog will like her."

"He would if it were the right girl. He isn't getting any younger. Other people his age already have children."

Fuyun was tempted to say, "You know why he isn't looking? Because there's room in his heart only for you!" But he couldn't say that, and his only outlet was to hit himself hard with his own fist.

"Have you gone crazy?"

"I'm just not in a good mood. I'm going to take a walk."

Fuyun left, but instead of going for a walk as he'd said, he went to the pier at the southern gate, feeling miserable. He wanted to cry, but the tears wouldn't come; he wanted to scream, but the sounds stuck in his throat. When a couple of boats passed by, he hitched a ride to Crossroads Township.

Golden Dog returned later that day, encountering Water Girl alone in the room, absorbed in her thoughts. His first question concerned Fuyun's whereabouts. They waited and waited for Fuyun to complete his walk, and eventually they began to feel uneasy. At last she blurted out, "I'll bet he's gone back to Stream of Wandering Spirits!"

Golden Dog was puzzled. Why, he asked, would Fuyun leave without a word?

Water Girl's tears began to flow. "Don't ask!" she whimpered. "Don't ask!" She said she wanted to go home too.

Since there was nothing else he could do, he said he'd take her home. They went to the pier, but all the boats and rafts were out on the river and they had to go back to town to take the bus to Zhou City that stopped in Crossroads Township. When they reached the village, Golden Dog said he wasn't getting off.

"You're almost at your old front door. Aren't you going to stop off at home?"

"No, I'm going on to Zhou City."

"Why the sudden flip-flop? Do you have business there?"

"No, I just feel like going."

The bus started up again, leaving a perplexed Water Girl staring after it. Golden Dog sat on the bus with his head bowed, as baffled as she was about why he'd decided to go to Zhou City.

The lamps were lit when the bus arrived there, and a chill permeated the air reeking of the river. His mind cleared a little, but when he started down the street, the flickering neon lights, the strange, unpleasant music emerging from the dance halls, and the cacophony of people and vehicles made him dizzy. He stood in the middle of an intersection, looking down the streets that came together and wondering if he should go to the newspaper compound or find a bar. He was tired and confused. He walked into a dance hall, but the minute he saw the fashionable young men and women, he decided to go see Shi Hua.

Her husband had taken their child to visit an out-of-town relative that night, and Shi Hua had gone out for a bath after cleaning the apartment. She'd just got back and was standing in front of the mirror putting oil on her hair when Golden Dog knocked at the door. "Come in!" she shouted. "The door's unlocked!"

He opened the door and entered. When she saw who it was, she gave a gulp of surprise and their reflections stood still in the mirror.

It was a quiet night, and a night of unbridled passion. The resentment that had occupied Shi Hua's heart like a block of ice melted into a flowing river of love that intoxicated her, dissolved her in its stream. Golden Dog was like an addict who knows the opium is killing him but craves it for the ecstasy it brings. The explosive release of passion left them like a pair of whipped dogs—or like a concoction that has lost its efficacy. They could hear the loud, crisp ticking of the desk clock.

"Have you missed me?" Shi Hua asked him.

"Yes."

"Then why did you leave Zhou City without a word?"

"I felt like it."

"Why did you come back?"

"I felt like it."

She hated this sort of masculine posturing, but with Golden Dog it was also the very thing that had made her fall in love with him. "Now that you're back, I won't let you go this time."

"I don't want to go. I'm going to get married and settle in Zhou City."

"Aren't you and that girl Yingying married yet?"

"I broke that off a long time ago."

"That's good. There's a girl who's been asking me to find her a husband. She hates weak, effeminate men. She's looking for a macho type!"

Golden Dog stayed at Shi Hua's home for three days, and during that time he met the girl. She was employed by the Zhou-Shen Limited Company. He also learned that Shi Hua had taken unpaid leave from the department store and with some other people had opened an advertising packaging company that had close ties with a business run by the son of a high official in the provincial government. The girl was impressed by Golden Dog, even though he was a little too rustic for her tastes and had an aging father in the countryside. But she figured those were flaws that would mend. She asked him if he wanted to go to the provincial capital to find work. Or, if he preferred, she thought they might go to Shenzhen.

Back at Shi Hua's home, Golden Dog blew up. "I'm supposed to work for the Zhou-Shen Limited Company, too? Like hell I will! Is everyone everywhere like this? Is this what life's all about? One great big network? Shi Hua, Shi Hua!" He called her name mournfully, and said over and over, "It's hard, so very hard!"

By now he'd found even Shi Hua repulsive, and he regretted coming to Zhou City and seeking her out. He was also dismayed by how disgusting he'd become.

He left Shi Hua and took a bus back to White Rock Stockade, his heart filled with the image of Water Girl. She was the last angel left on earth.

22

Golden Dog went home.

His father seemed to have aged a lot, and he'd developed a bad cough. All he talked about was Golden Dog's being unmarried. "Golden Dog," he said, "do you plan to remain a bachelor all your life? My health gets worse every day. What bothers me isn't so much that I won't have anyone around to take care of me but that after I close my eyes for the last time, I won't be able to face your mother. There isn't another person in Restless Hill, Stream of Wandering Spirits, or the other villages in Crossroads Township who doesn't have a wife. You decided you didn't want Yingying, so she married a military officer and she's already several months pregnant. I saw her down at the ferry landing the other day, and all she did was prance around and brag about her husband. Golden Dog, she was doing that to show me up!"

Downcast, Golden Dog heard him out without saying a word. When the old man was finished, his son said simply, "That's my business, Dad!"

What this answer produced, however, was reproaches and a demonstration of anguish from the painter. Knowing that there was no way to make the old man understand, Golden Dog retired to the ferry landing as dusk began to fall.

Han Wenju was gutting a fish on his boat when Golden Dog appeared. Four or five egrets were circling above Han's head, every once in a while swooping down audaciously and snatching pieces of offal out of his hand. The abbot from Restless Hill Monastery was leaning against the cabin hatch, his freshly shaved dome glistening as though it had been waxed. Han had made it clear that he didn't want to hear about Buddhism today; he said that all the abbot ever spoke of was *prajna* this or *bodhi* that, the Buddhist words for "wisdom" and "knowledge," and that no one could ever figure out what the hell he was talking about anyway. The abbot just chuckled before expatiating on the coarse, wild talk of mortals and on how far Han was lagging behind. It didn't take long for them to get into a good-natured argument, all over the decision to smoke or not to smoke. "Anybody who doesn't smoke or drink," Han affirmed, "is no better than a dog! You want to know who doesn't smoke? Rabbits don't smoke. Their mouths are split like triangles, so they can't hold a pipe! Turtles don't smoke. They're covered by hard shells, and the smoke gets in their eyes! Donkeys don't smoke. They can't hold a pipe in their hooves!" The nonsmoking abbot responded, "Of course rabbits smoke. Haven't you ever seen those little tobacco pellets they drop? And turtles smoke. Haven't you ever noticed how yellow their shells are? Nicotine stains. Donkeys smoke. Haven't you ever seen the tobacco pouches hanging between their rear legs?" Han was no intellectual match for the abbot, whose sophisms made even him laugh until he had trouble catching his breath. They broke off their banter as Golden Dog loomed before them. Han asked him if there was news from White Rock Stockade. "Any changes in policy?" he asked.

"Your ears are pretty long, Abbot; you must know what's going on."

"What would I know?" the abbot retorted. "I don't set policy. It's all too much for me. All I see is that the government is encouraging activity in every sphere and that everyone's making money hand over fist, which has driven up prices."

"Golden Dog," Han said, "let me ask you: has Dakong really made a killing? I haven't seen him around for a long time, but I hear that gold and silver are dripping from his fists. Like our ancestors said, 'If there weren't ten families getting poor, there wouldn't be one family getting rich.' Does the Communist party really say it's okay for one person to make so much money? I'll bet it'll reverse that policy."

Golden Dog laughed. "You've got a bent for running the country, Uncle Han. When they announced the new policy, you deplored the change. Now you can't wait for another change!"

"Uncle Han is prime-minister material," said the abbot dryly. "It's a shame you're tucked away at the Zhou River ferry landing. But don't worry, Wenju. Our historical forebear Jiang Taigong was fishing in the Wei River when King Zhou Wen sent the royal chariot for him to become prime minister. Be patient!"

Han deflected the irony amiably. "If my name were Tian or Gong, you might be surprised. When the day comes, Abbot, I'll send for you to become director of the Family Planning Commission!"

The abbot didn't return the jab, but Han Wenju, afraid he might feel the clap of the abbot's hand over his mouth, jumped to his feet. As he did, the egrets swooped down, scooped up sliced fish in their beaks, and flew off, leaving him there to beat his chest and stomp his foot in frustration.

As night fell, Golden Dog, wanting to keep clear of his father's badgering, asked Han to spend the night at his house and to try to get the old man to put his obsession in perspective. Golden Dog would stay behind and watch the ferryboat. He sat in the hatch of the cabin, surrounded by the black of night, and stared dreamily at the dense fog that rolled in, until the light reflecting off the waves vanished and everything was swallowed up by the lonely night. There was so much for him to think about, but at the moment he was weary of it all. The peaceful night was perfectly suited to his mood. He was very tired, and there were few opportunities to enjoy the luxury of a vacant mind; his head lolled on his chest as sleep overcame him. At some time during the night he woke up to the sounds of the bell at the Restless Hill Monastery wafting toward him. They seemed so deep and solemn, so special somehow, as they rose up to him from the surface of the water. The river was dotted with countless bright stars, like so many fixed gems. What a gorgeous sight, he reflected, and he had a sudden impulse to count the stars. He reached a hundred fifty the first time, a hundred fifty-eight the second, and was puzzled by the discrepancy. Just then he heard a swishing sound, which he assumed to be the wind, that invisible energizer that could be seen only when it made the leaves on the shoal rustle. His gaze moved silently back to the river, where the stars were set as deeply as before in the still surface of the water. The sound was getting louder; it was coming from the opposite shore.

"Ferryboat!" came a voice. "Hey, is there a ferryboat?"

Someone wanted to cross the river, but instead of shouting explanations, Golden Dog pulled the ferryboat out into the river. A man was standing at the water's edge alongside a bicycle.

"Thank you," he said. "I want to get to the monastery on the other side. Sorry to wake you up. I'll double the standard fare."

"Oh, don't mention it. Come, get on board."

The man lifted his bicycle and stepped onto the ferryboat. He was a middle-aged man wearing old but well-fitting clothes and a pair of glasses. He had a well-bred, suave look. An oversized leather valise was tied to the rack of his bicycle.

"You're not from around here," said Golden Dog. "Where do you come from?"

"No, I'm not from around here," the man agreed. "And I don't come from any place in particular."

"Are you going to the monastery to seek advice from the gods?"

"No, I heard the sound of the bell."

"Are you planning to spend a few days there?"

"I don't know. Maybe, maybe not."

It all sounded uncharacteristic of a pilgrim to Golden Dog, who said, "Since you're not going for the gods, and you don't seem to have any special mission there, you must just be looking for lodging. But it's awfully late, and it's a long walk to the monastery, so you're free to sleep on the boat if that's good enough for you."

"You're very sharp. I didn't reach White Rock Stockade until noon, and after a quick lunch I hurried off to Crossroads Township. But every place had closed for the night by the time I got here. When I heard the bell, though, I knew there must be a monastery nearby, and here I am. It would be great if I could spend the night on your boat, but I hate to impose on you."

"If you can sleep on a boat, it's no imposition."

Golden Dog made up the bed in the cabin for the man, who thanked him repeatedly before lying down and falling fast asleep, with a loud snore. Golden Dog sat quietly for a while listening to the peaceful sounds around him. There won't be any more passengers tonight, he thought, as the snores began to make him sleepy. He took off his shoes, loosened his clothes, and lay on the floor by the head of the bed.

Early the next morning, he woke to find Han Wenju sitting by the bed. "Golden Dog, who was here last night?"

"Someone passing through. He wanted to go to the monastery in the middle of the night, but I talked him into sleeping on the boat." He rolled over to reach up and wake the man, but the bed was empty. "Where is he?" he asked, surprised. "Has he gone?"

"He left a note saying he'd be back tonight, and asked you to keep an eye on his bicycle and valise."

Golden Dog got up and went out on the deck, where the bicycle and valise were in the bow.

"Who was he?" asked Han Wenju. "What's his name? What does he do? Where's he from?"

"I don't know," Golden Dog said. "But what a strange man he was, to take off so early and to leave his bicycle and valise behind!"

"You're too trusting, Golden Dog. What was he like? Did he look like an escaped criminal? Or a smuggler?"

During the years of operating the ferry boat, Han had seen all kinds of people, including, on two occasions, escaped convicts. He'd no sooner ferried them across the river than the police arrived on the opposite shore. And he'd seen smugglers who traveled around the countryside buying up old coins, gold rings, silver bracelets, and the like. Why, one of them had even wanted to buy those six old copper coins he used for divination. Han's questions planted doubts in Golden Dog's mind, so they opened the man's valise, which was filled with books and notebooks. The notebooks recorded the man's experiences in the various places he'd visited: there were entries on history, economics, politics, and local customs, as well as anecdotes. It all became clear to Golden Dog. "Uncle Han," he said, "he's a cultural worker on a survey tour. Survey tours like this have become very popular lately. Some of the people travel on foot, some on bicycles; some even sail up and down the Yellow River. They're either scholars or writers."

Han couldn't figure out how there could be people like that in the world, folks who had plenty to eat and good clothes to wear yet traveled around the country like mendicants. "Then you and he are in similar occupations. But what good do the surveys do? I'll bet he's not quite right in the head!"

During the day they busied themselves with their own work, with nothing much to say to each other. Toward nightfall, Golden Dog, looking forward to a long talk with the man on the survey tour, asked Han to sleep again at the painter's house. He prepared some food and made sure there was wine before sitting down to wait for the surveyor, who arrived just as night fell. Golden Dog introduced himself and explained where he worked, then came right out with questions about the visitor. The man was pleased by what he'd heard; he'd been on a survey tour for a year and three months, he said, through the provinces of Shaanxi, Gansu, and Ningxia. Finding the banks of the Zhou River interesting, he'd decided to tour the area, starting at the headwaters. It had taken him nearly three weeks to get this far. When he arrived in White Rock Stockade the day before, he was told that Crossroads Township was the pride of the county, so he'd pedaled into the night to get there, where, to his delight, he'd slept on a ferryboat. Golden Dog could tell by the way he spoke that he was no ordinary man. A background of considerable culture was clear. Offering the man some food and filling his glass with wine to promote a cordial atmosphere, he proceeded with the conversation.

"Your work must be tiring," he said, "but it sure looks interesting! I've been around the Zhou River all my life, but I've never traveled its whole length. What impressions of the area have you got from your time here?"

"The Zhou is the third largest river in the province," the man said. "But it has unique characteristics and the most personality. It wends through three provinces and forty-eight counties. It's two thousand eight hundred li long, deep in some places, shallow in others, as it twists and turns and keeps changing in myriad ways. It's the deepest, the longest, and the most turbulent river in this border region. The banks of the Zhou have some of the most spectacular scenery anywhere, and even though they're not rich in resources, there is considerable variety in their products. The people are poor, and their customs have a primitive simplicity . . ."

Golden Dog clapped his hands and marveled, "Wonderful! You've managed to capture the essence of the Zhou River in a few sentences. Why don't you stay on a few more days and get even more of a feel for the place? There have been tremendous changes in the villages lately, and it's no exaggeration to say that all the peasants have enough to eat even if lots of problems remain. Where did you go this morning? Was it a successful excursion?"

"I'm an early riser, and I didn't want to wake you. First I went into town and found a bar, where I sat and chatted with the owner about the history of the place and heard some of the local legends and some tales of extraordinary happenings. I also sounded out his economic standing. After that, I took a stroll through Eastern Wang Ditch and Jia Family Village, where I talked to four peasants."

Golden Dog listened to him relate the conversations he'd had with the four peasants, then asked him in what came close to being a reverent tone, "You've traveled all over and seen a lot. What are your views on the current reforms in China? And what do you anticipate in the way of developments? How does the Zhou River area compare with other parts of China?"

"I can see why you're a reporter. Those are the questions I wanted to ask you. My strongest impression is that when you talk to the people here, whether they're cadres, workers, or peasants, you discover how interested they are in national issues."

Golden Dog laughed. "This is a poor area, and the poorer the people, the more profoundly changes on a national scale affect them. There's something I've been thinking about lately. The current national policies have done a lot of good. Peasants at the subsistence level have made significant gains through the land contract system, and permitting, even encouraging, a market economy is a move in the right direction. But no sooner do some people set themselves up in business than they're rolling in money, and most of the new wealth has come through business practices that would give you the creeps. At this rate, individuals will get rich at the expense of the national economy, with inflation, serious graft and corruption, and a deterioration of public morality the result. Whether the recent innovations will become mainstream phenomena or not, and whether they're good or bad, I can't tell, but I vacillate between enthusiasm and despair, and I'm never quite sure what tone to adopt in my stories. Of course, in large part that's because of the gaps in my education, my insufficient knowledge, and a certain cultural deprivation. I'd very much like to hear your opinions, though."

"I'm impressed by your interest in these issues. They're the reason I'm on my tour. As I see it, the party's current policies are correct in their fundamental direction. Recent changes in China, particularly in the countryside, confirm that. Nevertheless, we're moving forward without drawing on past experience in a way that could benefit us. We're like someone walking through a twisting tunnel who knows he's heading the right way as long as there's a light in front of him. But each twist in our lives brings with it a number of problems, and if we don't work them out, we could be courting danger. In a word, the implementation of the reforms is not going to be easy."

"What do you mean?"

"China has a long feudal history, which has isolated her in the world. That changed at Liberation, when we became a socialist country, but features of feudalism remain deeply implanted in our society. We've worked hard to break free of our isolationist mentality, and a market economy has breathed new life into the people. It's like a wave crashing over the dike of tradition and spreading out in new directions. During the transformation, people's consciousness has emerged from hibernation. More and more people have become aware of their own significance and worth, but since they're adjusting to a new way of thinking, it's all too easy for them to be lured in the wrong direction and to go astray. That's why some people work only to enrich themselves, giving no thought to how they do it, even if it means cheating the collective and the country at large. What do you think, Comrade Golden Dog, am I making any sense?"

"What you're saying is that during a period of reform it's essential to exercise caution about how people reform themselves, right?"

"I like your way of putting it—clear and simple! This is your home, Comrade Golden Dog, and you're a reporter, so no doubt you know this place as well as anyone. If you have the time, I hope you'll come with me tomorrow and help gather some information."

Golden Dog jumped at the chance. Because he had had relatively little education, talking with the surveyor was probably more useful to him than years of reading would have been. It brought home to him how narrow his approach to social problems was and how superficial his thinking. He saw a chance to learn.

Over the next three days, he accompanied his visitor on a tour of five villages and towns, including Seven-Li Ditch, Xia Family Village, and Tea-Lane Township, where they interviewed people from forty-two households. Golden Dog hung on the surveyor's every word as he discussed problems with the people, and he made mental note of the angles from which the man came to the issues; his respect for the man's subtlety and penetration increased by the day. He arranged for the two of them to eat with the villagers during the day, but at night they returned to the boat, where he continued trying to gain from the surveyor's wisdom. It didn't take long for Han Wenju to realize that the surveyor was a learned man, and he joined the discussions, offering opinions on matters of national significance, giving views on Crossroads Township, and appraising the situation in Stream of Wandering Spirits.

On one clear, nearly moonless night when the river was calm, Han came to the boat with the yellow dog following on his heels. Once he got the dog into the cabin, the three men pulled the boat to the middle of the river, where they continued their conversation. After a while, they heard some barking on the opposite shore that began to disturb their conversation.

"I wonder who wants to cross the river," Han said, as he pulled the boat up to the shore. But there was no one there—just three barking dogs. "God damn it!" Han fumed. "There's no one here, so what are those damned dogs barking for?" He picked up a pole from the deck and threw it, hitting one of the dogs on the back. With a yelp, it ran off, pursued by the others. But as soon as he was back in the cabin, they were back on the riverbank barking for all they were worth.

"Golden Dog," Han said, "you're fast on your feet. Go drive those mangy curs away. We can't talk above the din they're making. They know me too well, since they come to the ferry landing all the time. They think they can do anything they damned well please here."

Golden Dog stepped onto the bank, but the dogs stood their ground, and he quickly realized that their yaps were being answered by the yellow dog on the boat. "Uncle Han!" he chortled. "You can brag all you like that everyone around here knows you and so do the dogs. But these dogs aren't looking for you; they're trying to get your yellow buddy on the boat to join them!"

The surveyor found this droll—but it embarrassed Han, who patted the yellow dog. "They want my yellow dog to join them, do they? They must be looking for a little romance." That pat was all the permission the dog needed to send it flying like a bullet out of the cabin, to leap to the bank and join the other dogs.

"Uncle Han," Golden Dog teased, "by watching you talk and joke all the time with your female passengers, your dog's become your protégé!"

"A real friend you are, ridiculing me in front of a visitor! But you're no match for a common mutt, Golden Dog. They know all about romance, but you're thirty-three or thirty-four already and haven't gazed upon a woman's body. You've wasted your life!"

Han was angry that he'd lost face in front of the surveyor. On top of that, his shot at Golden Dog about a wasted life had ricocheted. Since he was himself a confirmed bachelor, did that mean that he was no match for a common mutt either? Deflated, he turned to the surveyor and tried to retrieve matters with a smile. "How do you like dogmeat?"

"It's succulent, of course."

Han grabbed hold of the rope that tied his boat to the landing and jumped onto the riverbank.

"What are you doing, Uncle Han?" Golden Dog asked.

"I'm going to catch one of those wild dogs and serve it to our guest!"

"Do you know whose dogs they are? Do you really think you can catch one?"

"Of course I can. They're wild dogs, and horny, just like Tian Zhongzheng. Come on, give me a hand!"

They followed the dogs over to the shoal by the riverbank, where the three mutts had the yellow dog cornered and were yelping at it. Before long, the three began fighting among themselves and were oblivious to the approach of the men. With a shout, Han threw a lasso over the neck of one of them, the white one, which yelped and took off, dragging its captor behind it so that he skinned his hands and face. Golden Dog added his might, and together they grabbed the dog and carried it back to the boat. There they throttled it, skinned it, chopped off its head, and slit its belly. Han lopped off the dog's penis and said, "No more whoring around for you! This thing just cost you your life!"

Lapping sounds came from the water just then, like those of a boat on its way up the river. "Someone's coming," Han said, as he threw the dog's skin, head, and innards, as well as its penis, into the river. "Who's there?" he called. "Whose boat's that?"

"Is that you, Uncle?" came the reply from downriver. "It's me, We're back!" A boat appeared out of the mist. Fuyun and Old Seven were standing on the prow.

"You scared the hell out of me, Old Seven!" Han said. "If you hadn't rattled me, I'd have treated you to a dog's penis!"

Old Seven and Fuyun tied their boat up at the landing and joined the others on the ferryboat. Old Seven's eyes lit up when he saw the slaughtered dog, and he tried to think of an appropriately dirty rejoinder to Han Wenju. But he caught sight of the visitor, who looked suspiciously like a cadre, and he kept his mouth shut. After the introductions, the surveyor's interest was piqued, particularly by Old Seven and Fuyun's attire. "Old Uncle, Elder Brother," he said, "where have you sailed from?"

"From Purple Thistle Pass," Old Seven said. "We transported some cigarettes for a store in town. A light load."

"Where's Purple Thistle Pass? How far is it from here?"

"It's a port downriver," Old Seven replied. "Not far—about a day's travel with the current and a few hours more against the current."

"How come you're getting back so late?" Han asked.

"Ask Fuyun," Old Seven grunted.

Fuyun was already inside roasting the dog in a pot, following Han's instructions, and the flames had turned his face, neck, and chest bright red. Several days on the river, with the sun beating down and the wind carrying dust, had made his face more leathery than ever. He laughed self-consciously when he heard Old Seven mention his name. "Is Uncle Seven still griping about me? If I hadn't hung around Purple Thistle Pass like that, what stories would I have had to tell you on the way back when you wanted me to relieve the boredom?"

"What happened at Purple Thistle Pass?" Golden Dog pressed

him. "Tell us all. This comrade here is on a survey tour of the Zhou River, and it's things like this that he especially wishes to hear."

"A couple of years ago a boy from a mountain village fifteen li north of Purple Thistle Pass passed the college entrance exams and became famous around here as the first student from the area to go to college. Before he left for his studies he was engaged to a local girl, and he became one of the top students. He started writing things, novels or something, and made quite a name for himself. Some of his stuff was published in provincial newspapers and magazines and even won prizes. He had everything going for him. Well, there was a girl in his class, a professor's daughter, who fell in love with him. Oh, I forgot. When he left for college, he was wearing mountain clothes, and the other students all laughed at him. The professor's daughter called him Farmer Boy and made fun of him in front of everybody. But once she saw how well he could write, she changed her tune. She gave him money, bought him good things to eat and some new clothes, and when he got sick and was hospitalized, she sat with him day and night and cried because he was so sick. Eventually they went to bed. Later on he murdered the professor's daughter: he strangled her in bed, then held her in his arms and slept till noon the next day. Then he turned himself in."

"Are you finished, Fuyun?" Han asked. "That tongue of yours is made out of lead. You don't know how to tell a story!"

"You don't find it a moving story?" Fuyun asked. "I saw a poster in Purple Thistle Pass that said the boy was executed, but the poster was even simpler than my recounting, and it got me wondering. The boy must have been crazy!"

"What's there to wonder about?" Han said. "He was still in love with the girl in his village and had a guilty conscience over sleeping with the professor's daughter. Men always regret doing things like that. Since he couldn't free himself from her, he murdered her. Something similar happened with Gong Baoshan, but the ending was different. After Gong came to town, he fell in love with a student, though he hadn't got a divorce from his wife. He pressured her to file, and even brought the student home in order to raise her hackles. He'd come home late at night, and when his wife asked if he'd been at a meeting, he'd say no, he was out with his girlfriend! Well, she'd cry, and he'd take out a hankie for her to dry her eyes, but he'd tell her that the hankie was a gift from his girlfriend! His wife was the daughter of Zhang Shanzi, from Zhang Family Mountain, and she was so afflicted that she went and hanged herself. If she hadn't, the way things were going, I wouldn't be surprised if Gong Baoshan would have murdered her eventually!"

At this point in the story, Han realized that the woman Gong Baoshan nearly murdered wasn't just someone he was dallying with but his own wife—quite a different case from that of the mountain boy. But since he heard no protests, he didn't go into that.

"Everybody's talking about it in Purple Thistle Pass," Fuyun continued. "They say the kid didn't appreciate his good luck, that after he went to town all he had to do was break it off with the girl at home, since a mountain girl's no match for a city girl. But he went and murdered her, and that was the end of him! Some people said he'd always been stubborn, even as a kid, and never got into a fight he didn't expect to win. They all think he got what he deserved. Somebody told me that all the rivers in that area flow east, except the one where he's from, which flows west, and what could you expect from a place with a messed-up geomancy like that! His forebears were a wild bunch. His grandpa had been king of the mountain, and his daddy had caused trouble for a lot of people back in 1960 and went to prison for fomenting a rebellion. They overturned his sentence and let him out of jail, but that shows the kind of resolute stock he came from. A dragon's son is a dragon, a phoenix's son is a phoenix, and a rat's son knows how to dig a hole in the ground. So he murdered her!"

The surveyor, who had been listening intently, spoke up: "I don't understand every detail, but the way you tell the events, they sound extremely interesting. How do I get to Purple Thistle Pass?"

"Does the incident interest you enough to investigate it?"

"It sounds like something very much worth investigating. A boy from a mountain village goes to college, makes a name for himself, and the daughter of a professor falls in love with him. Those are the makings of a happy story. But then, after he and the girl get involved, he murders her. It sounds to me as if he lost control, went berserk! But I suspect there's more to it than meets the eye, because people with a narrow view of things only worry about personal gains and losses. If they're successful, they're proud of themselves, but minor setbacks make them paranoid, convinced that others are out to get them. Failure is the hardest thing for them to bear, and all they can think about is revenge . . ."

"You say these people take a narrow view. What makes them do that?"

"China has a long history as an underdeveloped economy, and there's a tremendous difference in wealth from one region to another.

The distribution of goods lags even farther behind. In lots of mountain districts there are also the problems of infrequent communication with the rest of the country and of conservatism, which easily lead to a narrow, rigid psychological makeup. Here you also have to take social psychology into account. What I mean is that after a major upheaval, changes in social attitudes invariably occur: the people grow agitated, begin to lose their sense of public morality, shun discipline, and grow more complacent about violence. That's what happened after World War II in Japan, and it's precisely what happened after the Cultural Revolution here. In the course of this tour, I've run into plenty of people who fall into the category of the socially disaffected. Nothing pleases them, nothing seems right. I often detect a desire for revenge, although even they don't know whom they want to seek revenge against. In fact, there isn't anyone. They just have a need to hate, to despise, to exact revenge. The only way they can secure a measure of peace is to release the turbulence inside them in some violent way. People like that are in constant need of a powerful stimulant."

The surveyor spoke with an eloquence that captivated Old Seven and Fuyun. Even Han Wenju knew he was outclassed by the man. They didn't understand everything he said, but the polish of his speech was enough to win them over, particularly with the richness of the vocabulary he was using.

"You're a learned man, Comrade. What level graduate are you?"

"College," the surveyor said.

"No wonder you know so much. You're a trained professional."

The surveyor smiled and said, "All this academic palaver must be boring you. I've traveled to a few places and seen a thing or two. I'm forever trying to figure things out, and when I think I've understood something, I can't stop talking!"

Golden Dog, who hadn't broken in once, had the distinct impression that everything the surveyor said was for his benefit, for the benefit of just one person from Stream of Wandering Spirits. When Fuyun took the lid off the pot of dogmeat to see if it was done, everyone cried out in unison, "Smells wonderful!"

But Golden Dog was too intent on the conversation to enjoy the aroma. "Your interpretation seems sound," he said. "How did you reach your conclusion?"

"If you look at the case of the mountain boy from a sociological rather than a strictly legal perspective, the court's determination that his act came of 'extreme individualistic tendencies' is incorrect, as is the idea that he was a callous murderer. That's because beneath the surface lies an easily discovered and very real psychological feature of the times, and that is the common consciousness of our specific historical environment."

"A psychological feature?" Golden Dog asked. "How do you view this feature?"

"The unique feature I'm referring to is the consciousness that pervades contemporary society," the surveyor said. "And we can take it back even farther. In the 1950s, the country was in a state of euphoria owing to our victory in the war, and the 'feature' was positive and eminently capable of propelling us forward. But our race is beset by an inherent failing, that of invariably transforming normal enthusiasm into abnormal stimulation, and of turning our confidence into irrational fanaticism. The mistakes of 1957, the setbacks of 1958, the sustained fanaticism of 1959, and the ten years of the Cultural Revolution are prime examples of that. Now that we've opened our eyes and taken a hard look at the world, we can see that we've fallen behind at least a century, but this awakened realization holds no psychological advantage for us, for our baseless national self-adulation has turned into a deep-seated national inferiority complex. So we've grown restless and confused, unable to decide what to do, as though we were in a fog five li thick. We trust nothing, we doubt everything, and everybody fights to display his own subjective consciousness, placing the emphasis on his own personal interests. Nothing seems right, nothing gives a sense of comfort, and in a flash what was once an unfounded idealism is transformed into nearsighted utilitarianism."

Golden Dog said, "But I believe there's a positive side to the confusion, in that it creates internal ferment. Just because people gripe and complain doesn't mean their demands are unreasonable."

"You're right, of course. The devaluation of a people results in the celebration and nurturing of self-worth by individuals. But there's a critical point in the pursuit of individuality that, if passed in chasing a sense of self-worth founded on a collective inferiority complex, is the gateway to a complete loss of the very sense of self-worth sought. The boy from the mountain village near Purple Thistle Pass probably suffered from that sort of psychological confusion."

Golden Dog was silent for a moment before mumbling, "What should we do, then?"

"You folks?"

Knowing that what he'd said sounded like self-interest, Golden Dog tried to cover his slip with a smile. "According to you, education is necessary in order to come to grips with the social consciousness of the time. But how do we ensure the right kind of education?"

"I'm working on an article on precisely that question. My personal opinion is that we should work on developing the Chinese people's most precious quality, which is their tenacious spirit."

What had begun as a discussion of the case of the mountain boy from Purple Thistle Pass had evolved into an examination of social problems by two kindred spirits—Golden Dog and the surveyor. Fuyun and Old Seven, having lost interest, had gone to take care of the pot of dogmeat. As for Han Wenju, he had reconciled himself to not being in the surveyor's league, or in Golden Dog's either, for that matter. Since he had nothing to add to the conversation, he went over and exchanged indecent stories with Old Seven and gave Fuyun a hard time about filling the bowls with dogmeat and the glasses with wine. "Golden Dog!" he butted in. "When you scholars get together, you talk a blue streak! Your mouths must be aching by now. Let your guest sample some of our dogmeat and strong wine."

Golden Dog held his questions and ushered his guest forward to join the others for something to eat. The fellow was an astonishingly good drinker, and after several rounds, when Fuyun and Golden Dog had started to have trouble staying upright, he seemed as sober and acute as when he began. Han dragged Golden Dog into the cabin and said, "This guest of yours can really pack the liquor away. Go to my house, and tell Water Girl to give you three more bottles."

"He's had plenty. If he drinks any more, he'll fall on his face."

"There's nothing wrong with that!" Han decided. "Since he likes to be among us, how can we stint on the wine? Getting our guests drunk is a local custom. Believe me, he won't mind; he'll be delighted. Go on. I'm not asking you to pay for it!"

Reluctantly, Golden Dog went for three more bottles. After Han filled everyone's glass, he said to the surveyor, "Allow me to toast you! We mountain folks aren't practiced at entertaining people. This wine's about all we've got, but if you don't think me unworthy, you'll accept my toast. Bottoms up!"

The surveyor stood and thanked him; then, holding the glass respectfully in both hands, he drank the wine down.

Han directed a raised eyebrow at Fuyun, Golden Dog, and Old Seven, and they each stood up and toasted the visitor in turn, three more full glasses for him. He drained every one.

After two of the three bottles had been emptied, Han stood up to drink yet another toast, but he lost his balance and crashed to the floor, drunk as a lord. Golden Dog was next, as dizziness and nausea overtook him. Fuyun listed to one side of his chair; he was motionless, and his eyes were closed. Old Seven was the only one among them who could still focus a thought. "What kind of hosts are you," he said, "tying one on before your guest? Well, it's getting late. We should get some rest." He helped Han over to the bed, leaving space for the guest. Then after getting Golden Dog and Fuyun settled on a straw mat at the foot of the bed, he staggered home.

Golden Dog slept fitfully that night, not being sure in the moments of wakefulness whether he was dead or alive. When he looked out the next morning, the surface of the river glinted with the rays of the morning sun. He looked about the cabin. Han Wenju and Fuyun were still in a deep sleep, but the surveyor was nowhere in sight. Golden Dog went on deck, and discovered that the boat was tied up on the shore opposite where it had been the night before. The bicycle and valise were gone. A note pinned to the cabin door read, "Thanks for your hospitality. I'll never forget it. I didn't want to wake you, so I'll say good-bye with this note. I hope you understand."

"Oh!" Golden Dog groaned. He walked to the bow and stood quietly watching the vast blanket of morning fog break up. There was a sort of emptiness in his heart.

He thought about nothing that day except his odd encounter with the surveyor. It had left him feeling both elevated and depressed: elevated because it had opened his eyes and unshackled his thoughts; depressed that there was so much that as a reporter he didn't know. In light of the surveyor's views, he began to rethink how things stood with Dakong and his White Rock Stockade City and Country United Trade Co. When he returned to the bureau office in White Rock Stockade, the first thing he did was to write to his young friends at the Zhou City newspaper office and in bureaus throughout the province, telling them about the surveyor and sharing the man's views with them. He ended with a challenge: *We're not trained professionals, and we have a lot to learn when it comes to theoretical nuances. But even though we came up from the grass roots or spend most of our time down at the grass roots, when we investigate problems we report only the facts. In order to lift our degree of cultivation, we young people should organize ourselves, gain all the knowledge we can, and share our thoughts.* He then spent three nights writing a story about Lei Dakong's business, but instead of sending it to the editorial office, he made several copies and mailed them to his young reporter friends to ask for their reactions. The key portion of the story went, "Speculation by illicit businesses has driven up prices in the marketplace. Petticoat influences within party and government institutions have increased bureaucracy. These problems are a direct threat to society, to current reforms, and to national stability. The incompatibility between the people's highly developed subjective consciousness and their cultural disadvantages has created the pervasive mood of turbulence China is witnessing today. This is something requiring serious consideration as reforms are implemented." In the accompanying letter, he wrote in a deadpan tone, "In all honesty, some of the terms I've used I really can't explain adequately—phrases like 'cultural disadvantages,' about which I have only a general sense. I guess that's proof of my own cultural disadvantages! I hope this gets us thinking more about the issues and triggers debate, the purpose of which is to smooth the way for and hasten our maturity, until we can all be reporters worthy of the name!"

23

Fuyun and Old Seven sailed the luckiest boat in the Crossroads Township River Shipping Brigade. Old Seven was one of the river's strangest denizens. During his youth he could polish off nearly a kilogram of rice at one sitting, and he'd always been as hard as nails. Now the oldest sailor in the brigade, he was a first-rate riverman who had never had an accident, even though he wasn't as strong as he'd once been. When he and Fuyun joined forces, Water Girl had said, "I'm glad Fuyun's sailing with Old Seven, who was born under a lucky star. At last my husband's bad luck will turn to good." Her prediction had been borne out, for in their months together, business had been good, the trips free of misadventures, and disputes virtually nonexistent. If there was any friction, it was over the importance Old Seven placed on his white snake. Twice a day he required Fuyun to pay homage to the snake, and when they sailed to White Rock Stockade or Purple Thistle Pass, they went first to the Smooth Seas Temple, where they lit incense, rain or shine. Back on the boat, Old Seven would milk the generational difference between them by stretching out to sleep while he sent Fuyun into town to buy food, always in two separate portions: roast pig's head and sesame-seed cakes for Old Seven and steamed buns for Fuyun, or noodles and meat for Old Seven and vegetarian noodles for Fuyun. Fuyun deferred to him like a father, and Old Seven had no complaints. But all that changed when they were drinking. The prerogatives of seniority went out the window, and they behaved like brothers. And always they sang drinking songs. Old Seven taught the younger man all the songs he knew, and when the river was calm, they'd let the boat drift along with the current as strains of music lifted into the air:

Le de, le de, Ready,
Set, *le de,*
We're ready, set to, *le de,* Go!
  Five chiefs! Seven skills!
  Up you go! Eight horses!
Elder brother's wine,
Little brother's cup,
When we finish this glass, it's *le de* time again!

Fuyun always lost when they sang this one. Wineglass in hand, he'd say, "Uncle Seven, you're drunk again. Instead of your calling me Elder Brother, I should be calling you Uncle."

"Those things don't count when you're drinking!"

All the boats sailing up and down the river had heard this exchange at one time or another, and they always laughed at the odd pair, but they envied the two as well, an old man and his young helper. When Water Girl came to the landing to meet the boat, she'd bring along two sets of clothes or shoes and socks she'd bought with the money Fuyun had handed her the previous time: one set for him, the other for Old Seven. And Old Seven, never the tightwad, would peel off for her most of what they'd earned on the trip. When she refused his generosity, he'd lose his temper: "I have food to eat and wine to drink. What do I need more for? To buy myself a coffin? You should be putting some of that aside, Water Girl. There'll come a time when you'll need it."

Water Girl, who was by now so big she could barely walk, missed the point and continued to decline the money. "Water Girl," Old Seven said, "let's see you take a couple of steps."

Bewildered, she nonetheless did as he said. "The left side's higher than the right when you walk. It's a boy!"

She was self-conscious. "Uncle Seven," she said, "if you're right, you'll have to teach him how to pole a boat when he gets older."

"Do you think his generation's going to be poling a boat like me?" His disappointment at the thought was contagious; it was time to change the subject. Just then they saw Tian Zhongzheng ambling toward the landing, and Old Seven turned and retreated into the cabin. The injury to Tian's foot had healed, and he no longer limped. But he always wore socks, no matter how hot it was, even with sandals. Feigning unawareness of him, Fuyun kept his head lowered and busied himself on the boat.

"Fuyun!" Tian shouted. "Just get back? Were you in Purple Thistle Pass?"

"White Rock Stockade."

"Safe trip?"

"Yes."

"That's good. I hear the dike at Sun-Moon Shoal collapsed, and the river was blocked. Be very careful!" He headed toward Han Wenju's ferryboat to cross the river and go into town.

Fuyun approached the cabin and said to Water Girl, "Tian Zhongzheng's sure being pleasant."

"The more agreeable he seems, the more evil he's got on his mind. It's all a performance. Just ignore him. Since we can't afford to offend him, we just have to stay out of his way."

The two men—one old, one young—were a good team: they worked well together, they got along well, and they were both on bad terms with Tian Zhongzheng. Most of the other boatmen in the shipping brigade had an affinity with them, until their influence was nearly as great as it had been in Golden Dog's time. Cai Da'an and Tian Yishen kept a watchful eye, and so did Tian Zhongzheng. Late one afternoon they sent for Fuyun. "Fuyun," Cai said to him when he arrived at the government office, "you've been doing a fine job ever since Dakong left. It'll soon be time to give merit awards, and after careful deliberation, we're prepared to put your name forward. In order to reward your exemplary record and make full use of your talents, we've decided to take you off the boat and have you assist me as a purchasing agent. How does that sound?"

It sounded very good indeed, but he said, "I don't think I've got what it takes for the assignment of purchasing agent. I'm not much of a talker, and I could never keep the books straight."

"We're not asking you to become foreign minister," Cai said. "I'll always be here. Maybe you're not much of a talker, and maybe you can't keep the books straight, but you've got two good legs, haven't you?"

Fuyun agreed to the proposal, but when he got home, Water Girl was skeptical. "They're just trying to split you and Old Seven up." Abashed that he'd been taken in, he blasted their machinations and started out the door to rescind his acceptance of the offer. Water Girl stopped him. "If you turn them down now," she said, "you'll give them the grounds they're looking for to accuse you of trying to stir up trouble in the organization. Go ahead and help Cai Da'an, and see what happens."

So Fuyun became a purchasing agent, and his fellow boatmen grew envious. They grumbled about how brute power was the only thing

Tian and his cohorts understood: having caused them trouble, Fuyun had now been promoted to a cushy job. As the days passed, Fuyun began to dress a little more fashionably, at his wife's urging. "A purchasing agent spends a lot of time around people. It's not like out on the boat. You have to look good, or people will make fun of us."

During July and August, the harvest products of the mountain villages at the upper reaches of the Zhou River matured. In Crossroads Township there was an open-air market every week; in Seven-Li Bay, some ten li west of town, there was one every three days, with the roads piled high with kiwi, peaches, plums, and hawthorns. The shipping brigade came to make purchases, then hired a tractor to cart what they bought down to the landing, where it was loaded onto boats and shipped downriver to the distilleries in White Rock Stockade and Xiangfan. At first, Fuyun did business in Crossroads Township; for two days he was so busy he was up before dawn and didn't get home until late at night. But then suddenly everything was sold out, and he had to turn to Seven-Li Bay, where he discovered there was nothing to buy, either. Because the shortage was unexpected, he asked around and learned that three families from Three-Li Bay had linked up to open a purchasing station alongside the road from the mountain. They had bought up everything coming to town. When he reported back to the office, Cai Da'an nodded his head. "I was going to tell you about that. By setting up a purchasing station, they used their geographical advantage to buy the stuff up, but they've agreed to deal with us. They've even promised not to sell to any other shipping organization. The new arrangement saves us the trouble of running around making individual buys."

"Individual purchases are more trouble, that's a fact, but they save money. This way we earn fewer profits, don't we?"

"We have no choice," Cai said. "We can't stop them from buying the stuff up! Back when you and Dakong were operating on your own, you competed with the river shipping brigade, didn't you?"

Fuyun was forced to go back to Seven-Li Bay and buy from the local purchasing station, but he wasn't happy about it and he made sure the goods he purchased were of high quality.

During one of his visits to Seven-Li Bay, he negotiated an agreement for fifteen thousand kilograms of crated Grade A kiwi fruit. But while he was weighing it, he discovered that the goods were below standard, that their size and weight were that of Grade B fruit, at best. An argument was inevitable.

"Don't take them if you don't want them!" the seller defied him. "Send Cai Da'an over!"

"I'm Cai Da'an's representative!" Fuyun argued. "These are Grade B, and if you won't sell them at the price of Grade B fruit, the river shipping brigade isn't interested!" He turned and stormed off, but when he got home, he decided not to say anything to Cai. The kiwi lay there for several days, until it began to spoil, and a third of it was sold to Scarface and some other independent shippers. As soon as Cai got wind of that, he went himself to Seven-Li Bay, where he bought up the remaining two-thirds at the Grade A price and had it shipped over. Fuyun was indignant. Why would Cai take a loss like that? When he told Water Girl, her suspicions were immediately aroused. She sent him to Seven-Li Bay to ask around and see what lay behind the purchasing station's arrogance. Her suspicions were on the mark. For he learned that it had been Cai's idea to set up the three-family operation. He had an agreement with it that let him pocket a quarter of the profits from the shipping brigade's purchases. Fuyun arrived at the purchasing station like a fury and confronted the people there with his information. Of course, they denied everything. So he went back and put the same questions to Cai; but by then Cai had already reported Fuyun's insubordination to Tian Zhongzheng, who had decided to fire him for incompetence, for "lacking aptitude as a purchasing agent."

Fuyun knew he'd been duped, but what could he do? He decided to see Tian and ask for his boatman's job back. Water Girl deterred him with the reminder that he had no hard evidence against Cai. She suggested that they'd been setting him up from the beginning. "What's done is done, so we'll just have to ignore them and make it on our own." The question was, How? He couldn't go out and sail a boat on his own, and the idea of gathering varnish in the forest behind Shaman Mountain worried Water Girl. They thought and thought, but nothing came to them except to go out and buy a half dozen piglets, since they knew that the price of pork had gone up over the past year and they'd heard that a number of families on the banks of the Zhou River had amassed wealth by raising pigs. After visiting one of the pig farmers to see what was involved, they devoted themselves to raising their pigs. But though the days passed quickly, the piglets grew slowly, and Han Wenju began to gripe that this was no way to make a living; he recommended selling off the piglets and buying grown animals. Since they had plenty of coarse grain at home, they could readily increase the nutritive value of the fodder to make it suitable for half-weight pigs and thus make a profit faster. So they disposed of the piglets at sale and went to the market in town, where they bought five pigs weighing between forty and fifty kilograms, which they took home. Three times a day they cooked fodder, and before long the pigs shed their immature red bristles, leaving their coats nice and shiny. Soon their bellies began scraping the ground, and in two months they had grown to full size. When two of the pigs weighed in at nearly eighty kilograms, they eagerly shipped them over to the purchasing station at Crossroads Township but were disconcerted to learn that there was a glut of pork in both the provincial and prefectural capitals and that no more pigs on the hoof were being accepted. All the White Rock Stockade purchasing stations were closed. Bemoaning their fate, they took the pigs to the purchasing station outside the city wall at White Rock Stockade, where the pork dealers formed a huge line. Water Girl had cooked up a potful of soupy corn mush for the pigs and for themselves, but by that afternoon, they could see that the two pigs were fading from hunger. The animals had already pissed three times and had three shits, which meant a loss of three or four kilograms at least, and they were tempted to plug up their assholes with stones. Just as their turn finally came, the purchasing agent hung out a sign that said, Closed for the Day—Will Reopen Tomorrow. Fuyun went up to the man and tried to prevail upon him to stay open just a bit longer, nearly fell to his knees, but the man said the station had reached its limit. They bought only as many pigs as they could kill in a day, and the sole cold-storage warehouse was filled to the rafters. Seeing that his pleas were getting him nowhere, Fuyun lost his composure and began to denounce the policy of encouraging the populace to raise pigs but then refusing to buy them. Did the planners expect him to keep his pigs at home forever? The purchasing agent argued back: "Either none of you people raise pigs or all of you do! It's monkey see, monkey do, with you mountain folk! Do you suppose we can buy all the pigs brought to White Rock Stockade, just to let the meat rot?"

"The goddamned government's playing games with the people!" Fuyun complained.

"Who are you to judge the government?" the purchasing agent replied.

Water Girl had to come up and make peace, and she and her husband had no choice but to find some shade where they and their pigs could get some rest. They decided to take turns going to a stall to get something to eat, with Water Girl going first. But when she got back, Fuyun, unequal to the two pigs, had dragged them into a public toilet and was sitting in the doorway to keep them penned. The pigs, nearly crazed with hunger, were eating shit from the toilet, while Fuyun was directing people away. He was in the midst of a heated exchange with a man who insisted on using the toilet.

The next day, however, they managed to sell off the two pigs and then returned to Stream of Wandering Spirits, where they slaughtered the four remaining porkers and sold the meat for sixty fen a kilogram under the previous year's mean price. What they'd hoped would be a chance to make some real money had turned out to be a pipe dream after all, and they were more dejected than ever. For the next several days, Han Wenju did nothing but mutter and complain. But then he had a bright idea: "You two worked as blacksmiths for Grandpa Pockface, didn't you? You may not be as good at it as he was, but there are no forges in Crossroads Township, and if you set up shop, I'm sure you'll make a go of it!" It was an idea they could accept, and they began making preparations.

Dakong visited Stream of Wandering Spirits in the spring to talk with Water Girl and her husband about the property they had let him occupy for his company. Since it would be impossible for her to live there, in the former blacksmith shop in White Rock Stockade, why not swap it for Dakong's house in Stream of Wandering Spirits? It had three rooms facing the street and several large rooms in back. This would work to everybody's advantage. But after the swap had been made official, Fuyun decided to dismantle Dakong's old property, and he used part of the material to remodel their own place; with what was left over he built a kitchen and a shed for storing firewood. They planned on opening their business under the sign Pockface's Blacksmith Shop. Of course, the address would have to be Crossroads Township, not White Rock Stockade. While Fuyun was working to get the house in shape, Water Girl went into town to find a place for the business, but it was soon evident to her that space facing the street in a decent location was hard to come by. Quarters that had rented for three yuan only a few years back went for twenty, since so many people had set up shops and driven up their value. She finally found something suitable across from the local supply and marketing co-op. After calculating that they could earn over a hundred a month if business was good, they signed an agreement with the landlord and began putting the new shop in order.

By combining all their savings they had barely enough to refurbish the old house, put up a shopfront on the rented property, and install a forge with all the tools they'd need. Water Girl was determined to do things right this time and set up a forge they could be proud of. They'd make Tian Zhongzheng, Cai Da'an, and their ilk sit up and take notice, and they'd show potential customers that they were firmly established. It was her idea to put in a full stock of steel and plenty of coal, give the front of the building a fresh coat of paint and varnish, and build a substantial counter and racks out of new wood. But when she added up the cost, it came to over a thousand yuan, and they fretted over how they were going to raise that much money.

Old Seven knew they were having trouble, so during one of his trips to White Rock Stockade he opened up to Golden Dog, who found their plans very exciting. Water Girl may be a woman, he mused, but you have to admire her self-respect and her drive to better herself. But that didn't lessen his concern over her financial pinch, and he handed Old Seven sixty yuan, telling him to convey it to her. He also sent word that he'd find a way to scrape together a great deal more in White Rock Stockade.

First he looked to his friends, but none were able to contribute much on the spot. One of them said, "Lei Dakong's a money tree, isn't he? All you have to do is give it a shake! Since you grew up together, why not borrow the money from him? It was you who got him out of jail, wasn't it?" But Golden Dog didn't like the idea. "All you want is a loan," the man insisted, "not a gift!"

Since there wasn't an alternative, Golden Dog went to see Dakong.

"Look here, Golden Dog," Dakong said. "I know you don't approve of what I'm doing, but they're trying to make a living by the sweat of their brow, and that's not easy. I feel sorry for them, the way things have turned out. I'll just give them a couple of thousand. I can't stand around and watch them struggle."

"You shouldn't be such a big spender of company money," Golden Dog said. "If she knew the money came from you, she wouldn't take it anyway. So let's do this. I'll borrow two thousand from your business and give it to Water Girl. Then I'll pay you back as I can."

"All right," Dakong agreed. "But you don't have to repay me."

"Debts have to be repaid. The business isn't yours alone. If something happened, we'd have trouble explaining ourselves. I'll give you an IOU, and you record the loan in your books."

Golden Dog wrote out an IOU and thrust it into Dakong's hand. That afternoon he went to the company's cashier and picked up the two thousand yuan, of which he used a thousand to buy coal and steel. Then he hired a boat to ship it to Crossroads Township, and personally handed Water Girl the remaining thousand. She was moved to tears by the kindness, but she refused the money. At that, Golden Dog summoned Fuyun and laid it on the line. "Take this thousand yuan. Opening a business is an expensive proposition. Besides, the baby's due soon, so you'll need a little extra. You can't let the new mother and baby go wanting. And you'll have to hire someone to help out for the first month or so. Take it. Once the money starts coming in, you can always pay me back, can't you?"

Fuyun took the money.

Animation surrounded the opening of the shop. Red congratulatory couplets were pasted alongside the door; red lanterns hung from the eaves. Han Wenju came from his boat to write out the honorable history of Pockface's Blacksmith Shop, all the way back to two generations before Water Girl's grandpa. He heaped accolades on the business until it occupied the first position in heaven and was unrivaled on earth.

"Uncle," Water Girl said, "don't go overboard!"

"You don't read the newspapers," he said, "so you don't know how people take out ads to toot their own horns!" When he finished the history he had Golden Dog's father paint it on the white outer wall. Old Seven led a delegation of boatmen in offering congratulations in the form of ten strings of firecrackers; to get the business off to a good start, they placed an order for seven hundred deck nails, three hundred rivets, and four iron anchors. Uncle Han laid out plenty of food and wine, and everyone ate and drank well into the night and staggered home good and drunk.

Since Pockface's Blackmith Shop had a long history and was being run by his own granddaughter and her husband, the presumption was that the tradition of quality work would be carried on. When people saw how husband and wife worked the forge, how they heated it up just right and used the hammers with precision, and how the picks, spades, shovels, and hoes came out exactly as they were supposed to and fit the jobs perfectly, the shop's reputation was assured and there was a steady stream of customers.

The highway from the provincial capital to White Rock Stockade ran right through Crossroads Township, so buses and trucks passed in front of the blacksmith shop every day; drivers stopped to eat in one of the cafés or to use the toilet. The break afforded them an opportunity for a little pleasure, and they came over and watched Water Girl and Fuyun work the forge. Fuyun would be naked to the waist, with an oilcoth apron tied around his neck, his face and arms tanned and red as he stuck his tongs into the forge to remove a piece of steel, his strong muscles rippling as he worked. Then he'd turn to the anvil, sending sparks flying, Water Girl, who was getting very big, wore a long shirt, and when she was too weak to wield the sledge, they changed places, with her using the smaller hammer. She had become a very practiced blacksmith. Townspeople there for the first time crowded around engrossed, and she'd invite them to take a seat where they could ask questions about her work and she could ask them what was happening in town. With the passage of time, the shop became a regular stop travelers made on the highway. It also became a place where fishermen, hunters, and peddlers congregated to sell their turtles, wild rabbits, and chickens and eggs to the people from the provincial capital. Water Girl often wound up in the role of sales representative for the locals. She'd hail a passing bus, which would stop, and the bartering would begin, one transaction after the other. There wasn't a soul anywhere around with mountain products to sell who didn't seek her out, and not a driver in the area who thought of her less than fondly. And eventually anyone heading to White Rock Stockade from Crossroads Township for whom river travel was too slow, including employees of the government offices and the cadres working in the township government compound, came to her, since she could get the bus to stop for them. It never failed.

Yingying seldom came to the shop, not because she was diffident but because she was ever so slightly envious. During business hours, if there were no customers in the co-op where she worked, she'd sit there, resting her head in her hands and gazing across the street at the blacksmith's with all sorts of memories running through her mind. She'd taken Golden Dog from Water Girl, but he'd left her because of Water Girl. *What a strange world it is. Golden Dog has hurt two women, and he deserves to die a thousand deaths!* One day, deciding to climb down from the lofty perch she was affecting, she sauntered across the street and stopped at the door. She leaned against the doorway and looked up and down at Water Girl's protruding belly as she put her hands under her own. "Say, old classmate, you're really something! Aren't you afraid of injuring him?"

Fuyun pulled a long face and ignored her, but Water Girl said, "I won't hurt him. He's not *that* delicate!"

Knowing that the jab had been polished for her benefit, Yingying blushed. But since to turn and leave would have acknowledged that a nerve was touched, she asked, "When are you due?"

"How about you?" Water Girl asked back.

"I've still got three or four months," Yingying said, "and look how big I am already!"

"The bigger the better," Water Girl said. "Then it'll be as strong as a dragon or as powerful as a phoenix!"

The comment had been intended as sarcasm, but Yingying took it as a good sign, and smiled. "Golden Dog didn't want this one and didn't want that one, and now there aren't any left!"

Fuyun, who didn't care for talk like that, picked up his hammer and brought it down with such a resounding blow on a piece of steel that Yingying took a couple of steps backward.

"You'd better be getting back to the store, Yingying," Water Girl said. "The customers are probably clamoring for you."

After Yingying left, Water Girl and Fuyun expended the rancor they felt on the metal for a while, until Fuyun said, "Who does she think she is, saying things like that about Golden Dog?"

"She was jeering at him. But it's true, Golden Dog isn't bringing any credit to himself by not getting married."

Fuyun said, "All the decent girls must be blind!"

Beginning to feel responsible for getting Golden Dog married, Water Girl and Fuyun, along with the painter and Han Wenju, began scouring Crossroads Township, four pairs of eyes looking for a girl who filled the bill. But whenever they thought they'd found someone, either the age difference was too great or it was clear that there'd be a personality clash. Then one day, out of the blue, a bus from Zhou City pulled up and Water Girl's attention was caught by the ticket taker, a girl with a face like a silver platter who smiled easily, bringing a glow to her eyes. From then on, whenever the girl's bus drove up, Water Girl greeted her warmly and plied her with tea. After watching Water Girl working the forge, the girl asked if she could give it a try. So Water Girl wrapped her hands around the girl's and showed her how it was done. Then she cupped her face in her hands and looked closely. "You have double-fold eyelids. That's good. The bridge of your nose is high. That's good. Your mouth's on the big side, but it's passable. Best of all, you have a mole between your eyebrows, which is a sign of nobility. It means you're destined to marry a talented, cultured man."

The girl was thrilled. "Just listen to you! If I said I was looking for someone like that, would you have one on the shelf?"

"You bet I would," Water Girl said. "Leave everything to me."

After the bus left, Fuyun said, "She says she's looking for a man. Do you have one in mind?"

"What do you think of her? Do you think she's right for him?"

"Are you talking about Golden Dog?"

"I'll explain things to her the next time her bus comes here. A string ties lovers together no matter where they are in the world. Who knows, maybe the Old Man upstairs sent her to us! The next time she drops by, I'll ask for a photograph, and I want you to take her bus to White Rock Stockade to let Golden Dog see her."

"Maybe this is the one!" said Fuyun excitedly.

They talked as they worked, agreeing that if Golden Dog and the girl hit it off, they'd take charge of everything: they'd choose the day to inform Golden Dog's father, they'd choose the month for the wedding, they'd arrange the wedding at the White Rock Stockade newspaper bureau office. Then, of course, there'd have to be a wedding party in Stream of Wandering Spirits, all in keeping with local customs, and a ceremony for the bride and groom to pay respects to the gods and to their ancestors, not to mention all the fun with the bridal chamber, the date they'd have to eat together, the lighting of cigarettes for the matchmaker and Fuyun . . . They were so wrapped up in their plans that they forgot to keep working, and Water Girl had to laugh. "What are we doing? You'd think everything was settled!"

Fuyun continued earnestly, "When the time comes, be sure to send Yingying an invitation. That girl puts her to shame. She's a flower, and Yingying's a lump of fermented bean curd!"

He turned and spit in the direction of the co-op.

24

The next time the bus came to Crossroads Township, Water Girl asked the girl for a photograph, but playfully she spread her hands and shrugged her shoulders, saying she wasn't in the habit of carrying her own picture around with her. Water Girl went inside and asked Fuyun to take the bus to White Rock Stockade, find Golden Dog, and lead him to the bus station to sneak a look at the ticket taker. And as soon as the bus arrived in town, Fuyun did run straight to the bureau office, but Golden Dog wasn't there.

Two days earlier, Golden Dog had gone to the provincial capital, having received enthusiastic reactions to his letter, from his young reporter friends at the newspaper headquarters and at bureaus in a number of provinces. Since they shared his viewpoint, they decided to form a Young Reporters Study Association, and they had chosen a date to get together in Zhou City to discuss plans and objectives.

The clever young reporters worked out the details of the association in a single morning of intense debate. The newspaper leadership announced its support, but when it came to financing it, they balked, saying the money simply wasn't there. The association thereupon decided to seek support from local entrepreneurs, and the members were asked to come up with other suggestions for supplementary funding. They also decided that since the membership was too dispersed to meet frequently, they'd keep in touch by means of written communiqués. On the fifteenth of every month they'd meet at headquarters to discuss current events, talk about what they'd learned from their studies, and subject each other's stories and the issues they dealt with to appraisal.

In the afternoon of the day of organizing the group, the first order of business was to canvass Golden Dog's article on Lei Dakong's

White Rock Stockade City and Country United Trade Co. After a day of invigorating discussion, Golden Dog took the bus home, stopping to rest in Crossroads Township. As soon as he stepped into the blacksmith shop, he was met by Water Girl's aggrieved tone. "You could have gone to Zhou City anytime, but no, you had to wait till something good was about to happen in White Rock Stockade before going!"

He was at a loss. "Something good? What was that?"

Water Girl took a quick look at the bus he'd arrived on. The ticket taker was a young fellow with peach fuzz above his upper lip, not the girl with the silver-platter face. "How come there's a new ticket taker today?" she asked Golden Dog.

"They're always changing shifts."

"One of them's a pretty, fair-skinned girl with a mole between her eyebrows. Do you know who I mean?"

"Do I know who you mean? Miss Ma, right?"

The answer delighted Water Girl, who lowered her voice confidentially. "What do you think of her? She's the reason I had Fuyun go look for you in White Rock Stockade. If you think it'll work, you don't have to do a thing. I'll be your go-between. She and I are close friends."

Golden Dog reddened, then chuckled. "Water Girl, don't make a move or you'll have people laughing at us. She already has a boyfriend, the son of one of our editors at the paper. I see her there all the time."

That took the wind out of Water Girl's sails. Her interest in the match quickly vanished, and she stood there glumly for a moment. "Ai!" she said in exasperation. "If you keep putting things off, all the good girls will be taken. Okay, forget this one. But I'll keep looking. And you'd better start worrying about it yourself. I can't believe that someone as well traveled as you hasn't found a girl he likes!"

He changed the subject as soon as he could, asking her about business at the shop. Then he reached into his bag and pulled out a package of sweets and some baby clothes. "I don't have time to go home and see Father, so you'll have to give him these sweets. The clothes are for . . ."

"When you're so thoughtful, you give me renewed hope that you'll land a wife before long."

"There's no hurry," he said. "Whoever she is, she's doing fine at her parents' right now."

The first thing he did upon returning home was make the rounds of local entrepreneurs asking for financial support for the study association. When the news reached Dakong, he came looking for Golden Dog. "If your association needs financial help, why haven't you come to me? You don't think I'm clean enough to deal with? I give handouts to those officials because I have no choice, but to you I'd give it because I want to. How much do you need? Would fifty thousand do?"

"You must be doing very well indeed if you can talk about a figure like that. We don't need that much. Ten thousand would be plenty."

"That's all? We'll go over to the office in a while, and I'll give it to you in cash. But I have one request."

"What's that?"

"Could you get the association to write something about my company?"

"The Zhou City newspaper already ran a story, didn't it?"

"That tiny article? People have been talking about the investigative reports. Can what I've heard be correct? I went to a jeans manufacturer in Zhou City—your paper ran a piece about it—that took orders for 120,000 pairs of jeans in a single month after being written up. I used to think that coverage in the paper produced only political rewards, but now I see the value of it in yuan. It gives us credibility among the readers, and the customers beat a path to our door. Any money we spend to get it makes its way right back to us!"

Golden Dog mumbled, "Now that you're a businessman, you think you're an expert on journalism." He went on, "We can't do that. If that's a condition I won't be able to take your money."

Changing his tone completely, Dakong said, "If it had been a condition, I wouldn't have used the word *request,* would I? If you can't write the kind of story I'd like, at least you can be sure to mention our support when you report the founding of the association."

"That goes without saying."

After wiring the money to the association, Golden Dog heard that Dakong had donated seventy thousand yuan to a middle school in the White Rock Stockade suburbs for construction of a reading room for the teachers and students. It gave him pause. Is he really trying to put some of his wealth to good use in society? he wondered. The next time he saw Dakong he asked about the gift. Dakong brought his head up close and whispered, "It's political capital."

"Nothing wrong with that," Golden Dog said. "The school gets the assistance it needs, and you get room to maneuver."

"Room to maneuver? Do you realize what people will do to support and develop the conditions necessary for advancement in the public sector? I'm laying a foundation to run for director of the White Rock Stockade Bureau of Trade."

Golden Dog couldn't believe his ears. "You mean you want to enter politics?"

"Gong Baoshan's son-in-law is no longer manager of the Zhou-Shen Limited Company. He's the new director of the Zhou City industrial bureau."

Golden Dog put it all together. "Then he must have been the one who advised you to donate the seventy thousand."

"What do you expect me to say? I thought it was the right thing to do . . ."

Golden Dog dropped the subject, realizing that Dakong was no longer particularly interested in his scruples. Although his White Rock Stockade City and Country United Trade Co. hadn't become a subsidiary of the Zhou-Shen Limited Company and continued to give bribes to the Tian family, it was the Gong family that pulled the strings. In the past, Dakong had been the victim of inhuman pressure; now he oozed corruption!

Wanting to gain an accurate picture of what the Tians had been doing while the Gongs were gradually infiltrating White Rock Stockade with their influence, Golden Dog paid a visit to the county party secretary.

Before he got there, Tian Youshan had been gazing appreciatively at a basket of fresh river turtles. They ranged in size from a dinner plate to a large bowl and were still alive and kicking. Eventually he turned the basket over and watched them crawl around the office, then began picking them up one at a time, placing them in a tub and covering it with a lid, which he weighted down with a rock. He was busy picking them up as Golden Dog walked in the door. He rolled them over with the tip of his shoe, then lifted them by holding one of the shell protrusions at the rear between two fingers, knocking their heads on the floor before tossing them into the tub. "Ah, Golden Dog!" Tian said. "You're good at catching turtles. These things can be vicious. Once when I was cooking some at home, I forgot to weight down the lid and one of them crawled out and bit my finger when I picked it up. It wouldn't let go until my wife ran in and cut its head off!"

"Turtles are afraid of thunder," Golden Dog said. "If one of them's got its teeth in you, it'll loosen its grip if it hears a crash of thunder. Are you planning on giving them away?"

"I'm going to eat them. The doctor says my kidneys are weak and advises a diet of these things. I've been eating them for six months, one every three days. Look at my hair. Remember how it used to be streaked with gray? Well, it's black again. Take some home. They're fresh—and delicious!"

"I wouldn't have a use for them."

Tian Youshan was tired and sweaty. He wiped his face and sat down on the sofa. "I guess not, since you're still a young man. When I was young, I didn't know the meaning of the word *tired.* But lately, if it's not pains here, it's pins and needles there. The doctor told me that when you're conscious of some part of your body, that's when it's got problems. He sure knew what he was talking about! I have problems with my health and problems with the county, and I'm fully aware of both. What have you been up to lately? Have you written any new stories? I'm glad you're here. I was planning on sending someone to look you up one of these days."

"Look me up for what?"

"Have you heard that we have a newsmaker here in our county?"

"Who's that?"

"The person you spoke up for a while back: Lei Dakong! We taught him a lesson, and now the penitent has come to set up the White Rock Stockade City and Country United Trade Co. He's a big success. Not long ago he donated the remarkable sum of seventy thousand yuan to a middle school in the suburbs. He's no ordinary rich man, he's a millionaire. There aren't many like him around here. White Rock Stockade has its river shipping brigade *and* a mammoth diversified trading company. That ought to be worth a story. We're a real two-fisted county!"

Obviously Tian was unaware of the penetration of the Gong family's influence and still expected to put the shipping brigade and Lei Dakong to his own use.

"Tian Zhongzheng established the model with his Crossroads Township River Shipping Brigade," Golden Dog commented, "and now we've got the trading company. A unique development like that is certainly worth writing about, but I've heard some disquieting rumors that the public is souring on the trading company. They wonder how it can do so well without any visible enterprises or technology."

Tian laughed. "No wonder you're a reporter. You understand things. But not everybody's disillusioned with the company, and among those who are, jealousy seems to be at the bottom of it. People find it hard to believe that a peasant could become so rich so fast, saying that even landlord families took generations in the old days to acquire the kind of wealth that Lei Dakong made in only a few months. But current government policy allows some people to get rich before others, and those people's interests must be protected if we're not to be accused of backwardness. It wasn't easy for a poor county like White Rock Stockade to develop something like the river shipping brigade, which is enriching lots of people. And when someone like Dakong makes it big, we should hold up his success as an example."

Lacking a reasonable rejoinder, Golden Dog went through the motions of agreeing. He returned home but decided not to write more about Dakong for publication. Tian telephoned twice to see if he had completed the story, and Golden Dog's stalling made him angry. He asked if Golden Dog was prejudiced against his former friend and reminded him that journalistic ethics did not allow a reporter's work to be compromised by personal feelings. Tian emphasized that he himself had no personal ties to Dakong and that Dakong had even brought charges against him once but that he was willing to forget all that in the interest of the reforms.

Golden Dog continued going through the motions of acquiescence to Tian, but he couldn't shake the idea of exploiting the antagonisms between the two families to bring one down and then starting in on the other.

Seeing that Golden Dog was stalling, Tian angrily ordered the news director of the county propaganda bureau to write a story on the party secretary's support for the operations of the shipping brigade and Dakong's trading company. The completed story, over seven thousand words long, went off to the Zhou City *Daily News*, which immediately splashed it over the front page.

It was a demonstration of how propaganda can work: the long piece had its effect. People throughout the province were lauding the White Rock Stockade party secretary as a leader of the reform movement, and Lei Dakong as a pioneer among the peasant reformers. Golden Dog, on the other hand, received a letter of censure from the newspaper for missing the wonderful opportunity of doing such a story himself. Could it be that he was too fixated on the dark aspects of society?

Put on the defensive, he fell into despondency, and even though the study association rose to his defense and forwarded to the newspaper leadership an edited copy of the article that he had circulated, it was shelved for not conforming to the requirements of social progress. The manuscript was not returned.

Tian Youshan moved about in an aura of triumph after this episode.

Until then, White Rock Stockade had ranked second from the bottom in the area, but at the next district meeting, Tian was up front, and as the leader of a progressive county, he proudly made his views known. Even the provincial party secretary thought highly of the article and had the provincial newspaper reprint it, accompanied by a short statement by him. Tian Youshan went around collaring high-ranking district officials in an effort to get Lei Dakong nominated as a model worker of the district. Gong Baoshan was left no option but to make a symbolic trip to White Rock Stockade to inspect Dakong's company. He balked, however, at naming Dakong a model worker: "We'll take it under advisement."

Not long afterward, talk spread through White Rock Stockade that Secretary Tian was to be promoted to the office of deputy district commissioner. The report was everywhere, and within days everyone in Crossroads Township had heard it.

The firing of Fuyun from the shipping brigade had not sat well with the boatmen. In discussions led by Old Seven some made open allegations of unfairness, and they went to the purchasing station at Seven-Li Bay to gather information on Cai Da'an's arrangement with the station's operators. Cai Da'an, realizing that he was sure to be exposed, ran trembling to Tian Zhongzheng and owned up to everything. Tian slapped him across the face, then went straight to Seven-Li Bay, where he ordained that the three families in charge were to take the responsibility for what had occurred and maintain that they'd given Cai a percentage of their profits in appreciation for his assistance. Tian next called a meeting of the shipping brigade and before all the members demanded an explanation by the Seven-Li Bay purchasing agents of their collusion with the purchasing station. He also ordered Cai to write a full report regarding his error of buying Grade B kiwi fruit at Grade A prices. Of course, that didn't placate the boatmen, who were making noises about taking the case to the county committee. It was then that rumors of Tian Youshan's imminent promotion began to circulate. Tian Zhongzheng and Cai Da'an bent their efforts toward driving a wedge between the boatmen. Old Seven was so disenchanted and saddened by this turn of events that he resigned from the brigade on the pretext of age and returned to his mountain home to settle into a new line of work.

Meanwhile, Lei Dakong, who was unaware of all this, had the article celebrating him blown up and framed. He hung it in the company doorway. He also reproduced over a hundred copies, which he passed out to business associates for promotional purposes. He was signing contracts right and left, and in no time the profits really began to roll in. But on his next trip home he learned what had happened with the Crossroads Township River Shipping Brigade, and he was appalled. He hastened back to White Rock Stockade. "What happened, Golden Dog?" he asked his friend. "How could things have got out of hand like this?"

"Dakong, I thought you were put out with me for withholding the publicity you wanted. I really didn't think you'd come to see me again. Yet here you are!"

"I don't hold a grudge for something like that. But I heard you wrote a derogatory article about the company, and *that* made me mad! But now things have gone too far, with Tian Youshan riding on my back to get a political promotion—and Tian Zhongzheng using that against Uncle Seven and some of the other boatmen. Damn it, I've become their pawn! What was my goal in setting up this business? What was my objective in seeking publicity? To undermine those officials, of course! I never dreamed they'd co-opt my success to make themselves look good and to climb even higher up the official ladder. What does that make me? How can I show my face in Stream of Wandering Spirits?"

He was on his feet, consigning eight generations of the Tian family to eternal damnation.

"I'm glad you're aware at last of the hard reality," Golden Dog commented. "But don't go to pieces now. Keep running that business of yours; just remember what I've said before: Walk the straight and narrow, and don't ever let yourself become vulnerable. Otherwise, they'll put you up on a pedestal when it suits their interest and knock you down when it doesn't."

But Dakong was a man who knew his own mind, and he scarcely heard Golden Dog's caution. All he could think was that it was high time to stop giving the Tians a purchase for manipulating him. He went to Stream of Wandering Spirits determined to drive the Crossroads Township River Shipping Brigade out of business: Tian Youshan would never again use it as a bootstrap for himself. Knowing how demoralized the brigade members were, he announced that his trading company was recruiting workers at a monthly wage of ninety yuan. Fifteen boatmen applied immediately; he hired ten of the strongest and hardest-working. There wasn't much for them to do, but he was happy to pay them to stand around, if necessary. He even contrived visits by them to Crossroads Township so that they could let the brigade members who remained know how well they were doing at the trading company. Gradually, the boatmen, increasingly discontented, either left the brigade for something better or simply went their own way. The group's unity had been destroyed. But not content with inflicting only that damage, Lei Dakong sought out opportunities to humiliate Tian Youshan. Whenever there was a meeting of entrepreneurs or specialized personnel at, say, ten o'clock, with Tian Youshan asserting his status by arriving five minutes late, Dakong would make a point of showing up fifteen minutes after the appointed time. At the conclusion of the meeting, he'd ensure that his car left before Tian Youshan's so that he could precede the party secretary down the street. Or if he learned that Tian was planning to see a new opera or movie in town, he'd buy up the ten rows at the front, then not show up and let the seats remain empty.

The talk in White Rock Stockade was that Lei Dakong enjoyed greater prestige than did the party secretary.

One day he met Golden Dog on the street. "How am I doing, Golden Dog?"

"You're a fiend in human form!"

"You have to admit that I traded my anger for status."

He threw back his head and roared with laughter.

BOOK THREE

25

Forty-one years earlier the Peace Preservation Corps of White Rock Stockade had surrounded the guerrilla forces of the Tian family at King Ma Gulley. On the previous day the guerrillas had lain in ambush beneath a ridge at the mouth of Flagstone Gulley, where they hijacked a truck from White Rock Stockade and made off with its cargo of over forty wooden cases. At King Ma Gulley, they were confounded by the discovery that the cases contained neither the anticipated guns and ammunition nor usable cloth and canned goods but all kinds of mirrors being smuggled by the garrison commander. Wrathfully, they smashed them in the gulley until the banks shimmered in the sunlight. But they hadn't come away empty-handed: the five guards' Hanyang rifles had been made part of their arsenal. They set up camp at King Ma Gulley, never expecting to be surrounded. The encirclement happened at midnight when they were fast asleep. Completely surprised by the sound of shots, the several hundred men broke up into four groups to attempt an escape. At dawn, Tian the Sixth, wounded in four places, broke out of the encirclement with his bodyguard Xu Feibao, a man from Zhechuan, in Hubei province. After stoning a landlord to death there, he had changed his name and fled, disguised as a cotton flufferer, to Zhou City, where he had been taken in by Tian. He was over a hundred eighty centimeters tall, with a face as dark as ebony; a particularly sharp-witted man, he soon became an excellent marksman and was devoted to Tian the Sixth.

Xu picked Tian up and carried him on his back to Chicken Gut Gulley under cover of the few remaining minutes of darkness. Tian recuperated from his wounds at a house in the gulley occupied by the Feng family, who treated his wounds with applications of pumpkin pulp. He was soon on the mend. Then one day at nightfall the daughter of the family burst in to announce that his presence had been reported to the Peace Preservation Corps in White Rock Stockade, that her husband had been arrested, and that a large contingent of troops had arrived at the mouth of the gulley. Fleeing, Tian the Sixth and Xu Feibao heard gunfire in the distance and scaled a ridge above the gulley, only to discover that it was occupied by forces of the Peace Preservation Corps. But since Tian's wounds had reopened and he could go no farther, he turned to his bodyguard and said, "Feibao, it doesn't look like we're going to get away this time. You try it alone. There's no reason for both of us to die."

Tears welled in Xu Feibao's eyes as he said, "Let me carry you on my back, Commander. We might make it. And even if we don't, we should die together!"

Tian slapped him across the face and rebuked him: "Bullshit! I told you to get out of here! If you don't get moving quickly, neither of us will make it! You came here to make revolution, not to commit suicide!" When Tian saw that blows and threats would never induce Xu to leave, he tried reasoning with him: "Look, since I can't walk another step, you hide over there on that side of the ridge, and I'll hide here. Maybe they won't find me. If they don't, come back and get me after dark. A year ago, I drew a tally at Eastern Omen Monastery in the mountains that said I'll live a long life. If you stay with me, we'll be too easy to spot, and you don't want to get me captured, do you?"

Xu reluctantly acceded to Tian's logic. After he was gone, Tian made a quick survey of the area around him and rolled into a dense clump of brambles; he was no sooner safely hidden than forces of the Peace Preservation Corps began sweeping the mountainside, fiercely stabbing the foliage with their bayonets as they came. From his shelter he could see two soldiers at the edge of the bushes poking at them with their bayonets. He'd already decided that if he was discovered, he'd use his pistol: if he got one of them, he'd be even; if he got them both, he'd be one ahead of the game. But the soldiers hunkered down and smoked a cigarette before sauntering off to join the others to search a different ridge. After nightfall, when the returning Xu Feibao had called softly and Tian had made his way out of the bushes, the commander said, "These brambles saved my life. After I accomplish what I've set out to do, I'm going to make them the king of plants."

Tian and Xu made their way back to Stream of Wandering Spirits, where they hid in the Restless Hill Monastery until Tian's wounds had healed and he had reestablished lines of communication with the other guerrillas who had fled at the same time he had. Later that year they returned to Chicken Gut Gulley, where they learned that after capturing the husband of Feng's daughter, the Peace Preservation Corps had punished him for Tian's escape by tying him to the boughs of two saplings they had bent toward each other; when they let the trees snap back, he was torn limb from limb. They had raped his wife on the kang, then slit her belly open with a bayonet. In anguish, Tian and Xu fell to their knees in front of the Feng home. They went on to cut open the skin on their right arms and drink their own blood as a way of sealing their vow to avenge the Feng family. Armed with sabers, they hunted down the people who had reported their presence in the village, and killed them all—man, woman, and child. They learned that the man who had led the troops over had moved to the banks of the Zhou River to open a dye works. That night, they captured him and brought him back. After pouring wine down his throat, they splashed cold water on his chest and cleaved it open with a saber. Then Tian the Sixth drove his knee into the man's abdomen, and his bloody, pulsating heart popped out of his chest.

Later, when the 25th Red Army passed through White Rock Stockade, Tian sent Xu Feibao along with Xu Haidong, hearing no news of him after that. Then in the 1950s a rumor swept White Rock Stockade that Xu Feibao had become the political commissar of a military region in Jiangxi, but no one was able to confirm the report. Invariably when people on the banks of the Zhou River spoke of the past, Xu's name was mentioned, until his military exploits became the stuff of legend. But the events about which the people reminisced had retreated so far into the past that no one dreamed that Xu Feibao was alive and well and that one day he would return to Tian's native province as the commandant of the regional command.

Commandant Xu was over sixty when he took up his command, but he was still an animated, vigorous man who, dressed in his military uniform, was as solid as a rock when seated and as tall and straight as a pine when standing. He was an awesome figure. During his frequent lectures in the local schools, he'd laugh heartily when he spoke to the teachers and students about the victories of the guerrillas on the Zhou River, but he'd curse mightily when he spoke of the guerrillas' defeats. When he related the death of Tian the Sixth, he'd weep without shame, his heart seeming about to break. When he was feeling particularly nostalgic, he'd travel to all the places in Zhou City and White Rock Stockade where the guerrillas had fought, in order to relive the experience and make offerings to the spirit of the martyr. His loyalty to Tian the Sixth still ran deep. On several occasions he had petitioned Tian Youshan to have the organization department prepare a revolutionary history of the Zhou River region. Tian Youshan eventually assented to the idea, and a book was brought out, but it met with vastly different receptions in Zhou City and White Rock Stockade. Members of the Gong clan were sadly disappointed, believing that it distorted history by playing up the Tians and slighting the Gongs. They commissioned what they considered the definitive version. The battle of the books completely polarized the survivors of the armed battles, and partisans of either camp refused to meet with those of the other or even to sit on the same bench. Commandant Xu, unaware of the animus, continued to live an exemplary life, fulfilling his personal obligations with single-mindedness and a pure heart and carrying out his official duties with solemn dedication. There was no doubt that the performance of good deeds was his overriding preoccupation. Then after dinner one night, alone in his room and lying in bed, he spotted the dim figure of a man standing at the window. The man didn't move when he summoned him or ordered him to leave, and Xu was becoming irate.

"Feibao," the man said, "things seem to be going well for you. You've been rewarded for your service by becoming a commandant!"

"Who are you?" Commandant Xu demanded.

"I am a wandering, drifting spirit of the wilderness. It's hard to believe you've forgotten the man who took you in when you were a cotton flufferer."

"Is it you, Commander Tian?" Commandant Xu exclaimed. He took a close look at the man. It was Tian the Sixth all right. But as Xu jumped to the window, Tian—astonishingly—vanished. Xu wondered if it had been a true specter or if the visitation had been a dream. The incident preyed on his mind for days. Finally, in order to ensure peace for Tian's spirit, he spoke of his experience to the White Rock Stockade county committee and asked them to request funds to build a memorial kiosk for Tian the Sixth, with a tablet to commemorate the spirit of the martyr.

At the time, Tian Youshan was suffering the disdain of Lei Dakong, and when the official realized the extent to which the power of the Gong clan had penetrated White Rock Stockade, he redoubled his efforts to get people to believe that he was about to be appointed deputy district commissioner. When approval and funding for the monument were received, he hired an architect from the provincial capital and some builders. Slightly over two months later, a completed octagonal memorial kiosk of classic design, with flying eaves, stood in a park in the northern suburbs of the town. The stone tablet was twice as tall as a man, and though there were no coiling dragons or flying phoenixes on the top nor reclining turtles or toads at the base, the seven-word inscription Eternal Repose to Martyred Tian the Sixth was chiseled in gold with scarlet borders on the monument's face, and the martyr's heroic exploits were memorialized in over two thousand seven hundred twenty ideographs on the back.

The dedication ceremony was scheduled for ten days later.

In White Rock Stockade, Tian Youshan convened four meetings of the expanded standing committee to determine the work assignments for the ceremony. Since none of Tian the Sixth's immediate family could be found, it was decided that Tian Zhongzheng would fill the dual role of nearest living relative and senior local official in representing Stream of Wandering Spirits, the martyr's birthplace. He wiped away tears as he accepted his assignment, as though during the preceding decades he had thought of little except his martyred forebear and had suffered incalculable guilt and anxiety over the want of a kiosk in his memory. Golden Dog had also been approached to participate in making the dedication a success, but he found Tian's display so disgusting that his skin crawled and he tried to slip away from the meeting. "Golden Dog," Tian Youshan called him back. "You failed us last time, but this ceremony, besides being one of the biggest events in the county's history, is considered important at the district and provincial levels. We expect you to write it up for the Zhou City paper, the provincial paper, even the *People's Daily.* We live in good times now, but that doesn't mean we can forget what made them possible. We must pay homage to, and carry forward, the revolutionary tradition!"

Promising to do his best, Golden Dog said he'd coordinate his activities with comrades from the White Rock Stockade county committee media bureau and the broadcasting station.

On the evening of the fourth day after that, however, he received a telephone call from his father, in Crossroads Township, telling him that Fuyun was dead.

"Dead?" Golden Dog boomed incredulously into the receiver, which he was gripping with white knuckles. "How can that be? How did he die?" He was sobbing.

"Water Girl told me to call you," his father said, "and to tell you to come right home. She'll fill you in when you get here."

Golden Dog hitched a ride to Crossroads Township that night and set off directly for Stream of Wandering Spirits, where Han Wenju's deserted ferryboat was tied up at the crossing. Without stopping to undress, he dived into the river and swam across. When he reached the shore he could hear in the distance the rasping sounds of Water Girl's sorrow.

Fuyun was dead all right, his body battered and torn. His abdomen was swathed in white cloth as he lay in the coffin they had managed to obtain for him; since it was too small to accommodate his long limbs, they had bent his legs inward to fit him in it. When Golden Dog neared the coffin, he saw that Fuyun's face had been washed and lightly powdered. Cotton had been stuffed in his ears and nostrils. Golden Dog couldn't suppress his explosive grief, and he had to be pulled away from the coffin so that it could be sealed with eight-inch nails. The thuds drowned out the sobs of the mourners. Regaining an outward composure, Golden Dog silently watched the motion of the hammers as they rose and fell, each blow seeming to drive a nail straight into his heart.

Fuyun had made those very nails in his blacksmith shop, and now they were giving the stamp of finality to his own death. The following day, at dawn, he was carried up the mountain and buried on a high crest.

Three days earlier Tian Zhongzheng had returned from a meeting in White Rock Stockade to announce that Commandant Xu and officials from the regional and provincial levels would attend the dedication of the memorial kiosk, and that in order to entertain the distinguished visitors properly, the county committee had decided to set a table with rare delicacies. He directed Crossroads Township to contribute a variety of wild game within a week. After consulting with Cai Da'an and Tian Yishen, Tian Zhongzheng distributed the assignments: Tian Yishen would organize a party to go down to the Zhou River and bring back some baby fish and turtles. Cai Da'an was to take a hunting party up to the woods around the gulley between the northern and southern peaks to bag some mountain goats, pheasants, wild boars, and a black bear. Tian Zhongzheng himself had a reputation as a fine hunter, but since his right foot, with the missing little toe, was subject to an infection that made it difficult for him to walk, he was forced to entrust the shooting expedition to Cai Da'an. He made it clear that the game was to be delivered within the week—no excuses. The despotic Cai Da'an went to each of the villages, where, administrative directive in hand, he selected the finest hunters for the three teams he was going to send up the mountain. Fuyun was working at the forge in his blacksmith shop on East Avenue when Cai ordered him to join the team.

"I'm no good with a gun," he protested.

"But you're strong," Cai Da'an countered. "You can carry a wild boar down the mountain on your back."

Knowing it was pointless to argue, Fuyun put down his work, threw a bag of rations over his shoulder, and followed Cai up Shaman Mountain.

The mountain was overrun with old trees and dead vines. Although there were fewer trees along the banks of the gulley, there was plenty of tall grass, as well as plenty of brambles, and they harbored hordes of black mosquitoes that swarmed over the men as soon as they came within range; when they tried to drive them off with their hands, they found themselves bloodied. They were all wearing hats and leggings, and they rubbed the ashes from their cigarettes on their faces, necks, and hands. As they began climbing the mountain, they handed their rations, clothing, and water to Fuyun, who was soon panting. Cai called him the pack mule. He gibed, "The quick-witted live by their brains; the slow-witted live by their brawn. Fuyun, since you're no good with a gun, you'll just have to work harder with your back. Even so—who knows?—you might get an audience with Commandant Xu."

"Who is this fellow who has such strange tastes in food?"

"The nobility eat noble food; young whelps eat buckwheat noodles. You don't think that communism means simply that you can stay home and eat Water Girl's spicy noodles three times a day, do you?"

Although the men hunted on the mountain all day long, they bagged only three pheasants and a mountain goat. Exhausted, they sprawled on the ground. "None of you can go home yet," Cai said to them. "How would it look to go back with this paltry trophy? It's bear paws we're after, bear paws!"

So they went deeper into the mountain, eating cold biscuits during the day and sleeping in a cave at night. And when nature called, they squatted in the tall grass, using a torch to drive away the mosquitoes. Fuyun's ass was a mass of lumps where he'd been bitten. During daylight, snakes menaced their feet as they tramped through the gulley; the poisonous serpents frequently hung from cliffs, looking like dead branches. Once, when Fuyun was tired, he sat down beside what he took to be a thin dead tree on a ledge and smoked three pipefuls of tobacco. When he was finished he knocked the hot bowl against the apparent tree, which suddenly began to squirm and slither away. On realizing that it was a huge snake, he was petrified; he just sat there openmouthed.

On the third day, they encountered the spoor of a bear, which made them jubilant. At once they split up to stalk the prey. Since Fuyun served only as a bearer, Cai told him to remain in the clearing. At last he heard gunfire coming from the gulley, followed by shouts of "Here comes one! It's coming down!" He stood up and peered into the distance, where a huge bear was crashing through the trees and bushes, heading straight for him. He swallowed hard, for he'd never seen a bear that big. The sight shocked and frightened him. Since the beast was aiming straight at him and he had no weapon, he threw down his ration sacks and shinnied up the nearest tree. As the bear closed in on the tree, it tilted its head so that its eyes remained trained on him. Excited by the sounds of gunfire and the human voices in the gulley, it bared its teeth and growled, then set to gnawing the bark of the tree until it was halfway through. Luckily the tree was a chinaberry whose bitter taste seemed to daunt the bear. It turned and went off toward a nearby mountain brook for some water. In a panic, Fuyun let himself down, but the bear heard him hit the ground, spun around, and charged back, in full throat as it came. It was too late. Fuyun felt a stabbing pain, was flattened by the powerful force, and was sent hurtling toward a precipice. He rolled over the edge. When he came to, he saw that the bear had leaped down, and the hazy thought came to him that bears won't eat carrion. He recalled someone's saying that if you tangled with a bear, it was best to play dead—that after nosing around, the bear would leave. So he lay there on his back with his eyes shut tight, holding his breath. The bear lumbered forward, and when it saw him supine, its ferocity began to subside. It drew up to him and circled him, nudging him with its paws. Fuyun didn't move a muscle. Then it began sniffing him at close quarters; Fuyun could smell its foul breath. It explored his smells from his toes to his head, with a special curiosity about his nose and mouth. One minute more, two at most, and everything would have been fine. But there was a hornets' nest nearby. The disturbed hornets poured out of the nest the bear had rocked, and one of them stung Fuyun on the face. He flinched involuntarily. At this, the bear swiped its paw across his belly, picked him up, and tossed him into the brambles. By the time Fuyun hit the ground, he was past knowing anything.

Before long, Cai Da'an led the others to the scene, but Fuyun was dead. His belly had been ripped open and his guts were draped over a bramble. The bear also lay there, dead, stung by thousands of hornets until its head was misshapen and swollen to twice its normal size. The hunters' eyes burned with grief. They took off their shirts to cover the torso of their companion, then lit torches and burned the hornets' nest to a crisp. Finally four rifles were aimed at the bear and twelve bullets were pumped into its carcass.

"Stop shooting!" Cai ordered. "You'll ruin the pelt. We don't want to come away with nothing when we skin it!"

Sickened that Cai's overriding concern was the bearskin, the hunters surrounded him menacingly: "You knew he was no hunter, so why'd you bring him along? Or if he had to come, why didn't you give him a weapon? And why'd you leave him alone in the clearing?"

Suddenly fearing for his life, Cai fell to his knees beside Fuyun's corpse and railed at the accursed bear, slapping his own face, and bewailing the impossibility of taking Fuyun's place in death. It was a convincing act.

Fuyun now lay in eternal sleep beneath the ground at the top of the mountain on the southern shore of the Zhou River. The black bear had been dispatched downriver to White Rock Stockade. For days, the whole of Stream of Wandering Spirits had been subdued by its grief.

But talk soon began to circulate in Crossroads Township that Fuyun and the others had gone hunting on a "mourning day," so that one of the hunters was fated to die, no matter what. As the idea spread, many residents turned their hard feelings from the Tian clan and toward fate. In Stream of Wandering Spirits, someone recalled that on the eve of Fuyun's death, owls had set up a terrible racket; someone else remembered that, on getting up to relieve himself, he'd seen a fireball fall from the sky and land on the hill behind Fuyun's house. But even if it was a "mourning day," why had Fuyun died rather than one of the men with him? That's when the whispers turned to Water Girl and to the death of her young husband in the Sun family. Is she a jinx? they asked themselves.

Han Wenju heard what people were saying, and so did Water Girl. It caught her off guard, and she searched her own memory for omens of Fuyun's death. She vaguely recalled that as she saw him off on the morning he went up the mountain, she'd heard a couple of popping sounds from the roof of the house. Had that settled his fate? Was it proof that she'd jinxed him? Deep in her heart she began to accept that explanation, and she did little but cry over Fuyun's bitter fate, and her own.

When the black bear was sent to White Rock Stockade, everyone commented on its size, its obvious strength, and its lustrous pelt. Party Secretary Tian decided to reward Tian Zhongzheng and Cai Da'an. "Zhongzheng," he said, "since you were responsible for bagging this bear, the skin's yours. It will make a wonderful bedspread!"

"I can't take it as a personal gift," Tian replied, "but I'll be happy to accept it on behalf of the township government."

Tian Youshan wanted to know everything about the hunting expedition, and Cai was obliged to describe the death of Fuyun. Tian's face darkened, and he kept shaking his head. Cai took the blame on himself, admitting that he had not behaved as responsibly as he should have and had not paid enough attention to safety.

"What a tragedy!" was all Tian Youshan could say. "Ah . . . the people are so good. So many sacrificed their lives in the revolution, and now . . . ah, the people are so good. That's why it's important for us cadres to take them to our bosom! Comrade Da'an, let this be a lesson to you, a tragic lesson. Don't ever forget it!" Then he inquired, "Who else knows about this?"

"Only a few people in Crossroads Township. No one in White Rock Stockade."

"We must see that it stays that way. Don't tell another soul, and above all, don't let Commandant Xu or any other high-ranking officials hear of it. Make sure all the arrangements are taken care of. Spend whatever you must to pay for the funeral and make sure his family is taken care of. And be sure to assemble everyone who knows about this and give them all a modest stipend."

Cai Da'an was back in Stream of Wandering Spirits in no time, to call a meeting of everyone who was aware of the incident, and to warn them to keep word of it from spreading further. If there was a leak, it would be on their heads. He gave each of them twenty yuan and took two hundred to Water Girl. But not only did she refuse it, she grabbed his arm as if deranged and screamed, "Is that what Fuyun was worth? Two hundred yuan? Give me back my Fuyun! I want my Fuyun back!"

At this she swooned dead away. They picked her up, laid her out on the kang, and gave her some water. After they sponged her forehead with cool water, she slowly regained consciousness. She began to weep. The sadness of Han Wenju, Old Seven, and some of the other men was mixed with wrath. They returned to the outer room and surrounded Cai Da'an, reviling him, spitting at him, and refusing to let him go. Water Girl, who by now had stopped crying, said to Golden Dog, beside her, "Let him go, Uncle Golden Dog. I don't want his two hundred yuan, because what happened represents not only Fuyun's bitter fate, but mine as well!"

"Water Girl, don't talk crazy. Have you been listening to the non-sense people have been spouting? How can an intelligent woman be taken in by that fatalistic talk?"

Turning her face to Golden Dog, Water Girl began crying again.

"If we place our trust in fate," he continued, "we should, logically, forget about doing anything at all. But even if that's what it comes to, and fate really is in control, it's our job to struggle against fate. Leave things to me."

He walked into the outer room and said to Cai, "You don't give a damn about the people. All you're interested in is toadying to your superiors. Don't you feel any shame at all? When you eat those bear paws at the banquet, your mouth shining from the grease, won't it occur to you that you might as well be eating Fuyun?"

"Golden Dog," Cai said, "you're a bright man, so you ought to know better than to level groundless charges. What makes you think I'll have a chance to taste those bear paws?"

"Okay, messenger boy. You can run back and tell Tian Zhongzheng and Tian Youshan that we won't let go until this matter is taken care of properly!"

That night Tian Zhongzheng called Tian Youshan for advice. He was told to offer an additional three hundred to Water Girl. But since he was too mortified to face her himself, he went to Golden Dog. "Fuyun's death was like a knife driven into my heart! And when Secretary Tian heard the news, he broke down and cried over the phone. He specifically directed us to ensure that everything possible is done to satisfy the family. He said that consultation over the details would begin right after the dedication ceremony for the kiosk, and he hopes you'll put your personal grief aside for now and go to White Rock Stockade early tomorrow morning. The ceremony is a big event for everyone in the county."

Early the following morning, Golden Dog lay on the ground in front of Fuyun's mountain grave, weeping over the loss of his friend, before making the trip to White Rock Stockade. When he arrived at the landing, Water Girl was there to see him off. "Water Girl," he said, "try not to let your sorrow defeat you. You have my word that I won't rest until this outrage is avenged! I'll call you with any news."

She nodded tearfully. Her pregnancy was so advanced that she could barely stand, so she sat on a rock beside the river.

Just before the boat got under way, Golden Dog murmured, "You must be strong, for you and for Fuyun." What he meant, of course, was that she had to protect Fuyun's unborn progeny. She understood perfectly, but as she turned to leave, tears were coursing down her cheeks.

People from all the work units in White Rock Stockade were engaged in a general cleanup, whitewashing the walls and painting the floors black. Welcoming banners for the VIPs had been unfurled above the four major thoroughfares. As Golden Dog approached an intersection, he perceived a cluster of people embroiled in a heated argument, which quickly drew a crowd of rubberneckers. The argument had started when a team of whitewashers had splashed paint on the signboard of a private bookstore; the irate proprietor was demanding restitution from the workers, who defended themselves: "Everyone was notified to cover up their signs with newspaper. Why didn't you do as you were told? So your sign got splattered; what are you going to do about it?"

"What am I going to do about it?" the proprietor hurled back. "I'm going to drag you over to the police station!"

"Be my guest," one worker said, offering his arm. "But I'll tell you here and now that once you walk into the police station, you can forget about coming out for a while. And you can count on losing your business license for this little bookstore of yours."

Someone in the crowd tried to defuse the situation by saying to the proprietor, "Forget it; just forget it! You're better off putting up a new sign. Be grateful you had your walls whitewashed without spending a cent or having to do the work yourself. You're still ahead of the game!"

"Screw you!" the proprietor shot back. "A few VIPs come to town, and the whole place is turned upside down!"

The bystander disagreed. "I'd like to see VIPs come to town every month. That way the town would be so neat and tidy we'd probably make the papers. You there, doing the whitewashing, how come you're only worried about the walls facing the street? If you really want to clean things up, maybe you'd better start by whitewashing Secretary Tian's intestines!"

The crowd roared. But Golden Dog, who felt too much bitterness to laugh, moved quietly away. He had walked about a block when a car pulled up and stopped. Assuming it was Dakong, he looked up to see Tian Youshan signaling him.

"Golden Dog," he said, "are you just back from Stream of Wandering Spirits?"

"I just got here."

"Have the funeral arrangements for Fuyun been taken care of? I still can't believe it happened. He just closed his eyes and left us. How is Water Girl going to get by? I hear she's going to have a baby. Well, at least he's left an heir."

"Fuyun died so Commandant Xu could enjoy a feast of game."

"Hunters die and get injured in accidents all the time," Tian said. "It's unfair to say he died for Commandant Xu. You're a reporter, and a party member. We can't forget party spirit when we speak. I've already called the government office at Crossroads Township and told them to take care of Water Girl's needs. And I've been wondering whether we should call Fuyun's death an act of martyrdom. Of course, only the county committee can act on that idea, but if he meets all the criteria, I'm for listing him as a martyr. That way, Water Girl and the unborn baby won't have to worry about getting by. For now, though, we must focus our energies on the business at hand. Consider how many people died during the war. If a martyr like Tian the Sixth were alive today, just think how high a position he'd in all likelihood be holding. But he died and doesn't even have a grave. Who did he die for? For the people, that's who. He died so we could have what we have today! The provincial officials attach great importance to our dedication ceremony. Why, even the former commander of the 25th Red Army, who went all the way to the top—the Central Committee—sent a telegram expressing his support. He even sent us an inscription in his own hand. So we have to make a success of this; we mustn't fail! I'd like you to go over and talk to the comrades in the news department to work out how best to report tomorrow's events. I'm on my way to the Chengguan Elementary School to check on the preparations of the Young Pioneers, who will be bringing the floral wreaths."

With that, the car sped away.

26

A bright sun appeared in the sky the following day, and the weather was perfect. Representatives from all the city bureaus and departments and from any other organizations that had a part in the event gathered early in the morning on the square in front of the park near the northern gate. The octagonal kiosk with the flying eaves was draped with couplets presented in calligraphy, the area surrounding it was covered with bounteous flowers and rare plants, the rows of cypress and pine trees to the left and right were draped with paper streamers, and floral wreaths in a riot of colors filled the spaces on both sides. The commemorative plaque was neatly covered by a sheet of red silk. A rostrum had been placed on the brick steps leading up to the kiosk, around which were an amplifier, a tape recorder, and shiny loudspeakers. Crisscrossed wires ran all over the area, as did a small army of people with Staff badges pinned to their shirts.

But the person in charge of the ceremony, the county party secretary, Tian Youshan, was nowhere in sight.

The Young Pioneers were dressed neatly in white shirts and blue trousers as they marched up, gongs clanging, drums pounding, and horns blaring; but when they saw that the ceremony had not yet begun, their sounds began to peter out and finally stopped altogether. The gate to the park was clogged with pushcarts whose owners figured that the swelling crowd promised a land-office business. But one after another they were dragged or pushed away by staff personnel who told them they weren't allowed to set up in the gateway, nor on the square in front of it. They had to move to the other side of the metal railing and observe the activities from there. They kept turning to look behind them as their steps took them all the way to the marketplace inside the northern gate. It was the sixth of the month, the second of three market days (the other two were the third and the ninth) for the county town, and that area was the most bustling section of town on those days. Everything from lumber, bamboo products, clothing and accessories, and household utensils to thimbles, earrings, buttons, and earpicks—in short, everything under the sun—was sold there. Donkeys, horses, pigs, goats, chickens, dogs, cats, and rabbits rolled around in the dirt, shitting all over the place, while auctioneers were hard at work indicating prices with their fingers shielded by their straw hats. The professional castrater brandished his knife boldly, a cloud of dust hung over the area, the din was deafening. Vegetable peddlers proclaimed the freshness of their wares and the accuracy of their scales in order to woo customers, whose shoes and socks were getting soaked by the filthy water dripping from the baskets the greengrocers had carried from the river, chock full of their produce. There were apologies all around. Snacks were available in the sidewalk cafés, where the stoves blazed and people fought over the tables and benches; bowls and plates clattered as arguments erupted left and right, then turned into fistfights that resulted in wholesale smashings of cutlery and spilled food. Pot liquor and slops were thrown everywhere. Hungry customers who wanted to avoid the tumult simply squatted outside the tents to eat and drink, and when they were finished, left their bowls and chopsticks on the ground and walked off. Once the crowd grew until there was barely room to walk and vehicles could no longer pass, the police appeared and ordered the café owners, vegetable sellers, livestock auctioneers, and peddlers of odds and ends to close up shop and take their wares over to the western gate if they wanted to continue to do business. Confused, the entrepreneurs said, "I paid my taxes already. Look, here's a receipt for administrative fees, here's one for sanitation fees, here's one for a business license . . ."

But the police were indifferent: "They're having a big ceremony in the park, and no peddling's allowed here today. Do you hear what I'm saying?"

"Let them take care of their ceremony," one of the entrepreneurs replied, "and I'll take care of my business. Well water doesn't get in the way of river water!"

"You're blocking traffic," the policemen said, "and ruining the atmosphere. If you don't leave, I'll have to confiscate your business license and you can debate the point at the police station."

That shut them up. They hurriedly gathered their stock and took off like a bunch of refugees. Their place was taken by sanitation workers who attacked the dust and filth with their brooms.

And still Tian Yousuan's car didn't arrive. Nor did the cars of the provincial and regional officials.

For a time, the audience sat somberly and quietly in the square, but soon it grew impatient. One person turned and looked toward the wall to the right of the park, three or four more heads soon followed, then dozens, then hundreds, until every head in the square was turned in the same direction. Unhappily, there was nothing to see but a patch of grass growing at the base of the wall. The turned heads snapped straight ahead. No one said anything; no one had to. The word *boring* was on everyone's mind; the assembly congratulated themselves on getting through another ten minutes. Then someone stood up to stretch his legs and take another long look at the memorial kiosk; he counted the tiles on the section of roof opposite, then calculated the total number on all eight sides. "I wonder how much this kiosk cost?" he said.

Thirty thousand, someone guessed.

Fifty thousand, someone else volunteered.

He clicked his tongue in wonder over Tian the Sixth's good fortune.

"Good fortune?" someone exclaimed. "If he were alive today, his private car alone would be worth 120,000! The geomancy of the Tian clan isn't as auspicious as the Gongs'!"

"Not necessarily," someone countered. "Rivers flow eastward for thirty years and westward for the next thirty. The members of the Gong clan are all still alive, but who knows if any of them will get a memorial kiosk."

Golden Dog, who was squatting down among the crowd of people, smoked one cigarette after another, five in all, before hoisting himself up and walking to the entrance to the square, where he asked a photographer from the news section, "Where's Secretary Tian? It's getting late, and the ceremony hasn't even started."

"Commandant Xu arrived in the region yesterday and called to say he'd be here with Commissioner Gong first thing this morning. Secretary Tian and several deputies went to meet them at the county line. I can't imagine why they haven't arrived."

Golden Dog smiled. "Being a party secretary is no bed of roses!"

"It sure isn't! I know for a fact that he hasn't had a decent night's sleep recently. He hasn't been able to set his mind at ease, because of all the arrangements."

Again Golden Dog smiled, then turned and walked from the park, to a bar tucked away inside the city gate, where he ordered some wine and sipped it slowly.

The proprietor's daughter, who was sitting behind the bar pouring wine and nibbling on melon seeds, was a pretty little thing whose eyes and brows reminded him of Water Girl. He was enchanted by her appearance. He ordered another round, and as the wine warmed his belly, his thoughts turned to Fuyun and his eyes began to mist. He sat there vacantly awhile, until the popping of firecrackers in the park awakened him from his reveries. He knew they were announcing the arrival of Commandant Xu. The memorial ceremony for Tian the Sixth was ready to begin. Two announcers from the broadcasting station—a man and a woman—were on the loudspeakers, telling about the activities that would take place at the site of the ceremony. He then heard Tian Youshan read the names and positions of the visiting dignitaries. That took a full twenty minutes and was followed by a eulogy by Tian Zhongzheng in his role as closest living relative of the martyr. Then it was Commandant Xu's turn to speak . . . Golden Dog walked out of the bar in measured steps and returned to the entrance to the park, where three or four men with Staff badges pinned to their shirts were hauling an old man away. He was struggling—dragging his feet on the ground and raising a cloud of dust. Golden Dog couldn't see the meaning of the forcible removal, and when he saw that one of the men carrying the old fellow was a chap he knew in the propaganda section of the county government, he walked over and asked, "What's going on, Little Li?"

But before Little Li could respond, the old man, whose nose was running and eyes were watering, grabbed Golden Dog's sleeve and pleaded, "You look like you understand what's what, sir. Tell me why I can't see Commandant Xu. Do they think he won't remember me just because he's become a commandant? Ask him. If he says he doesn't know me, call me a troublemaker. But if he remembers me, I have something to say to him."

Golden Dog at first wasn't sure what to think, but he questioned the old fellow. It turned out that he was a mountain man named Jiang Laizi, who had joined the revolution when Tian the Sixth and Xu Feibao were heading the guerrilla forces. For six months he'd been responsible for taking care of Tian the Sixth's horse, and since he had no weapon of his own, Tian the Sixth had given him a hand grenade, which he'd held on to for a long time. Then, during one of the skirmishes, he'd tossed it, but it had landed harmlessly, since he'd forgotten to pull the pin. But the horse under his care had thrived. In another skirmish, six months later, at King Ma Gulley, near the Zhou River, Tian the Sixth's horse had been killed by a stray bullet; without a horse to look after, Jiang had returned home to farm his land. After Liberation, virtually all the guerrillas became officials or, at the very least, received government pensions. He, however, was still a farmer. But he didn't mind, since he was illiterate and not qualified for a job requiring an education. But five years ago his son had gone up the mountain to gather firewood and had fallen over a cliff. He was now a mental cripple. On top of that, the old man's wife had been bedridden for years. His fellow villagers were always urging him to seek help from the government because of his past contributions, but the government and the county committee had ignored his requests. When the news came that Xu Feibao, who in the intervening years had become a commandant, was going to visit White Rock Stockade, it occurred to him to ask the commandant to intercede for him. But the staff had stopped him at the gate and refused to allow him entrance to the ceremony.

His voice cracking with emotion, Jiang Laizi protested, "I fought in the revolution. If I'd died along with Commander Tian's horse, I'd be a martyr today too and my grave would be decorated with floral wreaths sent by you very people. But because I'm alive, you'll have nothing to do with me. My name isn't Tian and it isn't Gong, but I was a groom for the Communist party! All I'm asking is for Commandant Xu to remember me, not for him to promote me to an official rank. I think I deserve something."

Golden Dog looked at the old man, in tatters, gaunt, pale, and clearly not some wily scoundrel. "You ought to let him see Commandant Xu," he said. "He might be telling the truth."

"Who knows what would happen if we let him see Commandant Xu?" Little Li said. "He's been to see Secretary Tian several times, always pathetic and creating a scene, even attempting a lie-in in the county committee headquarters. It could embarrass everybody if we let him close to Commandant Xu."

"I won't cause a scene," Jiang promised. "If Commandant Xu doesn't recall me, I'll walk away, no regrets, no blame—except for my own accursed fate."

"Commandant Xu is known for his commitment to the working man," Golden Dog said to Little Li. "And this fellow says he once fought alongside him. If that's true and Commandant Xu finds out you kept them apart, you might just bring his wrath down on your own head. Aren't you afraid of that?"

Li reflected for a moment. He decided to let the old man see Commandant Xu, but warned him of the importance of behaving decorously. They entered the site of the ceremony, and Jiang Laizi was taken aside to a tiny waiting room beside the memorial kiosk that served as the Zhou River Revolutionary Exhibit Hall.

At the end of the ceremony, Commandant Xu, Gong Baoshan, and Tian Youshan came to the waiting room for tea. Golden Dog, who saw Tian Youshan from time to time and was familiar with his normal coloring, could tell from his pallor that he didn't feel in his element. But as one of Xu's subordinates, he had no choice but to accompany him. While Commandant Xu was talking with Tian Youshan, Gong Baoshan had a strained, long-suffering look on his face, but he forced himself to smile and, now and again, to laugh with the others. When he spotted Golden Dog, he called to him and walked over.

"So you're here, too, Commissioner Gong," Golden Dog said.

"Duty, duty."

"Creating a martyr's shrine is another step in the education of the people of the Zhou River about our traditions," Golden Dog gushed shrewdly. "This will ensure that they never forget the sacrifices of our heroic forebears. Now that we have a memorial for Tian the Sixth, I wouldn't be surprised if pressure built for a monument in Zhou City for some other martyr. What we need is more memorials to the revolution!"

"Do you really think so?" Gong asked softly. "You have your ear to the ground. Is that what the people are saying?"

"That's what they're saying. At first I thought this kiosk would be erected in Zhou City and that you'd be in charge. You're the only survivor from your guerrilla squad."

Gong smiled, but it was a wry smile. He shrugged his shoulders. But then he said, "Golden Dog, they say you're at the White Rock Stockade bureau station now. Why don't you come to Zhou City more often? You should come over and see me once in a while. Have you written anything lately that I should know about?"

While he was replying to Gong Baoshan, Golden Dog heard the old groom call out to Commandant Xu, who looked up to see an elderly man. He smiled and nodded, then reached out to shake the old man's hand. "Are you here to participate in the ceremony, old-timer?" he asked.

"I'm back, Commandant Xu, I've come back!"

"It was a good ceremony," Commandant Xu said, "and well attended. It just goes to show that even during good times the people don't forget the martyrs who shed their blood for the revolution!"

Gong Baoshan, whose attention had been caught by the groom, said, "Golden Dog, who's that geezer?"

"He says he was a groom for the martyr Tian the Sixth. He's a farmer who went to see Secretary Tian several times for help, but nothing ever came of it. He's here today to see if he can get Commandant Xu to intervene."

Gong Baoshan's eyes lit up. "Let's go over and hear how it goes."

After the polite exchange of words with the groom, Commandant Xu turned back to his conversation with Tian Youshan. But the groom persisted. "Don't you remember me, Commandant Xu? It's me, Laizi. Commander Tian's groom. You and I slept in a haystack together on South Mountain. That night it was so cold and we were so hungry that we couldn't sleep, so we got up and fried some rice husks. Don't you remember how the next morning you were constipated and I had to use a piece of bamboo on you?"

You could hear a pin drop. Commandant Xu was no longer making small talk. He looked closely at the groom, and the recognition hit him. "Laizi, is it really you? Laizi! You're still alive?"

"Commandant Xu," Laizi said, "you remember me! Oh, how wonderful! Maybe you can stand up for me."

"Forgive me, Laizi, for not recognizing you right away. What are you doing now? Are you retired?"

"Retired, you say? I've been a farmer all these years."

"A farmer? How's your health?"

"These old bones have just about had it. I'm seventy-two this year. I have a son, but he's mentally disabled, and my asthma's so bad I can't get down off the kang when the weather turns cold."

Gong Baoshan pulled a stool over for the old groom to sit on. "You're still a farmer?" he asked in mock consternation. "Isn't the government taking care of you?"

"If it was, I wouldn't be asking Commandant Xu to speak up for me. I went over to the county committee, but they refused to believe my story, and I figured I wouldn't be granted anything for taking care of Commander Tian's horse all those months. I never thought the man upstairs would look down and send Commandant Xu to me!"

"Lots of people contributed to the revolution," Commandant Xu said solemnly, "and are still working on the front line of agriculture.

You have to admire their spirit. But we must take care of them if we're to be true to our national conscience."

Golden Dog sneaked a look at Tian Youshan, whose face was white as he nodded his assent with a shamefaced smile.

The groom turned to Tian and said triumphantly, "See there, Secretary Tian, Commandant Xu knows I'm not a phony!"

"Of course not," Tian said. "We'll look into your needs right away. It's our responsibility to make sure that elderly comrades who participated in the revolution live out their final years in comfort. Stay in town for the next few days, Old Jiang. We'll put you up in the county guesthouse while we begin working on your case. Little Li."

Little Li came in, and when he saw Tian Youshan talking to the old groom, he figured that he was chewing him out. "This old codger sure knows how to pester people," he groaned. "I only let him in because I had to."

"Take our friend, Comrade Jiang, to the guesthouse. Let him have a nice bath, and let him rest for a while. Buy three days' meal tickets for him. Do you have money with you? Here, I'll give you some."

Little Li was disoriented by the shifting winds. "I've got money!" he insisted. Then he turned to the old groom and asked gently, "Did Commandant Xu really remember you?"

Tian Youshan came over and saw the groom to the door, and when he reached the steps, he hissed at Little Li, "What the hell's the idea of letting such scum in here? When you get to the guesthouse, just tell him it's full. He'll have to go home and await word that will come from the county committee after we study his application."

Golden Dog found the incident both maddening and comical. After saying good-bye to Gong Baoshan he searched out the secretary of the ceremony in order to get a copy of the guest list for his story.

Commandant Xu stayed in White Rock Stockade for three days, and during that period the guesthouse laid out a sixteen-table spread at each meal, with mushrooms and bamboo shoots, sea cucumbers and squid. Tian Youshan was in constant motion, toasting his guests, filling their plates, and singing the virtues of local delicacies like turtle, baby fish, pheasant, and bear paws.

"Ha!" Commandant Xu said. "With excellent food like this, be careful you don't turn me into a glutton!"

"With these measly rations?" Tian said. "The last thing we'd intend is to lead you astray. The standard of living in White Rock Stockade is much higher than it used to be. All the people, in the villages as well as in town, have an abundance of food at every meal. Everything you see here is locally produced and didn't cost a cent. Taste this bear paw. We don't have a city-trained chef, though, so I don't know if it'll be up to your standard."

Commandant Xu picked a chunk up with his chopsticks and ate it, his lips shiny with grease. "Excellent," he said, "excellent. Where did this bear come from?"

"Up on Shaman Mountain. Old Blackie here was one strong bear but as dumb as they come. The hunter had his hand wrapped in bamboo, and when the bear grabbed the armored limb, it hooted with joy, laughing just like a human, and so hard it forgot everything else. That allowed the hunter to withdraw his hand from the bamboo and scramble up a tree. And while the bear was holding on to the bamboo in contentment, the hunter shot it dead."

"You mentioned Shaman Mountain. I once stayed in East Gulley for twenty days in the home of a mountaineer who fed me delicious corn mush at every meal. I haven't been able to get that flavor out of my mind for twenty years. I've never tasted anything like it. I tell people in the provincial capital to look at the mountain folk. City people are so concerned about their health that they get up bright and early to exercise, but not the mountain folk—and look how long they live. The mountain air's good, the food they eat is always fresh, and they can supplement their diet with bear paw . . . I told my wife that when I retire in a year or two, I want to move to the mountains."

Tian Youshan said, "It's very touching that you never forget your roots, Commandant Xu. The people of White Rock Stockade would be honored if you chose their county as the place of your retirement."

When their conversation turned to the people, Commandant Xu sighed and spoke with fervor, and the ever-attentive Tian Youshan added his own words of tribute. They finished off one of the bear paws, and followed that with its liver, its heart, and its lungs. Through the meal Gong Baoshan kept asking about Golden Dog. Tian left the table to call him up and reiterate that he was welcome to come over and eat with them. But Golden Dog declined; watching them slobber over that bear would have turned his stomach.

After Golden Dog finished his story and sent it by teletype to the Zhou City and capital newspapers, Tian Youshan had no more reason to come looking for him. So Golden Dog went to see him, to discuss the matter of Fuyun's death. The gate watchman barred his way, however, saying that members of the county committee and county government were reporting to Commandant Xu and other regional officials on local activities. On each of the next three days a crowd with complaints gathered at the gate of the county committee headquarters, but the staff was unable to do more than give uncertain advice, lecture the people, and when all else failed, send them home with soothing lies. Only one in the throng defied the lies and refused to leave: a forty-six-year-old dirty-faced woman with scraggly hair, who screeched and thundered at them and held on to the gate with all her might. She insisted on seeing Commandant Xu or Commissioner Gong, but Tian Youshan commanded her expulsion from the city. She was dragged to a car and driven twenty or thirty li out of town. But she was back that night, bringing with her a complaint written out on a piece of white cloth: during the Cultural Revolution, her husband had hanged himself after being falsely accused of corruption, and she was intent on having him cleared posthumously. The next morning she stood in front of the county committee headquarters and boomed at the top of her lungs, showing her cloth petition to those who would look and reading it aloud to the others. Everyone in town knew this woman, for she had been waging the same campaign for so long that many people believed her to be unhinged. But she always drew a crowd of curiosity seekers. Finally, Tian Youshan started badgering the public security bureau, and asked sarcastically if restraining one madwoman was beyond its capability. He told the bureau that the county officials were in the process of reporting to their superiors and reminded it of the effects a woman demonstrating in front of headquarters would have. She was arrested. But since she didn't belong in jail, the authorities locked her in an empty room in the compound of the bureau of agriculture and forestry, where for the next few days she ceased bawling and wailing only when it was time to eat her coarse buns and drink her water. They didn't release her until Commandant Xu and his entourage had left White Rock Stockade, and by then her filthy face was mottled and her voice so hoarse she could barely speak. When she was freed, she went back and demonstrated for three more days; then she vanished.

After Commandant Xu left White Rock Stockade, life reverted to normal. Golden Dog tried again to get in to Tian Youshan, but Tian begged off seeing him, pleading exhaustion after several days of overwork. Since Golden Dog was denied an audience with the man in charge, he looked up the office manager. As a writer, this fellow had no peers in White Rock Stockade, and he and Golden Dog had corresponded in the past; he was also the secretary's pet. Golden Dog went to his house but was told that he was in the hospital. That surprised Golden Dog. What could have happened to this specimen of robust health? In the hospital, Golden Dog found the office manager reclining in bed. His eyes were wide open, but he couldn't speak.

"What's wrong with him?" Golden Dog asked the attending physician.

"Insomnia. He hasn't slept in three days. He can't go on like this much longer."

"Comrade Golden Dog," the man's wife said tearfully, "look at the living corpse they've turned him into! For the visit by all those VIPs, the county committee demanded a detailed report on the work they've been doing, and he had to write every word of it. He was at it for five days and four nights, and he smoked ten cartons of cigarettes in the process. Now look at him! He's been here for three days, and he still hasn't slept!"

"The pills we gave him don't work," the doctor said, "so now we're going to give him a strong soporific intravenously."

The soporific did its job, for the office manager's eyes closed and he fell asleep. He didn't wake the next day, or the day after that, or even the day after that; but since he was breathing, he was obviously alive. At noon on the fifth day, he finally woke up. In view of the pitiful state of this man, the finest writer in the county, Golden Dog decided not to take up the subject of Fuyun's death with him after all.

Mulling over all that had happened recently in White Rock Stockade, Golden Dog's anger rose, and he sat down and wrote a story about the construction of the memorial to Tian the Sixth, in which he disclosed all the concealment that had been connected with it. But he was too smart to send the story directly to the Zhou City newspaper, knowing they'd never print it and that it would only bring him trouble. Instead he sent a letter to members of the Young Reporters Study Association to let them know what had happened and to make them alert to later developments, then mailed the story to Commissioner Gong, who had stayed behind in the White Rock Stockade guesthouse.

When Gong read the material Golden Dog had provided, he was filled with righteous indignation. At his behest, his secretary fetched Golden Dog to the guest house, where Gong subjected him to a grilling about details that the story had omitted. On the following day, when Tian Youshan came to lead Gong on an inspection of some of White Rock Stockade's factories and mines, he delivered himself from Tian's tour by saying that he wanted to visit his family home in Stream of Wandering Spirits. "I haven't been back in years," he said, "and since I'm so close, I ought to go take a look."

"You're right," Tian Youshan agreed, "you really ought to. The people there are always asking about you! I'll go with you."

Gong thanked him, but said he'd take Golden Dog as company in order to keep the visit unobtrusive. The prospect of Golden Dog's serving as Gong's guide to Stream of Wandering Spirits caused Tian misgivings, but what he said was, "Fine, that's a good idea." As soon as he reached his office, though, he rang up Tian Zhongzheng in Crossroads Township, directing him to put out the welcome mat—and to stick close to his guest.

The original plan was to leave the following afternoon, but Golden Dog suggested that they leave that very night, since Tian Youshan was sure to have been in touch with Tian Zhongzheng. The commissioner's car was on its way by the middle of the night, and they drove straight to Crossroads Township, where, instead of rolling into the government compound, they parked the car at the elementary school on the outskirts. At the ferry landing, Golden Dog called out to Han Wenju, who poled his ferryboat across. "Golden Dog," Han said when he drew up to the bank, "what are you doing here at this time of night?"

"I'm accompanying Gong Baoshan on a visit home."

"Gong Baoshan's here?" Han said. "Isn't he living the good life in Zhou City? What's he doing back here?"

Golden Dog told him what he was planning.

"Um-hmm," Han said with a nod. Then he eased himself off the boat and walked across the beach to welcome the visitor. "We thought we'd never see you again after you left, Commissioner Gong. I was just asking myself why I was finding it so hard to get to sleep tonight and why the mountain watchdogs were so quiet. I knew something was in the wind, but I never guessed it was your homecoming!"

"Old Brother Han," Gong said, "it's good to see you in such good health. Still poling your boat, I see. I've been meaning to come back and renew acquaintances for the longest time, but I'm so busy I barely have time to sleep. I heard what happened to your son-in-law, Fuyun, and it left me shaken. That was when I knew I had to come and see how things are. How's Water Girl doing? I hope she's taking care of her health."

Normally, Han was resistant to this kind of talk, but he was affected by the commissioner's comments. "She's fine," he said, "she's doing fine. It's good to know you haven't forgotten us. You're the only high-ranking official Stream of Wandering Spirits has ever produced, and everybody who lives here knows you're our protector!"

They boarded the ferry and crossed the river. Saying he wanted to go first to see Water Girl, Gong asked Han to let the Gong clan know he was in town so they could arrange his room and board.

"Commissioner," Han said, "I don't dare invite you to stay at our place, since it's so dirty, but I insist that you take your meals there. Water Girl's a wonderful cook!"

He walked off to notify the Gong clan.

Water Girl was sitting on the kang in deep thought when the visitors surprised her. Her apprehension quickly turned to pleasure. She didn't know who Gong Baoshan was, but Golden Dog whispered to her before making the formal introductions. When she set about gathering kindling to light the stove, Gong said, "Water Girl, you don't have to do that. I came to see you and tell you that I'll make sure the tragic circumstances of Fuyun's death won't be swept under the rug. When Commandant Xu came to White Rock Stockade, was it his idea to feast on bear paw? Absolutely not! Our senior cadres are decent, upstanding people. It's the people beneath them who give the party a bad name. If we don't act to straighten this mess out, what are these lower ranks going to turn into?" He spoke with passion and even took some of the blame unto himself. "I should have come back more often to get a handle on what was happening. But from now on, if you need anything, just write and tell me. I have a hundred yuan on me at the moment, which I'd like you to take. It's the least I can do as an official and as one of your elders. Take it, please. I only wish I had more with me."

Water Girl didn't want to accept it, until Golden Dog said, "Take it to show you appreciate the commissioner's concern. As for Fuyun's death, Commissioner Gong will make sure that the right steps are taken. After all, White Rock Stockade is under his jurisdiction."

"And if I can't do it by myself," Gong Baoshan added, "there's always the provincial party committee."

At the end of the short visit, Golden Dog, Water Girl, and Han Wenju saw Gong Baoshan out. They were so lifted by the experience that they stayed up and talked until dawn.

After breakfast, Golden Dog accompanied Gong back to White Rock Stockade. On the way, they stopped at the township government compound, where Tian Zhongzheng was waiting to receive the dignitary. The car's horn drew him out of the building, but when they explained that they'd already been to Stream of Wandering Spirits—had spent the night there—he recoiled. But he forced a smile to his lips and invited the commissioner inside to rest while lunch was readied. Tian volunteered to report on the work being carried out locally.

Gong just stood in front of his car and asked, "Are you party secretary of this township?"

"You don't get back here very often, Commissioner," Tian said, "so you don't know me. My name is Tian Zhongzheng."

"Ah, the name's familiar. Tian Youshan tells me what a good official you are! You'd like to report on the work being carried out locally? Fine. Tell me, how many people live in Crossroads Township?"

The question caught Tian Zhongzheng by surprise. "I have the figures inside," he fumbled. "Come in and I'll give you my report."

"I'd appreciate your answer now!"

"More than 2,340."

"But how many more? And how much land is there?"

"We're building lots of houses," Tian Zhongzheng muttered.

"How much forest land? How many well-to-do families? What's their average annual income? How many families are just getting by? What's *their* average annual income? How many families are below the poverty line? What's *their* average annual income? How many families are there on pensions? Hmm?"

Tian's face was florid and beaded with sweat. He stood there stammering. All of a sudden, Gong smacked his hand down on the hood of the car and roared, "What the hell kind of report is that? Let's hear your report on the rumor circulating around Crossroads Township that a certain someone is about to be promoted to deputy regional commissioner. Did someone tell you to start spreading it, or did you make it up yourself? What's the idea of misleading the people with rumors?"

Tian's face had passed from red to white. "I never heard such a rumor, and I've certainly never said anything like that. But believe me, Commissioner Gong, I'll get to the bottom of it."

"Fine. You do that. And you tell the people who are trying to stir things up that they'd better watch their step!"

He turned and jerked the car door open, gestured for Golden Dog to get in, and drove off.

Golden Dog had never seen Gong Baoshan that furious, and it was evident that he was still fuming. "He's scarcely worth your anger, Commissioner. Tian Zhongzheng's a nobody."

"I know it's bad to give someone like that the satisfaction of seeing me blow up in front of him, but I really couldn't help it. What kind of a commissioner am I if I lose control even of places like White Rock Stockade?" He paused, then went on. "When I see a township party secretary like that, who has no idea what's happening around him, I can't help blowing up! We'd be in real trouble if all the grass-roots cadres were like him."

They were driving along the bumpy, stone-covered road on the northern bank of the Zhou River when Gong Baoshan suddenly mused, "They say people are as greedy as a snake trying to swallow an elephant. Don't they know it's impossible for a snake to do that? You're a reporter, Golden Dog, what do you think?"

Golden Dog smiled but kept his own counsel. As the car sped along, they observed a squirrel washing its face with its paws and were taken by the sight. Gong told the driver to stop so he could try to catch the squirrel, but it was gone before he was out of the car. After they got moving again, Golden Dog mulled how Gong's metaphor might be altered. A snake may not be able to swallow an elephant, but they say that an elephant's afraid of a mouse and if one gets into an elephant's trunk, the bigger animal's done for. But this too he kept to himself and simply smiled.

27

Gong Baoshan lost no time in transmitting Golden Dog's material to the provincial committee, along with a letter describing his own visit to the family of the victim in Stream of Wandering Spirits. He stated his disapprobation in unequivocal terms. In reply, the committee ruled that erecting a memorial kiosk for the martyr Tian the Sixth was totally fitting and proper, but that the comportment of the White Rock Stockade county committee throughout the period was in contravention of party discipline. An investigative team from the regional organization department was authorized to go to White Rock Stockade to make a full investigation and take the steps necessary to set things right.

During the time of the investigation, Golden Dog returned to Stream of Wandering Spirits.

He suggested to Water Girl that she move to White Rock Stockade, saying he'd already spoken to Dakong, who agreed to hire her at the White Rock Stockade Town and Country United Trade Co. She was heavy with the child of her late husband and looked wan and sallow. With a vacant look in her eyes, she said, "Uncle Golden Dog, didn't you say that getting mixed up with Dakong was dangerous?"

"What choice do we have now?" he sighed. "With Fuyun gone, you're all alone here, and you have to look after Uncle Han. How are you going to manage? Dakong may be a devil in human form, but if so, he's a devil I know. A man with a peasant background like his can't make it in this world without at least a measure of the kind of spirit he has. Go on over for the time being to earn enough to pay back the money you spent on the funeral and to ensure that Uncle Han has enough to live on. Once things are on a more even keel, we'll go from there. Since you're pregnant, it's no good for you to stay in the house and cry all day. You ought to get outside more and try to occupy your mind with other things."

She talked it over with Uncle Han, and he agreed at once. "Golden Dog," he said, taking him off to the side, "Water Girl's had a tough life, and so have I. We were relying on Fuyun, never dreaming that he'd be gone one day, just like that. I've always treated you like a member of the family, and I haven't forgotten what it was once like between you and Water Girl. I hope you'll have compassion on us now!"

Han looked as though he were about to kneel in front of Golden Dog, as tears ran down his cheeks. Golden Dog had never seen him so racked by worry, and a sadness came over him. "Don't talk like that, Uncle Han. Where would I be today if it weren't for everything you did for me? Now that Fuyun's gone, I'm obligated to do everything I can. Don't worry. As long as I can manage to buy food, you and Water Girl will never go hungry! We have to go on living, and to live to our fullest potential!"

Water Girl went to Fuyun's grave, taking an offering of wine and spirit money to burn. She returned home, made some wheat noodles and other kinds for Uncle Han, then husked some rice and millet, before leaving for White Rock Stockade with Golden Dog. Dakong was as good as his word: he'd arranged for her to do some odd jobs around the company, at a preferential salary.

As for the blacksmith shop in Crossroads Township, there was no option but to close it and rent out the rooms to a family wanting to open a restaurant.

The investigative team went about its work with extreme thoroughness, and the Young Reporters Study Association kept the pressure on by prodding public opinion. Everything Golden Dog had alleged was confirmed. The team conveyed its report to the provincial committee, which reprimanded Tian Youshan severely. As for Tian Zhongzheng, he was not only reprimanded but also demoted to the post of administrative head of Crossroads Township.

The region was buzzing over these developments, and everywhere people were talking about Golden Dog, the bureaucrats' watchdog. The talk took an increasingly bizarre direction, until the idea gained currency that the reason for Golden Dog's influence—what had allowed him to become a steel pellet in the bureaucrats' craw, one they could neither chew nor swallow, one over which they could neither laugh nor cry, one they could neither abuse nor hit—was that he was not human after all but was a reincarnation of a mountain watchdog.

Mountain watchdogs suddenly became the rage. But the unique thing about mountain watchdogs is that you can't find them in White Rock Stockade or deep in the mountains or in the forests; they can be found only around Stream of Wandering Spirits. Some of the more opportunistic villagers began catching the birds and offering them for sale in the marketplace, demanding a price as high as that for a nanny goat. But when they were taken from their forest habitat and put into cages, they stopped eating and drinking, and pierced the silence day and night with their cries until they fell dead. But no matter where you went on either bank of the Zhou River, people were caught up in the frenzy of worshiping the mountain watchdog. In virtually every home, the altars to heaven, earth, gods, emperors, and ancestors were festooned with drawings of mountain watchdogs. Eventually, paintings of mountain watchdogs appeared on door frames to keep evil spirits away and on livestock sheds to deter wild animals. Sick people carried them in order to drive away disease and affliction, and travelers carried them for good luck and a safe journey; even the rat exterminators in White Rock Stockade, Purple Thistle Pass, and Zhou City began tacking up posters praising the efficacy of their Mountain Watchdog Rat Poison.

Golden Dog didn't know whether to laugh or cry.

He was, after all, a reporter assigned to the White Rock Stockade bureau station, which was under the jurisdiction of the county committee, and as his reputation spread, he came to be exalted irrationally by some people. That led to a number of problems in connection with his work. Virtually every story he wrote, whether it commended or condemned, incited a storm of protest, with people accusing him of serious distortions. Some went so far as to send warning letters to organizations or individuals in his name, and the letters they wrote were presented to the White Rock Stockade county committee and the Zhou City newspaper as proof that he was acting irresponsibly and committing all sorts of abuses of his position as a reporter.

Golden Dog knew who was behind some of his troubles, but not all. His boss at the newspaper forwarded letter of complaint after letter of complaint to him, admonishing him to be conscious of the impact of his actions. He also asked him to consider leaving the bureau station in White Rock Stockade to return to the main office or to be transferred to another bureau station. Golden Dog, however, always reaffirmed his innocence in these matters and insistently sought permission to stay where he was so he could prove himself free of culpability.

September rolled around, and with it Golden Dog's thirty-fifth birthday, his threshold year. Water Girl had already told him she planned to celebrate his birthday, and she mobilized as many people as possible to give him tiger-head caps and shoes and red underwear and belts to protect him from calamities during the year, which was assumed to be the halfway mark in his life. The goal of her measures was success, good fortune, and a happy marriage for Golden Dog. She'd bought a piece of red satin to make a stomacher for him and was already embroidering the vivid picture of a mountain watchdog on it.

The newspaper sent on another batch of letters to Golden Dog, mostly from readers in the area. They ran the gamut from unrestricted praise, to pleas for help in rectifying grievances, to defamation and slander. The last letter in the pile, with a Zhou City return address, was from Shi Hua. He was jolted by her writing him, since he hadn't been to see her since that time nor had he written a single word to her. The busier he got, the faster his past slipped from memory, until she'd dropped from his mind—except, that is, from his dreams, where she had put in several appearances. He often awoke in the middle of the night and was unable to fall back to sleep; he'd sit on the edge of his bed until dawn, overcome by his feelings and by an agitation that simply wouldn't go away. Sometimes he'd walk into the night, looking for a dark corner where he could jerk off, or wake up following a wet dream, which left him feeling spent and depressed. He cursed himself mercilessly, pulled his hair, and slapped himself across the face, in a self-loathing born of his lack of self-control and his baseness. It took a colossal effort of will, but ultimately he regained control, forced himself back to strength, and nursed himself to physical and mental health. He vowed never again to go to Shi Hua. But here was a letter from her, and all he could do was sit in his chair breathing hard and letting his mind roam over the past. He looked at the envelope as containing a visit from the devil, his predestination, his fate!

The letter was long and rambling, filled with mistakes and improperly formed characters but also with genuine emotion commanding attention. It began with recriminations and the accusation that he had no understanding of women or of human sentiments. It went on to recount how hard it had been to obtain information on his current situation or news about his role in the fall of the Tian family from power in White Rock Stockade. Then it turned to how much she missed him and how she and her husband were always talking about him at the dinner table, until both of them wound up losing their appetites, or in bed, until they found themselves unable to sleep the rest of the night. The second half of the letter was given over to news about her. She and the girl who had once fallen for him but whom he'd walked out on were now working for another private, and a very prestigious, company that had put up a commercial building in the provincial capital, where she was in regular contact with the children of high-ranking officials of the provincial party committee and government. Some were past hope and, since they had no chance of a grand future in official circles, were bending their energies to nothing more than making a financial killing. They were willing to try anything and use any means to get what they wanted. Money ran through their fingers like water. But there were also several who were very competent, who were always on top of things, and who were extremely clever and intelligent. It was her opinion that nothing could be accomplished in China without the involvement of the children of high-ranking cadres. "The next time you come to Zhou City, be sure to drop by my place and I'll introduce you to a few people. In all honesty, among all my acquaintances, you're the only one who's ever been able to stir my affections. But you haven't lost your small-scale, peasant-economy mentality, and you're hopelessly constrained by some powerful, invisible force. To be blunt, you're no politician! (Don't laugh at me for my language. I learned it from my new friends.) Your relationship with me, your sudden departure from the newspaper to go to the bureau station, and the bizarre way you left my house all go to prove that."

Golden Dog gave a short laugh when he reached this point in the letter: she was right, of course; she'd learned to see things through a different lens since the last time they'd been together. His thoughts drifted to the mysterious surveyor he'd met at the Stream of Wandering Spirits ferry landing. Yes, Golden Dog was no politician; he was simply a man who wanted to become a reporter worthy of the name. He had no regrets over leaving Zhou City; in fact, he congratulated himself on the decision. He hated to think what might have happened if he were still living in Zhou City and if his relationship with Shi Hua had continued. His aspirations would have been shattered. *Shi Hua, I'm* not *the son of a high-ranking cadre. I'm the son of a peasant, a powerless man on the lowest rung of the social ladder! I'm trying to do my best in a place you can't find on any map!*

In the final paragraph, Shi Hua mentioned that the company she worked for had recently established connections with the White Rock Stockade City and Country United Trade Co., and that she'd met and become acquainted with Lei Dakong at a dinner in the provincial capital. Her company had been working on a business deal with a forestry seeding company in Xi'an, but the negotiations had fallen through and they'd turned everything over to Lei Dakong. Dakong was grateful for the business, and during their conversation he'd revealed that he and Golden Dog were fellow villagers and friends. It was he who had told her what Golden Dog was up to these days. That explained how she knew to send her letter directly to the bureau station.

It's a small world, he mused. *The road curves even if the mountain doesn't. It's impossible to keep anything secret, and no one can hide forever.*

He couldn't sleep that night, for Shi Hua's letter had got him thinking about marriage. There weren't many men his age in White Rock Stockade who were still unattached, and in Stream of Wandering Spirits and Restless Hill, men of his generation were already fathers. The national policy was one-child families, and if it weren't for that restriction, most people would have three or four babies, like pigs. But most young men and women, even with all the responsibilities of marriage and the hectic pace of their lives, enjoyed their lot, no matter how dirty and ragged they were, and they laughed at bachelors and the deprivation of their lives. Golden Dog's father, the old painter, couldn't bear the villagers' ridicule, and had gone over to the monastery to do a painting with tears in his eyes. He was forever writing to Golden Dog begging him to hurry and get married. But where was he going to find a wife? As a man on the public payroll, who had achieved fame as a reporter, he couldn't very well go up on the mountain to cut kindling or follow behind some hens to gather eggs just to save up enough money to get married; and there was no way he could take expensive gifts to a matchmaker to find a girl for him. He was free to marry whomever he wished, and no matchmakers ever came to his door to offer their services, for they figured he must have a bevy of admirers following him wherever he went. But there wasn't a single girl to whom he could pour out his heart.

The people in Stream of Wandering Spirits—even the people in White Rock Stockade—found it hard to believe that Golden Dog didn't already have a girlfriend, except for those closer to the situation, who chided him for setting his sights too high. Who should I blame? he asked himself. He berated himself for the stupidities of his past, including those in his relationships with Water Girl, Yingying, and Shi Hua, and he simply wasn't interested in looking for someone else. He was in an especially low mood on this particular night—why he didn't know—so he went out walking and soon turned his steps to the offices of the White Rock Stockade City and Country United Trade Co. As he walked down the familiar old street where Pockface's blacksmith shop had been, he realized that there was still room in his heart for only one woman: Water Girl.

In recent days, she had been looking healthier than before, and she was getting bigger all the time. Late one night, Dakong told her that Golden Dog's efforts had at last resulted in Tian Youshan's and Tian Zhongzheng's being reprimanded by the party. She burst out crying. Dakong was uncomprehending. "What are you crying for?" he asked. "You should be cheering over wonderful news like that."

But her body continued to quake. The other employees came running in, thinking a disaster had struck.

"I'm laughing," she said through her tears. "I'm laughing!"

Dakong realized that she was crying for joy. She asked him about the particulars of the reprimands, then said, "Let's go to Golden Dog. Does he know?"

"I'm sure he knew before we did."

"Then let's go celebrate together. Uncle Golden Dog is a man apart, Dakong. He's really made a difference. They all talk about how hard it is to get anything done in China without powerful backing. But he did it; Uncle Golden Dog did it!"

Late though it was, they hurried to the bureau station and woke Golden Dog, then broke out a bottle of wine. Water Girl astonished the men by drinking four cupfuls, more than she'd ever drunk at one sitting before. "Uncle Golden Dog," she said, "you single-handedly avenged Fuyun, and I know that wherever he is, he'll protect you. Now his death wasn't in vain." They fell to their knees and called out Fuyun's name, then splashed the wine onto the floor.

Several nights later, Golden Dog wandered over to the White Rock Stockade City and Country United Trade Co., where he stood at the gate, looking up at Water Girl's room. Her light was still on.

She had nearly finished embroidering the mountain watchdog on the red stomacher. Suddenly her left eyelid began to twitch. She rubbed it and went back to embroidering. It began to twitch more obtrusively, and as she held the needle tight in her hand, her thoughts drifted. *When the right eye twitches, trouble's at hand; when the left eye twitches, a visitor's coming. Should I be expecting somebody at this late hour?* She laughed to herself and went back to the stomacher. But an uneasiness had begun to fill her heart. To calm herself, she got up to open the window for the breeze and the moonlight. But when she did, she spotted someone by the main gate.

"Is that you, Uncle Golden Dog? What are you doing here at this time of night?"

He reddened, grateful, though, that his discomposure wasn't evident in the dim light. He wanted to escape, but it was too late. "I . . . I was just passing by. Why aren't you asleep?"

"Uncle Golden Dog," Water Girl said, pleased, "come up and sit awhile. My left eye was just twitching, and I said to myself . . ."

He went to her room, where she'd already steeped a pot of tea. She asked him if he'd been out on an assignment and why he was returning so late. Had he eaten? He made up a yarn.

"I'm glad you're here," she said. "I was going to look you up tomorrow morning to see if there was anything you wanted me to take back to Stream of Wandering Spirits."

"You're going back? I guess you miss Uncle Han."

"That's one reason. Now that the weather's turning cool, I want to take him a jacket I made for him. I haven't been back for a long time—not since Tian Youshan and Tian Zhongzheng were reprimanded—and I want to visit Fuyun's grave and tell him about it. But mainly I have something to do for the company. Dakong went over to Purple Thistle Pass a couple of days ago to look after some business arranged through a company in Zhou City. He's selling ten tons of pine seedlings to some people in Xi'an. He sent a telegram today telling me to go to Crossroads Township to get Cai Da'an to schedule the river shipping brigade to transport them to White Rock Stockade, where trucks sent over from Xi'an will pick them up."

"So now you're doing liaison work!" Golden Dog said, with a pleased smile. "I didn't know you had the mettle to deal with Tian and Cai."

"What's there to be afraid of? You had the backbone to see that they were reprimanded, so why should I be afraid to face them now? I'm not easily intimidated! I'll deal with them as a company representative, and I'll be as forceful as I have to be."

"Marvelous! Our Water Girl's a new and improved woman."

"After Fuyun died, how could a widow like me make it in this world if I continued a shrinking violet?"

She glanced at Golden Dog, whose head was bowed and whose expression had darkened. She laughed and asked, "What would you like me to take home for you? You never go back there anymore. The last time I was in Crossroads Township, I saw your father and he complained that you'd forgotten him."

"That's why I don't go back. Now that he's getting on in years, all he ever does is jabber."

"Uncle Golden Dog," she said somberly, "I know what's on his mind. All he can think about is getting you married. Now I'm going to say something, and I hope it doesn't make you mad. How long do you plan to put it off? I know it's something that bothers you, but you can't go on like this. Maybe if you found the right girl, the past wouldn't be so hard to forget."

He looked at her without saying a word. Her eyes were fixed on him. Finally she lowered her head and went over to pour him some more water. He noticed how enormous she had become and how awkward her movements were, and he found himself thinking of Fuyun. A heaviness weighed on his spirit.

She brought the water and sat down across from him. Neither of them spoke under the bright overhead light.

Golden Dog was the first to break the silence, smiling shyly and saying, "Water Girl, are you doing okay here?"

"Everything's fine."

"Be sure you take care of yourself, and don't do anything strenuous. Let me know if there's any way I can help you."

She sat there looking at him, and before long a couple of tears slid down her cheeks.

Water Girl went to Stream of Wandering Spirits, where she made arrangements with Cai Da'an to have the pine seedlings shipped, then spent a few days at home. Han Wenju began wearing his lined jacket and lined pants, and Water Girl knitted him a sweater. In years past, she'd sit on the kang knitting several sweaters—one for Uncle Han and one for Fuyun, then one for Dakong. But now, once Uncle Han's sweater was finished, there was nothing more to do, and she couldn't help thinking about Fuyun, her ugly, shy, and totally lovable husband, who would never again put on a sweater she had knitted! She opened the cupboard and rummaged through the winter clothes he'd worn the year before, picking them up and holding them to her breast as she wept the sorrow of memories. When her tears dried, she went to a little shop, where she bought some hempen paper that she folded into the shape of a jacket and stuffed with cotton. That she took up the mountain to his grave site in order to tell him the news of Tian Youshan and Tian Zhongzheng's reprimands and to burn the paper jacket for him.

The grass on the slope had already turned yellow, and the standing wheat stalks had begun to wither and were making a metallic sound as they swayed in the wind. She knelt down at the head of the grave and burned the spirit money she'd brought with her, then did the same with the paper jacket. She gazed down at the surface of the water below. A line of boats and rafts belonging to the Crossroads Township River Shipping Brigade was sailing down the Zhou River to Purple Thistle Pass to pick up their load of pine seedlings. A crowd of people had gathered at the landing to see them off, and the sight reminded her of the past, when Fuyun was alive. Back then she'd always made dumplings for him before he set out; since they were eaten in a single bite, he wouldn't have to worry about trouble at home during his trip. Then, when he returned, she'd make him a meal of noodles, for which she was famous throughout Stream of Wandering Spirits; they were paper-thin, like threads of fine hemp.

"Long noodles keep your soul stretched. Are you afraid that I left my heart with those painted women in White Rock Stockade?" he never failed to say when he ate her noodles.

To that she'd reply, "The way you talk, you're quite a catch. I'd like to know who besides me could fall for you!"

Back and forth they'd go, sometimes keeping at it till dawn broke. Now she didn't have to worry, but the tingle of worrying was gone, too. She snapped her head back and stared full of hate at the dark, forbidding Shaman Mountain. That was where Fuyun met his death through the grapple of the bear. Such a horrible death! And all to entertain some people at a banquet. For *that* he lost his life! She despised that bear, and she despised the officials who had dined on its paws. Because of their part in the tragedy, Tian Youshan and Tian Zhongzheng had been reprimanded, but Fuyun wasn't around to savor the news or receive his friends' toasts. With such thoughts on her mind, she prostrated herself in front of the grave and wept convulsively.

The sound of her weeping startled Old Seven. Too old to sail with the younger men, he'd come up onto the mountain to make his living by cutting dragon-beard grass on the slopes. He would plait the grass like girls' braids, bundle it up ten braids at a time, a hundred at a time, hundreds at a time, then tie it all with a leather thong and send it rolling down the slope. He'd follow it down, throw it over his back, and take it into town to sell. When he spotted Water Girl on the slope grieving, tears came to his eys as well. Let her cry, he thought, it'll do her good. But after he'd tossed down two more bundles of dragon-beard grass, she was in the same position and her weeping hadn't let up. That worried him. He ran down the mountain and went to the ferry landing, where he said to Han Wenju, "Wenju, get up there, and bring Water Girl down. She's been at it too long. Don't forget she's pregnant!" Han scaled the slope and, after plenty of coaxing, persuaded her to leave the grave.

By the time Water Girl got home, her stomach had begun to bother her, partly because of her sorrow and partly because of the cold air she'd breathed. By her calculations, the baby wasn't due yet, so she wasn't worried. She made some hot soup, drank it down, and went to bed. But her stomach was still bothering her the next day, the pain coming in waves. "Water Girl," Han Wenju declared to her, "I won't rest easy if you go back to White Rock Stockade in your condition. Stay with me a few more days. Since your stomach hurts, we can't afford to take chances. I'll take you to the hospital across the river for a checkup."

She looked up at her aging uncle and decided to let him take her to the hospital in Crossroads Township. Approaching the hospital entrance, Water Girl saw someone in the distance who looked like Yingying, but she slowed to avoid meeting up with her. Yingying, whose belly was even more distended than hers, spotted her, however, and called shrilly, "Is that you, Water Girl? Are you here to see a doctor, too? Imagine! Both of us pregnant at the same time! Is the baby's position giving you problems too?"

Surprised at Yingying's openness, Water Girl was displeased by her own pettiness. "How long has it been since I last saw you?" she smiled. "You look so good. When are you due?"

"Late last month, but still no sign of labor. No way to tell if it's going to be a dragon boy or a phoenix girl! I hear you're working for Lei Dakong now. He's really gone off the deep end, from what I hear. They say he's bought himself four or five women! It made me wonder why you went there. How does he treat you?"

Water Girl wasn't sure how much of an insinuation Yingying meant by that, but she tried to squelch any gossip, on Dakong's behalf, telling Yingying how difficult things had been for her since Fuyun's death and how she'd decided to work for Dakong temporarily, at Uncle Golden Dog's suggestion.

Yingying smirked.

Water Girl assumed that Yingying would feel bitter toward Golden Dog because of his hand in causing Tian Zhongzheng to be reprimanded. It came as a shock when she said, "That Golden Dog's on the ball."

"What do you mean by that?"

"What I mean is, he's someone to reckon with. He finally managed to get my uncle into the soup. I thought all along that Uncle was no match for him—and I was right. It's no skin off my nose if Uncle's in trouble, since the way I see it, you can't trust anybody these days—especially if you're a woman. Have you noticed how all this becomes clear after you're married? I have to laugh when I recall what I was like when I was living at home. Is Golden Dog the same as always? Still not married?" She paused. "Water Girl, have you been spending any time looking at flowers during your pregnancy? Or at pictures of movie stars? They say that if you do, you're sure to have a beautiful child!"

A military man walked up with a basket of eggs. Yingying waved to him. "Hey, over here. Let me introduce you to Water Girl Han. Not bad, hmm? It's too bad life's treated her so roughly. First Golden Dog left her high and dry; then she married our village simpleton, Fuyun, and he up and died on her but not before placing his heir in her belly! This is my husband, Water Girl. He came home on leave to be with me. You be sure to eat the right food before the baby comes, like plenty of chicken broth, and you're sure to have a smart child."

Water Girl was surprised to see the change in Yingying since her marriage, although she wasn't sure if the changes were for the better or for the worse. She could hardly believe it was the girl she had known.

The encounter was still on her mind as she and Han started home from the hospital. "Uncle, can people's personalities change?"

"Maybe, maybe not," he said. "One saying goes, The heart is flesh and blood, like everything else. If so, then maybe you can change. But there's another saying that goes, It's easier to change the course of rivers and the lay of mountains than alter a man's nature. That suggests that you can't change."

"What about me, Uncle? Have I changed?"

Han's eyes widened. "Why ask me that, child?"

She had to agree that it was a pretty silly question. "It's nothing, Uncle. Let's go home." She began pulling the ferryboat across to the opposite shore.

28

Hen Wenju was still brooding about Water Girl's question that night. Since she wouldn't explain herself, that was all he could do. He sent word to her from the landing that he was going over to drink with Old Seven and wouldn't be home for dinner. She thought about what to cook, since she'd be eating alone. Not wanting the bother of lighting the stove, she ate a cold bun and went to bed early.

In the middle of the night she woke up with sharp abdominal pains unlike any she'd ever felt before—waves of pain. Then the back pains began, so she sat up and put a pillow under the small of her back. That was when she noticed the show of blood. She recognized that as a bad sign—that the baby was coming early. She was by herself, and the neighbors were too far away to help. So she threw back the covers and searched for her scissors in the sewing box. They weren't there. When the next contraction came, she fell back onto the straw mat. There were more contractions, worse than before. She thought she was going to die. Every muscle was as tight as a drum, her throat felt as though someone were choking her, she could hardly breathe. She fought with all the strength she had, but she was losing the battle. She pulled at her hair and didn't feel a thing; her face clouded, she was covered with sweat. She thought she saw Fuyun standing in front of her. Suddenly there was a loud burst and a gush of water, followed by placenta fluids and thick blood. A fleshy little life appeared in a hollow of the mat. Ignoring her pain, she moved so she could reach the sickle hanging on the wall that Fuyun had made to gather kindling on the mountain. Pressing her lips tightly, she cut the umbilical cord with the sickle. Then as she wrapped the baby in an old shirt, she saw a tiny little thing standing up between its thin, delicate legs, and she cried out, "Fuyun, you have a son!" She lay back exhausted, her face covered with sweat, tears, and a smile.

The yellow dog, which had witnessed the frightful birthing scene from start to finish, was running around in circles beside the kang. As Water Girl lay there, afraid to move, it began barking and pawing at the edge of the kang and running over to paw at the tightly shut door. "Dog," Water Girl said, "don't be afraid, Dog. You have a new master!" But the dog kept up its barking. "Are you worried because we're alone? Do you want to go bring Uncle back?" The dog stopped barking and ran over to the door again. Understanding what it wanted, she climbed out of bed and opened the door with her bloodstained hand, then wrapped her arms around the dog and said, "Uncle's over at Old Seven's house. Do you understand? Old Seven!" The dog ran outside like a shot. With her ebbing strength, Water Girl scooped a dustpanful of ashes out of the fire opening in the kang and spread it over the blood on the straw mat. Then she covered it with some old clothes, lay down, and fell into a restful sleep.

Han Wenju and Old Seven had just finished their first bottle of wine, and Han, who was feeling tipsy and a bit unsteady on his feet, was chiding Old Seven for not opening another. He then began execrating the officials responsible for Fuyun's death, and finally he slapped his own face for listening to his teacher in school, who had encouraged him to study hard and thereby ruined his chances of joining up with the guerrillas. Seeing Han drunk, Old Seven thought it best not to break out another bottle; instead he filled the jug with cool water and handed it to him. But drunk though he was, Han wasn't satisfied, and he dashed the jug to the floor. Just as things were beginning to heat up, the dog burst in through the door, barking like crazy. It sobered Han immediately. "Dog!" he shouted. "What are you doing here? Is something wrong at home?" The dog barked a couple of times more, then turned and scooted out the door. "Something's wrong at home, I just know it! Dog came looking for me!" He followed it out the door, trailed by the anxious Old Seven.

As he walked in the door, Han saw that the kang was covered with blood and Water Girl was lying at the head. He railed at himself, "Me and my damned precious wine! I've killed her! It should be me lying there dead!"

Old Seven stood next to the kang. "Wenju," he said, "are you out of your head? Water Girl's had her baby. You have a grandson!"

Han hung on to the kang, shedding tears of joy. He turned to Water Girl, who was just waking up. "Why didn't you tell me you were due? I should never have been out getting drunk!" At that, he clapped his hand over his mouth, pulled Old Seven into the other room, and exhorted, "Old Seven, run over and get Third Auntie Zhang to come take care of Water Girl. You and I have been drinking, and if Water Girl smells it on our breath, it'll dry up her milk!"

After Old Seven stumbled from the room, Han walked to the doorway, stuck his finger down his throat, and threw up everything in his stomach. Then he went inside, rinsed his mouth with vinegar, began kneading dough to make flatcakes, and put a pot of water on to poach eggs. Since Third Auntie Zhang had bound feet and Old Seven wasn't up to carrying her on his back, she was brought over by one of the young men in her family. As soon as she arrived, she straightened up the kang and cleaned the baby properly, wrapping him in a clean piece of cloth. "Water Girl," she said, "I don't understand you. Why didn't you tell me ahead of time? You uncle doesn't know about these things. But you're a brave little thing, the way you cut the cord with that sickle! Did it take very long?"

"He wasn't due yet, but he was so eager to come that it didn't take him long at all."

"You're lucky everything went so smoothly. My eldest son's wife had two babies, both breech births, and she was in labor all day and all night. The first thing that came out was a leg, and that scared us silly! Now lie back and take it easy. I'll stay with you for the next few days. What do you fancy to eat?"

Water Girl grabbed hold of the old woman and said, "Auntie, you're wonderful. I feel like my own mother's taking care of me. I was so scared. I don't know how I managed to get through it."

Uncle Han had dished out the poached eggs and flatcakes steeped in water, and as he watched Water Girl eat, he turned to his friend and said, "Everything's all right, Old Seven. The Han family now has somebody to carry on the line. You've been up half the night because of us. Why don't you go home and get some sleep?" Before seeing his friend to the door, he took a bottle of wine from the pantry and said, "Take this home with you. Count it as a bottle of celebration wine. Since we can't drink around here, drink it at home."

Third Auntie grinned and said, "Wenju, you're not to touch a drop during the lying-in month. The first thing tomorrow morning I want you to hang a bundle of threads over the door to keep people from coming in and scaring the baby. If that happens, he'll do nothing but cry for the whole month!"

Han gave his word and made a bowl of steeped flatcakes for Third Auntie.

He went out the next morning and bought two strings of firecrackers, setting one off by the front door and the other at the head of Fuyun's grave. When villagers came and crowded around the door, Third Auntie shooed the men away but let the women in to look at the baby, which was the spitting image of Fuyun, though everyone was too tactful to say so. Instead they remarked, "He looks just like Water Girl. When he grows up he'll probably be better looking than his mother!"

Water Girl called her uncle to her bedside. "Uncle, I want you to go into town and phone Dakong that I have to take some time off. Then call Golden Dog and ask him to come out here if he can get free."

Han made the calls. The first thought that crossed the mind of either Dakong or Golden Dog was to pass the good news on to the other. They came upon each other on the street and went to celebrate at a bar, where they ordered sliced chicken and two jugs of wine, drinking themselves nearly into a stupor. But before they reduced themselves to a sorry condition, they had agreed to buy a pile of gifts and go together to Stream of Wandering Spirits in time for the Day Ten celebration. So eight days after the baby was born, Lei Dakong and Golden Dog drove around town in Dakong's car buying all sorts of things, starting with baby wraps, booties and caps, and blankets. Then they bought food: ten boxes of milk powder, five bottles of orange nectar, ten catties of granulated sugar, and ten of brown sugar. After that, they bought an assortment of things for mother and son: clothes for Water Girl, baby bottles and nipples, a silk bandana for Water Girl, and some baby talc. Then they were off in the car to Crossroads Township with their diverse, colorful purchases, which filled several bags.

When the car drove into the township government compound, Tian Zhongzheng nearly fell over himself rushing out to welcome his visitors. He froze in his tracks when he saw Golden Dog and Lei Dakong getting out of the car.

"How are you, Chief Tian?" Dakong greeted him.

"Fine, just fine," the puzzled Tian Zhongzheng replied. "What are you two doing back here? I hope you'll accept some tea."

"No, thanks," Dakong said. "We're on our way to the village. Nothing will happen to the car if we leave it here, will it?"

"Of course not."

Dakong and Golden Dog hefted their bags and set out for Stream of Wandering Spirits.

News of their arrival preceded them to the ferry landing, where Han Wenju was ready with his boat. "Ah!" he greeted them. "Stream of Wandering Spirits is the birthplace of officials! When they belong to the Tian and Gong clans, they come by Jeep, but you drive up in a plush sedan. Hail the return of the conquering heroes!"

After they'd boarded the boat, their omission occurred to Dakong. "How could we have forgotten to buy a congratulatory gift for Uncle Han?"

"With all you've brought for the baby and Water Girl, there wasn't any need to get something for me."

"You're the proud grandpa!" Dakong said.

Han Wenju liked the sound of that. "In the long run, people need to go out into the world to make something of themselves," he said. "At home you were useless, Dakong, but now you've made it big and you speak sensibly."

"When your money belt's full, your words take on weight," Golden Dog smiled, making Dakong squirm.

Golden Dog, Dakong, Water Girl, and Uncle Han spent a good part of the day seated on the kang trying to come up with a name for Fuyun's baby. Uncle Han suggested several inelegant names for which the gods would take pity on the child and keep him from harm: Pig Child, Ugly Egg, Little Padlock, and Lumpy. Dakong favored a citified name, with a single character or with three characters, four including the surname. He said that the fad in town was to use Westernized names, combining both parents' surnames, then adding two more characters. Since Fuyun's surname was Guan and Water Girl's was Han, he recommended something like Guan-Han Dashan (Great Mountain) or Guan-Han Kangtiangong (Resist Field Consolidation), the latter a punning slap at the Tian and Gong clans. Water Girl asked Golden Dog for his opinion.

"These suggestions don't appeal to me," he said. "The way I see it, we ought to choose a nickname like Ugly Egg for the villagers' use, so that the more times they employ the word *ugly*, the better looking he'll seem. As for his real name, the one he'll use in school, nothing particular occurs to me. Let's get a dictionary and open it twice at random, choosing the first characters on those pages, and that will be his name."

"Golden Dog," he heard, "you're a born scholar. Your idea of appealing to a book proves it. When the child's big enough, we'll have to let you take him into town to start school."

So they took out a dictionary and flipped it open twice; as though an invisible hand had been guiding them, the first words on the two pages were *hong,* "swan goose," and *peng,* "roc," the names of birds known for flying long distances. It was an auspicious sign. When Fuyun married Water Girl he came into the Han family as a son, so his child would take the name Han. Word went through the village that the new baby's name was Han Hongpeng. With the baby named, the adults talked about how they'd celebrate Day Ten.

"I know exactly what you're feeling," Water Girl said, "and I also know that if there's life on the other side, Fuyun's with you right now and content with his fate. But, after all, he is dead—which means there's no one to take care of things here at home. Since, besides, you're very busy, I think we should forget about the Day Ten party. I can't believe that everything will be fine for Hongpeng just because we celebrate Day Ten or that everything will be unlucky if we don't."

"But that's why it's so important to make a big deal of Day Ten," Golden Dog said. "*It's because* Fuyun can't be with us. It's our chance to give the baby a decent start. You don't have to worry about things here at home. Uncle Han, all you have to do is greet the guests when they arrive. Dakong and I will make sure there's plenty of everything we need. You can invite all your friends and relatives, and as many neighbors as will come."

Seeing that Golden Dog and Dakong were determined to carry out the traditional observance, Han couldn't very well stand in the way. As soon as the duties had been assigned, they split up and got to work.

Many guests showed up for the party. Although Water Girl had few relatives, her schoolmates, Golden Dog's schoolmates and fellow soldiers, and Dakong's friends drifted in. They all brought gifts: baskets of dough fish painted in bright colors, a length of fabric, a pannier filled with wheat, a suit of baby clothes. On arriving, they set off firecrackers at the front door and greeted Han Wenju with hands cupped respectfully in front of their chests. After tendering the obligatory auspicious remarks, they crowded around the kang to take a look at Han Hongpeng. By that time, Water Girl was able to get down off it, and she stood dressed in the attire Golden Dog and Dakong had bought her, her hair done up with the silk bandana. Even though her face was still puffy, her fair skin had a rich luster, and as she looked at the growing pile of dough fish, steamed buns, fabric, and baby clothes on the cabinet, she was moved beyond words. Ten tables had been set for the banquet near a tent that had been thrown up for the three cooks who had been hired; smoke was already belching from the stoves. The cold appetizers were on the tables, and the seating was by age and generation. Han Wenju went from table to table toasting his guests, draining his cup after clinking it with theirs, and by the time he'd made the rounds, he'd finished off at least fifty cupfuls. He was in high spirits that had him talking nonstop, regaling his listeners with tales from China's legendary rulers, statistics on the course of the Zhou River and the peaks of Shaman Mountain, critiques of the current policies of the government, and narrations of the modern history of Stream of Wandering Spirits. Each time he opened his mouth, somebody teased him, and raucous laughter invariably followed. That slowed everyone's consumption of wine, so Han spoke out: "Why talk when there's wine to drink? You don't know how happy I am to see you all here today. The Hans are a humble family, and I've spent some time in school. Unfortunately, that kept me from joining the guerrillas, and that's why I've spent my life running a ferryboat. It may be a profession to look down on, but as the ancients said, even kings and noblemen are at the mercy of bridges and ferrymen. I'm past seventy, older than just about anybody here. When I look around, I can see that half of you women came here as brides on my boat, and you've all ridden it hundreds, maybe thousands, of times. Stream of Wandering Spirits is the birthplace of officials, and they all belong to the Tian or Gong clans, the big families, with money *and* power. But today you honor the Han family by coming to my house, letting me stand tall, and I've never been as happy as I am at this moment! Drink up, everybody. You can pass up everything else, but the wine's here to be drunk!"

Feeling that Uncle Han was rambling, Golden Dog came and whispered in his ear, "Uncle, you've had a lot to drink. I think it's time to serve the hot dishes, don't you?"

Uncle Han wrapped up his remarks. "All right," he said, "serve the hot dishes!" He slapped himself on the forehead and disappeared into the bedroom.

"Uncle," Water Girl said, "you sure had a lot to say out there. People were starting to smile at how you went on."

"I admit I've had a bit too much to drink, but I'm so happy. I didn't say anything out of place, did I?"

"You may be drunk, but everything you said was appropriate."

"I don't stack up to other people in most respects, but there isn't anyone who can outtalk me. Take Tian Zhongzheng, who fancies himself a party secretary. Well, now he's just the township head and nobody's fooled into thinking that what comes out of his mouth is anything but shit!" With that he leaned against the cupboard and fell asleep.

Outside, Golden Dog and Dakong were scurrying back and forth to put food on the tables.

"Golden Dog," someone said, "we've had enough wine. How many courses are we going to get? Will there be meat in any of them?"

"Twelve courses," Golden Dog answered. "You can dig in in just a minute. Two of the courses are braised meat, and when you've had your fill of them, you won't feel like eating again for days!"

They laughed. "You two haven't done badly this time. Golden Dog, when will we be attending your wedding banquet?"

Golden Dog was ruffled and didn't know what to say. Just then Water Girl came out with the baby in her arms. "Uncle Golden Dog," she pressed him, "why don't we plan on a spring wedding for you? You can send a truck over from White Rock Stockade and take us all out to one of the city's fancy restaurants!"

"Aha!" another guest bantered. "Has our Golden Dog finally found the right girl? Is she a city girl? Does that mean you'll start ignoring us country folk?"

Dakong chimed in, "She's a real beauty. Sitting still or walking, she's the quintessence of grace!"

"As pretty as Tian Yingying?" someone asked.

"This girl's a flower, not a chunk of smelly bean curd like Yingying!" Dakong rejoined.

Water Girl suddenly remembered something. She tugged at Golden Dog, and he followed her into the bedroom.

"Damn it," she said. "Damn it! How could I forget?"

"What is it?" Golden Dog asked, concerned. "What's upset you so?"

"Is today the thirteenth?"

"That's right."

"It's your birthday. I said I was going to throw a party for your threshold-year birthday, but the baby came along and made me forget my plans."

Golden Dog laughed. "Isn't a birthday party a chance to have a little fun and to celebrate an auspicious occasion? Could you want more fun than we're having today? And what more auspicious occasion than Day Ten for little Hongpeng? It's better than celebrating my birthday!"

Water Girl reflected for a moment and realized that she didn't want to disagree. Still she regretted not being able to give him the stomacher she'd embroidered. She reached up and took down a piece of red silk one of the guests had brought for Hongpeng, tore off a strip, and bid him tie it around his waist. When he balked, she, affecting a pout, walked over and bolted the door. Knowing it would be impossible to resist, he tied the silk strip around his waist.

When the meal was over, the guests sat around and talked until, upon someone's comment, "It's getting late," they began to drift off. Han Wenju had sobered up by then and was awake, so he went to the landing and ferried his guests. Golden Dog and Dakong stayed behind to clean up and to urge the cooks to dig into the leftovers. They themselves brought their bowls out and joined the cooks at the table. They'd just begun eating when someone called from the ferry landing, "Manager Lei!" Dakong walked to the door to look. Seeing someone from the company, he set down his bowl and went to hear what was up. Water Girl and Golden Dog were filled with conjectures, but when Dakong returned, he at first said only that the company had sent someone to take him back as soon as possible.

"What could be so urgent that they'd send someone to get you?"

"A company in Zhou City is demanding its money back. We had a deal to buy some color TV sets for them, but it fell through, and now they've canceled their order and are bellyaching for the return of their deposit."

"That sounds serious," Water Girl worried aloud. "Something like that could damage the company's reputation."

"Not to worry," Dakong reassured her. "Pass me that wine, Golden Dog. I need a drink. Nothing's important enough to go hungry or thirsty over." He gobbled a bowlful of rice and swigged half a jug of wine, then said, "Golden Dog, why don't you stay a few days more? I'll go back alone. And, Water Girl, you take care of yourself. We'll talk about getting you back to work after the lying-in month is over. When I get into town, I'll line up a nanny. That way you won't have so much to do when you come back." On his way out the door, he said to Golden Dog, "I'll send the car for you in a couple of days, all right?"

"No need for that. I'll hop a boat."

Dakong dashed away, saying something to a young woman along the road, who bent over, picked up a clod of dirt, and threw it at him as he moved on.

"Dakong's always hurrying somewhere or other, but he's good-hearted," Water Girl said.

"He's a good man," Golden Dog agreed. "Of course he is . . ." He didn't go on. No one understood Dakong better than Golden Dog did. He knew him like the back of his own hand and was sure of what was going to happen to him eventually. But the way society was, Dakong couldn't take all Golden Dog's advice, and there was nothing the reporter could say or do to fix that. As he watched Dakong's headlong passage down the road, he lit a cigarette and puffed it steadily, exhaling the smoke through his mouth and nose.

Water Girl, who didn't know what Golden Dog was thinking, piped up, "I've been so busy I forgot to ask him if the pine seedlings ever got there."

"That's all been taken care of," Golden Dog said. "The people from Shanxi sent six trucks, and they loaded up and were on their way home the first day we came here. Dakong told me the company made a profit of seventy-six thousand yuan on that one deal."

"That's good," Water Girl said. "But there's something I've been meaning to tell you, Uncle Golden Dog. Since beginning to work for Dakong, I've learned some things about their business practices. They seem to pull their profits out of the air. The man who came to get Dakong because the company in Zhou City wanted its deposit back—well, this isn't the first time something like that has happened. The transaction concerning the seedlings involves real commodities, and it helps the national afforestation plan. But that kind of deal, with goods actually transferred, is the exception rather than the rule. You must try to straighten Dakong out. He needs someone to watch more carefully what he's up to."

They sat talking until Han came back from the ferry landing. Golden Dog returned to his father's place, on Restless Hill.

When he decided to return to White Rock Stockade a couple of days later, Golden Dog came to say good-bye to Water Girl. She was alone, and after he had talked with her for a few minutes, his face flushed and he began, "Water Girl!"

She had been sitting across from him cradling Hongpeng in her arms and breast-feeding while she listened, but when she heard her name spoken so emphatically and with such urgency, she looked up. By then, however, he was flummoxed by his own tone, and he didn't continue. He leaned over and picked an ant from the floor, but he didn't kill it. "I'm going back to the bureau station."

"What's your hurry? You don't have any deadlines, so why not stick around until tomorrow?"

He looked at her and even opened his mouth several times to speak, but no words came out.

"Uncle Golden Dog, is there something you'd like to say?"

"No," he replied hastily. "I just dropped by to tell you I have to return to White Rock Stockade." He stood up and was about to go, but Han strolled in the door, humming a flower-drum song.

"Uncle," Water Girl greeted him, "Golden Dog says he's returning to White Rock Stockade."

"What's your hurry, Golden Dog?" Han remonstrated. "I haven't begun to pay you back for all you did for Hongpeng's Day Ten celebration. You're not going to leave just like that, are you? I won't let you go. I came back from the landing because I thought you'd gone to your father's. Old Seven has taken over for me on the boat, and I was planning to come and treat you to some wine. Let's get in some serious drinking today. The wine's ready, and so is the food. If we drink in the kitchen, Water Girl and Hongpeng won't be affected by the smell."

Knowing when he was beaten, Golden Dog deferred his plans to return to White Rock Stockade. While they were drinking in the kitchen, Han kept up such a stream of chatter that Golden Dog could barely squeeze a word in edgewise. Only half-listening, he drowned his sorrows in the wine, until his eyes began to glaze over and the skin on his face grew taut. He smiled from time to time, but his smiles came and went with little correspondence to Han's humor. Finally Golden Dog got shakily to his feet, insisting that he'd had enough and was going home. "What the hell's wrong with you today?" Han asked him. "Of course you've had enough—drinking as if everything was hopeless. Water Girl, you're not to let Golden Dog leave. If the old painter saw him like this, I'd never hear the end of it. Help him over to my kang so he can get some sleep."

"I don't want any sleep. Just let me sit for a while. If I sleep in there, Hongpeng will smell the alcohol on my breath."

Han brought a reclining chair from the other room and helped Golden Dog into it. Water Girl came in with a comforter, which she threw over him, and in no time he was asleep.

"You shouldn't have got him drunk like that," Water Girl scolded her uncle. "It's hard on his health."

"We didn't drink that much today," Han assured her. "Don't worry, he'll be fine after he gets some sleep. I'm going back to the ferry landing. Be careful he doesn't fall out of the chair. After he wakes up, boil him some hot water to drink."

As soon as Uncle Han left, Water Girl put Hongpeng to bed, then went to the kitchen to boil some water. Golden Dog was still sleeping when the water was ready, so she wet a towel and put it on his forehead. He's not himself today, she thought. *He can't spit out what he's trying to say, then he pours down the wine like a man with no future and winds up roaring drunk. He definitely has something on his mind.*

Golden Dog's eyes snapped open when she took the towel off to soak it in water again. She laid it back on his forehead. He tried to sit up.

"Uncle Golden Dog," Water Girl said to him, "I'm glad you're awake. You passed out!"

"I wasn't drunk," he proclaimed, turning his head as though about to throw up.

"Not drunk, you say! If you have to throw up, go ahead. It'll make you feel better."

He made a couple of retching sounds, but nothing followed, and he lay there staring blankly at Water Girl.

"You have something on your mind today. I know you have."

"No, I haven't."

"Don't think you can fool me. Why won't you tell me what it is?"

He stared hard at her. "All right, Water Girl, I'll tell you what it is. Sit here by me and I'll tell you."

As she moved closer to him, he took her hand and said, "Water Girl, I want to marry you!" He breathed a sigh of relief at having told her and looked straight into her eyes.

She had no presentiment that that was what she was going to hear, and she was stopped cold. When he gripped her hand more tightly, she let out a screech and jerked her hand back. "Uncle Golden Dog," she said in confusion, "you're drunk. You're drunk!"

He stood up, but his legs collapsed and he sat on the floor. "I'm not drunk," he said. "I'm not. I want to marry you; I honestly want to marry you. I'm not drunk, and I couldn't get drunk no matter how much I drank."

Water Girl began to tremble. "Uncle Golden Dog, how can you play with my feelings so cruelly? Are you trying to break my heart? I don't want to hear your drunken nonsense. I won't listen!" She fled from the kitchen into the courtyard, crying, "God help me! God help me!" She tripped and fell but scrambled to her feet and stumbled into her room, slamming the door behind her.

Golden Dog was heaving up everything, but even after he'd emptied his stomach, he felt nauseated. Soon all that came were bile and saliva, and he felt as though he might not stop until he brought up his guts in pieces. Vomiting had cleared his head a bit, but it also brought a sense of depression. He stared listlessly toward Water Girl's closed door, the handle of which was still swinging slightly, and he was overwhelmed by regret, shame, and helplessness. What magic power did wine have to let him say what he'd never have had the audacity to say sober? He loved Water Girl, he respected her, and he'd known for some time that he wanted to be with her. But he'd been afraid that she'd misinterpret his proposal as charity or pity, which would lower her self-esteem. She was no longer the Water Girl he'd once known. But under the influence of the wine, he'd made a mess of things, made his feelings seem base, made himself seem coarse and rash. She had every right to upbraid him bitterly and drive him away. He'd never be able to explain himself now.

He walked out of the kitchen, leaning against the wall to steady himself. Her door was still closed, and Hongpeng was inside crying. "Water Girl," he pleaded through the door, "I shouldn't have said that. I know I hurt you. Go ahead, hate me, revile me! How could I have turned into something like this?"

The yellow dog, which was crouching in the yard and at a loss about what had happened, began to bark as it followed Golden Dog's movements with its eyes. Golden Dog was shaking his head. "I'm not worthy of her, I'm not. I'm being punished by heaven." He walked off with a look of uncleansable shame on his face.

All this time Water Girl had been watching him through a crack in the door, and when she saw him lurch into the yard and disappear from view, she opened the door. "Golden Dog!" But even she didn't hear a sound coming from her throat. Her body turning limp, she crumpled to the floor in the doorway. She couldn't stop crying.

Golden Dog returned three times over the following month, bringing food and clothes for Water Girl and the baby, but he never breathed another word about his marriage proposal. She greeted him warmly each time he came, and when he left she cried. As soon as the lying-in month was over, Dakong fetched her and the baby. He had already hired a nanny for Hongpeng. Water Girl went back to work, and Han Wenju, who had been worried about his niece, made a trip to town to set his mind at ease. When he saw how healthy and well fed mother and son were, he saluted the goodness of Dakong and returned content to Stream of Wandering Spirits. Days turned into weeks, and it was New Year's, time for the spring festival. Dakong invited Water Girl to stay in town for the holiday and sent for Uncle Han to celebrate New Year's with them. Golden Dog went to be with his father on the first and second days of the month, then returned to the company office on the third, where the five of them, old and young, drank together in Water Girl's dormitory room.

Han, who once again drank too much, said, "I guess life is what you make of it. This place used to be the blacksmith shop, where the old man earned maybe one or two yuan a day. Now look at it: it's the home of a big business, with a river of silver flowing in. You can say Water Girl's had a life of hardship, but you can also say she's had a few breaks. Thanks to you two, if I died today I'd do so with no qualms about her well-being. Hongpeng will make it up to you when he grows up."

Mention of the building was painful to Golden Dog and Water Girl, for it stirred thoughts of the earlier days. Although they said nothing, Dakong guessed what was on their minds and said, "Back when the old blacksmith was still alive, I took plenty of meals in this place and drank my share of wine. This company wouldn't exist if it hadn't been for him. Since we're all here together, we should raise our glasses in a toast to his spirit!" The four adults fell to their knees, Water Girl holding the baby in her arms as she emptied her glass of wine slowly onto the floor.

29

After the fifth of the month, Dakong turned the daily operation of the company over to the assistant manager so that he could take a business trip to Guangdong. He was gone for over a month, although during that time he came back once for a few days and made a side trip to Zhou City. In March, Golden Dog was busy gathering material for a series on the Zhou River. He traveled from township to township preparing to launch a column called "Zhou River News." His plan had the unstinting support of his friends in the Young Reporters Study Association, and that gave him some confidence that it was worth the effort to try to air for the benefit of his readers many issues he'd been thinking about for a long time.

With Water Girl's two closest friends away from White Rock Stockade, she stayed inside and did her work, then went to the home of the nanny to play with Hongpeng. With the coming of spring, her health suddenly deteriorated. She suffered frequent headaches, for which she received injections from the traditional doctor in the district near the eastern gate. But they didn't help much, and he told her that the headaches were a consequence of the chills she had suffered during her lying-in. He told her to rest.

On the fifth day of the fourth month, something horrible happened near the landing at the southern gate, news of which hit her hard. There, where nondescript buildings lined the bank of the river, a young widow who lived in one of the huts drowned herself by jumping into the water from a window after weighting her body down with seven bricks. Since the landing was particularly quiet that night, with no boats passing, her death leap had gone unnoticed. The next morning, a woman washing vegetables in the river spotted something floating in the river, and when she tried to fish it out with a bamboo pole, she discovered it was a head of woman's hair. She moved it again, and a body floated to the surface, face up and bloated, like something in which yeast had been working. The horrified woman stumbled and fell. She was hysterical by the time she scrambled to her feet. The police came and dragged the body from the river and identified it.

The widow's death set tongues wagging in White Rock Stockade. Eventually it became known that she'd long been in love with a boatman from Crossroads Township who had drowned a few days earlier when his boat capsized at Sun-Moon Shoals on the way to Xiangyang. At the news of her lover's death the widow had wept for two days and two nights before taking her life.

Water Girl went over to see for herself and found that the woman was none other than White Fragrance, the mistress of Scarface, from Seven-Li Gulley. Confirmation of her worst fears saddened her enormously. It was rare for a woman living in such derelict surroundings to have White Fragrance's depth of feeling; it was too bad that her sensitivity wasn't matched by her fate. This thinking turned Water Girl's ruminations to her own situation, and before long, tears streamed down her face. She stole over to the river late that night and burned some spirit money for the poor widow.

Three days after the incident, a sickly woman living across from the company office ran a high fever, which resisted oral medication and injections. Eventually her eyes shut tight and she began to speak deliriously, alarming the people around her: She babbled in the voice of White Fragrance, talking about all those years she and Scarface had been together and how, even though everyone said she was loose, she'd never gone with anyone else but Scarface during that time . . . So-and-so had tried to get her for himself, so-and-so had tried to force himself on her, but she'd firmly driven them all away. They hated her for it and spread ugly stories and never paid back the money they had borrowed from her. She recited the names of people who owed her money, listing how much, and who had things that belonged to her. She requested that the money and everything else go to her mother. Then suddenly she changed her voice to that of an old man who was fussing that he hadn't had enough to drink but that King Yama had put him in charge of wine even though he wanted to work a forge, wanted his blacksmith shop . . .

When people heard her, they exclaimed, "Isn't that the pockfaced blacksmith?" They were enthralled. "She's become a medium! The souls of the widow and Pockface are drifting in hell!" Not everyone believed her, and the skeptics checked with the people who were cited as owing the widow money: every one of them admitted his debt and paid the woman's mother the full obligation that very night. The news spread through the town; it was the sensation of the moment. Meanwhile the medium kept babbling more and more frightful things. Because her husband was by now in a panic, he summoned a fortune-teller, who covered her head with a winnowing basket and lashed it with a branch torn from a peach tree, then used the same branch to pin down the middle fingers of her hands. That brought her around, and once again she spoke in her own voice, although she panted as if she'd dug up half the mountainside. She then fell into a swoon from which no one could awaken her. The fortune-teller instructed her husband to go to the widow's room, to nail a wedge to the wall, and to burn some spirit money. Later the same night he was to sneak to the compound behind the company offices and pin a magic tally to the chinaberry tree there, then spread chicken blood over the area and place in the crotch of the same tree a clay figurine representing the pockfaced blacksmith, with pins stuck all over its body.

Water Girl went into the rear courtyard early the following morning and saw the figurine. Enraged, she crossed the street to confront her neighbors. The husband, a big, burly fellow, responded that the soul of her grandfather was up to no good; he called her a shooting star, a floozy who'd caused Fuyun's death, before giving birth to his little bastard. She began pounding him with her fists. He kicked her in the stomach, and she crawled out of his house, rolling in the dirt. Seeing the violence, the assistant manager and some of the employees in the office ran over and grabbed the man, refusing to let him go and accusing him of spreading rumors and interfering with the operation of the White Rock Stockade City and Country United Trade Co. They dragged him off to the local precinct station.

Water Girl's stomach began to feel steadier around noontime, as she waited in the office to hear what had happened at the police station. But no one returned for several hours; finally several of the employees came in without the assistant manager. They paled when they saw her. "This is terrible, Water Girl, just terrible!"

"Calm down," she said, "and tell me what happened."

"The police have arrested the assistant manager! They said they were on their way to arrest him when he showed up at the station."

Flabbergasted, she grabbed one of the men's arms. "What's going on? Why would they arrest the assistant manager?"

They hadn't the slightest idea, but their faces were ashen, and a couple of them gathered up their bedding and hightailed it out of there; others took some products off the shelf and tucked them inside their shirts. Starting to panic, Water Girl blocked the door. "What do you think you're doing? Running off? Trying to make off with company property? Is this the way you people act when the boss is gone? Until this thing's cleared up, anyone who thinks he can make off with company property had better not plan on leaving through this door!"

The men, deeply ashamed, restored the stuff to the racks and left mutely. Once they were gone, she locked the showroom door and sat down to think. By noon scuttlebutt had reached her that Dakong was under arrest on criminal charges in Zhou City and that the White Rock Stockade City and Country United Trade Co. had been docketed as an antisocial enterprise. The jittery employees plagued Water Girl for reassurances. "It can't be true," she said to calm them down. "Somebody's spreading rumors—that's all. People are just envious of how well we're doing and are using smear tactics to ruin us." She went to phone the company office in Zhou City asking for Dakong. But before her call went through, the police charged in with a warrant to close down the White Rock Stockade City and Country United Trade Co., confiscate its business license, remove its books, and seal its safe, display racks, and warehouse. They dismantled the company sign over the front door and tossed it into the rear courtyard.

Water Girl watched all this happen in front of her as though her mind were a blank. The pain in her stomach returned. She leaned against the wall, at the very spot where it was covered by a silk banner awarded to the company. Her stomach muscles contracted, her legs grew weak, and she crumpled to the floor, dragging the banner down with her. It covered her like a small blanket.

The police were back the following day with their formal citation listing the grounds for putting the company out of business: the owners had falsified claims of reform activities and had damaged the socialist economy by engaging in corrupt business practices. The specific charge was selling useless pine seedlings to Xi'an, costing the buyers several million yuan and inflicting serious damage on the national afforestation plan.

It didn't take long for Water Girl to verify that the assistant manager had indeed been arrested, as had Dakong. Without even thinking about going to see her son first, she flew to Golden Dog, who was putting the finishing touches on the sixth installment in his "Zhou River News" series. He was aghast and just sat without moving for a long time. "Dakong's really fixed himself this time!" he finally said.

"What are we going to do?" she wanted to know. "The company was set up with the approval of the county committee, and Dakong received commendations from them and the government. How could they arrest him out of the blue? They say he was involved in illegal transactions, but county officials at all levels are implicated in his dealings. His notebook documents every bribe they took from him."

"Where's that notebook now?"

"He left it with me for safekeeping before he went to Zhou City."

"Regardless of who asks for it, don't give it away. It may come in handy. Don't be afraid. No matter how bad things get, you're not involved. Spend a little time with the baby over the next few days. I'll figure out what to do after I've snooped around."

His inquiries confirmed that Dakong was charged with selling a load of useless pine seedlings. During the negotiations, he'd slipped the buyer from Xi'an two thousand yuan, and after the seedlings had been delivered they'd been stored in a warehouse without being inspected. Later they were taken out and, except for a few acres of nursery land that were planted by hand, scattered by plane over thousands of mountain acres. The seedlings planted in the nursery failed to grow, and when they were dug up, the roots were covered with mildew. The people from Shanxi immediately went to the provincial capital to lodge a complaint, and the provincial party authorities were so incensed that they mounted an immediate investigation, vowing to bring those responsible to justice. Dakong had been arrested in Zhou City and returned to White Rock Stockade, where he was being interrogated.

Golden Dog could see that the days of high flying were over for Dakong. "He has no one to blame but himself," he said to Water Girl. "With the mess things are in now, you can't live on the company premises. It's best for you and the baby to go to the village for a while."

Five days after Golden Dog took Water Girl and Hongpeng to Stream of Wandering Spirits, it was his turn to be arrested. He was charged with accepting a bribe of twelve thousand yuan to give Lei Dakong the right kind of publicity—a clear contravention of the journalist's code of ethics. He was branded a blight on the journalistic profession.

Information about Golden Dog's arrest hit White Rock Stockade and the entire region like a bombshell. Water Girl was eating dinner when Golden Dog's father, apoplectic, reeled in with what he had just heard, and the two of them, with no idea what to do, just stood there and cried. Later that night, Han Wenju asked Old Seven to take them to White Rock Stockade in one of the boats tied up at the landing.

So this group of villagers arrived in White Rock Stockade, where they didn't have a friend in the world. During the day they ran from pillar to post trying to get the latest news; at night they returned to the boat. The situation was in constant flux. Finally they learned that Dakong had made a complete confession, obviating the need for further interrogations. He came clean with everything they wanted to know, his attitude and preparation showing that he'd expected this day to come sooner or later. His interrogators were astonished by the precision of his recollections. They were, at first, delighted, but their satisfaction soon became consternation, for his confession referred by name to twenty or so leading cadres, including Party Secretary Tian Youshan and the chief of police, as coconspirators. One of the interrogators banged the table and bellowed, "Lei Dakong, have you forgotten where you are? You're accountable for everything you say, so don't start going after people as indiscriminately as a mad dog!"

"You're right, of course," Dakong replied. "But since we're after the whole truth, I shouldn't leave you out, should I?" He proceeded to name the people to whom he'd given gifts in order to grease the wheels, and the exact dates of every bribe. When the interrogation record was handed to the chief of police, he scoffed. "This is where the class struggle turns to mischief. One kick by an accused criminal and the whole applecart is upset as he attempts to make laughingstocks of us Communist party members!" The chief of police shared the data in the interrogation transcript with Tian Youshan, then personally took over the questioning in order to get Dakong to extend his confessions. Dakong went on to reveal the relationship between his company and the son-in-law of Gong Baoshan in Zhou City. The plot thickened as the names of Commissioner Gong and the many members of his clan in Zhou City surfaced more and more frequently. When it was all over, the chief of police in White Rock Stockade and the party secretary went through the dossier, culling from the list the names of members of the Tian clan in White Rock Stockade who had taken bribes and sending only the remaining names off to their superiors. Almost immediately, people began talking about how Lei Dakong's tremendous successes had been possible only through the patronage of the Gong clan, nearly all of whom had taken bribes from him before conceding him advantages.

Golden Dog had been arrested because he was recorded in the company books as having taken a bribe of twelve thousand yuan. He defended himself by arguing that ten thousand of it had been a grant from Dakong and his company to the Young Reporters Study Association and the remaining two thousand had been a personal loan for which he had a receipt. But why had Dakong given the association a grant? Golden Dog replied that the journalists' association wasn't the only recipient of a grant from the entrepreneur—that there had been many others, including the school that had received seventy thousand, for which the county committee had given him a commendation and had mandated newspaper coverage. It was Golden Dog himself who had criticized Dakong in print, in a story that still languished at the newspaper office. All the members of the Young Reporters Study Association had read it and would confirm its existence. There was nothing the authorities could do but drop that particular charge, but they continued to maintain that what he called a two-thousand-yuan loan they had to consider a roundabout acceptance of a bribe. Since he had no documents to support him, it was only his word against theirs. They let him cool his heels in jail.

As reports of the official inquiries reached Water Girl, Han Wenju, and Golden Dog's elderly father, they grew more and more uneasy. Time and again they went to the police station and the courts, only to be rebuffed and ignored. On one visit to the police station, Water Girl was told, "Bring him some clothes. How come he's always sick? Why does he have such problems with his ribs?"

Near collapse with worry, she bought him clothes, some pastries, and a carton of cigarettes, which she handed over to the policeman. He took the clothes but threw the other items to the floor. "He's in jail," he barked, "not on a junket for his newspaper!"

When she returned to the boat, her face was bathed in tears. "As healthy as Uncle Golden Dog has always been, what can they have done to ruin his health so quickly? And the man said he's having trouble with his ribs. I know that means they've been beating him. Sooner or later they'll kill him!"

The old painter began to tremble, his lips quivering so that he couldn't speak. Tears flowed from his old eyes.

"Golden Dog offended too many people when he worked on Dakong's behalf that time," Han Wenju said. "He's rubbed lots of people the wrong way. Of course they're beating him now that he's in their hands."

"What are we going to do?" Water Girl asked. "We can't let them have a free rein with him!"

"Let's go see if Tian Zhongzheng will help," the painter said. "He's on good terms with the people at the county level. Maybe he'll intercede."

"Don't be silly," Water Girl answered. "Asking Tian Zhongzheng to help is like the chicken inviting the weasel in."

They fretted over their inability to devise a plan. Falling into silent depression, they sat there until the moon settled behind the uneven walls of the city tower.

"Get some sleep," Water Girl told the two men. "At your age you have to know your limitations. I'm going over to Uncle Fan's, near the eastern gate."

"This late at night?" the painter said. "What are you going to do there?"

"When Grandpa was alive," she said, "he often went to Uncle Fan's bar for a drink. I knew him pretty well, and he once told me that his cousin works as a guard at the prison. I'll see if he can help."

Han sighed and said, "Ai, what can a common staff worker do? But go ahead; we haven't come up with anything better."

The moon had fallen behind the wall by the time she stepped out of the cabin, and it was pitch black outside. Her clothes flapped against her in the wind; she felt a chill on her back. She shivered. As she crossed the plank at the bow of the boat, she saw the reflection of stars in the water that was flowing slowly by. She stepped onto the shore and looked up at the city gateway, which was unlit—dark and foreboding. Picking up a rock and holding it tight in her hand, she walked toward it, her eyes fixed straight ahead. As she drew near, she saw a sliver of light at the opening. There was a figure in white leaning up against the wall, who was being crowded by a dark figure, and both were moving slowly like bamboo stakes in the water . . . She stood transfixed for a second, but realizing what she was seeing, she cleared her throat to give notice of her presence. The figures separated, and vanished. Giggles emerged from the trees behind the gateway. As her thoughts were carried back to that night on the Zhou River shoal, she heaved the rock as hard as she could and heard it crash against the wall. Once inside the gate, she noticed the occasional street light ahead of her; in order to conserve electricity, only one out of every three or four was lit, glowing through a hazy blue mist like a layer of chimney smoke that blurred everything. Lights in the wooded areas lit up the bright green leaves and made them appear new and fresh; the lights themselves there seemed especially clean and bright. She walked on, feeling a constriction in her bosom. Hongpeng was still at the nanny's, and it was days since she'd last seen him. Her breasts had grown painfully full during that time, so she stopped beneath a tree and squeezed out the milk.

Water Girl returned to the boat as dawn was breaking. She told her uncle and Golden Dog's father that Uncle Fan had agreed to go to the prison, where his cousin had been promoted to warden and one of the men who cooked and delivered the meals to the prisoners was from the cousin's village. Water Girl and her two companions went into town for a hurried breakfast at a stall, then rushed over to Uncle Fan's bar.

Uncle Fan had gone to the prison early, and the three out-of-towners waited for him to return. Later that morning, he came in accompanied by his cousin and the cook. After the introductions, Han expressed his gratitude for their lending their ear and explained the injustice Golden Dog was enduring.

The warden said, "My cousin has made the situation clear. I met Golden Dog some time ago. He has a real temper, and this jail's no place for a man like him!"

Water Girl asked about the treatment Golden Dog was receiving and begged the warden to take him under his wing so far as he could.

"It appears that Golden Dog has offended a lot of people," the man said. "But try not to worry. I'll do my best to take care of him and keep him safe from his cellmates."

"Are you saying that it's the other prisoners who beat him?"

"With the kind of people in that place, whenever a new prisoner arrives, they gang up on him, beat him up, steal his food, and deny him the space he needs to sleep."

"Golden Dog isn't afraid of anyone," the painter said. "But he's not a fighter. I'm sure he's an easy mark for them!"

"That's why I brought the cook along. From now on he'll give Golden Dog extra rations. And I'll tell his cellmates that anyone who's physical with him is asking for trouble and that anyone who steals his food will go hungry for the day. Don't worry on that score. But a ruling on his guilt or innocence is in other hands."

Water Girl, Golden Dog's father, and Han Wenju spoke up together, thanking the two prison workers. They took out four bottles of good wine and handed two to each man. "This is all we have to show our appreciation."

"I can't take that," the warden said. "I'm doing this because you're my cousin's friends. For anyone else, I wouldn't do it for a thousand yuan. As for the wine, since my cousin runs a bar, I get plenty."

"Keep your bottles," said Uncle Fan. "We're all friends here."

Water Girl looked at the warden. "Could I see him?"

"That's impossible. Since his case hasn't been decided, he's not allowed visitors. If anything happened . . . My hands are tied."

Not wanting to impose on his kindness, she dropped the matter but asked if he'd give Golden Dog the pastries and cigarettes she'd bought. Again he made excuses.

Back at the boat, they were full of compliments for the warden and the cook.

"There are still decent people in the world," Han Wenju said. "But of course it's always easier to get things done when you're dealing with friends. As the saying goes, even an old rag can plug a hole in the dike. Who'd have guessed that Uncle Fan would help us like this? Ai! Golden Dog's still so young and inexperienced. He did too good a job, and that's why he's in the mess he's in today."

"Are you saying he shouldn't have done what he did, Uncle?" Water Girl asked him. "It's the Tian family that's doing this to him, even though he once saved Tian Zhongzheng's life."

"Ai!" Han sighed. "Life's more confusing all the time. You're a hero one minute and a bastard the next. First your face is red, then it's white. I don't know what's going on anymore."

Several days passed, and they still couldn't find a way to see Golden Dog or Dakong; they were powerless to help the two prisoners in any way. All Han did was drink and grumble; Golden Dog's father ate only a few bowls of rice and spent the rest of his time sighing and wiping away tears. Han went on and on, blaming fate for their troubles. People destined to become emperors, he said, wind up sitting on the throne, while those who aren't chosen by destiny can overrun the palace and still be denied the throne. He cited the case of the Ming rebel Li Zicheng, whose army was stationed on the Zhou River but who was routed and killed when he attacked Beijing.

Weary of Han's negativism, Water Girl spewed out, "Uncle, what's wrong with you? Instead of griping all the time, why don't you show a little concern for Golden Dog and Dakong?"

"A little concern?" he mimicked, in order not to have to admit to himself that Water Girl's jab had a basis. "What am I supposed to be doing?"

The old painter tried to calm Water Girl, reminding her that they all felt the same way but that, because they had been rebuffed at every turn, their frustrations were beginning to fester. Then he turned to Han Wenju. "Uncle Han, I think you ought to go back home. Someone has to run the ferryboat, and you can't stay away much longer. Water Girl and I can take care of things here." By then he was choking on his sobs and he couldn't go on.

"Why are you crying?" Water Girl asked. "Does it do any good to cry? Look. Both of you go home. I can take care of things here. As soon as I hear anything I'll let you know."

The painter was reluctant to leave, for it was his son who was in trouble and he felt bad about making Water Girl carry the full load. But she was adamant, knowing her mind as clearly as any man. For Golden Dog's father to stay, frightened and worried all the time, accomplished nothing, and was in fact a distracting burden.

"Water Girl," he said, "we can never repay what we owe you . . . If you're going to stay here be careful. I have eighty yuan on me. I'll leave it with you."

She didn't want to take the money, but he stuck it into her bag when she wasn't looking. On the boat with Han Wenju, he dabbed his eyes the entire trip to Stream of Wandering Spirits.

Water Girl went to the nanny's house and asked to stay there. She made daily trips to the prison in the hope of news about Golden Dog and Dakong. One day the warden came to her while she was there, closing the door behind him. He confided that the cases of Golden Dog and Dakong had been reactivated. The two prisoners were being interrogated daily, and Dakong, who had a fiery disposition, was forever hurling insults at his interrogators. On one occasion, they tied him to a post and went into another room to play poker, but he kept up his tirade until nearly everyone in the prison could hear him. To muffle him, they stuffed a rag in his mouth, leaving him bound and gagged through the night. Golden Dog didn't affront his interrogators with a wild insolence, but he refused to own up to his guilt and argued back, for which they called him obstinate and kicked him in the groin so viciously that he passed out for seven or eight hours at a time. Water Girl couldn't sleep. The next day she went to the jail's entrance wearing the light-colored shirt and straw hat of Uncle Fan's daughter and pretended that she, the warden's niece, had come to tell him that her mother was ill. The guard grilled her from every side before escorting her in, through three metal doors, to the rear courtyard, where the warden was standing beside a pond. At first he reacted obtusely, but then he saw through her disguise and was staggered. He had the presence of mind, though, to ask how her mother was. When the guard left, he said softly, "You've got more guts than I gave you credit for. What the hell are you doing here?"

"I beg you to let me see Golden Dog and Dakong!"

"You're out of your mind! Do you want us both to land in cells too? Out you go!" He turned to escort her away just as two armed guards brought a prisoner into the courtyard. It might have been better if she hadn't looked, for when she saw it was Golden Dog, the breath went out of her, and her momentary weakness drew the attention of Golden Dog and the guards. The warden paled but recovered to say, "Don't be afraid. He's just a prisoner on the way to questioning. Now, you go over to the hospital and take care of your mother. Tell her I'll come as soon as I can."

Water Girl, who had regained her wits, said, "Uncle, you don't have to come if you're too busy. If Mother gets worse, I'll be there to go for the doctor. I just came to let you know and to tell you not to worry. I'm sure she'll be better soon. All she needs is some bed rest."

Golden Dog, who heard her every word, was led toward the row of buildings at the rear. Water Girl wanted desperately to get another look at him, but the warden had an iron grip on her shoulder and was already guiding her out through the three doors. For the guard's benefit, he remarked, "Everybody gets sick once in a while. Your mother will be fine. I know there's a shortage of beds at the hospital, so I'll speak to the hospital director." He saw her out the main gate, turned on his heel, and strode inside without a backward glance.

At least she'd seen Golden Dog, and she expected that that would make her feel better. In fact, the result was the opposite: she was more anxious than before. She wondered what brutalities he lived under, whether the interrogators were still beating him, whether he had enough to eat, and whether, being a heavy smoker, he was in agony without cigarettes. As her worries fed on themselves, her heart felt as though it had lodged in her throat. A couple of days later she returned to the prison, and the day after that as well, but prudence kept her from trying artifices to get in to the warden. Instead, like anyone else, she stood before the brick wall, topped by its electrified wires, and gazed vacantly at its height. As night fell, she began singing a boat song from the Zhou River:

Waters of the Zhou River twist and turn,
One shoal after another,
Some with names, some without,
Inept sailors have trouble getting through,

A song emerges from a flooded shoal,
Boats fear songs like horses fear the whip.

She then sang the "Song of a Boat on the Shoal":

Yo—yo yo hai—yo—yo ao hai—hai—hai—hai—hai—hai—hai!

When she'd finished that, she sang "Free of the Shoal":

Hai hai—*don't let go*—hai hai—*move the tiller* hai
hai—*eyes straight ahead*—hai hai—hai hai—hai
hai—*move it—take a breath—it's nearly done—*
up—hai—hai—hai—*shout—!*

When that was finished, she sang "The Boat Weaves":

Yo *the song*—yo lao lao—yo *the song*—yo *the song*—yo *the song—up* lao lao—yo ao—!

She sang them all, one after the other: "The Hauling Song," "Furl the Sail," "Hoist the Sail, Pick up the Pole," "Pull the Lines," "Crossing the Street," "Weighing Anchor," "The Blockade," "The Meteor Song" . . . No matter how high the wall of the prison or how thick, and even though she couldn't see inside, her songs could get through. Which cells were Golden Dog and Dakong in? In that dark, cold place within those four walls, as long as they heard her songs they wouldn't feel alone; their hearts would commune with hers through the music. She sang until her mouth was dry and her voice hoarse, and even then kept it up, trilling songs that only Golden Dog and Dakong would know.

Late at night, when she was so tired she could barely stand, she dragged herself home, feeling at peace and fulfilled. Back when Golden Dog and Dakong were sailing boats and poling rafts on the Zhou River, she'd heard them sing those songs nearly every day, until she knew them by heart. But she'd never ventured them herself before, for knowing how bad her voice was, she'd always been too shy, even when they'd urged her to join them. Now the words had passed her lips, and she was surprised at the depth and strength of her voice. And that was only the first time. She came back nearly every day to sing the tunes over and over, and she felt that when she was singing, everything around her shared in the harmony, including the dark and forbidding wall around the prison. She knew that every note of her songs reached the ears of Golden Dog and Dakong.

It didn't take long for the townspeople to remark the woman who came every day to sing songs of the Zhou River. When they heard how well she sang, they came in droves to listen, and thinking she was there to make her living, they frequently tossed coins at her feet. But she always scooped up the coins and handed them back. Before long a passerby recognized her, and as word of the injustice that dogged her spread among the people, their sympathies were engaged, and the crowds grew larger. Soon even boatmen from the Zhou River—both private boat owners and members of the Crossroads Township River Shipping Brigade—came to sing along with her.

One day, while she was there singing, a stranger paused before her and asked, "Aren't you Water Girl Han?"

"Who are you?"

"What is it you're singing?"

"Just songs. Do you mind?"

"Who are you singing them for?"

"For myself, and for others."

"Like Golden Dog?"

"Are you a plainclothes policeman? Would you arrest me if I was singing them for Golden Dog?"

"Do you think he can hear you? And what good will it do if he can?"

Her eyes opened wide as the melancholy his remark had awakened swelled in her. But she didn't cry. "What else can I do? Who else will stand up for Golden Dog? You? Would you be tough enough to try?"

Struck by her question, he looked at her, stared at her. For the first time, she noticed a red-covered notebook sticking out of his pocket, on a corner of which appeared "Report—." She sneered, "Are you a reporter?"

"Yes."

"What about Golden Dog? Wasn't he one of you? He offended people by struggling on behalf of the people, but after he was arrested, not a single person came to his aid. It's not right!"

"Water Girl," the man said, "there are too many ears and too many loose tongues around here to be talking like that."

That incited her to contempt. "You're a reporter and you're scared? If that's the way you feel, you ought to throw your ID card into the Zhou River."

He eased his hand under her arm and led her away. "What do you think you're doing?" he chided gently. When they reached a deserted corner, he explained that he wanted to take her to a group of people who had assembled in Golden Dog's former office. More than a dozen young people were there when they arrived. They introduced themselves, and Water Girl realized that they were members of the Young Reporters Study Association. Upset by Golden Dog's arrest, they had gone in a body to the editor in chief to plead the reporter's case and ask the reporter's superior to intercede with the White Rock Stockade public security bureau. But he had been unwilling, holding that if Golden Dog was arrested, he must be guilty of something. Even though the prisoner had been cleared of wrongdoing in connection with Lei Dakong's contribution to the study association, his personal loan of two thousand yuan was a matter on which the newspaper management could not take a position. Besides, in view of the close relationship between Golden Dog and Lei Dakong, it would be rash for anyone to feel sure no other deals had been struck.

Rankled, the reporters, upon leaving the editor in chief's office, had dug out the story Golden Dog had written about Lei Dakong's company years before, and had hired a lawyer to represent him in the name of the association. They had come for Water Girl because they were preparing a detailed statement of what had happened, which they planned to present to the police, the procurator, and the people's court. After she exposed to them everything she knew about the personal loan, they produced a document entitled "A Report Concerning That Part of the Case Against Lei Dakong Involving a Charge of Bribery Against Golden Dog." The main point of the report was that Golden Dog could be defended against the charge of bribery on two grounds. First, his actions did not meet the legal definition of bribery as "illegally receiving payment to alter one's professional conduct so as to benefit another individual." As a reporter, Golden Dog's professional obligation was to write news stories, and he never wrote a story that benefited Lei Dakong's White Rock Stockade City and Country United Trade Co. or that personally benefitted Lei Dakong. Second, Golden Dog and Lei Dakong were childhood friends, and loans between close friends are a normal occurrence. Even though the money was lent by the company, Golden Dog gave a written IOU of his own volition.

The report was sent to the pertinent recipients in the name of the Young Reporters Study Association. It convinced Water Girl how hamfisted her own efforts had been. These reporters went about things just like Golden Dog, and through them she learned a great deal about the law and its effectiveness in a struggle. She recalled how Golden Dog had exploited the dispute between the Gong and Tian clans to bring down the Tian faction, and it was clear to her that his troubles were occasioned by the Tians' determination to get even for that. She wrote to the Zhou City authorities and told the whole story of the incident. When several days passed without a reply, she concluded that Commissioner Gong Baoshan's subordinates had intercepted the letter to prevent its reaching his desk. She went out and bought a colored banner, on which she wrote the words A Bright Mirror Hangs High. That she wrapped around her letter, and she sent everything off as a parcel to the commissioner, giving as the return address a certain member of the Gong clan from Stream of Wandering Spirits. She posted the package from the Crossroads Township post office and, afterward, took a bus to Zhou City in order to ascertain from the post office there that someone from the Gong family had indeed picked a parcel up. Relieved, she made her way back to White Rock Stockade positive that a response would soon come. But after ten days, after twenty, she had still heard nothing from the commissioner.

Instead she heard that Lei Dakong was dead, a suicide; he was said to have cut his throat with a razor blade. Water Girl, in a frenzy, went with Uncle Fan to see the warden. He confirmed that what she had heard was correct, but he didn't know exactly how it had happened, since the regional public security bureau had taken Dakong to Zhou City for trial, with the intention of restoring him to the prison in White Rock Stockade within four days. Dakong had killed himself on his first night in Zhou City.

"I knew Dakong as well as anybody," Water Girl insisted. "He wasn't a man who'd take his own life. It wasn't his nature to take an easy way out. And even if he'd wanted to, where would he find a razor blade in the Zhou City prison, of all places?"

"That's what everybody's saying," the warden acknowledged. "But that's none of our business. It's all being looked into by the competent authorities."

"This is a case of murder," Water Girl declared. "They killed him to shut him up!"

The blood drained from the warden's face. "You said that, not me. I didn't hear a word!" He bolted away.

"Water Girl," Uncle Fan said, "talk like that's going to get you into serious trouble. Dakong's dead, and there's nothing you can do to mend it. Since he didn't have any family, you can be the one to go to the police station and see what they plan to do about sending the body back from Zhou City."

"See what *they* plan to do? He was from Stream of Wandering Spirits, and that's where *I'm* going to make them send the body for burial. If we leave it to them, they'll pass his body on to the hospital for the anatomy lab and then dump what remains in a hole where the wild dogs will pick him clean." She paused, then nearly begged, "Uncle

Fan, since Dakong didn't make it out alive, you don't think that Golden Dog . . . ?"

"Don't let your imagination run wild," he counseled her. "I'll go see my cousin in the next few days and let you know what I hear."

After saying good-bye, Water Girl went to the post office, from where she telephoned Han Wenju to let him know about Dakong's death and to have him round up a delegation to come to White Rock Stockade to take the body home.

30

Lei Dakong's body was sent to White Rock Stockade the following day.

A group from Stream of Wandering Spirits, led by the old painter and Old Seven, arrived that night to take him home; Han Wenju didn't make the trip. Before the police released the body, they specified that the shroud was not to be opened and that no one was to mourn the death within the town. But as soon as the group reached the boat, they opened the shroud and everyone in the funeral party wept freely. Dakong's visage hadn't changed at all. Even after years of rich food and fine wine he looked the same, with perhaps a better complexion than before. He was wearing a suit and pointed leather shoes, but his socks were soaked with blood, since the rats had begun gnawing at his feet. Dried blood from the wound in his throat had soaked his chest, and maggots were squirming in the open wound. The painter swooned dead away when he saw the body, but Old Seven had the others take off Dakong's suit and dress him in the peasant clothes they'd brought with them. With his hands on Dakong's face, he lamented, "Dakong, Dakong, how could you kill yourself? How could you do it?" In the conflict of anger and sadness that he was experiencing he could shed only silent tears.

Dawn was just breaking when the boat arrived in Stream of Wandering Spirits. The men placed the body on a stone step at the entrance to the village, then went home for a hurried breakfast before returning to carry the body to a temporary crypt hollowed out at the base of the mountain.

After Water Girl's phone call, Han Wenju had put several people to making arrangements for Dakong's funeral. First they had to buy a coffin: it didn't matter if it was made of cypress or pine or a combination of woods; it didn't matter if it was built out of eight pieces of lumber or sixteen, or even thin strips, as long as it was found immediately. The next order of business was for the geomancer to select a grave site and pick a burial date. Arriving on a scrawny, hairy mule and holding a compass in hand, the geomancer examined Dakong's body, asked how he died, and studied his genealogy. "He has no living parents," he announced, "and leaves behind neither wife nor children, so there's no need to be choosy about the grave site. But because he died on an inauspicious day in a mourning year, permanent burial is for the time being inadvisable. There is no family to be endangered, but to protect the villagers of Stream of Wandering Spirits, it will be best to perform a floating burial."

Unlike a final interment, a floating burial is temporary; after the mourning year has passed, a body that has been given a floating burial can go to its regular tomb. Han Wenju, Water Girl, and Old Seven talked it over and decided that it would be preferable to lay Dakong to rest only once. But they ran up against opposition from the villagers, who wanted the geomancer's instructions carried out to the letter. Han Wenju and Old Seven, unable to devise a convincing counterargument, bent to the villagers' will.

On the day of Dakong's floating burial, the villagers paid their respects and stood in front of the temporary crypt commiserating with one another over life's uncertainties. Then they went home subdued, leaving behind Water Girl, Han Wenju, Old Seven, and the old painter, who volunteered to adorn the wall of the crypt with funeral designs; he wept as he worked. Water Girl, who had no more tears to shed, lay on the ground in front of the crypt, where she burned a packet of spirit paper, stirring it up with a damp willow switch to keep the fire from going out. "Dakong," she said, "you'll have to make do with this for now. Rest easy, you poor hero. After all the money you amassed, you died penniless! We wanted to bury you right away, but the day was wrong. And even if we'd gone ahead, right now I don't have the money to pay for a tombstone and a wake. Wait till next year, when the mourning year has passed, and I'll make sure you get a proper burial!"

Han wiped his eyes and said, "Water Girl, he can't hear you now, so don't make it any worse for yourself. Let's go home."

She neither answered him nor moved to get up but continued stirring the fire with the willow branch; the disturbed ashes swirled in the air like black butterflies. A flock of mountain watchdogs passed overhead in the bright sky, their cries of deathly loneliness striking trepidation in the hearts of the people below.

"Water Girl's overwhelmed by grief," Old Seven said, "so let's leave her alone for a while." He, Han, and the painter walked away with their heads bowed.

Water Girl sat there, her mind unfocused. Then she spotted someone walking toward her with a purposeful air, until she was only a couple of yards away. It was Yingying.

"Water Girl!" Yingying addressed her.

Water Girl stared at her woodenly.

"Dakong," Yingying asked, "—is he really dead?"

Water Girl still didn't respond. Yingying knelt beside her and reached for the willow switch in Water Girl's hand in order to stir the ashes of the burned paper for her. There was a brief flare-up of cinders, and the ashes floated up in the air more thickly than ever.

"I heard about it in town this morning from Tian Yishen. I never thought of Dakong as someone who could kill himself. I ran into the funeral party in town a while ago, and seeing them shook me up. It drove home that whenever I came, it would be too late to do any good."

"You came to see him?"

"I came to take a look. Water Girl, you can't bring someone back from the dead. But what about Golden Dog? What's his situation?"

"What aspect of his situation would you like to hear about?"

"Water Girl, you don't think I'd gloat over his arrest, do you? That would be a cruel thing to think. It's true that I wouldn't be taking any interest in him if he were prospering. But he's in jail! Just think, if things had worked out between him and me, wouldn't I be crushed now that this has happened to him? I'm married to somebody else, and I have a baby. And even if I'd married Golden Dog, we'd have fought like cats and dogs. I have no regrets. In all honesty, at first I didn't love him, but then when he refused to have anything to do with me, there was a time when I really did. That love, short as it was, is enough to make me pity him for the trouble he's in now. Why can't you believe me?"

Water Girl held her in her gaze for a long while, then threw her arms around her and broke into sobs. After all those days of tears that wouldn't come, how could the flow be such a torrent now?

Water Girl and Yingying left the crypt site and walked together toward Stream of Wandering Spirits. To Water Girl's description of

Golden Dog's situation, Yingying said, "I'll go see my uncle and get him to speak to the county officials. Dakong broke the law, but now he's dead, and I can't believe they want the same thing to happen to Golden Dog!"

"You don't have to do that."

"If he refuses to help, I'll threaten to break with him. He has to consider that he's dependent on my husband and me to take care of him when he grows old. Besides, Golden Dog once saved his life!"

Water Girl smiled understandingly and said, "Yingying, on Golden Dog's behalf, I thank you for your intentions. But you mustn't do anything. I don't want anything to do with that sort of plan, and I know Golden Dog wouldn't either. Even if renouncing your help means he'll die in prison, he'd hate you for doing what you have in mind and hate me for going along with it."

Yingying stood baffled as she watched Water Girl walk away.

That afternoon Tian Zhongzheng returned to Stream of Wandering Spirits from the township government office with a side of pork, nodding to everyone along the way, "Busy tonight? If not, come on over for some drinks and steamed pork!"

The villagers found his behavior bewildering. Why the sudden cordiality? It wasn't a holiday, nor, for that matter, was it his or Yingying's mother's birthday. Why, then, the invitation to drinks and steamed pork? Tian smiled. "Do you mean we're not allowed to enjoy good food and drink except on holidays? Come on, let's get together at my place for some serious drinking!"

They assumed he was celebrating the death of Lei Dakong.

After concluding the floating burial, Han Wenju and Old Seven went to Han's boat to drink themselves into oblivion. "Old Seven," Han said, "the way the world's going, I think we're finished—finished! As I see it, the geomancy of Stream of Wandering Spirits is at the bottom of the Tian and Gong clans but also of Golden Dog and Dakong. So things might have been expected to turn out differently. But the Tians and Gongs are triumphing the same as always, whereas Golden Dog and Dakong landed in jail, and Dakong died, supposedly by his own hand. Was he a man who'd kill himself? In the old days, he'd have taken to the woods to become a bandit chief or joined the resistance and become a guerrilla leader. He was the kind of man who wouldn't flinch if you put a knife to his throat. And he's supposed to have killed himself? Now that he's dead, I think Golden Dog's turn will come soon. Ai, what sort of government policy is this? First they tell us to go into business and make lots of money, then they can't arrest people fast enough for the money they've made. If that's what they want, then why all that rigmarole in the first place? Old Seven, I think this was in the cards for us all along. Crossroads Township belongs to the Tian family, and Zhou City belongs to the Gongs. To them we're nothing but so much straw. Come on, drink up; drink till you can't drink another drop! Have you read *Three Kingdoms?* Oh, I know you can't read, but you've seen the plays. Remember what Cao Cao says when he's drinking Dukang wine? 'To get rid of sorrows, one only needs Dukang.' Well, this isn't Dukang, but any wine can help you get rid of sorrows. Drink up. Why aren't you drinking?"

He refilled Old Seven's glass, then filled his own to the brim, and drank noisily. "Tian Zhongzheng bought a side of pork," he continued, "for a celebration at his house. Well, let him! It makes me so damned mad my teeth are about to bleed! But what good does it do us to get mad, Old Seven? If we died of a stroke, who'd drink this wine? Let them have their power, if that's what they want! We just have to avoid offending them and stay out of their way. Tian can't throw you and me in jail, can he?"

"I've had enough, Wenju. The more I drink, the worse I feel."

"Enough? Once you're drunk, you don't know if you're happy or sad. Getting drunk's the answer! An ant or a blade of grass is more important than a human being. Grass dies in the winter, then comes back to life in the spring. But Dakong's dead, and the world will never see him again! Ai, ai! Strike it rich, earn a fortune . . . Dakong had all the money a man could want, but now he's dead and can't spend a cent of it. With his talent, Golden Dog's struggled to get ahead all his life. So what good did it do him? The abbot over in the monastery has the right idea. Old Seven, mortal affairs make no sense."

"Wenju," Old Seven said, "you're drunk, and you're more discouraged than you ought to be. If I were twenty years younger, you can bet I'd raise some hell to set things right."

"How?"

"I'd go to Beijing and lodge a complaint even if I had to pawn my clothes to make the trip!"

Han laughed. "Who would you complain to? Water Girl sent a complaint to Commissioner Gong wrapped in a banner, and what good did it do? I hear his subordinates intercepted it and issued a directive that the matter be taken care of. So how was it taken care of? Old Seven, as old as you are, you still don't know how the world works!"

Old Seven didn't say anything. His chest felt congested, his head was spinning, and he just sat staring into the water. Han's nose was running and his tears were flowing as he filled and refilled his own glass and rambled on about the affairs of the world. As dusk fell, the son of the Lu family from Crossroads Township, who was carrying seven strings of three hundred firecrackers, boarded the boat.

"Where are you going, you little simpleton?" Old Seven asked him.

"Over to Township Chief Tian's. I bought these firecrackers for him."

Old Seven sounded like a firecracker himself when he heard this. "You're going to his celebration party? Why not take your sister Cuicui along?"

"My sister? . . . What do you mean by that?"

"What Township Chief Tian wanted was that little two-finger strip of tender meat of hers. It's no substitute to have you come over and kiss his ass. But while you're doing it, go ahead and bite those eggs of his!"

"I didn't expect crazy talk like that from you at a time like this!"

"Crazy talk? All I did was tell you what to do when you kiss his ass."

The Lu boy was too slow to manage a proper comeback, so he decided to let his fists do the talking. But he lost his nerve when he saw the bamboo pole in Old Seven's hand. With resentment in his eyes, he ignored the two old men.

Han Wenju's eyes were glazed by then. "Old Seven," he said, "let it drop. Why take it out on him? He's Tian's running dog. Things are bad enough already, so why get him riled?"

The boat pulled up to the bank, and Old Seven steadied it with his bamboo pole. But just as the Lu boy was jumping ashore, the boat gave a shudder and he fell head first into the river. By the time he pulled himself out, sputtering and exclaiming, the seven strings of firecrackers were soggy and ruined.

"Lu boy," Old Seven bawled at him, "you fucking idiot! Were you trying to kill yourself? You'd have drowned all for nothing, and now you've ruined Chief Tian's firecrackers! Is that what you had in mind? You fucking idiot!"

Instead of turning on Old Seven, the boy just shook his head in self-reproach.

And so Tian Zhongzheng had no firecrackers to set off that night, and very few villagers attended his party. Disappointed, he suggested to his wife that she go reiterate the invitation.

"Why do that?" she queried. "The fewer the people who come, the less we have to spend."

Tian threw his wife a disapproving look but didn't feel like arguing. Dakong's death and the arrest of Golden Dog had been momentarily exhilarating. But the satisfaction that he had felt soon turned to uncertainty and then to disquiet. He loathed Golden Dog and Dakong, but over the years he'd been forced to see them as formidable adversaries. Yet with everything they had going for them, they'd wound up dead or in jail. Their fall let him relax for a change but also made it clear that his hold on his own advantage as a "king in his castle" was tenuous. The world was now too complex for him to be able to feel impunity in acting like a tyrant in Stream of Wandering Spirits and Crossroads Township.

Seeing the dark look on his face, his wife compliantly went into the village to round up some more guests. To her face people reacted enthusiastically and thanked her for seeking them out. "We'll be right over," they said. But none of them went, and she was reduced to sending a go-between into town to invite some ne'er-do-wells. Old Seven ferried the emissary across the river, then pulled the boat back to the opposite shore and half-carried the helplessly drunk Han Wenju home to bed. Cai Da'an, Tian Yishen, and a motley crowd arrived on the far bank and signaled for the boat. Since there was no one to provide service, they stripped and swam across.

As Tian Zhongzheng had promised, he laid out an elaborate spread, with meat dishes galore. He went around filling his guests' glasses and toasting them. "Over the past few days Stream of Wandering Spirits has witnessed some tragic events, and everybody's feeling the strain. Maybe a few glasses of wine will help. There's no reason for you not to drink your fill. There's more wine than you can drink!"

"But there's also some reason for celebration," Tian Yishen countered. "Since Chief Tian's in an expansive mood, let's drink the night away! As the saying goes, the river flows east for thirty years, and west for thirty years. But this time it didn't take even three years. Things have turned around in less than one year. Dakong paid for his crimes with his life, and I say good riddance! Golden Dog may not be dead yet, but he can cool his heels in prison for a few years. Bottoms up!"

Glasses were hoisted, but Tian Zhongzheng brought his back down. "Stop gloating, Yishen! What the hell do you know?"

Then he raised his glass and drained it.

The rebuke put a damper on the party, since everyone had to wonder what was eating Tian. After discreetly emptying their glasses, they sat down and hardly moved. Tian just laughed. "Drink up!" he said. "Why is everybody so reserved?"

"Is something bothering you, Chief?" Cai Da'an asked him.

"What could be bothering me?"

Cai tried to liven up the party. "Chief Tian invited us over to enjoy ourselves," he said, "so let's relax. Come on, everyone, let's drink to our host!"

They laughed and uttered a few lucky phrases, then clinked glasses and drank a toast.

By midnight the wine had done its job on everyone. Tian Yishen was the first to sink toward stupor; Cai Da'an was next. The alcohol had driven Tian Zhongzheng's prickliness out of their minds, and without realizing it, they let their conversation return to Golden Dog and Dakong.

"Everybody out there's abuzz over Dakong. They all think there was something fishy about the way he died. It's a mystery to me what would make him commit suicide."

"Who cares how he died?" Tian Yishen rejoined. "What matters is that he's dead. You may not know that Water Girl Han sent a letter to Gong Baoshan, probably thinking she'd get some mileage out of helping him ruin us. The bitch had a good idea, but she couldn't know that Lei Dakong's days were numbered and that they'd end in Zhou City, not in White Rock Stockade! Do you understand, in Zhou City?"

"If only it had been Golden Dog who died!" Cai said. "He's the one who's always scared me—not Dakong."

"So Da'an's scared of Golden Dog!" Tian Yishen mocked. "No wonder you used to run around doing his bidding all the time. He wouldn't have become a reporter if it hadn't been for you—and you wouldn't have to be afraid of him now."

Cai shrank into himself and turned to look at Yingying's mother, who was standing nearby. She was getting fatter all the time, and as she looked at Cai she recalled his part in bringing off her marriage. "Hmph!" she snorted.

Without saying anything, Cai lowered his head and continued drinking. A few minutes later, he stood up and said, "A toast in celebration. Everybody, do me the honor. Bottoms up!" He walked around and toasted each of the other guests, holding his glass respectfully in both hands. But when he came to Tian Yishen, he passed by without so much as a nod. The drunken Tian was offended and let Cai know that he took the gesture to be an attempt to humiliate him. A loud argument erupted, during which the two men rehearsed all the grievances they had nursed against each other over the years, and before long they were letting their fists fly, upsetting the table in the process. Disgusted, Tian Zhongzheng walked up and slapped each of them across the face, quickly bringing the altercation to an end.

Cai stumbled toward home in the early hours of the morning, roundly cursing Dakong, Golden Dog, and Tian Yishen as he went along. All of a sudden, someone jumped him, getting on top of him in the darkness and pounding his face over and over. When the assailant stood up from his cowering victim, he began kicking him—a dozen times or more. The next morning Tian saw that his gate had been smeared with shit. Cai was lying near the entrance of the village covered with blood. Tian had no idea of the meaning of it all. A rumor spread that the drunken Cai had fouled Tian's gate but had collapsed as he was leaving the village. His pants were soiled with his own filth, and his head was bleeding. Tian suspected that there was more to what had happened than that, but he didn't want to voice his suspicions to anyone.

Water Girl stopped at Golden Dog's house on Restless Hill after breakfast and washed some clothes for the painter. After that, she went on to the monastery to see the abbot. She wanted him to predict whether Golden Dog was fated to suffer. The abbot, who was reading scriptures in the main hall when she arrived, had heard about Dakong's death and Golden Dog's imprisonment, and as soon as he saw her, he put down his book and motioned for her to take a seat beside him. "I heard about Golden Dog and Dakong," he said. "They were blessed to have you, a mere woman, exhaust herself in an endeavor to right the injustices they've suffered. The mortal world is a void, and the only way to deal with it is through self-cultivation and the Buddhist sutras. What good does it do to struggle and strive to be strong? Golden Dog wouldn't take my advice, and look what's happened to him! But I can see from your kindness that the Buddha nature is in you, like the clear sky. You have the ability to know what is to be known, and all will become clear and tranquil, inside and out. From within you will see all that is Buddha."

"Abbot, I don't understand what you're saying, but I know that Golden Dog's a good man. He wasn't struggling for his own benefit. Why do the good have to suffer? Tell me if he'll ever get his deserts."

"Seek repose," he urged her. "Say the first words that come into your mind, and I'll tell you what they mean."

The first word to come out of her mouth was *finished;* that was followed by *return*.

"Aiya!" the abbot smiled. "A wonderful sign! The top part of the character for *finished* is a roof, the bottom a son. The character for *return* is one individual around another. That proves that Golden Dog will be coming home, that he'll get married this year, and that he'll have a son."

Surprisingly, Water Girl pulled a long face. "Are you just saying that to cheer me? Even if he comes home, how can he get married and have a son just like that?"

"I'm as much at sea as you are. But that's the meaning that resides in those two words."

The earnest look on his face turned her sadness around. "If things do turn out as you say, it will prove that heaven has eyes after all! With Dakong dead and Golden Dog in prison, just look how smug the Tian family is."

"Was it you who beat Cai Da'an last night?" he asked her.

"I have no idea who did it, but I'm not sorry it happened. Let him spend a couple of weeks in bed, and I'll feel a lot better."

Just as the abbot was about to preach the Buddhist lesson of forbearance, she got to her feet and took her leave, her mind filled with the abbot's prediction. She was confused. There was no reason to doubt his interpretation, but she found herself too stimulated by her own thoughts about it to sit still in Stream of Wandering Spirits. So she took a boat to White Rock Stockade that afternoon, where she went straight to the bar near the eastern gate.

"I was about to go looking for you," Uncle Fan said when she walked in, "and here you are!"

"Do you have something new on Golden Dog?"

"My cousin came by at noon and said that there's been a ruling on Golden Dog's case. He's been sentenced to seven years."

Water Girl slumped to the floor as though from a heavy blow. Uncle Fan came to help her up. "Water Girl," he said, "it's my cousin's opinion that the Gong family in Zhou City was responsible for Dakong's death, and although there's no proof, there are circumstantial grounds for thinking him right. Golden Dog's sentence was ordered by the court on the recommendation of certain people at the administrative level."

"Why would they want Dakong dead? Was it the same people who recommended a seven-year sentence for Golden Dog? Why should they do that? I thought they were Golden Dog's supporters at one time, weren't they?"

"I thought so too," Uncle Fan said. "My cousin said that Dakong gave a list of people in Zhou City, including the Gongs, who'd accepted bribes from him. When the Tians sent the material on up, there was nothing else the Gongs could do to save their hides."

Water Girl bitterly regretted sending Gong Baoshan the message she had wrapped in the banner, regretted placing her trust in people like that. She had even suggested to the Young Reporters Study Association that they send a copy of their open letter to Gong Baoshan. "Gong Baoshan, the 'bright mirror hanging high'—hah!" Water Girl sighed. "I must have been blind!"

"Golden Dog refuses to admit his guilt and has filed an appeal," Uncle Fan said. "Expecting it to be turned down, he's smuggled a note out for you."

She snatched the note from his hand. "Go to Lane X on X Street in Zhou City. Have someone named Shi Hua try to get them to order an investigation of my case." She folded the note away, dried her eyes, and said good-bye to Uncle Fan on her way out the door.

31

Who was Shi Hua? Water Girl had never heard the name. She found the address written on the note and knocked at the door. It was opened by a stylish, attractive woman.

"Excuse me," Water Girl said, "I'm looking for someone."

"And who would that be?"

"The name is Shi Hua. Probably works for the newspaper."

"Who are you? What do you want to see Shi Hua about?"

"I'm from White Rock Stockade. It's very important."

With a skeptical look on her face, the woman invited her in. "I'm Shi Hua. But I don't work for the Zhou City newspaper."

Water Girl was stunned to discover that Shi Hua was a woman, and such a pretty, modish woman at that, and that she didn't work for the newspaper. Where had Golden Dog met her?

"Oh, I was under the impression that Shi Hua was a man, a reporter for the Zhou City newspaper. Golden Dog sent me to find you."

Shi Hua's expression underwent a dramatic change when she heard the name. "He's in prison. How could he send you?"

Water Girl took out the note and told her how she got it.

As Shi Hua held the note in her hand, she began to cry. "What's Golden Dog to you?" she asked Water Girl.

"I call him Uncle. Lei Dakong's dead, and there's nothing anyone can do about that. But what crime has Golden Dog committed to get him sentenced to seven years in prison? He had nothing to do with the business and never took a bribe from Dakong. Obviously the Gong family sacrificed him to protect themselves."

The note still held tightly in her hand, Shi Hua seemed not to have heard a thing Water Girl said. "Golden Dog wrote to me," she said. "He hasn't forgotten me after all!"

Water Girl, who had no idea of what that meant, pleaded tearfully, "Elder Sister Shi Hua, if Golden Dog sent this note, he must have confidence in you to think of something. There's nothing more my friends and I can do, so it's up to you."

Shi Hua reached out to reassure Water Girl. "Of course I will," she said. "I can't just let a friend die." She hung her head in silent reflection, then lifted it in a show of resolution and continued, "I'll do something—whatever it takes!"

"Elder Sister Shi Hua," Water Girl implored her, "tell me what to do. I'll go anywhere you want me to. I'm not afraid."

"You don't need to do anything. Go back to White Rock Stockade. I'll go to the office and arrange for a car to take me to the provincial capital tomorrow."

The first thing Shi Hua did in the provincial capital was appeal to the children of high-ranking cadres who worked in her company; she briefed them, and they put their heads together to try to come up with a plan to deal with the admittedly delicate situation.

"I've heard what happened to the White Rock Stockade City and Country United Trade Co.," one of them said. "What got it into trouble was its dealings with certain people, one or several of whom almost certainly had a hand in Dakong's death. This isn't going to be easy."

All of a sudden Shi Hua smacked her forehead. "How could I be so slow-witted? The son of Commandant Xu of the military region is a friend of mine. I'll see if he can get his father involved. If he can, the Gong family will have to watch what it tries with Golden Dog!"

"Are you talking about Xu Wenbao?" they asked her. "You mean that simpleton who gave you the gold necklace?"

"He *tried*, but I wouldn't take it," she said with a smile. "I don't think he'll say no if I ask him to do this for me."

Shi Hua went home to make herself up: eyebrows, eyeliner, rouge, face powder. She stood in front of the mirror, pleased to see that with a little makeup she looked as alluring as a young woman. She had no trouble getting in to see Xu Wenbao, who was so flattered by the visit, and so smitten by the visitor, that he agreed to her request without restriction. He went first to his father, but when the commandant rebuffed him, he appealed to his mother to intercede.

"What do you want from me?" Commandant Xu asked his wife. "Socialist laws are to be obeyed, and people who break them are duly punished. You can't expect me to lean on the courts."

"You don't have to go on about that," she said. "I wouldn't ask you for this if Wenbao were our own son. But it's Xu Tianwu's son we're talking about!"

Xu Wenbao was not Commandant Xu's natural son; the younger man's natural father had been one of Commandant Xu's comrades-in-arms in the 25th Red Army. After Liberation, Xu Tianwu worked alongside Xu Feibao in a southern province, and as soon as he had divorced his wife from an arranged marriage, he married a woman from the city, who bore him a son, Xu Wenbao. During the Cultural Revolution, Xu Tianwu, who had been sent down to do local work, was branded a capitalist roader and committed to prison. His wife, unable to bear the humiliation, hanged herself, leaving Xu Wenbao to fend for himself. Xu Tianwu was eventually rehabilitated and released from prison, but by then he was so ill with an inflamed liver that he lasted less than a year. The orphaned Xu Wenbao was adopted by Xu Feibao and his wife. His wife's mention of this chapter of their personal history took the commandant's thoughts into the past, and after several contemplative minutes he said, "The boy has suffered a great deal . . . Now peace has returned, and the people are living decent lives, but Tianwu and his family . . . Ai, the country owes them a lot."

Once his father agreed to help, Xu Wenbao went personally to tell Shi Hua. His price for the favor? A kiss. What could she do? She held out her hand and let him kiss it hungrily. "That's enough!" she said. "Now take me to see your father. I've written down all the particulars so he can familiarize himself with the case."

When they were standing in front of Commandant Xu, Shi Hua handed him the memorandum she had put together and lauded him as a man with high party consciousness who stood with the people. Commandant Xu smiled and turned his attention to the document. "Gong Baoshan seems to have had utter disregard for the law and for party discipline!" he observed sadly when he'd finished the report. "Shi Hua, even if you'd come straight to me instead of going through Wenbao, I'd have wanted to get involved in correcting this scandal. It's people like this who give the party a bad name! You needn't worry. I'll go to the provincial party secretary this very day and get the matter straightened out."

Xu Wenbao wouldn't hear of Shi Hua's leaving and insisted that she stay overnight. He filled her with good food and wine while they awaited his father's return. She was willing to stay since she wanted to see how things turned out. By the time they'd finished off about half the wine, Xu Wenbao was staring drunkenly at her. He fell to his knees and begged her to "have some fun" with him. That was precisely what she'd feared from the beginning, and she refused him. But he threw his arms around her and whined, "So you've just been toying with me! And after all I've done for you! Just what is Golden Dog to you that you find it so important to get him exonerated? You're going to do what I want or I'll see that the whole thing falls apart for you."

Shi Hua consented out of fear of what he might do. She asked for three sleeping pills and said, "Give me half an hour; then you can come to bed." She lay down, tears streaming, and after she had fallen asleep, Xu Wenbao heard her softly call the names of Golden Dog and her husband.

When Shi Hua returned, Water Girl was still in Zhou City. She had stayed so that she could come to Shi Hua's house every day to see if there were any developments. The sight of Shi Hua, who seemed to have aged overnight, with puffy eyes and a drawn complexion, alarmed Water Girl. At first, Shi Hua said only that she was sick, but when Water Girl kept at her, she told exactly what had happened. Water Girl fell to her knees and kowtowed to show her gratitude. But instead of helping her up, Shi Hua just stood there stolidly as Water Girl rose and walked out the door. She then crumpled to the bed, like a bundle of kindling untied, and dissolved into sobs.

As expected, the provincial committee and the provincial legal institutions organized a team to conduct an investigation in Zhou City and White Rock Stockade, and after two months of probing they concluded that the White Rock Stockade City and Country United Trade Co. had in fact been an unlawful business that deserved to be shut down, and that arresting the manager and assistant manager had been entirely appropriate. But they concluded that Lei Dakong's death was murder and that Gong Baoshan's son-in-law was responsible; he was arrested. Nearly a dozen other people in Zhou City were also named as having played a role, major or minor, in the affair. Gong Baoshan himself was severely reprimanded by the party and removed as commissioner.

Golden Dog was going to be released, cleared of all charges.

The assets of the White Rock Stockade City and Country United Trade Co. were impounded and the buildings that served as its offices returned to Water Girl. As she sat in the redecorated room, all sorts of emotions flitting through her mind, she became conscious of how fearful the place made her feel. When she heard that Golden Dog was to be freed in three days, she'd sat silent on a bench in the court's anteroom, drained of energy, instead of jumping to her feet. She left through the gate of the judicial compound, under a blistering sun, and gazed at the shaded moss in the cracks of the roof tiles on the houses along the street. The moss had been washed by the rain until it appeared to be painted a bright green. Suddenly she began running, like a madwoman, across the street, past one lane after another, bumping into pedestrians and peddlers' stalls along the way. When she reached the post and telegraph office, she dashed inside, picked up a phone, and shouted to the operator that she wanted Stream of Wandering Spirits of Crossroads Township. Golden Dog's father picked up the phone and heard her say, "Golden Dog's being released; he's going to be a free man; he's been declared innocent of all charges!" Next she ran to the bar by the eastern gate, clamoring for Uncle Fan long before she reached the door. When she barged in, she knocked over a stool just inside the door and sent a brass basin clattering into the street.

That night she went over and picked up Han Hongpeng, needing to hold him in bed. But she couldn't sleep—not in Grandpa Pockface's place—so she played with her son, kissed him, nibbled on him, hugged him, lifted him up in the air. When he giggled, she was happy; when he cried, she was also happy. She kept it up until he fell asleep from exhaustion, then sat there letting her mind wander. Golden Dog's release was one of the happiest occurrences in her life, but because he spent so long in prison for something he didn't do, and because he suffered so much, her happiness was mixed with sadness. She reflected on how, over the preceding years, he had failed to understand how bumpy and difficult the road of life was. Over thirty and having suffered prodigious setbacks in his career, he still wasn't married, and she wondered what his frame of mind would be upon leaving prison. Even though he'd been completely cleared, he'd spent a long time in prison. How would society view him? She thought back to how he'd proposed to her shortly after the baby arrived, and she realized she still regretted her reaction. His career had been flourishing then, and she was a widow with a newborn baby. She hadn't wanted to tie him down. But now, but now . . . Again she began to cry.

At noon on the following day a boat pulled up at the landing beyond the southern gate, where it discharged its load of passengers, who headed straight to the old blacksmith's shop.

Han Wenju was wearing new clothes, and when he saw how puffy Water Girl's eyes were, he asked, "Are you crying at a time like this?"

"Your eyes are failing, Uncle! Cry? I haven't stopped laughing! A speck of something got into my eye, and I've been rubbing it."

She saw that the abbot had come with them. "Your interpretation of the words was perfect," she said. "You're a true seer!"

"Not so fast," he cautioned. "Golden Dog may be coming home, but there's still the business of the wife and son."

"It'll happen; I know it will. We'll see what he says about your divination."

The abbot looked at her and smiled. "You're all right, Water Girl," he said approvingly. "You're all right. A perfect case of 'If the right land is found, the planter will appear'!"

Han Wenju interrupted. "Have you found a girl for Golden Dog, Water Girl?"

She hugged Hongpeng and colored slightly. "Don't ask, Uncle. You'll know soon enough."

The visitors busied themselves with buying food, killing chickens, and cleaning fish. They were going to throw a getting-out party for Golden Dog. Water Girl went and bought a set of new clothes for him to wear after he'd had a bath and a haircut. Han Wenju, always one for a bit of the unusual and in this case having an augmented desire to do something special, had decided he wanted to hire a horse, drape it with red bunting, and take it to the prison gate as Golden Dog's mount. The old painter, with only a string of firecrackers, made a show of opposing that pleasing idea. "Wenju, where are you going to get a horse? Don't go overboard. They won't allow a horse at the prison gate anyway."

"I've already arranged it with the photographer at the western gate. What's the difference if we spend a little bit more? Besides, there's no law against riding a horse. I'd organize an honor guard and let him ride back in style if I had a car."

None of them got any sleep. At the crack of dawn they were on their way to the prison, and when Golden Dog walked out the gate, they brought the horse up to him. Since it was a photographer's prop, it had a fancy saddle with colorful streamers and little brass bells. Golden Dog balked.

"Putting you on that horse," Old Seven said adamantly, "is our way of showing you've been rehabilitated!"

One man walked in front holding the horse's reins, two people took positions along the flanks, and the dozen or so remaining people formed behind Golden Dog, who looked like a bridegroom on his way to his wedding, or an old-time official on an inspection tour, or a general on a triumphant return! When passersby caught sight of the procession, they pointed: *That's Golden Dog! It's Golden Dog, the reporter the Gongs and Tians sent to prison on trumped-up charges!*

An old man crossed the street to them, grabbed hold of the reins, and brought the procession to a halt. "Golden Dog? Are you Golden Dog? Everybody says that the false case against you was overturned by an honest, upright official at the provincial level. Can you give me his name and address?"

For a moment people were confounded by the unexpected disruption. But Golden Dog jumped off his horse and asked the old man, "Do you want to register a complaint with this 'honest, upright official'?"

Tears came to the old man's eyes, who said he was from a township where the headman was one of Secretary Tian's lackeys. One winter day, five years before, the old man's wife had been out feeding a pig they were raising, when the township chief, taking it to be wild, shot at it. He missed, but the man's startled wife fell over the cliff and broke her back. She'd been paralyzed ever since. The old man's appeals to the party secretary's office were met by denials of any responsibility for the accident. For five long years he'd been fighting the case, but to no avail. Now he wanted to take his grievance to the "honest, upright official" who had freed Golden Dog.

"The only place you'll find an 'honest, upright official' these days is on the stage," Golden Dog said. "I don't know who did what, but if you'll bring me the evidence of your case, I'll look it over."

The old man was doubtful. "Can you really do something?"

"I can try."

The old man reached under his shirt and took out a cloth-wrapped bundle, which he opened to reveal a stack of dog-eared papers, from which he removed a sheet that he handed to Golden Dog with both hands; he then took out a cigarette and handed it to Golden Dog, again with both hands. Politely refusing the cigarette, Golden Dog asked the man to leave the material with him.

"Golden Dog," Han Wenju said, "you've scarcely had your own case settled. Why get involved with somebody else's problems? What can you do anyway?"

Golden Dog said only, "Let's go home!"

The procession continued on to the blacksmith shop, where a magnificent spread was waiting. As the visitors raised toasts to Golden Dog, his eyes misted. "All that's missing today is Dakong. Sure, he did ignoble things and made mistakes, but in the pages of history you won't find many peasants like him! He's dead now, and if we say he was born at the right time, we must also say that he died at the right time. I'm not bitter about sitting in prison for something I didn't do. The punishment was coming to me, if not for what I was accused of, then for something else. What grieves me is that I involved so many of my friends and neighbors. But knowing that I didn't lose your trust and confidence has given me renewed courage and the will to go on. Here's a toast to all of you!"

A dozen or more glasses were clinked, and Golden Dog drained his. As the warm wine settled in his stomach, his face flushed and he began to feel light-headed.

"Golden Dog," Water Girl cautioned him, "don't drink on an empty stomach. Let Uncle Han drink your toasts for you." But he drank a few more before withdrawing to the other room and lying on the kang; Water Girl followed him and sat beside him to massage his battered ribs.

"Water Girl," he said, "I only made it out of prison because of you. You've lost weight, and you're darker now . . ."

"When they told me you were beaten in there, you don't know how unhappy I was. Uncle Fan went to ask the warden to transmit a message to you because I worried you might break under the torture and take the easy way out."

"You actually thought I'd try to kill myself? You thought I'd be willing to die with those trumped-up charges still against me? My injuries aren't serious, and I'll be in the pink in no time. Go drink with the others—drink as much as you can. And tell everybody else to do the same."

She stood up, went out to the table, and made a general announcement. "This party will be a failure unless at least two of you keel over from drink. Abbot, you first. Here, let me toast you!"

The abbot's face was florid. "Water Girl," he said, "I've had enough. Toast your uncle. Look at him there, just look at him."

Han Wenju staggered up to them and said, "Some more for me. I'm not drunk. I could drink another liter if I wanted to. I'll drink if you won't. Water Girl, give me that wine of yours!" He took the bowl out of her hands and drank it down. Then he opened his mouth to express an afterthought, but he sank into a chair, his head lolling to one side. Whatever was on his mind never made it past his lips.

The old painter was the least drunk, so he helped the fuddled ones over to the kang or into a chair to sleep it off, then cleared off the table and gathered things for the trip home. "Let them sleep," he said to

Water Girl. "We can take the boat back later this afternoon. It doesn't matter when we get home. We can sail under the moon. Go get Hongpeng. Here's fifty yuan. Will that cover what you must give them for watching him?"

"Keep your money. I have plenty," she said as she went out the door.

The sun was setting when the people began waking up and hustling in order to get on the boat and leave for home.

"Golden Dog," Han Wenju said, "come back to Stream of Wandering Spirits with us for a month or two; then you can see if you want to go back to the newspaper in Zhou City. After we get home, I'll throw a party that really rocks."

"I don't want to go back just now," Golden Dog said.

"You're not thinking of returning to that job, are you?" Han asked incredulously. "Is it that important to you? You're supposed to learn from your mistakes. All this happened because you took your job too seriously."

Golden Dog addressed Water Girl. "You said you put Dakong's notebook someplace for safekeeping. Do you still have it?"

"I left it at home just in case. The police asked me if I had any company documents, but I didn't give them anything and I didn't tell them about the notebook."

"Then let's go to Stream of Wandering Spirits!"

"What notebook is that?" Han asked. "If it's so important, why didn't you tell me about it, Water Girl?"

Golden Dog answered for her. "A notebook in which Dakong recorded every bribe his company paid to members of the Tian family when he was starting out. That notebook will guarantee that the good times are over for them. So that this business can be straightened out once and for all, I'll fix it so that none of them can escape. They won't get away with breaking the law, then turning around and attacking their former coconspirators."

"Golden Dog, you've lost your mind!" Han howled. "Do you really think you can bring down the Tian family? Didn't you learn anything at all from those months in jail?"

"I don't care if it's the Gongs or the Tians," Golden Dog spit out, "or the Zhangs or the Lis. Anyone who abuses his power and position by feathering his own nest and who oppresses the people in the bargain is going to answer to me, whatever I must do!"

"You kept mum about the notebook when you were in prison," Old Seven said. "And now that you're a free man you're going to turn it against them. Golden Dog, you're bright. It's too bad Dakong didn't have your savvy. By telling them everything, he gave them a chance to destroy the evidence and kill him afterward. Dakong was a dog that bared his fangs, but Golden Dog's the dog that'll win the fight!"

"Old Seven, are you trying to egg him on?" Han asked. "Let the abbot have his say. Abbot, what do you think?"

"What can I add? Buddhism preaches Moke, Banruo, and Boluomi. *Moke* means 'great,' *Banruo* means 'intelligence,' and *Boluomi* means 'the distant shore.' When one reaches the distant shore, the ultimate has been achieved and the outcome has been revealed. By proceeding so, the heart expands and becomes capacious, thus containing all the heavenly bodies, all the land and waterways, all things that grow, all people, evil and saintly, and heaven and hell. But I doubt that Golden Dog has achieved that."

"If Crossroads Township and White Rock Stockade were one big monastery, I could be your acolyte in good conscience," Golden Dog said.

Han Wenju glowered at Golden Dog, then led the abbot, who had a hurt look on his face, into the cabin. "Maybe he doesn't believe what you say," he comforted, "but you've convinced me. I want you to teach me some more of that stuff."

Against a heavy current, the boat sailed slowly but steadily up the river between two darkened shores. It made Stream of Wandering Spirits shortly after cockcrow. After people had separated, Golden Dog and his father went to Water Girl's house to talk with her and Han Wenju. Water Girl brought out the notebook, and by candlelight Golden Dog began work on his exposé. Unable to dissuade him, Han excused himself and went to the ferry landing to sleep on the boat. The painter sat with Golden Dog and Water Girl for a while, but when he realized his inability to contribute to the project, he left for home, to get things ready for the guests he expected to drop by the following day; he didn't want to disappoint them. Water Girl sat wide-eyed, holding Hongpeng in her arms and watching Golden Dog as he wrote. When he finished, she asked, "Will you see Shi Hua when you go to Zhou City?"

He spun around. She had touched a nerve. Quickly adopting an attitude of indifference, however, he said, "I guess I should—at least to thank her."

"Who is she? She really knows what she's doing. Is she someone you met at the newspaper?"

Golden Dog nodded and mumbled yes.

"She thinks a lot of you," Water Girl continued. "When I told her what had happened, she burst into tears. She went to the provincial capital the very next day, and after taking care of things, rushed back to Zhou City. I called her the day before you got out of prison and asked if she'd be there to greet you. She said no, that she didn't want to see you, since she'd written to you several times but never received a reply . . . I didn't want to pressure her. She's a strange woman, Uncle Golden Dog. Is she married?"

He listened to her expressionlessly, his head bowed. When she finished, he answered, "She married a man from her work unit. They have no small children to worry about . . . Water Girl, it's getting late. I should be going home."

"It's still early," she said. "What's your hurry? Does it bother you when I'm around? You hardly ate anything for lunch. I'll make you noodles in clear broth. Here, hold the baby. He hasn't slept at all today."

Golden Dog dandled the baby while Water Girl was in the kitchen. He was struck by the resemblance to Fuyun, and the thought of the dead man saddened him. In no time Water Girl had cooked a bowl of noodles and brought them in; then she sat watching him eat, fussing over whether they were salty enough or too sour. As she lifted her blouse and stuck a nipple in the baby's mouth, Golden Dog noticed that the third button of her blouse was missing. "You've lost a button," he said casually, "but it was there when you greeted me at the prison gate. No doubt it fell off at the stove."

She raised her head and looked him straight in the eye. "I guess you're right. But you have a button of mine, don't you? Bring it here tomorrow, and I'll sew it on."

He recalled that night on the riverbank. It had happened long ago, yet he could relive every second of it. His eyes began watering as he looked at her, and when she came to him with her handkerchief, she fell softly into his arms, tears streaming.

The candle flickered and began to sputter. They could hear the sound of Hongpeng's even breathing. And they could feel the beating of each other's heart, which soon achieved a perfect synchronism. Neither spoke as they looked at the flickering candle. Was that a beating heart, too? they wondered.

A rooster crowed, and the paper over the window turned light.

"Are you leaving for Zhou City today, Uncle Golden Dog?"

"Why do you insist on calling me Uncle?"

"Elder Brother Golden Dog then . . ."

"I don't think so. Since I've just come back, there'll be a lot of villagers dropping by, and we haven't thrown a party yet."

"You should throw a party, you really should. And after lunch you should go see Dakong. We couldn't put him to final rest and had to do a floating burial over in the hollow. I'll go see Uncle later and get him to write a eulogy. He's the only one in Stream of Wandering Spirits who can write things like that. When he's finished, we'll go over and burn it for Dakong."

"You're right," he said, "I have to tell him that Gong Baoshan's son-in-law was arrested. A life for a life."

As Golden Dog had predicted, as many as a hundred people came to his father's at noon, more guests than the old painter had ever entertained before. Naturally, there wasn't enough wine or food, so he gave them more rice, and when the batch of noodles Water Girl had prepared was gone, she made another, which they also finished off in short order. She wound up making thirteen batches.

After lunch, Han took out the eulogy he'd written and passed it to Golden Dog. It was written in an ancient, elegant style. "There is surely no one but Uncle Han who could write something like this," Golden Dog smiled.

"Did you think you're the only writer in the area just because you're a reporter?" Han asked him. "I have an old book that tells how to write epigraphs and memorials. I'll teach you if you want to learn. Tell me if you think what I wrote has captured the essence of Lei Dakong's life."

Golden Dog read it through and said, "Don't you strike a note that's too discouraging? For instance, when you write of 'a heart that flies higher than the heavens but a fate thinner than paper' or that, 'losing his essential nature, he grew dizzy with success' or that 'he accumulated great wealth yet died a pauper' or that 'life, like a lamp, is extinguished; to whom can one complain of mortal chaos?' I think we should make a few changes!"

He sat down and began making careful revisions.

That didn't please Han, who became defensive. "It's a eulogy. It's gone as soon as you burn it. Things like that are written for the living, not for the dead."

"You're right, Uncle Han, but we can't let Dakong's death make us lose hope."

"Uncle," Water Girl said, "Golden Dog knew Dakong better than anyone. When one of the country's leaders dies, they hold a memorial service. But Dakong was a peasant, and writing a eulogy for him has the same function."

With the emended eulogy, Golden Dog went with Water Girl, and Hongpeng in her arms, to the place where the villagers had given Dakong a floating burial. At the site, they knelt on the ground, laid out some wine, lit incense, and burned spirit paper. Then Golden Dog read the eulogy:

> On this late afternoon of the x day of the x month of winter, 198x, I, your humble elder brother Golden Dog, in company with your unworthy younger sister Water Girl and your nephew Hongpeng, have come by lantern light with incense, spirit money, wine, and food to eulogize the soul of you, my younger brother Lei Dakong: Although these offerings are insignificant, in some small measure they represent our thoughts of you. You were born into an obscure family, but with a bright personality. Having lost your parents in childhood, you were not given to caution. We met under adverse conditions and linked our fates in suffering. Through years of rain and frost we struggled. Golden Dog went into the army, Water Girl moved away, you roamed in society. In Purple Thistle Pass, you sold rat poison; in Guangzhou, you dealt in silver and were forced to dress in rags like a beggar, scorned by all. Then the times improved. Business beneath Shaman Mountain began to flourish; river commerce thrived. You helped Fuyun sail his boat without mishap, standing impressively among the waves, helping Water Girl with her duties at home, respectful toward your elders and polite to your juniors, treating friends and neighbors with love and understanding, pulling together in whatever came along. But there were dark clouds looming, and dire times awaited you. Indignant over Water Girl's humiliation, you cut off the toe of your enemy in revenge, and for that you went to jail, where, haranguing the authorities and leveling charges at the evildoer, you experienced injustice. Your suffering hardened you against self-pity, while an enlightened government policy instilled you with great ambitions. Using loans from the state, you started a business, at which you excelled, moving easily in society. At some point your intelligence and ability took you into higher circles, where your wealth and influence were impressive. Trading straw sandals for leather shoes and work clothes for a Western suit, you kept your eyes on Tian and Gong, abandoning poverty to set your table with delicacies and live in plush surroundings. There was no pleasure foreign to you, no good fortune beyond your grasp. The populace of Zhou City was startled and envious when you contributed seventy thousand yuan to a school. So honest and frank, yielding to no one, someone to be admired, like the moth unafraid of the flames, heroic yet impestuous and simple, you sought, lamentably, quick success and instant fortune, and because of your single-

mindedness marched straight into the quicksand. You were a victim of the times; your experiences were written in your own blood. Ah! Over these thousands of years, throughout the length and breadth of the country, was there ever another peasant like you? You committed crimes, for which you must bear the consequences, but your glory as a peasant who made people sit up and take notice remains; your virtues are a mirror for those you left behind. Mud and sand are washed away by a flooded Zhou River, but boats sail easily. Turbulence surrounds the peaks of Shaman Mountain, yet they stand tall and majestic. Today your humble elder brother, your unworthy little sister, your infant nephew think of you, miss you, love you, hate you, resent you, pity you. Our hearts are filled with emotions that cannot be expressed in this simple eulogy. You should know that your murderer has been arrested and will soon pay the supreme penalty, his accomplices have fallen into the net, and justice will soon come to the remaining villains. The icebergs will melt away under the bright sun, and the Zhou River will wash away all the hidden shoals. You, my worthy brother, can rejoice in this news and fill the netherworld with your laughter. Time passes so quickly; several months have come and gone. If you are listening to me on the other side, worthy brother, eat the offerings we have provided, accept the money we have brought. Ah! We kneel beside our offerings.

Dusk had fallen by the time he finished reading. He set a match to the paper and looked heavenward, above the dark mountain peaks and the ribbonlike Zhou River, upon whose waters the sun's reflection rose and fell with the waves, as red as blood.

32

After decades of peace and quiet, boats had reappeared on the Zhou River, and from then on tranquillity had been lost. The number of people who made their livelihood on the water increased, as residents of Dongyang and Qingting counties, peasants from the countryside around Zhou City and hunters from the mountains, and peddlers who couldn't make ends meet in town converged on the Zhou River. The best sailors were from Crossroads Township, and the "wave-riding dragons" were all from Stream of Wandering Spirits. For several years those who made their living on the river had to snatch their food out of the pot of Yama, the king of hell, and though some did very well indeed, others lost everything; some did well for a while, then were wiped out, whereas others nearly starved at first, then suddenly did very well. In Stream of Wandering Spirits alone new houses had popped up all over the place, but they often changed hands. Sometimes whole families moved out to give way to new families; sometimes only the head of the household changed, as the river claimed another victim. Since most members of the Tian and Gong families worked elsewhere, it was people with other surnames who made it possible for the families of cadres to make ends meet during those years. Now, however, there were more youngsters from the Gong and Tian families than from the others. That could only be viewed as a tragedy. More and more people from Stream of Wandering Spirits viewed the Zhou River as a bane, even though they were still forced to earn their living on the water. Like red-eyed gamblers, they risked everything on one glimmer of hope. On the river, they staked their future, their fate, even their lives. Old Seven had been the first to give up that sort of life, not just because he was getting on in years but also because he was disturbed over the way things were going. Events at the Crossroads Township River Shipping Brigade had thrown a real scare into him. Renouncing the prospect of wealth, he went up the mountain to make a modest living cutting kindling and dragon-beard grass. As time went on, many of the older men and those who had suffered permanent injury on the river took up occupations at the periphery of river transport, setting up tiny cafés, or inns, or little grocery stores. Before long, the ne'er-do-wells, the thieves, the prostitutes, and the bums appeared, like flies on shit, and the banks of the Zhou River took on a completely new aspect. People locked their doors when they went out; they slept behind closed doors and protective screens; they raised dogs to bite at the slightest sign of disturbance. No one was exempt. Travelers were no longer greeted hospitably or invited in for a glass of wine or something to eat; rather, they were grudgingly allowed to sit on the rock by the door where the women washed clothes, under the steady scrutiny of hosts who eyed them suspiciously, afraid that letting down their guard for even a moment would result in the transient's stealing a broom, a bundle of tobacco leaves, or a string of dried peppers. Social morality deteriorated, relationships among people became strained, the quiet was shattered.

Han Wenju sat at the ferry landing enjoying a bottle of wine with the abbot as he studied the Buddhist scriptures; his appearance was solemn, his attitude serious. A boat sailed toward them and a voice lofted toward him. "Uncle Han, if you don't start noticing what's going on around you, you're going to turn into an immortal! Did you know that, in town, the daughter of Wang the Eighth was taken off by an outsider? As one of the elders here, you ought to be thinking of a way to help. Just because you're too old to care about women doesn't mean that the rest of us should be bachelors all our lives."

"There's nothing about the Wang family I don't know. They've disgraced their own name and disgraced all of Crossroads Township. There aren't many women in Wang the Eighth's family to begin with, so what was he thinking, taking a stranger in and giving him work? A callow girl and a young man: a perfect instance of throwing dry kindling into a roaring fire! Wang the Eighth must have been blind. Why couldn't a man who's always taken care to have enough grain to stuff into his face also have taken care not to let this happen? Well, he got what he deserved. Now that his daughter's run off with some wild stud, he can cry until he wets his pants and it won't do him any good. Anybody who feels like it comes here, and when they've seized what they want, they're off again. It used to be as hard to earn a living as it was to eat shit. Well, now the shit tastes just as bad as ever, but money's easy as long as you've got the wits. But remember this, youngster, you can only make so much money in this world. You suffer without it, but even when it comes along, remember, you can't take it with you."

"You're right, Uncle Han," the man said. "But that doesn't tell me why *you're* not doing anything about it. Why not talk to the party secretary? Since Tian Zhongzheng's no longer in office, ask the new secretary to straighten things out."

"You want me to take care of it? Sorry, I don't borrow trouble. The new secretary has his name in the book and collects his salary every month, but all he cares about are his career ambitions. With the hordes of outlanders on the Zhou River these days, what difference does it make who leaves? If you get into trouble, you suffer the consequences; if you do good, you reap the benefits. I let my sleeves flap gently in the breeze, and my heart's a void. That'll help me live longer. These days the wind blows the strands of our existence until you can't find a single end, and the only thing you see on people's faces is melancholy. Slow down, and the end will appear; rush ahead, and your freedom is gone!"

"Han Wenju, you old defeatist," the man scolded. "You spent your life trying to enlarge your power, but now that you're an old man all you do is parrot a bunch of weird sayings from that bald-headed mule, the abbot!" The man muttered so softly that Han couldn't hear what he was saying. What he did hear was, "That's easy for you to say, Uncle Han, since the three treasures of the Zhou River—Golden Dog, Silver Lion, and Spotted Deer—are yours, not to mention Water Girl, who's in White Rock Stockade. Since your family has it made, you can shut yourself off from the world around you and live a life of ease."

"Screw your goddamned old lady!" Han Wenju shot back. "It was because of Golden Dog, Silver Lion, and Spotted Deer that I came to know the abbot and the Buddha! You're too damned wet behind the ears to recognize that only the cooked yam is soft and that only the withered leaf is hard. Do you understand what I'm talking about? Everybody says how wonderful it would be to be an immortal, but they're not willing to give up the taste of wine or the feel of money!"

The men on the boat laughed derisively, and Han realized that he was standing there with a glass of wine in his hand. "What the hell are you laughing at? By *wine* I meant the loss of virtue through inebriation. Have you ever seen Han Wenju lose his virtue when he was drunk? Golden Dog has done well financially, but riches and health usually cancel each other. Water Girl was laid up all summer with a back so sore she couldn't stand up straight, and Hongpeng was in the hospital a month with diarrhea. If it hadn't been for me down here at the ferry landing storing up virtue and doing good deeds to make the world a better place, I'm afraid to think what might have happened to that family!"

The men on the boat, combating the loneliness of the river, were teasing him merely to divert themselves, and the last thing they expected was a torrent of nonsense from the old fellow. Uncomfortable with what they were hearing, they let out a call, signaled the other boats around them, and headed back down the river. Their departure didn't faze Han, who was busy reprehending the absent Golden Dog for not heeding his advice. He walked to the bow and shouted, "Baby Seven, Ox Boy, if you see Golden Dog out on the river, tell him to come home. It's been a year since Dakong's floating burial, and it's time to give him a proper tomb. And tell him that even if he's forgotten me, I haven't forgotten him. He'll be an old man someday too, and then he'll understand what it means to be put out to pasture!"

The boatmen scoffed. "You heap blame on Golden Dog one minute," Baby Seven called back, "and say how much you miss him the next. You're a useless old fart who says one thing and means another!"

Han watched the boats sail away, but he wasn't through pitying himself because of Golden Dog. "He's exactly what's ruined me. Who needs a son-in-law like that?"

The line of boats reached White Rock Stockade at dusk. They didn't see Golden Dog at the landing outside the south gate, but they did see Silver Lion and Spotted Deer. Silver Lion, who was from Crossroads Township, was only twenty-seven, but his hair was already white, and it glimmered in the sunlight. Spotted Deer was from a place called Du Village, beyond the northern gate. Having suffered from ringworm as a child, his face was pitted with scars. When the boatmen asked if they'd seen Golden Dog, Silver Lion replied, "Do you have business with our elder brother? He went to Zhouville the other day."

"He hasn't been home for a long time, and his father-in-law misses him. What's he doing way off in Zhouville? Arranging a deal?"

"Uncle Han's getting dotty. Golden Dog sends him money so he has plenty of food and drink, and as long as the abbot's around, he's never lonely. Golden Dog went to Zhouville to check out a motorized boat and maybe buy it and bring it back. Then Uncle Han can ride it all day and night if he wants, and we'll see if he's willing to give up that old tub of a ferryboat."

The boatmen's thoughts were occupied. *Golden Dog, Silver Lion, and Spotted Deer really are the wonders of the Zhou River. Now they're even going to buy a motorized boat!* One of the sailors, with a jealous edge to his voice, said, "Uncle Han's worrying that the period of Lei Dakong's floating burial is up, and he wants Golden Dog to come home and give him final interment. He hopes that Golden Dog's good fortune won't make him lose sight of his responsibilities."

Silver Lion missed the implication in the remark, but not Spotted Deer, whose face darkened. "Don't worry about that. Dakong was a Zhou River man, and he showed us the way. But he also deserved to be brought low. Nobody told him to put his own prosperity above the principles of the Communist party!"

The next day, Silver Lion and Spotted Deer went downriver to Zhouville to track down Golden Dog.

At the time of these events, Golden Dog had been sailing the Zhou River for a whole year.

After his release from prison and his compilation of the particulars in Lei Dakong's notebook, he'd gone straight to the public security bureau in Zhou City, for whom the material was a gold mine. The personnel there turned the data over immediately to the investigative team from the provincial committee and the various provincial legal branches, and the irregularities involving Tian Youshan in White Rock Stockade could no longer be concealed. The ensuing fight was extremely intricate. Tian sent someone to the military district headquarters to see Xu Feibao; Gong Baoshan sought to fortify his own position by revealing what had happened in conjunction with Xu's visit to White Rock Stockade for the dedication of Tian the Sixth's memorial. Both sides attacked and scrambled to find powerful backers, until the matter was a major scandal, stirring up public opinion and making it impossible for anyone to come away untarnished. Tian Youshan was removed from office; the party secretary of Qingting County was assigned to White Rock Stockade. Secretary Ma, who was called Camelback Ma because he was so thin and hunchbacked, knew how convoluted the situation was and how, even though there was no longer a Tian at the helm, grass-roots power continued to rest with the members of the Tian family. Conscious that even a powerful dragon is at the mercy of a snake in the grass, he asked permission to bring his own cadres to his new assignment. He arrived in White Rock Stockade with his own deputy secretary, county government chief, and head of the organization department. He replaced several mid-level cadres. Through his circumspect staffing, he broke the power of the Tian family. It was then that the Gong and Tian clans appreciated that when the dragon and the tiger battle, both get scarred. They laid all their problems at the door of Golden Dog, styling him a living demon, a vicious monster, and a reckless careerist.

After Golden Dog's success in unseating the members of the Gong and Tian families, they barraged the editor in chief of the Zhou City newspaper with letters of accusation against him, while behind the scenes they used the telephone to mount a smear campaign. The editor in chief called Golden Dog in, commended him for his courageous spirit in struggling against unhealthy tendencies, then took out the letters of accusation and the telephone log listing the calls that had leveled allegations against him. "Of course there are inaccuracies and exaggerations in the letters and phone calls we've received," he said, "but we can't ignore this outpour of public opinion. After careful deliberation, we've decided to transfer you to the reference department. This is out of concern and admiration for you. It's a good assignment, since you can use the opportunity to learn more about your profession."

Golden Dog flashed a comprehending smile and said, "I figured this was coming, and I accept your decision." He left the reporters' section that very day and turned in his reporter's ID card; he then went to White Rock Stockade to take care of the paperwork entailed by his transfer.

The treatment Golden Dog received did not sit well with his colleagues at the newspaper, many of whom urged him to appeal the decision of the paper's management. But he did not. The Young Reporters Study Association sent a letter to the district propaganda department, which responded that the decision was the responsibility of the work unit alone. Golden Dog served in the reference department for only a week before surprising everyone by requesting indefinite leave without pay. His request was approved with dispatch, and he returned to the Zhou River, where he had been born and where he had grown up. Two weeks later the policy permitting organizational cadres to take unpaid leave was rescinded. He was informed that he had to resume his duties in the reference department or see his employment terminated. He merely sniffed when he received the notice, and he decided neither to respond nor to return. His name was removed from the newspaper roster.

More and more boats were plying the Zhou River, and a river and highway transportation company was established in White Rock Stockade. Thirty-two reefs on the river were dynamited to open up the waterway to heavier traffic. It was then that two unfamiliar figures appeared on the river: Silver Lion and Spotted Deer, both educated, bold young men in their twenties who were better sailors than the best of the locals. When they learned that the renowned Golden Dog had come back to the river, they made three trips to Restless Hill to get him to affiliate with them. He wasn't home the first time. He turned them down on their second visit. But he began to waver on the third and spent the night talking to them. A rapport was established between them, and he finally agreed to their proposition. Silver Lion and Spotted Deer bit their fingers and wanted to form a blood-brother bond, with Golden Dog as the leader. But he said, "I'm throwing my lot in with you as an equal—all for one and one for all—and there's no need for an antiquated blood-brother vow."

"If you oppose the idea, that's that," Silver Lion acceded. "Although we have a notoriety beyond the Zhou River, it's undeserved. We're not men who think only of money, and we make our livelihood on the river because we feel we should be doing something worthwhile. We took the college entrance exams but failed all three times. We took jobs but found we were going nowhere. So we decided to come to the Zhou River to do what we do best. We've esteemed you and your achievements for a long time. That's why we wouldn't take no for an answer."

"I'm also a man going nowhere," Golden Dog said. "After knocking around on the Zhou River for years, I marched off to Zhou City with grandiose ambitions. It all seems pretty juvenile now. I decided to leave the newspaper and come back to the Zhou River since the months I spent in prison awakened in me the awareness that bureaucracy in China isn't going to be rooted out through a few campaigns or some editorials in the newspaper. It will disappear only when the people are well enough off economically to become more developed culturally. Economic betterment runs hand in hand with cultural progress, and only when the people reach a certain level will the foundation that bureaucratism requires collapse. For this, I believe we must retain the current political structure in its basics. It will help improve the means of production. At the same time, we must work to reform the political structure where changes can increase production and advance cultural development. Since we've joined forces, our first move must be to reject pie-in-the-sky schemes and instead to apply our skills to work on the river. If we do our job well, we can help the people on the Zhou River move ahead economically and culturally."

"Golden Dog," Spotted Deer said, "you're older than we are and more knowledgeable. We'll take your lead. If we succeed in bringing about a sound restructuring of the transportation industry on the whole of the Zhou River—who knows?—you might become the people's representative for White Rock Stockade, or the region, or the whole province. If that day came, people would arrive at a true appreciation of your talents, and—who knows?—you might become an official who did something important for the whole country!"

Golden Dog laughed dismissively. "That sounds better than what Lei Dakong had in mind, but talk's cheap. To think of becoming an official at this point is a joke. Under present conditions, anybody who sets out to be a decent, competent cadre will never get a thing done. We must learn a lesson from Dakong and always remember that the economic reforms in China today have nothing in common with the revolutionary battles of the past. It's immature and out of keeping with the times to chase the grandeur of tragedy. Knowledge and action are desperately needed now. Have you ever seen or heard of an outsider who came here on a survey tour?"

Neither Silver Lion nor Spotted Deer knew anything about the man Golden Dog was referring to. But Golden Dog told them of his encounter, relating the man's views and the personal knowledge he himself had gained over the years since then. He urged them to register for correspondence courses at a college in the provincial capital, spending part of their time doing course work that would benefit them and the rest of the time working on the river. In the end, the three men, working a single boat, transported more goods than anyone else, studied more books, traveled to more places, and accomplished more. When people spotted them on the river, they ran along the banks shouting, "Golden Dog—Silver Lion—Spotted Deer!" as a sort of homage.

Now Silver Lion and Spotted Deer were going downriver to Zhouville. The motorized boat hadn't been bought yet, but word about it had traveled on the wind to White Rock Stockade. The old painter, who had moved to White Rock Stockade, was up on the beam of the Smooth Seas Temple one day taking a smoke break before continuing his painting. Suddenly a string of firecrackers exploded outside the temple door and three boatmen walked in and placed a box with a white snake on the altar. Drenched from the rain, they knelt on the floor, lit incense, and kowtowed. Although the painter couldn't see their faces, he heard one of them pray to the deity: "River god, protect us! Before we set out down the river, we always come here to kowtow to you, so why have we lost another boat? Golden Dog, Silver Lion, and Spotted Deer never set foot in the Smooth Seas Temple, but nothing ever happens to their boat. Are they truly the three treasures of the Zhou River?"

The appalled painter knew that the three were from the Crossroads Township River Shipping Brigade. He knocked the bowl of his pipe on the beam and challenged, "Liu the Third, are you cursing my Golden Dog in front of the deity?"

Caught off guard by the voice, Liu the Third and the other men looked up and spotted him. "Is that you, Uncle?" one of them asked with a conciliatory smile. "Why would we be cursing your Golden Dog? We're just trying to find out if this deity is the real thing or not. We can't figure out why Golden Dog has such good luck all the time. His business keeps getting better and better, and now he's going to buy a motorized boat."

"Have you seen him? Is he really going to buy one?"

"You mean you don't know?" Liu asked incredulously.

"I know he discussed it with the others, but I thought it wasn't a good step to take. But who listens to me anymore? No wonder I haven't seen him during the past few days. All Water Girl says is that he went to Zhouville."

"You're a lucky old man," Liu said. "He didn't want to worry you. You don't appreciate how lucky you are. Uncle, when they bring the motorized boat home, they're going to be better off than ever, and since three people won't be able to handle it, put in a good word for us so they'll hire us as sailors."

"You must be joking. With all the people and boats in your shipping brigade, and all the influence you have, why would you want to sign on with Golden Dog?"

"We're not joking, Uncle!" Liu said, "Sure, there are plenty of people in the brigade, but our hearts aren't in it. When the Tian family fell from power, Tian Zhongzheng was reassigned to a government job in North Mountain Township, leaving Cai Da'an and Tian Yishen on their own, and they can't piss in the same bottle. They're at each other's throats all the time, and we're the ones who suffer. We have trouble finding cargo, and when we do, we can't sell it. Everybody's confused, and a lot of the men have already left the brigade. Boating's all we know; we can't do anything else. If somebody doesn't come along to pick us up, I don't know how we're going to make it."

The painter sat pensively on the beam, wanting to say something encouraging but feeling that he couldn't give assurances on behalf of Golden Dog. Liu the Third tossed him a pack of cigarettes, which he caught; he removed one, tucked it behind his ear, and tossed the pack down. "I could talk to Golden Dog about it," he said, "but there's no guarantee it'd do any good. You're better off talking to him yourselves."

"Of course," Liu the Third said, "of course. But sort of run it past him first." He fell back down on his knees and kowtowed, then picked up the white snake in the box and walked out of the temple to go back to the boat. As he went out the door, he said to the painter, "That Golden Dog of yours is all right, Uncle. All of us down there say the same thing. Now that the country allows for the democratic election of leaders at every level, we're going to nominate him for county head!"

The painter smiled contentedly and went back to work, finishing a dragon and a black panther before his thoughts gave him pause. "They can't elect Golden Dog," he said aloud. "I want him to have a peaceful life on the river."

It was dark by the time he returned home to the former blacksmith shop, where dinner was waiting for him. Water Girl was out back playing with the baby beneath the chinaberry tree. The leaves were yellow; the berries were falling to the ground with steady plops from the bunches and bunches on the tree. She was telling Hongpeng they were little firecrackers going off: "That one popped for your daddy, that one popped for your mommy, and that one popped for little Hongpeng." The painter looked out the back door, a bunch of vegetables he'd bought on the way home still in his hand. "Water Girl," he said, "what are you telling Hongpeng?"

Water Girl's biggest problem with the painter was knowing what to call him. As things stood, she should be calling him Father, but she'd got so used to calling him Granddad that that was always the first thing that entered her head. She smiled and said, "You shouldn't be bringing food home. If you take care of all the domestic work, what's left for me?"

After washing up, he took the baby from Water Girl, and she went into the kitchen to get food onto the table. By then Hongpeng was sitting on his shoulders, holding on to the old man's white hair, which he had mussed.

"Hongpeng!" Water Girl reprimanded her son, "you think you can get away with anything!" She lifted him down so the painter could eat. Then she sat, raised her blouse, and fed the infant. The painter was gratified by the way Water Girl treated him, and at times like this his heart swelled with a long-sought contentment. Savoring the good fortune of a family elder, he ate with a joyful spirit.

"Water Girl," he said, "I hear that Golden Dog and the others went to Zhou River City to buy a motorized boat."

"That's right. Didn't he tell you? The river's so navigable these days they figured they'd buy one to haul passengers and cargo from Crossroads Township to White Rock Stockade."

He realized that the purchase of the boat had been discussed with everyone but him, and this spoiled his happiness just a little. "None of you ever listen to me . . . Golden Dog and his partners are already very conspicuous on the Zhou River. They could be courting trouble if they got too prosperous because of the motorized boat."

"They want to play a pathbreaking role among the boatmen. As I see it, someday this place will be the hub for traffic all up and down the river."

"Water Girl," the painter dissented, "Golden Dog's cocksureness is coming out again, but instead of trying to reason with him, you're throwing oil on the fire! You haven't forgotten what happened to Dakong, have you? Why did Golden Dog leave Zhou City and come back to the river, anyway?"

"We've given a lot of thought to the kinds of things you're bringing up. But Lei Dakong broke the law, and I'm not worried about Golden Dog on that score. Don't forget, if it hadn't been for Dakong, the Gong and Tian families might still be in power."

Ill equipped to argue with her, he just shook his head. "I still think a peaceful, unaspiring life is best. We don't have any trouble getting by these days, and even if we were a lot poorer than we are now, we wouldn't have to go around afraid of our shadows. I've already heard talk about a movement afoot to elect Golden Dog to public office, and that terrifies me more than anything. They want him to be a government figure."

"That's a wonderful idea!" she exclaimed. "I know him well, and it's important for him to do something that makes a contribution. If he gained the support of the people on the Zhou River, that would be marvelous."

The painter finished three bowls of rice without saying anything more, then took Hongpeng from Water Girl so that she could eat. There were still traces of discontent on his face. Knowing full well what was going through the old man's mind, she said between mouthfuls, "You've raised your son; you must know his temperament. He's not someone who wants to hide in the crowd. Let him do what he has to do. You're getting on in years, and your health isn't as good as it used to be. You shouldn't let other people's doings bother you. Just work at the Smooth Seas Temple if you feel like it, and if you don't, stay home and rest."

He smiled and hoisted Hongpeng onto his shoulders to let him play again with his white hair. "Water Girl," he said abruptly, "now that we're all working in town, your uncle's alone in Stream of Wandering Spirits. You ought to go see him one of these days. If he takes to the idea, why not have him move into town with us? He and I always have something to talk about."

Mention of her uncle brought worrisome thoughts to her. Since moving to town, he was her only real anxiety; she was concerned that he'd be lonely down at the ferry landing. Time and again she'd asked him to move into town, but he'd always made excuses.

"You're right," she said. "I'll go see him again and try to talk him into it. Sooner or later he'll take me up on the offer."

One more time she took a boat to Stream of Wandering Spirits, and one more time Han Wenju declined to leave, saying he couldn't get used to living in town and that without his friends he'd die of boredom. She couldn't force him to come with her, and so she said, "Well, in that case, I'll stay here and take care of you for a few days." She stayed for five days, preparing three big meals a day and taking them down to the boat for him. The yellow dog had stopped running around the neighborhood and was content to tag along behind her the whole day, as affectionate as a well-behaved child.

One night, after she'd put Hongpeng to bed, she was cooking over a smoky stove when she heard the dog growling outside and then Cai Da'an's voice. "Why's this dog always trying to bite me? We must have been mortal enemies in a past life!"

Water Girl poked her head through the kitchen curtain and said, "Commander Cai, are you looking for my uncle? He's still down at the landing."

With an impertinent look on his face, Cai said, "You think you don't have to invite me in, just because your uncle's not home? Now that you live in town, we villagers don't count with you."

"You're not someone I have to fawn over, are you?" She told the dog to stop annoying him and asked him in.

"Why didn't you let me know you were getting married, Water Girl? Not a single word. Do you still bear a grudge against me? Back then I was living under Tian Zhongzheng's eaves, so I had to lower my head. Hmph! But the other day Yingying's mother asked me to get some mountain produce for her, and I just ignored her. A woman like that—I just turned and walked away."

"What was the point? Is that how you treat people as soon as they're out of favor?"

With a crestfallen look, Cai stammered his denial. He went on, "I heard you took sick after you moved to White Rock Stockade. Are you okay now?"

"I've been fine for a long time, Commander Cai. But you must be making this visit for a purpose."

"You don't have to call me Commander. Tian Yishen has made a mess of the shipping brigade, and I'm like a deaf man whose ears are nothing but decorations! I heard you'd come back, and I came over especially to see you. Water Girl, have Golden Dog and his partners bought their motorized boat?"

"You have the ears of a fox. You don't miss a trick. How did you know they were going to buy a motorized boat?"

"Everybody knows. You can't find anybody who doesn't look up to the three treasures of the Zhou River. When our boatmen heard about it, their thoughts began to shift from the brigade, and a lot of them are hoping to throw in their lot with Golden Dog."

"Then why don't you two commanders try to stop him? Won't the new boat spell the end of the shipping brigade?"

Not showing the slightest sign of feeling a reproach, Cai lowered his voice and said, "It wasn't what you think. It was all Tian Yishen's scheme. There he went running to the county transport company to see if they were going to permit Golden Dog to carry passengers. He and I had a terrible argument over his doing that. Who the hell does he think he is? Ever since Tian Zhongzheng was transferred, Tian Yishen has been working to reestablish the Tian authority around here. That's nothing but a pipe dream!"

Water Girl had figured out the motive for Cai's dropping by, and she said with calculated innocence, "Tian Zhongzheng has been transferred, and Tian Youshan has fallen from power in the county. But the power of the Gong and Tian families in Crossroads Township is as great as ever!"

"That's precisely why I've come to see you. I'd like you to tell Golden Dog that I'd be willing to join up with him. I was a fool before, and I lost sight of who was good and who was bad. If he'll take me on, I can bring a lot of people with me, and together we'll spell the end of the Crossroads Township River Shipping Brigade. There'll be a clean break between the Gong and Tian clans, on one side, and those of us who now have neither power nor authority, on the other. Once we get things going, no one will ever look down on us again. Tell him that Cai Da'an has no desire to command anything, that he'll do whatever he's told, whatever Golden Dog wants him to do!"

Doubt and confusion filled Water Girl's heart as Cai finished. She saw him out with a few innocuous pleasantries. When dinner was ready, she took it down to the landing and ran into Old Seven at the crossroads. After she told him what had happened, he spit on the ground and growled, "Cai Da'an is a son of a bitch who'll eat the flesh of anything that passes by. Tell Golden Dog that we'll take in anybody who wants to join us—anybody but Cai Da'an!"

"Aren't you overreacting, Uncle Seven? If Cai wants to join us, I say let him. There are good people in the world and there are bad ones. We can put his association with us to our own advantage as long as we don't forget which kind of person he is."

"Hai!" Old Seven sighed. "I'm having more and more trouble figuring the world out these days. Back when the land was distributed, the government allowed the peasants to use it any way they wanted, and I said to your uncle that good days were upon us as long as there wasn't another change in policy. It didn't take many years for chaos to set in and for all kinds of people to be engaging in every abuse you can think of. I've begun wishing for a return to the old ways."

"You really are hopeless, Uncle," Water Girl said. "What good would a return to the old ways do? Anyway, what would things be like if people weren't complaining about the mess they're in? And what could you do about the mess if there were a return to the old ways?"

"I don't know what's best, anymore," Old Seven said, dispirited. "Lately I've been resentful about everything, just like your uncle used to be—always yelling and cursing at people, until lots of them won't have anything more to do with me. But your uncle's turned over a new leaf. He doesn't get involved in anything, and nothing gets him sore anymore. He's a lot closer to the abbot than he is to me these days."

When they reached the landing, Water Girl gave Han his dinner and sat down to chat awhile. Old Seven, complaining about his own disgruntlement with everything, dragged Han over to his place for some wine, leaving Water Girl to watch the boat and to ferry any passengers who showed up.

She sat there alone until the sun had nearly set, and there were no passengers. A bit of wind came up and turned the night chilly, so she wrapped her jacket around herself snugly and sat against the cabin door, letting her thoughts roam, first to Golden Dog, then to Cai Da'an, and then to some of the things her grandfather and Old Seven had said. She was uncertain and restless. She too had trouble understanding what was going on these days; as soon as something became clear to her, something else made it melt back into confusion.

Finally she forced all these thoughts out of her mind and closed her eyes to rest. But a sound broke the silence, a very peculiar sound. Was it a motorized boat? she wondered nervously. She gazed downriver; sure enough, that's what was on the horizon. It was huge, at least ten times the size of a shuttle boat, and it was made of steel and painted bright red. The man standing on the prow looked like Golden Dog. The boat sailed up to the landing, placing Golden Dog squarely in front of her.

"Water Girl," he said, "take a good look. What do you think of it? Have you ever seen anything like this on the Zhou River?"

Agog, she asked how much cargo it could hold and how many passengers it could carry. His answers made her heart pound with anticipation.

A moment later Silver Lion was standing beside her and whispering in her ear, "Sister-in-law, there's even better news than that!"

"What could be better than this?"

"They held an election for county head in White Rock Stockade, and it looks like we're going to have to start calling you Madam!"

She didn't understand. "Why call me Madam?"

"There are lots of ways to refer to women," Silver Lion explained. "If you marry a peasant, you're his old lady. If you marry an organizational cadre, you're his wife. But if you marry a real official, everybody calls you Madam."

"Are you telling me that Golden Dog has been elected county head?" She looked over at Golden Dog, who merely smiled.

Spotted Deer said, "Sister-in-law, your Golden Dog has been elected county head. But it's not a case of, If everyone becomes an official, all officials are alike. Golden Dog, once you become an official, don't forget us common folk. The Gongs and the Tians were good people, too, until they became officials."

"If Golden Dog turned out like that," Water Girl said, "I'd leave him. What do you say, Golden Dog? Will you change?"

"Look at me," he said. "Do I look like an official?"

"No more fence sitting, Golden Dog," Silver Lion said. "Take the job."

"Silver Lion's right," Water Girl said. "It's because you weren't an official that you had no power. You became a reporter, but what happened in the end? You were forced out. Dakong wanted to do something big, but he left the straight and narrow, and if he had ever become an official, he'd have been just like the Tians and Gongs!"

Without another word, Golden Dog jumped back onto the boat, turned a switch, and started it up. He yelled to the others to come and sail downstream with him. Silver Lion and Spotted Deer helped Water Girl aboard as the vessel slid into the middle of the river. It gained speed until it seemed to be flying across the surface of the water. Water Girl began to get dizzy and nauseated: she threw up a stomachful. Turning the helm over to Silver Lion, Golden Dog held her in his arms, telling her to look straight ahead instead of down at the water. The boat sailed downriver in deep, clear water. Golden Dog, Spotted Deer, and Water Girl leaned over the side to scoop water out of the river, but damned if they didn't all fall in. She felt as though she'd fallen into an icehouse, or had had her skin painfully scraped by millions of tiny knives. When she finally floated to the surface, Golden Dog and the others were nowhere in sight. "Golden Dog! Golden Dog!" In screaming, she jumped to her feet, and she discovered that she was all alone on the ferryboat, surrounded by calm, with a river of stars overhead and gently flowing water beneath her.

Her eyes widened in fright. Was it a dream? she asked herself, as the sound of the night bell from Restless Hill drifted over on the wind, confirming her suspicion. She laughed lightly but couldn't dismiss the strange nature of the dream, and she went through it again in her mind. Suddenly a dreadful thought came to her, and she scurried home as fast as her legs would take her. The baby was awake and crying, his hands and feet thrashing. She picked him up and fed him, as thoughts of the dream swirled in her mind. She decided to go see the abbot at Restless Hill to get her dream analyzed and have him predict what lay in store for Golden Dog after he bought the motorized boat.

The monastery door was closed, and she heard the faint sounds of the clacking of a wooden fish. After several knocks, the door opened a crack and a shaved head peered out. She knew all the monks in the monastery. "Is the abbot meditating?" she asked.

"Would you like to see him about something?" the monk asked.

"Yes. Would you ask him to step outside for a moment?"

"The abbot went to North Mountain to beg alms. Before he left, he said that if you wanted to see him, I was to tell you to go to the fortune-teller at Cave of the Spirits village."

"How did he know I'd wish to see him?"

The monk smiled enigmatically, and with an "Amita Buddha," drew his head inside and shut the door. Water Girl went home marveling over the prescience of the abbot. Since he counseled her to go to the fortune-teller at Cave of the Spirits village, she knew something was up. When she got back to the ferry landing with the baby, Uncle Han still hadn't come from drinking with Old Seven. She left the yellow dog at the landing, untied the boat from the overhead line, and sailed toward Cave of the Spirits village.

The village was eight li downriver, where the southern bank of the river moves toward Shaman Mountain, then suddenly narrows like the waist of a hornet; on a jutting promontory stands a tiny village, behind which is a deep, slender cave with an opening at the top that allows the sunlight to stream in. A stalactite in the center of the cave is taken to have the shape of a multitude of spirits. It was said that long ago a roving monk with an alms bowl and a wide straw hat came and built a seven-story pagoda thirty feet tall, then climbed to the top and uttered a riddle: "There are no stories in the pagoda; there is sand beneath the Zhou River. Enlightenment exists in front of our eyes; there is no need to await the thousand-year blossom." He died on the spot. Then one day the tower was struck by lightning and the cave was laid waste. Later on, the monastery at Restless Hill opened, and the site had been neglected. But within the previous couple of years a fortune-teller had emerged from the village, an expert at geomancy, whose reading of characters and tallies had earned him a wide reputation. Water Girl poled her boat through the tempestuous Zhou River beneath the stone ridge and berthed it in a cove. She then followed a stairway of stone steps up to the village. Only five families lived there. A light shone in a window of one of the cottages; that was where the fortune-teller resided. Water Girl had had dealings of a sort with him before, for it was he who had selected the grave sites for Grandpa Pockface, Fuyun, and Dakong. But he had never seen her, for on her previous visits she had stayed behind on the boat while Old Seven went to call on him and Old Seven hadn't brought him down for an introduction. She hesitated at the door of the cottage but collected the courage to go inside, where she saw four or five people, who extinguished the lamp at once. In the reflected moonlight on the wall, she could see only their dark, shiny faces.

"Who are you?" someone asked her. "What are you doing here?"

Water Girl shivered. Obviously, these people were here to have their fortunes told. "I've come to see the fortune-teller," she said. "The abbot at Restless Hill sent me."

"We thought you were here to break this up!" one of them said, relighting the lamp. In the light she saw him clearly: he was tall and slim, with a protruding forehead, deeply inset eyes, and a large mole on his chin. It was the fortune-teller himself.

"Are you here to get a reading of geomancy or to avert some calamity?" he asked her.

Not knowing how to choose between the alternatives, she wondered for a moment whether she had been right in coming at all.

"Then you must be here to ask about something," the fortune-teller said.

Water Girl nodded. The baby in her arms started crying, and she sat down on a stone bench and stuffed her nipple into his mouth.

"Good," the fortune-teller said. "Sit there for a while." He turned and helped a woman pick up a large bamboo sieve, which they shook over a pan of fine sand. Everyone held his breath and craned his neck to watch the movement of the pan. Water Girl realized that they were performing planchette writing. She said nothing and looked around the house, listening to the indistinct mumbling incantations of the fortune-teller as they mixed with the sound of the Zhou River at the bottom of the hill.

The planchette writing was completed after the time it would take to eat a meal, and the visitors departed, leaving only the fat old lady and the fortune-teller, who asked Water Girl what it was she wanted to know. She told him about the motorized boat Golden Dog was buying and asked if it was good or bad to have motorized boats on the Zhou River, whether Golden Dog and his partners would succeed in their projected ventures, and whether Golden Dog himself could look forward to a future of good fortune or bad.

"You're Water Girl, aren't you?" he asked her.

"How did you know, Master?"

"I inferred that it was you when you mentioned Golden Dog's name. Everybody on the Zhou River knows Golden Dog! I'm aware that he doesn't place any stock in what I do, but you're here. Did he send you? In the end, humans are no match for the spirits!"

"Golden Dog has no idea I'm here," Water Girl corrected him. "I couldn't drive the confusion and anxiety from my mind, so I decided to come see you."

He said good-naturedly, "Golden Dog has no faith in what I do, and that's his business. But I'm no fraud trafficking in a pack of nonsense in order to swindle people out of their money. Here, look at this book of mine." He reached over and picked up an old, thread-sewn book from the table. Water Girl opened it to the first page and glanced at it under the lamp, where she read,

> The ancient philosophers said that the Way becomes clear through the text. The Way can be refined; it can be coarse. The text can be clumsy; it can be clever. If the words are sincere, the language will be correct. A thread runs through it all, illuminating all earthly phenomena. It accumulates spirit and light; it transmits government and education. The four styles of the *Book of History* extend to the far mountains and rivers yet encompass nearby flowers and birds; they extend through times ancient and modern, uninhibited and free, brighter than flames, leading the way better than streams. The sensibility of Zhou Dun and Cheng Xi, the rectifying power of Zhuangzi and Liezi, the candor of Zhu Xi and Lu Jiuyuan, and the profundity of Ban Chao and Fan Zhongyan incorporate every perfection, demonstrate all subtleties. The work of our forebears is the model to emulate.

Water Girl, who was not well educated, had no idea what it all meant, and wondered what sort of book this was.

"The knowledge in this book," the fortune-teller said, "is in no way inferior to what is found in that newspaper of Golden Dog's. In today's world many people scoff at us and attack us. But even if what you read here is called superstition, it has rescued countless individuals who had no other way out of their impasses. Humans are subject to hundreds of illnesses, which can be divided into two categories: those coming from the outside and entering through the mouth or on the wind, and those that are spiritual. The first kind can be treated with medication, but there's no medication that can cure illnesses of the spirit. Since you have come with questions about Golden Dog's undertakings, let's try some planchette writing and see what the Three Elders have to say.

"Who are the Three Elders?"

"Take a look at the images on the wall."

On the wall hung a New Year's painting, with Mao Zedong, Zhou Enlai, and Zhu De standing in front of emerald green pines and cypresses. The fortune-teller stuck three burning Front Gate cigarettes into an incense burner beneath the painting. "We must ask the Three Elders if Golden Dog's endeavors will benefit society. The Three Elders are the great spirits of our age. Kneel down, and concentrate on what you have come to find out. They will write out their answers for you."

Although troubled by doubts, she did as she was told, while he and the old woman picked up the sieve and held it above the pan of sand. It started moving slowly, and the needle hanging from the bottom began to make designs on the sand below. The movement stopped as quickly as it had begun.

"That's enough," the fortune-teller said, as Water Girl examined the sand, on which there were patterns that looked like writing. "Look, up in the left-hand corner, those large, vigorous characters. 'No problem.' Mao Zedong wrote those. The characters in the middle are much smaller and tighter. They say, 'Mission accomplished,' and were written by Zhou Enlai. That circle on the right is Zhu De's contribution. A circle represents 'Agree.'"

Taking a closer look, Water Girl thought she could see the similarities, and she smiled under the light of the lamp.

"The Three Elders will protect your Golden Dog," the fortune-teller assured her. "You can let him go ahead without any cares. He may do something truly significant someday."

Unsure if it was the spirits' message or something else that had restored her equanimity, Water Girl already had a renewed light in her eyes and brighter color in her cheeks. She asked how much she owed. "I take a fee from other people," the fortune-teller replied, "but not from you, because you were referred to me by the abbot and because you came on behalf of Golden Dog. I don't want your money." Water Girl took out five yuan, however, and handed it to the old woman, who accepted it.

As Water Girl emerged from the cottage and walked from the village, down the hill one stone step at a time, winds began whistling over the Zhou River. The baby was awakened by the impact of the cold gusts. To bring his tears to a stop, she spun around with him in her arms, asking, "Do you miss your father, Hongpeng? He went to buy a motorized boat, and he'll take you for a ride when he gets back. Toot, toot, toot—all the way from Stream of Wandering Spirits to White Rock Stockade!"

Her dandling had its effect, and he began saying, "Dada, Dada," as Water Girl pointed to the lower reaches of the Zhou River, where a solitary star hung in the sky.

"Your dada is there beneath that star, and tomorrow he's going to bring a motorized boat back for Hongpeng!" She looked up at the sky and perceived a drastic change. The dark clouds had turned orange, with traces of red, the color getting deeper and deeper, while the moon was encircled by a wide ring of color. "Is the Zhou River going to flood again?"

The river had flooded during the year Golden Dog went to Zhou City, and the sky had looked exactly like this for three or four nights before.

She sped down the steps, holding Hongpeng tight in her arms, stopping only once in her dash toward the rocky cove where she'd tied the boat. When she halted, on the cliff above the cove, she looked down at the river. The boat was gone! Winds churned the surface of the water, and moonlight flickered on the tips of the swells. Nothing but water and sky met her eye. A shriek left her throat as she tore down to the beach, where she found one end of the line still secured to a rock; the line had snapped in two, worn through by the jagged edge of a rock a few paces off. Still holding Hongpeng in her arms, she covered the length of the cove looking for her missing boat as water-whipped waves lapped the beach and crashed against the dark rocks on the shore, forming a subtle yet menacing sound. As she stood nearly petrified, she heard the barking of a dog, the sound drawing nearer and nearer and growing louder and louder. She looked upriver and observed the dog on the indistinct shore, a solitary shape barking at the river and running toward her. "Dog!" she screamed without a thought for anything else. "Dog!"

It was five nights before the Zhou River overflowed its banks for the second time in memory. It was midnight.